# *New* BEGINNINGS

A NEW BEGINNINGS
ROMANCE NOVEL
VOLUME ONE

## ANASTASIA DEAN

*For my readers who needed Mav and Javi bundled together.*

PART ONE

# On and Off The Field

*Ofelia*

CHAPTER ONE

OFELIA MENDEZ STARED BLANKLY at the large cutout of William Shakespeare contemplating where her life went so wrong. She suspected it was the moment she agreed to teach high school. The incessant nagging in her ear belonged to an irate parent droning on about her precious baby boy. By "baby boy" she meant her seventeen-year-old son and by "precious" she meant starved for attention. She desperately tried to follow the conversation, but thoughts of her mile long to-do list plagued her mind.

What Mrs. Davis didn't realize—or care to realize—was that Ofelia didn't *want* to be on the phone with her, hashing out the same conversation she had with Mrs. Davis about her son, Dustin, countless times before. It was her school district's policy to call home each time a teacher gave detention to foster a better parent-teacher-student relationship. She tried very hard not to notice Dustin's outbursts in class or the hallway—like *really* hard—but she couldn't just ignore it when he physically threatened another student. Unfortunately, his mother didn't share her views.

"Mrs. Davis," she said, attempting to sound both kind and unwavering. Mrs. Davis smelled fear. She fed upon emotions like a soul sucking vampire. "I apologize for yet another call. Dustin has

3

actually been a sweetheart in class these past few weeks. However, there was an incident in class today I needed to inform you—"

"Oh, this will be good," Mrs. Davis interrupted in a haughty tone she often adopted when talking to Ofelia. It made her feel like a child and since she was already one of the youngest teachers on campus, she hated feeling inferior because of her age. "So, tell me, what did Dustin do to deserve detention?"

"Well, Dustin yelled at another student and—"

"Oh, bless your heart," Mrs. Davis said in her southern drawl, making the hairs on the back of Ofelia's neck stand up. She only recently moved to Texas, but she understood what that phrase meant.

'Oh, bless your heart' was the equivalent of 'wow, you're a huge fucking idiot.' That was one thing about southerners, they were polite even when they were insulting you straight to your face. If the insult hadn't been geared towards her, she might have been impressed.

"Ms. Mendez, I'm not sure how they ran the schools back where you came from—"

"California."

"—but in Texas, we don't call home after every little mishap. They're children. They are still learning how to socialize and sometimes they do so inappropriately. It happens. I don't see why you needed to call me."

She kept her voice as neutral as possible, continuing before the evil witch could get another word in. "Mrs. Davis, my classroom is a safe zone for all students. Dustin threatened bodily harm on a peer. I had to deescalate the situation before a fight broke out. I do not tolerate bullying of any kind."

"Sounds to me like it was just a case of boys being boys. Let me ask you this Ms. Mendez: do you have any children?" Mrs. Davis inquired.

Gritting her teeth, she responded. "No, I do not."

"I can tell. I'm a boy mom, I have one in college and my

youngest is in middle school. They fight—it's what boys do. They don't know how to express their emotions, so they use fists."

"Mrs. Davis, are you insinuating I should have let the students fight?" She shouldn't be surprised, but she was. Did Mrs. Davis really teach her sons to bottle up their emotions and use fists as a coping mechanism? She tried her best not to be the type of person who judged mothers, but this didn't sit right with her.

"Of course not!" Mrs. Davis gasped, sounding shocked Ofelia would suggest such a thing even though Mrs. Davis brought it up first. "What I'm saying is that boys are different creatures than girls and they express their emotions in a way fitting for a young man..."

And that was where Ofelia stopped listening to the lecture because she knew from experience that it was better to just let them talk. She hated how this woman made her feel; small and out of control of the situation. The anxiety Mrs. Davis brought forth would be enough to fuel an entire therapy clinic. She had only felt so out of control twice before in her life and for things much larger than a helicopter mother. Once was at her mother's funeral and then again at what should have been her wedding day. Both monumental parts of her life, and yet Mrs. Davis worked her way into completing the trifecta of misery.

Wonderful.

Instead of listening to Mrs. Davis's ignorant ramblings, Ofelia tried to think of the one positive thing she was looking forward to today. Cheer practice. As a former cheerleader herself, she reveled in the bonds she made with her squad. Now as a coach, she strived to make her squad feel the same meaningful connection. Like with everything else in her life, Ofelia threw herself into coaching with passionate ferocity, spending countless hours creating and perfecting routines.

Although she put an insane amount of pressure on herself, she looked forward to coaching every Monday and Wednesday afternoon where she could hang up her teacher cardigan and don her whistle and yoga pants to coach a tight-knit squad. The stress of the day melted away during each practice.

No one could take that feeling away from her. She just needed to get her cheerleaders whipped into shape before the start of competition season...but in order to do that, she needed to end this phone conversation.

"Mrs. Davis." The woman was still in the midst of her soliloquy, but frankly Ofelia didn't care. She'd heard enough; anymore, and her head would spontaneously combust. "I hear your concerns, but I'm not sure we are understanding one another. Maybe you should contact our principal, Colbie Thompson, for a meet—"

"Oh I most certainly will, Mrs. Mendez. You can count on that. I'm concerned with how much attention you're giving my son. In fact, if I didn't know any better, I would say you were targeting him." With those parting words, Mrs. Davis hung up the phone, leaving Ofelia with her mouth open like a fish gasping for water.

What. Just. Happened?

This was not what she needed today - or any day for that matter. On top of her forever long teaching and coaching list, she would now have to add a meeting with Colbie and Mrs. Davis. She expected the conversation to go south, but she hadn't expected to be accused of "targeting." The call left her uncertain about whether she did the right thing. Ofelia *did* call Mrs. Davis more than the average parent, but according to her school's guidelines, she was simply following protocol.

Though perhaps she was being bothersome...

*No.* She refused to let Mrs. Davis get under her skin when she knew for a fact she did the right thing. If Mrs. Davis acted upon her threat, Ofelia was certain her principal would have her back. She had a good relationship with Colbie Thompson. If one woman could go head-to-head with Mrs. Davis and end up victorious, Colbie could.

As much as she loved her principal, she couldn't help but feel slightly flustered around the woman. The childhood fear of being sent to the principal's office after acting up in class still lingered, even years later.

Realizing the phone was still in her hands, Ofelia hung up as a knock sounded at her door. It was the end of the day, but she knew who waited at the other end. Bright red curly hair and a freckled face smiled brightly and waved manically in greeting.

Willow Clarke was just the person Ofelia wanted to vent to. Her teacher bestie always had impeccable timing. Ofelia swore she was psychic because Willow always appeared at her door holding chocolates after any inconvenience occurred. This time was no different.

"You look traumatized and in desperate need of wine," Willow said as soon as she let herself into the classroom, shutting the door behind her. She marched over to Ofelia's desk and for a horrible moment, Ofelia thought she had a bottle of wine to offer, but her eccentric friend pulled out a large Snickers candy bar instead. "You need this more than me," she said by way of explanation.

Willow was in her mid-thirties, married to a German man, and was the most free-spirited person Ofelia knew. The two of them connected almost immediately when she started in her current position as the English III and Creative Writing teacher at McKinley High. Willow said the reason they got along so well was due to their matching energies. Both women were insanely passionate, even to a fault, and preferred the company of each other over a large friend group.

"I think I made the top of Mrs. Davis' shit list. Ofelia groaned and reached for the proffered chocolate.

"Oh, that's right! I forgot you had to call that awful woman. I didn't realize Hell had cell service." Willow deadpanned.

Despite her best efforts, Ofelia laughed. The ball of anxiety brewing in her chest began to dissipate, but she still felt on edge. She was already behind schedule and when she glanced at the clock on her desktop computer, she realized practice started five minutes ago.

"Damn! I'm sorry Willow, I have to go. You didn't need something, did you?" She asked, frantically searching through her gym bag for her yoga pants and sports bra.

"Yes actually, but I don't think you're going to like it." Willow bit her lip, avoiding eye contact with Ofelia.

That was never a good sign.

"What is it?" A million thoughts ran through Ofelia's mind. Had she done her lesson plans? Had she somehow missed an observation or important deadline? She didn't think they were missing any books their English III students were reading because she had counted them herself this morning. She supposed it was possible that one of them accidentally got taken by a student but-

"It's about the gym."

Ofelia's blood went hot at the mention of her gym. The gym she had booked months in advance by attending every stupid meeting about the school's calendar and promptly submitting facility request forms. She even went as far as bribing the girls' basketball coach with a fresh batch of her famous empanadas, just to obtain an extra ten minutes of practice.

"What about the gym?" She couldn't hide the annoyance in her voice, trying hard not to aim her curt aggression towards Willow.

"Well..." Willow's voice went higher in pitch and suddenly seemed to find the pile of sticky notes on Ofelia's desk to be the most interesting thing in the room. Ofelia was trying really hard to keep her face curious rather than murderous.

"So, remember when you asked me to check if the gymnastic club had returned the blue mats?" Willow asked and Ofelia nodded. "Well, the good news is that the mats are there."

"But..?" Pulling teeth would have been less painful than getting Willow to speak. She loved her best friend, she did, but Willow had a way of dragging out the suspense.

"But...the bad news is that the gym was already in use."

"What?!" Who would have the audacity to take *her* gym during *her* scheduled practice hours? Especially with competition just around the corner. Although the other coaches didn't quite understand the importance of cheer and the scholarships her seniors could win if they placed highly at nationals, they typically respected her allotted time. Maybe if she finally brought home the big trophy, they might rethink their ignorance and even respect her sport.

"I think it was the baseball team because I didn't recognize the coach. You heard we got a new baseball coach, right? Old coach decided on an early retirement." Willow went on, oblivious to Ofelia's scowl. "So to be fair to him, I don't think he's been told about the calendar. Those things typically get overlooked during orientation."

Ofelia could accept that he was new and probably hadn't been told about the schedule, but she wouldn't allow him to take over her practice. The stakes were too high and she didn't need an audience while her cheerleaders were learning a new routine. They'd be distracted by the players and she needed their undivided attention.

"I'll just have to talk to the new coach then," Ofelia said, finally slipping on her yoga pants from behind her desk and discarding her chiffon skirt into her gym bag. "I'll deal with this, but thank you for telling me." She hoped her smile reached her eyes, but the exhaustion from today was pulling her down.

One more problem. She only had to deal with one more problem today.

Willow reached out and squeezed her arm, offering her a kind smile. "You are the most badass cheer coach and teacher I know. Don't let some guy come in and get you all shook up. Go take your gym back."

That was precisely what Ofelia planned to do. She hugged her friend before ushering Willow out, closing the door behind her. She finished changing and flung her gym bag over her shoulder with her head held high. If there was ever a day she needed a win, it was right now because it felt as if she was cursed. Or perhaps today was a test of her ability to keep calm under pressure. Except she felt like she was on the Titanic with no lifeboat and expected to keep the waters at bay. Oh, and just to add insult to injury, it was raining in this scenario.

*Bring on the storm*, she thought and walked out of her classroom.

The storm came in the form of two dozen teenage boys and an unfamiliar male. True to Willow's assessment, the baseball team - for some ungodly reason - decided today would be the perfect day to use the indoor facilities rather than their own field. Her squad stood outside the door, waiting on her expectantly to fix this mishap.

"Ms. Mendez, we should be practicing right now." One of her freshman cheerleaders supplied unhelpfully.

"I know. Just give me a moment to talk to him," she said, sounding more sure than she felt. Ofelia instructed her team to wait outside the gym while she went to speak to the coach. The baseball team sat in the middle of the floor staring at the back of the unfamiliar new coach. He sloppily wrote down different dates on a portable whiteboard, captivating his entire audience with the simple mundane task.

Ofelia must have made a sound, for every set of eyes in the room snapped in her direction. The man by the white board suddenly stopped writing to stare at her, giving Ofelia an unobstructed view of his entire profile.

Dear god he was one of the most handsome men she had ever laid eyes on. He was the epitome of "tall, dark, and handsome." His athletic body moved with such grace, reminding her of a sleek, black panther zeroing in on his target. She had never seen him before, because with a face and ass like that, he would have been the recurring star of all her wildest dreams. This man could easily fill in as a Michael B. Jordan stunt double.

He was tall, taller than her previous boyfriends, with muscles she only ever saw in movies or read about in books. Even behind his navy-blue t-shirt, she could see what lay underneath would be equally delicious. So much so that she wondered what it would be like to run her tongue along his—

No. Hell no. Stop that thought. Ofelia could not be lusting after this gym-stealing man in front of his team of smelly teenagers. This man was the enemy now, no matter how attractive he looked in those gray joggers...

"Can I help you, miss?"

He could do a whole lot more than help, but the words brewing inside her died on her lips as soon as she opened her mouth.

*Well shit.*

# Ofelia

## CHAPTER TWO

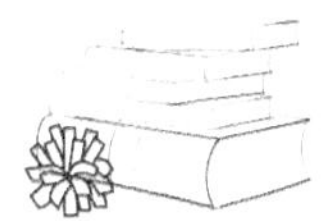

IT ONLY OCCURRED to Ofelia now that she'd been staring at the new coach this entire time, slack-jawed and silent. She hastily closed her mouth, face flushing with embarrassment. The students in front of him all stared expectantly, waiting for her to say something. Anything.

Words—she needed words.

After a few agonizing seconds, Ofelia found her voice. "Actually yes, you can." She tried to keep the full force of her annoyance out of her tone but was unsure how successful her attempt had been.

"I'm not sure if you glanced at the calendar, but on Mondays the gym is reserved for my cheer squad. Wednesdays too. We get the gym from four to seven. I'm afraid you're going to have to find somewhere else to hold your...well I don't exactly know what you're doing, but regardless you are going to have to move."

The man—she still did not know his name—raised a thick brow at her. His lips quirked into a smile, like he found the entire situation funny and didn't take her seriously. He poked the cheer momma bear, and he didn't even realize what he was about to unleash.

"Calendar? What calendar? I got to the gym at four and

nobody was here. Figured it was free for me and my baseball team to use." He shrugged.

"Well it's not. Free, I mean," Ofelia said, standing her ground. Every year she fought for her squad to get a practice space. The athletic department loved the funding her parents brought in, but they saw cheer as more of a hobby. Just a bunch of yelling and jumping around, people would say, dismissing everything she and her team worked so hard to accomplish.

"Anyways, wouldn't a baseball team want to practice outside? Where there are literal baseball fields for you to—" she gestured around at the boys' seated positions, "—do this?"

"Except our fields are currently undergoing last minute renovations for our first game tomorrow. So no, we can't do *this* outside. We need the gym for our team meeting and to run through drills," Coach Ass-hat said, not understanding the concept of a scheduled practice written in stone. Or, in her case, the official McKinley calendar.

Ofelia didn't give a damn about his fields. There were other perfectly good places he could go to get his precious practice in. Of course, she supposed he could make the same argument for her squad, but it was the principle of the matter. She had fought so hard for gym rights, and she would be damned if she let Coach Ass-hat waltz in and take her prize.

"I'm not sure how your fields not being ready is suddenly my problem," she said, earning some *ooohs* from the baseball team, their heads swiveling between the two teachers, watching a very chaotic tennis match unfold.

"Damn Ms. Mendez, you got some balls on you." One of the players called out. It was a familiar voice, but she couldn't quite place it.

"Cambridge! Take a lap. Don't speak to teachers that way."

"Aw, hell coach Wilson, I'm just messing around!" Nick Cambridge, who Ofelia knew from her second period English III class, complained as his buddies pushed him to his feet.

So Coach Ass-hat had a name. Wilson. She made a mental

note to learn everything she could about this man, one whose sole purpose seemed to be pissing her off.

Coach Wilson waited until Nick took off before parting the sea of baseball players to cross the gym floor and stand directly in front of her. Ofelia had to tilt her head up to see him properly. He was big, bigger than what she expected. He towered over her as if she were nothing more than a petulant child. Honestly, Ofelia sort of felt that way due to his presence. His very handsome and intimidating presence. Still, she refused to back up or give him any indication he affected her at all.

"I know jack about cheerleading, but isn't your season over?" He asked, confused.

That statement alone was far more than many people knew about her cheer season. And although yes, he technically was correct because Ofelia should have been prepping for the final competition, not their first, their season had been pushed back by a few months due to later school start. At first Ofelia had flipped out in the change of schedule, but then—after being reminded by Willow that this would give her more time to prepare—she eventually grew accustomed to the idea. Not like there was much she could do about it anyway.

"Later start date this school year. Competitions were pushed back to accommodate." She shrugged, but Coach Ass-Hat didn't appear to be paying attention to her anymore.

"Listen," Wilson finally said, dropping his authoritative tone. "I didn't realize there was a calendar. I was just hired and I didn't get the whole run down. Bottom line, I need this gym. The best I can do is split it with you, but I'm not leaving. It's for one practice. Do you really need the entire gym to skip around and belt out ancient cheers? Doesn't seem like that big of a deal."

"Excuse me?" Ofelia's blood boiled. Damn him for being like every other person who didn't see value in what she did. Who was he to dictate the rules of the gym during *her* practice? He might not understand what this meant to her, but Ofelia had a lot riding on this competition. She'd been a cheer coach for the past two years and hadn't placed at nationals yet. This *had* to be her year. "We do not skip or belt. If you believe that is all cheerleaders do, then you are sadly mistaken. You also sound like a misogynist, so please refrain from insulting me and my squad again."

A slight twitch in Wilson's brow was the only indication Ofelia got under his skin. Good. Let him stew in agitation. She had a younger sibling; she knew exactly how to slither under people's skin. Just ask her brother. If Wilson wanted to play the intimidating stare down game all day, she would gladly oblige.

To her satisfaction, Wilson looked away first. Ha! Victory! At least that was how she felt until he turned around and started to walk back towards his team. He cast one look over his shoulder and shouted, "Half the gym! Take it or leave it."

AFTER HER UNSUCCESSFUL attempts to win back the gym space, Ofelia left with what little of her dignity remained. She most certainly didn't look like the weaker dog that lost a fight and now had to retreat with her tail tucked between her legs. Nope, definitely nothing like that.

Except for the fact that was exactly what happened, and she feared it was written across her very tired face.

The moment she walked out of the gym door she stood face-to-face with her entire squad.

"So, why are we only getting half the gym?" Lacey, Cheer Captain and senior, asked. There was an edge of annoyance to her voice, which wasn't unusual for Lacey and her perfectionist qualities, but it still grated on Ofelia's nerves.

Unfortunately, she had no other explanation than the truth. She told her squad, hoping for an ounce of sympathy from the group but the verdict was split. Some looked perturbed and rightfully so, but she wasn't certain if their annoyance stemmed from the intruders occupying the gym or her inability to regain control over the situation. The others looked almost giddy at the thought of sharing the space with the baseball team.

Ugh, hormones.

It shouldn't be a big deal; she could easily waltz back inside and conduct practice like she always did. Except Coach Wilson would also be conducting his baseball meeting. Just the thought of the man sent shivers down her spine, which wasn't all from disgust. Damn, she seriously needed to get out more.

She had no other choice but to put on her big girl panties and take the initiative. Channeling her mother's 'take no shit' attitude, she said, "This isn't anything we can't handle. We'll ignore the boys, and they'll ignore us. It's one day and then the gym will be ours again. Pay them no mind."

There was still time to stick with Ofelia's original plan, which consisted of their series of warm-ups before they moved on running through their competition choreography. Their performance at regionals needed to be nothing shy of fantastic because it would set the tone for the remainder of the season.

Her plan had not come to fruition. The moment Ofelia walked back inside with twelve girls and two boys that made up her entire Small Varsity Co-Ed team, the mood in the gym instantly shifted. If she didn't know better, she would have thought they were the Montagues, stepping into Capulet territory.

Lacey scoffed, shooting daggers at a few of the baseball players unfortunate enough to be within breathing distance. "They aren't even moving and they already smell. Do you think it's a qualification to be a baseball player? You must smell like horse manure at all times."

"Shut up, Lacey, you're distracting me," Tony said, the only junior who could go head-to-head with Lacey and not shrink under her scrutiny. "You're talking is keeping me from admiring the muscled artwork in front of me."

Lacey scrunched up her face in disgust. "God, baseball boys? Seriously? You realize that baseball is like, the most redneck-y sport, and these 'bros' are most definitely exuding toxic masculinity."

"First off, that's an overgeneralization. Right Ms. M?" Tony asked, causing Ofelia to smile despite the situation. At least she knew some of her students paid attention in class. "Secondly, I'm pretty sure the most redneck sport is NASCAR. And thirdly, baseball players are sexy. I mean, think of how well they can handle their ba—"

"There will be none of that," Ofelia piped up before Tony finished his comment. The hardest part about being a teacher or coach was holding back laughter after a student said something funny and wildly inappropriate. She tried to disguise it with a cough, because seriously, didn't she think the same thing when she looked at the major league baseball players? Not that she watched much baseball. Her father and brother were soccer fans but watched the occasional baseball game from time to time.

"You aren't scared of a few baseball guys, are you Lace?" Came a teasing voice belonging to the only other male on the team. Devin was another senior who had been on the team since his junior year. Part of the reason he joined, Ofelia suspected, was to get closer to Lacey. Anyone could see just how bad he had it for her. Lacey pretended to be annoyed by his attention, but her eyes always wandered over to him when she thought no one was looking.

"Please, the only thing I'm worried about is the drool they will inevitably leave behind when they watch us warm up."

That was her cue to start practice, especially considering they wasted enough time dealing with Coach Wilson. Ofelia pretended like she couldn't hear the baseball team behind her as they also began to move into their workout routine, even when the gym grew exceptionally louder with the sounds of grunts and squeaky shoes. It was, however, nothing a little music couldn't dull.

Ariana Grande, to be exact.

The moment "Thank U, Next" hit her portable speaker and engulfed the room with Ari singing of lost love, Ofelia instantly felt more in her element. This was exactly what she needed after a long day of teaching, dealing with a deplorable parent, and fighting with the new hire. When she stretched, she could turn off her brain and let her body move of its own accord.

She led her squad through their normal warm up routine, slowly walking her hands down her body until she placed them firmly on the ground. One of her legs stretched far behind her while the other stayed rooted in front of her, drawing her chest close. Their breathing techniques came into play next. One long ten second inhale followed by a slow exhale while they pressed forward on their front knee, deepening the stretch. Ofelia felt the stretch in her hamstrings, bringing forth a delightful tingling sensation.

She was about to switch legs when the music stopped abruptly. "What—"

But a deep voice cut her off. "What are you doing?" He asked, his voice a mixture of annoyance and incredulity.

Ofelia didn't need to look up to see who stood above her, berating her. She may have only just met him, but the voice was permanently filed away under "Coach Ass-hat." Which is why she took her time getting up, feeling his eyes track her every move until she stood toe-to-toe with him.

Ass-hat's proximity reminded her how gorgeous this man truly was. His attitude should really fit his appearance. He was far better suited as a bridge goblin, or perhaps a lumpy troll.

"Is something the matter?" She asked innocently, getting a thrill from watching the man play through various stages of exasperation.

"Your music's what's the matter. It's distracting my guys. They can't hear me yell orders over the screeching."

"Would you prefer 'Take me out to the Ball Game?' I'm sure I can find a 2-hour loop version on YouTube if I tried."

That earned her a few snickers from both the cheerleaders and a few baseball players. It provided a small boost of confidence she didn't know she needed.

Ass-hat whirled around at his snickering players and ordered them to take a lap around the gym in typical coach fashion. It was so cliché that Ofelia nearly rolled her eyes at him, until he turned back to her and said, "No Ariana. No 'Take me out to the Ball Game.' You might be trying to relive your high school glory days, but some of us are trying to work. Just stick with your vapid cheers, and we won't have a problem."

Without another word, Wilson stormed away, going back to his side of the gym. He didn't glance back once; in fact, he seemed keen on forgetting Ofelia existed. She felt the stinging in her eyes, tears threatening to fall. She wasn't about to cry over some dick who never learned how to share. No, she wanted to cry because she was so frustrated with people always belittling her. This wasn't the first time a man disappointed her. Wilson was her colleague, not her superior. He had no right to tell her what she could and could not do at her own damn practice.

"Dang Ms. Mendez, who peed in his cereal this morning?" Tony asked, shaking his head. "Do you want me to egg his car? Because I can so egg his car."

"You can't egg his car, moron. Especially since you just told a teacher you plan on doing it," Lacey said, no real venom behind her words. Although they may bicker, the cheer squad was a tight-knit group, and no one messed with any cheerleader except for one another. That included Ofelia, which lessened the lump in her throat, knowing her team loved her as much as she loved them.

"As appealing as that offer sounds, Tony. We are just going to ignore him. To use your phrase, I don't know who peed in his cereal, but we aren't going to let that affect us. We can't control his actions, but we can control ours. So let's choose to be the bigger people. Coach ass-Wilson—" She coughed, stopping his nickname she created from slipping out. "—is perhaps having a bad day."

"He's about to have a really bad day when I egg his car after practice," Tony whispered loudly to Devin.

"No egging, Tony. I'm serious. Devin, you are on Tony duty after practice. Make sure he gets home having touched no eggs."

"You got it Ms. Mendez." Devin grinned, saluting her and playfully bumped his elbow into his friend's side. "You heard the teacher—no eggs for you."

# Maverick

## CHAPTER THREE

He was being a dick.

Maverick realized this the second he walked away from the wide-eyed cheer coach. If he had been a better man, he would have turned around and apologized right then and there. It was just music for fuck's sake and it wasn't harming anyone. Except she had to be playing *that* song. He didn't make it a habit to hate music, but that particular song had been one of her favorites and Maverick didn't need to be reminded of her. No, in fact, he needed to never think about that woman again.

Not thinking about her was harder these days. Breanna had been such a huge part of his life for so long, losing her felt like losing a version of himself. He did not know how to act. Breanna had called him at least a half dozen times since their highly publicized and messy breakup, but he never answered or listened to any of the messages she left him. Maverick have been tempted on more than one occasion, but it had become easier to delete and forget than rehashing a scenario neither of them could fix.

Instead of taking his anger out on the actual person who deserved every ounce of his vexation, he took it out on the pretty coach. What a way to make a fucking first impression.

Throughout the remainder of practice, or more accurately

work out since they couldn't use the field, Maverick continued to sneak glances at the woman. Her students called her Ms. Mendez, and they looked at her as if she hung the moon every night. He wondered if she knew how much her cheerleaders loved her when it was clearly written across all their faces.

Maverick was under no illusion he would ever be looked at by his players the same way the cheerleaders looked at Ms. Mendez. Even though they looked at him with awe, and some with pity, it was never out of love or respect. It was because he used to be someone. But his time in the spotlight had come and gone in the blink of an eye.

A year ago, if someone came up to him and said he would be teaching at a suburban high school in Texas, Maverick would have laughed in their face and then called security to get that person out of his line of sight.

Now he was nothing more than a glorified babysitter. Actually, babysitting might have paid more than this coaching job.

The only reason he came into coaching was due to his former manager taking pity on him. Maverick had been shunned, cast out of the major leagues just as he was working his way to the top. He could have been big, could have made a name for himself if only...

No, he refused to finish that thought. No good came from reliving those memories and opening still healing wounds. Keanon, his former manager, had made sure Maverick didn't fall on his ass when he plummeted from his high horse. "Listen man," he had told him the last day Maverick had been in Chicago, "I think time away will do you some good. My sister-in-law is an assistant principal or something down in Texas. They are always looking for coaches and I'll put in a good word for you. Don't you worry about housing or nothing. I got that covered too. I want you to focus on your damn self. Okay, man? Can you do that?"

It wasn't until he moved that he realized Keanon had been his only friend. He had people who wanted to be around him, sure. But did any of them ever reach out to him after that fateful night?

Or the day after when he found out only seconds before the public that he had been banned from the major leagues?

No. Only Keanon. Granted, Keanon had been his manager, so he was hurting from the ban as well, but the man at least made sure Maverick had other things lined up before leaving Chicago.

Keanon even texted him just to make sure Maverick was okay, but he was the furthest thing from okay. He used to wake up feeling like the king of Chicago. Now he felt very little at all. Each day was a series of tasks to complete, only to wake up and do it all over again.

This wasn't the life he wanted.

Yet he was here, and Maverick had to make the most of it. Teaching high schoolers wasn't glamorous, but it paid the bills and connected him to his past life.

"Coach Wilson," a voice called, drawing Maverick out of the past and back into the present. Damn, how long had he been working on autopilot? Only a handful of his boys were still in the gym. Three remained, his starting pitcher, catcher, and third baseman, sprawled across the bleachers. "You kicked our asses today."

No, he really hadn't, but that's what happens McKinley's team goes from an incompetent coach who couldn't tell the difference between shortstop and second baseman, to him, a former MLB player. He worked the boys through a series of warm ups mirroring his old routines. It got the heart racing, but wasn't meant to exhaust his players. To his team's credit, not a single one complained.

At least not to his face.

"Coach, do you think any of your old teammates will come and watch one of our games?" Dustin asked. Dustin was the third baseman, a tall, lanky kid who seemed oblivious to the art of proper conversation. His teammate next to him - Maverick couldn't remember the name since all the blonde kids blurred together - elbowed him in the side, a clear signal to shut up. Dustin, being Dustin, couldn't read the fucking room and glared at his friend. "What? Just because he's banned doesn't mean he doesn't have friends in the league."

Maverick wished he could say this conversation was the first time his ban was brought up by a student, faculty member, or any other asshole that stopped him on the streets, but sadly he'd lost count. Surprisingly enough, no one asked why. They were leeches who wanted nothing more than to ride on the back of one man's misery hoping it would make them feel better about their own wretched lives.

Normally Maverick would walk away or tell the person to fuck off but considering he was now employed at a high school; he doubted his administration would look kindly on either option. Also, from what he heard, Dustin had a rather aggressive helicopter mother who enjoyed picking fights with the school staff. Overbearing mothers were a good enough reason to not engage.

"Locker rooms. Shower. Now. I'm sick of smelling the three of you." Maverick ushered the boys along, unable to make out their faint grumblings. Fortunately, they didn't put up much more of a fight, immediately getting distracted by the departing cheerleaders. None of them returned the unwarranted attention, except a short, skinny male who decided to blow kisses in their direction.

High schoolers were a different breed.

Turning back around, Maverick caught Ms. Mendez from the corner of his eyes. She just finished folding up a giant blue mat and now attempted to pick it up. This gave Maverick a perfect view of her ass. The gentlemanly thing to do would have been to look away, but he already established he was no gentleman. The woman before him had a body meant to be worshiped.

No, he couldn't think like that. Not only was he recovering from a messy breakup of ten years, but he already ruined any chances he may have had with this woman. He regretted that now.

"Here, let me help you." The words left Maverick's lips before he had a chance to stop them. In three long strides, he closed the distance between him and Ms. Mendez – he really needed to learn her first name. She wasn't wearing a badge, so his fruitless search looked like he was checking out her chest.

Another dick move.

The cheer coach frowned, noticing where his eyes were currently located. Not only was he a giant ass in her eyes, but he was also a perv now. "I don't need your help, thanks." The woman said curtly, continuing to haul the blue mats to stack them in the corner of the gym. She lifted them high, giving Maverick a good show of her toned arms. How was it that this woman made something as mundane as lifting mats sexy?

Yeah, definitely not helping the perv thing.

Before he had a chance to dig himself deeper into a hole, she turned around, her hair whipping to attention as if it too were mad at Maverick. If her hair were snakes and she was Medusa, there was a one hundred percent chance that he'd be nothing but stone right now.

"If you ever embarrass me in front of my cheerleaders again, I'll bury you so deep in grievances you'll never see the light of day again," Ms. Mendez snapped, showing off a different side to the gentle persona she originally gave off. And damn if he didn't like fiery, passionate women. It was one of the reasons he was in his current predicament.

But they had successfully shared the gym, so she couldn't hold this over his head forever. He hoped.

"Noted. Grievances. Deep hole." He listed off, watching the smallest quirk of her lips. If he hadn't been studying her so profusely, he'd never have noticed the almost-smirk he elicited from her. He wondered what it would be like to earn a full smile from this woman for no other reason other than wanting to see her lips stretch into something other than a frown.

Maverick wouldn't be getting anything out of the woman though, for she pushed past him without so much as a goodbye. Her smell, vanilla and honey, lingered after she left. If he wasn't careful, Maverick could easily get distracted by a certain temperamental Latina woman. He made up his mind right there and then that the next time he saw Ms. Mendez, he would get her first name. There wasn't any harm in asking for a name. He couldn't keep calling her Ms. Mendez the rest of his employment.

There was absolutely no other reason Maverick wanted her name other than to get to know his coworkers. No other motive whatsoever.

Oh, how easy it was to lie to himself these days.

*Ofelia*

## CHAPTER FOUR

IT WASN'T every day you got to threaten the gorgeous, but definitely dickish, gym teacher with complaints, but today was quickly becoming a week of firsts. Did Ofelia regret her words or temper when he tried to apologize to her? Nope. The man definitely deserved her anger for how much of a tool he had been in front of a large group of students. It was completely unprofessional.

However, she couldn't help the wicked sense of pride that filled her stomach when she thought back to the way he looked at her. Never in her twenty-six years of life had she been more tempted to look back as she stormed away to check to see if Coach Wilson was checking out her ass. But she felt like that would have ruined the pissed off attitude she was trying to relay, so despite wanting nothing more than to turn around and peek...she didn't.

If that wasn't a testament to her willpower, then it most certainly would be surviving the rest of the week being the bad ass English teacher and cheerleading coach she was.

By the time Ofelia pulled into the driveway of her bright yellow craftsman Friday evening, all thoughts of Coach Wilson were pushed deep into the recesses of her mind. Mostly. She wasn't blind. The man was sex on a stick, but he'd be one stick

29

she'd stay far away from except when she was forced to cross paths with him in the hallway throughout the week.

Living alone had its perks. For one, no one was there to immediately attack her with questions about her day. Especially a day like today where she would undoubtedly lose the fragile control over her emotions. Ofelia was an ugly crier, the less who saw it the better. Her past roommates compared her to a wailing banshee. Which...harsh, but accurate.

So no, no human greeted her at the door, but two furry creatures did. Leila, a beautiful, chubby calico cat, brushed against Ofelia's leg. No doubt depositing all her fur into that one spot. Her other cat, a beautiful gray tabby named Stella, continued to rest peacefully atop her couch. The only acknowledgement Stella gave to Ofelia's presence was a slight raising of her head, then right back into nap mode.

"Hello, my babies," she spoke in that high pitched voice most people reserved for infants and toddlers. Yes it was annoying, but no one was here to judge her. "Did you miss mommy today? 'Cause I missed you soooo much," she cooed and bent down to scoop up Leila. The cat in question was not light and tried, unsuccessfully, to escape her loving embrace. But Ofelia had a hard day and she just wanted to be loved, dammit! Eventually, Leila accepted her fate and leaned into her nuzzling, purring in contentment.

Yes, she was a crazy cat lady who loved literature. She knew damn well she fit all the cliches, but after moving thousands of miles away from her family, Ofelia was fine taking solace in books and cats. It made the pain of leaving her home state of California a bit more bearable.

Knowing she put Leila through enough emotional abuse, she finally released her onto the couch, where she swatted at her sister until both were curled up together.

Not having the energy to cook, she declared today an Uber Eats sort of night. The question was, what type of food did she want to drown her sorrows in? Mexican food was good for cleansing the soul, but something about Chinese food always provided a certain level of comfort when one was wallowing in self pity.

Hmm, decisions, decisions.

Ultimately, and to no one's surprise, Ofelia went with Chinese food. The only Mexican food she truly wanted was that of her mother's, but her mother passed away nearly five years ago, taking away the most loving and supportive person in her life. Mexican food didn't measure up when her mother wasn't the one to cook and serve it. It made her regret not paying better attention to her mother when she attempted to teach Ofelia how to make some of her classic dishes. As much as she tried to replicate her mother's cooking, it never quite tasted the same.

An hour later, Ofelia was showered, dressed in her coziest pajamas, and lounging on her couch with her shrimp fried rice nestled neatly in her lap. The tv was showing some reality TV series about couples from different parts of the world and the absolute shit show their relationships were. There was something cathartic about watching other people's drama unfold and real- izing your life, in comparison, wasn't all that bad.

Ofelia's life wasn't bad. Not really. She had a job that she loved and adored which allowed her to teach a subject she loved. She had friends, or rather *friend*, whom she loved as much as a sister. And she had a cozy home, close to work. She was truly grateful for these positive accomplishments, but that didn't stop the ache in her heart each time she thought about home and all she left behind.

For starters, her father, brother, and two-year old niece still lived in California. Her mother was buried at the cemetery near her childhood home, a quick ten minute walk from her brother's current residence. Family was everything to her and leaving them had been one of the hardest decisions of her life, but a necessary one.

California held memories that she once held dear, ones that now cut like a knife. Because her favorite coffee shop back home was no longer a place she could go when she needed to escape into a book. She couldn't enter the grocery store near her childhood home without looking over her shoulder because she was terrified she would run into *him*.

She was even more terrified when she eventually ran into him —because in her small town it would only be a matter of time— he'd be happy. For her, the pain of the fateful evening still felt so raw, a festering wound too stubborn to heal properly. A wound she could not discuss to even her best friend, despite the fact it had been five years since it happened.

Ofelia shook her head, placing what remained of her dinner on her side table. She would not allow herself to succumb to the sadness haunting her from that day. Not when he didn't give two shits about her and was probably balls deep in whatever body warmed his bed this week.

Fuck, she was doing it again: thinking too hard that she was bound to hurt her own feelings.

Needing a distraction, Ofelia searched the couch for her phone. The copious amounts of pillows and blankets stacked around her like a personal fort seemed good at the time, but now it had eaten her phone.

"Damnit, where did-ah!" She broke her sentence off with a triumphant yell, raising her phone as if she had just found the holy grail. To her, at least, it was. It provided her a way to see her family and nothing was more important to her.

Scrolling through her contacts, Ofelia hovered over her father's number. She hesitated, wondering whether or not she should call Javier instead. She knew it ultimately wouldn't matter since her father and brother lived at the same house and she would end up talking to her father regardless. She adored the man, but sometimes Ofelia felt that their love only ran surface level. Her father loved her because he was her father and fathers were supposed to love their children. Just as daughters were supposed to love their fathers. It was an easy role that both of them fell into, but provided very little room for anything other than pleasantries.

To hell with it though. After her day, she would be willing to talk to a third cousin, twice removed if that meant she could speak with family.

Ofelia clicked on her father's contact and then pressed the FaceTime button. She watched as her face engulfed her screen, making sure she looked presentable and not like she just had a shitty week dealing with entitled assholes.

It took two rings before her father answered, showing only the top of his head. He sported a new cut, shaved close to his head. He must have dyed his hair recently because there were no longer gray stands weaving throughout the black ones. "Hola, mija."

Despite her earlier uncertainties, Ofelia's eyes stung with tears that she desperately tried to hold back. "Papá." Ofelia smiled widely. "Papá, hold the phone down so I can see you."

"Qué?" Her father asked, jostling the phone some before he understood. "Ah, okay. Can you see me now?" He asked, his thick Mexican accent sounding like home. She really needed to go up and visit soon.

"Yes papá, I can see you. How are you? How's work?" She asked. Her father was technically retired but still occasionally took on an odd job and babysat so her younger brother Javier could work. From what Javi told her, Camilia was a full-time job. Much to her dismay, she had only seen her niece through Facetime, but even she knew Javier had his hands full with his spitfire daughter.

"Busy, all day busy. Ella is...cómo se dice salvaje en Inglés?"

"Wild?"

He nodded, looking very much like a bobblehead as he did so. "Sí. Wild. Just like your mother. Scary too when she's angry."

Ofelia laughed at the image of a tiny two-year-old making a grown man cower in fear. Ofelia might have a precarious relationship with her father, but he was a fantastic grandfather to Camilia.

"How are you, my little *maestra*? Are the kids good?" Her father asked and she just shrugged. Ofelia didn't want to get into school.

"Fine. Everything's fine."

Her father nodded, getting distracted with something in the background. Knowing him, some sport was playing. She tried not to let it bother her, but was it too much to ask for five minutes of uninterrupted visiting? She knew they did not have many things in common, but they were still family. That had to count for something.

"Oh hey, don't you have one of your first dance thingies coming up?" He asked and Ofelia did her best not to roll her eyes at his "dance thingie" comment. She had only been going to *cheer competitions* since she was a little girl.

"In a few weeks, yeah. I sent you over the dates to all of our competitions. Why?"

"I'd like to come."

Ofelia could not have been more shocked if her dad had burst out into interpretative dancing, complete with a pink tutu and a matching tiara. She was gaping, and almost certain she blacked out for a second because there was no way her father, the man who never made it to a single competition in her life, was suddenly willing to fly thousands of miles to watch her high school team perform. This did not sound like her father at all. Not even a little.

She waited for the *'just kidding* or *got you there!'* But it never came. "You're serious?" She asked, her voice laced with disbelief.

Her father clearly did not realize he successfully broke his daughter with one statement. "Yes I'm serious. Javi said I should go."

She did her best not to deflate after hearing that the only reason he decided to finally come to one of her competitions was because Javi put him up to it. He knew how hard it was for her last year not to have her mother there to support her coaching career. She imagined he spoke at length with her father until he got tired of hearing Javi pester him and just agreed. Still, it was better than nothing.

"O...kay." Ofelia said slowly, allowing him one last chance to back out. When he didn't take it, a hesitant smile began to form on her lips. "Well, wow. Okay, so I'll have Javi help you with tickets. I'll send over information about the hotel. Wow Papá, this is exciting!"

Since moving down to Texas two years ago, none of her family had been able to make it down for a visit. This hurt her in the beginning, but she realized her selfishness. Her brother worked and had a child. It wasn't easy for Javi to do much of anything, much less get time off from work to take the entire family down to Texas. He wasn't in the financial situation to do that and her brother was too stubborn to ask for help.

Stubbornness was definitely a shared family trait.

"Papá, is Javi home from work yet? I want to talk to him, and I'll mention you're interested in coming down to watch the competition." Like he did not already know.

"Si, mi amor." Her father rose from his spot at the table, looking all too eager to pass her off so he could get back to watching whatever game he had on. The screen suddenly went dark as soft and undecipherable mumbles filled the line.

Then a lamp flipped on, illuminating a small bedroom. Javier filled the screen, looking tired and rumpled, as if she had just woken him up from a nap. Before she could apologize, Javi put his finger to his lips in a universal "be quiet" sign. He untangled himself from his bed and only then did Ofelia see a small lump curled up in the blankets.

Camilia.

"Sorry, just got her to bed. Little brat won't sleep in her own bed these days," Javier said, but when he spoke of his little girl, there was nothing but fondness in his voice. It was so beautiful to see her little brother become a father. Camilia had changed him, changed all of them. She also saved Javi after the death of Estella, Camilia's mother.

"She's so big, Javi. How can she be so big when she was so tiny last week?"

Javier laughed. "Shit, I dunno. I ask myself that daily. I feel like I'll be moving her into college next week."

"Oh god, don't say that. Do you know how old I'll be? Forty-three. Forty-fucking-three. I'm not going to be the young, hot auntie anymore."

"I wasn't aware you were the young, hot aunt now." Javi teased.

"First off, pendejo, that was rude as hell. And secondly, just because you're somebody's father now doesn't mean I won't kick your ass the next time I see you."

Her very serious threat was meant by a loud snort, followed by laughter. Yup, that definitely didn't help her ego, but it was worth it to hear his laugh. Javi rarely laughed these days. Not since the accident.

"So, what's on your mind? Did you call to threaten me?" Javier asked, his focus back on Ofelia. Typical for him to get straight to the point.

"Not to threaten, but I do have a question. Papá just said he was interested in coming down to my competition this year. He's literally never been. You wouldn't happen to know anything about that, would you?" She stared at him pointedly.

Javi put on his best clueless face and shrugged, though a small smile creased the corner of his lips. He would never outright admit he did something nice for her, but that was all the confirmation she needed. "Any other reason you called?" He asked, clearly not going to answer her.

"I just...missed you. All of my family."

Javi adjusted himself and moved closer to the camera. His eyes bore into Ofelia's, causing her to stir. Damn him. She knew what those eyes were searching for. Breakage. Any signs to indicate that Ofelia was moments away from a full on ugly cry. Even though she was supposed to be the big sister and take care of him, Javi always reversed those roles and did it without complaint.

"Tell me what's wrong," he said, leaving no room for argument.

Ofelia had none. She opened her mouth to speak, but the only thing that came out was a rather embarrassing whimper. Her warm brown eyes filled with tears. She seriously hated crying, but her emotions needed a release. In retrospect, today hadn't been entirely terrible, but it was the straw that broke the camel's back.

This camel had come to Texas damaged too, so she had already been at a disadvantage.

"Do you think I made a mistake? Leaving town?" She asked, feeling vulnerable and a little silly to finally say the words constantly plaguing her thoughts. "Did I make a rash decision to leave like a coward?"

Javi let out a deep sigh, his face softening at her words. There he went again, being the best damn little brother ever when she knew he was fighting his own demons. Who was she to dump more trauma on him?

"I'm sorry Javi. I shouldn't—"

"You should." He interrupted before she could tell him to just forget about it. "You should come to me and talk about your problems. I'm your brother, Ofi. *Familia.* You know I'm here to listen."

Despite her tears, she couldn't help but let out a weak laugh. "We sound like a scene from a Hallmark channel."

Javi smiled at that and nodded. "Yeah, probably a bit. It's true though. Listen, Ofi. You needed to get out. It wasn't an easy decision, but we all understood why. We wanted to see you happy and if moving to Texas did that for you, we weren't going to stand in your way. It was brave as hell, honestly. Something mamá would have done. You deserve a fresh start."

A fresh start.

That's what she had called it too when she left a little over two years ago. When her life had come to an abrupt stop. She remembered that day vividly, for it felt like an out of body experience. She saw herself in the hotel room, sobbing into her pillow. There were a few others in there with her, mostly family and even his sister. Ofelia remembered *his* sister, Analucia, attempting to comfort her, but she was so lost in her own grief. She snapped at the woman, blaming all of her brother's sins on her.

It wasn't fair and she wasn't proud of her behavior. Analucia didn't deserve her wraith. Her brother Hector did.

"Have you seen him around?" *Is he still hurting or was mine the only heart to break that day?* Was the question Ofelia truly wanted to ask, but she was afraid of the answer.

Javi looked uncomfortable, which only confirmed her suspicions.

So he *had* seen Hector. Why was he so unwilling to talk to her about it? Was it because Hector wasn't alone? Was he with someone else? It had been two years after all, and just because she hadn't dated since the day he left her, didn't mean Hector also stayed single. Did she care if he was dating someone else? Yes...no...fuck she didn't know.

"Yeah, I saw him." Javi finally admitted. "And Analucia a few times. Hector steers clear of me each time he sees me. Which is smart. I swear if I ever get that bastard alone, I'll—"

"Do nothing. You'll do nothing." Ofelia reprimanded. Not out of loyalty to her ex, but out of concern for her brother. "Call him all the dirty names in your mind. Hell, imagine kicking his ass, but under no circumstances will you engage. Do you understand me? He's not worth it. Camilia doesn't need to see that side of her father." Ofelia didn't actually think her brother would lay a hand on Hector...probably. He wasn't a fighter, at least not in that way. He had never been one for petty drama or relish in his own superiority. He was, however, extremely protective and would defend his family. Perhaps not with fist, but if Hector threw the first punch, she doubted her baby brother would just sit there and take the beating.

Despite having her heart ripped out by this man, Ofelia didn't want to see any harm come his way. It was a terrible burden to have such a good conscience.

"Whatever. No hurting that asshole. I'll just glare at him until he spontaneously combusts."

"Seems fair." Ofelia agreed, smiling at her brother.

"Is there anything else on your mind? Or did you call to see my sexy face?"

Ofelia made a retching sound, which she was sure made her look like a cat hacking out a hairball. If she were next to her brother, she'd playfully shove him. "No, you dummy. I just had a long day at work so far."

"Evil parents?"

"The evilest!"

"I'm no English teacher like you, Ofi, but even I know that evilest isn't a word."

"Actually it is," Ofelia said, ready to dive into the history of etymology, but Javier pretended to fall asleep. Her useless knowledge on words and their origins never got the proper respect it deserved.

"Anyways," Ofelia continued, her voice raising an octave to get his attention. Javier opened one eye, a smile playing on her brother's lips. "I just called to vent about crazy parents and an asshole coach."

"There was an asshole coach?"

"Yeah. Truthfully he just annoyed me and was being a bit of a jerk. It was just a lousy way to end my day. I probably shouldn't be keeping you any longer though." Ofelia noticed the time at the top of her phone. It was only a quarter past eight, but her brother woke up even earlier than her. His job was pure physical labor. He tried to hide how tired he was, but she had the sneaking suspicion he could fall asleep right now if he tried.

"Give Camilia a big kiss for me and tell her *tía* Ofi loves her so much." Ofelia felt a surge of emotion in her chest, something she always got when speaking about her niece. It was a mixture of regret, longing, and love. Even though she was far away, she wanted Camilia to know she was so important in Ofelia's life. "I love you, Javi. I'll call you soon."

Javi's smile lit up her camera screen. For a brief moment, she could still see the nine-year-old little brother in him that equally annoyed and delighted her. "I love you too, Ofi. I'm just a call away." He winked and then Ofelia was no longer looking at her brother, but the background on her phone.

The ache in her chest eased only a fraction, but it was enough for her to wind down from the day. Getting up, she placed the remainder of her Chinese dinner in the fridge to have for lunch tomorrow, checked her school email once more to make sure nothing urgent awaited her, and finally moved into her bedroom.

Ofelia fell asleep the moment her head hit her pillow, plagued with dreams of a certain hot coach with a bad attitude.

# Maverick

## CHAPTER FIVE

SLEEPING ALONE WAS new for Maverick.

He used to have a partner. Now he only had memories of their time together to haunt his dreams. These days Maverick went to sleep alone and woke up alone. There was once a time in his life when he complained he didn't have enough room in bed. Breanna had insisted she needed the middle of the bed, out of fear of rolling over and falling out of bed. Maverick never understood how a grown woman could have problems staying in bed, but he never pushed it.

He grew used to Breanna and her *unique* tendencies long ago. They had grown up together. In elementary, their friendship began, like most childhood friendships do, at recess. Where the other students had cowered at the bottom of the monkey bars, Breanna had been fearless. Each monkey bar she grabbed was like watching someone compete in the junior olympics.

That was all it took for five-year-old Maverick to fall in love.

Of course, his and Breanna's love story didn't start until freshman year of high school. It wasn't until the homecoming dance that Maverick finally got the courage to ask Breanna out. As much as he wanted to say he had game and was smooth with the ladies, Maverick was fairly certain he blacked out when he asked her to be his date. Smooth, he was not.

Even with his piss poor game, Maverick still scored the hottest and smartest girl at school. Their relationship survived high school, moving on to college where he received a full ride to the University of Miami. Breanna agreed to accompany him; she even received her own Volleyball scholarship to the university.

When he was drafted to Chicago, Maverick promised he would make an honest woman out of Breanna, but neither one of them were in a hurry to schedule a date for their wedding. They both agreed the right moment would come eventually.

Except that moment never came.

Looking back, there had been signs. He had just refused to accept them. He didn't acknowledge the way Breanna smiled when she looked at her phone, or the way she started to dress when she went "shopping." No, Maverick could ignore those things as long as the sex was good. Because if the sex was good, then there was no possible way their ten-year relationship was crumbling around them.

He couldn't remember when sex became more of a competition, rather than a form of expression. Or perhaps he did and once again his mind refused to dive any deeper. His brain knew before his heart and tried to protect him for as long as possible.

When the dam finally broke, releasing a flood of secrets and deceit, Maverick lost everything. His life, his future wife, and his career.

So yeah, he was still getting used to sleeping alone. The world spun too fast and Maverick couldn't plant his feet firmly under him.

Rolling over, he reached out blindly into the dark until his hand connected with his phone sitting on his nightstand. He braced himself for the unholy glow his phone cast in the dark before checking the time. It was five in the morning. His body wanted nothing more than to stay in bed, but his mind was alert and functioning on full power. Nothing unsettled him more than being alone with his thoughts. That and the red notification awaiting for him in the corner of his screen indicating he had another voicemail from Breanna.

Over the past few weeks, he had gotten really good at emotional avoidance. Unfortunately, in exchange, he turned into an asshole. Or so people tended to think. Maverick didn't possess the emotional capacity for idle pleasantries and frivolous conversations.

He was tempted to delete this notification along with the numerous other ones she had left for him. Something stopped him this time and curiosity won him over. He clicked on the green icon and it took him into his voicemails. Before he could stop himself, Maverick pressed play and a familiar voice filled the room.

*"Maverick. I know you aren't taking my calls, which I get. I'm not even sure if you are listening to these but we have to talk. I don't like how things ended between us and I want to make it right-"*

He deleted the voice message immediately. It had been foolish to even indulge himself and for what? To get angry for no goddamn reason? Breanna could want to make it right all she wanted, but it wouldn't change the fact that she not only ended their relationship, but ended his career. Even now he felt his blood begin to boil and knew he needed to get up and use this misplaced energy.

Forcing himself out of bed, Maverick stretched and did his best to put thoughts of Breanna on the back burner. An early start to the morning wasn't the worst thing. He had spent the weekend being lazy, the least he could do was wake up early on a Monday. For once, he could take a long warm shower without feeling crunched on time. He desperately missed his shower back in his old high rise with its multiple showerheads and settings, but he made do with the new, more traditional shower located at his current residence.

His former manager, Keanon, clearly didn't believe vacation homes should have all the latest updates. People didn't understand what they were missing if they never experienced a deluxe shower. It was heavenly, big enough for at least four people. The amount of times he fucked Breanna against the wall, hearing nothing but the sound of his dick moving inside of her and the breathy little moans she would make right before she—

Fuck.

She always popped back into his mind uninvited. His cock didn't receive the memo they were no longer together because it stood in full attention, hardening against his control. No matter how low he fell in life, he refused to jerk off in the shower with thoughts of his ex.

Fuck that.

Instead, Maverick stood under the shower head, turning the water on as cold as he could bear it. He let the cold water run down his body, watching it pool at his feet as the drain struggled to do its job.

For as long as he could stand, Maverick let the water fall until he trembled from the icy drops. Only then did he reach out and turn off the shower. The one good thing about being a high school coach was that no one gave a shit what he wore to work. When he played professionally, each work outing had an approved outfit, sometimes two, strictly enforced by some unknown assistant tasked to make the team look good.

Funny enough, Maverick was now allowed to wear whatever he wanted. No one looked at him anymore. Not even the tabloids had much to say about him these days. He didn't expect that last one to hurt as much as it did.

Once dressed in clothes he would normally only wear to the gym, Maverick gathered his phone and lunch before heading out the door. He was still early, with some time to spare. At that moment, there was only one thing he desired.

THE SMALL, local coffee shop was located approximately five minutes from the school. It was partially hidden from the road and Maverick only happened to stumble upon the cafe after a sleepless night resulted in a midnight drive to clear his mind. Pecan's Coffee was the only shop in town open twenty-four seven. Maverick had been surprised to see other restless souls taking refuge inside.

Pecan's Coffee always had a steady line of customers, but no drive through. Their motto read, "don't let the little moments pass you by!" Which translated into, come inside and buy your coffee, we don't serve people in cars. As it happens, they were definitely worth getting out of the car for.

Maverick entered the shop, greeted by the warm smell of coffee beans and the soft instrumental jazz humming through the speakers. A few tables were occupied with people, mostly college students desperately trying to finish last minute homework. He was too busy reviewing the day's specials to pay attention to his surroundings.

Maverick collided with a body, tripping over his own large feet in the process. Instinctually, he reached out to grab the person he ran into before they made contact with the floor. His strong hands fastened around a small waist, bringing a soft body against his chest. The woman's scent hit him, sparking a flame of recognition. He smelled that perfume before. Was it yesterday? It had been on-

"You can let me go now," a haughty voice spoke, breaking his train of thought.

He knew that voice. It was the same voice he thought of last night before he went to bed. Dammit, she was going to think he was following her or something.

Maverick looked down in his arms, only to find a very perturbed woman staring back at him. Ms. Mendez had the stern teacher expression down perfectly. He felt like a student who'd just been disciplined for being in the wrong place at the wrong time.

When he didn't make an effort to move, Ms. Mendez pushed at his chest, putting distance between them. From her expression, Maverick noticed she was just as flustered as him. He watched as she wrapped her arms around herself, forming a protective barrier between the two of them. Their collision caused quite a stir; a few people looked up in annoyance, blaming him for the disruption to whatever mundane task they were working on. Others looked on, wondering if they should intervene.

The last thing he needed was unwanted attention. Maverick was no celebrity, but his name held a new reputation from his abrupt dismissal from baseball. The headlines would read "Former MLB player harasses young woman at local coffee shop." His name would be splattered all over disreputable news outlets again.

He needed to placate the few onlookers. He plastered on his camera worthy smile, the same one he wore before any press conference or meet and greet with fans. It seemed to work; the few still staring at him nodded in return before going back to their coffee. The only person still glaring at him now was Ms. Mendez.

Realizing he still hadn't addressed her, Maverick promptly said, "I'm sorry. I didn't see you there."

She snorted, and he'd be damned if that wasn't the cutest sound he'd ever heard. "Clearly. I didn't suspect you run into people out of fun. Then again, judging by your behavior last time, I wouldn't put it past you."

She had sass. He liked a girl who could dish it out just as well as she took it...in more ways than one. Not that Maverick was thinking about this woman like that. No, absolutely not.

"Yeah, about that," he chuckled softly, running a hand down the back of his fade. "I need to apologize again. I was out of line. The baseball fields weren't ready for practice and I didn't want my guys missing out on another practice. I didn't realize the gym was a hot commodity."

"It is. I sat through all the calendar meetings battling the athletics department, band, and drama club for time in the gym.

You threw me off. I didn't appreciate how you talked to me in front of my squad."

By squad, he suspected she meant her cheerleaders. That was fair, he hadn't exactly been quiet or kind when he addressed her. He knew what it was like to feel out of control of a situation. He hated that he made her feel that way, but also had it been that difficult to share the gym with him? Her squad wasn't exactly large and the gym had ample space to accommodate them both.

"Then I should probably warn you, I'm going to be in the gym again this week."

Shocked silence followed his breaking news. Her slightly parted lips soon pressed into a thin line as her expression changed to full on anger. It was as if he had just admitted to killing her sweet grandmother rather than admitting he'd be using half her gym on one of her scheduled gym days. If he wasn't gearing up for an earful, he might have thought her passion for her sport was extremely alluring.

"But you just apologized for how you acted the last time you stole my gym!"

"I did and I am. But that still doesn't change the fact that I need the workout equipment to get my boys in shape. They've been sitting pretty for too long."

"Can't you just have your team run around your field for exercise?"

Maverick did his best to hold back his laughter. He didn't think she would appreciate that right now. "I need weights. Running is only half the workout."

Ofelia knuckles whitened around her cup, dangerously close to snapping the styrofoam in two. Between her manicured nails, Maverick could make out a word written on the cup in black sharpie. *Ofelia.* It had to be her first name. Ofelia Mendez, the teacher who wanted to bury him in grievances. Fortunately if things worked out like he wanted, he wouldn't be around long enough to receive them.

More people came through the door, exactly where Maverick

and Ofelia stood in their silent battle. He was getting more glares from the coffee addicts and he knew from personal experience that nothing good came from getting between a person and their caffeine for the day.

"If it helps at all, we will only be there until six on Wednesday. You say you have the gym until seven? That's one glorious hour without us." He tried to raise his brow in a teasing gesture, but it did not land well with her.

Ofelia bristled with annoyance. It was clear she had not wanted to negotiate her time in the gym at this godforsaken hour. Maverick couldn't blame her. Neither one of them had their coffee yet.

"Just make sure to stick to your side of the gym and don't interfere with my practice. We have competition coming up and my squad needs to focus." She relented.

"Wouldn't dream of messing that up for you, coach." He winked and swore she saw her tremble. "Have a good day, Ms. Mendez. I look forward to avoiding you in the gym tomorrow."

Ofelia mumbled something unintelligible under her breath, but Maverick was pretty certain it was not flattery at his expense. She stormed past him, her damn hair hitting his shoulder as she left the building.

He was fairly certain that was strike two for him. Without another word, Maverick got his coffee and headed out to another full day of coaching.

## CHAPTER SIX

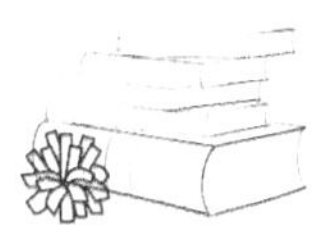

IT WAS a rare day in public education when every single student actively paid attention, but one swift glance around the room confirmed just that. Each group formed a circle and was passionately discussing *Fahrenheit 451*. Ofelia's little teacher's heart swelled with pride. English wasn't everyone's favorite subject, but the times she managed to enrapture her students made her feel successful. It proved that her efforts weren't fruitless after all.

Specifically for her English III class. Her students were a diverse group, each ranging in their learning abilities and interests. They weren't easily won over and getting them to talk proved nearly impossible. Who would have thought *Fahrenheit 451* would be the solution to all her problems? Her dystopian unit was one of her favorites; she looked forward to it every year.

Every year this book was a mild success. Her students seemed to like it and the themes sparked conversations, which is why she kept the book in her curriculum. However, she never received a reaction quite like this and from a typically silent class, nonetheless! Damn, she actually felt like a good teacher.

"The bell is about to ring," Ofelia hollered over the chorus of voices to get their attention. "We are going to have to finish up tomorrow." she grinned, causing the class to groan. Only this time they complained because they didn't want to stop.

"Ms. Mendez! You can't have a book end like that!" A student called from the back of the room.

The bell rang just as she said, signaling the end of class. "Alright everyone, go ahead and leave your books on your desk. We will continue next class." Ofelia called out over the rumpling of papers being squished into already full backpacks and the scrapes of chairs on the worn off-white vinyl flooring. Most students rushed past her, eager to visit with their friends for a brief moment in the hallway. A few others lingered behind to ask questions or to talk about theories.

When the last student finally left, Ofelia felt as if she could float. She did that! She made her students care about what they were learning. If only the evil Mrs. Davis could see her now.

*Ha! Suck it, you witch!*

Ofelia took a seat behind her desk, surveying her classroom. From her assessment, all books were accounted for and her room wasn't a complete mess. She looked over at her computer, happy to see that no emails were awaiting her either. Yes, today would be a good day, she thought to herself, reaching for her mocha. Her coffee had cooled to room temperature, but she was still milking the last few drops.

Her mind wandered back to the strange encounter with Maverick this morning. She was still bitter about it, but had he seemed nervous to talk to her? Of course not. Men like Maverick didn't get nervous around women. He held himself like a man used to getting what he wanted. He knew he looked good and used that to his advantage.

"Ofelia?" A familiar voice called out, startling her out of her chair. Ofelia had been so immersed in her own thoughts that she hadn't heard her principal, Colbie, walk in.

"Wow, really? Usually the keys are a dead giveaway." Colbie laughed, gesturing to her jostling key ring that held far too many than any normal human should ever need. "Sorry about that. I wanted to touch base with you about Mrs. Davis."

*No, no, no, no.* Ofelia groaned inwardly because her day had been going so well! If you discounted the Maverick situation, that is. She had been riding a teaching high, but just the sound of that woman's name sent her falling fast into the ground. Today's lesson almost made her forget about Mrs. Davis's claim of targeting her son.

Colbie took her earpiece off, disconnecting her radio. "I need people to stop needing me for two seconds," she said and planted herself down in the seat in front of her. To say that Ofelia's heart beat a little faster than normal would be an understatement. As much as she liked Colbie, being around a principal was still an intimidating experience.

*I'm not in her office. She is in my classroom. Completely different. Normal even.* Her brain attempted to rationalize.

"Anyway, I thought I would come by rather than say this all in an email. I got a call from Mrs. Davis." Colbie started as Ofelia's heart sank to the floor. Something in her expression must have alerted Colbie to her dread, and she quickly hurried on. "I know how much of a hassle she's been this year. I also know what type of teacher and person you are."

"Did she demand my head on a stake?" That was the only option that would remotely satisfy that woman.

Colbie's hearty laugh echoed around the room. "Get in line, Mendez. There's a whole fleet of poor saps ahead of you." Well, at least she wouldn't be headless alone. "No, I think I talked her off a cliff, mostly. I informed her that you were doing your job and notifying home when a problem arises, just as you do for any student. I also let her know how much progress he's made in your class."

"Why do I feel like there's a but at the end of this sentence?" Ofelia asked, knowing Mrs. Davis wouldn't drop something so easily.

"Fantastic question. I think it's time for some restorative practices. Now hear me out—" Colbie said, putting her hands up to stop Ofelia's eyes from rolling. "It wouldn't hurt to try to restore the relationship between you and the Davises. I'm aware that you are not at fault here, but I'm hoping you and I can be the bigger person in this situation."

Ofelia would rather do anything else, but she had to be willing to give this shattered relationship one last ditch effort. "Okay. Do you have any suggestions? Because I'm honestly at a loss of what I can do at this point."

"Actually, I do." Colbie grinned. She got the distinct impression she would not like whatever Colbie had planned. "I hope you don't have plans tonight because I have the perfect solution to your Mrs. Davis troubles."

As Colbie told Ofelia what she needed to do, she knew tonight would test her very soul.

Universe, you son of a bitch.

OFELIA STOOD in the school's parking lot, measuring the distance between her car and the baseball field. Maybe if she walked at a snail's pace, she'd make it just in time to see only the last inning. No one could say she wasn't there because she had undeniable proof her car was parked, and her body was near-*ish* the fields. That had to count for something.

There was the slight problem of her cheerleaders waiting for her to arrive and Willow doing her best to corral a bunch of teenagers. Football games were a given for cheerleaders, but baseball? What the hell were they supposed to do at a baseball game? Wave their poms in the air until someone in the crowd got fed up and threw lukewarm hot dogs at them?

She understood why Colbie suggested Ofelia attend tonight's game along with her squad, but it didn't mean she was happy about it. For one, Dustin was on the team, and she wasn't mentally prepared to see Mrs. Davis. Secondly, the cheer moms were finally showing their claws and questioning Ofelia's coaching abilities and choices about tonight's event. Honestly, she was surprised it had taken this long for any of the cheer moms to start complaining about her.

She could do this. She needed to do this. Colbie assured her this would bring in more school spirit and wasn't that what she wanted? The alternative meant dealing with Mrs. Davis' absurdities all year. At this point, she was willing to try just about anything to get the woman off her back.

With that in mind, Ofelia made her way towards the bleachers. Dozens of people were already seated, talking animatedly amongst their family and friends. A few younger kids stood by the dugout on their tiptoes, trying to get the attention of the baseball players. The other team, a high school from about thirty minutes away, warmed up on the field, throwing balls back and forth.

In the middle of it all sat her squad, all tightly pressed together at the top of the bleachers.

After Colbie left, Ofelia immediately called Willow to help gather her cheerleaders. Willow took it as far to make sure they stayed in her classroom after school until the game started so Ofelia could attend her department chair meeting.

Willow spotted her first and sighed in relief. "Thank goodness you're here! Get up here, now." Willow waved her arms frantically, gesturing for Ofelia to get her ass up the bleachers.

Ofelia picked the wrong day to wear her brown, heeled boots. Her feet screamed in protest with each clunk of her heel as she maneuvered around families and various other obstacles. The last thing she needed was to take a header directly into the bleachers. There would be no living that down.

Willow reached for her at the last step and pulled her up. Her friend wore her hair in a twisted knot atop her head, a tell-tale sign she entered panic mode. From what she could see, all her cheerleaders were here, albeit looking aggravated, no pissed off parents stood nearby, and no one was bleeding. So what was the problem?

Judging by the look on her best friend's face, Ofelia prepared for the worst. But Willow just gestured wildly at her squad, as if she should have picked up on this problem too.

"Words, Willow. I need you to use your words." She loved her friend dearly, but sometimes it felt as if she were communicating with a toddler.

"You don't see it? How do you not see it? Look at them!" Willow gestured in the general direction of the squad. "Their clothes! I remembered where you keep the uniforms in the gym, but when I checked they weren't there."

"Okay, first breathe," Ofelia said, going into cheer coach mode. As far as problems went, this hardly qualified. "I only keep the uniforms in the gym at the beginning of school. The squad all have their uniforms, but I didn't think it necessary to dress out. We didn't know we'd be asked to come and support the baseball guys tonight. You managed to get everyone in a McKinley High shirt, which is uniform enough."

"Uh, Ms. Mendez? What is it that we are doing here?" Ofelia looked past Willow to see Devin leaning forward. He sat at the end of the bench, next to Tony and Lacey. Tony looked to be the only one of her cheerleaders excited to be here. He spoke to another cheerleader, no doubt ranking the hotness of the baseball players.

"We are here to support our team! That's why we're here!" She pushed the enthusiasm a little too much, but she needed them to buy in.

"Okay, but why?" This time Lacey spoke, her cheer caption. If Ofelia could get her on board, she knew Lacey would get the others to participate. "We've never cheered at a baseball game before. Is that even a thing? This definitely isn't a thing."

"Of course it's a thing! We're making it a thing. All I'm asking is for you to cheer when they hit the ball and run the little... squares." Ofelia encouraged, getting snickers in return.

"Oh no. You did NOT just say little squares. Ms. M, seriously? Do you even know baseball?" Nadine, one of her new freshmen, giggled.

It was blatantly obvious that Ofelia knew very little about baseball. In her defense, growing up her house only had two sports. Soccer and cheerleading. Watching the former was a religion. The TV was on nonstop during soccer season. Her father and brother tolerated cheerleading because it meant a great deal to Ofelia and her mother.

Baseball was rarely, if ever, on at the Mendez house.

"Apparently I don't. I need everyone to be my hype squad. When it seems appropriate, cheer loudly for our players. Can you do that? I'm not above bribing you with donuts."

"Donuts?" Tony grinned, tearing himself away from his conversation. "I will do anything for donuts."

"Jesus Tony. You're so weird." Lacey rolled her eyes. There was no real malice behind her words, everyone knew Tony was her best friend. "Fine, Ms. Mendez. It's only because we love you and donuts."

"Pretend I'm hugging all of you really tightly right now. I love you!" Ofelia beamed, giving her squad a dorky thumbs up before Willow pulled her down into the open seat next to her. In a matter of minutes, the bleachers filled with people. A dozen or so more brought their own chairs, propping them up in the grass, while more seemed content to stand.

"Why are there so many people here? Is this normal?"

Willow gave Ofelia a strange look. "Sweetie, do you think I frequent boys' baseball games? Because I don't. I'm only here because my best friend needed help."

"You owe me, by the way," Willow continued, giving her a pointed look. Her wild red hair, stacked high upon her head, illuminated by the bright lights of the field, giving her fire goddess vibes. "But I suspect they're here because of the new coach."

"New coach...you mean Maverick?" She asked, unable to keep the confusion out of her voice. Why in the world would so many people want to show up to a high school game to see a coach?

From her spot in the bleachers, Ofelia squinted to make out the faint shadow of Maverick. If the surplus of fans in the audience concerned him, he did a great job of concealing it. In fact, Maverick wasn't paying the crowd any mind at all. He stood in deep conversations with his players, rubbing his shadow of a beard, and Ofelia couldn't help but admire him in his coaching uniform.

Uniform was a loose term for what he wore. He wore slim fit pants, the color reminding her of a dusty desert. His black top stretched across his chest in a sinful manner, doing little to hide the chiseled muscles laying underneath. McKinley High Baseball was embroidered into his polo, complete with a matching hat.

This man was the definition of delicious. If he were ice cream —and not her biggest rival at the moment—she'd have her tongue all over his-

"Did you hear what I said? Are you paying attention to me?" Willow's voice cut through her scandalous thoughts. She flushed with unexpected heat, and she silently cursed her body for betraying her. There was no other reason for this lust other than she had not been with a man for two years, her body ached for touch. Her lady boner seriously needed to get a hold of itself *now*.

Crossing her right leg over her left, she smiled sheepishly at her best friend. "Sorry, my mind is all over the dam-dang place."

"You can say damn, Ms. M. It's a damn good word!" Tony piped up from behind her, causing her to jump. She hadn't seen him move. "Sorry - sorry I'm not listening! Carry on!" He grinned before pushing past them to talk to a few other cheerleaders.

"I said that I heard some hot gossip about our new baseball coach. I told you that eating in the teacher lounge pays off occasionally. They hold nothing back in there." Willow laughed and then pointed a slender finger at Maverick. Ofelia leaned in, like they were about to share a secret. "Apparently the new coach used to be a professional baseball player. Up until recently. But people are saying he got kicked off the team. Or banned...I don't remember the correct terminology, but you get my point."

Despite Willow's serious words, Ofelia couldn't hold back a laugh. The news was absurd! Maverick? A baseball player? Or, rather, a former baseball player? Because according to the rumors, he no longer played professionally. Willow did not appear amused by Ofelia's outburst and narrowed her eyes slightly. "Laugh all you want, but it's true. Get out your phone and look it up. Actually, here."

Instead of waiting for her to take her phone out from her purse, Willow thrusts her bright yellow one into Ofelia's lap. With one of her rainbow nails, Willow tapped on the phone screen, gesturing for her to hurry up.

"Fine, fine." Ofelia acquiesced. "What do I look up? Also, this feels a little creepy. He's literally right down there."

"So? You think his Spidey-Sense will start tingling, and he'll run up here to confiscate my phone? Just like, google his name. Maverick...uh, I don't know his last name."

"Wilson." Ofelia said automatically, earning a raised brow from Willow. "I only know because he was a bit of an ass-hat yesterday when he took over my gym."

"Hold up. What?!" Willow's raised voice stirred unwanted attention. "He was an ass-hat? Did he apologize? Why am I just hearing about this? Oh my god, are you keeping things from me? You're keeping things from me. I'm shaking right now."

God, if anyone ever missed their calling, it was Willow. With her constant display of dramatics, she could have pursued a career in acting. After all, Willow never got upset with her or jealous when Ofelia forgot to share something. She liked making a scene; this outburst was purely theatrical.

"Would you keep it down? Yes, he kinda apologized at the coffee shop I ran into him at. Right before he told me he'd be using my gym again. That's it, nothing exciting, so you see why I didn't tell you. I honestly forgot all about it!"

Okay, that was technically a lie. Every moment her brain wasn't in teaching mode, it switched over to the Maverick station. But that was not something she was willing to tell Willow...or anyone for that matter.

The answer placated Willow, and she nodded, giving Ofelia

the opportunity to pick up her friend's phone. She knew the passcode by heart and unlocked the phone, only to be greeted by a cute picture of Willow and her husband, Karl. What disturbed her though were the number of red notifications clogging every app. Ofelia would have a heart attack if her phone had so many messages, emails, and voicemails she needed to catch up on.

Ignoring the clutter for now, Ofelia touched the internet app, pulling up the search bar. Her fingers hesitated over the keyboards as she mulled over what she should do. It felt like an invasion of privacy to search up details about a person, especially when they were a few yards in front of her. If what Willow said was true though, would it really be an invasion of privacy if his business was on the internet for anyone to see?

Her curiosity won out and Ofelia quickly typed in Maverick's name and pressed enter. She watched impatiently as the blue bar slowly loaded. And loaded. And loaded.

"Ugh, Willow, your cell service sucks." She held it up above her head as if the cellphone gods would cast their light upon her, giving her the 5G she rightfully deserved.

What felt like an eternity later, the screen finally lit up with unfavorable news articles and pictures. "Aha!" She brought the phone back down and quickly scanned the first page. Headline after headline greeted her.

**He's Out! Former MLB Player Hangs Up Bat**
**Maverick Wilson: What Went Wrong?**
**Banned in His Prime: What's Next for Chicago Baseball Player?**

More of the same articles came up, some with small pictures of Maverick decked out in his Chicago uniform smiling at an invisible audience. Others showed a stern looking Maverick in dark clothing, eyes black with malice. Yet there was also sadness behind his expression, if one stared long enough. This was the man she was familiar with, the man she had met just a day ago in the gym, who used his dickish behavior as a shield.

What surprised her most is that none of the articles listed the same reason for his ban. Some said it involved an altercation between him and his coach, going as far as obtaining statements from said coach's publicist. One claimed Maverick went berserk after his fiancée broke up with him that he destroyed an entire locker room, accidentally hurting teammates in the process. The only common denominator in the articles mentioned the ongoing investigations into this incident.

"Holy shit," Ofelia whispered once she closed out the last article. "Have you read some of these?"

Willow nodded, tucking a strand of hair that came undone from her bun. "I did. Yesterday, after one of the math teachers mentioned it. Turns out, a few parents made a stink about it and complained to Colbie. I think she listened to appease them, but there's no reason he can't be coaching. No legal reasons anyway. Besides, I think he is winning over parents by the looks of this crowd."

Ofelia swore the crowd had nearly doubled in size since she had started diving into the articles over Maverick. She didn't know what to make of the situation. It explained why he was such an ass to her the other day, though it did not excuse his behavior. She would be wound tight too if she had to deal with the details of her life plastered all over the internet.

"This is a lot to take in. It's also making me hungry. How bad do you think the concession line is right about now?" Judging by the size of this crowd, she assumed the line would be astronomical.

"The game is about to start, so it's probably dying down. Will you get me a sausage wrap? Thanks." Willow smiled, giving her air kisses. "Oh, and a diet coke? I need caffeine if we're staying here for the next few hours. I'll save your spot!"

Ofelia nodded, giving final instructions to her squad, reminding them to cheer energetically when the game began and to make sure they enunciated their words. Nothing worse than a cheer team that sounded like dying cows.

Weaving through the wall of people had not been one of her

best moments, but she managed to reach the bottom without tripping or falling to her immediate death. She turned back to give Willow a thumbs up before making her way to the concession stand. Willow had been right. The line wasn't wrapped around the field as she initially pictured. Only half a dozen people stood in front of her, all on their cellphones.

Ofelia took her place at the back of the line, reading over what they offered...which wasn't much. Luckily, they had Willow's sausage wrap. There was nothing worse than a hungry Willow. She needed to keep her friend fed for both of their sanities.

As Ofelia looked over the menu, she felt someone come up behind her. She didn't think anything of it until she heard a long exhale with a voice that could curdle milk. "Ms. Mendez, funny you should be here, of all places."

*Oh fuck. Oh no, no, no. Think happy thoughts. Puppies. Rainbows. Unicorns.*

When Ofelia turned around, she wore her best 'I'm Totally Not Afraid Of You' expression and the biggest fake smile she could muster. "Hi, Mrs. Davis! How are you?"

# Maverick

## CHAPTER SEVEN

THERE WERE a lot of damn people.

You would think he'd be used to the crowd by now, but Maverick felt each set of eyes on him, heard every hushed whisper said between friends, and he couldn't shake the feeling of multiple phone cameras pointing directly at him.

He schooled his face into the most neutral expression he could produce, but if anyone looked close enough, they could see the cracks in his armor. Clenched fists. Stiff shoulders. Eyes that couldn't focus on one thing for longer than a few seconds. The evidence was right under everyone's noses; they just had to care enough to look.

"I've never seen so many damn people." A short, stout man named Benny Sanders said, working his way over to Maverick.

When told he would be given a coaching assistant, Maverick expected someone less...Danny Devito-esque. Benny barely reached Maverick's chest, so he had to look down when they spoke. Benny was older than Maverick by at least twenty-years, meaning Benny pushed fifty. He was balding, with small tufts of salt and pepper hair on the sides of his head. His tiny legs made it hard to keep up with the baseball players and Maverick couldn't help but imagine a waddling penguin amongst sea lions.

What Benny lacked in athletic ability, he made up in spirit. He never once balked at a single task given to him, even when it was clear he struggled. He was the first to cheer on the team and made sure each victory, however small, was celebrated. Ironically, Maverick supposed they made a good team. He was the rules, tactic, and leader, while Benny provided encouragement and...that was about it. Still, it worked.

"I take it this isn't a normal Tuesday night crowd?" Maverick asked, though he already knew the answer.

Benny snorted. "Are you kidding me? We can barely fill up a third of the bleachers. Now there's not a single spot open and people are spread out across the grass. They are here because of you."

"Yeah, that's what I was afraid you'd say."

But Benny had stopped listening to him, far too enthralled by the size of the crowd to hear what Maverick had to say. Another stark reminder people cared less about what he said and focused more on what he could offer. Apparently Maverick offered a big ass crowd.

For the first time that night, he let himself take in the crowd, never lingering on one face for long before he moved on to the next. It took him a moment to realize he was looking for someone. His damn brain couldn't shake off his earlier encounter with Ofelia at the coffee shop and the dreaded practice they'd have to endure together. It did not seem rational, but his mind flipped through many things right before a game.

Just as that thought crossed his mind, Maverick caught a glimpse of two people walking back from the concession stand. He swiveled his attention back, noticing one middle-aged woman and a familiar younger woman.

Ofelia.

Maverick puffed out his chest like a damn peacock attempting to lure in potential mates. The sight of Ofelia both excited and terrified him. It was like he wanted to impress her, but he didn't understand why. They'd had nothing but complicated encounters since their gym run in.

Ofelia didn't seem to notice him staring. She was locked into an intense conversation with the older woman. Maverick thought she might be one of his player's mothers, but he wasn't sure. He had not been formally introduced to the parents and hadn't made it a priority to remedy that.

Ofelia, to her credit, looked engaged in the conversation. She nodded along with whatever the woman said, but her smile was set in a thin line. She looked uncomfortable, eyes darting around, as if looking to make a swift exit.

"Hey, Benny," Maverick called, nudging his assistant in the shoulder. Benny had been with the school district for twenty years which resulted in making many friends in the community. If anyone would know who Ofelia was talking to, it would be Benny.

"Yeah? What is it?"

Maverick tilted his head up and gestured to Benny's right where Ofelia rounded the dugout to head back towards the bleachers. "Do you know who that is?" Benny had been in the district for years and lived in the town even longer than that, if anyone would know, it would be him.

"Ofelia Mendez? Yeah, she's the Eng—"

"No, not her." Maverick did his best to hide his annoyance. "The woman next to Ofelia. Do you know who that is?"

Benny squinted his eyes and took off his hat, as if that would make him see any better. "Oh yeah." He grimaced. "That is Cheryl Davis. Dustin's mother. She's a *real* Karen, that one."

"Karen?"

"Yeah, you know, a 'let me speak to the manager' type of person. An 'I'm holier than thou' type of person. A—"

"Yeah, I got the idea." Maverick interrupted before Benny went on. "Is she friends with Ofelia?"

"Ha! Friends!" Benny barked out a laugh but Maverick couldn't see the humor. "Sure, they are as friendly as the Starks and Lannisters. That's a *Game of Thrones* reference, by the way. Which is to say, no they aren't friends. But hey, no bloodshed between them yet. That's a good thing!"

Maverick should have left it alone. He didn't know Ofelia well enough to insert himself into the situation. Not to mention he was minutes away from the start of the game. His players were finishing their warm up and slowly trickling into the dugout. He needed to get himself ready for the game, which was the logical thing to do.

But he had not been logical a day in his damn life, so why start now?

"Hey, make sure the guys read the lineup. Have the first three get their helmets and bats. I'll be right back." Without waiting for a response, Maverick found himself jogging towards the fence nearest first base. *Stupid, this is stupid!* The rational part of his brain chanted like a mantra, over and over again. He pretended like he couldn't hear it as he approached the fence.

The tone of the crowd shifted, changing from curiosity to excitement with Maverick within speaking distance. A few tried to grab his attention, but he ignored their calls. Especially when the one person he wanted to talk to turned around and saw him. Ofelia's eyes widened in surprise.

"I'm just saying it's extremely odd that you happen to show up to Dustin's game, a day after our phone call. I have a right to be concerned. You—"

"Excuse me," Maverick spoke confidently, falling easily back into an old role. Mrs. Davis's attention snapped to the side, an angry retort on the tip of her tongue until she saw who spoke. It was almost comical to watch such an angry woman turn into a gaping fish, moving her lips but no sound coming out. "I'm sorry for interrupting. I wanted to make sure I got the chance to thank Ms. Mendez."

It was Ofelia's turn to gape. "You...what?"

He had no idea what he was saying or doing, but he also didn't want to give Mrs. Davis any other opportunities to berate

Ofelia. Benny hadn't been the first person to warn him about Mrs. Davis' helicopter mom tendencies. He hoped she would play along.

"I said I wanted to thank you," he reiterated, staring her down. He willed his eyes to speak what his mouth could not. *I'm trying to save you, go along with it!* "For making sure all my guys had water before the game." It was the only thing that came to his mind. He had watched her walk back from the concession stand, which inspired his lie.

Ofelia didn't answer for a second, her eyes moving back and forth between Mrs. Davis and him. If she didn't speak soon, she would make them both look like idiots. "I uhm," She started, her hazel eyes finding Maverick's dark one. "Right, yes, yes of course. It was my pleasure."

Smart girl.

"And thank you for showing up to support the team. I know you probably have a family who needs your attention."

Shit. It never occurred to Maverick that Ofelia might have a family. Did she have a boyfriend? A husband? No...not husband. He didn't see a ring on her finger. That still didn't mean she was single.

But the slight wince from Ofelia, as if he had physically struck her, told him all he needed to know. She was alone. Like him. A ghost of a smirk crossed his lips. There was absolutely no reason for him to be this pleased about this new discovery, but he was.

"It's really not a problem." Ofelia smiled, recovering from earlier words. "My cheerleaders are here to pump up the crowd and show their support?"

Mrs. Davis had been surprisingly silent throughout the exchange. It could be all in Maverick's head, but he swore he caught her looking at Ofelia with a newfound respect. He blinked and the look vanished, replaced with a frown. "Seems out of place for cheerleaders to come to a game."

Shit. He hadn't thought about that, but Mrs. Davis was right. Baseball didn't have cheerleaders. They had mascots that would occasionally pump up the crowd, but that was the extent of their cheer section.

Luckily Ofelia's brain worked faster than his because she recovered faster. "No, it's definitely unique, but we want all of our student athletes to know their peers and teachers support them."

All Maverick could do was nod his head like a lifeless bobblehead.

Mrs. Davis eyed them both, sizing them up. They apparently passed her inspection because she nodded and said, "Yes, very sweet of you. Let's hope this new streak of honorable deeds remains. Good luck coach Wilson; us booster club moms are rooting for you."

With that, Mrs. Davis walked away, towards a group of women that all shared the same haughty expression and haircut. No doubt they would dive into gossip the moment Mrs. Davis arrived. When she was out of ear shot, Ofelia mouthed "Why?" Which was a fair question. He had gone out of his way to help a stranger. No matter that he thought of her constantly since meeting, Ofelia was still a stranger to him.

"Payment for the gym." He winked, watching her roll her eyes at him, but he didn't miss the small smile she tried to hide. She turned from his gaze before he could properly commit that image to memory, climbing back up the bleachers and straight towards a red-headed woman.

"Mav!" Benny screeched, drawing Maverick's attention away. "Let's go. Game is starting!"

Knowing Ofelia was in the crowd, a new swagger appeared in Maverick's walk to third base. His cocky demeanor stayed firmly in place throughout the entire game, even when his team was down in the 5th inning.

The excitement of the crowd was palpable during the 6th inning, with bases loaded. Maverick assigned a senior as his clean up batter, knowing this player had a reputation for his home runs. Just as expected, the senior hit the first ball out of the park, earning the team's first grand slam of the season.

During the 7th inning, the opposing team wasn't able to bring any runners home, ending Maverick's first game in a victory. Mckinley's first victory in the past few years.

After his team stormed the field, jumping up and down like a group of overly caffeinated toddlers, their attention moved to Maverick. Two dozen teenage boys sprinted in his direction. There was no escape. Maverick had no other choice but to let it happen. Somehow Benny got swept up in the tsunami of teenagers and was half dragged, half carried towards Maverick. He had never seen someone so happy being manhandled.

In a matter of seconds, twenty-four bodies crashed against him, nearly knocking him down onto the golden dirt of the field. He didn't even need to move his body, the movement of his team propelled him off the ground as they jumped in celebration. It was like they had just won a war, rather than a high school baseball game. It made him grin like a fool.

The celebration continued off the field. The moment he got away from his team, their parents struck. He couldn't help but notice that in front of the parent line, was his apparent new best friend, Mrs. Davis. A foul ball must have hit her square in the head, changing her entire personality. It took him closing his truck door for Mrs. Davis and her son, Dustin, to finally leave him alone.

For the first time in a long time, Maverick felt happy.

MAVERICK DIDN'T RETURN HOME until close to midnight. After their victory his entire team stormed the field.

Flashbacks of his time with his former team plagued his thoughts, reminding him he too once had friends as close as family who celebrated every victory and mourned each loss with. Very few relationships came close to that of a well-functioning team. It took every player and every coach to create an atmosphere where everyone felt valued and appreciated, no matter how small their role.

Maverick fucking did that.

He took a group of a few dozen dysfunctional boys in a matter of weeks, and he made them a damn team. They weren't perfect, but their strengths outweighed their deficits. Their first game put things into perspective for Maverick. He now knew they needed to work on infield plays and batting practice. Despite this, his guys played hard, and it paid off in the end.

By the time he stumbled into his rental, Maverick's adrenaline died down. He took the fastest shower known to man, mostly, so he could scrub sweat and dirt off his body before falling face first into his bed. He didn't even bother getting dressed first. The moment his head hit the pillow, he was out in a dreamless, blissful sleep.

Until his phone rang early the next morning. He apparently remembered to put it on the charger but neglected to silence the damn ringer. Before he reached it, the ringing cut off abruptly, and he sighed in relief. He could get a few more moments of uninterrupted sle—

***Riiingggg. Riiinggg.***

Dammit. Why he ever thought an old-fashioned ring tone would ever be soothing or pleasant was beyond him. He flopped around ungracefully until his naked body unwound from the blanket burrito. Once he freed his hand, Maverick reached for his phone. His annoyance from being awoken unexpectedly went away when he noticed the caller. A new emotion took its place, and his heart began to race in anticipation. "Hello?" He answered, holding his breath.

"Mav! How are you, bro?" Keanon's overly jovial tone came across his speaker.

Maverick released his hold on his breath and sighed. Trust Keanon not to check the goddamn time before he called. "Exhausted. It's six o'clock in the morning. Do you not own any damn clocks? I know your lame-ass has an Apple watch. I was there when you bought it."

"I always love catching you in a good mood, but to answer your question, yes. I know it's early, but don't you work today? Teaching the youngins."

"Not until nine."

"Oh." Keanon paused, papers shuffling filled the line. No doubt his friend and former agent had printed out the school's bell schedule and was now confirming Maverick's words. "Oh, I see that. My bad, man. I just wanted to make sure I caught you before you went off to work. I have some news about your case."

And there it was. The reason Maverick's anxiety spiked the moment he saw Keanon's name flash across his phone screen. He knew Keanon referred to the appeal. Before Maverick left – more like fled – Chicago, Keanon agreed to help him overturn the ban. Maverick hadn't put too much stock in it, but his friend was adamant he could find someone to help plead his case. Keanon was the only person who knew the entire story and wholeheartedly believed his removal from the MLB was wrongfully sentenced.

Now after months of radio silence, Keanon had information, but was Maverick ready to hear it? Did he *want* to? A few months ago, he would've jumped on the chance of any news about the future of his career, but now? Perhaps not knowing made him believe in a future. If he got a definitive answer, there was the potential of him realizing baseball would never be something he'd get back to. He would forever be a disgraced household name.

But if there was a chance that someone would take his case, where did that leave him? Would he be investing in a fruitless journey where all that waited on the other end proved more disappointing? There was always the alternative, which was the possibility of winning the case. He would have his old life back.

"Mav? Are you there?" Keanon asked, sounding like this wasn't the first time he called for him. Maverick had been too distracted with his own thoughts to realize his friend continued to speak.

"Yeah, sorry. What'd you say?"

"Remember that lawyer I was trying to contact? The one who has taken on many professional athlete cases and has a reputation of being an overall badass?"

Keanon had mentioned a lawyer by the name of Lloyd Gilmore who specialized in sports law. Out of desperation one night, Maverick googled his name and found a case from ten years ago where he defended a baseball player who had been banned for allegedly violating his contract. The details of the article were fuzzy, probably because Maverick had been highly intoxicated while reading it, but he remembered Gilmore had found a loophole, proving the player in question did not violate any parts of his contract.

Maverick was under no delusions that his case would be simple, though. Still, his curiosity got the best of him, and he answered. "Yeah, Gilmore. What about him?"

"I just got a call from his secretary. I sent over your information and gave him a quick rundown on your situation. He says he is willing to meet with you, but he wants to know more before he takes that case." A new excitement laced Keanon's tone that hadn't been there prior. "This is a good thing, Mav. A damn good thing."

"When does he want to meet?"

"I think his secretary will reach out to you soon. They have your information, so it's only a matter of time. Listen Mav, I gotta go. Meeting in five, but keep your head up, man. We got a fight ahead of us." Keanon said goodbye and then the line went dead. Maverick dropped the phone back onto the bedside table.

His groggy and sleep-deprived brain was slow to process the entire conversation. On one hand, hearing they potentially bagged a big time lawyer like Gilmore would be a huge step in getting back everything he lost. Yet he couldn't silence the insistent whisper in the back of his head telling him he didn't belong in that life anymore.

Why wasn't he more excited? This was everything he hoped for.

For now, Maverick needed to silence all thoughts, good and bad. He kicked off the last of his blanket and got out of bed. There was nothing quite like a good morning run to clear his head. Since Keanon got him out of bed so early, he had time to get two miles in before returning home to shower and get ready for work. If the universe wanted to throw him another bone, he would have time to stop at Pecan's Coffee.

The thought of a fresh brew was enough to get him out the door.

# *Maverick*

## CHAPTER EIGHT

WEDNESDAY PRACTICE BROUGHT with it a new level of comfortability and unity that had been lacking previously. Not even Maverick was immune to the positive energy encompassing his team. A newfound respect began to mold and even Benny had commented on the functionality of Mav's team after their first game. He said he'd never seen the guys work so hard together. They had never been a sloppy team, or so Benny believed, but they also hadn't been polished. Winning their first game of the season provided the confidence boost his team needed.

The lists and sets he had written across the old-school white board did not intimidate his team as he thought it would. At the very least he was expecting a few groans or push back, but was instead greeted with a chorus of 'yessirs' and 'you got it, coach!' He felt as if he were living in The Twilight Zone.

He was halfway through helping his third baseman with proper lunge form when the side doors to the gym burst open. Ofelia strutted in as if she owned the place, which she technically did at this time, with her hair pulled back in a high ponytail, bright neon pink leggings and a black tank top with the words "Cheer Boss" across her chest. Her gaze met Maverick's for a beat

73

before going back to the female student next to her, nodding at whatever Ofelia said.

"Damn, is this our present for winning, coach?" Dustin asked as he watched nearly a dozen girls and two male cheerleaders walk in. The urge to hit the back of the boy's head was strong, but willfully Maverick stopped himself. He didn't think his mother would take kindly to that, even if she was his current bestie after last night's game.

"Don't be a creeper, Davis," he barked at Dustin. "We're sharing the gym one more time, so you boys better be on your best behavior." Maverick said to the group within earshot. He got a few grunts of confirmation, all too focused on their sets for the day to pay him much mind right now.

He needed to heed his own advice about not being a creeper, especially once Ofelia began to lead her team through stretches. He was no better than a teenaged boy, but at least he pretended not to stare at a certain English teacher's ass. He wasn't completely without class. It was much easier to keep his mind engaged with his team when he had to coach them through certain exercises, correct their form, or help ease sore muscles by showing them what stretches they could do to help the affected muscles.

It was sweet torture, but for an hour practice went on without a hitch. Even the music Ofelia started to play did not trigger him like it did the first time he heard Ariana Grande play through the speakers. This time he was listening to snippets of their competition music and Ofelia's voice yelling out orders.

It wasn't until the second hour he noticed their side of the gym had mysteriously shrunk in size. He was constantly running into boys and his team had little room to devote to their training. Sometime within the hour, the cheerleaders had managed to push his baseball players into the corner. The cheerleaders were sitting pretty with over half the gym at their disposal. Alas the fragile truce between them had crumbled. He needed to speak to a certain cheer coach about it. And Maverick definitely shouldn't feel as excited as he felt to rile up Ofelia.

Excusing himself from his team, with orders to stay on task, Maverick crossed the invisible line into enemy territory. Ofelia's back was turned to him, but her cheerleaders noticed his arrival. As if sensing a disturbance, Ofelia turned around and visibly groaned when her eyes locked on to Maverick. "Lacey! Take over the counts for me. This will be one second," she called and a girl —presumably Lacey—began their counts from the beginning.

"Hello, Coach Wilson, to what do I owe this pleasure?"

So she wanted to do it like that. He could entertain her sass.

Plastering on what he knew from experience was a 'panty-melting smile,' Maverick watched her stiffen. Good, he wanted her on pins and needles. "Ms. Mendez, I'm afraid we have a problem."

"Yes, we do. I'm glad you finally realized that. Are you going to leave now? Maybe do your practice, oh, I don't know, outside?" She said, a false sweetness in her voice.

"You would like that, wouldn't you?"

"Very much so. In fact, I would personally escort you and your boys outside so you don't get lost," she said and fluttered—actually fluttered—her eyelashes at him. A fire roared inside of him and Maverick licked his lips.

Ofelia took in a deep breath of air, her eyes traveling down to Maverick's lips. He watched her breath hitch before she pulled her gaze back up to his, but by then it was too late. He had seen the desire etched across his features. Her cute blush as she avoided him made Maverick feel far too many unsuitable for work feelings. The air around them was thick and he had to remind himself they weren't alone. And she didn't like him.

Though that wasn't the truth, was it? At least not entirely. Ofelia might have found him annoying or an asshole, but her body felt very differently.

"Anyway," Ofelia said, taking a step back slowly. The tension still lingered, but it was not as all-consuming as it had been only seconds before. "What is that problem you wanted to talk to me about?"

Problem? He had a problem. Oh, right, his cozy corner. Seemed rather unimportant now, considering he could hear his team doing just fine in the space they had. So what if a few elbows touched during weight lifting? They'd survive. Instead, now that he had her attention, he needed to ask her about something that had been on his mind since Monday night. "Why were you at our game?"

The look of confusion that crossed Ofelia's face indicated she had not thought he would ask about it. Honestly neither did he, but her being there had been a surprise. Especially since she brought her cheerleaders.

It only took her a moment to recover before she reluctantly said, "Colbie asked me to come."

Colbie. Their principal Colbie. "Why?" He had no business asking, and yet he still did.

Instead of telling him to fuck off like he expected, Ofelia sighed. "Because of restorative practices."

He blinked once. Twice. But nothing. "Is that supposed to make sense to me...?"

"Well it should, but you probably haven't been versed in the fun world of restorative practices. Basically I'm trying to get on a certain parent's good side. He happened to be on the baseball team and Colbie suggested I take the squad."

"Would that person happen to be the woman I saw you walking back from the concession with? Mrs. Davis?"

Ofelia nodded. "Yeah, and you did manage to help some. So... thank you for that."

Because he was an asshole and couldn't just accept the thank you, Maverick found himself smirking, "How badly did that suck to say?"

"Honestly I feel like I need a cleanse after that," she dead-panned, earning a wolfish laugh from him. "But in all seriousness, it got the desired effect so thanks."

"Happy to help. Besides, we won the game so it's sorta like you and your squad are our good luck charm."

"Don't expect that to happen again. There's no way I'm ever going to get my squad back out there. Except for Tony, he'll be your one-man cheerleader."

He opened his mouth to say something else, but one of his players called his name. "Looks like you need to head back," Ofelia said, already looking towards her squad. "Will this be the last time we share the gym?"

"I believe so." And for some reason that thought saddened him. "Benny found some equipment out in the shed we can use on our fields. We won't need the weights in here anymore."

"Perfect. Enjoy the rest of your practice, Coach Wilson. I'm sure you have a lot on your plate right now." She said the last part as if she had personal experience with it. Once again his curiosity got the best of him and his mouth responded before his brain could.

"Know something about being busy?"

The smile that came across her lips was purely self deprecating with no signs of humor. "Between parents, teaching, cheer, and cheer moms...yeah, I would say I know a thing or two."

He wanted to pry more. He felt like a baby bird who was just offered his first worm. He needed more to be satisfied. Yet before he could ask more, he was called again by one of his players.

"I'm on my way!" Maverick said, hopefully not too bitterly. He offered Ofelia an apologetic smile but she had already started walking away from him to rejoin her team. He sighed and tore his gaze away, finally rejoining his team. Yet all throughout practice, he couldn't help but wonder what responsibilities were weighing so heavily on the all star teacher.

# Ofelia

## CHAPTER NINE

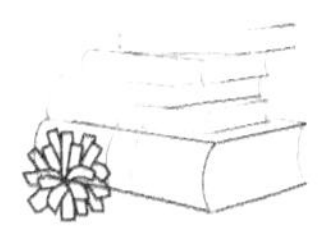

OFELIA COULD COUNT on a single hand how often she had been late for work. She couldn't remember how many times she snoozed her alarm, only that she remembered picking up her phone and shooting out of bed because she had exactly thirty minutes before she needed to be on campus.

Which meant no makeup, no hair products, and absolutely no coffee. If Ofelia could get away with wearing leggings, she would. Instead, she found burgundy pants that she paired with a mustard-colored top. It was all she could gather this Friday morning after neglecting laundry all week. She slipped on the closest pair of shoes she could find, checking twice to make sure they matched before running out to her car. In the seconds it took her to walk from her front door to her car, she managed to put her hair up in a messy bun.

It would have to do.

Since she arrived so late, the parking lot was already crowded with staff and student cars. Ofelia had to forgo her usual front parking for one all the way in the back. Which would have been fine if her room wasn't on the complete other side of the building and on the second floor.

By the time she reached her door, her breath came out in

short, labored pants. She doubled over in attempts to get her breathing under control before fumbling with her keys. She found the right one and pushed open the door when Willow rounded the corner. Upon spotting her best friend, Willow laughed at her disarrayed appearance.

"I would say you had a good night last night and are now suffering from the D effect, but I know you too well," Willow smirked.

"D effect? Really? You sound like the students." Ofelia pushed her door open but didn't shut it behind her. Willow followed. Since she ran so late, she silently thanked whatever divine entity listening that she set out all her materials the previous day. At least she wouldn't have to scramble like a chicken with its head cut off while making copies.

"So, I thought of a way you could repay me, your best friend, for helping you out on Tuesday."

Ofelia raised a brow, wondering why Willow felt the need to add in the best friend qualifier. Knowing her, it wasn't anything good. "Okay," she said slowly, "What are you thinking?"

"We're going out!"

"Come again?"

"Ofi!" Willow said dramatically, perching her ass atop the closest desk. Ofelia gazed longingly at the coffee in her friend's hand as if it were the last drops of water in the middle of the desert. "When was the last time we went out?"

"Uh, never. That's why we are friends. We don't go out. We have pizza nights where we drink too much wine, eat too much, and watch crappy hallmark movies. It's kinda our thing."

"So I'm proposing we do something different tonight," Willow said matter-of-factly, like she was commenting on the weather rather than a nighttime activity that involved being social after a day of teaching high schoolers.

"Karl left for a business trip and will be gone for a week. He wants me to pick up someone at the bar for a one-night stand and immediately FaceTime to tell him all about it. Don't worry though, he's planning on doing the same."

She would never quite understand Willow and Karl's swinger endeavors, but she didn't need to understand to support her friend's interests and kinks. As long as both parties were consenting and into it, Ofelia saw nothing wrong with it. Not that Willow needed her approval for what she did in the relationship or in the bedroom.

"We'd need to go shopping after school because I feel like going out in a new outfit. Plus, you haven't bought anything nice for yourself in God knows how long. We are getting you something sexy and slutty, but classy because you are an educated lady."

"Willow," Ofelia groaned inwardly. "This is so much more than what I asked you to do! Are you crazy? Do you know how tired I am? I'm late because I physically could not get out of bed. This week I've dealt with practice, parent meetings, and tutoring. Now you want to not only go shopping, but go out clubbing-

"Oh god no. Not clubbing. To a bar."

"Fine, a bar." Ofelia rolled her eyes. "No. I love you, but no."

Those words woke the dragon in Willow. She narrowed her eyes, putting her hands on her hips, staring down Ofelia. Ofelia flinched under her scrutiny. "First off, it was a courtesy I even asked. This isn't up for negotiation. We are going, and secondly, you are going to have so much fucking fun, you aren't going to know what to do with yourself. Maybe some good dick would perk you up a bit."

"You did not just say that."

"Yes, I did, and I'll keep saying it until you agree. Good dick good dick good dick good dick good di—"

"Okay!" Ofelia shouted, throwing the first thing she found, an expo marker, directly at Willow. "You're seriously so annoying."

A devious smile played across her friend's lips. Willow knew she bested her. "So you're in?"

"Clearly. I don't get a choice."

"Nope, you do not," Willow squealed, unable to hide her

excitement. "Okay, we'll take your car after work and go shopping and then tonight we'll hit the bar. Ah! I'm so excited. This is going to be fun! You'll see."

*Famous last words*, Ofelia thought.

WHEN WILLOW WALKED out of her classroom, exclaiming she would meet Ofelia as soon as the bell for the last period rang, she pushed all thoughts of shopping and bar visits to the back of her mind. Maybe, if she hoped really hard, Willow would realize how tired she was after a long day's work and their typically Friday night pizza binge would be back on the table.

For the rest of the day, Ofelia threw herself into her lessons on *Fahrenheit 451* and the needs of her students. During her planning period, instead of taking a nap like she really wanted to, she started making her lecture slides for next week. What she couldn't finish, she knew Willow would piece together. She also made sure that all the copies needed for next week were on route to the school. How she managed to function at all without coffee was a mystery to her.

When the last bell rang signaling the end of the day, Willow burst through her classroom doors faster than her students could leave.

"How do you have all this energy still?" Ofelia groaned before sinking onto her pink swivel chair as the last of her students filed out. "I feel like I was run over by a bulldozer."

"Because I'm about to go shopping with my best friend! Then I'm going to get absolutely wasted at a bar. We are in our twenties and deserve to let loose." Willow was already tidying up Ofelia's classroom without being prompted.

Seeing her friend so excited over something so small made Ofelia feel a little guilty that she wasn't as into it as Willow.

Willow had a point. They were still young, and it had been a long time since Ofelia did anything for herself. Yes, she was tired, but nothing a strong cup of coffee wouldn't fix. Maybe subconsciously she was avoiding bars, not because she didn't like to go drinking every now and then, but because it was where she had met her ex. Hector had loved going to bars for playoff games, friend's parties, and after work to unwind. He would often drag Ofelia along and she would go without complaint because she wanted to be close to him.

Then he started leaving her behind. Slowly at first, giving Ofelia excuses about wanting a boys' night. She remembered the moment he stopped bringing her entirely. They had a huge fight over something trivial, probably about the laundry since he was so careless with his, and Hector stormed out saying he needed a break. Ofelia took that as a break from their relationship. She remembered sobbing in the kitchen, elbows on the table with her head in her hands.

That was how he found her, eyes puffy from crying and hair disheveled from anxious fingers. Hector swayed, clearly so drunk that even standing proved difficult. He had apologized and said he didn't want to fight. Ofelia had been young and her love for Hector clouded all her better judgment. She allowed Hector to take her back to bed and make love to her. He had passed out, arms holding her tightly as if he were afraid he'd lose her.

Or afraid she'd run.

But Willow didn't know that. All Willow knew was she left California after separating from Hector before their wedding. Because she was still too scared to tell her best friend what really happened. It was silly, she knew, to completely avoid bars simply because it reminded her of him. This could be her one opportunity to reclaim that part of her life, the life where she didn't fear going out with friends and hanging at bars. Willow, her best friend in Texas, would be there too.

She could do this.

Ofelia, now determined to make the most of tonight, stood up. Perhaps a little too abruptly because she caught the attention of Willow. "Is everything okay?" She asked hesitantly.

"Everything is perfect. I'm just ready to go, but our first stop has to be coffee."

Willow cocked her brow and stared at her like Ofelia had just been abducted by an alien. Ofelia could practically see the thoughts going through Willow's mind right now. *Who are you and what did you do with my best friend?*

"O...okay," Willow said slowly, elongating the "oh" sound. Realizing that Ofelia was actually serious Willow beamed, her smile lighting up the room. "Right! Okay, let's get some coffee!"

One hour, two long red lights, and one frantic coffee stop later, Ofelia and Willow arrived at a small independent boutique. The store was packed full of clothing all ranging from evening wear to sleepwear. Immediately several dresses caught her eye and she imagined slipping a few on, just to take a look. If she got a new dress, then she would obviously need to get a new pair of shoes...and accessories. If they were going out, she might as well go all in.

"Those print jumpsuits are calling my name." Willow maneuvered her way through the racks of clothing, leaving Ofelia by the entrance. The older woman by the register smiled at her with kind eyes. "If you need any help sweetie, you just let me know. Changing rooms are in the back."

"Thank you." Ofelia returned the woman's affectionate smile before wandering off towards the back. The entire left side of the boutique was full of dresses for every occasion. What she needed was something she could wear out that didn't look like the rest of her teaching attire. She didn't want to go out looking like Ofelia, the teacher, but rather Ofelia, the single woman.

All of the maxi dresses were cut from her list, even if they were adorable. She had plenty of those back at home. The dresses that hit mid calf would also not work, but she was getting closer. The dresses left fell under two categories. One being the "legs for days" and the other being "did my ass just pop out?" She wanted to look sexy, but not at the expense of flashing half the bar in the process.

"Legs for days" dresses would have to do. She jumped through one hurdle only to come across another. What color of dress did she want? She could go with a fierce, loud pattern that demanded attention. Or she could choose a solid color that wasn't quite as loud but provided a level of mystery and sophistication. She knew exactly the dress she would have chosen if she were still dating Hector, the bold cheetah print that hugged her ass a little too tightly, pairing it with red pumps.

But she wasn't that person anymore and she didn't want to choose a dress in hopes a man would notice her. She wanted a dress for herself. To look and feel good. She deserved that, dammit!

Her mind made up, Ofelia picked out a little black dress and headed back towards the fitting rooms. Willow was already there, holding a very Willow-like jumpsuit in front of the mirror and inspecting it. "What do you think about this?" She asked, turning around only to notice the dress in Ofelia's arms. "Hell yes. I don't even need to see it on you to know it's going to be your dress."

There was no way Ofelia was leaving with a dress she hadn't tried on. The last thing she needed was buyer's remorse. Still, she appreciated Willow's enthusiasm. "Let me take a look at yours," she said, instructing her friend to hold up so she could look it over. It was a vibrant green jumpsuit with jaguars and roses as the print. It shouldn't have worked as well as it did, but instead of looking tacky, the jumpsuit looked chic and trendy. It also screamed Willow. "I actually love it."

"I actually love it too!" She shrieked, her voice raising an octave as she did a little happy dance. "Wait, wait." Willow stopped suddenly, mid dance. "We need to try them on first. Let's not get too excited until we see how we actually look in them."

Ofelia didn't mention how she thought Willow was already too excited, but instead smiled and nodded. They took up the only two changing rooms in the boutique and Ofelia shut and locked the door behind her before turning her back to the mirror. She didn't want to spoil the look before it was completely on. She stripped out of her clothes, leaving on her bra and panties, and placing them in a neat pile on the bench.

Now to tackle the dress.

There was no zipper, so she pulled it over her head and shimmied inside of it. Once her head popped free, and she could see again, she made sure to adjust the bottom of the dress so it hit mid-thigh. It was short, but she didn't feel in danger of it accidentally showing off her goods. With only the briefest of hesitations, Ofelia turned around to see how she looked in the mirror.

The dress hugged her body tightly, framing her curves in the most delicious way. She was a proud Mexican American woman, so she had ass, tits, and hips and nothing was going to hide that fact. She embraced those parts of her body long ago. What she liked most about the dress though was that it wasn't sleeveless. The sleeves billowed around her arms in sheer fabric giving the illusion of sleeves while putting more skin on display. It cuffed at her wrists, small black satin ties to keep the ends in place.

She was completely and irrevocably in love.

"Ofi, you done? Come out, I wanna see," Willow called impatiently on the other side.

When she opened her changing room door, Willow had her back turned to Ofelia, checking herself out in the full-length mirror. Ofelia had been correct in her assumption that the jumpsuit was made for Willow. No one else could pull off a bold animal print jumpsuit quite like her and look hot doing it. The moment Willow's eyes met Ofelia's in the mirror, however, her friend stopped what she was doing and immediately turned around to gap.

But she didn't say anything. Ofelia was starting to feel like a circus attraction. Maybe the dress didn't look as good as she thought. In her worried state, she quickly tried to rationalize her choice. "I know I'm not wearing the right bra for this, and the sleeves are probably not everyone's cup of tea, but—"

"Shut. Up."

Ofelia did happily.

"Shut up!" Willow said again, girlish giggles leaving her lips. She circled Ofelia like a farmer assessing his prized sheep. It did nothing to quell the nerves inside of Ofelia. When her friend made a full 360, Willow finally said, "You look so hot right now. Like, so so hot. Am I tearing up? I feel like I'm tearing up. You just look so incredible and ugh! Okay, no, I am not going to cry in the middle of a boutique. Stop it, Willow!" She scolded herself.

It made Ofelia's heart warm with love for her best friend's giddiness at that moment. "Thank you," she said, trying to convey so much in those two words. Thank you for being my friend. Thank you for taking me out. Thank you for getting me out of my comfort zone. "You look so incredible too. I'm sure if Karl were here, he wouldn't be able to keep his hands off you."

"That will be someone else's job tonight." Willow winked, clearly still set on her plan to find a hookup partner. "So it's settled. We are both buying these. But a sexy little black dress needs an equally sexy pair of heels. Oh, and accessories."

"You are speaking my language, bestie. Those black strappy shoes on display demand my attention." Ofelia beamed. For the first time today, Ofelia was excited for tonight. She still wasn't ready to invite someone back to her house for a one-night stand, but she was ready to let loose. Just a little bit. Because she deserved it.

# Ofelia

## CHAPTER TEN

HER MIRROR WAS BROKEN. That was the only explanation she could come up with. The woman looking back at her was not Ofelia. Maybe Ofelia's long-lost hotter sister, but definitely not her. The woman looking back at her had prominent cheekbones and sultry hazel eyes. Her lips were the color of a freshly ripened apple, full and pouty. In her ears, Ofelia chose a set of silver hoops and a matching elegant silver necklace to wear. The strappy black heels completed the look.

"So, what do you think?" Willow asked from the perch of her bed, barely concealing her excitement.

After shopping, they agreed to head back to Willow's home and get ready. It came down to who had the bigger bathroom and Willow's house undoubtedly won out. Which was fine by Ofelia because cramming into her tiny bathroom would have been a nightmare. Plus, Willow had more makeup and transporting hers would have been a pain.

"I've never felt more beautiful in my entire life," Ofelia admitted, blinking back the stinging sensation in her eyes. The last thing she needed was to cry and ruin an hour of Willow's hard work. "Thank you, Willow. For everything."

"Don't you start. If you start, I'm going to start." Willow

waved her hands rapidly in front of her eyes, as if the constant air motion would hold the tears at bay. "You deserve this." Willow fluffed her already bouncy, red hair, giving herself a quick look over in the mirror. "No more crying, it's time to drink."

Because they were both two responsible adults, Ofelia ordered them an Uber. "I don't recognize this address, where is it again?" Ofelia asked.

"It's new, I think it opened a month or so ago. It's one of the few bars in the area that isn't a sports bar. I think it's more upscale," Willow replied, grabbing a tiny white purse and stuffing her wallet and phone inside. "Do you think I should take my can of pepper spray? Yeah, I will. Better to be safe than sorry." She answered her own question and stuffed her blue key chain pepper spray into her purse.

"Car's here. You ready?" Ofelia received the notification just as a blue Camry pulled into Willow's parking lot. Her friend nodded and ushered them both out of the house, locking the door behind her.

"I sent a selfie to Karl earlier to let him know we are about to go out and I am determined to give this man some major blue balls. He wants me to text him a play by play," Willow said as she slid into the back seat, followed by Ofelia. "Not for long though, we have an old college friend he's seeing tomorrow that's also into —" she cast a look at their driver, a middle-aged Asian man, before whispering. "You know."

Ofelia loved the wild, care-free spirit of her best friend and the relationship she had with her husband. It was one of the healthiest she had ever seen, even though it wasn't considered traditional. "Of course he will. You look so good. Make sure to send him many pictures and videos from tonight."

The drive to the bar—Willow called it Cloud 9—only lasted ten minutes. Their driver pulled up to the curb so they could get out. "Thank you." Ofelia smiled, making sure to remember to go back and write a good review for this man because he had to listen to Willow babble on and on about her plans for tonight.

Cloud 9 was located on the edge of a large shopping outlet that catered to both high end and every day shopping. From the looks of people entering the bar, they catered to an eclectic clientele, ranging from people in their early twenties, all the way to mid-fifties. The building was a large one story, with cute black and white brick covering the exterior.

As soon as they walked inside, Ofelia realized too much time had passed since her last girl's night out. Her belly bubbled with a mixture of anxiety and excitement. Her body buzzed, unsure whether to throw up or start dancing.

Inside the bar, top hits played loud enough to dance to, but not so loud that someone couldn't hear the person next to them. It was still relatively early in the evening, about seven, so Cloud 9 was only starting to liven up.

Willow found them a high top table towards the bar area, big enough for two people to sit comfortably. It took some skillful maneuvering for Ofelia to climb the tall chair without exposing herself to the crowd. Luckily the lighting was somber, and she doubted anyone would truly be able to see up her dress.

"I'm going to buy our first round of drinks in celebration of doing something outside of our normal Friday night routine," Willow declared, grabbing her wallet from her purse. "I'll leave this here and be right back." She blew Ofelia a kiss and headed off towards the bar.

Ofelia took the moment alone to breathe.

She was out and determined to have a great time with her best friend. Didn't she deserve that? Two years was a long time to get over someone, perhaps too long, and in that time she neglected this part of her. The fun, easy-going socialite who enjoyed entertaining and hanging out with friends. She found it easy to lie to herself these past two years by pretending she was introverted and suppress her extroverted tendencies by hiding inside, away from people.

Although that was half true, it wasn't entirely who she was. She would never be the girl who wanted to go out every weekend, but she was a girl who liked having a tight-knit friend group who planned the occasional outings and trips together. She could have that again, if she stopped letting her past haunt her. Part of healing was finally telling her best friends of two years why she really left California two years ago. At that moment, she felt the last chain holding her back began to crumble. She was finally ready. She had needed this final push from Willow to get out of her comfort zone and tonight had done just that.

Ofelia had been so deep down into memories that she didn't hear Willow approach until she placed a giant frozen strawberry margarita in front of her. "You're thinking really hard over there. Should I be worried? You aren't about to ditch me, are you?" Willow asked, her smile not quite reaching her eyes. "Look, if this isn't your thing, we can leave after—"

"No." Ofelia stopped her before Willow could finish her thought. She reached across the table, grabbing for Willow's cold hand. "I'm so happy you made me come out tonight. Not just now, but after school when we went shopping. Then getting ready and listening to old boy bands. I can't tell you the last time I've done any of those things."

"It's a typical Wednesday night for me."

Both women laughed, the tone shifting into lighter and easier territory. Ofelia took the first sip of her margarita and moaned. "Ugh this is the most delicious thing I've ever had in my mouth. Don't make a dirty joke out of it," she said before Willow could make a crude comment.

Her friend only smirked. "Wouldn't dream of it," she said, feigning innocence. "I'm curious about what you were thinking so hard about. If you wanted to share, that is. I won't push you, of course. Just know that I'm always here to talk to. And not only about school stuff. Anything."

Willow's words sounded almost shy, bordering on cautionary. Ofelia felt her heart lurch in her chest. How many times had Willow poured her heart out to Ofelia? Entrusted her with information she probably didn't give to many others aside from Karl? What had Ofelia given in return? Not a whole lot.

Willow knew of Hector and their messy break up, but Ofelia never went into detail. Most of her life was still a secret from Willow and it wasn't fair. Willow would never demand details about Ofelia's personal life, but she realized she *wanted* to tell her best friend everything. To lessen the burden and get it off her chest to someone other than her family.

"I was thinking about my ex," she confessed, searching Willow's face for surprise, but all she found in her friend's expression was compassion. It gave Ofelia the strength to carry on. "We were engaged, you know."

But of course she didn't know. Ofelia never told her. Willow sipped her margarita with wide eyes, speaking only when she pulled away from the straw. "I didn't want to pry. You always tensed up when I mentioned any of your old relationships, so I just let it be. Damn. Ofi. What happened?"

Two years ago, that question would have nearly incapacitated her with grief for the life she thought she lost. Now it only filled her with shame and embarrassment for falling prey to Hector's game. She couldn't blame him for everything; a small part of her had been aware their relationship wasn't working. Ofelia desperately wanted to ignore all the red flags and believe love would overcome everything. Love conquered all in books, so why not real life too?

"We were having problems. I was trying to get through college to become a teacher and my last few semesters were really stressful. He was used to having my attention all the time and I couldn't give that to him anymore. Hector had the emotional range of an egg; he couldn't process not being my number one priority. Which resulted in him going out...a lot. Sometimes he'd drag me to bars, but then he started going out more often and coming home drunk. We would get into the worst shouting matches and—"

Willow's hand shot out, gripping Ofelia. She hadn't realized she had a death grip on her drink. Slowly, Ofelia released her glass, pulling back but not out of Willow's grasp. "Did he lay a hand on you?"

Ofelia's eyes went wide. "Oh god, no! Nothing like that. Sorry, I know it sounds that way. No, Hector never hit me," Ofelia quickly assured, watching Willow visibly relax.

"Thank god. I was about to drive up to California and kick some deadbeat's ass."

The image of an eccentric Willow who preached love and self-expression, beating up Hector who stood six feet tall with tattoos covering his arms, was comical to Ofelia. She laughed, unable to unsee the image. "He's a jerk, but he isn't physically abusive. He respects women, having grown up in a household of only women. They would skin him alive if he ever touched a woman aggressively. Trust me, he wouldn't dare."

Estella had been a single mom, raising two kids. Her twin sister, Maria, moved in when Hector was eight and his sister Analucia was four, to help raise her niece and nephew. Estella and Maria had been good to Ofelia, even after they broke up. It devastated her more than anything that she wouldn't be marrying into his family. She adored Hector's family, and they tried to reach out when she moved, but Ofelia ignored all their calls, unwilling to bring her past to Texas.

This was the embarrassing part, and it still left her sleepless on rough days. The pain healed long ago, but the shame and distress lingered. Telling Willow felt like the final stage in the healing process. The baggage she carried for so long could finally dissipate.

"Despite all the fights, he proposed. We both thought that was what we needed, and I couldn't have been happier. On the day of our wedding, I was getting ready with his mom, aunt, and Analucia, while my brother and dad were supposed to be getting ready with Hector. When we were the first to arrive at the chapel, I knew something was wrong. Analucia tried calling Hector and I tried calling Javi, but neither of us could ever get anyone to pick up.

"Until about an hour later when Javi and my father walked in, both staring at me the same way they did when mom died. Sadness and a little pity. I thought something happened to Hector. I remember demanding they tell me or take me to him. But neither of them said a word. I think they were silently trying to decide who would be the bearer of bad news.

"In the end, it was Javi who told me Hector left. Gone. He told Javi he couldn't do this, couldn't go through with marrying me. He didn't love me and wasn't willing to give up his fast life-style to settle down and start a family.

"So instead of doing the right thing, Hector ran and left me at the altar. His mother and aunt were crying, and Analucia tried to comfort me, but I couldn't look at them. I didn't have anyone to blame, and I took it out on them. It's not one of my prouder moments, but at that moment I was nothing but rage and despair."

There. It was out. Willow knew everything and the last few walls Ofelia erected around her best friend had finally been breached, as they should have been years ago.

Willow didn't speak for a few, long moments. She took everything Ofelia said in. Which to be fair, was a lot. Especially at a bar. She didn't plan to tell her best friend her tragic left at the altar story here, but the moment appeared, and Ofelia seized it. It felt damn good to get that off her chest too, having someone else to confide in.

On the opposite end, Willow looked close to shedding a few tears for Ofelia's ruined love life. "Oh, Ofi. That is so awful. I hate that you went through that, I can't even imagine how you felt. I'm so sorry."

"I'm not." It shocked her, just as much as it did Willow, to say those words. Where would she be now if she had married Hector? Not happy, she knew that for certain. They were two different people and were going to extreme lengths to make their relationship work. Trying to get blood from a stone was fruitless and ineffective.

"I'm not," Ofelia repeated herself. "Him leaving saved me from a life of a loveless marriage. I got the opportunity to figure out who I am and what I'm capable of. I was heartbroken at the time, but I can't help but be proud of the woman I've become. I've made a life for myself and worked my ass off to achieve what I have in my career and personal life. I found the best friend a girl could ask for." She smiled at Willow. "So yeah, I'm not sad about it anymore. Maybe a little embarrassed, but I think that will fade in time as well."

"Thank you for trusting me." This time Willow got up, fighting back tears, and hugged Ofelia, who happily accepted. "I'm so proud of you. Ugh, I'm not going to cry. No, I worked too damn long on this mascara to mess it up." She said and untangled herself from Ofelia. "But I will get us more to drink."

Ofelia must have been chugging her margarita during her story since it was completely empty minus a small puddle at the bottom of her glass. "Fine, but the next ones on me."

"Oh honey," Willow laughed. "If we have to buy any more of our own drinks tonight, then we are doing something wrong." With that, Willow fluttered away, back towards the bar.

After the second drink, Ofelia started to feel a warm tingling in the pit of her stomach. She felt lighter and found herself laughing louder each time Willow told a funny story about Karl or work. Cloud 9 continued to fill up as people and friend groups trickled in. They had been lucky enough to secure a table because now people were claiming wall space to visit and drink with others.

The first time a round of drinks was delivered to their table, Ofelia had been shocked. Neither her nor Willow ordered from the bar. "A round of beer from the two gentlemen over there." The waitress had pointed vaguely over to the corner. The cramped area was dimly lit, making it hard to make out faces. She thought she saw someone raise their hand and give her a wave, but she wasn't sure if it was meant for her.

"You like beer?" Ofelia asked when Willow picked up the glass.

Her friend shrugged and said, "I do when it's free." Then brought the glass to her lips and drank.

Now they were on their fifth round and somehow Willow coerced Ofelia into dancing. Cloud 9 played a killer soundtrack, full of old pop hits she loved in middle school and high school. It would be a sin not to dance when they played Usher. Instead of feeling insecure about dozens of eyes on her, Ofelia didn't hesitate when Willow dragged her over to a small crowd of people.

Song after song, Ofelia danced like nobody was watching, even after Willow was whisked away by an eager dance partner. The dryness in her throat eventually couldn't be denied though, and she made her way through the dancing bodies to quench her thirst. If she remembered correctly, there had been a self-serve water station at the end of the bar. She could feel the alcohol getting to her head and it made the room spin.

When she located the water station, she was happy to see an open bar chair next to it. Her feet cried out in pain. The damn shoes were cute, but her feet throbbed with each step. Beauty is pain had never been a truer statement.

Ofelia filled up a cup of cold water, chugging it down in one go. Her dry throat satiated at last with the cool liquid. Filling it up once more, she took a seat in the unoccupied bar stool, hoping to take a few moments alone to sober up.

Her precious break was cut short when a shadow darkened her view. Ofelia looked up through half-lidded eyes at the strange man before her. He was taller than her, but still on the shorter side. His brown hair was shaggy and cut close to his shoulders. He wore form fitting blue jeans and a collared black shirt he tucked in for some ungodly reason. He wasn't unattractive, per se, but not Ofelia's type. He also seemed to be older than her by more than a few years.

Ofelia offered him a tight smile, one that she hoped convey she wasn't interested in whatever he had to say. She went back to sipping on her water, which she pretended was the most inter-esting thing in this bar. Unfortunately, black shirt didn't get the memo and plopped his body down on the seat next to her, scooting close. Way to close for comfort.

That was when she realized she was alone. *Fuck! So stupid!* She thought to herself. That was the number one rule in outings! Don't separate from your friend group. She was on the opposite side of the bar, and she couldn't make out her friend's red hair amongst the sea of dancing people. If she walked away, she had the feeling the creep would follow her.

"What's a pretty lady doin' all alone in the corner over here? Tryin' to hide from me?" Mr. Creepy asked, offering her a smile that matched his nickname. She watched as his eyes raked over his body, taking in every inch of her bare skin. Ofelia felt like she stood naked in front of him and did her best to pull her dress lower down her thigh.

"I'm here with someone, just getting water," She said curtly.

The man laughed, a low throaty sound that made her think of nails on a chalkboard. "Don't see nobody here, sweetheart. I guess it's my lucky day. Say, how 'bout you let me buy you a drink? What's your poison, darlin'?"

"No, thank you. I'm fine with water."

*Fuck!* This was bad. So, so bad. Of course the bar creeper would hit on her. She just had to wander away from Willow to find water. Her heart pounded harder in her chest, signaling a flight or fight response. But the bar was so crowded, there was no way the man would try anything...right?

"Awe, come on, sweetie! Let me buy you a little somethin'. How about a shot then?" This time when he spoke, he placed his hand on her thigh. Her bare thigh. She tried to pull away from him but his hand gripped her tighter, causing a tendril of pain to shoot down her leg.

"Don't touch me," she growled, trying to put on her best pissed off expression. She narrowed her eyes, but she felt like a frightened animal cornered by prey. Her body wanted to run, but her tipsy brain was still trying to process the severity of this situation. It left her immobilized, unable to do more than scream internally.

"Don't be like that sweetheart. I just wanna buy you a drink." Mr. Creepy grinned and leaned closer.

Fear overrode every sense in her body, making her helpless to do anything but stare at the man. Before he could lay another hand on her though, a deep voice sounded from behind Ofelia. "You have exactly one second to take your hands off her." The hairs on the back of her neck stood on end. She knew that voice! His deep, sensual baritone sent shivers down her back, sending warmth between her thighs. She pressed her knees closer together. Not once since they met did she ever think she'd one day be so thankful for his presence.

When she turned towards Maverick, she was greeted by the full wrath of his stare and *oh god* it did wonders for her nether regions. Because not only did Maverick look ready to draw blood, but he was doing it all for *her*.

She was in so much trouble.

# Maverick

## CHAPTER ELEVEN

MAVERICK DESERVED A DRINK.

Baseball practice ended up running an hour past what Maverick originally intended. They were finally out in their fields and time had gotten away from him, but none of his players noticed either. Maverick only realized the time when a few freshmen parents started to show up looking frazzled and impatient.

Benny and Maverick began to load up the school's golf cart so they could transport their practice equipment back to the storage room in the gym. Benny, who insisted on driving the damn cart, waited for Maverick to take the spot next to him. "Why do you always insist on being the driver?" Mav asked, once inside.

Benny shrugged. "I don't know. It's fun." Maverick couldn't argue with that solid logic, so he nodded as Benny began to drive them back towards the gym. "So, Friday night, huh? What does a young single man do for fun on a Friday night?"

Maverick resisted the urge to roll his eyes. He liked his coaching assistant, but Benny saw anyone ten or more years younger than him as a child. He had a grandfatherly quality about him that was both endearing and slightly bothersome. "I think I'm going to find a spot for a drink. Any recommendations?"

Benny seemed to light up when Maverick asked for his opinions. He doubted they would frequent the same place, but since Benny was a long-standing member of this town, he should be able to recommend a place with good drinks.

"I don't take you as a western saloon type of guy?" Benny pondered, looking over at Maverick's scowl. "Ha! I'll take that as a no. Okay, well there's a few restaurants in town that serve drinks, but if you are looking for more of a bar scene, I'm not entirely familiar. Wife and I don't often drink and when we do, it's at home."

Well, that was slightly disappointing, but Maverick could easily google bars in the area.

"Oh wait!" Benny piped up once they stopped at the back of the storage room. Maverick hopped out to open the overhead door. "I read in the paper about a new, modern bar that just opened up not too far from here. It's supposed to be hip and trendy with young folks. I think it's called Cloud...something. Cloud Sign? Cloud Five? Damn, I forgot, but I know that it started with cloud."

Of course Benny would still get his news from a printed paper. Everything about the man screamed dated. Still, Maverick liked Benny. Even if he was a bit dated.

"Cloud something. Got it," Maverick said, committing it to memory.

He finished lugging the last of the equipment inside the storage room. It was as if a damn tornado went through this room, several times, obliterating everything in its path. One of his biggest pet peeves was disorderly sports equipment, but there was no way his ass was going to sort through all the football mess piled next to his baseball equipment. He made sure his small corner of the room was orderly, all his equipment packed up and readily accessible when he needed it.

"Alright, Benny I think we're done," Maverick said, stepping out of the garage to shut the door. He made sure he secured the lock before pocketing the key. "Imma hit the showers, so I'll lock down the gym tonight. And thanks for the rec. I'll see if I can find the bar you mentioned."

"Sounds fine to me boss. I better get home to the misses before she sends out a search party." He laughed good-naturedly and for a second Maverick wondered what it would be like to have a love like that. To be excited to go home because you knew the person waiting for you loved you with every fiber of their being.

Mav once thought he had that.

"See ya Monday, Mav!" Benny called, waving goodbye. He made sure Benny got to his car before heading inside.

It was a known fact that schools at night were creepy, especially with no one else around. Maverick walked a little faster than normal to the gym showers, half expecting a murderous clown to pop out and chase him. Luckily, none appeared as he stepped into the boys locker room for a quick shower.

Once finished, he grabbed a pair of light-colored jeans from his gym bag. This morning he had worn a button up white shirt, with a gray blazer over top. They weren't his usual attire to work, but the Yearbook class had wanted to take pictures of the team after their second win last night. Mav had wanted to appear professional in the photos, even if his team teased him mercilessly about it.

*Those fuckers,* he thought fondly, bringing a smile to his lips.

Maverick slung his training duffel bag over his shoulders, searching through it for his phone and keys. The crisp chill in the air assaulted his skin the moment he walked out of the building and straight to his truck. Yes, truck. A huge, almost luminescent white pickup. It wouldn't have been Mav's first, or third, choice in a vehicle, but Keanon insisted Mav borrow his truck while he stayed at his home, since Breanna kept the car.

Which meant Mav's latest drive was The Beast, as he dubbed it. If he weren't tall, he'd need a running start to pull himself into the monstrosity. Keanon was six or seven inches shorter than him. He couldn't imagine how his friend managed to pull his body into the driver's seat.

Now, Maverick needed to figure out where to go in this town for good booze. What had Benny suggested? Maverick vaguely remembered and began to type in cloud on his phone. A few results quickly came up. Cloud Dreams, which happened to be a sex store, Cloud Knight - they sold insurance - and finally Cloud 9.

Cloud 9 was the obvious winner, so Maverick let his GPS navigate him. When he arrived twenty minutes later, Mav was surprised to see a packed parking lot. The thrumming music hit his senses instantly once his door opened. It had been a long time since Mav was in a crowded place, outside of school functions. In the back of his mind, he wondered how many people would recognize him and how to handle it if someone approached him in a negative way.

Gathering all the swagger of his former self, Maverick put on the face of a confident man and walked inside. Judging by the parking lot, he had expected bodies to be packed close together, but that wasn't the case. There were a lot of people in Cloud 9, but the bar was spacious and provided ample space for drinkers and dancers. All the tables were currently occupied, but he didn't need one. Maverick didn't plan to stay long; he just wanted a sense of normalcy and a strong whiskey.

The bar was dead center, and he had to weave his way through dancing bodies and full tables. A few times he thought he heard his name, but no one tried to come up to speak to him or ask him for a selfie. Fading into obscurity was something he had not expected to like as much as he did.

With the bar only feet in front of him now, he scanned the chairs for an open seat. There was one tucked away in the corner, next to a couple. At first glance, they seemed enthralled by each other. The man leaned close, hand resting on her thigh, laughing at something she said. Mav thought the woman, just from a quick glance, was far too pretty to be with a man who looked as if his mother still picked out his clothes. But who was Maverick to judge? Love happened in mysterious ways, or some shit like that.

However, the longer he stared, the more he noticed the woman's rigid posture. She leaned away from the man, not towards him. The hand on her thigh, which Maverick had interpreted as affection, was an aggressive attempt to keep the woman from moving. Her body language screamed her discomfort and Maverick knew he needed to step in; he just didn't want to scare the woman any more.

There was also something extremely familiar about the woman too. Deep chestnut colored hair, hanging in spirals down her back. Long, gorgeous legs that came from years of athletic training. Curves he could lose-

"Don't fucking touch me."

Everything inside Maverick tensed, heat flashing through his body at Ofelia's voice.

How dare the man think he had the right to touch a woman, especially *this* woman. His body reacted before his brain contemplated a course of action. He zeroed in on the fucking bastard touching Ofelia, and Maverick found himself moving forward at a brisk pace. The man noticed him before Ofelia did, and he saw the flicker of fear in the man's eyes. Maverick's own voice was foreign to him, husky and full of disdain for a man he didn't know. "You have exactly one second to get your hands off her."

Ofelia's head shot back, looking at him with a mixture of shock and something else he couldn't quite place. He didn't have time to analyze that now though. Mav stepped in front of her, putting his body between Ofelia and the man in front of her. The pervert took his hand back, stumbling back like a coward. "I..it was nothin' man...I was just messin' around. Didn't know she had a boy-"

"Doesn't fucking matter." Maverick was done listening to this pathetic excuse of a man. "You shouldn't have touched her, period. I swear to God if she's bruised from your touch, I'll—"

"Maverick." Ofelia's soft voice called out in warning. She reached for his hand, trying to uncurl the fists he didn't know he made. He relaxed, but only slightly, as she slipped her hand into his and squeezed. "Don't make a scene. Just let him go."

Let him go? That was the exact opposite thing he wanted to do to this perv. He wanted to take away the man's sense of safety as he did with Ofelia and countless other women before her. The man was weak, trying to make himself seem superior by scaring women into submission. Yet when Maverick turned his head, Ofelia looked at him with worry in her eyes. Worry that he caused. It was like icy water being poured over his head, alerting him to Ofelia's needs.

Only because Ofelia was safe and unharmed did Maverick take a step backwards, casting one last heated glare at the perv. The stranger turned around, taking this opportunity to leave before Maverick changed his mind. Smart guy. Maverick's eyes followed him until he got lost in the crowd; lost in the sea of bodies.

"Are you okay?" Maverick finally asked, once capable of speech that wasn't laced with profanity. His eyes dropped down to where she still held his hand.

Ofelia must have realized at the same time as Maverick because she blushed before letting him go and tucked a strand of hair behind her ear. "I'm okay. Thank you. He didn't hurt me." They both heard the unspoken yet, but Ofelia didn't seem like she wanted to push the matter. "Why are you here?"

Maverick laughed, letting the air in his chest deflate some. His body still felt ready to take care of a threat, even though Ofelia was safe now. "Me? I should be asking you that. Why are *you* here, Ofelia?" More importantly, why was she dressed like she was out on a date? That black dress did all sorts of things to his mind and body. She could stab him with a bar knife and Maverick would thank her. That was how much this damn woman affected him.

Ofelia looked a little offended by his question; he saw her tense up and fold her arms over his chest. Which was a terrible move because it only pushed her large breasts up, causing Maverick to exert all his focus on keeping his eyes from glancing down. "I'm here with Willow. She's dancing and I was thirsty. I didn't ask for that man to harass me, Maverick."

No, of course she didn't. Logically, Maverick knew that. The last thing he wanted to do was blame her for the actions of another. There were far too many men that blamed women for what they were wearing, or their levels of alcohol consumption and Maverick refused to be that person. The anger built up in his chest began to subside. He let out a deep breath, sounding like a kettle letting out steam.

"I'm sorry. I know. I'm sure you could have handled him yourself but—"

"No, no, thank you." Ofelia cut him off, shaking her head. Her beautiful curls bounced around her face as she moved. "To be honest, I was getting worried. I can usually hold my own against assholes, but my body froze. I think I was in shock. So, thank you for stepping in. I feel like I owe you a drink." She laughed, trying to break the tension between them.

"Nah, you don't owe me anything. Mind if I sit here?" He indicated to the seat beside her. When she nodded, Maverick pulled the seat close, but left enough room to give her personal space, as he waved down the bartender. "Are you drinking anything?"

"I really shouldn't."

"But if you were?"

"It would be something light, like a mojito, but I'm buying."

Maverick ignored the last part and turned his attention towards the bartender he flagged down. "Your best whiskey and a mojito," he requested and quickly threw in a "please." Once gone, Mav swiveled his body to face Ofelia, resting his arm on the bar to prop himself up. This was the first time Maverick was able to get a good look at the woman. Before, his thoughts were preoccupied with making sure the man got his hands off her. But now...

Now he indulged himself.

Ofelia held herself with confidence he hadn't yet seen from her. That dress demanded it. There was no way anyone could wear that sexy, form fitting number and not feel anything less than a goddess. He hadn't considered himself a leg man before, but damn if he didn't want to run his hands up and down them. "You look fantastic." The words slipped out before he stopped himself. Sexy was the word he wanted to use.

"Don't I, though?" Ofelia beamed and God if that wasn't the single fucking hottest thing he had ever heard. He loved a woman that owned her own sexiness. "You don't look half bad yourself. You clean up nicely for a...what sport do you coach again?" There was no mistaking the sly look on her face as she spoke.

"You know exactly what sport I coach."

"Do I?" A teasing smile played on Ofelia's red lips. "Hmm, must have slipped my mind."

Maverick knew damn well that it didn't. Was she flirting with him? No, of course not. Why would she? They hardly knew one another. And yet...

"Your drinks," the bartender said, placing two glasses in front of them. "Holler if you need anything else." He smiled before moving on to the next customer.

"You never answered my questions," Ofelia said, reaching for her martini, soft pink nails reflecting in the light. "What are you doing here? Waiting for someone?"

Mav shook his head. "Not exactly. I came because it's been a roller coaster of a week. I don't know how teachers like you do this every day, year after year. I'm exhausted and it's only been a few weeks."

Mav earned a laugh out of Ofelia. He found that he liked the sound, low and seductive without trying. "Teaching isn't for the weak, but you've seemed to pick up coaching well. I've heard a few students say some pretty nice things about you. Trust me, coming from a high schooler, that's like an academy award."

"Glad to know they don't think I'm completely incompetent," Mav mused. "Your turn. What are you and Willow doing here?"

"Ah, well." Ofelia's eyes flickered down, and Maverick heard the slight hesitation in her voice. "Willow thought we needed a girls night. Something other than sitting at home and eating pizza. We went shopping for new outfits, got ready, and came here. She's somewhere..." Ofelia gestured to the crowd dancing. "Over there. I think she's been hitting on the same woman since we've been here."

"Sounds like Willow's getting a lot out of tonight. And you? What are you getting?"

Ofelia looked over at Maverick with confusion etched across her features. "What do you mean?"

"Well, Willow seems to be here to have fun and maybe more. Why did you come here? Boyfriend gone?" It wasn't the most eloquent way for Maverick to ask if she was seeing someone, but he was rusty. How did he use to pick up girls? Didn't people come to bars if they were looking to meet people? Maybe that's why she was here.

His question clearly flustered her. "B..boyfriend?" She said the word like bitter vinegar on her tongue. "Oh, no. No boyfriend. No. I don't date."

"Correction, she doesn't date yet!" A familiar voice rang shrill behind them. Then arms wound tightly around Ofelia, familiar red hair catching Maverick's attention first. He was happy to see Willow tear herself away from her dance partner long enough to come and find Ofelia.

"Maverick!" Willow greeted him as if they were old friends rather than coworkers who have had only a few interactions during lunch duty. She untangled herself from Ofelia and then went over to hug Mav like it was the most natural thing in the world. He awkwardly patted her back, thankful she moved away quickly.

"If we are talking about Ofelia's love life, then as her best friend, I must be here." Willow declared to no one in particular.

"We are most certainly not talking about that, or lack there-of," Ofelia said, thrusting water into Willow's hand.

He didn't have any right to know, but it didn't stop the seed of curiosity planted within him. "Why not? Sounds like a delightful topic to me."

Ofelia glared at him. "Because it's none of your business!"

"Ofi!" Willow whined, dragging out the last syllable. "Let loose, just a little. You deserve it," Willow said, sloppily kissing Ofelia on the forehead. "Gotta go. I got a sexy brunette waiting for me. Enjoy the rest of your date."

"Oh my god, Willow, this isn't a date!" Ofelia shouted after her friend, but Willow no longer paid attention. She groaned, rolling her eyes. "Ugh, sorry about her. She becomes overly affectionate when she drinks. This is why I keep her corralled at my house on the weekend. Wait, why are you smirking at me like that?"

Was he smirking? Yes, he most definitely was. He needed to remember to thank Willow later, for inadvertently giving him the perfect opening. "Nothing, it's cute that she thinks this is a date."

"Yeah, she's a mess—"

"Because I would never bring you to a bar for a first date. That dress is wasted here."

"What?" He watched Ofelia straighten up, his words slowly washing over her. He scanned her face carefully for any hints of anger or fear, but he found none, only shock.

This made him brave. He played a dangerous game, one that had the potential to end badly if he didn't play his cards right. They had played this game before, but under different circumstances. Now he was going to push her like he always wanted to. Not a teenager in sight. "You heard me, Ofelia. I said I wouldn't take you to a bar and call it a date."

"Why would you think I'd ever let you take me out on a date?"

She was toying with him. Good. He piqued her interest, despite her hesitation. He fucking loved that she knew her worth and questioned his. As confident as she appeared, Maverick couldn't help but notice the apprehension in her gaze and the way her eyes darted around nervously. This was new to her as well, or so Willow implied. They were both in a strange limbo, uncertain what the other thought. He hoped he gave her the same butter-flies she had been giving him since he arrived.

"Because you're curious. You'd want to know what a date with me entails."

Maverick watched Ofelia bite her lip. He couldn't help but think about what it would be like if he was the one biting her lip, sucking, and tasting her. What sounds would she make when he kissed her, pulling her close to his hard body? He bet they would be the sweetest damn sounds he'd ever heard.

"You are awfully cocky for someone who doesn't know a thing about me," Ofelia said, spinning in her chair until she faced him. Her knee brushed against his and she left it there. He'd place a wager that it was purposeful. "I don't like cocky men, Maverick. That's a strike against you. Three strikes and you're out." She held up a finger, signaling his one strike.

Fuck, she wanted to do baseball references now? He hadn't been this aroused and intrigued by a woman in so long. Even with Breanna. Towards the end, they had lacked the spark they once had and Maverick craved a woman who could not only please him physically, but mentally and emotionally as well.

"I'm not cocky, sweetheart. I'm confident and I know what I want. I suspect you do too, deep down." Maverick said. "I'm also attracted to confident women. The way you wear the dress, how you command your cheerleaders so effortlessly, it's an amazing quality about you. How am I doing?"

"Not bad." Ofelia tried for nonchalance, but Mav saw the smile quirk her lips. "Tell me about this date you'd take me on if I were to agree."

"Where do you take any English teacher? The bookstore." He grinned and Ofelia laughed. He felt that was a safe answer, but what else would he do? Mav was rusty when it came to dating, but he wanted to impress this woman. "After, we'd head to a restaurant and-"

Another finger went down, leaving only her pointer finger up. "You were doing so well with the bookstore, but a restaurant?

That's not very original of you. Try again but be careful. You only have one more chance to impress me."

This woman was evil. Pure, and unadulterated evil. But he loved this game they were playing. It was fragile and could break at any moment, but he wanted to play it until the end. "Did I say restaurant? You must have heard me wrong. I meant to say that I'd cook for you."

"You cook?"

"Not a bit, but I'm a fast learner." Maverick smirked, earning a laugh from Ofelia. Good, he wanted her to enjoy herself and see him as a possibility. What did either of them have to lose?

"So, a bookstore and homemade dinner. How could a girl pass that up?" Ofelia asked, her ring finger swirling over the top of her empty glass, as if pondering something. Maybe the fake date scenario?

Before he could ask more of her, Willow chose that moment to make another reappearance, slithering in between them. Maverick had to move back in his chair to make room for her. She seriously had the worst timing ever. "We have a major problem. Ofi, we need to leave. Now."

"What?" Both Maverick and Ofelia said at the same time. Ofelia pulled Willow to face her, running her eyes up and down her friend's body. Not in the way Maverick had looked at Ofelia earlier. She assessed her friend for any signs of maltreatment. Exactly what Maverick had done to Ofelia after the man harassed her.

"My contact! Mascara got into my eye, and I tried to rub it away, but I ended up ripping my contact in half and now my eye hurts." Willow's voice turned whiny. He didn't know how many drinks Willow consumed, but he assumed more than her body could handle.

Ofelia seemed to sense the same thing and got up. "Yeah, that's awful babe. I'll get our ride here. We'll take you home." She already had her phone up, clicking through the app.

Maverick was not about to let two young women get into a

stranger's car while intoxicated. Even if Ofelia wasn't as drunk as Willow, she had still had a few drinks. "I'll drive." He offered, waving down his waiter to pay and close their tabs.

"You really don't have to do that."

"I'm not letting you walk out of here without me. I don't trust a stranger to get you both home safely. It's not up for discussion; I'm taking you home." Maverick didn't wait for her to argue. He paid his bill and dug his keys out of his pocket. "Bring her to the front, I'll bring the truck around."

Not wanting to leave them alone for too long, Mav jogged to his car and soon pulled up at the front doors. Ofelia had just gotten Willow through the door. Mav left the truck on and hurried to help Ofelia lift Willow into the back seat. Willow flopped on her back, giggling and murmuring unintelligible words. Ofelia struggled with her buckle, but eventually clicked it into place.

"She's going to have the worst hangover in the morning," Ofelia said, shaking her head. "Willow isn't a lightweight. I can't begin to guess the number of drinks she had."

"We'll get her home safely," Maverick assured.

The drive back to Willow's house was silent, minus the incoherent mumbling from Willow in the back. The silence in the car wasn't awkward or tense, but comfortable. Maverick liked not having to fill the time with idle small talk. Even though there was still so much he wished to know about Ofelia, this was not the time.

When they pulled up to Willow's house, only a five-minute drive from his own, Maverick cut off the engine. "Do you want me to help you carry her inside?"

Ofelia shook her head, unbuckling her seat belt. "No, I can do that. But can you help me get her out?"

"Of course," Maverick met Ofelia on the passenger side. She had the door open, attempting to coax Willow out like a child with promises of pizza and cupcakes. He reached in to unbuckle her seat belt. Between the two of them, they were able to pull Willow out of the car and plant her feet firmly underneath her.

It then took her approximately two seconds to escape their grasp and run towards the door. "I'm going to be sick!" She yelled, stumbling inside. Maverick was amazed at how fast a drunk Willow could run.

"I should probably go check on her," Ofelia said after a beat passed between them.

A wave of disappointment overcame him. He had been enjoying his night and then it had been cut short. He felt like he missed his moment. "Yeah, you probably should."

Ofelia began to walk away, but when she made it halfway to the house, she turned around and looked back at him. "You never told me how that date would end? The hypothetical one."

A smile crossed his features. He wasn't the only one that had been thinking about the fake date. "I'm a gentleman when the time calls for it, Ofelia. I would take you home and walk you to the door. Before you turned away from me, I'd pull you to my body and kiss you like you deserve to be kissed."

He swore he heard an intake of breath. It was too dark to see her expression, but he imagined her flustered. When she spoke, her voice was a little breathy. "That's your idea of a gentleman?"

"Sweetheart, if you read my thoughts, you would see that is the most gentlemanly thing I want to do right now."

"Oh." Was all she said and for a moment, Maverick thought he lost her. Then her voice pierced through the silence. "When would this date take place?"

As much as he wanted to say tomorrow, Maverick didn't want to rush her. "Next Saturday?"

"Can I have a night or two to think about it? Before I give you my answer?"

"Yeah, of course." He would have preferred an answer now, but he was thankful it wasn't a no. "Let me give you my number."

They exchanged numbers in the dark. Ofelia handed him the

phone back first, his fingers lingering a second longer than normal, before pulling back. "I'll hear from you soon?" He asked.

"You will. Goodnight, Maverick."

"Goodnight, Ofelia."

He waited until Ofelia locked herself inside the house before getting in his car and driving home.

The smile he wore the entire way home never once disappeared, even as he slept soundly that night.

# Ofelia

## CHAPTER TWELVE

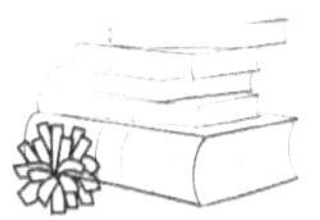

Willow had not been a fun friend to be around last night. As soon as Ofelia came back in from saying goodnight to Maverick, she found Willow hunched over a potted plant, puking her guts out. "Oh Willow! That's not...oh, never mind." Ofelia had said before coming up behind her friend and pulling back her hair. They stayed like that for an hour, Ofelia rubbing her friend's back as Willow apologized profusely.

She wasn't upset though. She was worried about her friend, but mostly her head was still clouded with thoughts of Maverick. Hot, sexy Maverick. The same guy who had been a dick to her the first time they met, but had been nothing but sweet since. Was she actually considering a date with Maverick Wilson? Was she crazy not to?

Luckily Willow had needed her full attention last night and Ofelia's mind had no time to think about just how yummy Maverick looked. She was definitely not thinking about the way he stepped in to rescue her from Mr. Creepy, feeling his hard chest against her back. She would also not think about the palpable chemistry brewing between them and the way he ignited a fire in her core.

No, those were things she definitely wasn't thinking about as she helped Willow get herself showered and hydrated. Many times her friend tried to apologize, but Ofelia was hearing none of it. They had a great time and she was happy they went out, but she did lecture her friend on knowing when it was time to switch over to water. They weren't in college anymore and couldn't drink like they used to.

After making sure Willow was tucked into bed with water and ibuprofen on her bedside table, Ofelia meandered into the guest bedroom down the hall. Since their usual Friday nights took place at Willow's and Ofelia typically had one too many glasses of wine to safely drive home, she began to store some clothes over at her friend's house. Within twenty minutes, Ofelia had showered, brushed her teeth, and put her phone on the extra guest room charger before slipping into bed. The moment her head hit the pillows, she was out.

It was only when her body rested and her thoughts roamed freely, that Ofelia dreamed of Maverick. Her thoughts started innocently enough, simple things like getting coffee with him or what it would feel like to cuddle on the couch. Her mind drifted into more dangerous territory when she thought about the strong, protector side of Maverick and how that would transfer to the bedroom. Her dreams quickly become R rated when she pictured them in bed together; her writhing and begging for more. Just as Dream Maverick was going to give her exactly that, a vibrating sound rattled the bedside table, causing her to wake up.

Dammit! She had been in the midst of probably getting the best orgasm of her entire life and her damn phone ruined it. Yes, it had been a dream but it felt so real. Her body was on high alert, aware of every tingling part of her. She wanted nothing more to take care of the ache between her legs, but her phone vibrated once more, signaling an incoming text.

Curse her curious nature and her inability to not obsessively check her phone as soon as a notification came in. She groaned and reached for it, seeing a missed FaceTime call and a text, both from Javi. There was nothing more of a buzz kill than having your brother interrupt your sex dream. It was exactly the cold water she needed dumped over her body to kick the horny demon to the curb.

Ofelia pushed herself up into a sitting position on the bed. She was sure her hair was a crazy mess; it was the reason why she hated going to sleep with wet hair. Her head was pounding slightly from the alcohol. Even though she hadn't been wasted, she still had more alcohol than she normally did. Poor Willow, her friend must be absolutely miserable. She hoped Willow saw the medicine she placed near her bed and took it as soon as she woke up. Knowing Willow, it would be a few more hours.

Her brother would just have to deal with her looking like a swamp monster. She clicked on her brother's missed FaceTime call and her face, a very tired and slightly hungover face, stared back at her. It only took two rings until her brother picked up, Camilia snuggled up happily in her daddy's arms.

"Oh my goodness, is that my Camilia? Hi, baby girl!" Ofelia cooed, unable to stop the warm smile her niece brought to her lips. There was still an ache in her heart each time she saw Camilia because her niece was so far away. She felt like she was missing out on her life.

"Tía Ofi!" Camilia said and pointed to what Ofelia guessed was the tv. "I watch Bluey!"

She had no idea what the hell Bluey was, but Ofelia smiled all the same. Her sweet niece climbed off her father's lap and ran off screen, Javi pointing at some toy she was asking for. "Sorry, sis. She's on to her baby dolls now."

"Well, I can't compete with baby dolls." Ofelia laughed, before asking. "So, what's up? Why did you call me at the butt crack of dawn?"

"It's 10am." Javi laughed, rolling his eyes. "And I wanted to make sure you didn't wake up dead or with a weird ass guy you met at the bar last night."

"Javi, you can't wake up dead. You're dead. But also, how did you know I went out to the bar last night? Are you tracking me?"

Javi didn't look apologetic as he shrugged. If anything, her brother looked smug with his cocky grin. "I have my ways and of course I'm tracking you. I didn't want you to end up in a ditch somewhere." It was Ofelia's turn to roll her eyes, but secretly she liked that her brother loved her enough to make sure she got home safe. "But no, Willow told me." He said, stunning Ofelia.

"W...Willow told you? As in my best friend Willow? Since when have you and Willow talked?" Ofelia was honestly confused. She had mentioned her friend a few times to her brother and introduced them over FaceTime a year ago, but that was the extent of their communication. Or so she thought.

"Don't be so shocked, Ofi. You think I'm going to let my sister move across the country and not check in on her from time to time? You got it twisted. Besides, it is hella easy finding people on social media."

Well, that was new. Ofelia wasn't sure how she felt about her brother and Willow talking behind her back. Of course she understood the need to make sure she was okay, Ofelia felt the same way about her family. She couldn't get mad at him for caring, but she could be bothered by the secret exchange. This was definitely something she was going to grill Willow about later.

Since he knew, she supposed there was no harm in telling him about last night. She could actually use his advice on the whole Maverick issue. "It was really fun." She admitted, running a hand through her highly matted hair. "It had been a long time since I allowed myself to let loose and have fun. But, something did happen. And don't freak out!"

She knew immediately she said the wrong thing. Javi's relaxed posture on the couch grew rigged as he sat up straighter, bringing the phone closer to his face. "What the hell happened, Ofelia?"

Yeah, she definitely shouldn't have phrased it like that because she alerted the guard dog inside of him. Too late to take it back now. "There was a creepy guy hitting on me at the bar and getting a little too handsy."

Javi cursed under his breath and Ofelia heard Camila "ooh" in disappointment. "Sorry baby. Papa will put a quarter in the jar," he said to his daughter, before giving his attention back to his sister. "Did he hurt you? What happened?"

"No, Javi. No one hurt me. Or at least no one got the chance to hurt me. Maverick stepped in before the guy could do any real damage."

"Maverick. Who is Maverick?"

Oh right. She hadn't really kept her brother up to date with what was happening in her life. She knew that was common in most siblings, but Javi was one of her best friends and she told him everything. It was unusual that she kept anything from him. She blamed this on her busy cheerleading schedule that consumed her every free minute.

"Maverick was the asshole I kinda started to tell you about, but it's good now," she said quickly, before more steam could pour out of her brother's ears and nostrils. "He's apologized since then. Anyway, he happened to be there that night and scared the jerk away. Then we sorta ended up talking for the rest of the night. Actually, I think we were flirting. No, no we were most definitely flirting."

"Oh," Javi said, his shoulders relaxing. He didn't look ready to fly down to Texas and tear the dude's head off, so Ofelia took that as a win. "Wow, that's great Ofi. Do you like him?"

If that wasn't the world's most loaded question. Yes, she did like him. Maybe. But did she like him enough to end her two year dry spell? Was she really ready to get back out there? "I...yes? Maybe? Fuck, I don't know." She groaned miserably. "Help, Javi. I haven't been in the dating scene for years. I'm rusty as hell. Not to mention jaded."

"You are preaching to the choir, sis." Javi laughed, but his smile didn't quite meet his eyes. Instantly, Ofelia felt guilty for complaining. She was only left at the altar. Which sucked and she wouldn't recommend it, but Javi had found his person. He created life with her and was getting ready to plan their wedding. Until Camilia's mom got into a horrible car accident and died on scene. So yeah her situation was shitty, but what right did she have to complain when Javi's love died?

As if knowing what she was thinking, Javi shook his head. "Stop it. I can handle you complaining to me about things like this. I'm just happy that you are even considering dating again. That's a big step, Ofi."

This was why she loved talking to her brother so much. He knew exactly what to say and what she needed to hear. He could be her light in the fog and she really needed that right now. "I'm scared," she admitted.

"What are you scared of?"

"I...I guess I'm scared to open myself up again. To go on a date, which is essentially like a job interview. First dates are the absolute worst things in existence. There is so much judging going on. What if he's not the person I thought he was? What if he is and I really like him but he doesn't like me? There are so many unknown factors and it's driving me a little crazy," Ofelia said, words pouring from the deepest parts of her insecurity.

Javi didn't judge; he just nodded. "Yeah, I think those feelings are natural though, you know? Dating is fucking terrifying. But that just means you like this person and want to see where it can lead. Maverick is obviously interested, which is why he asked you out. The hard part is out of the way. The date is something you both can enjoy."

"What if he turns out to be horrible? Or thinks that a microwavable dinner counts as a meal? What if we have nothing in common?"

"But what if you do?"

Ofelia groaned. "Javi! You can't answer my question with a question. I need you to tell me what I should do!"

"You know I can't make the decision for you, sis." Javi laughed as Ofelia deflated. Things would be so much easier if people could just make all the hard choices for her. "But I can support you in whatever you choose. I don't think there is any harm in going on one date with Maverick. But if you don't think you are ready to hit the dating scene yet, then that's also fine. There's no timeline that you have to follow."

Just the one that she set for herself. At twenty-six, Ofelia thought she would be married by now, with a child. Her life had changed so drastically from the girl who wanted that life. She enjoyed the path she was on now and knew if she had gone through with her marriage to Hector, she would be miserable. Maybe now was the perfect opportunity to see what other options she had. Like Javi said, she didn't have to put any expectations on the date. She could just see where things went.

"How about this," Javi spoke again, after a beat of silence passed between them. "You go on the date with Maverick. An hour in, I'll call you with some fake emergency. If you feel overwhelmed or things are going badly, answer it and I'll make up some reason for you to leave. But if things are going well and you are having a good time, just ignore my call. I'll take that as a sign that everything is fine."

"Javi, you are a genius!"

"About time you picked up on that." He smirked.

Ofelia loved the idea of having a choice to leave the date if things weren't going as she wanted them too. This would make the anxiety she felt about the date lessen considerably. "Okay. I think I made my decision. Holy shit, I'm going out on a date!" Ofelia said with a sense of giddiness. Yes she was freaking out, but she couldn't help how excited she was about it. This just seemed like another step in the right direction for her. Like she was finally in control of her life again. She just needed to text Maverick that they were on for next week.

"Thank you, Javi. You're the best. I think I should go and text Maverick back—"

"I'm proud of you, Ofi. I'm glad you are doing something for yourself for a change," her brother cut in, smiling. Ofelia felt her cheeks flush as pride swelled in her chest. "Listen, I gotta take Camilia to the park, but tell me how things go. Keep me informed."

"You know I will. Thank you, Javi. For everything. Wait! Before you go, how's dad? He's still coming to my competition, right?" Ofelia wondered, since the last time they spoke her father had shocked her by dropping that bombshell.

Javi looked confused. "He talked about going?"

Dread began to set in, but she kept it at bay. If there was one thing her father was bad at, it was communication. "Yeah, I was under the impression you put him up to it honestly. But he said he wanted to fly down to see my competition. I think he feels bad since I don't have mama to come watch me. I sent him all the information."

"Right," Javi said slowly, still confused but plastering on a smile. "I'll talk to him about it later and see what's going on. You just worry about your date, but I gotta go before your niece destroys my house due to her impatience." Her brother offered her one last wink before ending their conversation.

With newly found elation and slight trepidation about her father, Ofelia got out of bed. There was one thing she needed to do before checking on Willow. She grabbed her phone and scrolled through the contacts until she landed on Maverick's name. Her fingers flew across the screen without hesitation. She pressed send, watching the blue line move across her screen, disappearing once it was sent.

*'You've convinced me. I would love to go out next Saturday."*

Ofelia didn't wait to read his reply. She tossed her phone on to the bed and went off to tell a very hungover Willow all about her exciting morning.

# Maverick

## CHAPTER THIRTEEN

THE NEW SCHOOL week went by in a blur. Maverick finally found his footing and developed a routine. He juggled between coaching off-season boys and mentoring his baseball team. Both were rewarding in their own way but left him with little time to do anything else during the actual school day. He never realized how needy teenage boys could be. They were like chicks to a mother hen, flocking to him each time a problem arose.

And Maverick loved every fucking second of it.

Since when did he become such a damn softie? He not only helped teenage boys run through workout routines or baseball plays, he also helped them in their personal lives too. Sometimes his players would come to him when they had homework. Maverick didn't know shit about algebra, but he knew how to google. At times, he would have the whole damn team in the gym, sprawled out across the floor and working on their core classes. If they didn't pass, they didn't play. He couldn't preach the importance of academics without supporting their studies.

His office in the gym turned into therapy sessions when his guys needed someone to talk to. They told him far more than he would have ever told any of his teachers or coaches in high school. Maverick didn't think he was qualified to give high school boys relationship advice, but he could listen and impart some wisdom from his own experiences.

Over a short period, he had been able to make strong impressions and relationships with his students, but it also meant he rarely left the gym. It killed him knowing he worked in the same campus as Ofelia but was unable to see her during the day. After her text accepting his date, Maverick's mind hadn't been able to think of anything else.

They started texting each other more and on Wednesday, Ofelia had sent a picture of her, draped dramatically over a stack of what he presumed to be student essays. She had that sexy librarian look going on again, with her hair styled in a messy bun, wearing a sweater dress he hadn't seen before. She looked beautiful and Maverick had to do everything in his power to stop himself from finding her room and kissing those pouty lips until they were both breathless.

The only thing keeping him sane was their date on Saturday. An entire day to impress her and finally spend time alone that didn't involve needy teenagers or drunk friends. He wondered if she thought about him as much as he thought about her, since she plagued his every dream.

More than once this week, he woke up hard and had to relieve himself in the shower. It was pathetic, but also incredible. If just the thought of Ofelia made him throb with need, what would it be like when, or rather if, he got her into his bed?

Maverick was getting ahead of himself. He needed Saturday to go well before he started down this road he'd be unable to turn back from. For now, Mav, like many other important things in his life, packed Ofelia and their upcoming date into a neatly wrapped box, shoving it far back into his brain. If he agonized over this, no work would get completed. There was only an hour left in the school day and he wanted to make sure he completed all of his tasks.

Maverick sat down in front of his computer, fully set on updating his grade book and making sure everything was in order for their game next week, when his phone rang. He groaned, fishing around in his pocket until he found it. Breanna's number flashed across the screen and he saw red.

It had been several weeks since she tried reaching out and he had naively thought her calls were finally going to stop. Clearly he needed to take care of the problem himself and it did not involve answering the phone to rehash the past. No, his method was quite simple. He blocked her. He wasn't entirely sure why it took as long as it did, maybe he had been holding on to a pathetic hope they would rekindle once he was ready.

But he knew he never would be ready, so he went back through his call log and finally blocked Breanna. A sense of peace came over him and he was about to put his phone down when it lit up again.

An unknown caller flashed across the screen with a Chicago area code.

He frowned. A part of him wondered if a reporter found his number and was looking for an easy story. It had happened so often directly after his ban, but had slowly become less frequent. Normally he'd ignore it, but he remembered Keanon mentioning someone from Gilmore's firm might be reaching out to him about his case. Or maybe it was Breanna again, calling from a new number, but that didn't seem likely either. She had never once tried contacting him by any other number other than her own and her area code had never switched over to Chicago.

At the last possible second Maverick picked up the phone. "Hello?"

Someone cleared their throat on the other side, away from the speaker. "Maverick Wilson?""

"Speaking."

"Mr. Wilson, this is Lloyd Gilmore from LG Law Firm. A Mr. Keanon Jermaine contacted my firm last week regarding your case. Is this a good time to talk?"

*Holy shit.* Maverick thought he'd speak to a secretary or an intern. Not Lloyd fucking Gilmore himself. He definitely wasn't prepared for this phone call, but he couldn't demand Gilmore call him back at another time. Maverick's body tensed as he spoke. "Yes, of course. Thank you for taking the time to look at my file."

"It's been a long time since I've dealt with an MLB ban, so I'm intrigued. I had some questions for you before I agreed to take on your case. Now, from what I'm seeing in your file, the reason for your ban is disorderly conduct with a coaching professional and conspiring to fix the game outcome. Is that correct?"

Maverick gritted his teeth. He heard the reasoning a multitude of times, but it never got easier to hear. Gilmore was one of a handful of people who could read the charges without disgust or superiority in his voice. Mav couldn't help but to be a bit unnerved, even though it was quite literally, the man's job to be neutral until he accepted his case. "That is correct."

"This was brought to the Office of the Commissioner by Grant Adams, coach of Chicago Rays, after an altercation took place between you, your former fiancé Breanna Homes, and said coach."

It wasn't a question but Maverick answered anyway. "Yes, sir."

"There isn't a detailed record of what transpired between the three of you. This may be hard to talk about, but it is important for your case. I don't need the long, drawn out story, but I do need the important facts. Do you think you can give me that?"

Did he? He wasn't sure he understood that night and it had been replaying in his head almost daily since it happened. It had gone so wrong, so quickly. If Maverick hadn't stayed late. If he hadn't gone in search of Grant Adams. If he didn't bring Breanna to his practices....so many ifs and all completely out of his control. He could, however, control his own narrative of the sequence of events that happened that night. He needed to get his thoughts in order because they were racing as fast as his heart.

"I understand this is hard to talk about, but it is really important. I could call back later-"

"No, no. It's okay," Maverick assured, not wanting to agonize over this for any longer than he had to. Gilmore was his best shot at getting his old life back; he needed to play along. "Coach Adams had the team come in for conditioning training. My fiancée at the time, Breanna Homes, came with me so she could hang out with the other wives and girlfriends. I was already hesitant to go because I was getting over a mild case of food poisoning and I didn't want to push my body."

"Did Breanna go with you to all your practices?" Lloyd asked. Maverick heard the click of a pen and knew the man was writing down their conversation.

"Not at first. She didn't like one of the other wives, but my last three months playing was when she really started to come to each practice."

"I see. Continue," Lloyd said.

"I started to feel nauseous and my trainer told me to hit the showers. He didn't want me to push myself anymore. So I left practice early and headed down to the locker room."

"Is there an office in the locker room?" Lloyd asked, interjecting again.

"There is, though Adams rarely used it," he said, remembering how his coach hardly visited the locker rooms. "But when I got down there, I saw the light on in the office and then I heard a grunt. I thought someone was hurt or in trouble. When I walked in..." Maverick stopped. This was the hard part. A piece of him died that day, perhaps his innocence. He had been naïve enough to think love was enough, but it wasn't. And it hadn't been for a long time.

When he continued, he closed his eyes and remembered the scene. "Breanna was bent over his desk, naked minus her bra. Grant Adams was behind her, pants down around his legs. He was...inside of her, and they were in the middle of having sex and neither noticed me. Breanna saw me first and-" He would never forget the look on her face. It shattered any hopes of a future with her and this team. "She looked part relieved and part smug. I got the sense this had been going on for a long time, but I was too much of an idiot to notice."

Lloyd didn't change his tone as he spoke, but Maverick detected a softness to his voice that hadn't been there before. "According to the report, you attacked Grant Adams and struck Breanna? Is that true?"

A bitter laugh left Mav's lips. "Hardly. The man attacked me first. He had the audacity to be pissed at me when I walked in on him fucking my fiancée. He lunged and I defended myself. Breanna tried to pull me off, but she got caught in the crossfire. I'm not sure which one of us pushed her back, but I didn't slap her. She hit her face on the desk when she fell. I screamed, said things I'm not proud of. I was angry and hurt. Breanna told me they'd been sleeping around behind my back for months."

"And Grant Adams, he's a married man is that correct?" Lloyd asked.

Maverick nodded, even though the man couldn't see him. Grant and his wife had been married for over twenty years. She was a former beauty pageant queen turned doctor. Arguably more of a success story than her husband. "He's married to Geneva Adams."

"I see. This is starting to make more sense. Adams claims you forced your fiancée on him, to manipulate him so you have more field time. Not sure how that equates to fixing the outcome of the game, but I'll dive into that. The other claim, disorderly conduct, will be harder to overturn. But from what you've told me, I think we have a pretty strong case in your favor."

"Wait, are you saying you'll take my case?" Maverick was stunned. At the beginning of his fall from grace, Maverick had reached out to countless lawyers. Only a handful ever got back to him and only to say they wouldn't represent him. Grant Adams was so lawyered up that no one was willing to risk their career for a case that seemed like a losing battle. Yet Lloyd offered his services, despite the risk to his career.

"I'll be honest, Maverick. Your file interested me and believe it or not, you have not been the first to reach out about Grant Adams. You are, however, the first I see with a solid case. If you are willing to proceed forward, then so am I." The man said, throwing the ball back into Mav's court.

Maverick had waited to hear those words for so long. He had a case. *Finally.*

He thought he would feel a sense of satisfaction, but he just felt slightly queasy, and he couldn't understand why. Still, he knew, even if his body said otherwise, this wasn't an opportunity he could afford to pass up. "I'm ready. What do you require from me?"

"In about a day or so, I'll have my assistant send over a contract and a few other documents I'll have you read over and sign. I don't need anything from you right now while I start building your case. When it's time, you'll need to come back to Chicago for your hearing.

"Once the process starts, it can go fast. I reckon Grant Adams's lawyers will be eager to get this case out of the way in a hurry," Lloyd said and then went over a few details of his contract and payment plans. Once he finished describing the nuts and bolts of the contract, Lloyd finished by saying, "I'll be in touch. Keep an eye out for my call and check your email."

The call ended, leaving Maverick in a stew of his own mixed emotions. This is what he wanted. He wanted to clear his name and get back to the life he had worked so hard to obtain. Baseball *was* his life. His purpose. So why did he have to convince himself of that?

Maverick started to pack up his duffle, unable to think about work now. He needed to go home and call Keanon about what happened. Slinging his duffel over his shoulders, Maverick headed for the door. He looked back once, to make sure he didn't leave anything behind, before turning off the light. He shut his door, locking it before turning around, preparing to walk out to his car, and...

He ran straight into Willow, startling her. "Oh! Maverick, don't sneak up on me like that! You nearly gave me a heart attack."

Maverick just stared. "Willow, you're in my gym. Quietly

stalking outside my door. How is it that I'm the one getting yelled at?" It was strange to see the woman here. Maverick had only ever seen her come in here with Ofelia, but even then Willow never stayed long, and she most certainly didn't come alone. "Did you need something?"

"Actually, I did, and I know you are eager to get home, so I'll be quick." She said as her face changed from friendly to what he assumed was meant to be intimidating. It was as effective as a puppy with a knife, cute and maybe a little spooky, but mostly comical. "You're taking Ofelia out on Saturday—"

"Yes, I'm aware of that."

"I'm not finished." Willow did not appear pleased at being interrupted. "Let me start over. What I came down here to say is that Ofelia is very special to me. I love her like my own sister. I don't know if you know how big of a deal this is for her to agree to go out with someone. I don't want to see her get hurt. You understand?"

Maverick did. He smiled, trying to reassure her friend. Willow looked on the brink of crying, and he didn't handle tears well. "Willow, calm down. I know Ofelia is your best friend. I wouldn't do anything to intentionally hurt her. I like her and I want to see where this goes. I promise, I'll be a perfect gentleman." Well, mostly. There were a few things he wanted to do that were not very gentleman-like.

Thankfully his words seemed to ease Willow. She let out a deep breath and the tension in her body visibly eased. "Good. That's good. Because if you hurt her, I will sic my husband Karl on you and....actually no. Karl would think you were cute and then I would have another problem on my hand. My point is, don't hurt her or I'll make sure you get bus duty for the rest of your days."

"You wouldn't dare." He smirked.

"Oh, I dare! I dare so hard. I'm watching you Maverick." She did a weird hand gesture, signaling she had her eyes on him. "Also don't tell Ofelia I threatened you. Make sure you pick her up at her house. Don't have her meet you anywhere, that's not classy enough for her. I have a few ideas on where you can take her, so I'll be in touch."

With that last ominous threat, Willow gave him one last piercing glare before walking out the gym. She stopped when she got to the double door to scowl at him once more for good measure and then disappeared entirely.

Today was shaping up to be more eventful than he anticipated. He didn't think he could handle another intense phone call or strange encounter, so he walked to his truck a little faster than normal and drove away without looking back.

OFELIA WAS SWEATING. It was so damn hot in her bathroom. Not only were her mirror lights shining spotlights on her but coupled with the heat of her curling wand, made the space unbearable. Also her arms hurt, like a lot. Which was pathetic but they burned from exertion. *Note to self, stop skipping arm day in favor of butt day.*

"You should have gone with the curlers," Willow said unhelpfully. "I told you it will save a lot of time and you'd be on to makeup by now. But no one listens to me."

"You have my curlers, Willow!" Ofelia glared at her phone. "And besides, I'm almost done. Stop distracting me."

"Why did you FaceTime us both if you don't want us talking to you?" Javi asked, distracted by his video games. She knew Camilia was napping because there was no way her brother could play his games in peace.

"Because," Ofelia threw her arms down, a bit too dramatically because her phone fell into the sink. "Ah shit. I just needed to give my arms a break, not drown you both in my sink," she mumbled, grabbing her phone to perch them up against the mirror once again. "Sorry. Anyways, I called you both because you are the two people I love most in this world and I'm fucking nervous. I need to see friendly faces while I get ready and I need you both making sure I don't talk myself out of going."

Today was her first official date with Maverick. The nerves set in the moment she woke, and they nearly consumed her. It didn't make any sense, since this was the first time all week she started feeling anxious. She talked to Maverick daily since last Friday night. Never on the phone, but rather they texted each other dumb memes and mundane life events. It was so easy to talk to him, but it was easy to talk to anyone with a screen dividing them.

Today Ofelia wouldn't have the luxury of a screen between them; a concept that both thrilled and scared her. It was silly to be this nervous, especially since they had spent a great deal of time together last Friday night. It still didn't have the "date" word attached. Now she actually had to try putting herself out there. What did one talk about on a date?

"Your arms have rested enough. Now back to curling. You are almost done. Maverick should be there in thirty minutes," Willow piped up after she deemed enough time had passed.

"Thirty minutes! What the hell! I don't have time....wait." Ofelia paused, narrowing her eyes into little slits as she glared back into the phone for the second time in five minutes. "How do you know what time Maverick is coming?"

"You think I'm going to let my best friend go out with a stranger, albeit smoking hot, and not get his number? Javi has it too." Willow smiled triumphantly.

"Javi!"

Javi threw his hands up in a 'don't look at me' gesture, feigning innocence. "Hey, don't be mad that we care for you."

Despite her best efforts, Ofelia couldn't stay mad at the two of them. Annoyed...but not mad. "Do not text or threaten him. I don't need him thinking I associate with crazy people."

"Sweetie, he saw me shit faced and crying over my contact. If he doesn't think I'm crazy by now, nothing will." Willow had a point. "There's nothing wrong with us having his phone number. Just in case."

"Fine, whatever," Ofelia acquiesced, finishing her hair. "Let me go get dressed first. Stay here."

"Where the fuck else would we go?" She heard Javi calling after her, but Ofelia was already deep within her closet.

It wasn't a particularly cold day, but a slight chill hung in the air. A skirt was out of the question...unless she paired it with one of her thick tights. That could be cute, if only she could find her brown corduroy skirt. It only took a few moments of searching before she found her skirt and the long sleeved, black bodysuit she typically paired it with. Would it be a pain in the ass to pee today? Yes, yes it would. But she also looked cute as hell, so she was willing to risk it.

It took Ofelia approximately five minutes to get dressed, which she hoped left her enough time to apply some makeup. When she walked back into her small bathroom, she was surprised to hear her brother and Willow chatting about the best toppings for pizza. She had no clue how they arrived at this conversation, but it was cute to see her best friend and brother getting along.

"So how do I look?" Ofelia asked, hating to interrupt their very intense conversation on whether pineapples went on pizza. They didn't, in Ofelia's opinion.

Willow and Javi looked over at her at the same time. She watched as their eyes widened, looking at her as if she just sprouted angel wings on her back. Neither one of them spoke though and it didn't help her nerves one bit. "Someone needs to say something now before I call this off."

"Ofi, you look beautiful, just like mama when she was younger." Javi's voice spoke up first, sending unexpected emotions coursing through her body. Hearing that made Ofelia feel like her mother was still here, that she carried her wherever she went. She fought back tears at his comment.

"Sweetie, you are beautiful, but you have about ten minutes until Maverick gets there. No time for tears! Makeup. Now!" Willow's command ended the sweet moment. Her friend smiled at her encouragingly as she started listing off what Ofelia needed to do. Brows, concealer, mascara, and blush. She didn't have time to do a full face, but she could enhance her natural beauty.

Ofelia finished applying her lipstick when her doorbell rang. She let out a sound of surprise, eyes wide in terror. "Holy shit, he's here! What should I do?"

"Well, personally, I'd answer the door, but that's just me," Javi said, smirking. He was trying to lighten the mood, but Ofelia felt on the brink of a panic attack. Was it normal to be this nervous before a first date? Was it too late to cancel?

"Yes! It's very too late to cancel and I wouldn't let you do that!" Willow said. Ofelia hadn't realized she said that out loud.

"Remember Ofi, we have a plan," Javi spoke, his soothing voice was exactly what she needed. "In an hour, I'll call you. Then you can decide if you want to answer or not. You have options, don't forget that. Now hang up and go answer the door. Remember, have fun."

Both Javi and Willow waved goodbye before disconnecting, leaving her alone. She could do this, deserved to do this. It would be a shame to waste a good outfit and hair day. She repeated her silent pep talk as she walked to the door.

Taking a big breath and before she could chicken out, Ofelia opened the door a little too forcefully because Maverick took a step back in alarm. "Uh, sorry. Hi." *Great start*, she thought miserably. "I guess I don't know my own strength."

Maverick chuckled, probably at her expense. "No worries," he assured as his eyes swept down her body. His gaze landed on her feet and slowly made their way back up until he met her gaze. He looked at her as if she were art on display, his smoldering gaze hot and assessing. "You look beautiful. Wow."

His words brought on a faint blush but also boosted her confidence. Since he allowed himself a once over, it was only fair she did the same. She had never seen him outside his uniform or work out gear. Today he wore faded jeans that looked expensive, but Ofelia couldn't be sure. She knew virtually nothing about men's fashion. His black and white shirt fit his torso nicely. He paired it with an oversized army green jacket. When she finally reached his eyes again, Maverick was smirking.

The man exuded sexual energy, leaving her hot in all the right places.

Heat soared through her body, going directly to her core. Great, now she was nervous and horny. If she made it out of this date alive, it would be a miracle. "Are you ready to go?" Maverick asked.

"Let me go get my purse," she said, disappearing back into her house and returning a moment later with a small, over the shoulder purse. "Now I'm ready."

As they walked to the truck, Maverick's hand hovered near the center of her back. She could feel his phantom touch, and she had the urge to stop walking entirely so she could feel his body against hers. She resisted though and Mav opened the door to his truck for her. She didn't remember the vehicle being this obnoxiously tall. Maverick had to give her a little boost before getting in on the driver's side. "I didn't take you as a truck man."

"Trust me, I'm not. I hate this damn truck. The gas mileage on it is shit and I feel way too tall when I'm driving," Maverick said, buckling up. "It's not mine though. It belongs to my friend Keanon. I, uh, am currently living in his vacation home and this happened to come with the house."

That was an interesting tidbit about Maverick. She wondered if she could ask more about it, but maybe they weren't in the hard questions portion of the date yet. She could file that for later. For now, she suspected it better to keep the conversation light. "So, do I get to know where we're going today? Or are we sticking to the fake date scenario we made up last week?"

"So I should probably get this out in the open before we officially start our date," Maverick said, causing Ofelia to raise a brow. Nothing in his tone raised alarms, but the statement piqued her interest.

"Okay...should I be scared? If you are about to tell me you

have a furry kink, I'm going to have to leave this truck. Not to kink shame you or anything, live your true self."

Maverick's expression turned positively wicked. "Are you already thinking about me in bed, sweetheart?" He all but purred, melting her panties right off her.

Oh shit, she definitely walked into that one. Her cheeks flamed with heat because she *had* thought of him in bed. Multiple times. Having him so close brought back those dirty dreams and the bleak reminder that she hadn't had sex in two years. "No! No, of course not. I was just—"

"I'm messing with you, Ofelia." Maverick laughed, stopping her babbling. "For the record, no. That is not a kink I have but maybe I can fill you in on those later." He winked and Ofelia felt like she could explode at that very moment. "What I was going to say is that I was completely on board with the whole cooking thing even though I'm terrible at it. So I bought stuff to make pizza."

"Sounds easy enough."

"That's what I thought!" Maverick agreed. "But just to make sure, I decided to make a tester pizza, to see if I could do it. And...let's just say I'm so glad Keanon has a fire extinguisher under the sink because it could have ended badly."

Ofelia stifled her laugh with her hand. A cooking Maverick was an adorable image but hearing he nearly burned down his entire house because he was attempting to make pizza for her, was both incredibly hilarious and sexy. Why was burnt food turning her on? She seriously needed to get her priorities sorted.

"So, to spare you from any fire damage, I am going to have to insist that I take you out somewhere. This way, I can assure your safety and your sated appetite." He grinned, showing off his white teeth.

Ofelia pretended to think about it, biting her lip in concentration. "Hmm. I accept. However, I insist that for our next date, I will cook you an authentic Mexican dinner. I haven't had the chance to cook for many people since I've moved to Texas and I miss it."

"Second date, huh?"

"Of course that is what you got from that." Ofelia rolled her eyes but couldn't hide the smile twitching at the corner of her lips. "Do we have a deal?"

Maverick didn't hesitate. He put his truck in drive and took it out of her driveway. "Sweetheart, if that means more time with you, I'll agree to just about anything."

# *Maverick*

## CHAPTER FIFTEEN

MAVERICK HAD BEEN nervous about picking Ofelia up. He couldn't remember the last time he felt so tongue-tied around a woman, but Ofelia rendered him senseless. He was surprised he had the capacity to string two words together, let alone a sentence.

Was it cliché to say she took his breath away?

Ofelia rested her arm on the middle console, right next to his. A few times, Maverick ran his knuckles against hers and from the corner of his eyes, he swore he saw her smile. It made him feel bold and like he actually might not seriously fuck up their date.

Their first stop was an indie bookstore Maverick extensively researched last night. It took up most of his time because only big book retailers popped up in his search, but Maverick didn't want to take Ofelia somewhere she had been a dozen times. He wanted a spot that would be more cozy and intimate, where he wouldn't have to battle crowds for Ofelia's attention.

Which is why he settled on a family owned bookstore called Quills, Books, and Coffee. He knew he'd made the right choice when Ofelia's beautiful face lit up in wonder. "I've never been here before. Oh my goodness, it's so cute!" She said and exited his truck before he could cut off the engine. By the time he was out of the car, Ofelia waited at the front door for him.

"You are about to let a bookworm roam freely in a cute little bookstore. Are you ready for that responsibility?" Ofelia asked. Maverick thought she was teasing, but she waited expectantly for his answer.

Maverick patted his jeans pocket and gave her a thumbs up. "My wallet and I are prepared for this. We've been preparing all week actually."

"Oh, I don't mean you have to pay—"

Maverick reached for her hand, effectively silencing Ofelia as she glanced down at their interwoven fingers. Her hand was warm in his, molding perfectly to his own. He half wondered if she would pull back, but Ofelia seemed to relax her body after the initial shock passed through her. "I know you don't mean for me to pay. Despite my current job—" he faltered, unsure how much she knew about his time before coaching. It was something he would need to bring up when they were at dinner. "—I have money. And I would love nothing more than to buy you tattooed shavings of dead trees."

That earned him a laugh and a playful shove. "Oh hush. But don't say I didn't warn you," she teased before leading him inside, their hands still clasped firmly together.

He couldn't boast about not being strapped for cash because he didn't want to come across as cocky, but Maverick didn't hurt for money. He made a decent amount from baseball and his sponsors. Even though his current income was only that of a high school coach, he had enough money to live comfortably for the rest of his life.

It was only when Ofelia began to take books off the shelves that his hand fell to his side as she paged through a thick book. He wasn't much of a reader. He had never enjoyed it as much as some of his other friends and family. Part of his lack of reading stemmed from his short attention span and the need to be moving and doing something. When he played baseball, his mind and body were always occupied, and he felt completely at peace. He missed that feeling.

As Ofelia browsed, Maverick soon became the designated book carrier. Which he didn't mind at all. He liked seeing the various titles and covers she enjoyed. Most of the covers she put in his basket were colorful with cartoon people on the front. "You really like these types of books. What are they?"

"Romance books," she said, tossing another one in the basket. "I find them empowering and a way that I can freely express my romantic needs. I've learned a lot about myself from reading romance books. Like the fact that I cannot stand miscommunication. It happens a lot in some romance genres and it frustrates me beyond belief each time."

"My ma has a huge stack of romance books by her bed. She calls them bodice rippers." He shuddered.

"Then your mother is an empowered sexual lady and should be proud of that."

Maverick didn't want to think of his mother as anything sexual and left the comment at that. Ofelia took that moment to enter a new book section. "Fantasy?"

"Oh yes. I love a good fantasy in between my romances. The world building is spectacular and I love quests. Game of Thrones is my all time favorite fantasy series, but they are massive."

"I've only seen the show."

This time it was Ofelia's turn to cringe. "Oh Mav, there is so much I need to teach you."

He smirked. "Word around town is that you're a pretty good teacher, Ms. Mendez."

She beamed with pride which made Maverick want to make her feel like that always. "Aren't you lucky?"

He was. Oh so very lucky.

They continued like that for a while. He'd ask her questions each time she handed him a book and she would go on a long tangent of how excited she was to read it and what drew her to the book. The way she described her stories and reading was nothing short of magical. He hung on to her every word, finding himself agreeing or nodding as if he too were a reader.

By the time they finished, Maverick held nine books and a bullet journal as Ofelia fussed over which books to put back because she couldn't possibly let him spend his money on so many. Maverick did what anyone in his situation would do: turn towards the register and ignore her protests.

By the time Ofelia approached him, the cashier handed him his large bag of books. She tried giving him a reproachful glare, but he wasn't buying it. Her bouncing feet and cute lip bite said differently. "Thank you." Ofelia murmured, giving him a swift hug before taking the bag.

They headed back to the car and thirty minutes later found themselves sitting at a locally owned, authentic Italian restaurant. Admittedly, this place had been Willow's suggestion. After the fiasco of his pizza, Maverick wanted to make sure he took Ofelia somewhere she liked and Willow assured him Ofelia would melt. The interior of Stefano's Italian Cuisine was cozy. It was small, but intimate. Each table had a thick white tablecloth with flowers and wine waiting for them. The lights were low, giving off a romantic ambiance.

Hanging on the walls were intricate art pieces by Italian artists, family photos, and photography of Italy. A small fountain decorated one of the few free walls. Small stone cherubs forever immortalized in dancing positions lined the edges. Their table sat directly in front of the fountain and Maverick noticed the abundance of coins littering the bottom.

"I have been dying to come here," Ofelia said once they were both settled at the table, a fresh basket of bread was placed in front of them, alongside a small plate of olive oil. "I'm so okay with you burning the pizza now."

"If I knew a burnt pizza would get you out on a date with me, I would have burnt hundreds by now." Maverick mused, reaching for the bread. He wanted to know more about the gorgeous woman sitting in front of him, but he didn't know where to start. He couldn't ask her anything he was unwilling to answer himself.

Maverick landed on the safest option he could think of and

asked. "So, I heard you lived in California before Texas? Why the switch?"

Apparently that was the worst fucking question he could ask because he watched Ofelia tense up. She seemed locked in a silent battle with herself and Maverick mentally kicked himself for asking such a dumb question.

*Why do people move, dumbass? To start over.* He never wanted to take a question back so badly, but before he could dig himself into a deeper hole, Ofelia surprised him by answering.

"To escape. I was engaged at the time, but my ex left me on our wedding day." She admitted, looking at him as if he were the one that needed pity.

A pang of jealousy shot through him upon hearing Ofelia had been so close to getting married. Anger for the stupid prick who left her came next. It was illogical for him to feel jealous and angry when he had also been engaged to someone else. Even so, he wanted to throttle the man that broke this woman's heart, but also thank him for getting himself out of the picture.

His brain was a confusing place.

"Sorry, I didn't mean to make things awkward. I'm over it! Mostly, but definitely over *him*," Ofelia said quickly, probably thinking she was the reason for his silence.

"No, please don't apologize. I was just thinking about how idiotic this man sounds. I hope that isn't too forward of me to say."

Ofelia waved his comment away. "You're right, it took me a while to reach that mindset, you know? So long in fact that you are the first guy I've been out on a date since."

He liked knowing that he was the first person she had dated since her breakup. She trusted him enough to agree to this date and Maverick couldn't help but feel prideful along with a fierce sense of need. "I like knowing that I'm your first, sweetheart." He said it because he knew she would blush and it would color her cheeks like he liked it. She did blush, but this time she never took her eyes off him. Her comfort around him was growing. Good.

"What about you? Any skeletons in your closet, Mav?" Ofelia bit her lip and Maverick felt it straight down to his cock. She looked so fucking sexy, biting her lip and looking at him as if she knew exactly what she did to him. Under the table, he swore her leg rubbed against him. All the blood from his body headed south.

Trying to readjust himself covertly, Maverick leaned against the side of his chair. She had given him the perfect opportunity for him to talk about his past. He wanted to be able to clear up any misunderstandings. "Did you know I used to be a Major League Baseball player?"

She nodded.

"So you also know I got banned."

Another nod.

"What exactly have you read about me?" Maverick shook out his napkin, giving his nervous fingers something to do while he waited for her answer. He smoothed the cloth over his lap, trying his hardest to keep his expression unreadable.

"Just that. I know that you were in the MLB, but I'm not clear on the reason. You have to forgive me because my knowledge of baseball is nonexistent. The more I looked into it, the less everything made sense. Then I realized how much of a creeper I was being, so I stopped looking. I figured I didn't need to know." She shrugged, offering him a sympathetic smile. "I heard that you were good."

A wave of sadness overtook him, darkening his features. Maverick didn't think it would ever get easier to think about his past, but the pain had dulled to a slight ache rather than a sharp cut. "I was," he said after a moment, not fully present. Ofelia didn't try to stop him or encourage him on and Maverick liked her all the more for that. She was willing to sit there and listen. The only comfort she gave was placing her hand over his, squeezing it gently as if to say, *I'm here.*

After that, the words began to tumble out of Maverick. He told her everything. How he met Breanna to how they became high school sweethearts and eventually engaged. He spoke about slowly losing the love between them and the fateful night he found Breanna with his coach, leading to his downfall. And how he finally began to work with a lawyer in attempts to right the wrongs of his situation.

When he was finished, he dared to look up and noticed the entire time he had been talking, Ofelia had tears in her eyes.

"Mav," she started gently after Maverick poured his heart out. "I'm so, so sorry. I can't imagine the pain the situation has caused and the anger you must carry because of it. What happened to you is wrong and you were unfairly pulled from a game that means the world to you. Please don't feel like you need to carry this baggage alone. You aren't alone. If there is anything I can do while you are dealing with the legal actions, let me know. I can make some pretty fantastic comfort food if you want to eat your feelings."

No one had ever said those words to him before. Keanon was the only other person who understood Maverick's struggle and offered up his home and car. Maverick would never forget his kindness, but they didn't talk about how Maverick felt. Not past surface level emotions, at least. Ofelia offered the emotional piece he had been missing for years, a confidant he could bare his soul to. This beautiful woman couldn't possibly understand how much those words touched Maverick.

"You don't know how badly I want to kiss you right now," he said unabashedly, his piercing gaze staring into Ofelia's hazel ones. She didn't look away or blush like Maverick expected her to. The magnetic pull between them became almost palpable.

"Perhaps you should show me then."

Fuck yes. He would jump across this damn table, pull her lips to his and kiss Ofelia until she was breathless. Until she begged him for more. Maverick wouldn't stop until she was unable to take any more pleasure. He desperately wanted her in his arms, bodies melding together until they fit perfectly as one.

Except none of those things happened. Reality came crashing

down when their waiter, a portly man with a thick mustache, placed their dinner in front of them, breaking the spell they were under. Maverick didn't remember ordering, but they clearly had.

Dammit! He had never been cock blocked by food before, this was a first. Luckily, he wasn't the only one that was disappointed. Ofelia grimaced when the waiter chatted with her briefly, eyes flashing back to Maverick in silent apologies.

Even though the raw sexual tension between them simmered down to a light flame, their conversation didn't stop. It flowed freer and without restraints now that their past was laid out on the table. Never before did Maverick find himself wanting to learn every small detail about a person before. Where did she go to school? Did she always want to be a teacher? What music does she listen to? Maverick asked all these questions, soaking up the new information like a sponge.

Ofelia asked him questions too, mostly about his baseball career and his family. He surprised himself by finding he wanted to talk about growing up with baseball. How he started when he was only four years old in T-Ball and how that slowly progressed into his full time career. She was a good listener, always nodding and smiling at the appropriate times and laughing at his dumb jokes. She would take time to ask him questions as well as answer a few of his own.

The food in front of them lay untouched for quite some time. When Maverick finally remembered he had a bowl of pasta, it had already gone lukewarm. Neither of them seemed to mind, far more invested in learning about each other's lives than the delicious food they ordered.

By the time the check came, two hours had passed by in a blink of an eye. Their date was reaching an end, but Maverick wasn't ready to say goodbye. When they got up to leave, Ofelia reached for his hand, a simple gesture but one he didn't take for granted. He leaned down, pressing the faintest kiss to the top of her head, letting his lips linger for a second longer than necessary.

Ofelia leaned into his touch, and he silently cursed the fact they were in the middle of a restaurant.

"I guess I should get you home." Maverick said, pulling back just enough to see her face.

The idea didn't seem to thrill Ofelia either, but she nodded reluctantly. "Yeah, I think you're right," she said, but made no movement to start walking first, so Maverick took the lead.

This time when he helped her in the truck, his hands lingered on her hips, feeling her soft curves underneath. He let go all too soon and made his way over to the driver's seat. He tossed Ofelia his phone, already unlocked. "You pick the music this time."

Her eyes lit up, and he saw her instantly click on his Spotify. From the corner of his eyes, he saw Ofelia scroll through the music before landing on her chosen song. Or so he thought a song would start playing over his car speakers, but he was greeted by haunting music and then a crisp female voice.

Ofelia laughed at his expression and put his phone down in the console. "I do like music, but I also love murder mystery podcasts. This podcast is about a serial killer that got away with his crimes for two decades, even though the people of his small town suspected him for years. So many were terrified to speak up because they thought they'd be next."

Morbid, but damn if he didn't get sucked right in the crazy story, hanging on to the woman's every word of the bizarre and frankly fucked up descriptions of the man's poor victims. The podcast made their twenty-five minute drive back to Ofelia's home pass too quickly. By the time he pulled into her driveway, the episode was nearly finished. Naturally, they both sat for another five minutes to see how it ended.

"Okay, I'm hooked," Maverick said as soon as it ended. "I didn't expect to hear about chopped up remains on our date, but you know. First time for everything."

"I already favorited it for you, but you need to go back and listen to the first two episodes and report back. Hearing about the man's upbringing is honestly outrageous and makes so much sense as to why he turned out the way that he did."

The truck then grew quiet, both of them realizing they were completely alone and in close proximity. Both unbuckled as soon as Maverick put the truck in park. Maverick's hand was close to Ofelia's thigh. Just a few more centimeters, and he could have his hand splayed across it. The same heated urgency from earlier hit him in full force.

Maverick cleared his throat, needing to break the tension before he did or said something out of line. "I should—"

"I want you to kiss me," Ofelia blurted, stunning them both into silence. She bit her lip, as if contemplating what to say next before she did. "I want it, but only if you do. And if you don't want it that's cool too, but I—"

His mouth was on hers, cutting off the last of her ramblings. She squeaked when his lips pressed against hers and his large hands cupped her face in a feathery light caress. Ofelia didn't kiss him back right away and for a second, Maverick thought he might have scared her. Until she leaned into his touch and kissed him back, sighing softly.

The sigh was enough to drive Maverick crazy. He deepened the kiss, his tongue running along her bottom lip. When she opened for him, Maverick wasted no time exploring her mouth, needing the taste of her on his lips. His tongue flicked across hers and elicited the quietest of moans. Ofelia moved her hands up to rest on Maverick's chest, rubbing her hands along his shoulders.

"Fuck, baby girl." Maverick panted. "I need you closer."

"You, wha—?" Ofelia said breathlessly, but Maverick was already pulling Ofelia over the middle console and into his lap. She giggled in surprise, but eagerly helped move her body closer to his. Soon her legs straddled his thighs and his hands moved down her back, hovering over the curve of her ass. Ofelia shifted her body, grinding down over his hardness.

If she noticed his hard cock against her ass, Ofelia didn't say anything nor did she pull away. Instead, she leaned down and kissed him this time, putting her entire body into it. They groaned in unison, Maverick bucking up, creating more fiction between them.

The woman was going to be the death of him. Or his rebirth. He was still unsure of which.

"Mav," she moaned his name, so breathless and full of lust. Fuck he was never going to get the sound of her moaning his name out of his mind. Her flushed cheeks, looking as turned on as him, made his cock harden painfully in his pants.

"Tell me what you want, baby girl," he murmured against her smeared red lips. No doubt he was supporting his own set of red lips as well.

She did that thing again, where she bit her lip and looked at him like there was nothing in this world she wanted to devour more than him. "You," she whispered.

With every fiber of his being, Maverick wanted nothing more than to indulge Ofelia's request. He wanted to hear her moan his name again. To feel her tongue all over his body. He wanted to look into her eyes as they reached their peak and came down from their high together. And if Ofelia were anyone else, he wouldn't hesitate taking her to bed, no problem.

But she wasn't anyone else. Ofelia was someone who was starting to mean a lot to him, and he didn't want her to get the impression that he only wanted a quick lay. "Ofelia, I think—"

"Oh shit." Ofelia lurched back, hitting the steering wheel. Her eyes were wide, full of panic. "I messed this up. I pushed too hard, too fast. I'm sorry, Mav." Tears were pooling in the corner of her eye as she frantically reached for the handle, attempting to flee Maverick.

Maverick reached out, placing his hand over hers to hold her in place. "There is absolutely nothing more I want than to take you inside, strip you naked, and taste that sweet little pussy, baby girl." Ofelia sucked in a breath, eyes fluttering close for a brief moment. "But, and I hate myself so much for saying this, I don't think either one of us is ready.

"When I take you Ofelia, it's not going to be in the front seat of this ridiculous truck. It'll be when you are truly mine and we are both ready for it." Maverick finished, leaning in to give her a soft kiss on her lips. "Tonight when I get home, I'll think of all the ways I wish to ravish you as I get off to the thought of your legs wrapped around me, moaning my name."

Ofelia shuddered and warily nodded her head in agreement. He should leave it at that, but he had a clearly needy female on his lap and if one of them didn't come in the next ten minutes, it would be a waste.

He could give her exactly what she needed, a final thing to remember him by, all while not lifting a single finger.

Ofelia went for the door, prepared to leave his car, but Maverick was faster. He grabbed her wrist, holding it in place. "Do you want to get off, baby girl?"

"I thought you said—"

"I know what I said. Answer my question. Do you want to get off?"

She was already so close as it was, he could see the way her chest heaved and the flush along her cheeks and down her neck. Slowly she nodded. "Yes," she whispered.

He waited for her to change her mind, but Ofelia continued to stare at him expectantly. He brought her hands to the hem of her skirt. "Let's see how well you listen." He murmured. The moonlight hit her so perfectly that he could make out just enough of her. "Push up your skirt."

"You aren't going to do that for me?"

He smacked her ass, causing her to gasp in surprise. "I'm not touching you, baby girl. But I'm going to watch you get yourself off for me before I drop you off at your door."

She glared at him, but he could see the eagerness in her eyes. Maverick normally wasn't this dominant and he doubted Ofelia was one to fuck her date in the front seat of his car on the first date, but there was an undeniable rightness about this moment.

She did as she was told, pulling her skirt up around her waist.

She had on leggings, but didn't ask her to take those off. He wanted her to have some semblance of modesty in case they were caught by a nosy neighbor. "Show me what you would do if you were alone," he said.

Ofelia's hand shook. For a moment he thought that she would call this off and Maverick would have stopped immediately. Except she didn't do that. She moved her hand and let it disappear into her leggings. He knew the moment she touched her clit because a low moan left her lips. His dick had been hard before, but now it painfully pressed against his jeans and her ass. "Tell me how wet you are."

She did not hesitate this time. "Very. Very wet." She moaned, as her hand moved faster underneath her leggings. It was a new kind of torture to watch someone masturbate before you, but not actually being able to see it happening.

Her needy moans began to increase and Ofelia moved her head to rest against his forehead. "Mav…"

"Let it out, baby girl. Make yourself come," he whispered, unable to stop himself from bucking up against her core.

That was exactly what she needed because he watched her body tense up, her breathing hitch, and listened as she moaned longingly in his ear as she came for him. They stayed like that, pressed together, forehead to forehead, and breathing heavily for a few minutes.

"You didn't get off," Ofelia said after a moment, breaking the silence.

"This wasn't about me. It was about you."

"But—"

"Next time." He assured her, silencing any more protests with a swift kiss to her lips. He then began to help her fix her clothes, just enough so that she could walk out of this truck without it looking too scandalized. He found her blushing each time he would look at her, but he did not see regret or embarrassment in her eyes.

"Do you regret it?" Maverick asked, needing to be sure.

Ofelia shook her head, loose curls falling down her face. "Not even a little bit."

"Good." He smirked before finally opening the car door to let them both exit.

They walked in peaceful silence to her door, Maverick stopping at the entryway. Ofelia turned to him. "I had such a fun time tonight, Mav. And...thank you for stopping us before we got too carried away. I am not a one night stand type of person. I wouldn't have wanted you to feel that way. What we did was incredibly hot and enough."

Maverick also didn't want one night with her. He wanted plenty...when they were both ready and knew what they had between each other was more than lust. "I only hate myself a little for stopping us, though I did enjoy the show immensely." Maverick smiled and laughed with Ofelia.

"Goodnight, Maverick. I'll text you tomorrow?"

"I'll text you tonight." He winked and stepped forward. He leaned down, bringing his lips to hers one last time. He kept it light, knowing he wouldn't have the strength to stop himself for a second time. "Goodnight, sweetheart."

"I prefer baby girl," Ofelia quipped.

"Noted," he said, grinning like a fool. He lingered while she opened the door and led herself into her house. Ofelia gave him a small wave goodbye, which Maverick returned, before closing the door.

As Maverick walked back to his car with a newfound lightness to his steps, he realized that he was still smiling so hard his cheeks were hurting. Ofelia Mendez was one of the first good things that had happened to Maverick in this new post baseball life. Tonight had been just a taste, but he was determined to see where this could lead.

<h1 style="text-align:center">Ofelia</h1>

CHAPTER SIXTEEN

TWO DAYS LATER, Ofelia's lips still tingled from Maverick's warm kisses and her body heated each time she thought of his commanding tone. She had waited to feel some sort of guilt or shame over their intense interaction in his truck, but it never came. At work today, she all but strutted in, stopping by the teacher's lounge to leave a box of donuts she bought for no particular reason. She told herself that she most definitely didn't buy the donuts for the lounge because it was located across the hall from the gym. That was only a bonus. If she happened to spot Maverick from the door window, it would simply be fate's doing. Not her own.

She was not ashamed to say she peeked inside the gym when walking by. The basketball team was running drills while Coach Campbell blew his whistle to bark orders. *Damn.* Not the coach she wanted to see. Her good mood faltered, but she knew coming by would be a long shot. Instead of pouting, she decided to head back to her room and-

The air rushed out of her as she ran directly into the person who silently stood in front of her. Strong hands came up to grip her arms, keeping her from embarrassing herself even more. "Ugh, I'm sorry! I wasn't—"

157

"Were you looking for me, baby girl?" A low whisper tickled her ear. A pleasurable shiver went through her body as she timidly looked up at the man she ran into.

She sent up a silent *"Thank you, Fate!"* as she met Maverick's deep brown eyes. He smelled of peppermint mouthwash and fresh laundry. He wore his standard black joggers and an old school shirt someone from the office must have given him. This man looked delicious enough to eat.

"Why would I be looking for you?" Ofelia played coy, wiggling out of his grip. Maverick gave her one last squeeze before taking a step back, putting some distance between them. It was for the best; she didn't need to jump his bones at work.

"Because you were staring pretty hard through that window. Unless you're checking out Campbell over there, I'd say it's safe to say you were looking for me."

"Maybe I was looking at Campbell. Would that make you jealous?"

"Incredibly so."

Ofelia beamed. "Then I totally checked out Campbell. It's the salt and pepper hair and the beer gut that get me going."

Maverick sighed melodramatically. "It's always the beer gut." He made an adorable drama queen and Ofelia couldn't help but laugh.

"Maybe I hoped I could catch a glimpse of you, so I brought donuts. They're in the teacher's lounge if you want one," She said, noticing a few students began to trickle in. The first bell was still forty-five minutes away, but she had a few coming in for tutoring this morning. "I need to head back to my room, but if you have C lunch today, you can join Willow and I."

Maverick gave an apologetic smile. "B lunch. Let's have dinner after school?"

Ofelia felt her heart race in excitement. Could someone die of giddiness? Was that a thing? If it were, she'd be patient zero. "Perfect. I have a cheer meeting after school, but I was hoping to have dinner together tonight?" She suggested, thrilled with the prospect of potentially seeing Maverick later.

"Of course, where would you like to go?" He asked, sliding his hands into his pockets.

"Actually, I was hoping I could cook for you," she said, her cheeks warming.

Maverick raised a brow, a slight smile pulling at the corners of his lips. "I would love that."

"Great!" She said a little too loudly, earning weird looks from a few passing students. "I uh, will text you tonight."

More students began to filter in, walking towards the cafeteria for breakfast or headed to teacher tutorials. She couldn't kiss him goodbye and had to settle for an awkward wave with their hands brushing as they walked past each other. She didn't look back, even when she felt eyes watching her as she made her way to her room.

The kiss would wait until later. She had writing workshops and cheer moms to get through first. Upon entering her hallway, Ofelia was shocked to find ten students waiting outside her door. "Oh my goodness, I'm sorry y'all. I didn't mean to keep you waiting." She fumbled with her key and unlocked the door, immediately turning on the lights. Her students all filled in behind her, slugging their backpacks down on desks and rifling through them for their work. One by one, Ofelia went to each student, going over what each needed to work on and answering any questions they had. Five more students entered and waited patiently for their turn with Ofelia.

It was the start of a long day.

By the time the last student left her morning tutorials, Ofelia's first period class began to trickle in. The cycle started anew because this week was every English teachers' nightmare. Essay writing week. A minimum of five paragraphs over a subject the kids knew well, but when presented with the prompt, everything they learned magically disappeared.

At Lunch, Ofelia took slight comfort in seeing Willow come into her room looking like a walking corpse. Her classes weren't going much better, and she had an angry email from a parent stating that their child was grievously injured from the amount of writing this school was forcing upon him. "What does that even mean?!" Willow complained. At the end of the day it was Ofelia's turn to deal with parents. Not just any parents, cheer moms.

Back in December when Ofelia scheduled the parent meeting, it seemed like a great idea. Her dumbass-self believed she was being proactive. Ofelia would lay out exactly what their first tournament would look like, detailing everything out from the expense to the time they left for San Antonio, and ending with competition schedules. Now she knew it was only an added, unnecessary task she put upon herself.

After changing into her cheer coach uniform and putting her hair up in a bun, Ofelia started down to the gym. There was nothing terrifying about these mothers. They were just...a lot. One wrong move meant an unflattering post on their not-so-secret Facebook group. Since she was already running a few minutes late, she had minimal room for error.

Parents were still making their way into the gym and on to the bleachers by the time Ofelia arrived. Lacey sat in the front row with her mother, a woman who tried a little too hard to cling to her youth. She wore a top, one likely stolen from Lacey, with a plunging neckline. Her boobs spilled over the top and Ofelia wondered what type of bra she wore and where she could get one of her own.

"Ms. Mendez," a high-pitched southern voice called, effectively dragging Ofelia's eyes from Mrs. Steward's cleavage. Inwardly Ofelia groaned when she caught sight of the woman standing in front of her; the cheer mom's fake southern charm in full effect. One would think it was snow storming outside rather than a crisp seventy-degree day, for Mrs. Roberts was decked out in her best winter attire. Long sleeve shirt with a white, pleated vest over top. Dark jeans with tall brown boots.

Mrs. Roberts was the mother of one of Ofelia's juniors, Gabbie Roberts. Without her mother's influence, Gabbie could be a sweet girl if she weren't weighed down with crippling anxiety and the need to always be perfect. It was obvious to everyone but Mrs. Roberts how badly her daughter craved her approval, but Mrs. Roberts was obsessed with her family's image. If they weren't the best, they were nothing. It pissed Mrs. Roberts off that Gabbie hadn't made cheer captain when she tried out at the beginning of the year.

Because Ofelia was nothing if not classy, she smiled at the woman. "Mrs. Roberts, it's so nice to see you again. I'm glad you could make it."

"You know I never miss an opportunity to hear the latest news firsthand. Besides, I have a few questions and concerns I was hoping you'd be able to answer."

Shocking, but Ofelia kept her expression neutral and nodded. "Of course. There'll be time for questions at the end. Go ahead and take a seat, and we will get started immediately."

She could tell that Mrs. Roberts wanted to argue, but Gabbie pulled her mother into the stand. Ofelia waited as the last few parents took their seats, waving at Tony's mom as she entered. Gianna was the only mom Ofelia was on a first name basis with and the only mom that supported anything Ofelia planned.

Why was it so easy to talk in front of a group of teenagers but debilitating when it came to talking in front of peers? She had to emit queen bee energy, even if these bees stung back. A lot.

"Hello McKinley cheer parents. Thank you so much for taking the time to be here today so we can discuss our first competition in San Antonio this upcoming weekend." Ofelia took a moment to pass out the itinerary to all the parents and cheerleaders. Her squad already knew this information, so really it was for their parents and their need to track every minute of every day.

Ofelia walked them through the detailed four-page document; she even color coded the schedule. She made it idiot proof so none of the parents could come back and blame her for not knowing time or location.

They would meet at school on Friday morning at 5am. From there, the squad would board the charter bus and take the two-hour drive down where they would immediately check into their hotel. At ten, they would walk across the street to the convention center and sign in. Their performance time wasn't until 2:15pm so the team could go for brunch before warming up.

Ofelia walked the parents through the second day as well, making sure they realized they performed twice that day. "Then on Sunday we get our results and see if we placed. We will start heading home around one or two." Ofelia took a deep breath; mouth dry from talking for the last thirty minutes. Miraculously not a single person interrupted her. Unfortunately, she would still have to take questions. As soon as she asked if anyone had any, most hands went in the air.

"Yes, I do." Mrs. Roberts piped up disregarding every hand in the air. There were a few glares from some other parents as their hands slowly went down. "Will you be asking for parent volunteers? Some of us have a lot of experience with these things and it might be beneficial to you if you had some of our expertise."

Ofelia pursued her lips. She couldn't jump a parent, that was unprofessional and wouldn't set a fitting example as a leader. But seriously, Mrs. Roberts always had to flaunt her knowledge of cheerleading and overlook everyone else. It didn't matter that Ofelia had been in cheer since she could walk. It didn't matter how many state championship trophies she won or that she went to college with a full scholarship for cheer. She could hold up all her awards and accomplishments, but none of that would phase Mrs. Roberts. She would still find fault in something.

Ofelia had to brush her comments off and deal with the question laced between the sass. Admittedly, she asked an important question because she did need parent support. "Of course, I'm so glad you brought that up," she praised, as she would with any challenging student. Mrs. Roberts looked pleased with herself.

"Parent chaperones are highly encouraged. All our fundraising efforts only provided us with enough money to cover the hotel rooms for the team and me. If any parent would like to attend, they would need to purchase their own room. They can, however, ride up with us in the charter if they want."

"Oh, that shouldn't be a problem for most of us, Ms. Mendez. Don't you worry about that. Where do we sign up?" Mrs. Roberts asked, a big, fake smile plastered across her face.

"You'll see a QR Code on the last page of your schedule. Just hover your camera over it and the website will pop up. Fill out the information and you'll receive a text message confirming your sign up."

Much to her squad's dismay, almost all the parents flipped to the last page and scanned the QR code. It was a relief to have this many hands-on-deck, even if those hands belonged to some questionable characters. Mrs. Roberts was tolerable at big functions, as long as they were winning. It was poor Gabbie who would have to suffer her passive aggressive attitude if she didn't perform at top tier.

"Ms. Mendez, can you give me more information about the hotel? Is it the one directly adjacent to the convention center? How will the girls—and Tony and Devin—room?"

For the next hour, Ofelia fielded questions from all the parents. Would dinner be provided? Did the parents have to pay for admission? What happens if there is a wardrobe malfunction? Ofelia answered to the best of her abilities, even if some questions seemed improbable. Mrs. Roberts and Mrs. Steward grilled her the most. Lacey ended up dragging her mother away from the conversation. "Seriously, mom. You'd think this was your first damn competition." Lacey growled.

Mrs. Roberts finally ran out of obscure questions and Ofelia adjourned the meeting. She smiled and said her goodbye to each parent. There was no way they were going to write a shitty post about her on Facebook after this.

Gianna was the last to walk down from the bleachers with

Tony. "You handled that excellently, Ms. M. Totally crushed it." Tony said, sipping on his iced coffee.

"He's right, those parents were out with claws tonight. You'd think this was a Botox convention."

"Mom!" Tony said but giggled. "Okay true. Those foreheads weren't moving!"

Gianna rubbed her son's head affectionately. "I'll be coming along as a chaperone, so I'll run interference. Don't stress about that. You're doing great. Tony tells me all the time you are his favorite teacher. It's so easy to see why your team loves you. Plus, it takes a special type of person to deal with these cheer moms. I think the only thing worse would be dance moms. Maybe football moms."

"I understand. They want what's best for the kids, they just don't have the best ways of approaching," Ofelia said, not able to blame the parents for their consistent nagging. It stressed her out to no end, and she vowed that she would never be that type of mother, or at least she hoped she wasn't the type of mom most teachers avoid. "Even Mrs. Roberts, as...difficult as she is. I know deep down, very deep down, she loves her daughter. She just shows it differently."

"Girl is two types of crazy, no sir. Her husband must be—" Tony started but was cut off by his mother, nudging his shoulder.

"Hush boy. That mouth of yours is going to catch up with you one day."

"And it will land me a fine husband and I'll finally live out my dream of being a trophy husband." Tony smiled, looking all too smug about his future. He winked at his mother before strutting through the door, leaving Ofelia and Gianna as the last two remaining.

"Love that boy, but he's going to be the death of me." Gianna shook her head, but affection colored her face. She loved her son, and it showed in everything she did. "Anyway, I know you are eager to go home. This momma has your back this weekend. Let me know if you need anything."

Gianna hugged Ofelia goodbye, leaving her feeling good about the meeting, even if only one person thought so. Everything was planned to the T, her father would come, and she had enough chaperones to lighten her load. So tonight she could simply enjoy her evening with Maverick.

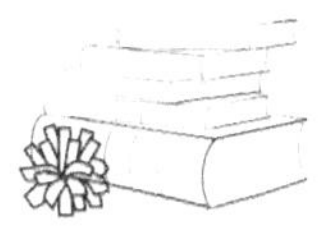

# Ofelia

## CHAPTER SEVENTEEN

THE POP of the sizzling grease made Maverick jump back despite her many warnings to stand clear. "Listen, if you want to get burned, keep it up." Ofelia smirked and nudged him out of the way of her stove with a light hip bump. A deep laugh caressed her senses, sending a delicious tingling sensation straight to her core. Something that happened a lot when Maverick was around.

"Maybe I like knowing you'd nurse my wounds if I get burned," he said and Ofelia rolled her eyes. He had her pegged though; it was exactly what she would do. Any excuse to have her hands all over him again. Thoughts of their time in the car rushed back and she blushed for a completely different reason.

"So how do you make it so the corn tortilla doesn't fall apart when you roll it?" Maverick's question brought her back to the moment. Just in time too because the flautas she was currently cooking reached the desired golden brown color, signifying they were ready to take out. Maverick stepped back as she maneuvered the hot flautas to a napkin to drain all the excess oil.

"You just put the tortillas in the microwave to let them warm up before you try handling them. My mamá taught me that," she said, creating four more corn tortillas stuffed with shredded chicken and dropping them into the pan. Maverick had offered to help, but she had watched him demolish and shred two tortillas already and burn their first attempt at spanish rice.

A chef he was not.

Not that Ofelia minded. She loved cooking and it had been a long time since she had someone other than Willow to make dinner for. Although she forbade Maverick from touching any food currently out on her counter, he watched the process and asked tons of questions. She liked answering them and sharing a bit of her culture with him.

After another fifteen minutes, she finished dressing up their flautas with pico de gallo and Mexican Crema while Maverick set the table. She soon joined him, pushing his plate in front of him. This was her favorite part. The part where she watched someone try her food for the first time. She liked seeing the different emotions play across their faces as they took their first bite.

Sensing her anticipation, Maverick didn't hesitate when he took the first bite of her meal. A low groan left him as he licked off sour cream from the corner of his lips. He took another bite, this time shoveling rice in his mouth. He made sounds this time which Ofelia believed to be words, but she couldn't decipher their meaning.

"I'm not fluent in stuffed mouth language. You are going to have to translate for me." She laughed, watching as he quickly chewed the remaining food.

"I said," he coughed, clearing his throat. "That this is the best damn meal I've had in a long time. Thank God I didn't have this food around me when I was in the major leagues. I would have pissed off my trainer and nutritionist." He laughed, but soon stopped as if realizing what he just said.

This thing between them – whatever it was – was still new, but Ofelia quickly learned that Maverick didn't like talking about his baseball life. He would share a few details of his time playing, but the conversations never lasted long and she got the sense he didn't want to talk about it with her. It stung a little, but she understood his need for privacy, especially when half of his life was plastered on the internet for anyone to see.

"You really miss it, don't you?" She asked softly, afraid that Maverick might close up on her. She saw him tense slightly and noticed the rapid tap of his finger on the table while he tried to decide what to say.

"I do." His voice was barely above a whisper. "It's what I know. I dedicated my entire life to baseball and I just wish..."

What did he wish? Ofelia wanted to know so badly, but she could see Maverick deflecting with a slight shrug to his shoulders. "I suppose it's in Lloyd Gilmore's hands now. But enough about me. I want to hear about your cheer meeting. How'd that go?"

Ofelia highly doubted he wanted to talk cheer, but it was clear Maverick was ready to change the subject back to something safe. She obliged him, if only to see the lingering sadness leave his eyes.

"I regret holding a meeting instead of sending out the competition information in an email." It had been so foolish to think she'd be able to run a quick meeting and be out in time to get her house cleaned before Maverick came. But of course the mothers had kept her for over an hour past the scheduled ending time.

She told him all about the snide cheer moms and their obnoxious questions about her preparedness thinly veiled behind fake concern. Of the countless reminders that Ofelia hadn't been able to obtain a win at nationals yet and the pressure the parents placed on her this year to be perfect. Maverick nodded and commented at the appropriate times, actually listening and taking an interest in her day. It was...refreshing.

"The one good thing that came out of the meeting is now I have chaperones for the competition and one of them is Gianna, Tony's mom. She helped me deal with the high demands of the parents last year and kept me sane throughout the entire competition weekend via texts." It was a small relief a friendly face would be joining, but a relief all the same.

"You're amazing," Maverick said after a beat of silence between them. His words were so unexpected and she didn't know how to respond. Surely he couldn't be talking about being amazing from simply dealing with parents? It wasn't that impressive, but she appreciated the sentiment.

"It's really noth—"

"No, it's not nothing. You are amazing." His words came out strong and he stared at her as if daring Ofelia to argue with his assessment. She didn't. "It's not just the meeting, though I could never deal with that many mothers at once. No, you're amazing because of your passion and dedication to your students and squad. You make a difference in countless lives every day. That's why you are so well loved and respected by those who have the honor of knowing you. I won't be convinced otherwise, baby girl."

When he spoke like that, a weird fluttering sensation happened in the pit of her belly...or was it her chest? Maverick rendered her speechless with the naked honesty of his words. He actually *did* think that about her. How he saw her each time he looked at her.

What did one even say after such high praise? Thank you felt inadequate and no other responses came to her. She hated that they were separated by her kitchen table when she wanted nothing more than to use her body to convey how she felt; to say the words she couldn't.

Luckily she didn't have to try coming up with a suitable comment because Maverick soon continued. "And you mentioned your father would be there, yeah? That's kinda a big deal, isn't it?"

It was a huge deal and she had mentioned that to him before. Maverick didn't know all the details about her strained relationship with her father, but he did know that she struggled to connect with him. Growing up it had been a constant fight for his attention and even when she got it, it was never undivided. Sports, Javi, or work would take precedence over her. She was made to feel inadequate and that she didn't deserve her father's love.

"I just hope it works out and we can finally spend some much needed time together." Before her thoughts spiraled into anymore gutters, Ofelia cleared her throat and smiled, wanting to change the subject. Clearly Maverick wasn't the only one avoiding hard topics tonight. She glanced down at his plate, realizing he must have finished sometime during her story and she hadn't noticed. "Oh. Are you still hungry? There's plenty more."

"Nah, I'm good, but I'll take leftovers," Maverick said. She liked that he enjoyed her food enough to have it for lunch the next day. She could get used to cooking for him if it meant she got to share her kitchen with him and learn more about Maverick.

"Where are you going?" Maverick asked as Ofelia got up to find Tupperware for the leftovers.

"I'm just going to tidy up the food really quick and make you a plate to take home. It'll only take a moment." But Maverick was already shaking his head before she finished talking, wrapping his hands around the arms of her dining room chair and pushing himself to his feet.

"Later. Right now I would very much like to sit on the couch and put a movie on so we can pretend we are actually watching it, but really we are just waiting for the other to make their move so we can make out like teenagers."

Ofelia let out a bark of undignified laughter. His words were not only funny but true as well. How many times had she thought about kissing him each time his tongue licked his lips clean? Far too many for one night.

"I'll help you clean up before I go. Just give me an hour?" Maverick stuck out his bottom lip like a child begging his mother for the shiny new toy. How could she say no to that face?

She couldn't.

She allowed herself to be led into her own living room and pulled down next to Maverick on the couch. They lasted approximately five minutes before Maverick initiated the first kiss.

And the second.

And the third.

Despite the stress from the day and knowing that tomorrow would be the start of her weekend tournament, Ofelia had never felt more at ease. Not only did she have this amazing night with Maverick to replay over and over again, she knew everything was planned to the T. She had all her ducks in rows for the first time in a long time, everything was working out perfectly.

# *Ofelia*

## CHAPTER EIGHTEEN

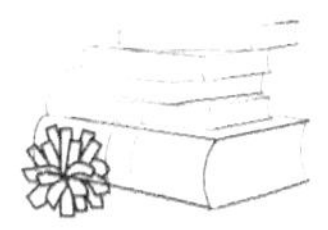

Everything was going wrong.

Friday morning arrived like an unexpected house guest, far too early and full of complications. For starters, Ofelia slept past her alarm clock and woke up with only thirty minutes before she needed to leave. She hadn't packed her suitcase yet. She had every intention of doing that last night, but dinner with Maverick consumed most of her evening.

She thankfully remembered to do her laundry the other morning and began to toss unfolded, wrinkled clothes into her small suitcase, not caring how disorderly she was being. Ofelia mentally went through her checklist, knowing she had her clothes, but needed her bathroom accessories. She darted into her bathroom, nearly slipping on the tile but righted herself by holding on to the sink.

Ten minutes later, with only two to spare, Ofelia ran to her car, like an overzealous Olympic runner. She tossed her suitcase and purse in the backseat and placed her phone in the console. It had been vibrating for the past ten minutes and Ofelia knew parents were wondering where she was. If she wasn't fifteen minutes early, she was late.

Major panic sat in when Ofelia pulled up to the school and no giant white charter bus awaited her. "What the hell?" She hissed, gripping her steering wheel hard. She grabbed for her phone only to realize now that the charter company tried to contact her. Several times and left a voicemail, which she promptly listened to. Apparently there had been miscommunication about the bus's arrival time. They promised to have a bus out ASAP, but it could be another twenty minutes.

This was fine. Totally fine. No reason to freak out. She needed to remain calm when she told the news to her squad, half of which already stood on the curb waiting for Ofelia to hop out of her car. Devin gave her a tentative wave as Lacey glanced up briefly before putting her nose right back into her phone.

After returning the call from the charter company and hearing a bus was in route, Ofelia felt more confident walking over to her team. From the squad, she received a lot of smiles and a few hugs. The only person missing was Tony and his mother, but Gianna always ran a little later than everyone else.

"Ms. Mendez, where's our bus? My mom is having a meltdown, so I made her wait in the car," Lacey questioned, clearly the adult in the situation. If it weren't for her cheer captain, Lacey's mother would wreak havoc, more so than the other two moms on her list.

"So I got a call from the bus company, and they said there was a bit of a mix up." She started as the protests began and the panic started to seep in. Sometimes she wondered if she directed the drama troupe rather than coaching cheerleaders. "But your amazing coach, AKA me, planned for some delay in our schedule. We will still get to San Antonio with enough time to check into our hotel rooms and change before we need to be at the convention center."

"You are sure we will make it on time?" Gabbie asked, looking around nervously.

"Of course we will. If worse comes to worst, we will check into our hotel later. Don't panic," she said, just as Gianna's car pulled up.

Tony ducked his head out of the window with a big grin. A song from *Hamilton* loudly played on the speakers as Gianna tapped along to the beat. Tony paused for dramatic effect before saying, "Ladies and Devin, we brought donuts."

Suddenly everything was better.

Twenty minutes later the charter bus arrived and everyone piled in while the parents loaded the luggage. Ofelia counted heads, making sure everyone was there. Only a few parents wanted to ride up with the bus while the rest promised to follow along in their own cars. It was quite the parade as a large white charter with six various cars and trucks followed close behind. They were finally on the road.

Now that she had a moment to herself without teenagers or parents breathing down her neck, Ofelia texted her father. She knew he would be boarding his plane in an hour and wanted to catch him before he got on. "I'm so excited to see you, Papa! Call me when you land." He hadn't responded since last night, but that wasn't unusual for her father. He was notorious for ghosting his children and then having the gall to get upset when people stopped texting him. She spoke to Javi as well, but he had not seen much of their father due to his busy work schedule.

The next message was for Maverick, just saying they took off and that she missed him. She debated that last part, not wanting to seem clingy. She decided she didn't care and sent it anyway. Almost immediately, Mav responded with "Stay safe. I miss you too." He included a green heart emoji at the end, which made her inexplicably happy.

For the duration of the ride, Ofelia popped her earbuds in and listened to a fantasy series Willow recommended to her about ancient vampires and gods. Romcoms were more her speed, but she promised Willow they'd discuss it soon. Ofelia retreated into her imagination for the next two hours, only stirring when someone poked her. Nila, an upbeat freshman, looked down at her, as if waiting for Ofelia to answer a question.

"I'm sorry, what did you say?" Ofelia apologized, stopping her book and removing her earbuds. The bus was stopped, which explained why Nila was up and walking around. She straightened up in her seat to peer out the window.

"I said we're here. The bus driver wants to know if he should park or wait," she said before bouncing back to her seat, joining the rest of the squad in an off-key rendition of Justin Bieber's classic, "Baby."

"We can park. Thank you," Ofelia said to the driver, who nodded and made his way to the parking garage. The bus zone was bare, meaning they had to be one of the first schools to arrive, which pleasantly surprised her. She was glad that they made it early, even with their late start. By the end of the day, the zone would be filled with various buses from all over Texas. The same thrill Ofelia got before each performance started racing through her body, making her giddy. It was amplified now that she coached a kick ass team.

Said kick ass team were quickly becoming squirrelly and impatient. "Does everyone remember who they are bunking with?" Ofelia asked, rifling through her oversized purse in search of their reservations and school credit card. Of course it hid all the way at the bottom of her bag, causing a near mini heart attack. It would have been just her luck to leave the important documents at home, even though she checked her bag religiously the day before to ensure they were in there.

"Yes, Ms. Mendez," a chorus of voices said. The bus was a whirl of activity as everyone gathered their personal items. The parents sitting in the back of the bus began to shoo her cheerleaders forward, getting them off the bus.

"When everyone has their suitcase, meet me in the lobby. I'm going to go check us in," Ofelia called over the noises of moving bodies and luggage, making her way towards the hotel, seeing a steady line of patrons ready to check in.

This year's hotel was a big upgrade from last year because Ofelia actually knew what the hell she was doing. She booked their rooms at the end of last year, as soon as she got approval from administration. She learned waiting a few months before a huge cheerleading competition to book a hotel left very slim pickings, which resulted in her finding one thirty minutes away. It had been hell packing up each time they needed to go anywhere near the Riverwalk or the convention center.

By the time Ofelia made it to the front of the line, most of the squad had wandered over towards her. An older gentleman greeted Ofelia as she placed the yellow folder full of their reservation information on the table. "You must be here for the competition?" He asked pleasantly.

"We are. I've bet you've seen a lot of us," she said conversationally, handing over her ID when he asked for it.

"Y'all have been arriving steadily, but I suspect it will pick up in an hour or so." The man typed a few things into his computer, taking her reservations. It took only ten minutes to sort out the rooms and the keys. "Your rooms will be located on the tenth floor, but we couldn't arrange six rooms right next to each other. I did my best to make them all relatively close. If you have any problems or questions, the front desk is open twenty-four hours. Feel free to come down or call. Oh, room 1045 is the only room with a single bed."

Which made it her room by default. When they got back in the evenings, she would make sure her squad was locked in their rooms, and she could hide away in her fluffy hotel bed and read whatever romcom she had loaded on her kindle. "Thank you for all your help." Ofelia smiled and went to rejoin the rest of her team.

Her squad all looked at her with the same expectant expression when she made her way towards them. "Alright squad, gather round." Ofelia gestured for everyone to move closer, so she didn't have to yell. "I have our keys, and we are on the 10th floor. It is currently-" she checked the time on her phone. "9:25. We need to be at registration by ten. Let's be ready to head over to the convention center in twenty minutes."

"What about brunch, Ms. M? I am two seconds away from being hangry," Tony said.

"And nobody wants to see that," Devin agreed. "Especially me. I'm rooming with him. A Hangry Tony is a Scary Tony."

"Of course, we will pick up food after. There are places in the convention center to eat, but they will probably all be crowded. We can walk the Riverwalk and find the food court by the mall. They'll have plenty of options for everyone." Ofelia suggested knowing her team was full of picky eaters. For dinner, they were going to have to split up with their parents and go to different restaurants because Ofelia didn't want to fight that battle.

"So meet back out here in thirty?" Nila asked, arm and arm with her best friend Faith. "In full uniform?"

"Yes to meeting back in thirty minutes and no to the competition uniform. Wear our cheer shirts and the black wind joggers. Hair needs to be competition ready and full face of makeup. Pack your competition outfit and your makeup in a duffle. We will lock it in our assigned room."

After handing out keys to the assigned roommates, her squad all made a beeline to the elevators, but Ofelia stayed back. By now, her father should be in the air, only an hour before landing. She hadn't heard from him yet and worry started to settle in. It wouldn't be the first time her father left her high and dry. Much of her childhood had been a sequence of disappointments when it came to her father attending her cheer events. Work always took priority for him. It was why she was closer to her mother than anyone else.

Ofelia was still going to give her father the benefit of the doubt. If he said he was coming to support her, then he was. She would allow herself to be excited because she was no longer a child anymore, and he no longer had work obligations. At least not a full time job. For some ungodly reason, his father still liked picking up odd contracting jobs from time to time. For now, she checked her phone for updates and hoped her father would show up in the nick of time.

~

REGISTRATION WAS MUCH MORE of a streamlined process than last year. Getting her team out of the convention center and across the street to take the stairs down to the Riverwalk had been something else entirely. She felt like a rancher, wrangling in her unruly animals and trying to get them to the same location at the same time. Honestly high schoolers were just larger toddlers with more attitude.

At the food court she released her squad and many flocked towards Starbucks and McDonald's. Ofelia decided on Little Tokyo and found Gianna sitting away from the rest of the parents. Tony's mom was young and many of the other mom's looked down on her since she had Tony when she was fourteen. Ofelia admired the woman's tenacity and ability to raise another human being when she was still being raised herself. To her, Gianna embodied strength and perseverance.

"Thank you again for agreeing to chaperone." Ofelia said once she sat across from her. "It's nice to see a friendly face amongst-"

"The sharks?" Gianna supplied.

"Well...yes. That."

"It's cool. Tony is so excited and it was cute, you know? I wanted to be here and see him perform. I didn't get to come last year and I know he was super bummed about it, even if he won't admit it. Bad mom move."

"Hey, you're here now and you helped out so much last year," Ofelia encouraged. Gianna's eyes flickered over to Tony who was deep in conversation with Lacey. It still shocked her the two of them were best friends, but Ofelia loved that. Lacey needed a Tony in her life. "Tony is thriving. So you are doing a good job, mama."

Gianna smiled and it only enhanced the woman's natural beauty when she did, making her appear younger than her early thirties. Many people thought Gianna was Tony's sister. "Thanks, Ofelia. You're doing great too. Seriously, you are handling these parents with so much patience. I know you don't see it, but they truly respect you. Before you came here." She shook her head, letting out a low whistle. "Let's just say the poor woman couldn't leave for summer fast enough. I'm fairly certain they ran her out of town."

The parents were difficult, yes, but she had grown up in the cheer world so many of their comments and attitudes didn't phase her as much as they would someone who hadn't been part of this world since childhood. When she didn't run away after one year, Colbie knew Ofelia belonged in this position.

Was she thriving? Ofelia wasn't sure thriving was the right word, but her team was damn good and worked as a unit. They teased each other and fought occasionally, but at the end of the day they were family. Family took care of one another and that was what her squad did too. It wouldn't have been possible without her gentle push.

So maybe she *was* thriving. It certainly felt like that at this moment.

While Ofelia ate, Gianna talked about her job as a correctional officer. Ofelia was content to listen while her friend spoke. Every so often, her father would pop into her mind and the string of anxiety wound its way a little tighter around her heart. Judging by his flight schedule, he should have arrived thirty minutes ago. There was still a chance that he would come, but hope was fleeting.

After two years of not being able to see her family, Ofelia had let herself become excited with the notion she would soon be reunited with her father. It would be the first time he saw her coach and for inexplicable reasons, she wanted his approval. It was such a childish thing to want, but Ofelia craved it.

As if he knew she was thinking about him, Ofelia's phone went off. Her heart lurched as she looked to see who called. Her father's picture illuminated the screen. "I'm sorry Gianna, I need to take this. I'll be right back," Ofelia said, all but jogging away to find a more secluded and quiet area to answer.

"Papa, hi!" She answered with too much enthusiasm, denying what her gut told her was coming. "Did you land yet? Do I need to send a car?"

*"Mija,"* her father spoke, and she could hear people in the background talking in Spanish. It sounded like he was outside, surrounded by a lot of commotion. "I am sorry, *Mija,* but I'm still in California."

As soon as he said those words, her heart shattered. The hope she dared to have died, leaving a heavy sadness in its wake. Breathing became harder because she felt the sob trying to break free. If she let herself cry, she didn't think she'd ever stop. The only thing her body knew as a defense mechanism was to go numb. Numb off all feelings and emotions. If she didn't feel the pain, she couldn't hurt. It was as simple as that.

She didn't need to listen to her father as he gave her another bullshit excuse as to why he couldn't be here. She caught a few words, "exchanging tickets," "job," and "bad cell phone service." He chose a random job over her and didn't have the common decency to tell her beforehand. She was two seconds away from a mental breakdown in front of her kids during one of the most stressful times in her career.

Her father was still talking when Ofelia cut him off, no longer caring to hear his pathetic excuses. "You know what papa? I don't care. I don't care that you picked work over your own daughter again. I don't care that you never gave a shit about my life. I shouldn't have even asked you to come in the first place. It was always mama supporting me, and I was foolish to think you would give up one weekend for me."

She hung up and immediately silenced her phone. It took everything in her power to hold back the angry tears ready to fall. Later she might regret her harsh words, but right now she meant what she said. This was so typical of her father, but she had still fallen for one of his neatly dressed lies! She would pay for her foolishness later, but she had to put on a smile to go out and be a coach to her cheerleaders. Her problems would have to wait until later.

Doing a quick glance in her phone's camera, Ofelia made sure she looked presentable and not the miserable mess she felt on the inside. There were cracks in her barrier, her eyes were watery and her smile didn't quite meet her eyes, but otherwise she appeared fine. Gathering the last of her strength, Ofelia held her head high and walked back over to the rest of her team.

Not many of them saw her leave to take the call, but Gianna had. She clearly had been watching and noticed something was wrong. "Is everything okay?"

And damn if Ofelia didn't almost break her fragile composure and let the tears spill. She swallowed back a sob and controlled her face into what she hoped was a reassuring smile. She failed because Gianna winced, looking even more concerned.

"Everything's fine. All good," she said, her voice sounding strange to her own ears. "But we should go. It's time to start warming up and I'm sure you all want to find the best seats to watch the performance."

"Are you sure—"

"Yes," Ofelia said too quickly, loving Gianna but wanting to throttle her at that moment. She just needed to keep busy and not think about the horrendous phone call she just had. "Will you help me gather the team? Thanks."

She didn't wait for Gianna to reply. She simply left her behind, pushing the pain deep, deep down and focusing all her attention on her squad. Ofelia didn't need her father to be the best coach she could be for her team. She just needed to be here and clear-headed.

If there was ever a time she needed comfort, it would be now. She wished Maverick was here.

# Ofelia

## CHAPTER NINETEEN

OVER TWO HUNDRED schools traveled for the cheer competition, raising the stakes from one hundred fifty teams last year. They needed to do more than shine to get the judges' attention, especially since they wouldn't be performing first. The judges had to sit through nearly three dozen schools before McKinley would enter the stage.

Normally, Ofelia found herself giddy with anticipation right before her team took stage. She was a picture of perfect composure because her squad depended on her to be their rock during their storm. After her phone call with her father, Ofelia found it difficult to muster up a smile. Her father's words played through her mind on repeat, reminding her why she shouldn't put her faith in him, knowing it was in his nature to disappoint.

What was worse, Ofelia started to feel bad about some things she said to her father in the heat of the moment. Years of pent-up resentment came to the surface, and she spoke without thought to his feelings. But what about her feelings? Didn't he give a damn about how his actions affected her? Maybe he was so used to disappointing her he was unconcerned with how she would take the news. Fuck her conscience and its inability to stop caring.

Right now, her cheerleaders needed her full attention.

Tears came to her eyes as she watched her babies, aka full grown high schoolers, run through the routine so flawlessly and effortlessly. Tony landed his tumbling pass perfectly for the first time. Faith finally nailed her two-to-a-standing-full instead of her usual layout. Lacey's smile illuminated her entire face, looking entirely the cheer captain she was meant to be. The squad's pyramid stunt sequence went off without a hitch and their cheer section bursted with crowd-leading energy.

All the moving parts to the routine Ofelia spent countless nights meticulously creating came together in a way she couldn't imagine. Even if the judges hadn't seen the great strides her cheerleaders made this year, Ofelia could, and she was going to make sure each of them knew how incredibly proud she was to be their coach.

Ofelia screamed the loudest, to the point her throat became scratchy with overuse, at the end of their routine. So much pride radiated off her body.

When she found her squad after, Ofelia jumped, hugged, and cried along with them. Not once did she think of the heavyweight burden on her heart placed there by her father. She didn't think about him when the team went out for dinner, all miraculously deciding on one location on the Riverwalk. Nor did she think of him when she told her team how proud she was of each and every one of them.

She didn't think about the ache in her heart as parents took pictures of the squad, nor when they complimented her, suggesting they always suspected Ofelia would lead their team to victory. She didn't think about it even when they made it back to the hotel and locked the students into their room for the night.

She only allowed herself to give into the sadness once back in her room, showered and changed into her fleece pajamas. Ofelia had half a mind to call her father up now and demand answers. Anger wouldn't accomplish anything other than making her feel better.

She could call Willow, but Karl recently came back from

working out of town. She knew her best friend, and they were probably going at it like rabbits, potentially with another couple in their bed. Good for them. Her brother Javi would also be asleep or getting Camilla down, and she didn't want to interrupt their nightly routines.

Then her finger hovered over the last name. She stayed up well past ten to text Maverick before; he was a night owl like her. He would be awake and would answer.

Yet she wondered if he really needed her drama at the moment? She didn't know what they were yet or if calling him would even be appropriate. What they had was new, and she desperately wanted to continue the dinner dates, the lingering kisses, and the deep conversations where everything else faded away, leaving only the two of them.

Ofelia wasn't willing to let that go. Still, for every reason she shouldn't, a reason she *should* also came to mind.

Before she could talk herself out of it, Ofelia pressed Maverick's name to video call and her phone started to ring. As she suspected, Maverick was still awake and answered after two rings. His gorgeous face and torso filled the screen. He was shirtless and looked so fine. He laid in bed, the light from the TV in his room lit half of his face. He smiled up at her as if he had been waiting for her call all day.

Something on her face gave away her emotions because Maverick's smile instantly faded, and he sat up. He momentarily went out of frame and soon a light brightened the room. When he looked back at the screen, Ofelia saw worry crease his brow. "What's wrong?" There was no hesitation in his voice, only the need to try and fix whatever was broken.

He couldn't fix this though, no matter how hard he tried. Ofelia lost her last bit of composure, and the tears started to fall freely until they turned into heaving sobs. She couldn't form words to tell him what was wrong. All her body seemed capable of was trembling and crying. A dam broke inside of her, and she didn't know how to fix it.

To Maverick's credit, he didn't shy away from Ofelia's ugly crying face. He murmured soothing words, not asking her to talk about it or telling her to stop crying. He promised not to get off the phone until she felt better, even if he needed to stay on all night. Ofelia wanted to thank him, but each time she opened her mouth to talk, another sob came out.

God she was so fucking pathetic. He probably thought someone in her family died or she got fired. Not that her dad stood her up. Without context, it would seem like she was overre-acting, but this was something Ofelia had dealt with her entire life. Her mother had always supported her, up until college when she passed away from breast cancer. She had been her comfort and security and without her mother, she hoped her father would pick up the role in her absence.

So no, she didn't cry simply because her father didn't show...again. She cried because she no longer had someone to share this huge part of her life with. Last year Javi was able to video chat in. He couldn't be there in person, but he promised Ofelia he'd still be here for her in this form. That had been enough then. This year, she wanted more.

Fifteen minutes of waterworks, Ofelia's crying turned into small drunk-sounding hiccups. She had a tentative grasp of herself, or at least she didn't feel like she was about to start sobbing again. Small victories.

"Just breathe, baby girl. That's great. You are doing excellent," Maverick encouraged, breathing with her. Each time she tried to speak, Maverick would shake his head and make her continue the breathing exercises until the small hiccups went away and her cheeks dried of all tears.

"Good," he said at last. "Now you can tell me what happened. If you're able to."

When Ofelia spoke, her voice sounded small and scratchy. "He didn't come."

Maverick cursed under his breath; she didn't even have to say who *he* was, she knew he already guessed. She mentioned countless times about how excited she was for him to come and admitting he didn't show was embarrassing. "My father didn't show up because he chose to pick up a random job over me. Again. For once in my life I just want someone—other than my mother—to show up and support me."

"Did you call your brother?"

"No. I didn't want to talk to Javi." An unspoken, *'I wanted you,'* hung heavily between them. It scared her how much she needed Maverick's comfort, especially when she didn't exactly know where they stood yet.

Maverick looked like he wanted to jump through the phone and pull her to his chest. She would gladly take solace in his arms. "I'm sorry, sweetheart. I know how much you wanted him to show up. I have half a mind to go pick up his ass and drag him to San Antonio."

A small smile crept across her features. "I wish you could."

"I do too," he admitted. "Fuck, I would do anything to see you smile. He would have been proud to see you shine today. How did your squad do, by the way?"

Ofelia was thankful for the change in topic because she didn't have any more energy, or tears for that matter, to continue to discuss her father and his lack of commitment. He was not going to ruin the amazing performance her team put on.

Instead of dwelling any longer on her father, she told Maverick all about her day and how proud she was of her cheerleaders. She explained all the amazing comments from the judges, mostly about their contagious energy and the execution of their pyramid stunt.

"Damn, I didn't realize I'm talking to a badass coach." Maverick grinned once she ran out of steam. "Did you record it?"

"Uhm, of course I did. This isn't my first rodeo. I had a parent record them. Why? Did you want to see it?" She asked hesitantly.

To her surprise, Maverick nodded eagerly. "Of course I do. I want to see what your long nights resulted in."

Seriously, she could kiss him right now. Why hadn't they'd

been able to go out again so she could do just that? She desperately wanted to kiss his sexy face until they were both breathless and in need of much more. Damn her horny thoughts when he was so far away. "I'll send it to you as soon as we hang up."

They talked for an hour about nothing and everything all at once. When their conversation came to a natural end, Ofelia couldn't hold back her yawn. She had another early morning tomorrow, and she needed sleep. "Maverick? Thank you for letting me ugly cry to you, and thank you for listening."

"I like being the one you called, baby girl. Regardless of the reason. Call me again tomorrow and tell me about your day?"

"Of course. Bye Mav."

Ofelia smiled when she hung up her phone and put it on the charger. The moment her head hit the pillow she fell into a peaceful sleep with thoughts of Maverick's voice.

# Ofelia

## CHAPTER TWENTY

THE FOLLOWING MORNING, Ofelia awoke before her alarm. Much to her surprise, she didn't wake up with any residual sadness from yesterday's disappointing call from her father. A familiar excitement crept in, stemming from today's events. Crying to Maverick had been the best thing for her, who knew! She couldn't remember a time when she felt this good after a phone call.

A low rumble from her stomach reminded her of how little she ate yesterday. She'd kill for a few breakfast tacos at the moment but would settle for the continental breakfast her hotel offered. As long as they had something hot and savory, she couldn't complain. Oh, and coffee. A lot of coffee because today would be the longest day of the competition.

Bring it on.

Stretching out her long, tired limbs, Ofelia groaned as she worked the knots out of her body. Her dirty mind thought of a few ways Maverick could work the knots out of her body...and speaking of Maverick, she needed to text him a "thank you" for last night. He had no obligation to listen to her pitiful story, but he stayed on the phone through it all.

For now, Ofelia needed to focus on feeding herself before her stomach went on strike. She kicked the feather down comforter off and rolled out of her bed. Today's coaching outfit consisted of a navy-blue polo shirt with cream colored pants. She dressed pretty modestly compared to some of the extravagant outfits coaches wore.

By the time she made it down for breakfast, Ofelia was surprised to see that everyone else beat her there. She thought she got up early too, but she hadn't been the only one starving. "Y'all better have left some food for me."

Devin, whose plate was piled high with eggs and bacon, spoke between bites of food. "No promises, Ms. M. Tony—" he glared at his friend, who wore a *who me?* expression, "—woke up in the middle of the night and ate all my snacks. All of them. Do you understand how much I brought? He saved me one pop-tart, but he even took a bite out of that!"

"Yes, I did, and I would do it again. Next time don't challenge me by saying I couldn't eat half the snacks you brought. Let the record show, I, in fact, ate all." He said smugly, looking around as if he had adoring fans and not just Lacey who laughed at Devin's expense. "But don't worry, I promised I would buy him lunch. So he can't stay mad at me."

"I'm pretty sure I still can."

"But you won't. We are too sexy to be mad at each other."

Devin shot Tony a confused look. "What does that even mean?"

"As exciting as this conversation is," Ofelia interjected, stepping away. "I'm going to grab my plate before Tony eats my food too. Lacey, hold him back," she said to her cheer captain, but apparently 'holding back' meant attack, because Lacey threw herself at Tony, so he wouldn't run for more food.

"I'm not seeing what I'm seeing." Ofelia threw her hand up and walked away from the unruly children. The smell of sausage and eggs permeated the air around her and once again her stomach gave a loud grumble. "Alright, alright, I'm feeding you," she mumbled, grabbing a disposable plate and piling it high with potatoes, sausage and gravy on biscuits, and a fruit salad. She made her coffee, adding a little cream and sugar, before taking a seat with her team.

Per Ofelia's orders, everyone at the table had studied the schedule numerous times, but Gabbie asked if Ofelia could go over it one more time. A few of the others groaned, but she shot them a look to quiet them. "That's a great idea, Gabbie. Let me walk you through our day one more time. There's been a slight change," she said and upon hearing that, her team all scooted in a little closer.

The change wasn't a major one, but required them to sign in at ten today, rather than eleven. They would be performing at one and their last performance wouldn't be scheduled until midday if they advanced. Lunch would be provided by the convention center, though Ofelia didn't know what that entailed. She would find something she wanted to eat, she wasn't picky, but she hoped the rest of the squad would also find something. If not, the parents would have to make a food run.

Day two would be their most physically demanding day, but she hoped today would also be the most memorable for her team, especially her seniors. If they didn't place in the top fifteen percent, they wouldn't be on the track to nationals. Their year would end abruptly, and Ofelia wanted so much for her seniors. If they didn't advance to the finals, she would have all four of her seniors to console.

After her last bite of eggs, Ofelia looked around the table only to notice she had been the last to finish and everyone waited for her to leave. "Alright team, I think this is the time I give the big pep talk before we sign in, yeah?"

"You could," Lacey said, elongating the final syllable. "Or I could." She said it nonchalantly. Ofelia blinked slowly, making sure she heard Lacey correctly. The girl wasn't one for big declarations of teamwork, though she was great at inspiring the team individually. Ofelia couldn't help the pride that began to swell in her chest.

"Okay, go on," she encouraged, allowing the captain to take over. Every eye turned in Lacey's direction, waiting expectantly for what she had to say.

To Lacey's credit, she didn't shy away from the attention. She thrived. Inwardly, Ofelia did a little 'yaasss queen' dance as her second in command began to speak. "So, I'm proud of us, or whatever. We did a great job yesterday and that set the bar for today. We can't screw it up now, because us seniors aren't ready to put up our poms quite yet. Right, guys?" Two senior girls and Devin nodded, all giving her thumbs up. "We gotta be better than we were yesterday and play on our strengths. We go in confident, like the badasses we are—sorry Ms. Mendez—and we leave those judges wanting more."

As far as speeches went, it wasn't earth-shattering, but clearly got the job done. A chorus of "McKinley High" chants erupted around Ofelia, much to the dismay of the handful of guests who unfortunately booked the hotel over competition weekend. They were probably seriously regretting that choice now.

"Okay, okay!" Ofelia laughed once the chant started to die down. "Let's sign in. Battle faces ready, team."

# *Maverick*

## CHAPTER TWENTY-ONE

MAVERICK MADE up his mind the moment he hung up the phone last night. She didn't ask him, he wasn't entirely certain she'd want him there, but he knew one thing for certain. There was no way in hell he'd let his woman suffer another day.

His girl needed him, so he'd show up.

Fuck her father for not understanding how lucky he was to have Ofelia as his daughter. He didn't deserve her, but Maverick would prove that *he* did. He'd fix the man's mistake.

Everything Maverick needed for a night away fit in a small duffle bag that he threw in the backseat of his truck. His plan, one he thought of last night, was to sweep into the competition unannounced and then attempt to locate his girl. If Ofelia needed someone to show up for her, he was going to be that person.

He would need to ask around to see where McKinley practiced and if he was allowed backstage. He'd have to play it smooth so the parents or her cheerleaders didn't think much of it, other than Ofelia called in Maverick for backup.

Believable? Maybe.

Okay so that part was weak, Maverick was going to have to improvise. Who knew romantic gestures took so much time and careful consideration? The men in the movies made it seem so effortless, while he tried to remember if he packed a toothbrush. He was fairly certain he did.

The drive down to San Antonio wasn't bad. The problem came when he found the convention center and realized quickly how much of a nightmare parking was going to be.

The first two parking garages were completely full, causing him to drive further away in desperation, hoping some unlucky fool would give up their parking. Eventually Maverick did find parking, in a sketchy McDonald's parking lot. He paid the man sitting outside twenty dollars to allow him to park, and he couldn't be certain that was even the man's job. It made the man leave him alone though, going off to find his next victim, so Maverick thought it was a twenty well spent.

He'd have to come back to his truck at some point, so he left his overnight bag inside, shutting and locking the door. In the far-off distance, he could still see the convention center on the horizon, but he had to be at least a mile away. Nothing like showing up to his own romantic gesture smelling like sweat. If he was lucky, Ofelia might be into the smell of a musky man.

Maverick hoped he wasn't making an ass of himself. What if when she saw him, Ofelia looked horrified? Or worse yet, she might stare at him with pity. Here comes Maverick, the dumbass that thought he could play the hero. Hadn't he learned his lesson on surprising people at inopportune times? He refused to let his mind drift off into that dark place, so he picked up his pace. No sense in chickening out now.

As expected, the convention center was flooded with people, an introvert's worst nightmare. Even Maverick, who was used to stadiums full of people, couldn't help feeling out of his element within the sea of cheer fanatics. But nobody paid him any mind. He may as well have been a ghost for all the attention he got. Many people around him were primarily female, young and old, all clumped in groups talking amicably to one another or consoling crying cheerleaders.

No signs indicated where he needed to go, and if there were, they were covered up by groups of people. Maverick needed to locate the damn sign-up station so he could ask....well he wasn't entirely sure what he would ask yet. The more he thought about his plan, the less confident he was about surprising Ofelia. He knew from experience how testy she got during practices.

Not to mention he was fairly certain the sign-up station, if such a thing existed, would not let a random man know the whereabouts of a group of high school students. If he were still somebody, he could have cajoled someone into giving up that information, but even that would have been risky.

Maverick needed a new plan of attack, one that required a lot less unknowns. He first needed to get out of the middle of the damn convention center so another person wouldn't "accidentally" bump him as they walked by. Navigating through the crowd proved easier said than done. It wasn't so much where he wanted to go, but where the mass led him, and they led him straight towards a small cafeteria area.

He decided to just text Ofelia and hoped she had her phone with her. If not, his search would continue. He quickly typed out a simple message, hoping it got a prompt response. "Where are you?" He pressed send. There, now he just needed to wait on—

Immediately his phone began to buzz. "Fuck, she's fast," he murmured, since her name, along with the picture she sent this morning, filled his screen. There was no way in hell he could hide from the cacophony of sounds around him, but maybe she wouldn't notice if her side was equally loud.

Maverick answered and put the phone to his ear, trying to cup his hand around the speaker and his mouth to keep the sound at bay. Before he could speak, Ofelia beat him to it. "What do you mean, where am I?" She sounded confused and slightly apprehensive. There was definite apprehension in her voice. *Fuck.*

Ofelia wasn't buying his bullshit. Maverick heard her whisper something to someone and moments later the surrounding sound all but vanished. Had she walked into a utility closet or something? "I feel like I should ask where *you* are, Mav."

So much for surprise, but Maverick thought this might be better. He could at least find her without having to walk every square inch of this place. "Oh, you know, San Antonio."

"What?!"

"I'm in San Antonio."

"No, I heard, but...*what*?"

"I'm not sure how to answer that." Maverick laughed awkwardly. "Uh, I guess more specifically I'm at the convention center."

"You did not drive two hours to come to our competition. Tell me you didn't do that."

Maverick still couldn't tell if Ofelia was happy or furious and it unnerved him. "I mean, I did, but if you'd rather I not—"

"Tell me where you are! Now. I'll come find you."

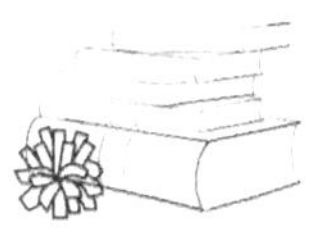

MAVERICK WAS HERE. *Here.* As in he drove all the way to San Antonio on a Saturday morning after she sobbed her eyes out to him last night. Who the hell does that? Maverick, apparently. Ofelia needed to see him this instant to make sure this wasn't a dream because there was no way Mav came. Right?

Ofelia had no problems leaving her team in the capable hands of the parents. She told Gianna an impromptu coach meeting sprung up, which was the quickest lie she could produce. Thankfully, Gianna didn't question her; if she had, the lie would quickly unravel.

Maverick described his location next to multiple vending machines and self-serve pizza stands. Ofelia knew right away where he was. The convention housed many small eateries, but only one served pizza on the first floor. She clutched her phone tightly, as if it were a lifeline connecting her to Maverick as she raced to the escalators. The first teams of the competition had already begun to perform, making this area less busy than usual.

When her feet touched down on the bottom story, she went through a mental map of the layout. Yes, she had memorized the entire layout of this damn building in case she lost a cheerleader or needed to get them from point A to point B as fast as possible. She didn't also know that it would come in handy now.

As she got closer to where Maverick should be, her heart began a funny lurch in her chest. She was feeling a mixture of emotions, most notably one she had not experienced in years. Ofelia couldn't put a name to it, not yet. She wouldn't allow herself to think of that word now. Still, she felt deeply and eventually she would have to face her emotions.

Ofelia finally arrived at the eatery, stopping dead in her tracks as all the breath in her lungs left her. Standing only a few feet in front, with his back turned towards her, was Maverick. He'd come. He showed up after one of the most important men in her life let her down. She couldn't begin to form words now because she nearly burst with emotions.

Maverick must have sensed a presence behind him because he turned around. The moment their eyes met, he beamed at her, a rare smile he reserved solely for her. One minute he was across the shop and the next Ofelia was in his arms, kissing him passionately. She didn't know who moved to whom, but she frankly didn't care. All she wanted was her lips on his with her body planted firmly against Maverick, creating a new type of heat.

Maverick let out a low chuckle from the back of his throat, vibrating through their kiss. "Shit, baby girl. I take it you're happy I came?"

"Happy? Maverick I'm fucking losing my mind. I don't know if I want to kiss you, or cry, or climb you like a tree!"

Maverick's eyes went dark, and Ofelia swore she saw lust within him. "Hmm, if I had known that was an option, I would have waited for you in your hotel room."

"You're staying? In my room?" Ofelia didn't care if she sounded over eager. She had no sense of chill, and she was okay with that. Maverick didn't seem to mind.

Maverick didn't want to assume, but he would also need to find a hotel fast. Booking a room hadn't been part of his grand gesture plan. "I can find my own room, but yeah, I wanted to stay and make sure you had someone here for you," he said softly, reaching out to tuck a stray curl behind her hair. She leaned into his touch, closing her eyes to let this moment truly sink in.

"Nonsense. You'll stay with me." Then, almost reluctantly Ofelia pulled back, but just enough to look into his eyes. "But I won't be back in my hotel room until tonight. I can give you a key if you want, I have an extra. My squad is probably performing twice today, so I'm not sure when I'll be back in the room. You can wait in there for me though. You'll just need to be kinda secretive. I can't have the parents finding out I'm housing a man in my room."

Maverick looked at her as if she were speaking a different language. "Sweetheart, I'm going to watch your cheerleaders perform. I came here knowing you'd be busy, but I wanted you to know there was someone in the crowd for you. I'll take that key though, for later. I'll make sure no one sees me sneaking into your room."

It was official. Ofelia was never going to let Maverick get away from her. He officially proved himself to be a permanent fixture in her life. He didn't know how wonderful he was. "Thank you. Here, take my room key," she said, fishing through her back pockets to hand it over. "The room is written on the back. I'm on the tenth floor. Are you serious about staying to watch?"

Maverick nodded and Ofelia thought he looked genuinely excited. It was cute. "Yeah, I am. These people look like they are going to go to war, and I don't want to miss that. Where should I sit?"

"Just take this escalator up and head right. You can enter the arena from there and find a seat with a decent view of the stage. My phone is with me if you need me. Tonight is all yours, I promise." Ofelia grinned, lighting up like a kid on Christmas, except instead of a Barbie as her gift, she had a super-hot baseball player. Honestly, it was the definition of an upgrade.

"Don't worry about me today. I'm here for support. You text me if you need me. I've got nothing but time."

Speaking of time, she was quickly running out. Her team would be expecting her back soon, and she still needed to run through the first routine once more. Even though she wanted nothing more than to stay next to Maverick, she was needed elsewhere. One last time before tonight, she leaned up to press a soft, yet deep kiss to his lips. "Tonight. And remember, don't let anyone see you." She promised, basking in his piney scent, before reluctantly untangling her arms from around his waist.

"Tonight," Maverick repeated.

When Ofelia walked back to her team, she did so knowing the man she was falling deeply for would be sitting in the audience.

# Maverick

MAVERICK HAD NEVER SEEN anything quite like this. Baseball tournaments were a given because of his familiarity with them. The crowd would burst with pent-up energy as they waited for their favorite teams to enter the field. Each play would be taken to heart and if the desired outcome wasn't achieved, the umpire was bound to hear a chorus of boos and threats.

None of that compared to the utter spectacle taking place in front of his very eyes. This crowd wasn't just invested; they acted like their very souls were in the hands of Lucifer, and if they didn't give the perfect performance, a giant pit would open in the center of the floor and drag them down to the fiery depths of hell. That wasn't an exaggeration either. Maverick witnessed plenty of interactions between cheerleaders and their overly involved parents to make him want to call up his own parents and thank them for never becoming *those* parents.

Maverick understood the dedication and pressure these young people put upon themselves. Didn't he do the same thing when he was their age? He hustled and worked his ass off to be the best. It paid off in the end, but the small voice he was seriously beginning to despise reminded him that he lost it faster than he earned it. He wondered how many of these young cheerleaders would watch their dreams slowly fade away into obscurity.

And that was enough self-deprecation for the day.

Luckily the dark place in his mind didn't stay active for long; it soon became enamored with the routines he witnessed. These squads didn't come to mess around and Maverick began to worry slightly for Ofelia. His girl was good, but he hadn't seen her team in their elements. They would have to be completely badass to stand a chance against some of their opponents' routines. He was fairly certain one team had their own blow horns and Bluetooth speakers.

As it turns out, Maverick had no reason to worry about Ofelia and her team. When McKinley walked on stage, owning it like a damn catwalk, Maverick was glued to their every movement. So much happened, and he didn't know whether to look at the ones back flipping or the ones soaring through the air after being tossed by their teammates. Gravity evidently hadn't been invited to watch their routine. There was no physical way the squad could pull off so many flips, flies, and jumps if Newton's law of universal gravitation was involved.

When McKinley's first routine ended, Maverick sprung to his feet, cheering like a proud father. Apparently, he was no better than the loud mothers sitting around him, for many of them turned to give him a look indicating their annoyance. Not that it mattered much to Mav. It felt like the right type of justice after what those very moms put him through only minutes ago with their loud wails and obnoxious crying.

After McKinley's second and final routine of the night, which was somehow even more impressive than their first, Maverick's stomach began to protest. He heard a deep rumble despite the cheering crowd. He hadn't eaten since that morning and Maverick was ready to consume an ungodly amount of calories. He quickly sent off a text to Ofelia, letting her know he was going out to pick up dinner for them and would meet her back at the hotel.

Dinner wasn't a hard choice. Since he was in San Antonio, a

place full of amazing Mexican culture, he needed authentic food. Maverick settled on a restaurant called *Mi Tierra*, a place that not only sold amazing Mexican dishes, according to the online reviews, but also a variety of baked goods. He made sure to stock up, knowing Ofelia liked to sample a mixture of foods and Maverick was hungry enough to eat the entire restaurant.

Getting back to the hotel was simple enough. It was located directly across the street from the convention center. Finding parking for said hotel was a different story. He should have remembered the parking fiasco from this morning. It took an entire thirty minutes of driving through the garage, getting frustrated and cursing like a sailor before he found a car finally pulling out of a spot.

He wasn't surprised he beat Ofelia back to her room, but was glad that he didn't run into anyone from McKinley. When he checked his phone, she had texted him only ten minutes ago saying she was picking up pizza for her squad and would be back after. Her parents offered to arrange a movie night for the teens in the hotel's media room while Ofelia got some much-needed rest. If things went the way he hoped they would tonight, Maverick didn't expect either of them would be resting much.

He couldn't deny wanting Ofelia. The need to have her in every way possible only strengthened from their first night in the truck together. He had done the right thing when he said they shouldn't go any further that night, but the feel of her soft skin against his and her sounds of pleasure had stayed with him ever since. He wanted to know what she sounded like when she came undone in his arms and not just by her own hand. When she withered in pleasure as he moved inside of her, moaning his name. When she...

Fuck. He was hard again. His body heated at the mere thought of her and him together. He needed to cool himself down before she got here and saw him sporting a hard on while he sat in her bed. Fortunately for him, his stomach took this opportunity to growl in hunger again, giving him something new to focus on other than Ofelia's naked body.

Thirty minutes and four barbacoa tacos later, Maverick heard a faint tapping sound of a key before Ofelia peered inside. Her face instantly lit up when she saw Maverick. She was glowing from today's achievements. At that moment, hair slightly askew and clothes rumpled, she looked more beautiful than Maverick had ever seen her.

"Are you hungry?" Was all he was capable of asking. All other words left him when he realized he was alone with Ofelia in a room with a bed. He reverted to a caveman, only able to think in simple sentences. *Man have woman. Man have bed. Man take woman to bed.*

Ofelia shook her head, coming into the room and shutting the door behind her. "I had a slice of pizza, but I'll definitely be taking some food later," she said, shrugging off her bag and kicking her shoes off. She crossed the room in a few long strides before dropping herself into Maverick's lap. Her ass ground down on him until she was comfortable, and Maverick had to hold his breath for his body not to react to her.

"You came," she whispered, snuggling up to him. It was only two simple words, but they packed a punch. He had come when her own father let her down. This wasn't a simple act and whether he meant it or not, it spoke on their relationship and how much Ofelia meant to him.

"I came," he repeated into her hair, moving his hand to take out the elastic. Her bun toppled over, and he ran a hand through her hair, working out any tangles. "And you were brilliant. Your squad was amazing. I don't think you understand how impressive you are." He murmured, hoping his breath didn't smell like onions.

If it did, Ofelia didn't seem to mind. She tilted her head up and leaned forward until their lips touched. It started off tender, simple with no real heat behind it. It was perfect. She was perfect. Ofelia didn't know it, but she had Maverick securely under her spell. He'd do anything for her, including but not limiting to driving two hours to sit in a massive crowd so she knew someone was there for her.

"Thank you." He heard himself say the moment Ofelia's lips moved away from him.

She looked at him oddly, tilting her head to the side and flicking her tongue out to lick her bottom lip. Maverick had half a mind to bring that lip between his teeth and suck on it until she begged him for more.

"Thank you? For what? I should be the one thanking you." She asked, bringing his attention away from her lips and back up to her eyes.

"For..." Maverick hesitated. The words were on the tip of his tongue, he tasted them, but something held him back from effectively communicating the raw emotions he felt. How could he say what he needed to without scaring her away? What were they to begin with? Maverick wanted to be more than a guy she casually dated, but was Ofelia ready for that?

The words soon began to tumble out of him, unexpectedly and without hesitation. "For being you. For listening. For trusting me enough to call me when you were at your lowest. God damn, Ofelia, for just existing. When I took this job, I was miserable and couldn't see past my own pain. I gave up, and I was going through the motions of day-to-day life, but I wasn't living.

"The moment I saw you at the coffee shop after our first encounter, I left feeling something for the first time in God knows how long. When I saw you at the bar with another guy, all I could see was red. I hated that man because I wanted to be the one next to you. After our first date, you were all I thought about, and I haven't been able to go a single day—no, a single moment—without thinking about you. You provided the sun when I was in the storm and when you called me, I felt like I could be your sun. Like I could be worthy of you."

For a long moment after he finished his emotional soliloquy, Ofelia didn't say a word. She looked at him with wide eyes, eyebrows raised nearly to her hairline. Then she did something unexpected, causing Maverick's heart to lurch. She pushed off him and stood.

*Fuck!* He blew it. He word-vomit scared her. He couldn't take back the words even though he desperately wanted to turn back the clock and go back to their kiss. Back before he screwed it up with his fucking feelings and his inability to read the room. "Ofelia, I'm sorry—"

Ofelia shushed him by holding out her hand, looking down at him. Now he saw the tears in her eyes and his increasing anxiety only heightened. How could he say so many wrong things in such a short amount of time? Was he truly so unlovable or intolerable that the thought of him caring about her made her want to cry?

"Come here," Ofelia said when Maverick made no attempt to get up or speak. This time she smiled at him, and he swore there was a new warmth in her eyes that hadn't been there a moment ago. "Please Mav. Come here. Stand up."

He wasn't going to argue with that. He stood, nearly bumping into her with how quickly he picked himself up from the chair. Ofelia stepped forward and wrapped her arms around his waist. "Remember when we were in your truck?" She asked. Maverick nodded because it never strayed far from his mind. "You asked me what I wanted, and I said you. But you said you didn't want our first time to be in your truck and not until we were both ready."

Maverick watched as Ofelia took a step backwards. The dim lights in the room made her look ethereal, playing on her skin to illuminate the best parts of her. She locked her eyes with him and didn't hesitate as she lifted her polo shirt over her head, tossing it down on the ground. She stood in her white bra, showing off her toned stomach. "Well, I'm ready. I think you might be too. And if memory serves, I remember you saying you wanted my legs wrapped around you while I scream your name. Is that still true?"

Maverick's entire body heated up. His cock strained against the front of his pants uncomfortably. For a brief moment, he saw

Ofelia's eyes dip down, taking in his bulge. Color reddened her cheeks before she looked back up, waiting for Maverick to speak. Although she looked confident, there was a shadow of insecurity in her eyes, and he wondered if she thought he'd reject her.

"I believe my words were something along the lines of needing to taste you when your legs are wrapped around my shoulders." His voice was deep as he took a step forward. Ofelia shivered. She stood abnormally still as he circled her; a hungry wolf ready to taste the little lamb. He stalked up behind her, placing one large hand on her lower abdomen and the other on her hip. "Tell me what you want, baby girl."

He said those words before, but this time he wasn't planning to stop. He intended to devour her if that's what she desired. Ofelia leaned back against him, and Maverick was certain she felt his erection pressing into her ass. "You," she said breathlessly.

They had been down this road once before, but neither had been ready to take the plunge. Until now. Maverick dipped his head lower, his lips finding the crook of her neck and nipped. Ofelia let out a little frustrated whimper, causing Maverick to chuckle at her impatience. "Don't be a brat, baby girl. I already told you that when I get to have you, I'm taking my sweet time with you."

"Mav—"

Maverick located the clasp to her bra and undid it. He slid the straps down her shoulders until the bra was nothing more than a discarded memory on the ground and her soft brown breasts were bared to him. He brought both hands up, taking her breasts into them and squeezing gently. Ofelia gasped softly, her sensitive nipples pebbling at his touch. He ran a thumb over her delicate flesh, earning himself another moan.

"I always pegged you as an ass man," Ofelia said, attempting humor but Maverick heard the shakiness to her breathing.

"Would it be cheesy to say I'm 'your' man?" Mav smirked.

"A little. But it's working for me." She laughed as Maverick spun her around. He took in the beautiful woman and once again thanked his lucky stars for putting Ofelia into his path. He kissed down her collarbone until he got to her breast. He pulled her nipple into his mouth, running his tongue along the hardened nub. She arched into him, and Maverick wrapped an arm around her waist to keep her up.

"Why are your pants still on?" Maverick murmured around her nipple. Ofelia's eyes flickered open, looking over Maverick who was still fully dressed. He read the question in her expression, but he shook his head. "No. My clothes stay on. For now. Take off your pants, baby girl. Let me see what you are hiding underneath."

Ofelia splayed her fingers out across her waistband. Her thumbs dug into the sides, waiting for his reaction. Maverick didn't give any, he simply waited, motioning for her to continue. "Pants, Ofelia. Off."

"You are bossy in the bedroom." Ofelia giggled and Maverick thought she didn't know the half of it. If she knew the dirty things running through his mind right now, she would call this request vanilla. Ofelia did a cute little shimmy as she pulled her slacks off. She then stood in nothing but a lacy black thong. Maverick raised a brow in question and Ofelia shrugged. "Thongs don't leave panty lines in pants. Plus, I paid way too much for these and I'm going to get my wear out of them."

"Trust me, baby girl, I'm not complaining. Those are going to stay on. For now," he said, getting a full view of her body. Her body was soft and toned from years of cheerleading. She was what he liked to call "thicc," plump in all the right places with thighs for days. How one woman held so much power over him was beyond him. The tentative control he had over this situation was slipping rapidly.

Still, he needed to remember this wasn't about him right now. It was about pleasing the goddess of a woman in front of him. He closed the distance between them, leading her back until the back of her legs hit the bed, and they both stumbled into it, Maverick on top. He pinned Ofelia underneath him. She was so small compared to him, but not meek. In fact, he'd never seen her look stronger than in this moment.

"I've been thinking about how you taste, sweetheart," Mav purred. Ofelia tried to reach under his shirt to feel his torso, but her hands kept getting stuck in the fabric. Her attempts amused him, so he took pity on her. "I think you've earned this." He lifted himself up momentarily, stripping himself off his shirt before laying back on top of her. "Better?"

"It would be better if you were naked. I want it, Mav. Please," she begged him, reaching for the fly on his jeans. She managed to get it halfway down before Mav playfully swatted her hands away.

"Soon." He promised her, kissing his way down her stomach. He slowly made his way further down, kissing the apex of her panty covered thighs. They were drenched and Maverick inhaled deeply, taking in her aroused scent. "Beautiful," he whispered. "And entirely mine."

"Yours." She echoed as Maverick hooked a finger through the crotch of her panties and pulled them aside. He was serious when he said he wanted those to stay on. He wanted to enjoy them a little longer before he ripped them off her body.

Maverick took a slow, long lick down her center before parting her and flicking his tongue out to meet her clit. "Holy shit!" Ofelia gasped, clutching the bedding as her body spasmed under his first touch.

"I couldn't agree more." He smiled mischievously, taking her clit between his teeth as his tongue relentlessly teased her. She tasted sweet, like he thought she would. He moved to swipe one finger through her wetness, rubbing it against her lips, spreading her arousal all over her bare pussy. Maverick groaned before pushing in a single finger, feeling her tightness. "So fucking tight baby girl."

Ofelia said it had been at least two years since she had been with a man and Maverick was also going through a dry spell. This felt like coming home, buried deep between her legs. When he felt her adjust, Mav then pushed in a second finger, groaning when she tightened around them.

"Mav!" Ofelia moaned, rubbing her sweet pussy in his face. "Yes, please, please don't stop! Don't stop...yes!" Her words ended in a scream as he tongued her clit again, feeling her squeeze around his fingers. "Maverick...don't stop...don't stop! I'm going...going to..."

Mav was relentless with his sweet torture. He took care of her clit while finger fucking her until she became a puddle underneath him. When Ofelia orgasmed, she screamed out his name as she came all over his tongue. He licked her until she came down from her high and immediately Maverick pushed away to claim her mouth.

Their lips met in a warm, wet embrace. Ofelia's climax still on Maverick's tongue, but she didn't shy away from tasting herself. "More. Mav I need more. I need you," she pleaded and this time when she went for his pants to finish what she started earlier with his zipper, Maverick didn't stop her. Ofelia clawed at his jeans until he helped her kick them off. The last to go was his boxers and her panties, joining together on the floor.

They were both naked, laying flushed against each other. Ofelia reached down to grip Mav's cock in her hands, moaning. "You're so fucking big." She panted, each stroke driving him absolutely wild. "I want it. Please Mav." Her begs were like candy to him, sweet and addictive.

"What do you want to do with this cock? It needs you." He wanted to be inside of her, but he wanted to do it in a way that she liked. He hadn't had to learn what someone liked in bed in so long, it was actually fun discovering what made Ofelia moan.

There was no shyness in his girl's voice, only complete understanding of what she wanted and needed. "I want to ride you."

How could Maverick say no to that request? He would be a fool otherwise. They moved together until they switched positions. Maverick was laying on his back, his head on the pillow as

Ofelia climbed on top of him. His cock was throbbing, painfully so, but he needed to last for her.

"Do you have a condom?" She asked like the question just dawned on her.

Maverick came prepared. He reached for the bedside table, grabbing his wallet. He opened it up and pulled out a silver wrapper. Ofelia immediately stole it from him, ripping it open with a devious smirk. "I want to do the honors."

"You don't need an excuse to touch my cock, baby girl. Touch away." He winked. Then watched as she took the condom out and rolled it down his impressive length. He took the base of his cock into her hand and hovered over his length before slowly bringing herself down.

Ofelia hissed as the first few inches went inside of her and Maverick reached out to grab her hips, stopping her before she could go any lower. "Are you hurt? Did I prep you well enough?"

Ofelia's features softened as his concern, but she shook her head. "You're so big, Mav. Just give me a minute. I'll adjust." She murmured and leaned down to plan a soft kiss to his lips. Ofelia kept his lips on his, inching herself down on his cock. When he was fully seated inside of her, she gave off a soft gasp. "I've never been this full before," she panted gently.

"Move when you're ready. I want to see you please yourself on my cock." Maverick couldn't keep the moan out of his own voice. It was enough to make Ofelia start to move for him. It took everything for Maverick to remain focused and not let his lust consume him out of fear he would take over in a frenzy. He didn't want to hurt her.

Ofelia seemed to be playing a battle of her own, shifting on top of him so he rubbed deeper inside of her. He watched transfixed as she rubbed herself against him, the movement providing a natural up and down movement. Her eyes flickered halfway closed and soon Maverick's name was leaving her parted lips in a series of moans. Maverick's own face mirrored her own.

He couldn't stay still anymore though. On their own accord,

his hips lifted and slammed into her. He felt himself hit deep inside of her and Ofelia cried out. Not in pain but pleasure. "Yes! Oh, Mav...rough. I want it rough."

She knew what she liked and Maverick was going to give her just that. He met her thrust for thrust, a string of colorful expletives leaving his lips. Ofelia was on top, but Maverick oversaw their pleasure. Her hand snaked between her legs and began rubbing her clit. Maverick tsked. "Fuck no, baby girl. When you are with me, I take care of your clit. Do you understand?"

"Yes. Oh, fuck yes I do." She nodded enthusiastically and all but grabbed Mav's hands to move between her legs. He began to stimulate her clit, giving more pleasure. His own began to build, and he didn't know how much longer he could last in this state.

"That's my girl. Fuck, you drive me crazy. That tight little pussy of yours is going to be the death of me. I'm so fucking close." He opened his eyes, making sure she was as consumed as him.

She was.

"Mav...oh god, Mav—"

"God has nothing to do with this, baby girl. It's my cock that is making you crazy. My cock that is nestled deep inside of your pussy. Cum for me baby. Cum all over my cock." The dirty words left his mouth just in time for her to scream out as she toppled over in her orgasm. Maverick finally let himself go, coming hard inside of the condom.

Ofelia milked him until he went soft inside of her and then pulled out of him before falling into his arms, panting. "That was..."

"I hope you say nothing short of amazing." Maverick's own breathing was labored from their activities.

Ofelia grinned and kissed his chest. "Exactly that." Then a sly smile crossed her features. "And to think, it's only the start."

That made Maverick cock his brow. "The start?"

"Oh yes, the start," she said as if it were the most obvious thing in the world. "You awoke something in me, Mav and I want to make you feel as good as you've made me feel. I hope you'll be ready for another round...after tacos of course."

And damn it if his cock didn't twitch in anticipation at her words. "What can I say, I'm captive to your every need. We have all night."

That was precisely what they did too. They finished off the last of the food Maverick had bought before going in for another hot and sexy round between the sheets. When they finished for the third...or was it fourth?...time, Maverick held Ofelia as they fell asleep with their limbs still entangled.

## *Ofelia*

### CHAPTER TWENTY-FOUR

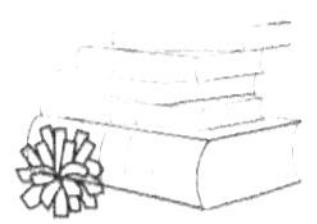

OFELIA WOKE up with the most delicious ache between her thighs, a parting gift from last night's activities. Her body was extra sensitive; she felt the soft caress of the sheets against her naked body. Big, strong arms held her tightly against a firm chest. Maverick's chin nestled atop her head and Ofelia wondered if his mouth was full of her unruly hair.

Last night was nothing short of spectacular. Maverick worshiped her body, treating her like a sacred deity he wanted to please. And please he did, many times. To say her sex life previous had been lacking, even when she was with Hector, would be an understatement.

For so long Ofelia believed something inside of her was broken. Hector and her had good sex, but it had taken her so long to reach orgasm and it hurt Hector's feelings. It wasn't that she wasn't attracted to him, she had been and loved him desperately, but Hector struggled to reciprocate in bed. Often Ofelia ended up working out her own tension.

Her lack of orgasm hadn't been ideal, but Ofelia had thought the problem was entirely her own fault. If she gave Hector pleasure, then her own didn't matter. How stupid her thinking had

215

been back then. Maverick, in only one night, had found the most sensitive spots and drew out her cries of ecstasy.

Sex wasn't supposed to be like that, was it? Fucking spectacular and earth-shattering. Hadn't Ofelia read countless books and spoken to a few friends who all agreed their first time with their significant other was less than stellar? Ofelia had thought that until Maverick completely rocked her world.

Home run. Knocked it out of the park. Grand slam. All puns included.

Maybe they were just the rare match that instantly clicked. There was no embarrassment or shame Ofelia felt during or after, quite the opposite. She felt empowered and sexy, capable of bringing grown men to their knees. Maverick falling between her thighs would be etched deeply into her brain for the rest of her life.

The thought made her smile and cuddle back against Mav, her back resting against his chest. She wiggled slightly to readjust herself, effectively grinding into his crotch. Something was definitely awake, even if Maverick was not. His morning wood pressed against her ass, and she nudged back against him again, biting her lower lip.

"If you keep doing that, I will be forced to retaliate, baby girl." Maverick's gruff voice whispered into her ear. So, he was awake, not just her new favorite part of him.

"Who, me? I'm afraid I don't know what you mean." Ofelia feigned innocence and moved back against him again. Which promptly earned her a low groan and a swift spanking on her ass, causing her to yelp. "What was that for?" She asked as if she didn't know. Ofelia also made a mental note that she really liked being spanked, and she would need to demand more of it the next time.

Maverick didn't answer her. Instead, he rolled her around until they were chest to chest. He snaked an arm around her thigh and hiked her leg up around his hip. The head of his cock pressed against her entrance, teasing since Mav made no attempts of pushing in further. "Good morning, beautiful." His voice was deep and husky with sleep. She didn't think she had ever found him more attractive.

"Morning." The word came out more breathlessly than she anticipated. Maverick must have noticed for he reached down between them and dragged the tip of his cock down her seam. A moan escaped her lips, and she suddenly no longer cared that she was still sore from last night.

Ofelia had the foresight to grab their last condom from the bedside table before reaching down and halting his movements, a sly smile on her lips. "Did you sleep well?"

Ofelia didn't give him a chance to answer as she ripped open the condom, rolling it over his hard length. He plunged his thickness deep inside of her, filling her up completely. They both hissed in surprise and pleasure, Maverick squeezing her thigh draped around him.

"I could get used to this," he murmured as he started moving. These were not the hurried, almost frenzied movements from last night. No, this morning Maverick moved almost lazily with no regard to time. Ofelia found that she liked it a lot.

"Waking up with my hair in your mouth?" She grinned, feigning naivety.

Maverick chuckled and shook his head. "Your hair is beautiful and none of it got in my mouth. I'm talking about waking up with you next to me."

"It's...nice." Ofelia's last word left her lips in a soft moan. Maverick had quickened his pace but kept his movements gentle. Nice didn't describe how she felt, not even close. She couldn't yet put those feelings into words, but the thought of waking up alone or with anyone else other than Maverick caused a deep ache in her chest she didn't want.

"Nice is one way to describe it. Fucking euphoric would be another." That's when their conversation ended, and their lips met in a passionate embrace. The kiss communicated far more than Ofelia could articulate; she only hoped Maverick understood what she conveyed in that kiss.

They made love slowly and fervidly. The searing caresses started a flame deep within her belly and it built and built until the flames erupted into a full-on inferno. They toppled over at the same time, holding on to one another until their fire fizzled out, leaving nothing but immense satisfaction in its wake.

Again, just like last night, three tiny words played at the tip of her tongue. Small in stature but heavy in meaning, they begged to be released, but her fear of ruining this precious thing between them stopped her from voicing how she felt. In time, she would work up the courage. She wanted to be sure anyway, perhaps when Maverick wasn't seated inside of her, and her brain wasn't full of lust and satisfaction.

Ofelia's alarm began to go off, ruining the moment. "Damn," she muttered, untangling herself from Maverick to reach for her phone. It occurred to her that in an hour, Ofelia would have fourteen cheerleaders and their parents starting to wake up, and it seemed incredibly salacious to have a naked Maverick next to her. Slight panic began to course through her body. Maverick needed to leave.

As if reading her thoughts, Mav rolled to the edge of the bed, bracing his feet firmly on the floor as he stretched his back. "I suppose that's my cue to leave."

"I'm so sorry Mav, it's just that if anyone found out we were together right now—"

Maverick silenced her by reaching around to pull her in for a quick kiss. "Trust me, I'm not offended. I know I'm not your booty call." He winked and stood. His entire body stood on full display and Ofelia thought she'd get used to seeing all the hard lines and strong muscles, but she definitely wasn't. The man was built like a damn gladiator and Ofelia had rode that man! Multiple times!

Damn it felt good to be her right now.

Ofelia blatantly and unabashedly stared at her man as he got dressed. Maverick seemed to eat up the attention, winking at her as he slid up his jeans. "Do you want me to stay around for the results?" He asked.

He was sweet to ask, but Ofelia knew nothing exciting happened today. She could easily text him if they were moving to nationals. This competition was a stepping stone to bigger things. "No, it's fine. Go home and rest. I'll text you later and let you know how we did."

Maverick was fully dressed and disappeared momentarily to brush his teeth. When he finished, Mav walked out carrying his overnight bag. Ofelia still laid in bed because she desperately needed a shower so she didn't reek of sex. Not that she was complaining, of course.

"Thank you again, for coming. I'm so happy you did." Ofelia tilted her head up as Maverick walked over to her, stopping in front of her. "Does this mean we are serious?" Ofelia wasn't sure what prompted her to ask the question right then, but she needed to know. She didn't make it a habit of sleeping with men that didn't mean anything to her, not that she was against hookups. Mav meant something to her, and she needed confirmation he felt the same.

"Baby girl, I've been serious. I'm glad you are finally on board." He grinned and leaned down to kiss her gently. "You're mine, Ofi. You're mine and I don't like sharing what is mine. And I'm yours. You are stuck with me."

"I wouldn't say stuck. Happily committed, more like." Ofelia smiled like a fool but didn't care. She was happy, happier than she had been in years. All because of a stupid gym fight. Amazing how that could be the best thing to ever happen to her. "Text me when you are home?"

"Not a minute later." Maverick agreed, hovering above her. Unsaid words hung heavily between them and for a second, Ofelia thought Maverick might say what she couldn't. The stretch of silence lasted only a few more seconds until broken by a kiss from Maverick. "Bye, Ofelia." With that, she watched her man walk out of the room. An embarrassing giggle left her lips the moment she was alone.

She had it bad for Maverick Wilson.

# *Maverick*

## CHAPTER TWENTY-FIVE

*HAPPILY COMMITTED* WAS the perfect way to describe how Maverick felt. The ridiculous grin he wore hadn't left his face since he left the hotel. Stranger yet, Maverick couldn't shut the hell up when he passed someone walking back to his car, forcing polite conversation with everyone he passed.

There was only one reason he acted like a social butterfly starving for attention and that was because of what transpired last night—and this morning. It would have been easy to slip back into bed and spend all day together wrapped up in each other. They were both adults and had adult things they needed to do, but Maverick wouldn't mind ignoring the outside world for a little longer.

The drive home wasn't bad. Maverick only stopped once for gas and to pick up a gas station burrito he was certain he'd regret later. Traffic was nonexistent, but he pitied the poor souls who would leave once the competition ended. He imagined that would be one hell of a nightmare.

As soon as he walked through his front door, Maverick texted Ofelia knowing she wouldn't answer until she was on the way home. He tossed his overnight bag by the door leading into the small laundry room.

221

As Mav moved further into the house, passing the small office and the guest bathroom, he headed straight for the living room to relax as his phone started to vibrate. He figured Ofelia texted back, but the vibration didn't stop. A Chicago number glowed across the screen. Through all the excitement of the past couple of weeks, Mav had nearly forgotten about the lawyer Keanon set him up with.

Before the screen flashed to black, Maverick answered by clearing his throat and saying, "This is Maverick Wilson."

"Mr. Wilson, glad I caught you. This is Lloyd Gilmore again. Is this a good time to talk?" Even without introducing himself, Mav remembered Gilmore's voice. Just like the first time they spoke, his body grew tense. He felt like he navigated life as two different people, baseball star Maverick and humble Coach Maverick. Gilmore served as a reminder that his old life was still within reach.

"Yes, hello Mr. Gilmore. Now's a perfect time," Mav said as he moved to sit on the couch, legs wide apart as he leaned an elbow on his thigh. Whatever Gilmore was about to say, Maverick braced himself.

"Fantastic. I took the liberty of moving ahead with your case and I must say, we have solid evidence in your favor. Remember when I said that you weren't the first of Grant Adam's unfortunate victims? There seems to be a connection between you and the two other banned players because of a complaint posed by Adams.

"Unfortunately, there's not much I can do for the others, but this does help your case. The petition we filed has been accepted, which means our case is eligible to be brought in front of a judge. Are you with me, Mr. Wilson?" Mr. Gilmore paused since Maverick hadn't made so much as a noise.

To say Maverick was stunned was an understatement. He wasn't privy to the dealings of court, but he didn't expect his case to be picked up so quickly. It felt like yesterday he was signing contracts for Mr. Gilmore for the man to represent him. Though looking back, he supposed a few weeks had passed since then. Still, everything was moving so fast. "I...think so," Maverick said hesitantly. "But I guess I don't understand what happens next."

"Ah yes, well that's why I'm calling. I've already gotten multiple letters from Adams lawyers, and they want to flush this out quickly and privately." Meaning that they didn't want the press to catch wind of this. Even if Maverick lost, it would still reflect badly on Grant Adams.

"I must request you fly back up to Chicago at your earliest convenience." Gilmore continues as if he were commenting on a weather change rather than asking Maverick to jump on the nearest plane to get his ass back to Chicago. "The proceedings will take place in two days' time, and you are required to be there, as is Grant Adams. If this time frame doesn't work for you, I could try to change the date, but I highly advise against it. The sooner we get this done, the better. We've taken his legal team by surprise in getting this far. What would you like to do?"

The pitch was on the table and Maverick had to be the deciding factor. The best option, at least according to Gilmore, was to get to Chicago as fast as possible. Was he prepared to face his past? His coach? Worse yet, would Breanna be there? He wasn't sure he could see her and face all the emotions he buried so deeply. It wasn't a clean break and Maverick was content with leaving it as is, even if a small part of him would have preferred closure.

"Mr. Wilson, are you still there?" Gilmore asked, making Maverick realize he had been quiet for longer than appropriate.

He wished he had more time to make the decision, but he wasn't given the luxury of time. Waiting any longer would only postpone the inevitable. It was better to jump in feet first and hope for the best.

"I'm in. I'll be there by tomorrow night."

"Wonderful." He heard the smile in the man's voice. "I'll have my assistant give you the details about our meeting and perhaps help arrange a flight." Gilmore paused before adding, "You are making the right choice, Mr. Wilson. Be ready to fight like hell. Your name and your career are on the line."

Not to mention Gilmore's career as well, but Maverick didn't think he needed to point that out. Losing this trial wouldn't damage Gilmore's name and reputation but winning could skyrocket him further.

"Thank you so much, Mr. Gilmore. I'm eager to get this over with," Maverick said and Lloyd said his final goodbye before switching Maverick over to his assistant. She helped coordinate their meeting times and locations. She went as far as helping him find the first flight into Chicago, a flight that would be leaving at six the following morning, and a room at a hotel located in the center of downtown.

It was done. Just like that. He felt like he should be more excited about this, or at the very least relieved. He did feel a sense of excitement, but it was mixed with conflicting emotions of indecision. Gilmore said he needed to make sure this, meaning lifting the ban and getting a chance at his old life, was what he wanted.

If someone asked him a month ago, there would be no hesitation. But now? Now he felt as if he finally started to connect to his new team. The small suburb of Austin was growing on him, and he liked the atmosphere of it.

Plus, there was Ofelia, his main reason for the hesitation.

It was silly to base his entire life on a new relationship, but he couldn't deny he was falling for her. Hard and fast. Yet...there wasn't any harm in going through with the proceedings. At the very least, he could clear his name and wouldn't be looked upon as a failure. Baseball would be an option again, not a distant memory. He could make that choice when he heard the final verdict.

He would need to let his work know he'd be out and try to find a substitute. Laundry needed to be completed and then packed. He needed to call Keanon and fill him in on what was happening.

And finally, he needed to let Ofelia know. He regretted not

having enough time to tell her in person, but he'd be gone early in the morning. Gilmore said Adams' team wanted to get this over quickly, so he hoped that meant he wouldn't be gone for more than a few days.

He hoped his new streak of luck wouldn't run dry now.

## Ofelia

### CHAPTER TWENTY-SIX

THE WEEKEND CAME and went like petals in the wind, disappearing before Ofelia could appreciate its beauty. San Antonio had given her what she needed and provided her with so much more than she hoped for. Her cheerleaders far surpassed her expectations and performed their little hearts out. She could see all the hard work her squad put into their season pay off in their performance. They never lacked in school spirit or camaraderie. Seeing their smiles when the judges announced McKinley would be moving on to nationals fed her soul (and her energy) on their ride back home.

From there, everything else was much of a blur. She texted Maverick they'd placed and headed to the next competition in about a month. When she arrived home, Ofelia stripped out of her clothes to change into something more comfortable. Then thought to herself a nap was exactly what she needed and put her head down on the pillow. The next thing she remembered was waking up to the sound of her alarm.

Perhaps it should have worried her that she had slept her entire Sunday away and didn't stir once during the night. She hadn't stopped to think about how much she did this weekend. From shuffling kids around, making sure her cheerleaders felt prepared for their routines, placating parents, and her time with Maverick, Ofelia had to be constantly "on." Her body needed to crash and recoup.

Especially since she experienced a marathon of sex with Maverick and each time more intoxicating than the last. She so desperately wanted to spill, in great detail, everything that transpired between them. Willow would freak out and demand a play by play, which Ofelia would gladly provide. Over the past two years, she heard all the dirty details of Willow and Karl's sexual endeavors, so it only felt right she returned the favor. Now that she finally had a sex life to talk about.

Unfortunately, her mood changed once she picked up her phone and saw she had a notification from Maverick. The time stamp was around nine last night, meaning Ofelia had been dead to the world. It was a short message, but still shocking.

She typed out a quick response and although she had a million questions, she didn't think Maverick needed any extra stress while he was dealing with his unjust ban proceedings. A small, selfish part of her wished he asked her to go along, even though that was utterly crazy. Not just because he received the news last night, but also because Ofelia was nowhere prepared to leave her class in the hands of a sub.

Still, Maverick was all she could think about on the ride to school. He hadn't texted back yet, but he had mentioned his plane took off at six. She didn't expect a response until he arrived safely in his hotel room. It wasn't as if she had ample time to check her own phone at school. Especially today when she would be in the midst of essay revisions, also known as her own personal purgatory.

Even if she wouldn't be seeing Maverick's beautiful face today, she knew she had the next best thing: a quirky best friend she was ready to divulge all her secrets to.

～

"SHUT UP! Shut all the way up!" Willow screeched, looking like a flightless chicken as she flapped her hands in excitement. Ofelia had to admit it was nice being on the receiving end for once. Usually it was Ofelia getting excited over Willow's sex adventures. She resolved herself to a lifelong term of being the single friend. Until today.

Thank God that ended.

Ofelia had been bursting with the news of her and Maverick all day, but she had been unable to catch her friend's eyes. Willow was called into a student meeting before school and they didn't share the same off periods on certain days. Lunch was their only time to catch up and Ofelia wanted to tell her so much about her night (and morning) with Maverick and his hasty departure to Chicago.

When Ofelia finally got her best friend alone, she shut her door to ensure their utmost privacy before immediately jumping into the events of the weekend. Willow's jaw dropped to the floor and in a very Un-Willow like fashion her friend didn't speak once while Ofelia shared every juicy detail of her night with Maverick. It wasn't until she recounted the morning he left did Willow find her voice.

"Was it good? Can he locate where the clit is? Maverick seems like a guy who could but looks can be deceiving. Oh! Please tell me you little love birds were safe, because—"

"Willow, oh my god." Ofelia couldn't help it. She busted out laughing. "I'm not some horny teenager who hasn't been taught about contraceptives. I'm on the pill and Maverick used a condom. Well, all his condoms actually."

"SHUT UP!"

"Willow!" Ofelia hissed but couldn't conceal her slight smirk. "Use your indoor voice, please."

"Don't use your teacher voice with me, Ofi," Willow said but made a show of lowering her voice down to a reasonable level. "I can't believe you had sex with a steaming hot baseball player! Or former, but you know what I mean. Ofi, do you know how freaking cool you are? How many women would die to have their chance with Maverick?"

Willow paused for a second before her face scrunched up in something that could only be read as disgust. "Ugh, I take that back. Does Maverick know how lucky *he* is to have *you*? You are smoking hot and have the perkiest ass I have ever seen. You are a freaking catch! Maverick better understand what he has. As your best friend, I am obligated to beat his ass if he hurts you."

Ofelia looked over her petite friend. Willow didn't scream threat, especially when Maverick stood well over six feet and had at least sixty pounds on her. Willow was, at best, an angry teacup chihuahua; small but packed a mighty bark. Ofelia wouldn't want to be on the receiving end of that.

"Well thank you and if he does, I'll let you loose on him. But I hope it doesn't ever get to that point. I really like him, Will. Like a lot. Far more than I should. Like I feel I'm moving too fast."

"Pfft!" Willow rolled her eyes dramatically. "It's not too fast at all. I'm honestly surprised it has taken you this long to get some D from him. Trust me, girl, you aren't moving fast."

Easy for her to say, considering Willow married Karl after three weeks of knowing him. Willow and Karl's romance was the kind authors write about. Several summers ago, Willow took a summer vacation to Germany with a few friends. The first night there, she met Karl in some dingy pub and fell in love. Right then and there. Willow described it as coming home after a long and strenuous journey. When their eyes met for the first time, Willow claimed the room parted, giving them space to run into each other's arms.

It was all very fairytale and fantastical, but Ofelia liked to believe it happened exactly as Willow described. Where her friend was more of a dreamer, Ofelia usually kept two feet on the ground. She wasn't ready to go off and profess her love for Maverick yet, even if her heart felt sure.

"So where is he today, anyway? I had to make copies after my meeting and when I walked by the gym, I saw an ancient looking grandpa as his sub. Did you bang him into a coma?"

Despite her best efforts, Ofelia barked out laughter at the absurdity of Willow's statement. "You are so vulgar sometimes." Willow didn't even attempt to look contrite, not that Ofelia expected her to. "No, Maverick texted me last night when I was asleep. He left for Chicago."

Willow's eyes widened at that. "Chicago? What's he doing there?"

Ofelia realized she hadn't been keeping Willow in the loop. To be fair, Maverick didn't talk to Ofelia much about his sudden departure. From previous conversations, Ofelia knew Mav had been contacted by a big shot lawyer named Lloyd Gilmore to represent him in his ban appeal. However, for Willow to understand the severity and unfairness behind his band, she would be required to tell Mav's story, even though it wasn't her story to tell.

Willow was her best friend though. Ofelia told her everything and if anyone would be on Mav's side beside herself, it would be Willow. Besides, his business was already out into the world, albeit wrongly reported, so it seemed only fair that Willow knew the true story.

"Fuck that guy and his cheating fiancée! That is absolutely deplorable. No wonder why Maverick was such a hard ass before. It makes so much sense now." Willow exclaimed as soon as Ofelia finished retelling the events. As expected, Willow reacted as Ofelia thought she would.

"Right? But I guess Mav was just as shocked as I was when he told me he had to leave. They want to settle this quickly and his lawyer feared that prolonging it wouldn't work in his favor."

"Wow. This is...a lot." Willow seemed to deflate into her swivel chair. She plucked a grape from her bento box, popping it into her mouth. "So how do you feel about all this?"

"I mean, I want to support him of course. This is all new territory for me, so I'm just trying to keep an open mind. Mostly I want to make sure Mav is okay. I don't know if he's thought about it, but there's a good chance he will see his ex. I don't know what type of emotional toll that will take on him, but I want to be prepared for anything."

Willow nodded, seeming to consider everything Ofelia said. She appeared calm on the outside, but her insides were churning with worry and self-doubt. Worry because she didn't want Maverick to feel like he needed to go through this ordeal alone and self-doubt because she was unsure if she was doing her part as a supportive girlfriend.

How much did he need from her? She didn't want her presence to become overbearing, but Maverick shouldn't feel isolated either. Plus, and she would never admit this part to Mav, she was a little concerned about Mav seeing Breanna again.

Okay, maybe a *lot* concerned.

Maverick would never do anything to violate her trust, but she didn't trust Breanna. There was no telling what that woman was capable of. In her mind, Breanna was a beautiful seductress keen on making Mav as miserable as possible. Whether that was the truth was completely irrelevant to the unease beginning to blossom within her.

"So, let's say that the judge overturns the ban and Maverick is then allowed to play again. Where does that leave you in this equation?" Leave it to Willow to ask the very question Ofelia tried to avoid. Those thoughts had crossed her mind one, two, or ten times since Mav texted her this morning, and she honestly didn't know how to answer that question.

Luckily, Willow appeared to realize the question struck a nerve with her friend, so she waved it off, downplaying the severity of it. "You know what? It doesn't matter. That's a 'cross that bridge when you get there' sort of thing, yeah? Anyway, I wanted to ask you what you were planning to do for Spring break. It's coming up in a few weeks. Freaking finally."

Ofelia appreciated the subject change and the light tone that came with it. "Well actually, I planned on finally going back to

California to visit Javi and Camilia." She conveniently left out her father because she was still upset about his last-minute ditching.

Willow choked on the grape she was eating, having to pound her chest and chug water to stop the coughing hysteria. When she composed herself, Willow melodramatically said "I'm sorry. I just thought I heard my best friend say she was going to go to California. The same California she has been avoiding for the past two years. Are pigs flying?"

"Yes, why I just saw a few fly over my car this morning," Ofelia deadpanned.

Willow looked around her desk, probably trying to find something to throw at Ofelia, but she came up empty-handed. "You make fun, but this is a big deal. You've never talked about going back, only trying to get your family here to visit. What changed suddenly?"

Saying Maverick would have been too cliché and made Ofelia seem like she was only willing to change for a man. Maverick had unknowingly been a big part of her decision, but Ofelia had been the one to break free from the fear that consumed her so viciously for the past two years. It had kept her from her family, and she didn't want to go another year without seeing them.

"I guess I just realized the reasons for not going weren't as important as the reasons to go. I'm tired of letting something hold me back and it's a lot easier for me to travel than it is for them. I'm just one person and Javi is dealing with a toddler and my father, which is essentially the same thing as a stubborn toddler." Even if she was pissed at him, a large part of her wanted nothing but to be wrapped in his warm embrace and smell the scents of home on his t-shirt.

Willow finished her last grape and stuffed the bento box into her lunch bag. They only had a few more minutes of peace before their students began to fill the hallway at the sound of the bell.

"I think that's wonderful, and I fully support this. Are you going to bring Maverick with you? You know, meet the family and such." Willow pretended to ask casually, but Ofelia could see the wicked glint in her eyes.

Her cheeks reddened as she shook her head adamantly. "Of course I'm not. I know you literally fell in love and married your husband in less than a month, but we don't all have Disney love stories. It's too soon. I want to be one hundred percent certain this man will be in my life for the long run before I commit to anything. Besides, he does not need to experience the knockout my father and I are destined to have."

Willow nodded in understanding. What she liked most about her talks with Willow was that she'd actually listen and give great advice. She wouldn't just say what Ofelia wanted to hear. At one time that annoyed her to no end, but now she enjoyed getting another perspective. Even if it sometimes hurt.

"Even though I think it is more than appropriate to take Maverick to meet your family, I also agree you deserve this time alone. I know how much you miss them and I'm just incredibly happy you've decided to go back home for a few days." Even though a whole desk sat between them, Willow leaned over and reached for Ofelia, bringing her in for a hug. "I'm so proud of you."

Ofelia's eyes began to sting, the threat of tears nearby. She hugged Willow back a little harder than normal and if her friend noticed, she didn't comment. Instead, she hugged Ofelia back a little tighter too. "Good things are happening for you and I couldn't think of a more deserving person."

If the bell didn't ring at that exact moment, Ofelia was certain she'd cry. Since it did, she let go of Willow and ran a finger underneath her waterline, wiping away tears that fell in the process. She smiled at her best friend, thanking her again before she headed to her room, prepared to sit through grammar revisions for another three hours. Tonight she would get to talk to Maverick and hopefully learn more about what was going on in Chicago.

# Maverick

## CHAPTER TWENTY-SEVEN

MAV REGRETTED LEAVING SO SUDDENLY and without seeing Ofelia once more. It wasn't as if he had much choice on the matter though; he had needed to get to Chicago and put this case to rest as quickly as he could. Still, he would have liked to hold her once more before he had to pack up and leave abruptly for an unknown length of time. He was hoping his stay wouldn't extend past a few days, but even he knew that was wishful thinking.

Maverick landed in Chicago around eight thirty in the morning and was promptly whisked away to his hotel. A man in an expensive looking black suit drove him to a ritzy hotel nestled deep within downtown Chicago. It was the type of hotel his team might have stayed at if they were having a stellar season, where the interior was impossibly white and complimentary champagne awaited in every room.

Unfortunately, Maverick didn't get to explore the hotel past his room. He only had enough time to change for his meeting with Gilmore. He had talked to many attorneys over the years, mostly dealing with his baseball contracts, but never something as world changing as this meeting.

Maverick was nervous and several other emotions he couldn't quite place since arriving back in Chicago. He turned every corner with trepidation, wondering if this would be the moment he ran into someone from his old life. To Adams or Breanna.

It was the first time his old life had mixed with the new Maverick and already he started to see some substantial changes. For example, his old self wouldn't have thought twice about having a personal chauffeur drive him to and from an overpriced hotel to a prestigious law firm. He definitely wouldn't be as unsure and anxious as he was now. No, his former self was a bit arrogant, if he was being honest. The world revolved around him and baseball...until it didn't.

Until it started being about coaching his high schoolers, supporting his off-season athletes in their wellness journey, and spending as much time as he could with the woman who was consuming his life.

Mav's phone buzzed, effectively reminding him he needed to be at the law firm in the next fifteen minutes. He grabbed his wallet, phone, and hotel key before leaving his room and heading down the long, dimly lit hallway that reminded him of a modern castle: sleek and the color of stone.

He made it back to the lobby half expecting professional dancers to burst out from one of the expensive vases and began a slow waltz. Sitting patiently on a sofa was Jared, his driver. "Ah, are you ready to go, Mr. Wilson?" The man asked, pushing himself up.

"Call me Maverick and yeah, I'm ready," he said. Jared nodded, though Mav had the inkling suspicion the man would continue to call him Mr. Wilson. He opened the back door for him again, even though Maverick was very capable of opening his own door. Since Jared seemed almost eager to do it for him, Maverick kept silent.

Jared ran around the black car and got into the driver's seat. He glanced up, meeting Mav's eyes in the mirror and smiled. "A Mr. Keanon Jermaine will be meeting you at your destination," he informed him as he started the car.

It shouldn't have shocked Maverick that Keanon would want

to be in there for the meeting, because of course his agent would. Keanon often said Mav excelled at tuning out what he didn't want to hear and only relaying the information that behooved him. Which was...accurate. Knowing his friend would be there lessened some of the knots in his stomach.

Jared, somehow miraculously, made the drive through downtown as painless as possible, getting Maverick to the firm with three minutes to spare. "Damn, you're good. That traffic was no joke, man."

Jared tilted his head back and winked. "Thank you, Mr. Wilson. Driving for as long as I have, you pick up some tricks along the way," he said, pulling up as close to the curb as possible. He put the car in park and before Mav could argue, Jared was out of the car and opening his door, holding out a small card. "Here's my number, sir. When you are done with the meeting, just send me a text and I'll be right back here to pick you up."

"Thank you." Mav pocked the man's card, tilting his head in goodbye. The firm was exactly as Maverick pictured it, a tall executive building, bustling with interns eager to get their foot in the door. The first floor was spacious and quiet, with a bulky secretarial area, a sitting room, and a small coffee bar. Seated on a large leather couch was Keanon. His dark complexion contrasted starkly with the white interior. In fact, the only color in the room was Keanon and Maverick, which shouldn't have surprised him. True to form, Keanon was busy responding to something on his phone. It took him a few moments to realize he was being watched.

Keanon's gaze traveled from his phone to land on Maverick, still standing in the doorway. His face changed instantly from serious businessman to excited friend. "Mav man! My dude!" He hopped up, crossing the room to pull Maverick into a one arm embrace. "It's good to see you. You look good. Really good," Keanon said as he pulled away.

Despite his reservations and anxiety about the meeting, Maverick smiled. It was good to see one of his oldest friends and the person who had continued to be a friend even after Mav lost everything. "You have a good feeling about this?"

Keanon's smile soon turned into a smirk. He was all predator at that moment and Mav wondered if his friend knew something Maverick didn't. He was almost certain he had stayed connected with Gilmore, not trusting Mav enough to fill in all the information.

"I do, Mav, but we need to prepare for war. Let's talk to Gilmore and see where we're at. Is it cool if I come in with you?"

Maverick didn't want to face this alone and was grateful Keanon had probably cleared his busy schedule to support his friend. Money aside—Maverick had been the one bringing in the most money for Keanon—he knew his friend was there for support rather than obligation.

"Fine by me. You can keep up with all the boring legal shit."

"Glad to see you haven't changed a bit," Keanon teased.

The men then walked up to the receptionist behind a large desk with "LG Law Firm" plastered in front. She directed the man to the eighth floor and promised to inform Mr. Gilmore they arrived. Maverick and Keanon took the elevator up, only to be greeted by another woman once the doors opened. She was an older lady, if Maverick had to guess, he would assume she was in her sixties, but looked like the no nonsense type. She strangely reminded him of his grandmother, not that Mav would ever tell this woman that. He valued his life too much.

"Mr. Wilson. Mr. Jermaine," she greeted them stiffly, but not unkindly. "My name is Constance Barber, head assistant to Mr. Gilmore. Would either of you want something to drink before I bring you back to Mr. Gilmore?"

Maverick shook his head, but Keanon asked for a coffee. Constance Barber looked down her wire frame glasses at him, her expression not changing as she pointed to a small coffee station. "Then make it yourself, young man and make haste."

Both men exchanged a quick glance. Maverick unsuccessfully tried to hide his smirk as Keanon whispered, "Ooookay..."

Constance Barber continued to stare at him pointedly until she compelled Keanon over to the coffee pot, leaving Maverick alone with the woman. Maverick didn't know what to say and Constance didn't seem like the chatty type, so they stood there in tense and awkward silence.

Silence that broke once Keanon rejoined them. "Good, good," Constance Barber said and turned on her heels to walk in the direction of Mr. Gilmore's office. She was a petite woman, but insanely fast. Her sensible heels clicked behind her as Maverick and Keanon struggled to keep up with her. She soon stopped in front of a door located at the end of the hallway and knocked twice. A gruff voice answered, and Constance took that as permission to open the door.

"Mr. Gilmore, your ten o'clock is here," Constance said once the door opened. Neither man moved until the woman shot them a glare that could have turned them to stone. "Please, Mr. Wilson and Mr. Jermaine, do come in."

Maverick quickly entered, too intimidated by Constance Barber to disobey. Keanon looked much the same, nearly jumping when the door shut abruptly behind him. Mav wished Mrs. Barber was his lawyer because no one would want to challenge that woman in court, if they showed up at all.

Lloyd Gilmore's office was nothing short of spectacular. The room was spacious, filled with bookcases full of pristine books, half of them with no titles and the other half not in English. Mr. Gilmore sat behind a grand mahogany desk with a glass top. Two comfortable looking chairs sat unoccupied in front while Mr. Lloyd Gilmore sat in the expensive looking swivel chair behind the desk. Behind Mr. Gilmore was the best part of the office, in Maverick's opinion. The entire wall was constructed with floor to ceiling windows, giving a breath-taking view of Chicago.

Lloyd Gilmore wasn't what Maverick expected him to look like. Mav had imagined a heavy man in his mid-forties, balding with an impressive mustache. How he conjured that image, Maverick didn't know, but the Lloyd Gilmore sitting in front of him looked nothing like the man Mav envisioned. This Lloyd Gilmore was not balding, but in fact had a full head of perfectly shiny black hair, styled back. The man looked extremely athletic and prided himself on his appearance. He also had no facial hair and Maverick spotted a tattoo creeping up his neck.

On Mr. Gilmore's desk, Maverick saw a few personal photos. One of a big, but friendly looking greyhound with a brindle coat. Two other photos were of Gilmore and another man, holding a little girl. They were both in the other picture as well, but on the beach this time. He suspected they were his husband and daughter.

"Maverick Wilson," Gilmore said in a way of greeting, a smile curling at the end of his lips. Even his voice, which sounded so gruff on the phone, held a lighter, more friendly note in person. "It's a pleasure to finally meet you in person." He got out of his chair to reach across his desk to shake Maverick's hand. Then turned his attention to Keanon. "As well as you, Keanon. Good to put faces to the men I've been talking to. Please, sit down." He gestured at the two chairs in front of him.

Maverick took the chair on the left, his body molding to the soft backing and cushion. He felt at ease in Gilmore's office. It wasn't stuffy or daunting, which he suspected was the point. Gilmore looked like the type of man that wanted to make sure his clients felt comfortable and relaxed in his office.

"Shall we get started then? I'll have you fellas out of here by lunchtime," Gilmore assured, rifling through some folders on his otherwise meticulously organized desk.

"Before we start Mr. Gilmore—"

"Lloyd, please. Call me Lloyd."

"Lloyd." Keanon nodded, offering a small smile. "Does my boy Maverick stand a chance? I don't want to cause anymore unnecessary drama and drag his name through the news again. I would rather you tell us straight, so we don't go into this without a chance."

Lloyd nodded in understanding. Instead of addressing

Keanon, his gaze flickered over to Maverick. "Listen Maverick—is it okay if I call you Maverick—good. I don't often deal with MLB bans because most cases wouldn't stand up in court due to lack of evidence. But I firmly believe that Adam's legal team is going to have a tough time digging themselves out of the hole we are about to dig for them."

Both men's attentions piqued. Mav raised a brow. "So there's a chance we can win?"

Lloyd didn't answer. Instead, he laid out four manila folders on the desk before them. He pointed at each one and began to name them off. "Harvey Black, 2000 for assault against a team member. Issac Rodriguez, 2005 for conspiring to fix the outcome of the game. Donnie Wellbringer, 2011 for substance abuse, and Tito Walker, 2017 for violating contract. Do you know what all these men have in common, Maverick?"

Maverick didn't, so he shook his head. "I don't. Is this relevant to my situation?"

"Oh extremely," Lloyd said, with a certain flair that made Maverick wonder if he rehearsed this speech before. "You see Maverick, these men were coached by Grant Adams. All star players in their prime who fell from grace abruptly. Just like you. Grant Adams is named as the accuser and witness of the deeds in which they were tried for, and each man banned from baseball; their contracts voided immediately. And each time, Mr. Adams came into a healthy chunk of money from the MLB for his part in it."

Keanon was thinking the same thing as Maverick because he spoke up first, voicing Mav's thoughts. "So they were set up?"

"Hmm, seems like it. Doesn't it?"

"And no one seemed to have noticed this? No one thought it was odd that this happened every few years and Grand Adams got a payout?"

"Oh, I'm sure one of these men did. Which is probably the real reason a few of them aren't playing today. I'm sure others started to notice as well, but like I said, Grant Adams' legal team is nearly indestructible." Lloyd shrugged, looking relaxed and completely at ease. Not like a man who just suggested they would be going against a dragon with nothing but steak knives.

Maverick began to get nervous. Adams had a team and he had Keanon and Lloyd. They were good, but they were two people against an entire legion. Maverick was the only one showing any outwardly dejection though. "I don't understand. You say I have a chance, but then claim that Adams' legal team is indestructible-"

"Nothing is indestructible," Lloyd said, not reassuring Maverick at all. "I'm not saying this is going to be easy and I can't guarantee a win, but what I can guarantee is a chance. A pretty big chance at clearing your name. I'm poking holes in the narrative his team tried to spin, but there are so many inconsistencies and coincidences that can't be overlooked. Plus, you've never fully told anyone your side of the story, and this will give you a chance to plead your case in front of the big wigs on the MLB panel."

Maverick was still skeptical, and rightfully so. What made Lloyd think he stood a chance when so many others failed? Was Maverick just asking for more drama when he could be saving himself a lot of media attention? And how would this affect his life going forward?

No one spoke for a moment, all giving Maverick a chance to come to terms with what would soon take place. Keanon only waited a beat longer before saying, "Remember when I told you that this man—" he pointed to Lloyd, "—was good? I wasn't lying. He can prove that you and the other banned players were used as a money tactic. People love a good scandal and there's money in that kind of exposure. You were used to line Adams' pockets and now Lloyd is willing to fight for you. I'm willing to fight for you too. But we can't do anything if you aren't one hundred percent on board with this. It's your call, man, but now you have people who want to see you succeed."

This was no longer just about Maverick, though his name would be attached. This was about righting a wrong that went deeper than just him. Yeah, he was scared shitless. He didn't like not knowing how this would play out, and he hated knowing the press would catch wind of this. He would be the center of the sports news again. Mav barely made it through the first time, could he seriously go through that all again? But could he also stand to walk away because he was afraid?

He thought of Ofelia. His beautiful, level-headed woman. If there was ever a time he needed to talk to her, it was now. He wanted her opinion, but a part of him wondered if she would understand his situation. She had never been with him while he was in the spotlight. Could she handle that life? Especially since there would be reporters itching to learn more about her when they got wind of their relationship.

No, he needed to make this decision by himself and owed it to himself to at least try to clear his name, even if that was all he did. He missed playing and his team. He missed the life he once had, despite finding happiness in his new life. If he didn't take it, he would always wonder if he would have been able to clear his name or not.

Lloyd and Keanon still waited patiently for his answer. He put the poor fools out of their misery by nodding his head and saying, "I guess we are going to do this, aren't we?"

A collective sigh of relief went around the room and both Lloyd and Keanon smiled. Keanon patted Maverick on the back, assuring him he was doing the right thing. "Good. This is going to be fast and furious. We are waiting for approval for the court date, but it will be this week. You are going to have to stay in Chicago until the end of this. You haven't bought a plane ticket home yet, have you?"

Maverick had thought about it, but he decided against it. He was now glad he did. "No. No return ticket."

"Great. Then I will have Mrs. Barber get into contact with you and Keanon tomorrow by mid afternoon. We should have a date set by then. Before you go, do you have any questions for me?"

Maverick did. But just one. "Will I see Grant Adams?"

Lloyd looked like he expected this question, and he nodded slowly. "Yes. Not for long, but you will see him in court."

Maverick expected as much, even if he had naively hoped against it. He suddenly wanted a glass of whiskey so he could take all this information in. Keanon stood and shook Lloyd's hand. "Thank you again Mr. G-, Lloyd," he corrected. "Mav and I will leave you for lunch, but we will eagerly be awaiting your call."

Maverick stood up last and shook Lloyd's hand. Gilmore looked directly at him and said, "Things are going to change, Maverick— because of you. After this week, this will all be behind you, and you can rest assured that you did everything in your power. If we are lucky, which I'm hopeful we will be, you'll have your old life back by the next game."

That was the thing though, wasn't it? Maverick now had to decide what version of himself he would choose after this week.

And come to terms with the idea of losing something he loved, regardless of the outcome.

APPARENTLY KEANON HADN'T JUST TAKEN the morning off to attend the meeting with Maverick. The man had completely cleared his schedule and took it upon himself to drag Maverick around town. It was as if Maverick had never set foot in Chicago, despite having lived in the area for several years. When he asked why they were playing tourists, Keanon just shrugged him off and demanded he enjoy himself.

That was exactly what they did, and it had taken his thoughts away from the upcoming week.

Nothing had changed in Chicago over the last few months Maverick had picked up and left. Keanon desperately wanted to take him to a new jazzy brunch place a client took him to. He liked it so much he came back once a week and even had his own table. Maverick wasn't much of a brunch person, but he even had to admit the food was fantastic. Bottomless mimosas didn't hurt either. Keanon drank his weight in them, and Mav was happy they had a driver.

After brunch and countless hours exploring Keanon's favorite spots around town, he finally released Mav back to his hotel. It was close to eight at night and Mav felt as if he'd been run over by a dump truck. Repeatedly. He was both emotionally and physically exhausted, but he remembered his promise to Ofelia.

He was still torn about what would happen after the hearing, but he didn't want to think about the complexity that would undoubtedly follow if his ban was overturned. There was nothing he wanted more than to hear her voice at this moment.

First, he needed to get out of his suit. He grabbed a pair of sleep pants and hung up his suit after stripping. He didn't bother with a shirt since he often slept without one. He hated the way it would bunch up in the middle of the night and rub his skin the wrong way.

After completing his nightly routines, Maverick stepped out of the bathroom and into the main room. There was a small kitchenette with a table set for two. Past this room was his bedroom with a decent sized TV mounted on the wall.

The king-sized bed was piled high with a multitude of blankets. Maverick peeled layer by layer back until he reached the sheets and slid in, working up the nerve to call Ofelia. Deciding on a video call, Maverick dialed. Almost immediately, she picked up and Maverick stared into what he guessed was the ceiling. He heard another voice whisper, "Is that Maverick?" Followed by Ofelia shushing them.

From the corner of the screen, he saw a head peak over and recognized her as Willow. Her curious expression turned into a full bloomed grin as she said, "It *is* Mav! How cute...wait. Are you naked? Oh my god, is he calling for phone sex! Ofi, am I cock blocking you?!"

"You are literally so embarrassing right now, you know that," Ofelia hissed and Maverick could imagine she was blushing. He didn't know for sure though, because Willow had stolen the phone.

After a few moments of phone wrestling and the sound of a door locking, Ofelia's beautiful face illuminated his screen. He couldn't help but smile though she looked thoroughly scandalized.

"Are you in the bathroom?" Maverick laughed, thinking he caught a glimpse of her shower curtain.

Ofelia groaned. "Unfortunately. Willow is trying to sabotage this call. I had to lock myself in the bathroom, and we only have a few minutes before she finds a way to break in."

"Damn, I guess no phone sex," Maverick teased, but it got a pretty blush from Ofelia. She sputtered something unintelligible, and Maverick took pity on her. "I'm just playing, baby girl. I like the real thing better."

"You are a tease, Mav." Ofelia said, finally able to find words. "How is it going? How are you?"

Leave it to Ofelia to make sure he was doing okay. He quickly filled her in about his meeting with Lloyd. Avoiding all discussions on what would happen if he won. He didn't want to go down that path yet.

After taking a moment to process everything, Ofelia let out a long exhale. "Wow. That's a lot...but good. Right? It seems like this Adams guy has been a problem way too long and it's time for him to deal with the consequences of his own actions. Your name would be cleared. That's amazing, Mav. It really is."

He wondered if Ofelia was thinking the same thing he was but unsure of how to ask. The "what happens next" discussion hung heavy between them and Maverick knew this would be his opportunity to bring it up and invite her into the conversation. Yet, he couldn't quite bring himself to broach the subject.

*Coward.*

There was a loud knock on the door, and it took Maverick a moment to realize that it came from Ofelia's end. "Oh my god." She groaned dramatically. "Willow is about to break down my door. I should go, and it looks like you could use the sleep. Text me tomorrow?"

The moment to talk about the future passed and Maverick sighed in relief. "Sure. I'll catch you up when I can."

Ofelia seemed ready to hang up, but then stopped, looking back at the camera. "Oh, and Mav? Please don't think you need to go through this all alone. I'm here for you. We're a team, okay?"

A team. He wanted that to be true, wanted that more than anything, but he couldn't shut up the annoying whisper in the back of his mind that said Ofelia held no place in his old life. He saw firsthand how it corrupted people and he didn't want that for Ofelia. He also didn't want another Breanna situation for himself. He tried to keep out the uncertainty in his voice as he repeated. "Right. Team."

Ofelia looked as if she wanted to say more but the pounding came again, only louder. "Oh my god, Willow!" She yelled, saying something in Spanish he didn't understand but would have guessed wasn't pleasant. "I'll check in tomorrow."

Then the phone went blank, leaving Maverick to stew in his own troubling thoughts until sleep finally claimed him.

*Ofelia*

CHAPTER TWENTY-EIGHT

IT WAS Thursday evening and Maverick was still in Chicago. Ofelia did her best to be there for him, even though they were states apart, but the conversations between them dwindled from video calls to the occasional text message. Logically, she understood Mav was caught up with his legal team and didn't have much spare time to sit and chat with her. He needed what little time he had for himself to sleep, or so she told herself.

But she was worried.

On her first and last video call with Mav, she told him they were a team. Maverick could get in his head and because he was prideful, he didn't always know when to ask for help or when it was okay for him to lean on other people. Ofelia understood what it felt like to feel hopeless, like every situation was out of your hands.

Though perhaps she looked too deeply into something she manifested inside of her own head. Maverick cared about her, and she damn well cared about him. So much. So all she could do in this situation was pick up the phone when he called. No matter the outcome, she planned to stick by his side and prove to him she didn't care what walk of life he chose, because she *chose* him.

Ofelia stayed after school far past her contract hours. Willow

249

came to check on her before she left, wondering if she was going to leave soon. When she told Willow that she planned to go to the baseball game, Willow offered to go with her. It was a sweet gesture, but Ofelia knew Willow only asked to be kind. Besides, she didn't really want company, unsure of her own emotions at the moment.

Which was how Ofelia found herself alone in the bleachers without Willow or her cheerleaders. She was thankful that her principal's suggestion of cheering at a baseball game was only a one-time deal. Judging by the mood of the crowd and the long faces of McKinley's team, she almost wished she brought her squad though.

Unlike her first game, the bleachers were sparse instead of packed with eager fans. The crowd consisted of a few parents and a few students that came to support their friends or boyfriends. Other people had shown up before the game started, but left when they realized Maverick wouldn't be coaching tonight. Poor Benny was all on his own. He was a nice man, but he was no former MLB player. Seeing people leave in waves made her happy she decided to be an extra body in the stands.

The McKinley boys needed it too. They were playing a school they historically did well against. However, the sixth inning began and the score was 4-0, with McKinley in last place. She could see in their faces how frustrated they were each time they made a bad play on the field. Maverick wasn't there to encourage them, and Ofelia wasn't sure if he had let them know he would be gone.

The painful game stretched out for another three innings before the umpire called it in the rival school's favor. She watched as the opposing school jumped in celebration, basking in their win, while the McKinley boys looked like sad, kicked puppies. It was hard to watch. For his part, Benny tried to console and cheer up his team, but not even his lovable personality conjured so much as a smile from their faces. One by one, the players began to trickle out, heads hung low, leaving poor Benny to deal with the rest of the equipment.

Ofelia hurried down from the bleachers and jogged over to the home dugout. Benny saw her as he reached for a discarded catcher's mitt. He smiled but it didn't quite meet his eyes. "Hey, Ms. Mendez. Thanks for coming out tonight, I know these boys appreciated it."

She doubted the boys even knew she was there but nodded politely regardless. "I'm sorry about the game, Benny. You did so well coaching. It was just an off night."

Benny laughed mirthlessly and Ofelia was certain that was the first time she ever heard Benny sound anything less than friendly. There was a certain clip to his voice as he spoke. "You can say that again. Say, have you heard from Mav at all? The boys and I are wondering where he went. I asked Colbie, but you know she's buried under mounds of...whatever the hell principals do." He shrugged.

Although she wondered if Maverick had reached out, she at least assumed Mav would tell Benny where he was, even if he didn't give the specifics. "He's in Chicago, Benny. He's, uh, dealing with some personal things at the moment." She didn't want to put his business on blast if Mav wasn't ready to tell people.

Benny was a smart guy though. She saw the wheels turn in his mind and realization struck. "Ah," he said, his voice carried a hint of sadness as if he had already come to his own conclusions about Mav's future. "I see. Well, I suspect we'd need to be looking for a new coach soon."

"Oh, no Benny. Mav, wouldn't abandon the team. He is just — "

Benny shook his head, putting his hand up to stop her. "C'mon Ofelia. You can't honestly believe that. If this man had the option to go back to his baseball career, you really think he'd give it up to come back here to coach high school boys? Let's be realistic now."

Hearing Benny say it gave power to all the doubts swirling around in her brain. She loved teaching, but she wasn't sure

Maverick would want to stay in this career. He never planned on being a high school coach, and she doubted very much this would be something he would want to do in the long run.

Benny picked up the last bat, stuffing it into his bag as he began to walk it back to the golf cart. Ofelia followed behind him silently, still thinking about his earlier words. "Listen," Benny finally said once he heaved the bag into the back seat. "If you talk to him, will you tell him to give me a call? I just want to know what's going on, so I can prepare."

"Yeah, of course."

"Thank you." Benny smiled, getting himself into the driver's seat of his golf cart. "Wanna ride back to your car?"

Ofelia shook her head slowly. "No, I can walk, but thank you."

"Suit yourself, but I'm not leaving this spot until I see that you made it to your car."

She gave his arm a quick squeeze and then made her way back to her car. Her mind was still fogged with questions of Maverick when she unlocked her door and slipped inside. Off in the distance, she heard Benny's cart drive away.

# Maverick

## CHAPTER TWENTY-NINE

THIS WASN'T A COURTROOM.

In his mind, this room would have been a courtroom with a judge presiding over today's hearing. Off to the side would be the jury. On one side Maverick would sit with his legal team and on the other side would sit Grant Adams' team. The scene would play out as a classic trial; both attorneys pleading their cases as they tried to one up the other. It would end with Maverick walking away a free man.

Well, at least that is what they did on murder trials, but he supposed getting banned was a far cry from killing someone.

It shouldn't have surprised him that they waited outside a large conference room, awaiting their moment with the Office of Commissioner. It was a mouthful, but essentially it was a board of people who oversaw the entire MLB operation. Lloyd had mentioned the board was made up of three high executives, a few lawyers, and a judge that dealt specifically with MLB. It had all the fixings of a trial without it feeling like one.

Surprisingly enough, Maverick wasn't nervous, or at least he hadn't been until he noticed a familiar figure in the corner of his eyes. Mav's attention immediately snapped to the newcomers in the room, and he sucked in a deep breath. Grant Adams appeared just the same as he did months ago, only this time he didn't have his pants around his ankles.

He half expected to see Breanna on his shoulder, but he was accompanied by an older, pretty woman. Mav recognized her immediately; his wife. Their postures were stiff, like they weren't comfortable being around each other. Mrs. Adams looked to be here out of obligation rather than a wife concerned about her husband's wellbeing.

Why would she care? This creep cheated on her constantly. Maverick didn't know if Mrs. Adams had other lovers or not, but she could very well be a victim herself in this situation.

Adams looked up, registering for the first time Maverick was seated mere feet away from him. A nearly imperceptible twitch to his jaw gave Maverick everything he needed to know. Grant was nervous. As he fucking should be.

Maverick felt a comforting hand on his arm, and he turned to see Keanon give him a reassuring smile. It wasn't until then that Maverick realized he was clenching his fists so hard, his nails dug into his palm..

The doors to the boardroom opened shortly after that, sparing them further awkwardness. Lloyd got up first and led Mav and Keanon inside. Strategically, Lloyd and Keanon placed Mav in between the two of them, so he'd be boxed in by a friendly face on either side. It was thoughtful, and he gave Keanon a look of gratitude. His friend nodded back, taking his seat.

Adams and his crew came in next, forcing the poor secretary to conjure up a few more chairs rather than forcing some of his people to wait outside. Lord knew he could spare a few.

Once the chair situation was settled and everyone had a glass of water or coffee in front of them, an older gentleman with a receding hairline cleared his throat. Maverick recognized him from press conferences and online interviews. Every baseball player would know his name. If baseball had a god, it would be this man.

"Good morning everyone. We appreciate your ability to be here on such short notice," the baseball god spoke mechanically. Maverick was tempted to turn around and see if a teleprompter sat behind him, but he forced himself to continue staring ahead. "My name is Jeff Manuelo and I serve as Commissioner of Baseball for the Major and Minor League. We are here today to discuss the recent ban of Maverick Wilson which involved his coach, Grant Adams. Today Maverick's legal team, led by Lloyd Gilmore, would also like to discuss Mr. Adams' history with former MLB players. Is that correct?"

"It is, Mr. Manuelo. We've come with documents I faxed over a few days ago for the board to review," Lloyd said evenly, far more so than Maverick could have sounded in his situation.

Jeff Manuelo didn't comment but nodded his head. He then fixed his stare on Adams and his legal team. "Mr. Adams, you have been an active coach in the MLB for close to twenty years and within that time, five bans were brought forward to us, all petitioned by you. Is that correct, Mr. Adams?"

Adams didn't answer. The young-looking man, reeking of luxury, spoke in his stead. "Good morning, Mr. Manuelo. My name is Timothy Sheppard, part of Mr. Adams legal team. Your assessment is correct. Mr. Grant has rightfully petitioned five players to save the validity and heart of the game, which you are meant to uphold, Mr. Manuelo. These men committed crimes and Mr. Grant made sure that was the case before bringing their offenses to you."

Mr. Manuelo continued to look emotionless, unfazed by the slight jab Timothy gave him. Was he applying that Mr. Manuelo wasn't upholding his duty to the game? Perhaps he had gone lax over the years, and it finally came back to bite him in the ass. Whatever the reason, Maverick hoped Manuelo and his team would conduct a thorough review.

When Maverick's attention went back to the Commissioner, Mr. Manuelo stared directly at Maverick. He offered no clue as to what he was thinking, nothing but a blank canvas yet to be completed. He appeared to be saving all his emotions for the end verdict, whatever that may be.

"Mr. Wilson," Mr. Manuelo began, gingerly wetting his finger, and flipping to the next page within his folder. His eyes scanned the page before glancing back up. "According to the official records, Mr. Adams stated you attacked him in a fit of rage and jealousy. That you and your fiancée at the time, Breanna, arranged sexual relationships between Breanna and Adams in exchange to get extra playing time. When Mr. Adams tried to deny your fiancée, she threw herself at him and you attacked. Is that correct, Mr. Wilson?"

Of course it wasn't correct! How many times had he tried to set the record straight until he realized that no matter what he did, no one believed him? They avoided him like the plague, as if they too would catch whatever unluckiness fell upon him by association. This was the moment he could change the narrative that had been thrust upon him without his consent, but his throat felt so damn dry. His story was lodged deep inside, and he didn't know how to coax it out.

The silence must have stretched a beat too long; Keanon turned slightly, an unasked question in his expression. Lloyd cleared his throat and leaned closer to Maverick, talking into his ear. "Take a deep breath and tell your story. It's my job to tell the others, but this is your opportunity Maverick. Choose yourself."

Choose yourself.

Could it be that simple? At this point, what did Maverick have to lose? Ofelia was the only name that popped into his mind, which he promptly pushed aside. When he thought of her, his judgment began to cloud, and he couldn't think of anything else. A hard knot began to form in the pit of his stomach as doubt began to form.

Despite the growing tension all around, mostly radiating from Keanon and Lloyd as they held their breath, wondering what Maverick would do, a newfound strength began to take hold.

"No. That is not correct." As soon as the words left his lips, both Keanon and Lloyd exhaled, some tension easing away. It escaped and found a new host: Adams and his legal team. It was their turn to fester under the light of uncertainty. For some reason, that thought made him extremely happy.

Mr. Manuelo cocked a brow and shared a wordless glance with one of his own men. The same man dug through his briefcase sitting on the floor next to him and pulled out a legal pad and a pen, no doubt prepared to write down Maverick's version of the events. "Please go on, Mr. Wilson. My colleague will be taking notes," Mr. Manuelo prompted.

Maverick found that as soon as he began to speak, the words flew out of him like a caged bird escaping. He didn't care that his words were being recorded and would be public knowledge. He shared his truth, taking the Commissioner through his entire day, leading up to the scandal. How he was blindsided by the news and in a fit of rage, attacked after Grant Adams struck first. He didn't know how long the affair had been going on and frankly Maverick didn't care to.

A few times throughout his explanation Maverick was stopped so Mr. Manuelo could ask clarifying questions. None of the man's questions were ever geared towards one side or the other; he was truly a man that straddled the line of neutrality like an umpire.

When he came to the end of his story, Maverick finally felt as if he could breathe a little easier. The pressure didn't go away entirely, but it lessened immensely. His story might not change a single damn thing, it might not even get him unbanned, but it was out and now people could poke holes in Grant Adams' story.

Even though his story ended, Lloyd picked up where Maverick left off. He circled back to the four other men Adams had connections with. Lloyd had filled him and Keanon in on what he would say at the meeting so Mav had a chance to tune him out and check on everyone's body language. The men sitting in front of them were expressionless bobble heads, nodding after every few sentences to prove they were paying attention.

As for Grant and his small army, they appeared completely composed, as most legal teams would be in stressful situations. However, Maverick saw the cracks peeking through, fidgeting with pens, the occasional hushed whisper to one another, white knuckles from clenching a hand too hard. Perhaps it was naïve of Maverick to think this was the start of the collapse of Grant's empire, but clearly he was scared. Why else would he bring in an entire legion of lawyers?

Lloyd seemed to be in his element and Maverick was more than okay with taking the back seat. Lloyd held his own against Adams' team, never wavering or faltering when they would rebuke one of his claims or ask for more proof. Lloyd seemed to have prepared for all the possible scenarios and was always one step ahead of the others.

It was official, Lloyd ranked amongst Mav's favorite humans. He shouldn't have doubted Lloyd, for he had gained quite a badass reputation in the sporting community, but seeing him hold his own firsthand was different. He fielded all the questions Mr. Manuelo asked Maverick or tore down any explanation Grant's team had brought to the table. It was like watching a fencing match, but instead of battling with foil, they fought with wit. Far more entertaining, in Maverick's opinion.

The conversation lasted a total of two hours with Lloyd getting the final word in. "Look, Mr. Manuelo, we can discuss until we are blue in the face, but the fact still remains. There was a huge payout for each ban. Money that mysteriously wound up in Mr. Adams' possession when it should have gone to finding and funding a new player to fill the spot of the former. Not only that, but most files from the previous banned players have little to no evidence supporting such a punishment. I know you recently just stepped in as Commissioner a few years back, but Mr. Adams has been pictured multiple times with your predecessor. It's not frowned upon to be friends with the Commissioner, but it does give you pause when you take into account that the two men are in external business together."

"Mr. Adams is not involved in any form with your predecessor, Mr. Manuelo. All tie—"

Lloyd placed a photo out on the table of two men, one very obviously Grant Adams and the other less familiar, but Maverick still recognized him as Darren Jacobs, the man who used to serve as Commissioner. "Unfortunately, that isn't true. This photo is from last week in Mexico. I received this from an anonymous reporter who overheard Mr. Adams and Mr. Jacobs discussing a new business adventure on which they plan to collaborate."

Whatever Adams' team prepared to say was cut off when Mr. Manuelo held up his hand. "I've heard enough for today," he said, his voice leaving no room to argue. "Here is how we will proceed. My team and I will look and read through all the documentation you brought us today, as well as conduct our own investigation into this. Expect an answer within the next few days. Until then, we ask both parties to remain in or near Chicago so we can settle this."

Mr. Manuelo left no room for further comments. He stood and shook hands with both parties before leaving the room while his colleagues trailed after him. Maverick wondered if Grant would say anything, now that Mr. Manuelo left. Grant's team began to trickle out, but Grant and his wife were one of the last to exit. Although Grant didn't speak to Maverick, his former coach shot him a glare so vile, he nearly choked on the animosity. Yet he didn't flinch; he wasn't going to give him the satisfaction.

Lloyd and Keanon stood. Keanon stretched his back while Lloyd gathered his briefcase. Mav stood last. "So, we just wait?" He asked once alone.

Lloyd nodded at him. "We wait. It could be a few days or longer. I don't want to alarm you, just prepare you. However, I do believe we will get an answer sooner rather than later. Can you extend your stay at your hotel?

"If he can't, Mav knows he can stay with me," Keanon supplied. He was grateful Keanon didn't ask him to stay at his house rather than the hotel. He loved his friend, but Keanon had already done so much. Plus, Mav wanted time to himself just to think and process.

Sometime during the trial he had made the executive decision to keep the trial to himself. He didn't want to share the details or the outcome with Ofelia because he had the sinking suspicion he was going to hurt her if they won. He would have to leave Ofelia in his old life. He couldn't afford another distraction or scandal if he was invited back to play.

"It's settled then," Lloyd said, standing tall once all his possessions were gathered. "I'll keep in contact with you and call you as soon as I hear something. You did good today, Maverick."

Maverick was certain it was the other way around. Lloyd had been the star of the show, but he thanked him nonetheless. "Now I guess we play the waiting game."

# Ofelia

## CHAPTER THIRTY

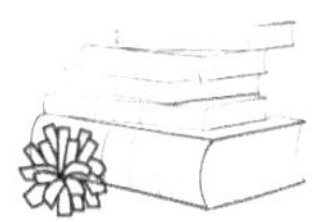

THE TILE in the kitchen sparkled under the bright lights and the air around her smelled of artificial lemon with a dash of bleach. There wasn't a speck of dust to be seen in her too small galley kitchen. No dish clogged up the sink either. Ofelia had forgone the dishwasher and scrubbed the pile completely by hand. She then dried them and stacked the dishes neatly away in the appropriate cupboards.

Ofelia took a step back to assess her work in the kitchen, surveying each inch for imperfections. Damn, her kitchen was completely spotless. Which normally would be a good thing, but now her distraction ended. Maybe a run would clear her head. But she wasn't a masochist and didn't want to put her body through a strenuous activity when her week had been full of cheer practice.

Her cleaning frenzy started early this morning, getting out of bed with enough energy and determination to clean the entire house top to bottom. What else did a tired teacher have to do on a Saturday morning when their boyfriend was gone and not responding to texts? Not that she was thinking about him of course. Nope. Definitely not.

If she were, Ofelia would probably worry that going nearly a week without contacting your girlfriend might be considered a red flag. She might have blamed it on her phone for not sending messages properly, but Maverick had read receipts on, so she knew he was getting all her texts. He simply decided not to respond. Another red flag.

But luckily, Ofelia was definitely not thinking about any of those things or risk feeling a sense of dread begin to stir in her belly. Everything was perfectly fine and, in a few days, when (if?) Maverick returned, he'd probably have a completely logical explanation for his lack of responses and she would feel silly for having over thought it.

She needed to chill out. She couldn't work herself into a tizzy over something she had literally no control over.

"Leila. Stella. Tell momma what she needs to do." Ofelia groaned, looking over at her cats who were both peacefully sleeping atop her dining room table. Leila completely ignored her because she was a bitch (whom Ofelia loved with her entire being,) but Stella perked her head up, vaguely interested in hearing Ofelia's voice. But since she was a cat, Stella responded by putting her head down and falling back asleep.

"You both are no help," she muttered under her breath. She supposed she could do some grading, but Ofelia worked hard all damn week and really didn't want to grade during her days off. Besides that, she wasn't in the right frame of mind. Grading essays was stressful enough and she didn't want to add that stress on top of everything else.

There were no rooms left in her house to clean and Ofelia didn't want to be by herself with nothing but her own thoughts to keep her company. She should call Willow and ask her to come over. Typically, her best friend was busy on Saturdays but since Karl just left, Ofelia doubted Willow had much on her schedule.

As if thinking about her name summoned her, Ofelia's phone rang. Her heart lurched as she made a mad dash to grab it. She deflated when she noticed it wasn't Maverick, but then felt guilty because it was Willow.

Ofelia answered the phone, putting extra cheerfulness in her voice in hopes of sounding normal and not a tired mess. "Willow! Hi!" Okay, so maybe she overdid the enthusiasm a bit. Ofelia took an audible breath and started again. "Hi. I was about to call you —"

"Well hell yeah you were! This is freaking headline news, Ofelia. I'm kinda pissed you didn't tell me anything, but maybe for legal reasons you couldn't. You could have at least attempted to tell me. I'm so good at keeping secrets. Also, it is a known rule in the universe that you are allowed to tell your best friend anything because even if someone said, 'don't tell anyone,' they don't mean your best friend."

Willow talked a mile a minute and usually Ofelia didn't mind. Today was not one of those days. Mostly because she had no idea what the hell her friend was talking about.

"Whoa, Willow. I'm gonna need you to slow down," she said, speaking over Willow who blabbered on about the importance of not keeping secrets from your best friend. "Let's pretend I have no idea what you are talking about." She wasn't pretending because she didn't know, but that would only lead to more questions from Willow. "And slowly tell me what you think I'm keeping from you."

"I'm talking about Maverick, of course!" She blurted, sounding like she had been waiting for this moment all day. It felt like an inside joke that Ofelia should be a part of, yet she couldn't think of a single thing about Maverick she kept from Willow.

"Hon, I don't know what you are talking about. I tell you everything and Mav—"

"Oh, don't play coy!" Willow sounded affronted. "I had to find out on the news just now. You know I like my afternoon news, so I turned on Channel 8 and BAM! Maverick in my face. Looking pretty sexy I might add...Ofelia? Hello? Are you still there?"

An icy chill washed over her body and Ofelia found breathing difficult. She felt a light on her feet, swaying from side to side. She reached out to grip the wall to steady herself. When she spoke, her voice sounded shaky, unable to hide the hurt within. "Willow, what about Maverick?"

She heard Willow suck in a deep breath on the other end of the phone, realization donning. "You seriously don't know." It wasn't a question, but Ofelia nodded her head nonetheless, even though Willow couldn't see. "Shit, Ofi. I'm so sorry. I thought he would tell you. Seems like something he'd keep the woman he's dating aware about."

But Ofelia was done with the guessing game. She couldn't continue this conversation without Willow telling her what she knew about Maverick. "Please, just tell me what you are talking about." Deep down she knew. What hurt the most was Maverick didn't want to share the joy in this monumental life moment with her. She would have been happy and cried tears of joy with him because...

Well, because she loved him.

"Turn on your TV now. Channel 8 is airing the story." Willow's voice was soft like a gentle caress. It didn't soothe the knots in her belly though.

Ofelia, in a daze, walked to her living room and dropped down on her green sofa. The remote was still wedged in between the cushions from last night when she accidentally fell asleep before moving to her own bed.

She turned on the TV and flipped robotically through the channels until she reached the news. The news anchor spoke, looking directly into the camera but Ofelia couldn't hear a thing. All she saw was a photo on the right side of the screen. A photo of Maverick with two other men, all smiling as they left some building. Underneath the picture, floating across the screen, were the words **"APPEAL APPROVED: WILSON'S BAN OVERTURNED."**

"Oh my god." Ofelia's voice cracked. She hadn't meant to say the words out loud and forgot that she was on the phone with Willow.

"Ofi, I'm so sorry. I thought he was keeping you up to date on all this."

The news should be one Ofelia celebrated. The tears that had stubbornly fallen down her flushed cheeks should be tears of joy rather than pity. Her feelings were hurt. She wasn't crying over Maverick; she cried for herself and the doubts forming in her brain.

Yet she couldn't quite voice these insecurities, afraid that by voicing them she would give them life. Even speaking her fears to Willow seemed scary to her.

"Ofi? Are you okay?"

"I'm just...really happy for him," she said. It wasn't a lie; Ofelia *was* happy for Maverick. Mav went through hell and back, had his name shredded in the media, and lost things he loved along the way. She related to loving a sport so much that it became an integral part of you.

"Ofi," Willow said cautiously. "It's okay to be upset with him because he didn't tell you himself. And also proud because of how badly he wanted this."

Willow spoke the truth, but Ofelia had been blindsided by the news. It was all happening so quickly, and she had no time to take in any of this information. She didn't want to rush into anger when she was already this emotional.

"You should call him," Willow continued. If only she knew how many times Ofelia had tried to call him, only to be met by his voicemail. "Call him and talk. Do you want me to come over, love?"

"No, no. It's okay." It had been what she wanted earlier, but now all she wanted to do was attempt to get Maverick on the phone. She didn't want Willow to see her pathetic attempts to contact him. "I'm fine—"

"Ofi, you are certainly not fine."

"Okay...true. So I'm not fine, but I will be okay. Just let me call him and get answers." Ofelia reached for the remote and turned off the TV. She didn't want to see her boyfriend's name and picture plastered in front of her. She wanted to hear Maverick's voice and get the news from him.

Still, Willow seemed hesitant to leave her in such a state. "Okay..." She spoke reluctantly. "But it will only take a call—not even a call, a text—for me to get my ass in my car and head over. Okay? I'm serious, I don't want you to be all sad by yourself."

She loved Willow so much and was thankful for her gregarious and loving nature. Her resolution to drop everything she was doing to come and sit with a crying friend on her day off. "Thank you, Will." Ofelia smiled, hoping Willow felt her appreciation through the phone. "I'll make sure to request the biggest tub of ice cream if I call you over for a sad party."

"As you very well should! Just a call away, don't forget!" Willow reminded her before they said their goodbyes.

Instead of immediately calling Maverick like Willow suggested, Ofelia got up and headed back to her kitchen. If there was ever a time for wine, it would be now. She didn't typically recommend self-medicating using alcohol, but this seemed like an appropriate time, so she could calm her racing heart. She grabbed one of the shiny glasses she recently washed and grabbed a red wine from her fridge. She poured herself a hearty glass, indulging in her vices.

After grabbing her wine and a snack from the cupboard, Ofelia went back to her couch. She placed her wine on the wooden table beside the arm rest and grabbed her gray Sherpa blanket from behind her, letting the material fan out across her body. Now she was ready to face this phone call.

Ofelia picked up her phone and ran through her contacts, stopping at Maverick. Her stomach lurched; Ofelia shouldn't feel nervous calling her own boyfriend and shouldn't have to question if he would pick up or not. Their relationship was still new and she didn't want to cross any lines with him. She also didn't know where Maverick would be. How old were the pictures the media were using? For all she knew, Maverick could be caught up in press meetings...or something of equal importance former banned baseball players did when they got reinstated to the game.

She was stalling. Ofelia swallowed her pride and clicked on Maverick's name. The phone began to ring.

And ring.

And ring.

And—

"You've reached Mav—"

"Shit!" Ofelia cursed and aggressively hung up her phone. Her call had gone to voicemail. If he thought she would admit defeat after only one call, Maverick had another thing coming. He was going to talk to her one way or another.

Ofelia did what any other pissed off girlfriend would do. She called again. And again. And again. By the fifth call, she started to believe Maverick was never going to answer and her attempts would have been in vain. Until on the last ring of her fifth time calling, he answered.

"Ofelia."

No greeting, no 'how are you doing.' Just *Ofelia*. His clipped tone bordered on anger, which...understandable. She had called him five times in rapid succession, which was annoying, but it was more annoying to not be updated about a major life event. It was more annoying not to have contacted her for an entire week.

"Really? That's all you have to say to me, Maverick?" So much for not being angry.

"I'm kinda busy right now."

*Yeah, no shit.* She was barely able to contain her anger but managed to swallow it down. "I understand that Maverick, but I just saw the news. Is it true?" It was a stupid question, considering a major news station was running his story, but she still wanted to hear it from him.

Maverick sighed and she imagined him rubbing his head impatiently. "Yes."

"Then why don't you sound happy? Mav, this is amazing

news!" Ofelia tried to cover up the fact he hurt her by not telling her about the news first.

"No, it is great. It is...it's..." Maverick trailed off and Ofelia heard a male voice call out for Maverick. He must have been holding his hand over the speaker because she heard a muffled 'one second!' before he spoke to her again. "Listen, I know I should have told you. There's been a lot going on and I'm trying to sort through some stuff."

"What stuff? Maybe I could help you with it?"

"No, you can't." The words hit like a bullet, hitting their mark perfectly. Ofelia flinched at the coldness in his voice. "Sorry. I mean I'm stuck in my mind and I can't do this over the phone."

"Can't do what? Mav, you aren't making any sense."

"Yeah, I know. I'm sorry." And he truly did sound sorry, but he also sounded like a man who carried too much on his own. "Listen, I'm coming back to Texas tomorrow. Can you meet me at my house, and we can talk? I want to see you when I talk to you."

Ofelia took a little comfort knowing he was coming home and wanted to see her. She couldn't help but feel a wedge grow between them and Maverick was distancing himself from her. Maybe he was also still processing the news and here she was demanding he talk about it. She could wait one day if that meant she got to hear the entire story.

"Yeah, of course. What time tomorrow?"

"Four. Let's meet at four."

"Four it is then," she said and then tried to lighten the mood. "I miss you. I'm excited to see you tomorrow. We could go for dinner and-"

Ofelia didn't get to finish her sentence. Maverick cut her off and sounded like he hadn't been listening to what she had suggested. "Great. I gotta go, Ofi. I'll see you tomorrow. Take care."

Then the line went dead.

Ofelia had never been more confused. She should be excited to see him, but why did it feel like she was about to say goodbye to him? Anxiety. That was all it was. Tomorrow, she would be back with Maverick, and they would get through this patch. That's what couples did. Not everything was happy and perfect all the time. Real relationships had their struggles and problems. It was how they decided to respond to those challenges that made couples strong or tore them apart.

Sunday couldn't come fast enough.

# Maverick

## CHAPTER THIRTY-ONE

Chicago spring was different from Texas spring. Texas had two seasons: summer and hellish summer. There was no in between. Maverick hadn't even lived in Texas long, but he had experienced the scorching hot days and the days that required a light jacket in the morning and a tank top in the afternoon. Unlike Texas, Chicago had seasons. He hadn't been out of the city long, but he forgot that spring still had a chill in the air.

The past few days had been a whirlwind and Maverick still was in a state of shock. It was as if he were having an out of body experience. He could see the smile on his face as he got the news, the joy in his eyes when he learned that Mr. Manuelo sided with Maverick and called his ban "unjust and completely unethical." He saw the calmness wash over him when he did his first interview last night with a big network as he robotically fit back into the role he had known for years.

Yet it still didn't feel real. His time had come to an end, and he could no longer ignore the decision he needed to make. There were only two options. Maverick couldn't have parts of his old life back and integrate it with the new life he had made sans baseball. Those were two different worlds and as far as Maverick was concerned, two different people.

Which is why he needed to head back to Texas and talk to Ofelia. Make her understand the decision he was making had everything to do with him and nothing to do with her as a person. They had fun and he was thankful for their time together, but nothing more could come from it. She didn't belong in his old world and maybe a part of him wanted to shield her from the darker parts of being in a relationship with a professional baseball player. She had to understand. She just had to.

He glanced at his watch, he had two more hours before his flight to Texas took off. O'Hare Airport could be a bitch to get through on a good day, so he needed the extra time to make sure he could get through security. There had also been a surplus of people wanting to come up and ask for his autograph and picture. Suddenly everyone was his fan again because he mattered. It was like everyone simultaneously cut him out of their lives when they thought he soured the name of baseball.

It came with the territory though. Fans would only remain loyal if you didn't fall from grace and could make them happy. That was simple and familiar and that was exactly what Maverick needed right now. There was no room for second guesses. It was the motto he repeated to himself the entire way to the airport.

All through the plane ride and up until the moment he reached Keanon's home in Texas. If he continued to lie to himself, he could believe he wasn't going to regret breaking the heart of the most loving woman he had ever known.

He kept telling himself he was doing this for her benefit. That she would be better off without him. He fed himself these lies until he started to believe them. He had done the right thing not including her in his trial and his decision...hadn't he?

He was a baseball player. He belonged on the field, not at a school teaching teenagers. Ofelia was better off without him. She deserved stability and he could not provide her that right now.

Perhaps one day this decision wouldn't cut like a knife.

# *Ofelia*

## CHAPTER THIRTY-TWO

THE COZY ONE-STORY craftsman sat snugly at the end of the cul-de-sac. Even in the uncomfortable heat spring days brought, the grass was still a vibrant shade of green, no dry patch in sight. It was also recently mowed, giving off the fresh smell of cut grass. The one tall oak in the front provided a decent amount of shade.

She had been to Maverick's—or rather Keanon's—house on numerous evenings when they would cook dinner from scratch and cuddle on the couch as they settled in to watch a movie. Ofelia always got to choose, and Maverick never complained, even when her choice usually consisted of heartwarming romance.

Standing outside now, waiting for Maverick to unlock and open the door felt different. It was exactly four o'clock, the time Maverick suggested they meet. Ofelia clutched her purse tightly to her side, fidgeting with the zipper. She gazed down at her watch. Only twenty seconds had passed since she rang the doorbell, but the seconds were passing agonizingly slowly.

Ofelia moved to ring the doorbell again when the door suddenly opened. The abruptness of it unnerved her and caused her to jump, nearly slipping on the welcome mat. Before she fell on her ass though, strong hands reached out, grabbed her waist to stop her before she embarrassed herself. Maverick looked just as frazzled as Ofelia felt. His hands lingered on her hips longer than necessary. When he realized he was touching her, he took a step back and put distance between the two of them.

Maverick cleared his throat, rubbing the back of his neck awkwardly. "You definitely know how to make an entrance, baby girl."

The term of endearment had to be a good sign, right? At the very least, it loosened some tightness in her chest. "I guess you could say I'm falling for you." She smiled at her own cheesy joke, trying to lighten the mood. Maverick's delayed smile looked more like a grimace. "Sorry, that was awful."

"It was pretty awful," Maverick said, not unkindly. He then stepped to the side and opened the door wider, allowing Ofelia to squeeze past him and enter the house.

Two suitcases sat in the middle of the hallway, but Ofelia didn't find that unusual since he had just returned from Chicago. What she did find unusual was the lack of *Maverick* around the house. His favorite sweater he hung up on the back of a dining room chair religiously wasn't in its spot. His few baseball caps that hung on the wall were bare. The one family photo Ofelia had seen of Maverick and his parents, that typically sat on an entryway table, had been replaced with a new photo of a cute dog in shades and a sun hat.

"Did your trip inspire you to redecorate?" She asked, her voice sounding strained, even to her. When she turned back around to face Maverick, he looked everywhere but at her.

"Not quite," he mumbled. "Can I, uh, get you something to drink?"

Although her throat had gone dry, Ofelia shook her head. "No, I'm fine. I would rather talk about your big news." *And why you didn't tell me*, she thought but didn't add. They were already dangling off a cliff's edge, one more slip up would plunge them down to the rapids below.

A soft smile, the first real smile she had seen from Maverick since she got here, crossed his features. "Yeah," he said slightly breathlessly, leaning back against the front door. "I'm sure you've heard on the news."

"I heard from Willow. But I'd much rather hear it from you."

"A new investigation is underway with Grant Adams. The board found numerous money links going straight into his account over the years and that was enough to disprove anything he had against me. He'll go to trial soon and the courts will decide his fate."

"I don't understand how the deception went on for so long and nobody knew," Ofelia said, not fully understanding the operation but knowing the ploy couldn't have been easily done.

Maverick just shrugged. "The old Commissioner of baseball was his friend. He was involved too and will also be facing charges. Lloyd found a whole damn chain of people. The baseball world is pretty shaken up and will probably take a bit to recover."

She wasn't sure how an organization recovered after that, but she imagined policies would change as more information came out. She seriously needed to study up on her baseball knowledge because Ofelia had no idea what a Commissioner did, but it sounded really important.

"Wow," Ofelia said after a beat of silence passed between them. "That's incredible, Mav. You helped a lot of future players by doing what you did."

"Nah, it wasn't me. It was Lloyd. The man's a genius."

"No, this was you." Ofelia shook her head adamantly. "It was no easy feat to stand up to those who wronged you and tell your story. That took a hell of a lot of bravery. Don't sell yourself short."

She could have been imagining it, but she swore a new softness in Maverick's expression appeared. He looked like a man who had hardly slept at all this week and was forced into making too many decisions in a short amount of time. Ofelia wanted to reach out and hug him. She couldn't take his worries away, but she could provide comfort. Unfortunately, she didn't know if that would make the situation worse or better.

Ofelia didn't know what to say next. She felt like she was trying to tiptoe through a minefield and hoping her next step wouldn't end in catastrophic destruction. God, she hated feeling this way. Especially with Maverick. Why couldn't they go back to before Chicago—before things got complicated? She knew where she stood with him then, but now Ofelia didn't even know if Mav wanted to be in the same room as her.

Thankfully Maverick finally spoke up, sparing her. "My old team offered my position back with a pay increase to compensate for lost time. I can finish out the season and renegotiate my contract at the end of the year. I've already got offers from other teams for next year as well. I have options, Ofi. For the first time in a long time, I have full control over my future. Do you know how much I've craved that?"

She thought she did, but maybe she hadn't fully understood the extent of his feelings. At the beginning, she knew how hard the adjustment was for Maverick. She had thought though, over time, it had gotten better. Maybe it was a bit too conceited to believe she was the reason for his happiness in his fresh start and severely underestimated how miserable he had been.

Although she was afraid of what might happen next, Ofelia still tried to smile. Though things were tense between them, she still felt happy for Maverick. "That's incredibly exciting, Mav. I'm so happy for you. You've worked so hard for this and to see it pay off..." She trailed off and reached to squeeze his hand.

Almost immediately as their hands connected, Maverick jerked away. Ofelia flinched as shock and disbelief etched their way across her features. Her eyes followed Maverick as he strode past her, rubbing his hands together. He stopped when he got to the end of the hall and turned back to face her. Nothing familiar remained in his features, only a blank stare as he looked her over.

"Don't you get it, Ofi? Or are you seriously as clueless as you look right now?"

Ofelia stepped back as if he struck her. This wasn't her funny and kind man she had fallen for. This man was quickly becoming a stranger before her eyes. "What the hell is that supposed to mean?" She tried to sound angry, but her voice came out smaller than she anticipated.

"It means I'm taking back what I never should have lost in the first place. I'm not meant to be a high school coach or live in this godforsaken town. This was never meant to be my life, Ofelia. I never asked for it. All I have ever wanted was to play baseball. I'm not going to lose it. Not again."

"You don't have to!" Ofelia shouted back. "No one is asking you to do that! I'll support you in whatever the hell you choose, I just want to be part of that decision-making process. This affects both of us!"

"There is no us!" The words reverberated around them, stopping time itself. Ofelia froze like a statue, her eyes widening as tears pooled in her eyes. Maverick blinked twice, his words settling in. He had the decency to look ashamed and when he spoke again. His voice quieted, but there a new firmness remained. "Look, we had fun. A great time even—"

"Don't."

"—but that's all it was ever going to be—"

"Stop."

"—we have our memories— "

*"ENOUGH!"* The scream erupting from her was a breaking point she never expected to reach again. "Don't fucking diminish our relationship to a good time. Don't you dare say our relationship is a fling. Not when I fucking allowed myself to love you!"

The word "love" hung heavy in the air between them. Maverick's eyes widened to a comical level and in any other situation, Ofelia would have let herself laugh. But there was nothing funny about handing your heart over to someone and watching it fall and break into a million different pieces at their feet.

"Ofelia...no. You don't lo—"

"Don't you fucking dare tell me how I'm feeling. Don't tell me what I feel is one sided because I know you feel it too. Can you honestly look me in the eyes and tell me you don't feel a damn thing for me?"

Maverick was the man that brought her coffees in the morning. The one who would help her with dinner. The man who would kiss her until she was breathless. The man who went out of his way to make sure she had someone in the audience for her team's cheer competition. That was love. She felt it. He couldn't say he didn't feel the same because Ofelia saw how happy she made him.

This was his chance to take it back. She could forgive him for his outbursts because he had been through an emotional week, but he couldn't push her away because things got hard. He would need to learn to trust her as she trusted him. He could say 'sorry' and all this would be behind them.

But that wasn't what happened. Unfamiliar hazel eyes stared back at her, devoid of all emotions as he said. "I don't love you, Ofelia. I never loved you. I can't love you."

The dam broke and she fought back sobs. The walls were closing around her once again. This was just another failed love story. She had repaired her heart and given it freely to another person, only for it to break all over. But this time was so, so much worse. Because Maverick wasn't leaving her for another woman. No, he was leaving her for a fucking sport.

"Ofelia, I'm sorry," Maverick said, almost looking like the Maverick she loved. He reached out, as if going to hug her when not seconds ago he had been the one to cause this pain.

Ofelia snapped out of his grasp, taking two large steps backwards. "Get my name out of your mouth." Maverick stopped moving, but Ofelia hadn't. Her back hit the front door, and she reached blindly for the handle. "You don't get to leave me. I won't go through this again because this time, I know my fucking worth. You can lie to yourself all you want, but I know you cared for me. I don't understand why you are doing this and when I look back at this moment again in a few years, it won't be me that I pity. You will have to live with the fact that you could have had everything you ever wanted but you decided to throw us away because you were scared."

"Ofelia—"

"I'm not finished!" She hissed, her entire body shaking as she did her best to keep herself together for one more minute. "I love you, Maverick. But you don't fucking deserve me." And with that, Ofelia opened the door and walked out of Maverick's house for the last time.

He didn't follow her and for some reason that stung even more. She managed to get into her car and drive a few blocks before she pulled over and called Willow. The moment her best friend picked up, Ofelia gave in to her misery and openly sobbed for the future she once saw with Maverick. Gone, like the rest of her withered heart.

# Ofelia

## CHAPTER THIRTY-THREE

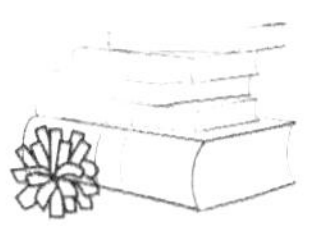

PEOPLE SAID time mended a broken heart and to those people, Ofelia wanted to send a fresh, hot bag of dog turd. Only two weeks had gone by since Ofelia offered her heart to the man she loved as a final effort to save what might have been the best relationship of her life, only for Maverick to say she had no part in the path he chose.

After breaking down in her car minutes after the breakup happened, Willow had tracked her location and found her doubled over the steering wheel. She didn't remember how Willow persuaded her out of her car and into Willow's Buick, but the next thing she remembered was collapsing on her friend's couch as another round of wracking sobs took over her body. Willow had rubbed her hair soothingly, not talking for once as Ofelia cried herself to sleep.

In the morning, Ofelia had found a note saying Willow took the liberty of arranging a sub and the only thing Ofelia needed to do was stay and rest. She didn't possess the energy to care about her classes falling behind with state testing only weeks away.

One would think getting your heart ripped to shred for a second time, only a few years apart, would become easier. It didn't. Not even a little. It came with new regrets and self-loathing. Ofelia blamed herself for letting it go too far. She should never have agreed to their first date or any date that came after. She should have guarded her heart more fiercely and not been so eager to dive into bed with the first man who showed her an ounce of decency.

Javi had called her multiple times over the last two weeks, but Ofelia hadn't had the energy to talk to him. She didn't want to talk about being dumped...again. Eventually Javi had stopped calling and started texting. He knew Maverick had broken up with her because Willow spoke to him. That relieved Ofelia because it spared her from having to talk about it.

Javi started to text her daily, just to check in and make sure Ofelia knew she wasn't alone. She appreciated his efforts and always tried responding, even if it was with an emoji. Some days that was all she was capable of, but her brother never pushed her. Willow didn't either, but she did hover. She knew her friend worried and believed any minute Ofelia might dissolve into a puddle of sad tears, but Ofelia's tears had dried up on Monday night.

It was surprisingly easy to fall back into the work routine. Her body was on autopilot, and she went through the motions of day-to-day life, always trying to keep busy. She feared the sadness and pain that came with breakups would rear its ugly head the moment she allowed herself to relax.

Thank goodness for coffee. Most nights, Ofelia forced herself to stay up and keep busy until she could not physically keep her eyes open. Then and only then did she allow herself to fall into bed and sleep. She worried if she laid down too soon, she would lay in bed and replay the break up over and over.

During this time, Maverick hadn't reached out to her once. Ofelia wasn't sure how to feel about that. She should be happy to never talk to him again and consider that part of her life a lesson learned. On the other hand, she desperately wanted to know why. Why was he pretending he didn't feel the same about her? Why was she not enough for him? She wasn't sure she was in a place to hear the answers to those questions.

Ofelia felt her thoughts slipping into forbidden territory and mentally shook herself as if that would also shake away the darkness settling over her mind.

It was now Friday and school had ended ten minutes ago. All through the day her students had been antsy and full of pent-up energy. That's how they always got before a break, so Ofelia did her best to go with the flow of each class. Nothing major needed to be completed today so if students wanted to share what they were doing for spring break or where they were going, Ofelia would happily indulge.

Hearing their stories made her smile. She took solace in knowing others were feeling happiness and excitement for their upcoming week. She was too, but she pictured her homecoming a little more...celebratory? With losing Maverick and being on shaky ground with her father, the thought of going home didn't hold the same appeal now. Her plane tickets were already purchased and Javi was looking forward to seeing her, so there was no backing out of it now. Not that she would anyway.

A gentle knock on her classroom door nearly sent Ofelia tumbling out of her chair. The door opened slightly, and Willow's apologetic face peeked around the corner. "Sorry! I thought you saw me coming. You were staring right out the window."

Was she? Ofelia had been inputting grades earlier and then blanked after that. "No, it's okay. I'm just spacey today."

Willow nodded understandingly, unable to keep the pity out of her eyes. It wasn't her friend's fault, Willow meant well, but she hated that look of pity. It only reminded her she failed again, and everyone knew it.

Willow stepped further into the room and shut the door behind her. She perched herself up on a student desk close to Ofelia's teacher desk, letting her maxi dress billow out around her. "So, I just got back from talking to Colbie," Willow said after a brief pause.

Ofelia raised a dark brow questioningly. Her principal noticed the change in her and had stopped Ofelia to ask if she was okay, which resulted in complete word vomit and the unfolding of the truth. Colbie had been extremely understanding and checked in on Ofelia from time to time.

Still, she was weary as to why Willow spoke to her.

"I wanted to ask her if we had the funding to send me as an extra chaperone on the next cheer competition. I know it's still a few weeks away, but I didn't want you to go alone. Don't argue with me, Ofi." She said, cutting off any protests Ofelia might have had. "We do; so, I signed myself up to go. It'll be fun!"

"Willow, I'm not fragile. I can handle going by myself," Ofelia said, not meaning to come across as ungrateful. She didn't need Willow tiptoeing around every aspect of her life. "You should have come to me first."

"I know but—" Willow bit her lip, debating on her next words. "Your cheerleaders have noticed a change in you," she admitted. Ofelia's eyes widened. Had her carefully curated mask failed her? It wasn't surprising since she spent a lot of time with her squad, even on non-practice days. They were in her room a lot, either storing personal items, getting prepared for a school event, or simply coming in to talk. She should have known they would see right through her mask.

"And they are worried about you," Willow continued, searching Ofelia's face. "They know you haven't been yourself and a few of them came and talked to me. I didn't tell them anything, only you are going through something personal right now. Then they asked me to come along to their next competition, so you weren't alone. Lacey didn't want you stuck with 'exhausting parents that have nothing better to do than to live vicariously through their offsprings.'"

Ofelia laughed because it was such a Lacey response. She wanted to hug her and thank her entire squad for caring. It was sweet, and she was foolish to think she could hide her pain and fool her cheerleaders, some of whom she had known since they were freshmen. Willow also deserved a hug because she was being the best possible friend she could.

"I appreciate that. Thank you, Will. I've probably been the least fun person to be around these past two weeks, but I want to thank you for everything you've done. I would love it if you chaperoned. It'll make the entire experience much better." And then Ofelia did get up to hug Willow, who seemed surprised at first but hugged her back hard. She had needed that as much as Ofelia had.

When the two finally pulled apart, Ofelia was surprised to see tears in Willow's eyes. Now it was Ofelia's turn to be concerned for her friend. "Will? What's wrong?"

"Nothing." She all but choked out, a tell-tale sign she was moments away from full-on waterworks. "It's just been so hard to see you so sad and I hate that I can't grab He-Who-Must-Not-Be-Named and shake some sense into him. But it wouldn't matter because dick head doesn't deserve you."

"Oh, Willow." Ofelia couldn't hide the genuine smile that crossed her lips. "What would I do without you?"

"I imagine you would forever live your life in darkness because I'm the light of your life. You are like, my most favorite person in the world. Don't tell my husband."

"Your secret is safe with me." Ofelia assured, crossing her heart to show Willow she met business.

Her phone began to buzz, alerting her it was time to leave. Her flight was set to take off at nine forty-five in the morning and Ofelia had so much laundry she needed to do, not to mention the last-minute errands to pick up her medicine from the drug store and a few toiletries.

"Are you still certain you can drop me off tomorrow? I really don't mind calling an Uber," Ofelia said to Willow, gathering up her lunchbox and purse.

"Uhm, of course. I'm not letting you into an Uber by yourself. You never know what sicko could be driving it. What time did you want me to be by your house again?" Willow wondered. It wasn't as if Ofelia had told her friend numerous times, nor did

Ofelia send her several text reminders on when she should be at her house.

"Seven thirty. Seven if you want me to buy you coffee from Starbucks," Ofelia said, knowing Willow would never be able to pass up coffee. It was a teacher's entire life force. Plus, Ofelia craved the lemon pound cake.

"You know my weakness," Willow sighed, following Ofelia out of her classroom. Ofelia set her trash can outside her door and turned off her lights.

She turned to Willow and gave her one last hug. "You're the best. Thank you again," she said before leaving, ready to tackle the mound of laundry waiting for her at home.

# Maverick

## CHAPTER THIRTY-FOUR

THE BUSY STREETS of Chicago were full of the hustle and bustle of a typical Saturday morning. It was simple to pick out the tourists from the native Chicagoans. Residents of Chicago didn't stop and gawk at any shiny thing the sun touched. There was a sense of ease in their walk that only came from knowing your city like the back of your hand. The tourists traveled in packs, pointing out different shops or vendors as they walked through town.

When Maverick first got to the city, years ago when he was still new to professional baseball, he had been much like the tourists. He and Breanna had spent countless hours exploring their city, neither one ready to believe this was their life. They tried to find places the locals kept secret from tourists and discovered so many amazing restaurants and bars.

Maverick hadn't realized how much he missed the feeling of discovery until it was too late. That was the thing about self-reflection, it only ever happened in the moments one least suspected and oftentimes it was too late to fix the mistakes made in the past. All he could do now was hope he didn't make the same mistakes in his future.

Yet, as he stood by the window in Keanon's high-rise, overlooking the city while only half listening to his friend drone on and on about Maverick's return to the game, Maverick couldn't quite shake the feeling that he had just made the biggest mistake of his life.

Mav didn't regret choosing baseball. It was his passion and a once in a lifetime opportunity to rejoin his old team. What he regretted, even if he couldn't quite admit it to anyone but himself, was choosing baseball *over* Ofelia. The look in her eyes as he watched the moment he broke her heart still haunted him. The utter betrayal and helplessness that radiated from her was almost enough for Maverick to fall to his knees and beg for forgiveness.

He should have begged for forgiveness.

But he hadn't done that. He let her walk away from him, thinking she meant nothing more to him than a quick lay and fun time. Why hadn't he stopped her? What had been holding him back?

"Maverick? Have you been listening to a thing I've been saying, man?" Keanon's voice rang through the fog in his brain. "What's up with you, man? You're not acting like yourself."

Maverick mentally shook himself before turning around. Keanon was sitting on his large symmetrical corner sectional. He had his feet kicked up and resting on the white pillows, looking at Maverick with a hint of annoyance.

Admittedly, he was being shitty company, and he wished he matched his friend's enthusiasm, but he couldn't quite muster it. "Fuck man, my bad. I'm distracted. I'll be good. What were you saying?"

Keanon looked at him like he didn't believe a word he said. "Is it about that girl? What was her name? It was kinda Shakespearean, yeah?"

"Ofelia. Her name is Ofelia and it's nothing. I'm fine. Or I will be fine." There was no way in hell he'd be able to concentrate on tonight's game if he couldn't force his brain to shut her out.

His friend opened his mouth, no doubt ready to argue with him, but then a phone rang. At first, he thought the sound came from Keanon's phone, but when Keanon didn't make a move to answer, Maverick realized it was his phone ringing. His heart lurched as he read the name. Disappointment came when he realized it wasn't Ofelia trying to call him. Why would she? Maverick thought about sending the unknown number to voicemail when he decided at the last minute to pick it up since he had been getting an influx of important calls from unknown numbers.

"Hello?"

"Maverick."

Everything around him came to an abrupt halt. He couldn't hear anything but his own heart rapidly beating, threatening to jump out of his chest. He knew that voice; had heard that voice for the better part of his life. The reason he had been through hell and back in the first place.

Breanna.

"Don't hang up. Please. I just want to talk."

Anger. Resentment. Hurt. These were all the emotions he was battling, on top of an already emotional past few weeks. He hadn't had 'your ex calling unexpectedly' on his bingo card, and he hated how his breath hitched at the sound of her voice. He didn't love her, not anymore, but the history they shared didn't just go away after a few months. There was a time when this woman meant everything to him and now, she was little more than a stranger.

A stranger he had blocked weeks ago.

"Mav, you good, man?" Keanon sat up, ready to take the phone from Mav if he asked. Although he was tempted, he couldn't help the curiosity starting to form.

He nodded reassuringly at Keanon before excusing himself into the next room, which happened to be the room Maverick had been staying in while he settled back in Chicago. Closing the door to make sure their conversation was private, Mav gritted out. "What do you want, Breanna?" He hadn't guessed she would use a friend's phone to call him, but he should have been prepared for this to happen. He wasn't.

"I saw you were back in Chicago and that you are no longer banned. That's amazing news, Mav."

"No thanks to you," He snarled before he could stop himself. The box he had carefully constructed labeled 'Breanna,' where he filed away every memory and every ounce of pain, finally exploded. There was no stopping the onslaught of harsh words coming out of his mouth. If he were a better man, he'd have the decency to hold back. But he wasn't a better man.

"You turned my world upside down, Bre. The only reason I was banned in the first place was because you slept with my damn coach behind my back, and I was unfortunate enough to walk in on you. If you were so damn unhappy, why didn't you leave? Why did you have to ruin everything? Did you fucking care about my feelings? Or were you so far removed from our relationship you didn't care if you hurt me or not?"

There was a long pause on the other end of the line after his angry speech and Maverick thought for sure he had scared Breanna off. But a moment later, he heard a loud exhale and then Breanna's shaking voice. "I deserved that," she said softly. "That's the reason I called. Will you give me a few minutes to explain? I promise, I won't contact you again, but I owe you an explanation and an apology."

He so desperately wanted to hang up and ignore her as he had done every single time before. But instead he found himself relenting. "Fine. You have five minutes."

"Thank you," Breanna said, sounding grateful. Maverick didn't comment, simply waited for her to continue. "I handled things the wrong way between us and for that I am sorry. For nearly costing you your entire career, I'm sorry. Truly Maverick, I have lost sleep knowing the only reason you were banned was because of me. I couldn't make it right because Grant threatened to sue me if I so much as looked in your direction. I was scared.

"Our relationship had been dying for a while," Breanna continued. "That is not an excuse, just a fact. It had gotten to a point where neither of us could stand to be around each other because it resulted in arguing and resentment. Hell, Mav, we didn't sleep in the same bed half the time. We were falling out of love with each other and both were too scared to do a damn thing about it."

"So you cheated on me because you were scared and didn't love me?" Maverick deadpanned. "Wow, I feel so much better now. Thank you so much-"

"Stop, no. That's not what I'm saying. Or maybe it is, I don't know," Breanna said with a frustrated sigh. "I'm not saying what I did was right, but Grant made me feel like you used to back when everything was new. I got swept up into his fast-paced life and seduced by the lavish presents he rained down upon me. With Grant, I felt like a person. But with you...I just felt like a baseball girlfriend. I didn't know how to be anything different because I had never been anything other than a baseball girlfriend.

"We both deserved to be happy, Mav, and at the end of the day we weren't making each other happy. Were we?" She asked him.

Some anger from earlier slowly started to deflate. Even though he didn't agree with what she did, he understood the reasoning. It just didn't make it right. "No. I suppose we weren't happy anymore."

"We were so afraid of stepping out and trying something new; we decided to stay in a loveless almost-marriage. Mav, we could be married right now and freaking miserable. We both deserve better. I'm so sorry that things happened the way they did. If I could go back and change them, I would. Grant is an asshole, I know that now. I was an asshole for cheating, but at the time I thought you were an asshole for not appreciating me."

"Breanna, I never not appreciated you, I just—"

"Fell out of love with me. I know that now, but I didn't always know that. My biggest regret is hurting you and putting you through so much pain. I can't begin to imagine how miserable and lonely you've been since."

"I wasn't."

"W...what?" Breanna sounded confused. Understandably so.

The truth was, Maverick had been exactly that, miserable and lonely when everything first happened. Having your entire life uprooted would do that to a person, but to say he had been miserable and lonely the entire time would be false. He found a woman who showed him true happiness he had not experienced in a long time. A woman who cheered him on, even though she didn't know a damn thing about baseball. A woman who would text him about the books she was reading or the new podcast she was listening to.

The woman he left in Texas.

"I found love again. I guess I wouldn't have found her if it weren't for what we went through."

Maverick swore he heard sniffles on the other end of the line, and he didn't think Bre cried because she wanted him back. She cried because she was happy for him. The joy in her voice only confirmed it. "Oh Mav, that's amazing. You deserve it. So much. She must be one special woman."

"She was...is," he said, trying to swallow the lump lodged in his throat. "But we're over now. It's for the best."

"Maverick Jarrell Wilson, don't you dare do this to yourself." Breanna's attitude towards him did a complete 180. One minute she seemed over the moon about his news and the next minute she seemed ready to murder him. "You're self-sabotaging. You throw everything into your career and cut people out. It's like you have to be two different people and eventually you get tired of one act and fall back into your cocky baseball routine."

"I don't do that," Hh said indignantly.

"You do," Bre countered. "I admit to my faults, but you weren't perfect either. You always felt like you needed to pick baseball or a personal life. Like you wouldn't allow yourself to have both. You can, you know. Have both. What's the point of your career if you have no one to share your successes with at the end of the day?"

Breanna sighed and Maverick almost saw her rolling her eyes. "Listen, I didn't call you to lecture you about your new relationship." She said, changing the topic before Maverick could say anything. Not as if he had much to say because, and he deeply hated admitting this, but Breanna was right. "I called to say congratulations on your win. I don't want any bad blood between us anymore. I'm not saying we need to become friends, because I don't think either of us are ready for that, but I would like to leave this phone call with a sense of peace between us. Can you forgive me?"

For so long, he had hated Breanna, blaming her for every single problem he had after their split. Never once did he sit back and reflect on his own shortcomings. It was a lot easier to blame the bad on someone else than coming to terms with his own vices. Breanna was right about something. He was exhausted. Carrying anger and resentment for someone became a burden. One he didn't wish to carry any longer.

There was only one thing Maverick could say. "I forgive you." And he truly meant his words. He was finally ready to let it go.

"Thank you. You didn't have to, so I appreciate it." Bre said and Maverick sensed the smile in her voice. "Oh, and Maverick? One more thing?"

"Sure, but I make no promises."

"Get your head out of your ass and get back the woman you lost."

And damn if he hadn't heard a better idea that entire day.

# Ofelia

## CHAPTER THIRTY-FIVE

"Just close your eyes. I'll get you there in one piece. Scout's honor," Willow said, abruptly swerving into the next lane and cutting off the car behind them. The succession of angry honking that ensued afterwards was enough for Ofelia to sink lower into her seat.

When Willow agreed to drive her to the airport, Ofelia hadn't expected she'd need to fight for life. With each abrupt turn and lane switch, Ofelia clutched her seat belt a little tighter, remembering why she never let Willow drive them anywhere. She quite liked living and Willow was apparently hell-bent on killing them both. Of course when Ofelia mentioned this, Willow would take her eyes off the road to glare at her, so she gave up and did as Willow suggested. She closed her eyes.

The airport was thirty minutes away, but Willow made it in twenty. "Southwest, right?" Willow asked as she pulled her car into the passenger unloading zone. In the process, she almost hit an elderly couple crossing the street, earning two very stern glares that Willow dismissed. "We are here, you can open your eyes now."

"Here as in I'm in heaven because my best friend killed us on the way to the airport? Is that what you mean?" Ofelia slowly opened one eye, just in time to see Willow roll her eyes.

"Ha, ha. Very funny. I got you here, didn't I? And you are still very much alive. So you're welcome," she mused, all to please she scared Ofelia half to death. Willow reached for a button next to her steering wheel and the trunk popped open. "No more stalling. Let's get you on your way so Mr. Fugly security guard stops motioning me to go."

Ofelia looked up to see a burly man, dressed in an airport security uniform, stare at the car. They were in a no parking zone, but if the engine was running and you were actively getting your luggage, it was fine to stall to drop off. He probably had seen the reckless abandon in which Willow pulled in and wanted her to leave before she became a liability. Ofelia understood that completely.

Giving him an apologetic wave, Ofelia got out of the car. She heard the driver's door shut, signaling Willow followed her out. "You don't have to grab my stuff." Ofelia argued as Willow dug through her messy trunk to find Ofelia's suitcase and backpack.

"Nonsense. I didn't want you to get lost back there," she said, searching through her messy trunk before handing Ofelia her things. "Okay, you have to promise to call me as soon as you land. I want to make sure you get there alright."

"It will be late. I have a long layover in Denver, but I'll text you when I arrive at the next airport." Ofelia promised.

Willow seemed happy with that answer. After a heartfelt goodbye and a few more promises to keep in touch, Ofelia was on her way to check in. She was thankful they had got there as early as they did because the lines to check in baggage and TSA lines were astronomically long. Clearly she was not the only one who had the idea to travel in April. California would be a popular destination, since it was a hot spot for spring breakers.

It took one hour to weave through both of her lines, giving her exactly one hour before boarding started. She was gate twenty-five and began to maneuver her way down the terminal. Ofelia was thankful she already had her coffee fix once she passed Starbucks and the crowd of people all waiting for their drinks. She couldn't help but notice many of the couples standing hand in hand, in deep conversation as they ignored everyone else around them.

Ofelia's heart ached at the sight, jealous of literal strangers. She walked a little faster down to her gate number, doing her best to avoid noticing anymore couples or families. In a few hours, she would be home with hers and all this silly pain she experienced at the airport would soon be forgotten.

Gate twenty-five bustled with people, as Ofelia assumed it would be. Tired-looking parents attempted to wrangle their rambunctious toddlers, while people in business suits rapidly spoke into their phone about important deadlines needing to be met. It was oddly refreshing to experience such mundane and trivial things, though she couldn't quite place why. Maybe because it made her feel a little less alone in her own problems.

Since seating was limited, Ofelia couldn't be picky and ended up seated between a woman talking amicably on her phone and a man watching something on his tablet. A familiar face caught her attention and Ofelia turned her head to the side so quickly, she nearly gave herself whiplash. The man with the tablet turned to her slightly, raising a brow. "Sports fan?" He wondered, taking an earbud out of his ear.

At first, Ofelia was helpless to do anything other than stare at his screen. Two sports commentators talked excitedly amongst one another. Ofelia didn't need to hear what they said, the man's picture in the corner was a dead giveaway. The picture must have been taken a few years prior because Maverick looked younger, more baby-faced, and he wore his team's uniform.

Today would be his first game and all Ofelia felt was numbness.

"Chicago might actually win a game now. It's been a rocky season without Wilson. You think he's going to whip them boys into shape?" The stranger asked, oblivious to her conflicting thoughts.

The picture should have sparked joy. Maverick was in his element, doing what he loved best. Instead, it reminded her yet again he made a choice and it had not been her. He must be coping a lot better than her.

Realizing the man waited for her to answer, she gave him a half smile that didn't meet her eyes. Coming up with something nice to say about Maverick proved to be more challenging than she initially thought. Finally, she settled on, "I think he's probably happy to be back."

The man seemed satisfied with her answer and nodded. He then proceeded to spend the next hour until they boarded, giving her a full and extensive history of Maverick and his baseball career. If only he knew just how familiar she was with him.

THE MOMENT she stepped into the San Francisco airport, it hit her for the first time in two years, she was home. She had expected to feel like a stranger amongst the sea of Californians, but she didn't. Soon she would be reunited with her brother and the thought of seeing Javi made her giddy. She texted him the moment the plane hit the ground, and he promised to be on his way.

Ofelia followed the crowd until they reached baggage claim. The process was never speedy, but gave her time to catch up on her texts. Or rather text. Willow had sent her a GIF of a confetti bomb after Ofelia had texted her earlier, right before she boarded her final plane. She sent a quick text to her friend, letting her know she made it home. It was the middle of the night back in Texas, so she didn't expect a reply anytime soon.

Once the conveyor belt began moving, Ofelia made her way to the front and watched the luggage go by until she found her bright yellow suitcase. It had been a wise investment to purchase the neon yellow because it stood out. She pitied all the fools who thought black was the way to go.

As she made her way outside to pick up, she watched as families reunited and young couples got into Ubers. She searched the crowd, hoping to see Javi's car pull up, but it was dark and all the headlights were giving her a headache. She reached for her phone again, only to have someone grab her wrist. She shrieked, whirling around, getting ready to hit them with her backpack...and then she heard laughing.

"Javi! You jerk!" Ofelia's fear soon turned to excitement as she jumped into her laughing brother's arms. Javi stood right in front of her. The tears began to fall freely. "I can't believe you are here!"

"I can't believe *you're* here, chica." Javi gripped her tightly and didn't let go. If Ofelia looked up, she would bet Javi had tears in his eyes too. Two years was a long time to go between hugs and Ofelia was going to have her fill. Javi smelled like home.

When Ofelia managed to pull herself away from her brother, she wiped the lingering tears in her eyes and laughed. "I almost hit you!"

"With your luggage, no less. Very dangerous." He teased, and she realized how much she had missed that.

"What are you doing out of your car? I thought you were going to pull up out front?" Ofelia asked, taking another look to see if she missed his car in the lineup, but nope. It wasn't there.

Javi shrugged. "Well, I planned on surprising you inside, but parking was a bitch. When I finally found one, I saw you walking out, so here I am."

"Here you are," she agreed, smiling brightly.

Javi took her suitcase from her and gestured across the street to the large parking garage. "I'm in there. Let's go, I bet you're tired from traveling."

Ofelia was downright exhausted and wanted nothing more than to fall into bed and sleep until she was woken in the morning by homemade breakfast. "I'm so ready to sleep."

"Camilia knows you are coming over, so she is sleeping in the guest room waiting for you. That cool?" Javi wondered, approaching his black pickup truck. She always thought the thing was too big, but since he worked in construction, he needed the truck to maneuver his things to and from workplaces.

"Uhm, duh. I need all the love from my niece. I just want to squeeze her." Ofelia couldn't stop grinning. She hadn't felt this happy in weeks and knew she should have made the trip back earlier. She was here now though and that's what matters.

"Then let's go. Be prepared for the most Mendez crazy spring break you've ever had." Javi grinned, winking at his sister before his expression became serious. "It's so good to have you back, Ofi. We've missed you."

"I missed you all so much. I'm so sorry it took me so long to come back." Her family understood her reasons, but it didn't make separation any easier.

Javi winked. "You are here now," he said before sliding into his car.

Ofelia followed him in, and for the first time in a long time, she was excited to see what the week had in store for her.

# Maverick

## CHAPTER THIRTY-SIX

"So let me get this straight," Keanon said, rubbing the stubble on his chin. He hadn't moved from his spot on the couch, but mentally Maverick knew he was pacing back and forth as Keanon took in everything. "You don't want to play tonight?"

"No."

"And you don't want to play for the rest of the season?"

"That is also correct." Maverick nodded.

"But you still plan on playing next season, if the team allows?"

"If my plan works out the way I hope it will, then yes," Maverick assured as Keanon looked at him like he was seeing him for the first time.

Honestly, he couldn't blame Keanon for his reaction, considering how hard Lloyd and Keanon worked to clear his name. Maverick would be eternally grateful. It wasn't as if he were deciding to never play again, making all their work for naught; he simply couldn't continue with this season after he royally fucked up his new life.

"I just don't understand, man. Help me understand." Poor Keanon looked out of sorts, rubbing his eyes as if the answer would mysteriously appear in front of him. "I thought this is what you wanted. One call from your ex and suddenly everything has changed?"

"It's not because of Breanna, but she did help me recognize what I wanted and what I didn't." Maverick briefly explained Breanna's call and the impact she had on him. "She's right though, Keanon, I do see in black and white. I can have this, but not that. Or I can be this, but I can't be that and I'm so damn tired of it. My time with Ofelia—god you'd love her—made me the happiest I had ever been in such a long time. Even when playing. I fucked up, man. I fucked up bad."

To his credit, Keanon didn't immediately react and lecture him on the choice he made. Instead, he did something that surprised Maverick. He nodded his head and said, "I agree. You fucked up."

Maverick, too stunned to speak, stood there with his mouth open; something his mom used to lecture him about all the time when he was younger. She said he was bound to swallow a bug one of these days if his mouth was always open.

"Don't look so surprised." Keanon laughed, clearly enjoying himself. "I'm a ladies' man. A romantic. This shit is straight up Hallmark." Normally Maverick would jump at the chance of making fun of Keanon for watching something as sappy as the Hallmark channel, but he decided to let this one pass. Especially since he needed his support.

"Listen, when you first told me of the idea—"

"Thirty minutes ago."

"Shut up." Keanon glared before continuing. "I was hesitant. You've been put through the wringer these last couple of weeks and I wanted to make sure you weren't doing this for the wrong reasons. I'm team love, man. I've never met this girl that has you wrapped around her finger, but I already know she's too good for you." Maverick smirked because he couldn't agree more. Ofelia was entirely out of his league. "As a friend, I want you to be happy. As your agent, I can see the benefits of you starting next season. I can already see the offers coming in. Everybody will be trying to snag you before the season starts. It's brilliant if you ask me. Besides, I think you've outgrown Chicago. You need to set your sights elsewhere."

The tension in Maverick's body eased. He didn't realize how much he needed someone else to affirm his actions. It wasn't exactly a solid plan, there were many factors against him. The biggest one being if Ofelia didn't take him back. She had every reason not to, but he selfishly hoped with enough groveling, she'd at least consider taking him back.

More so than Ofelia, though she was the main reason for his decision, another factor came into play. He was a coach with a real responsibility to his high school baseball team. How shitty would leaving them now be. After all the work he had put into the team, he couldn't give up on them now. Benny and his guys deserved better.

"Alright, I'm fully on board with operation: love, but what the hell is your plan? Going to barge back to Texas and ask for her forgiveness?" Keanon asked.

Well, it *had* crossed his mind until he realized that Ofelia wasn't in Texas. She had mentioned going to visit her family back in California. This complicated things...a lot. How the hell would he find her in California? He couldn't call her and demand her location. Ofelia probably had his number blocked and if she didn't, she wouldn't pick up if she saw his name flash across the screen.

No, if he was going to win her back, it wouldn't be through a phone call. He had to see her, face to face, and apologize until he was blue. Maverick needed to figure out how to do that. His girl was a romantic, even if she tried to hide it. She liked acts of service, or so Maverick had gathered from their time together.

Then something occurred to him. He laughed because if anyone knew how to track down Ofelia, it was Willow. Keanon looked at him as if he had gone mad, but Maverick shook his head and said, "I know what I need to do. Help me out here because this woman is going to be pissed."

"Who are you calling? Pissed women aren't really my specialty, but I'm a smooth talker." Keanon made a show of dusting himself off, full of himself and his ability to talk to women.

"Her best friend, Willow."

"Fuck, best friends are worse than girlfriends. Alright, let's get this shit done." Keanon sat up straighter, looking like a man preparing for battle. Maverick thought the call would be more of a slaughter but thought it best not to let Keanon know how much tiny Willow terrified him.

Although he didn't have Willow's number saved, he did have access to the faculty directory at school. He pulled up the PDF file the principal sent out and searched through the list until he found Willow's number.

Maverick would be lying if he said he didn't hesitate for a few moments, his pointer finger hovered over Willow's number a beat longer than necessary. Keanon knocked his shoulder against him, his way of telling Maverick to hurry up and call. Keanon would soon realize why Maverick was nervous, and rightfully so.

Before he could chicken out, Maverick touched her number and his phone began to ring. "Speaker. Put her on speaker," Keanon urged in a hush whisper and Maverick listened.

Both men waited in tense silence as the phone rang repeatedly. After the fourth ring, Mav was certain Willow wouldn't answer. He'd have to try later or think of a new plan. Before he could enter panic mode though, his phone stopped ringing and a familiar voice answered on the other end. "If you are a scammer, I will make your life a literal hell."

"I'm a lot of things, Willow, but scammer wouldn't be top of the list," Maverick said in a way of greeting, hoping to ease some awkwardness and hostility that was bound to happen. Which he deserved.

The silence that stretched out between them spoke volumes. Maverick had to tap his phone screen to make sure Willow hadn't hung up on him. She didn't; she just wasn't saying anything. "Erm, it's Mav—"

"I know who it is, dickhead. I'm deciding if I want to take the high road here and hang up on you, or completely rip you to shreds for hurting the sweetest person on the planet."

Keanon snorted, holding back a grin. Maverick shot him a look, but all his friend did was shrug innocently.

"Please don't hang up," Maverick begged. "I would rather you rip me to shreds, but I need to talk to you."

"And I need my best friend to have never met you, jerk face, but both of us are at a loss!" Willow yelled into the phone and Keanon had to grab a pillow to stifle his laughter.

"You aren't helping." He gritted through his teeth, covering up the microphone so Willow didn't think he was talking to her.

"You have some nerve calling me, Maverick. Can you hear how much I want to punch you in the throat? Because there is nothing I like more than some good throat punching, you spineless prick."

If Maverick wasn't so terrified of Willow literally murdering him, he might laugh at her ability to call him every bad name in the English language. There was no use in trying to reason with her. Willow was fired up, and he knew from experience that when she felt passionately about something, there was no stopping the words that tumbled out of her mouth.

Keanon, bless his soul, decided to jump in when he realized Maverick wasn't going to speak any time soon. He cut Willow off mid curse, mustering up all his charm as he said, "Good morning, Willow. I'm sorry to interrupt, because I'm enjoying your monologue, but I wanted to introduce myself. I'm Keanon Jermaine, Maverick's agent."

"Is that supposed to mean something to me?" Willow huffed, her anger shifting courses. For his part, Keanon seemed to handle himself well. "If you are in association with dickwad, then you are also the enemy."

"I like her." Keanon mouthed to Maverick with a grin. Of

course he would hit it off with the scary chihuahua-like woman. "I agree that Maverick is a dickwad, as you say, but he's a lovesick dickwad. Which is why he is reaching out to you. This is all part of operation: love. Basically, we are inviting you to be part of that."

Silence remained on the other end as Willow took in his words. Keanon eyed Maverick as if to say, *"see?"* and smugly relaxed back on the couch.

"Is he serious?" Willow questioned after a moment. "I want to hear it from you, Maverick."

"I am. Very serious," Maverick chimed in. "I thought the only way I could have my old life back was if I left my new life behind. I understand how stupid that sounds now, but things started happening so fast and I felt like I needed to make a decision. I was...scared for what it meant for me and Ofelia. And instead of dealing with our relationship, I broke it off. I was afraid one of us would get hurt."

"One of you did get hurt. Majorly hurt," Willow argued. "Ofelia called me after she left your house. She had to pull over because she was crying so hard and so violently. I held her that entire Sunday while you gallivanted across states to get back to your precious baseball. Now you decide that it's convenient to have a girlfriend? Please," She scoffed and Maverick imagined her rolling her eyes.

Hearing the utter devastation he left for Ofelia to handle on her own, gutted Maverick. How could he fuck something up so horribly and expect her to take him back after all this? But if he didn't try, then Ofelia would forever believe he didn't love her. He couldn't do that to her.

"I'm not making excuses. I was an ass and I acted without thinking. I let the woman I love slip through my fingers because I was scared and rushed into a decision. I hate that I hurt her, more than you'll ever know." Maverick took a long breath, his hand gripping his leg tightly so it would stop nervously bouncing up and down. "I decided I wouldn't play for the remainder of the season. I want to go back and finish my coaching job before I choose where I want to end up. And I need to tell Ofelia that the only life I want is one where she's in it. Because nothing matters if I don't have the girl I love by my side. But I need to make things right with her first. Which is why I need your help in finding her. You know where she is in California. Please, Willow, I'm begging you to tell me. Let me make this right. If she never wants to see me again, I promise I'll disappear. But I refuse to strike out without at least trying to fight for her."

It was up to Willow now. He would be devastated if she decided not to give out Ofelia's information, but at the end of the day he had no one to blame but himself. Even Keanon seemed to be holding his breath, waiting for Willow to put them both out of their misery.

What felt like an eternity later, Willow sighed softly, sounding tired and not convinced she was doing the right thing. "How do I know you aren't going to hurt her again?"

Fair question and it wasn't a flat-out no. His plea hooked her and now he needed to reel her in, sealing their fate. "Because I have never been more sure about a single thing in my life until Ofelia. She made me better, Willow. When I was at my lowest, she gave me a reason to wake up every day and I can't lose that. Not without a fight. I think...she's my person, Willow. Please, let me tell her how much I love her to her face."

For the second time that day, Maverick swore she heard sniffling on the other end of the phone. "Shit, that's romantic as hell. Damn you, Maverick Wilson. Ugh, I can't believe I'm doing this. But fine." A new gentleness laced Willow's words, but hesitation remained. Maverick would have to work hard to get Willow to trust him again.

Judging by the smugness on Keanon's face, Maverick knew he must look like a grinning fool. "Thank you, Will—"

"On one condition."

Her words cut Maverick short as he sucked in a breath. He

doubted he'd like this one condition, but he didn't have any other options. "Alright. What?"

"I will give you her brother Javi's number. You talk to him to get the address. And just so you know, Javi knows everything. So good luck."

*Well fuck.*

*Ofelia*

CHAPTER THIRTY-SEVEN

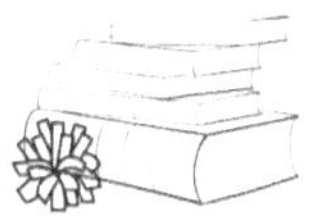

LAST NIGHT WAS by far the best sleep Ofelia had in months. By the time Javi picked her up from the airport and drove her back home it was well past midnight. As soon as Javi brought in her suitcase, Ofelia hugged her brother goodnight and snuck off to her room. True to his words from earlier, a small mound lay in the middle of the bed, curled up with a pillow and a pink stuffed dragon.

After taking care of her business, Ofelia skillfully maneuvered her sleeping niece over, closer to the wall so she could get in next to her. Camilia didn't wake up, not even when Ofelia pulled her close, kissing the top of her little head. She was already thinking about all the fun the morning would bring them when Camilia realized her auntie was finally here.

Unfortunately, Ofelia's body didn't get the memo she was, in fact, on break. So naturally she woke up promptly at seven the following morning. During the night, Camilia had somehow shifted so that laid towards the end of the bed, curled up in her Mickey Mouse blanket. Quietly, as not to disturb her, Ofelia slowly rolled out of bed, needing the bathroom.

Sound from the kitchen soon drifted down the hallway and

309

the familiarity of it made her smile. Vicente Fernández's melodic voice filled the space, and the delicious smell of breakfast made her stomach growl in protest. Ofelia pictured her mother in the kitchen, swaying as she prepared breakfast for the family. Even though she was no longer here, someone carried on her morning tradition.

When she finished in the bathroom, Ofelia made her way to the kitchen. It was surreal to be back in her childhood home after so many years away. There were still touches of her mother's decorating, but Javi had fixed up most of the house and made it his own. Her mother's yoga studio was now Camilia's room, complete with a toddler bed and all the toys a little girl could want.

Ofelia expected to see Javi cooking breakfast this morning, but the man humming along to the music wasn't Javi, but her father. Ruben Mendez finished adding the chopped-up corn tortillas into the hot pan after having sautéed the vegetables beforehand. It took him a moment to realize his daughter stood right behind him. When he saw her, his face immediately lit up and grinned widely. "Mija."

Ofelia was conflicted. On one hand, she wanted to run into her father's arms and hug him tightly. She wanted him to rub her hair and tell her how much he missed her and how happy he was for her to be home. On the other hand, Ofelia still held anger with him for bailing on her in San Antonio. The problem was rooted deeper than that one instance, but it had been the tipping point. So as much as she wanted to run into his arms, her anger at him held her at bay.

When Ofelia didn't respond, her father sensed something was wrong, and he dropped his smile. She wondered if he too was thinking about San Antonio and the last phone call they shared. It had been the last time Ofelia had spoken to her father, and she didn't have many pleasant things to say to him. At the time her father deserved her anger, but a lot of the things said were in the heat of the moment. She regretted her tone, but not the words.

"Papa, we have to talk." Ofelia didn't like unresolved problems, and she most certainly didn't want any with her father when they both should be enjoying her time in California.

Her father nodded and gestured for her to sit down at their family table, nestled into the corner of the kitchen. The vintage lace tablecloth her mother had loved still decorated the table. In the center was a large vase of fake poinsettias, another one of her mother's favorites. The beautiful red flowers weren't in season; her mother would put them out during December to decorate the house. Ever since she passed, her father had kept them out year-round because the flowers made him feel like her mother was still here.

When Ofelia sat down, her father sat directly opposite her. He looked so small and too frail. Age hadn't been kind to her father, but she wondered how much of it was grief and how much of it was physical labor he still put himself through. She was tempted to forget the whole ordeal...almost. But if she simply pushed another incident aside, the unresolved problems between them would only continue to stack against them.

Summoning her courage, Ofelia took a deep breath and then began to speak. "Papa, I wanted to apologize for the things I said to you the last time we spoke on the phone. I was angry and hurt. Even though I needed to get those things off my chest, I didn't go about it the right way. You just...it hurt, papa. It hurt so much because I felt like a kid again, waiting for her daddy to show up to my cheer events, but you never did. I hoped with mom gone that I could have you there. Then you completely blindsided me."

This wasn't something she often did with her father; talk about her feelings. He came from an older generation of Mexican immigrants who taught him many things, but never put value on mental health and emotions. It wasn't something they talked about, and her father had followed in their footsteps. When her mother was around, she was able to get him to understand their children had emotions, and they were important. As parents, they needed to listen to them and help guide them through life.

But she wasn't here anymore. Ruben and Ofelia only had each other, and both were sailing uncharted territory.

To her utmost surprise, tears began to roll down her father's face. She had only ever seen her father cry once before and that was at her mother's funeral. Everyone had been in tears, so her father's grief hadn't stood out amongst the rest. His tears now didn't make any sense, and they only seemed to fall harder and faster; his entire body shaking with silent sobs.

Did she manage to break her father?

"Oh, papa." Ofelia moved out of her seat and over to her father's side, pulling his too small frame into her arms. She hugged him tightly, trying to comfort him. His tears opened her own flood gates and soon they both cried while holding each other as they mourned different things.

After ten minutes of silent sobbing, firm hugs, and her father getting up to take the food off the burner, Ruben finally rubbed the last few tears out of his blood shot eyes. She was unsure if she should hug him again or sit back down. Ofelia eventually decided to stay standing, keeping some distance between them but still close enough if they needed another hugging session.

"Mija, I..." Her father started but choked on his own words. This wasn't natural for him, and Ofelia appreciated the effort he put forth to save their relationship. "I'm sorry. I'm not always good at showing how much I love you. When you were little and your mother was pregnant with Javi, your mom and I made an agreement. She would be at home with you kids, and I would work to keep a roof over our heads and food on our table. I took every job I found. No matter how exhausted or tired I was. All I had to do was pull out a photo of the three of you and I remembered why I worked so hard.

"I wanted to give you both the best life I could, even if I wasn't in it much. Even if I missed things your brother and you did. The only reason we could afford to keep you in sports was because I worked like a dog every day." Her father looked up and met her eyes. "I know you think I didn't care about your cheerleading, mija. I did. But it was expensive, and your mother told me how much you loved it. How good you were. I knew I couldn't be the reason we couldn't afford it anymore."

"You worked constantly because you never wanted us to go without," Ofelia said softly, as if this reason just occurred to her. In truth, it did. As a child, you never thought about money or the cost of things. All this time she had thought her father wasn't interested in her hobbies, but it turned out he had always been her biggest supporter. He just did it in a way she couldn't see at the time.

"I don't understand what that has to do with last month and you not coming down to Texas. If it was about the money, papa, I would have bought your ticket." She still could not understand why he changed his mind at the last minute.

"Your brother is too proud to tell you this. He is a lot like me when I was his age. He took Camilia to a cheer clinic a few months ago and your niece fell in love. Not surprising because she's a lot like her tía." Ruben smiled at his daughter and Ofelia's chest swelled with pride. She hoped Camilia would love cheer as much as she does because Ofelia was ready to be the biggest and most involved cheer aunt ever.

"Javi is a good man. Supporting me and Camilia. He works too hard as a single parent and I see how badly he wants to give his baby girl everything, just like I wanted to give you. A love between a man and his daughter is the purest thing in this world, mija. I instantly thought about you, and I wanted to help Javi. I can't work much, but I can do some. When I got this job, I took it without thinking how badly you'd be hurt. Your mother would have set me straight." He smiled sadly, still so much pain as he spoke about his wife.

"She's not here anymore to keep me from being a bad father —"

"Oh papa." Ofelia's heart broke. She couldn't have her father thinking he was a bad dad. He was the furthest thing from it. He pushed her buttons, but she never thought he was a bad father. "You are a good man. The best man I know. I don't think you are a bad father."

Ruben reached out to his daughter and squeezed her hand gently. "Thank you, mi amor," he said and kissed the top of her hand. "But I am sorry. I didn't think how upset it would make you. I should have gone because it was what your mother would have done. I pride myself on being a man of my word, but I always break it with you, mija. You are so much like your mother and sometimes I forget you might still need me."

Fresh tears began to spill from her eyes as she stepped forward and hugged her father. For the first time in a long time, she felt like she understood him. That they were finally on the same page. "I will always need you, papa. Forever. I'm so happy you told me this. I wish you had told me before, but it doesn't matter."

Ofelia got more than she anticipated. She got to see a different side of her father and it made her reevaluate what she thought she knew about him. He had come a long way and it was never too late to make the most of their time now. They could make new memories, and she could put more of an effort into keeping him updated on her daily life. As long as he did the same.

"I love you, princesa, and I'm so glad you are here," her father said and leaned in to kiss the top of her forehead, just like he did when she was little. "Whatever you want to do, just tell me. We'll do it."

"You know what dad? There's nothing more I want than to help you make breakfast. Teach me how to make your special tortillas?"

With the biggest smile she had ever seen from her father, Ruben straightened up and began to explain, in Spanish, how to create fluffy and butter filled tortillas. By the end of breakfast, Ofelia and Ruben were covered in flour, laughing at the mess they created.

It had taken a lot for both of them to open up, but now she felt as if she could reclaim their relationship. She still had one parent left and now more than ever, Ofelia needed her family. She hoped this was the start of the healing her mind and soul needed.

*Ofelia*

CHAPTER THIRTY-EIGHT

SPRING BREAK at Casa Mendez went off without a hitch after Ofelia and Ruben buried the hatchet. In fact, Ofelia had never felt closer to her father and that filled her with warmth after being so cold towards him for so long. She feared what would have happened if they never had this talk and how much of each other's lives they would miss out on.

When Camilia woke up her niece attached herself to Ofelia's side. It didn't matter they had never met in person; their weekly FaceTime calls had been enough for a strong bond to form and made Ofelia less of a mysterious figure. Hugging her sweet niece for the first time was not something Ofelia would forget anytime soon. The smell of her sweet baby shampoo filled her nose as she nuzzled the top of her head, baby curls bouncing at the action.

The first day Ofelia wanted to do anything Camilia wanted, even though Javi advised against it. "How am I possibly spoiling her? I haven't had the chance!" She argued with him, but her brother just smirked and shook his head. That was all the permission she needed to take her precious niece out for a fun day. Javi stayed home on Ofelia's insistence since he looked like he hadn't been getting enough sleep. Papa came with, offering up his car, which Ofelia appreciated.

317

The three of them went to an ice cream shop Ofelia's mother used to take her and Javi to after school on Fridays. She always called their outings a little treat for being so good during the week. It had been their thing for years, even when Javi and Ofelia were too old for ice cream dates. On rare occasions when their father wasn't working, he would join them.

The first time her father had come to their weekly ice cream outings was the first week both Ofelia and Javi had been in school. She remembered how shocked she had been to see her father waiting at their usual table with two brand new backpacks. Hers had been Hello Kitty. She remembered that because she had been obsessed with the cat and brand; she was fairly certain she cried after seeing it. They enjoyed ice cream together after that and remembered going home to play board games, even though her father was absolutely horrific at games and her mother was far too competitive.

It was one of Ofelia's most treasured memories as a family.

She had planned on taking Maverick here to share stories of her mother. How the ice cream shop connected Ofelia to her and she had hoped she'd create new memories with Maverick. Thinking of him sent daggers straight to her heart.

Although Camilia was too young to understand the significance of this simple ice cream place, Ofelia knew her father understood why she brought her niece here. A sad smile crossed his face when they entered the shop. "I haven't been here since your mother passed."

The ice cream shop hadn't changed much since her youth. A new coat of green paint decorated the wall, but the same small circular tables with the rickety wooden chairs still filled up the area. Camilia pointed to four different ice cream flavors she wanted before running off to climb on top of a chair. "I wait here," she said cutely, kicking her little feet up and down.

"She only likes chocolate," her father whispered and Ofelia ordered a kids cone for Camilia, cookies N' cream for her father, and a rich chocolate shake for herself. After the onslaught of sugar, Camilia's energy spiked, and she bounced eagerly in her seat.

"Is that children's museum downtown still open?" It opened when Ofelia was old enough to babysit. The museum had been a great way to spend a sweltering summer day indoors and all the young kids she brought there had loved it. She was certain Camilia would feel the same.

"Yes, Javi took Camilia there a year ago. She probably doesn't remember," her father said.

He had been right. When Ofelia pulled up to the large, kid friendly museum, Camilia gasped as if she had just seen a real unicorn and not a pretty building. "We go there?" She asked excitedly, pointing to the horse fountain out front.

"Yes! We're going to go inside to play!" Ofelia was definitely going to win aunt of the year. Camilia's energy was contagious and even her father seemed excited to explore inside.

The museum was set up for smaller children and everything was interactive. There were a few demonstrations going on, one about bubbles seemed exciting, but Camilia didn't seem interested in watching a demonstration. Instead, her niece ran straight to an area set up like a mini grocery store, complete with carts, isles of food, and cash registers run by other little toddlers.

Camilia wasn't shy, despite being an only child. She inserted herself into a group of toddler shoppers and started talking a mile a minute. Whatever they were talking about seemed important. Toddler language wasn't something she was fluent in, but by the looks of it, Camilia was having fun.

After the grocery room, which they spent at least an hour in, Camilia was ready to go on to the next place. They toured the dinosaur exhibit and "extracted" dinosaur bones from a pile of sand. Then they made their way to the insect room where Camilia got to paint her own butterfly. They ended in a diner room where Camilia pretended to be a waitress and served plastic sandwiches to Ofelia and Ruben.

By the time they left, Ofelia was ravenous. Her two companions were fast asleep by the time she pulled out of the parking lot, so she settled on a drive-thru for burgers, picking up extra food for when they awoke. It was nearly 5pm when they got home, and that was only day one.

Day two consisted of the beach. She missed California beaches and yearned to be back in the water. Or more realistically, to lounge in the sand while sunbathing and reading a romance novel.

Javi, now well rested and off from work, decided to tag along. Which was fine by Ofelia. After one day of caring for her niece, she was already exhausted. It amazed her that Javi could do this every single day and never complain. Being a single, working father was hard, but her brother managed to do it with a smile on his face daily.

Ofelia loved watching the two of them interact in the water. Camilia was all smiles and Javi looked at her like she was the very air he breathed. From the corner of her eyes, she watched her father constructing a sub sandwich, big enough to feed an entire army. It only needed to feed the four of them, but her father didn't understand portions.

It was another late evening before they arrived home and Camilia was barely keeping herself awake. Like her father, she was stubborn and didn't want to miss a single second. "I'll give her a bath. You two relax," Papa said and neither her nor Javi put up a fight.

Javi suggested they sit outside on the porch. Her mother's and father's old rocking chairs sat unoccupied, and Ofelia remembered many late nights her mother or father would rock her outside until she inevitably fell asleep in their arms.

Ofelia didn't notice her brother slipping inside the house until he came back with two blankets, handing the lavender colored one to her. She thanked him and then nestled herself into the rocking chair, humming contently.

Javi glanced over at his sister, a warm smile spreading across his face. "You look happy."

"I am," Ofelia said automatically. Her eyes flickered open, and she tilted her head to see Javi better. "Being home makes me happy. Being back with my family is exactly what I needed."

"After Maverick?" Javi asked softly, stealing the breath from her lips. He was bound to come up at some point. Javi had been just as invested in her relationship as Willow, but unlike her best friend, Javi didn't have the full story. He only knew they were no longer together and whatever Willow told him while she had been inconsolable in her own grief.

"Listen, I don't mean to bring up his name and cause any problems," Javi said. "I know how much he meant to you. Do you think there's a chance you'll get back together?"

Despite her best efforts, Ofelia couldn't help but laugh. It wasn't Javi's fault, he didn't know, but there was no way Maverick would ever come back into her life. He made that perfectly clear. "He made his choice, Javi. I can't keep crying over a man who didn't love me enough. The only thing I am grateful for is that Maverick taught me my worth. If nothing else, I got that out of our relationship."

Javi glanced down at his phone, the screen lighting up with a text message. He seemed to only be half paying attention to her, which was a little annoying since he started the conversation. "Am I boring you with my boy problems?" Ofelia teased, poking his side.

"You're my big sister. You always annoy me," he chided, flipping his phone over to give her his full attention. "What if he asked for your forgiveness? Then what?"

Ofelia wasn't sure where this was coming from. She honestly didn't know what she would do in that situation, but considering it was incredibly unlikely, she simply shrugged. "I guess we will never know." She was done with this weird turn in conversation and wanted to change the topic. "Enough about my pathetic love life. I heard Papa mention that Camilia is interested in cheerleading?"

Her brother's teasing smile faded as he blinked. He retreated into himself, the same thing he always did when the discussion of money wasn't far off. "She's two. She's interested in everything."

"True...but mama started me in cheer when I was about her age. It's a great way to make friends and have fun," she said gently. "Papa said you took her to a free clinic, and she loved it. Why don't you sign her up?"

"Because cheer costs money," Javi answered, forced patience in his voice. Javi rarely got like this, unless she hit a nerve. He wanted to give his daughter everything, but everything cost money. "And before I put her into anything, I want to make sure that this is something she will stick with."

"If it's about the money, Javi, you know I'll help."

"I don't take charity."

"Oh hush." Ofelia smacked his hand lightly. Her brother was so prideful that he couldn't see an act of kindness without strings attached. "This isn't charity. This is my niece and my money. I would love to help pay for lessons on a temporary basis. If she doesn't like it anymore, I'll stop." She shrugged nonchalantly, hoping he'd see the value in her offer.

One of Javi's fears was turning into their father. Working too much and not being able to be there for the little things that meant the most. Neither one of them blamed their father, at least not anymore, but it wasn't a life that either would choose for themselves. Javi worked enough as it was, but he was always there in the evening to play with his daughter and read her to sleep.

A resigned sigh left her brother's lips. "You said temporarily?"

Ofelia did her best to conceal her smile but did a horrible job at it. "Temporarily. Until she decides she doesn't like it or until you can take over the payments."

"Six months."

"Hmm?"

"Six months." Javi repeated. "You pay for six months and if Camilia still likes it, I will take over the payments."

"Javi, we don't have to assign a time frame. It can be for however—"

But Javi cut her off. "Six months. That's my compromise."

It was the best that she would get so Ofelia nodded. "Alright then, six months."

Javi put his hand out to shake, sealing the deal between them. In six months, Ofelia would try to convince her brother again that she was fine with paying. For now, she celebrated that her niece would be following in her footsteps. "I'm going to need a lot of pictures. You are going to be the best cheer dad there is."

Javi's goofy personality came back, leaving the man who stressed about money behind. "Pictures of me or Camilia?"

"Both, of course." She mused, just as Javi's phone went off again. "Damn, you must be pretty popular tonight. Hot date?"

She had hoped that would earn a laugh from her brother, but he didn't hear her. He typed back a message to someone on his phone and then put his phone away in his pocket. "Sorry, that was...dad. Camilia is ready for me to tell her bedtime story."

"Since when does dad text?" Ofelia asked confused, able to count on one hand the times her father had ever texted her. One of those times had been accidental.

"Since now, I guess. I'll be right back."

"Do you want me to read her a bedtime story? Then you can relax."

"No!" Javi said a little too quickly, causing Ofelia to raise a brow in suspicion. Her brother grimaced. "Uh, sorry. I just enjoy this time with her. How about you do it tomorrow?"

"Okay," Ofelia said slowly, still unsure what to think of her brother's outburst. "I guess I'll wait here for you then."

"Okay, yes perfect," Javi said and leaned down to kiss her cheek. "If you need me, text me." Before she could ask questions, Javi went inside, leaving Ofelia on her own.

It was a beautiful night; there were worse ways to spend her evening. The sun was setting, and Javi's active neighborhood of children was finally quiet. No more kids played on the street and cars weren't coming to and from work. It was almost as if she were the last person left on the block, not ready to let go of today's events.

Ofelia pulled the blanket tighter around her, sinking deeper into the rocking chair as headlights illuminated the street. She didn't think anything of it, until the black car came into view. The car nearly drove by the house but pulled over to the curb at the last minute. Ofelia sat up, confused. Had Javi invited someone over? Or was she about to be kidnapped? Also, was it still called kidnapping when you were an adult?

Before Ofelia's brain could finish considering the term adult-napping, a shadow stepped out of the car. It was tall and lean, standing at least half a foot taller than her. She couldn't make out the person's figure, but they were walking this way.

Damn the sun for going down so quickly. Just a minute ago she was admiring the beautiful sunset and now she was sitting in complete darkness as a stranger walked up to the house. It wasn't until he got closer that the shadow triggered the light, illuminating the stranger.

Ofelia heard her breath hitch in her throat as familiar brown eyes stared back at her. The last time she stared into those eyes, they were cold and empty. Now they were full of uncertainty and hesitation. Her body stood without her permission, taking an involuntary step towards him.

For a second, his face looked full of hope. Something in her expression must have made him feel like there was still a chance. But then the pain of the day he left her came rushing back and this time, it was Ofelia's turn to stare at him with cold eyes, keeping the tears at bay.

"Maverick," she whispered. She didn't know how he found her or why he was here, but she told herself she didn't care. "Leave." The words left her lips so quickly that she couldn't take them back even if she wanted to. And a part of her didn't want him to leave, but the logical part of her mind knew his visit meant nothing but more heartache.

If she didn't turn around now, she never would. With great

effort, she turned her back towards Maverick and was prepared to leave him behind. Until she heard his voice.

"Ofelia, please," Maverick said, still behind her. She didn't think he moved at all to allow her space. Smart man. "Please, I only need five minutes. Let me explain and if you still want me gone, I'll go. Please Ofi. I know I don't deserve another chance, but I don't want you to think that I never loved you. That I walked away because you aren't important to me."

"I think you said enough the last time we spoke. There's nothing more to say."

Maverick visibly paled. He looked caught between letting her go and getting down on his knees to beg for time with her. It made her heart hurt, but he had thoroughly ruined her. Made her feel small and unimportant, despite the fact that he knew just how much leaving hurt her. How much it took to open her heart to someone else. She saw a future with Maverick, but he had chosen something else over her. She was tired of being cast aside as if her emotions didn't matter.

"I know I fucked up." There was a slight tremble in his voice as he spoke. She wondered if there were tears in his eyes, but it was too dark to tell. "And I deserve your scorn. I fucked up majorly. Please just give me five minutes, but if you want me gone, I'll go. I'll fucking hate it, but I'll leave you alone if that's what you choose."

His words gave her pause, her hand hesitating over the handle. After a few minutes, she turned to face the man who shattered her heart right before her eyes. Perhaps she should let him suffer like she had suffered. She should turn around and never see him again. It would save her a lot of pain later.

But Ofelia didn't do any of those things. Instead, she crossed her arms over her chest and said, "Fine, speak."

THROUGHOUT THE ENTIRE plane ride and five-hour layover, Maverick thought about what he would say the moment he came face to face with Ofelia. In his head, he'd rehearsed different speeches where he spoke eloquently and won back the love of his life. Now that he was here and she was waiting on him to say something, anything, all his well rehearsed lines left his brain. Javi had given him the chance to plead his case and he was fucking it up by becoming tongue-tied.

To his surprise, Javi hadn't immediately hung up on him nor had he called him every name under the sun, both of which he would have completely deserved. Instead, Javi listened and agreed Maverick fucked up. "Listen, I'm not her keeper. Ofelia is a grown woman and can make her own choices. Plead your case with her and then accept whatever outcome she chooses." Had been his words right before he sent the address.

That had been his second win, and he held on to that feeling all the way until he landed in California. His mood shifted dramatically. What was once quiet excitement soon changed to dreaded anxiety. Was Maverick doing the right thing? Should he leave Ofelia alone and let her get on with her life? Would she forgive him? Maverick was afraid he might have just lost the woman of his dreams.

Ofelia stared at him expectantly, while his thoughts became a tangled mess of uncertainty and fear. His mouth went dry, and he felt like a middle school kid about to admit his feelings for his crush. Except this was one hundred times worse because her answer would legitimately affect the rest of his—or rather *their*—lives.

"Your brother knows I'm here." He didn't know why he started with that, but it seemed important. Realization washed over her, and Maverick saw the moment she started piecing together the puzzle.

"He was distracted on his phone tonight...I thought it was a friend, but that was you?" She asked, unable to believe it.

"Yeah. Willow—"

"She's involved with this too? Actually, that's not surprising." Ofelia shook her head, looking jostled. Maverick wanted to reach out and hug her. To reassure her that everything was going to be okay, but he didn't think it was his place anymore. At least not yet. "What are you doing here, Maverick? You should be in Chicago at your game."

Clearly she hadn't watched the news this evening. Keanon had fed the media the story of Maverick sitting out for the rest of the season. He'd be back again next year and more than likely with a new team. Keanon said Maverick had affairs he needed to put in order before he dedicated his life back to the game. Which was true, but the biggest "affair" was getting his girl back.

So far he was striking out in that department.

"I decided not to play for the rest of the season. The game will be waiting for me next year. I have more important things to take care of," Maverick said.

Ofelia's brow creased in confusion. "But...why?"

"Do you even have to ask?" Obviously she did because he had done a shitty job at making his feelings known. Maverick sighed and took a step forward. Ofelia didn't back away, but she did tense which made him stop in his tracks. "I was an idiot, Ofi. I was a scared idiot who thought I couldn't have the girl and the dream job. I was so afraid you'd resent me if I brought you into my old life. I was scared that what happened with Breanna would happen again. So I made the cowardly decision to break it off before you could hurt me.

"It doesn't make sense and I took that choice away from you, but baby girl, I have never loved someone as much as I love you. I thought I could walk away from you because I felt like you'd be better off without me. But I'm fucking miserable without you and I shouldn't have made that decision for you. When I was getting ready for my game, which should have been a happy moment for me, all I could think about was you. How badly I wanted you next to me to share this experience.

"I also realized that I have a life in Texas. One that I made for myself and it's a pretty good life. I couldn't just walk away from it without tying up loose ends. I can't leave my team and I most certainly can't let the best woman I had the pleasure of loving think she was nothing more than a fun time to me. I love you, Ofelia. I love you so goddamn much and I was a coward to walk away."

Maverick felt breathless by the time he finished his speech. It had gone so much better in his head; he fumbled over words and wasn't explaining himself well. Being around her made him nervous because he couldn't help but wonder if this was the last time he'd ever get to be close to her.

After a long, stretched out silence between them, Ofelia finally took a step closer. She was still at the top of the porch and Maverick was on the bottom step. They were nearly eye to eye this way and though she closed some of the distance, he still felt worlds apart from her. He desperately wanted to close the gap, but had he done enough?

"Why the sudden change of heart?" She asked and Maverick was unable to decipher her tone.

It was an easy answer though. He didn't have to think about

it. "I might have been told that I see the world in black and white. That I make no room for anything to overlap. It has cost me everything, but I finally realized I don't have to choose one thing or the other. I have the ability to make decisions and compromises with people I love and want in my life. I'm the biggest idiot for letting my dream girl walk away and I don't expect you to forgive me, but on the off chance you do, I swear I'll do anything in my power to make it up to you."

"Anything?" She repeated, and he swore he saw the sides of her mouth quirk up into a smile.

"Anything. You name it." Maverick held his breath, anxiously awaiting her answer.

Like a starved fish, she dangled the worm in front of him, too far to reach. It was torture, but the kind that he deserved. If she asked him to walk away, Maverick would. It would be the hardest thing he ever had to do, but he would do it knowing he had put his heart on the line.

Ofelia descended the last two steps, stopping once they were chest to chest. She didn't reach out for him, so he kept his hands trained at his sides, even though everything in him told him to hold her. He had come this far, and he wasn't about to mess it up anymore.

"I want to be an equal partner in this relationship," Ofelia said, eyes fixed on him. "You don't get to make decisions for both of us anymore. I want to be part of them, even if you think I can't handle it. I'm stronger than you give me credit for. I want a relationship that will last a lifetime, so if you aren't in this for the long run, spare us both the heartache and leave now."

Her words were like a challenge, and she waited for his next move. If Ofelia thought her words would scare him off, then she underestimated how deep his feelings ran. He would offer his heart on a silver platter if she asked him too. "Baby girl, I want to be one of those old couples who still does the nasty at the nursing home."

That earned him a genuine laugh. God, it was so good to hear her laughing again. He thought the last sight he would have of Ofelia would be her crying after breaking her heart.

"So, what are you waiting for?" Ofelia's next question caught him off guard. She smirked at him knowingly, but he hadn't a clue what she meant. She saw the confusion on his face because she continued, "Isn't this the part in romance movies where the guy kisses his girl within an inch of their life? I'm feeling a little cheated on that front."

All the nerves, all at once, left his body. He was left with nothing but immense relief and a giddy feeling starting in the pit of his stomach. "How foolish of me."

"How foolish indeed. I'm waiting, Romeo." Ofelia grinned.

There was nothing left to be done other than pulling Ofelia into his arms tightly and crushing his lips to hers as if his life depended on it.

He wasn't fooled into thinking everything was perfect between them now. He still had to make it up to her, but right now, the stars aligned, and the world was perfect.

He was home.

# Ofelia

## CHAPTER FORTY

OFELIA DIDN'T REMEMBER MOVING, but they must have because the next thing she knew her back hit her front door. How she didn't trip and fall on the stairs would forever be a mystery to her. Her brain still tried to process everything and with Maverick's lips on hers, he made it impossible to do so.

Maverick.

He was here. Kissing her like she was the only woman left in this world, and he needed her kiss like a starving man. So many emotions ran through her mind, but the most prominent one was love. Love for a man who came back and admitted to his faults. Was everything suddenly perfect between them? No, but that didn't mean she wasn't willing to give this another shot. She owed it to herself and their relationship to give them another try.

This time she wouldn't let Maverick walk away out of fear. Not again.

His hand shot up the front of her shirt, hand curling around her hip. He squeezed, making her involuntarily sigh. This man's mouth was wicked, and she thought of a few other naughty uses for it.

Before she could tell him just what she wanted that mouth to do, the door behind her opened. Ofelia yelped, flailing her arms as she desperately tried to gain her balance. Before she fell on her ass, Maverick's hands shot out and grabbed her, pulling her flush against his chest. "Are you okay?" He asked, and she was pleased to see him slightly breathless from their kiss.

Ofelia assured him she was fine and then whirled around to see who interrupted them. She supposed she shouldn't have been surprised to find Javi, a knowing smile on his face. Nor should she be surprised to see her father only a few steps behind her brother. She was embarrassed all the same and heat rushed to color her cheeks.

"Please tell me you weren't there the entire time." Ofelia groaned, wishing the floor would open and swallow her whole. Even though she was a grown ass woman, there was still something about knowing her brother and father watched her hungrily kiss a man that made her stomach churn in horror.

"You think I'd leave my sister with a man that broke her heart unsupervised? Nah, princesa. What type of brother do you think I am?"

"One that stays out of my love life," she said with mock sweetness. She wasn't truly upset with Javi; he was the reason Maverick was here. He could have easily hung up on Maverick and made the decision for her, but Javi wouldn't ever interfere in her life like that. He trusted Ofelia to make her own decisions and if she asked him to escort Maverick off the premises, he would do just that.

"Mija, who is this young man?" Her papa said from behind Javi.

Ofelia felt Maverick tense behind her. She reached behind and took his hand, giving it a gentle squeeze to reassure him. To his credit, he didn't back away or wait for Ofelia to introduce him. Instead, he squeezed her hand and then stepped in front of her. He offered his hand to shake, smiling at her father. "I'm Maverick Wilson, sir."

"You look familiar." Her father said, taking his hand to shake "Hijo, doesn't he look familiar?"

"Sí, papa. He plays baseball for Chicago."

Ofelia was surprised her brother knew that. Both the men in her family were soccer fans; she didn't think they paid attention to anything else. Her father's eyes lit up in recognition though, so evidently they dabbled in other sports as well. "Ah, sí." She swore he sounded slightly disappointed, but if Maverick caught on, he didn't show it. "You are dating my daughter then?"

Once again it would be a perfect time for the ground to open and swallow her whole. Javi choked back a laugh, enjoying this far too much. One day she would be able to get him back, but right now she wanted to kick him.

Maverick turned back and smiled at Ofelia encouragingly. It was nice to know that one of them was in control of the situation. "Yes. I am." She heard him say. "As long as she wants me, that is. And if I have your permission, of course."

There was no hesitation in her father's voice. Only pride and happiness when he spoke of his daughter. "If she chose you, then consider yourself the luckiest man on this earth. My girl is perfect."

"That I can agree with." When Maverick turned to wink at her, Ofelia felt weightless.

It took an hour before they escaped into Ofelia's room. Her father refused to let Maverick go to bed without a meal. It was how Mexican families showed their love, so there was no fighting it. Her father made Tostadas, piling it high with beans, shredded chicken, lettuce, tomato, cheese, and topped off with Mexican crema and guacamole.

Both Maverick and Javi managed to eat three while Ofelia and her father settled on one. Thankfully, Ruben was too tired to serve dessert, making escape possible. Ofelia kissed her father goodnight and hugged her brother. Both men seemed eerily calm about allowing a strange man to stay the night, but clearly Willow and Javi had been talking a lot behind the scenes. Ofelia imagined Javi spoke with her dad about it as well.

When she got Maverick alone, Ofelia locked the door and

turned to face him. Mav looked over her childhood room, eyes roaming through the photos on the dresser. One caught his interest and he picked it up. It was a photo from ten years ago. Ofelia was a teen, and her mother was beaming at the camera. It had been taken during one of her competitions because she was still in her cheer uniform. "Is this your mother?" Maverick asked softly.

A familiar heavy lump stuck in her throat. Except she didn't feel the need to burst into tears at the mention of her mother. She wanted to share this small memory about her with Maverick. "It is. We had just won in our division and my mother was so excited. This was taken after we accepted our medals."

"She's beautiful. You look exactly like her."

Ofelia had been told all her life that she resembled her mother. It was the best compliment anyone could have given her. "Thank you. She was a wonderful woman. She would have loved you."

"And do you?"

"Do I what?"

"Love me?"

"You know the answer to that," Ofelia said as Maverick slowly closed the gap between them. He cupped her face between his large hands, tilting her head up. His heated gaze was so intense and she almost wanted to look away, but no other man had looked at her with so much. He looked at her like he'd been searching for her his entire life.

"I love you, Ofelia. I love you so damn much. I'm sorry for all the pain I caused. I'm sorry—"

He had apologized enough. Ofelia broke off the newest apology with a kiss. If he wanted to make it up to her, he'd do so now. In this room. It was time for her to take what she wanted, and she wanted nothing more than Maverick. Judging by the smoldering look he gave her once Ofelia pushed him back, he wanted it just as much as she did.

"You're the first man I've ever brought in here." She hummed, lazily taking off her shirt. She was thankful she decided to wear a nice bra today and not one of the old beige bras she sometimes wore. Maverick's eyes burned her skin as he took her in. She liked the way he looked at her, full of desire and need.

"Am I? I'm one lucky bastard," he said, taking the hint and pulling his own shirt off. A body like his shouldn't be covered up but kept on display.

Ofelia was inclined to agree with his assessment. She clucked her tongue, hands moving down to her jeans zipper. She made quick work of the zipper and soon peeled them down her legs, leaving her in nothing but her bra and panties. They didn't match; she didn't know Maverick was going to be here, and she certainly didn't know she'd be having sex tonight. But at least they were cute.

Maverick clearly didn't give a shit if her bra and panties matched. He reached for her, pulling her towards the small, full-sized bed. Maverick was too big for her small bed, but he made no complaints. Even when he had to wiggle precariously at the edge of the bed to get his own jeans off.

"Can you be quiet?" Ofelia purred, once he rolled back over. It was dark, but she knew he still wore his boxers. If she wasn't mistaken, she could see an impressive bulge in the front, begging to be touched. "Because I have my father and brother on either side of us. I doubt they'd be thrilled to know you are seducing me."

"Says the temptress that brought me in here and locked the door." Maverick grinned. "If anyone is seducing anyone, it's you baby girl. But yeah, I can be quiet."

"Why don't we test that, yeah?" Ofelia didn't wait for a response; she started her descent down his body with kisses. She heard Maverick inhale deeply, his body trembling from the touch of her lips. She flicked her tongue out to tease his nipple on her way down. So maybe she was being mean, but Maverick deserved a little evil in his life.

"You aren't playing fair." He groaned, running a hand through her hair. He gathered up her locks and held it tightly behind her head, which she was thankful for. There was only so much hair a girl could have in her mouth before sexy time turned disastrous.

"Maybe not. But you deserve a little torture." Ofelia finally kissed her way down to his waistband, feeling the heat radiating off his body. She brought her hand up to cup his growing erection and Maverick hissed. "Shh, Mav. You have to stay quiet."

She didn't know where the sudden bravado came from, but she liked being in control of Maverick. He also seemed perfectly fine giving her free-range to do as she pleased. With careful precision, Ofelia began to pull Maverick's boxers down, letting them fall around his feet. He managed to kick them off the rest of the way and Ofelia nestled between his legs, staring down at his massive erection.

Giving head hadn't always been Ofelia's favorite thing to do, but she found herself wanting to please Maverick in this way. He didn't make her feel like a warm mouth to fuck or inferior in any way. In fact, she felt quite the opposite. In her eyes, she felt like the most powerful woman kneeling between the legs of the man she loved. Maverick's next words only confirmed it. "Fucking goddess, baby girl."

Fucking goddess was correct.

She took Maverick's length down in one go, earning a low moan from her man. It spurred her on, giving her an extra boost of confidence she needed to begin bobbing her head, taking him inch by inch. She used her tongue to trace around his pulsing vein, already tasting the saltiness of his precum.

"Shit, Ofi." He panted, pulling the pillow over his mouth to stifle his moans. When he began to buck his hips, Ofelia let her mouth go lax to give him the space to move. Dampness began to pool between her legs as she grew excited for him. Reaching between her legs, Ofelia began to tease herself, circling her clit with her thumb. The added pleasure sent vibrations through her entire body.

"I'm close, baby girl. You gonna take my cum?" He asked, but Maverick's control was slipping. Ofelia pulled back just enough to tease his tip while still pleasing herself. They came together in a rush of pleasure. Maverick gripped her bed so hard his knuckles turned white from the force.

Ofelia pulled away, licking the last of him off her lips. "Evil woman," She heard Maverick say, his voice deep from his orgasm. "We proved I can stay quiet, now it's your turn. I also distinctly remember informing you that your clit is mine to take care of." He grinned before grabbing her hips and flipping them over before she registered what happened.

Two thick fingers rubbed her entrance, parting her lips. He dipped his fingers inside of her, gathering up her wetness to lubricate her. "So wet for me, baby girl," he purred happily. Ofelia was extremely turned on and almost frenzied. She needed him desperately. She whimpered impatiently underneath him but that only delighted him.

"Tell me what you want, Ofelia," Maverick said the words slowly. He didn't stop the teasing to her clit, circling his thumb over her lazily. It was pleasurable but his strokes were too slow, keeping her on the edge but never pushing her forward. "Tell me exactly what you want."

What did she want? She wanted him, of course. She wanted to feel the connection between them, to remind herself that Maverick was here and real. That he wasn't going anywhere. How did one put all that into words?

Her face had been an open book because Maverick's face softened, and he stopped stroking her. His free hand came to rest on the side of her face, forcing her to keep eye contact with him. "I'm not going anywhere, Ofi. I love you. I was afraid to say it before and now I'm afraid you don't understand how much I love you."

It was what she needed to hear. Still she needed more. "Show me," she said, her voice barely above a whisper. "Show me how much you love me."

Maverick understood what she needed. Ofelia was almost

positive he needed the same thing. He kissed her, in a frenzy, like she would disappear at any moment. Then he was inside of her, taking and giving exactly what she wanted. Her hands roamed his body, touching everything they could reach, imprinting herself on him. It was quick and hard, but exactly what they needed to go over the edge once again.

The second time he made love to her, they took their time, no longer afraid at any moment one of them would disappear. In the single act, more words had been communicated than either could verbally say. But Ofelia had no doubts that Maverick loved her. Only a man who loved a woman as much as he did could make her feel this way.

It was late into the night when they finished for the last time, sweaty and spent in each other's arms. The moonlight flickered in from a gap in her window, illuminating a small corner of her room. Even though she couldn't see Maverick, she could feel him and that was enough for now.

"You don't regret sitting out this season for me?" Ofelia found herself asking, despite the wordless exchange they shared.

To his credit, Maverick didn't seem bothered by her insecurity. "Not even a little. There's always next season. I want to finish out the school year coaching and take the summer to decide what we want to do next year. We have time. We don't have to make decisions now."

And they did have time. She knew there would be many tough decisions ahead of them but those were decisions they were going to make as a team. It included both of their futures and Ofelia didn't want one without Maverick. They could make this work; she just knew it. She could teach anywhere, even online. Or she would become a full-time cheer coach. All those things were possibilities, but none of them had to be chosen now.

For now, she could simply enjoy the man in her bed and know they had the rest of their lives to make these big decisions. "I love you, Mav."

Not missing a beat, Maverick took her hand in his, lifted it up to his mouth and placed a gentle kiss on her palm. "And I love you, baby girl. Forever."

Forever would have to do.

# *Epilogue*

"Ugh! Ms. Mendez, this stress isn't good for my skin. I read online that stress can make you wrinkle prematurely," Lacey said, obsessively looking at herself in her phone's camera. Tony snickered, earning himself an elbow to the gut.

"Lacey you aren't going to have any friends if this is how you treat them," Willow said, just as nervous as Lacey.

Ofelia would be forever grateful for Willow who agreed weeks ago to accompany Ofelia and her cheerleaders to nationals, their final competition of the year. Willow threw herself into the assistant coach role with ease, going as far as leading some warmups allowing Ofelia an extra thirty minutes to get ready in the morning.

"Oh, we aren't friends, Mrs. Clarke. Lacey and I tolerate each other at best. It's more of a reluctant friendship, if you will," Tony said.

Willow shook her head. "I will never understand teenagers."

"Well, I'll never understand teachers. Like, why would you willingly go back to high school? It's like a never-ending nightmare." Tony shuddered, like the thought was too grim to bear.

"With all due respect, Mrs. Clarke, and no respect for you at all Tony, I need you both to stop talking so I can panic in silence,"

Lacey stressed, peering from backstage to look at the judges table. They were still deep in conversation and Ofelia understood the apprehension from her seniors.

This was their last competition as high school students. Not only that, but a hefty scholarship was on the line for the top five schools. Ofelia knew how much that money would help a lot of her seniors. At the very least, it would cover a semester at their chosen institute.

"Any news?" A voice came from her phone. Ofelia shook her head, looking down at the tiny screen where Maverick, along with a few of the other baseball players, stood on a field.

"Not yet, they are still debating. There are tons of teams here, so it could take a while," Ofelia said, biting her lip. The anxiety wafted off her cheerleaders and settled in the pit of her stomach. She wanted this win just as much as her squad.

"Damn, does it usually take this long? I feel like this is the longest Maury show ever, and we are waiting to hear if we are the father or not," one of Mav's boys said. She thought his name was Garrett, and he was dating one of her cheerleaders.

Upon coming back from California, Maverick had taken back his position as head baseball coach. Surprisingly enough, it had not taken near enough groveling and apologizing as Ofelia initially thought it would to win the boys' trust back. They seemed happy to have their coach back; Benny most of all. His coaching assistant didn't know how he would survive the rest of his season alone, especially when tournaments were just around the corner. He all but kissed Maverick's feet when he returned.

The tournaments were the reason Maverick couldn't join her. Ofelia was bummed she was missing his games as well, but they had video chatted an exuberant amount this weekend, making it feel as if they were truly taking part in the other's events.

Maverick would be there when she returned home. Considering he moved in with her after California. They hadn't planned for that to happen, but after Maverick stayed a few nights at her house, Ofelia wasn't about to tell him to leave. It was more fun to have him there.

"What about y'all? Still in the bracket?" She asked. It was a new term she learned from Maverick. The more they won, the further they moved in this imaginary bracket until only two teams remained. Then the final two teams would play off and the winner would be crowned champion.

"Yup. Next game is in two hours. They should be at lunch." Maverick glared at the few guys around him, but none of them seemed intimidated by his stare.

"Hey, my girl is on the other side of that phone. I gotta hear what happens," Garrett said.

"Yeah, well my girl is holding the phone and you all are ruining our call," Maverick shot back and was meant by a chorus of whistles and jests.

It was now common knowledge that Maverick Wilson and Ofelia Mendez were dating. If it was up to her, she wouldn't have put their relationship on blast since her students were insistent with their questions. Unfortunately, that choice was taken from her when the press caught wind of them and a few articles about her surfaced online. Nothing bad, but Ofelia was still new to this world, and she was adjusting to public scrutiny. She felt as if she were handling that public side of their relationship better though.

"Oh my god!" Lacey suddenly shricked and Ofelia nearly dropped her phone as a chorus of "whats!?" rang out through her phone. "He's moving! The balding judge is moving. Oh my god they are about to name the top five squads. Somebody hold me— not you Tony!"

"We want to see!" A voice hissed from Ofelia's phone, but she barely paid attention. She looked towards the stage and watched the judge meet the announcer with a sealed envelope. The whole auditorium went quiet, as if everyone collectively held their breaths. Her squad should really be in their seats, but she couldn't stop them from coming behind the stage and no one had kicked them out yet.

There was another long pause as the competition announcer broke the seal on the envelope. He didn't look at the card immediately like anyone else would have in his situation, instead he launched a drawn-out speech on the importance of sportsmanship and hard work. Ofelia swore Lacey's head was going to explode at any minute. That or she would run up on the stage and snatch the envelope from him.

Just when Ofelia thought she'd have to hang up the phone to keep Lacey at bay, the long-winded announcer finally began to call out the top five schools, starting with 5th place.

"Bayview High school!"

Bayview stormed the stage accepting their metals while their seniors veered left to hold the large check of scholarship money.

"I'm going to have a heart attack." Willow whispered, gripping Ofelia's free hand tightly.

"It's okay. There are still four more—"

"Deer Valley High School!"

"Okay, make that three," Ofelia muttered as the announcer named another school. The tension between her squad was palpable now.

These were the hardest moments as a coach. Her squad did an absolutely amazing job, but the competition was fierce. Everyone here was looking for a win and the reality of the situation was not everyone here would be leaving a winner. She didn't want to have to end the season off on a bad note, but she would remind her team how amazing they did this year. It was a successful season they should feel proud of.

Two more schools were called, leaving one left. Mentally, Ofelia already thought of the speech she would give her squad and parents if this went south. She turned to Willow, but her friend looked to be at her breaking point and Ofelia didn't want to add another layer of stress. She could deal with this. They had never not placed, but this could be a humbling experience. There had to be a way to turn this around.

Ofelia was deep in her own thoughts, so she didn't hear the

announcer say the last school. What she did hear was the loud screams coming at her in every direction, including from her phone. At first, she thought someone had gotten murdered until Willow began to shake her and jump around in a little circle. "Why aren't you celebrating!?" Willow yelled, clearly mystified as to why Ofelia wasn't reacting.

"Celebrating what? What happened?"

"You didn't hear? Oh my god, look!" Willow pointed, causing Ofelia to notice her team was no longer standing around her anymore. That was because they were now on stage accepting their trophies while the seniors got a huge scholarship check.

"Oh my god!" Ofelia repeated Willow's words, nearly sinking to the ground.

They did it! Her squad won! The long months of practice, dealing with whiny parents, and all the fundraising had finally paid off.

Willow had run off to celebrate with the parents, leaving Ofelia alone with Maverick. Through the chaos of the last minute, she had accidentally dropped her phone on the ground when Willow hugged her, so she quickly retrieved it. Maverick was alone now, smiling widely at her. She didn't know how he ditched the rest of his team, but they were no longer in the frame.

"You did it, baby girl!" Maverick grinned and his happiness was genuine. He was proud of her and that made Ofelia melt a little inside.

"They did so amazing! Oh, Mav, they worked so hard! They deserve this."

"And you deserve a warm bubble bath and a nap."

Ofelia laughed. Those things sounded heavenly to her. "Are you offering to run me a bath?"

"Hell yeah. As soon as you get home. I'll be your bath boy."

She liked the sound of that. It was a five-hour drive home, but she had Maverick's upcoming game to keep her entertained on the ride back. "I'll meet you on the field in two hours?" She asked since he always propped up his phone so she could take in most of the infield.

"And off, baby girl. Get your sexy ass home as soon as you can, and we will have our own celebration."

Ofelia didn't have to ask what his celebration would entail. She knew and her body grew hot at the thought of it. Sometimes when she thought about her life, she couldn't believe this was the path she was on. She wouldn't change it for the world, not even the small breakup they went through. Because even that taught her what she was worth and what she deserved in a man. It taught Maverick to trust and not to let fears or insecurities get in the way of a good thing.

Her love story wasn't a typical fairy tale, but it felt like the only story worth reading about. So much was still left unwritten, but together, they would create their own happily ever after. Ofelia couldn't ask for anything better.

*Bonus Chapter*

THERE WAS A PERFECTLY logical explanation as to why her period was late. Ofelia had taken on more at school, because apparently coaching cheer and teaching teenagers wasn't enough. No, now she needed to add debate club to the mix. That coupled with impending state testing added a whole new layer of stress.

Plus, they were also in the middle of a huge move across several state lines. Ofelia was leaving behind the life she created pre-Maverick. Although she was excited to follow the next chapter of her life, she couldn't help but mourn the students and friends she'd leave behind.

The decision to move back to California was challenging—especially for Maverick who spent weeks going back and forth with Ofelia and his manager, Keanon, on whether or not he'd accept the spot offered to him in The Golden State. As soon as the news broke that Maverick and Ofelia were moving back home, her family were overjoyed. Yet, Willow had been heartbroken, even if she tried to put on a brave face about her best friend leaving.

Since then, Willow had come over every day to help Ofelia pack up different areas of the house. It was always her favorite time because she got to laugh, joke, and cry with her best friend about the upcoming move. The two shared so many memories in her tiny craftsman home, but it was evident they needed something bigger. This house was set up for her, but not the family they wanted.

Ofelia also had to deal with the publicity that came with being a wife of a well-known baseball player. She wasn't a celebrity by any means, but every once and awhile, she would catch a person taking their picture in public and stumbling upon it in a pop-up ad the next day.

She had a hell of a lot of stress on her plate. According to her extremely reliable online searches, it was normal for a period to be late since it interrupted hormone production.

But still, she couldn't ignore the tiny voice asking *"what if"* in the back of her mind.

Ofelia was a planner and enjoyed the process of organizing her time and thinking about the future. In none of those plans did she ever consider herself pregnant, however.

Sure, she and Maverick had discussions about starting a family and Ofelia wanted to have children, but now wasn't an ideal time. Baseball season was starting, meaning Maverick was going to be away a lot and adjusting to a new team. They were in the midst of a major move and none of these things were conducive for a baby.

Honestly if she stressed and grappled with the what if's for any longer, Ofelia knew she would spiral into uncharted territory and there was really only one thing she could do right now.

She needed answers.

And her best friend.

Ofelia put down the pan she was washing to reach for her phone. As if sensing she needed her, Willow's face lit up her screen, a photo taken at Ofelia's wedding. Cheesy smiles captured forever.

She answered on the second ring to her best friend already speaking, "Ofi! Please tell me you're not doing anything. Karl is working and I'm bored out of my mind. I'm not meant to be caged up in the house on a perfectly good day."

Ofelia wasn't doing anything other than panicking. "I need moral support."

Ofelia heard shuffling around on the other end and a door closed. "More packing? Not exactly what I had in mind, but—"

"My period is late," she blurted, effectively silencing her best friend on the other end of the line. She had to check and make sure she hadn't accidentally disconnected from Willow. She hadn't; she just managed to render Willow silent.

"Did you hear me? I said—"

Willow squealed, loud enough that Ofelia almost dropped her phone. "No fucking way! Okay, stay there. I'll be over in ten minutes. Don't move and don't pee." And just like that, the line went dead, leaving Ofelia's head spinning. She wished she could bottle up Willow's excited energy and horde it for herself.

For the next ten minutes, Ofelia made herself keep busy. Cleaning was usually her go-to when she needed to keep her mind occupied. She wiped down the kitchen counters and put away the clean dishes from the dishwasher. She was about to start moping when her front door opened and a flurry of yellow and red scrambled inside.

Willow's red hair was barely contained within the messy braid down her back. Her sunshine dress billowed around her like a cape as she ran to Ofelia, pulling her into for a hug. "Sorry, I'm late! Kinda like you're period—too soon?" She giggled, pulling back. Despite herself, Ofelia smiled.

"This is a happy thing, isn't it?" Willow asked, breaking away from Ofelia.

"The timing isn't ideal. Mav and I want kids, but I don't want to be pregnant during our big move and the start of his season. I'm so conflicted, Will. I want to be excited, I really do, but there's like a million things I need to get done before I have kids."

Ofelia wanted to be a mother, there was no question about that. Ever since she was a little girl, she dreamed about having her own family and doing everything her mother did for her. Reading bedtime stories before falling asleep, cooking big family meals, and singing and dancing in the kitchen as if the music lived inside of them.

"Is there ever a perfect time to have a baby?" Willow asked gently, placing her hand on Ofelia's arm. A beacon of calm in unsteady shores. "I mean, I'm not a parent, but I'm not even sure the most well-meaning people are ever truly prepared for a new life. It completely changes everything and you won't know how much or in what ways until they are here."

"But it's not just me, Will. I have Maverick to think about and his career. I don't know if this would derail that."

"Have you talked to him about this?"

"Well, no. You're the first person I called."

Willow sighed, squeezing her shoulders. "Ofi, I love you dearly, but you have the tendency to overthink. You are a grown woman in a loving and stable relationship. If there is anything I have learned about you in the years I've known you is that you're resourceful. You are capable of hard things, with or without a plan."

"Since when did you become so logical?" Because what Willow said made sense. Ofelia could plan and plan for the arrival of a new baby, but would she ever truly be ready until she was thrown into motherhead feet first?

And it wasn't as if she was in a precarious situation, like Willow mentioned. She had a loving husband, ability to support a newborn, and she'd be close to family. So maybe it wasn't as bad as she initially thought?

But Ofelia was getting ahead of herself. She didn't even know if she was pregnant yet. All of this could be her overreacting due to the stress of the move.

Something in her expression must have tipped Willow off that Ofelia was opening herself to the idea of pregnancy because she smiled and tossed a grocery sack on the counter. "Okay, I came armed."

With that, she dumped the contents of the sack out on the

counter and a half dozen pregnancy tests scattered across the counter with a few falling to the ground. "Holy shit, Willow, did you buy up the store? How many people are we testing here?"

"Well I grabbed one of each. I didn't know which one was the best, but I figured you can pee on a few of these. They can't all be wrong," she said, sorting through each one. "Maybe I went a little overboard, but we have them now for the future."

"One baby at a time, Willow," she chuckled, and sifted through a few of the boxes. Ofelia was at a loss of where to start as well.

As Willow and Ofelia discussed which tests would be the best to try first, neither woman heard Ofielia's front door open until it shut loudly. Both women jumped apart like they were both toddlers caught by their mom with their hands in the cookie jar.

Except it wasn't a mother. It was Maverick.

And Ofelia wasn't holding a cookie, but a pregnancy test.

For a moment, no one budged. They were caught in a game of forced freeze tag and nobody wanted to be the first one to move. Willow finally broke the spell and started to laugh. A high pitched laugh that sounded like a cartoon witch. It was a nervous habit she sometimes did in awkward situations.

Maverick's eyes traveled down to what they held in their hands. "Are those..."

"So, I'm going to wait in the living room. You two have your moment," Willow giggled, still nervous, but probably also a little amused at Ofelia's expense. She waltzed out of the room with the same energy from earlier.

"Baby girl?" Maverick asked once they were alone.

"I didn't think you'd be home until late," Ofelia blurted the first thing that came to her mind.

Maverick eyed her wearily. "I texted you saying Keanon had to leave early for some meeting. I take it you didn't get it?"

Ofelia cursed softly. "No, sorry. I haven't checked my phone since..."

"Since a bunch of pregnancy tests landed in your possession?" There was no anger or malice in her husband's tone, not that Ofelia thought there would be. If anything, he seemed a little amused, but mostly confused. "Are these tests for you or Willow?"

The fear and uncertainty from earlier came roaring back and she hated those were the first emotions that flooded her. Societal pressures coupled with her own anxiety didn't bode well when it came to pregnancy.

"Well...they're for me," she said after a moment, her eyes never leaving Maverick. She knew she would fold at the slightest hint of discomfort, but she found none. In fact, she didn't find much of anything in his expression. His silence made her continue to babble. "My period is late, but it could mean nothing. I'm just not usually late. Like ever and I've been feeling weird these last few mornings and—"

Maverick's lips found hers. She hadn't even seen him approach her, but here he was. Holding her close and kissing her like he just couldn't get enough. That was all it took for Ofelia to melt into his arms.

When he finally released her, she was left feeling dizzy and slightly breathless. "Go take the test, baby girl. Let's see if we are starting our family early."

Relief washed over her like a tidal wave. Hearing the excitement and love in Maverick's voice went a long way to ease her anxiety. "The timing isn't great, are you sure you're okay with this?"

"Okay with this? Baby girl, fuck the timing. We make our own timing, and of course I'm okay with this. My wife might be pregnant, I'm fucking excited." He grinned, reaching behind him for another test to hand to her. "I'll be out in the living room with Willow. Come out when you're done and we'll wait for the results together."

"I love you so much." Ofelia beamed, kissing him one last time before disappearing into the bathroom.

She knew the basics of pregnancy tests; she wasn't entirely ignorant about them. Still, she read the instructions on both boxes twice before she started. Peeing on both sticks was a humbling experience and she pretended as if she didn't get any pee on her hand. As soon as she was done, she placed the tests down and scrubbed at her hands until they were clean.

Willow and Maverick awaited for her on the couch, conversation ending as soon as they spotted Ofelia. "It's done. We only have to wait about three minutes. This one will either have a positive or negative symbol and this one will say pregnant or not pregnant," she said and placed both tests on the table in front of them, moving to occupy the space between the two.

She felt safe, surrounded by two people she loved most in the world. All that was missing was her brother and her father. If her mother were still alive, she knew she'd be in this room with her, holding her hand and telling her stories about her first pregnancy.

She missed her so much.

Maverick's strong arms pulled her close, grounding her in the present once again. Her gaze kept shifting to the clock above the entertainment center, but each second went by agonizingly slowly.

"Ugh, this is the longest three minutes of my life. I just want to know if I'll be a tía!" Willow groaned, legs bouncing up and down. She impatiently looked at her watch, murmuring something about centuries.

Ofelia had set a three minute timer on her watch after she had taken the test. The chimes she set for it went off, signaling her time was up.

"What was that?" Willow asked.

"That means it's time to look." Ofelia took a deep breath and looked at Maverick. "You ready?"

Maverick's dark eyes bore into hers. "I'm ready."

She took a moment to collect herself, knowing that whatever she saw on the test would change everything. She wasn't sure if seeing not pregnant would be a relief or utter devastation.

Willow was practically buzzing with excitement and Ofelia knew if she stalled any longer, her best friend would explode. She grabbed the test, both sets of peering eyes behind her looked over her shoulder, just as eager to see the results.

The answers were in her hands, but her mind was slow to process what she saw. Willow bursts into tears next to her and Maverick squeezed her. The room erupted around her, but her mind was working too slow.

On one stick two faint lines. On the other were the words 'pregnant.'

Pregnant.

She was pregnant.

"Oh my god." The tests dropped to the floor as she flung herself into the arms of her husband, pulling Willow in with them. "I'm pregnant!"

"You're pregnant!" Willow echoed, happy tears streaming down her face. Ofelia hadn't realized she was also crying until Maverick wiped away the tears on her cheek.

"We're going to be parents, baby girl," Mav said, his face lit up with the biggest smile. Ofelia had only ever seen him this happy on their wedding day.

"I'm going to be a mother," she whispered as different emotions overtook her. Fear, excitement, joy, and love.

"And you are going to be the best mother ever to your little boy or girl," Willow beamed and Ofelia hugged her tighter.

Ofelia had never been excited for the unplanned or unknowns, but she was beginning to realize there were exceptions to that rule.

"You ready to take on long nights and early mornings?" Maverick asked playfully and Ofelia thought back to the moments he spent with their niece Camilia and how good he did with her. The first time Camilia fell and scraped her knee in front of them, Maverick was quick to render aid. That moment had only solidified her choice in a partner.

"I can't think of anything better." Between her husband, supported best friend, and an amazing family, Ofelia couldn't wait to add another into their lives. It was about time Camilia had a cousin to play with.

# PART TWO

# Fixed Up Ever After

# Lola

CHAPTER ONE

Lola Roberts managed a feeble smile at her sister's engagement news, even when Marisol announced she would be marrying Archie, Lola's ex-boyfriend. It was fine. Totally and completely fine. In fact, Marisol did her a favor. No woman in their right mind would voluntarily agree to marry a guy with the first name of Archibald, as if they were living in their own little version of Bridgerton.

*Sir Archibald of Douche Baggery and Lady Marisol of Back Stabbery.*

Honestly, they were a match made in hell. A business exchange disguised as two people happily engaged. Or as happy as Marisol could be. She rarely saw her sister smile and for most of her life, Lola didn't think Marisol was capable. Except someone turned up the wattage inside her brain and her radiant smile lit up the room. She clung to Archie like pet hair to black clothing.

Their manufactured happiness disgusted her.

Not as much as her mother's over-the-top reaction though. Her stone-hearted mother openly wept over the news and expressed how proud she was of Marisol. Their mother, Luciana, thrived on material goods and a well-rounded image. Lola, her youngest daughter, had never been able to fit into the box crafted for her.

Her hair was too unkempt. She was too fat. Her clothes weren't by the right designer. Her job didn't scream luxury. She didn't befriend the right people. The list went on, but thinking anymore about all the ways she came up short in her family would make her spiral. And she couldn't do that without a strong drink in her hand.

No one noticed as she left the table, too consumed with admiring the giant rock on Marisol's left hand. It was a miracle her petite sister could even carry it on her slender finger without breaking a bone. She wondered if the ring had originally been made for her when she believed Archie would propose, but like everything else in Lola's life, the ring and the man went to Marisol.

"They sure are good-looking, aren't they?" the bartender asked. Unconsciously, she had made her way over to the open bar, the one positive thing her family did at special dinners.

"Sure. If you can look past their superficial facade, then I guess they look good together." So she was feeling petty, but her sister marrying her ex would do that to a person. She deserved to be a little bit of a bitch.

The poor bartender fumbled for something to say, but clearly, his classes on mixology had not prepared him for Lola's particular brand of sulking. She spared the man by requesting whatever beer he had on tap. He fluttered away, all too happy to get away from her.

The gray cloud in the room.

As far as Lola was concerned, she had two options right now: she could sulk and drink away her sadness, or she could do something brave to wipe her mind of the last hour.

Sulking was always a safe option. She could throw herself a literal pity party back in her hotel room—complete with ice cream, pizza, those little street tacos she liked so much, and cake because every party deserved cake. Basically she wanted all the foods her mother would normally chastise her about while never letting her forget how many carbs and calories she was consuming.

*"Dolores, do you think you'll magically lose the baby fat if you keep eating like a high school boy?"* Her mother would constantly nag, no matter how many times Lola asked her not to. The "baby fat" was just fat at this point. She was twenty-four, but her mother still treated her like a teenager who lived under her roof.

Thank goodness she didn't. Lola had been put through enough fad diets under her mother's watchful eye to last a lifetime. Her mother couldn't fathom how Lola liked her body. As if bigger bodies weren't worthy or desirable.

Lola was far from cocky, but she knew she looked good, even with her thick thighs, soft belly, and heart-shaped face. It took her a long time to appreciate the body she had, but when she stopped hating herself for simply existing in a bigger body, her life got tremendously better. She found clothes that showed off her curves. Learned how to style her thick curls and watched countless YouTube videos of plus-size beauty influencers doing their makeup until she found a routine that worked for her face structure.

She was thriving. Until she'd met Archie and lost the woman she was in order to become the woman best suited to be on the arm of a future CEO of a multimillion-dollar company.

If she were a character from one of those superhero movies her father enjoyed so much, this would be her villain origin story.

A cold, pale beer was placed in front of her, giving Lola a reprieve from her wayward thoughts. The bartender disappeared, as if afraid she'd rope him into another off-putting conversation. "Coward," she mumbled under her breath, bringing the beer to her lips and taking a sip. The rich coldness of the beer sent a jolt of electricity through her, stiffening her spine.

It was exactly the shock her body needed to get out of the funk this whole engagement dinner put her in. She still couldn't believe she voluntarily got on a plane from Florida to fly to where her sister lived in California, only to walk into this messy disaster. No one seemed to care how she felt, so why should she give these people power over her? It was time to pull up her big girl panties and take matters into her own hands.

She needed a way to leave this crappy family function because there was no way she could spend another second watching Archie and Marisol pretend to be in love. What she needed was a good, old-fashioned hookup. And thanks to the wonderful world of dating apps, Lola did not have to search far.

With newfound vigor, she swiped up on her phone, letting face recognition unlock it. Her finger hovered for a second until she remembered what folder she put the dating app in. "Dating app" was probably not the best name because she doubted anyone had found love amongst a pack of horny people. Its purpose was hookups and that was what she needed.

The app opened under her manicured finger. It had been months since she last used it. The last two times had been a week after Archie broke up with her and again when she learned he had started dating her sister. So she had a few security questions she needed to answer before it restored her profile.

The red dot at the bottom of the screen indicated she had unread messages in her inbox. After a quick scan, she determined they were all over two months old and promptly deleted them. They served her no purpose now. Instead, she fell down the rabbit hole of endlessly swiping left on countless men.

There was a whole damn sea of them. She didn't consider herself picky, but she could only handle so many profile pics of men holding fish. Most of these men were as white as her father and definitely didn't want a plus-size half-Mexican woman.

No, she needed a man who could handle all of her for one night.

Out of the legion of men, only one caught her eye. His name was Javier and his dark eyes held a certain warmth that drew her in. His golden-brown skin stood out against the white of his shirt, pulled taut at the chest. He sat alone in his photo, smiling wide at whoever took the picture.

Scrolling through his brief bio, Lola discovered he was adventurous, enjoyed video games, and loved horror movies. Next to the job box, he stated he worked in construction. That was evident in his well-toned biceps, which were covered from wrist to shoulder with tattoos.

Lola was a sucker for a man with tattoos. It was one of her weaknesses. Which made her relationship with Archie so odd. He was as vanilla as they came, and yet she had bent over backward for him, lost in her weird, out-of-character obsession.

A boisterous laugh from the table brought her attention back toward her family. Her father's pale cheeks were a bright tomato red from laughing at something Archie said. Marisol laughed politely, still hanging on his shoulder. Next to her father stood her mother, fussing over Marisol's hair. Lola tried not to make eye contact, but Luciana was a damn lioness, sensing prey from miles away. Their eyes met briefly and then Luciana bent over to whisper something in her father's ear before making a beeline for Lola.

Before her mom got too close, Lola sent off a quick message to the stranger on the app. She cut straight to the point, not wanting to waste their time, and mentioned she was only here for one night. Once the message went through, she clicked her screen off.

"Dolores, what are you doing all the way over here? You should be with your family, congratulating your sister. This is a very important day for her." Her mother's posh voice grated on her nerves.

Luckily, Lola had a wonderful poker face. She plastered on the same fake smile she wore in most of her staged family photos. She did a decent job at convincing people she was happy because no one ever questioned her. "They're getting quite enough attention without me, Mom."

"Oh, please, don't be like that," her mother chided. "Don't

start a scene or ruin this night for your sister. If not for her, do it for me."

Now she really had to hold her tongue. Did no one remember that Archie had been Lola's boyfriend first? How they were together for almost two years before he cut her out of his life like an expired coupon, only to immediately get into a relationship with her perfect sister not even a month later?

But of course, *she* was the one causing a scene. Typical. Fortunately, she was used to being the black sheep of the family.

Lola opened her mouth to say something that would only dig her into a deeper hole when her phone chimed. She looked down and read the notification that popped up. A smile crept over her features.

> You don't have to ask me twice. I'll be there in
> an hour.

"Dolores, are you listening to me?" Her mother's patience ran thin, but for once she didn't care.

"No, sorry. I have to go. A friend is waiting for me."

"A friend?" Her shrill voice suggested she didn't believe Lola was capable of making friends. Which, ouch. "This is your sister's engagement dinner! What friend could be more important than this?"

"A new friend. Goodbye, Mom. Give Marisol my best."

Luciana sputtered incoherent nonsense as she left the overly priced private dining room. Not once did she look back.

She had a hookup to meet.

# Javi

## CHAPTER TWO

THERE WERE times in Javi's life where he had done questionable things, like the time he set a dumpster on fire to see if it truly did smell as bad as his friends said it did. Spoiler alert, it smelled worse.

Teenage Javi was a terror and had no reason to be so feral. But since becoming a father who worked full time to provide for his six-year-old daughter—who was only getting more expensive as she aged—he thought he had become a more mature, well-rounded person.

Certainly not the type of person that downloaded hookup apps, dropped his daughter off at his sister's house, and drove forty-five minutes to a fancy hotel in the rich part of town to get some action.

Except that was exactly what he was doing.

How the hell had he become so desperate? Well, he knew the answer to that, though he hated to think about his time with Estella. He had fallen so head over heels in love with her, he planned on making Estella his wife.

That was five years ago, but the grief never fully left him. In many ways, Javi felt responsible for Estella's death, no matter how many times his sister or father told him there wasn't anything he could have done. He didn't believe their lies, but appreciated the comfort they attempted to give him.

Since Estella, he hadn't pursued another relationship. He had many excuses as to why, most notably his lack of free time. He juggled being the best father he could be to Camilia and the rest of the time was spent at his job.

As if working hard, long days would allow him to escape any emotions still lingering after Estella's death. The minuscule amount of free time he had was spent with Camilia, who was growing so fast. Javi didn't want to be an absent father like his own father had been. He wanted Camilia to have memories of him at all her important life events and never doubt how much he loved her.

Going out tonight was a big fucking deal. He wrestled between guilt and acceptance. He deserved a night of fun without feeling like he was a bad dad for leaving his daughter behind. He wanted—no, *needed*—physical touch from a woman who desired him on a simply superficial level.

So all of that to say, he might have been feeling lonely. He hadn't been celibate since Estella's passing—he was no monk—but the last time he took a woman to bed had been over a year ago. The urge for sex had been easy to ignore, but suddenly it was getting harder to block out those urges. Seeing how happy his sister was with her husband and their new son made him miss the touch and comfort of another person.

That was the only reason he pulled into the labyrinthine parking garage. He shoveled out an exuberant amount of money just to leave his car behind so he could meet a woman named Dolores.

Actually, he was going to do a hell of a lot more than meet with her, and that unnerved him.

Javi was not a one-night stand sort of man. He was not sure what kind of man he was, but it was not this. Maybe teenage Javi, but that had changed after Estella. Then changed again once Estella died. He was an anomaly.

A fucking horny anomaly.

The hotel looked like something he'd only ever seen in spy movies, where the millionaire criminals hid amongst the unsuspecting wealthy. The building had to be at least twenty stories high, and from that vantage point, probably overlooked the entire city. He always wanted to see what downtown San Francisco looked like from a bird's-eye view. At night it would be lit up, twinkling beneath him like millions of tiny stars.

Javi knew this place was fancy when a literal doorman greeted him on the way. His job was rather unnecessary considering the doors were automatic, but he smiled at the man nonetheless.

"Where is the bar?" Javi asked, stepping inside.

The blond man smiled and pointed his finger to the right. "If you see the restaurant, you've gone too far."

"Thank you." Javi made his way through the lobby and off to the right like the man indicated. Nerves began to set in, but so did an undercurrent of excitement. He was about to taste a forbidden fruit. He shouldn't indulge, but why pass up the fruit when both parties consented and wanted to feel good for one night?

His phone buzzed in his pocket and he pulled it out to see a message from Dolores. He clicked on the notification, quickly scanning the message.

At the bar. I'm in pink.

Another text popped up, but this time from his sister who was watching Camilia. It was a photo of Camilia and her two-year-old cousin Arturo wrapped up in a *Paw Patrol* blanket. The corners of Javi's lips pulled up into a smile and he saved the photo before pocketing his phone.

The bar was hard to miss. A giant horse fountain indicated he had found their arranged meeting spot.

Not many people occupied the stools: an elderly couple sipping champagne, a man in a full tuxedo with his tie askew, a middle-aged woman with twin boys running around her feet, and finally his eyes landed on the woman dead center.

She wore a blush-pink eyelet dress that went down to her mid-thighs. He only knew the term "eyelet" because his mother had been into sewing and mended plenty of clothes. The woman's beautiful golden-brown skin shined under the chandelier. She was giving him a sneak peek at her legs, and Javi couldn't tear his gaze away from her thighs. He drifted closer to get a better look.

After what was probably an inappropriate amount of time staring, his gaze slowly traveled up the dress, to where the thin fabric strained against her hips and chest. When he finally reached her face, she was staring back at him. Her muddy-brown eyes challenged him as if to say, "*Can you handle me?*"

God, he hoped so.

If she wanted to honor him by suffocating him between her thighs or working him past his breaking point, then Javi would say he'd experienced a life well lived. He couldn't envision a better way to go than with this goddess sitting on his face.

"Have you decided if you are staying or leaving yet?" a sultry voice spoke, going through him like molten-hot lava as it settled in his core. She said the words so carelessly, but her searching gaze told him she wasn't nearly as confident or relaxed as she pretended to be.

Because he was an idiot, he still didn't respond nor made any attempts at moving forward. *Good fucking job, Javi. She's going to think you're a virgin who is about to see tits for the first time.*

Her gaze darkened as she took another sip of her cocktail. "You're Javier, right?" she asked.

When his voice decided to come back to him, he nodded once. "Javi. Are you Dolores?" She obviously was, but his brain decided now was the time to do a full system reboot.

"Lola," she corrected, "I just go by Lola." She gestured to the spot next to her, repeating the question from earlier. "Now that you've seen me, are you staying or leaving?"

His brow furrowed. What did she mean by that? He saw her

in her photos and she caught his attention on a purely superficial level. He read her bio and she seemed like an amazing woman, but he knew this arrangement was only for tonight. He didn't want to invest in a woman he would no longer see.

She was so fucking beautiful. His treacherous body was already reacting to her. "Why would I leave?" He took the spot next to her and called the bartender over to order himself a whiskey. He needed some liquid courage to give him the confidence he was lacking when faced with a sexy woman.

Dolores—no, Lola—looked surprised by his answer, but shrugged. "No reason," she said and took another long sip of her cocktail. It was already half gone; he would need to drink his own quickly because he didn't want to keep her waiting.

A long moment of awkward silence stretched out between them. When he found his voice, Lola opened her mouth to speak and Javi's words turned into a weird, whistled groan. Lola at least had the decency to pretend that she didn't notice his nerves. "So, you should probably know that I don't normally do things like this."

The tension in his shoulder subsided and he sighed in relief. Of course, he would not judge her if she hooked up with strangers often, but it felt like solidarity to know he was not alone in this. "Neither do I."

"And I'm not going to ask you the reason you agreed to…"

She made a weird gesture with her hands that made Javi raise a brow. "Sex?" he supplied.

The faintest blush heated her cheeks, but was gone a second later. "Yes, sex. So I think we should set some ground rules before I take you back to my hotel room."

The conversation came to a natural pause as the bartender placed Javi's drink in front of him. He picked it up, just as a flash from a camera went off. Lola unabashedly had her phone out and was pointing it right at him.

"Did you take my picture?"

"I did," she said, typing out something on her phone before

placing it down on the bar counter. "And I sent it to my best friend so if you are planning on murdering me, she'll send your ass to jail so quickly that my body will still be warm when she finds me."

At that, Javi nodded. "Your friend's a cop?"

"No, baker. Why?"

"No reason." It was his turn to smile, hiding it behind his crystal glass. He probably should have asked the price of this whiskey, but it was too late now.

"Anyway, I needed to threaten you. Do you feel threatened, Javi?"

"Oh, most thoroughly. Go on, what is your next rule?"

"This is a one-night thing. After tonight, I'm deleting the app. It will be easier if we both agree on this to alleviate a messy situation for after."

That was easy enough to agree with. It was the reason he was here. Javi was still not in a place where he could handle a relationship and from the looks of it, neither was Lola. They both had an itch to scratch and they were each other's backscratchers. That was it.

"I'm pretty much open to anything, but I don't like being blindfolded or called derogatory names in bed," she added. "Tied up is fine though, but I doubt it will come to that."

Just then a vision of Lola, lips slightly parted, chest heaving, and tied spread eagle to the bed, emerged in his brain. He imagined her panting and begging for him, demanding him to fuck her until both of them passed out from sheer exhaustion.

The thoughts went straight to his dick and he cursed. The last thing he needed was to be walking around with a boner, announcing to the entire hotel what they were about to do. He tried to readjust himself covertly, but Lola's eyes trailed down his body, straight to his crotch. His cock stiffened as if to say, "*Hello.*"

*Fucking hell.*

With a sly smile on her lip, Lola brought her attention back up. "Is anything off the table for you?"

He racked his brain hard—pun intended—to come up with some sort of answer to her very reasonable question, but not even five minutes ago, he was prepared to die by thigh suffocation. There wasn't a whole lot off the table for him.

He settled on, "Nothing comes to mind, but if it does, I'll be sure to tell you."

Lola nodded. "Wait, did you bring a condom?"

"I brought several, actually." He said, ignoring the glare from the elderly couple who heard Lola say the word condom. They were young once. They should know how it felt. And honestly, they should be happy that they were being safe. Safe sex was never a reproachful topic.

Taking the final sip of her cocktail, Lola placed her glass on the table before pushing off her high chair. Her dress rode up to dangerous territory and Javi didn't know he was staring until he caught her smirk.

"Well let's go. The night isn't getting any younger and I need a good distraction after my hellish day."

Javi did not get the opportunity to ask what she meant, because Lola was already walking toward the elevator. "Are you coming?" she called over her shoulder.

He wasn't coming yet, but he intended to by the end of the night.

Javi downed the last of his whiskey, ignoring the burn down his throat. He threw money on the table, hoping it would cover the cost, before racing after Lola.

# Lola

CHAPTER THREE

FAKING confidence was a skill Lola learned at a young age. Chubby chicks always had to exude extra confidence for simply existing. The moment she let her guard down, someone always had to remind her that she was fat. As if that was a secret and not the reality of Lola's everyday life.

Over the years, her feigned self-assurance morphed into acceptance. No, she was not conventionally skinny, nor did she fit societal beauty standards like her mother and sister, but her body was a damn temple and she was a goddess. Even Aphrodite had rolls and she was considered to be the most beautiful goddess of them all.

It did not matter what her parents, sister, or anyone at that damn engagement party thought of her. Right now the only important opinion was her own and Javi's, since she was taking the very hot and muscular man back to her room. Teenage Lola was freaking out because Javi looked like a member from one of the countless boy band photos she hung up on her wall like a religious shrine.

He was wearing a skintight, black, long-sleeved shirt, rolled up to his elbows. Decorating both arms were beautiful and intricate tattoos that she wanted to study. His hair was cropped short and styled with more product than she probably used in her own hair. He had a beard and whispers of a mustache trimmed close to his face. Lola's dirty thoughts conjured up the feeling of those fine hairs brushing her between her thighs. It sent a delicious jolt down her spine.

Even if the sex sucked she would forever summon the image of him for her spank bank for months to come.

Her overpriced hotel room was a gift from her father for flying from Florida to California in order to attend her sister's engagement party. She had not known that at the time, and wouldn't have agreed to come if she did. No doubt her mother made her father keep it a secret since she was certain they had known.

Opening the door to her room, they were greeted by an extended hallway leading toward another area in the suite. Off to the left was the bathroom with a large walk-in shower and a claw-foot tub, adding a vintage element to the space. She reached back for Javi's hand, leading him down the hallway and into her bedroom.

Floor-to-ceiling windows took up most of the wall. The view was pretty, though not as nice as the view from the main room, and Lola did not bother with the curtains because they were too far up for anyone to see them. The moonlight shining in through the windows provided enough light for them to see each other without having to turn on the harsh, unnatural lights of the room. It seemed less intimate this way.

That was the kind of vibe Lola was going for. She wanted no confusion over what this was and what they would be doing. Javi did not seem like the stalkerish type or a man that overstayed his welcome, but she had been wrong before when it came to making assumptions about a beautiful man.

Lola reached down to unclasp her heels before kicking them off and turning to Javi who was still taking in the extravagant room. Sometimes she forgot that not everyone was in her father's tax bracket and she appreciated when people humbled her. She never wanted to lose touch with reality like her parents.

Or her sister.

"Do you want a tour, or do you want to take my clothes off and rail me?"

Her crude words made Javi blink, swiveling his head back toward her. A small smile creased the sides of his lips and Lola felt an invisible pull toward him. She wondered how many panties dropped for this man when he smiled at a girl like that. Did he know what power he possessed with those lips and that smile?

"Nah, I've seen enough. I choose the second option," he said and stepped closer to Lola. She took an involuntary deep breath at his proximity. She probably should feel embarrassed about it, but there was a certain freedom in knowing she would never see this man again. She did not have to put on an act and that alone was refreshing.

Lola leaned in, but then stopped once her plump breasts grazed his pecs. "You don't have a wife and baby at home, do you? Or a girlfriend?" She didn't know what possessed her to ask, but she couldn't go through with this if she would be Javi's dirty little secret.

She watched his face, waiting for the lie, but it never came. His eyes remained kind, albeit lustful, and his voice never wavered. "No wife. No girlfriend."

He did not say anything about a baby, but that was the least of her worries. If she was screwing a dad, then so be it. Even fathers needed to let loose once in a while. Or so she assumed. She had no children or nieces or nephews herself, but she imagined parents had a lot of pent-up frustrations and sex was the perfect outlet.

"Well, lucky me." How no one had snatched this sexy man up was beyond her, but Lola was going to take full advantage of this situation. She pressed against Javi, feeling his hard muscles underneath his clothes. He felt like the type of guy that could handle every inch of her, every curve, and not think twice about throwing her around.

That was exactly what she needed right now. To be thrown around and told what to do. She was usually the dominant one in the bedroom, but after her day she did not want to think. She wanted to be told what to do and be called a good girl when she obeyed. She wanted pleasure for the sake of pleasure and judging by the hungry gleam in his eyes, she guessed Javi wanted the same thing. Or why else would he be here right now?

Lola opened her mouth to say something else, anything to break the increasing tension between them, but her words were swallowed up in Javi's kiss. Thank God. She was prepared to make the first move to get Javi to loosen up, but she was glad she didn't have to. His mouth was warm and wet, tasting of spearmint and whiskey.

A needy moan left her as his arms wrapped around her hips, hands resting on her ass. His large hands engulfed her cheeks, kneading them. If he was determined to drive her wild within five minutes of getting to her hotel room, he succeeded.

"Turn around." Gone was his light, teasing demeanor from the bar; in its place was the deep baritone of a man who knew what he wanted and took it. If he asked her to get on her knees, Lola would have shattered both kneecaps with eager compliance.

She did as she was told, turning away from him. Javi ran his hand up her back, finding the zipper to her pink dress. He was careful of her hair, which Lola appreciated, making sure it was twisted out of his way before he pulled the zipper down to the top of her ass.

Her puffy sleeves slipped off her arms, exposing more of her brown skin. Unlike Javi, her skin was free of tattoos, mostly because she was too afraid of needles and far too impatient to sit and wait for the tattoo artist to finish.

Lola let the sleeves fall completely before pulling her arms out. The dress was too low cut to wear a bra underneath it, so her large tits were on display. The room was cold, causing her brown nipples to perk up in response.

Javi made an appreciative sound from behind her. She

expected him to reach up and cup her breast, but he no longer touched her. She could feel the heat radiating off his body and sense his eyes all over her, but his hands were nowhere to be found.

"Take off your dress, Lola." His hot breath hit the back of her neck. Her panties flooded with moisture at his command and she shimmied out of her dress leaving on her lacy pink panties—ones that left little to the imagination.

Finally, she turned around to face him. Javi bit his bottom lip and the need to tease him grew strong. She was a flirt by nature and appreciated it when people enjoyed her body. It made her want to put on a show.

She cupped her own breasts and then pinched her nipples between her thumb and forefinger. Javi groaned and stood still, his gaze piercing her as if he were afraid to miss even a second of her show.

"You have far too many clothes on, big guy. Why don't you change that?" she purred. She could tell her voice went straight to his cock, because of the bulge forming in his jeans. It gave her a confidence boost and Lola backed up to the bed, easing her body down gracefully.

Still, Javi did not move. It was as if he were in a trance, unable to break the spell he was under. She chuckled and spread her thighs, panties barely covering her most intimate places. It had the desired effect, though, because Javi snapped out of whatever hold he was under and finally peeled the black shirt off his body.

And hot damn was he an Adonis. An actual living, breathing Adonis and all hers for tonight. She licked her lips, wanting to lick down his chest to his happy trail to discover the prize that lay beneath.

Javi shucked off his pants while she continued to play with her breasts, moaning. In a matter of seconds, he was on top of her, pinning her down to the bed, with nothing but a thin layer of boxers on. They did little to hide the indent of his cock from her. Her mouth watered, actually watered, for a taste of him.

"Javi…" she whined as he leaned down to kiss her neck, one of the most sensitive parts of her body. She impatiently reached for the waistband of his boxers, tugging them down. But before she pulled down any further and exposed his beautiful cock, Javi caught her hands and pinned them above her head.

She huffed indignantly, which earned her a satisfied chuckle from Javi. "You seem like the impatient type, Lola. Impatient and spoiled. Do you always get what you want, preciosa?"

Her cheeks reddened at the nickname. Her Spanish was minimal, but even she knew that was a term of endearment.

"Not always," she said, but couldn't keep the whine from her voice. So what if her father spoiled her to compensate for her mother and sister's general shittiness? She liked it and she was not going to apologize for it.

Javi laughed again. "Just most of the time." He said what she didn't. He leaned down so his nose touched hers and when he spoke, his lips brushed hers. "And what is it you want right now?" he whispered.

"You." The word came out breathy and far too quick, but Lola did not want to take it back. She wanted him badly. Wanted to feel nothing but pleasure and his cock pumping deep inside of her until they both reached their peak.

Javi seemed to consider her words and then he nodded, finally releasing her arms. She wasted no time tugging off his boxers and freeing his erection.

"Fuck," she hissed once he was completely exposed to her. "You carry that weapon around with you all day?" She was panting, but she didn't care. She had good dick before, but never the size or girth of Javi's. Would he even fit?

As if reading her thoughts, Javi said, "You'll take it just fine." Clearly, he had more confidence in her abilities than she did, but she was willing to test that theory.

He reached down and ran his thumb along the seam of her panties. Lola ground down on his thumb, desperate for some pressure on her clit. It wasn't enough and she made her dissatisfaction known. Javi took mercy upon her and pulled the lacy number off, discarding it on the floor next to his boxers.

The first swipe of his thumb down her center sent her toes curling. She gripped the bedding, balling it up in her fists to keep from arching too high off the bed.

"So wet for me, preciosa." He purred, one finger diving deep inside her folds. It slipped in without resistance. Another one quickly followed, moving in and out of her at a slow, teasing pace. His thumb continued to circle her clit, bringing her to the edge of orgasm and pulling off before she could take the plummet.

"So damn cruel—" she hissed, just as Javi pinched her bundled nerves again. Her words ended in a loud moan as her legs widened for him.

She thought he would back off again like he did each time she got close, but he didn't. He picked up the pace of his fingers and let his thumb circle her clit until her legs quivered and her back shot off the bed.

Her orgasm came on suddenly, engulfing her body as Javi continued to tease her until she was putty in his arms.

"Your turn," she said and reached her hand down to rub between his legs, stroking his throbbing erection.

Javi grunted and shook his head. "No. I don't want to finish in your hand. I want to be inside of you."

Lola could not argue with that. "Where is your condom?"

Instead of answering, Javi pulled off her, the cold air hitting her exposed body and sending shivers down her back. "On your knees, Lola. Hands on the headboard."

"Yes, sir." Her words were automatic, but she knew Javi liked it because he smirked and slapped her ass when she got up to do as she was told.

"Good girl." She felt Javi move away from the bed and come back a moment later. She heard him rip the foil, tearing the top off to get the condom out. She imagined him rolling the rubber down his thick cock and her body shivered with anticipation.

Javi didn't know this, but she loved being taken from behind.

It was both sexy and mysterious. She liked not being able to see because it heightened her sense of touch. Plus she liked how deep men could get from this position.

She felt the first touch of his cock at her entrance, teasing her. She ground against him, her ass pressing back into his hips. "Fuck, Lola, your ass is going to be the death of me," he moaned. Her name sounded so good on his lips. She wanted to hear it again, so she ground back harder.

"Lola." This time her name came with a sting across her left cheek. The mix of pain and pleasure nearly flooded her.

Javi used this opportunity to press into her. Her pussy hugged him tightly. It had been so long since she had gotten any action that did not involve her battery-operated boyfriend. But Javi was so much bigger and deeper and he was only halfway in.

"Fuuuuckkkk," she moaned, her head flopping back to land on his chest. Javi wrapped his arms around her, hands finally going to her breasts, holding them in his very capable hands.

"So tight, Lola. So eager for my cock," he groaned right into her ear. She felt the vibrations of his groan straight down to her core. "Just a little more. You can take it," he said again.

Lola wasn't sure she could, but before she could overthink it, Javi thrusted hard, sending her body pitching forward. She grabbed the headboard harder to keep herself from falling on her face.

Apparently, she could take him all.

She had never been so full before. She did not know where she began and he ended. She also didn't fucking care. Her pussy was stretched, bordering on pain, but she loved every moment of it. To his credit, Javi did not move, knowing she needed a moment— or a century—to adjust to his size.

To distract her, or drive her further into a sexual frenzy, Javi came back to her neck, kissing and biting. He was going to leave his mark on her and she found herself wanting it. A small reminder of what happened tonight, even if that reminder only lasted a few days. Her memory would last a lifetime and she already knew she would not forget sex with him easily.

After a moment, her body grew accustomed to him and she tested out her tolerance by moving her hips. He pulled his cock almost all the way out of her before she pressed her ass back against him. Both of them groaned at the movement. She felt Javi shake and she knew he was doing everything he could to hold himself back.

"Do that again," he commanded.

So she did, but this time faster. She rotated her hips, feeling him hit new spots inside of her, spots she did not know she had.

But then Javi took over and once again, she had no complaints. He moved his hips at a punishing speed, leaving her gasping. She never considered herself loud during sex, but he was bringing out a lot of things she did not know about herself.

"Play with that pretty clit. I want to come with you," he said, taking one of her hands off the bed frame and moving it between her legs. He kept his hold on her wrist, as if afraid she would disobey. Little did he know she was far too gone to even consider being a brat right now.

Her finger went straight to her clit, rubbing small circles in time with his thrusts. She couldn't believe she was going to come again so soon. But the pressure inside of her, the slapping of her ass, and playing with her clit was all too much. "Javi, I'm going to —"

"Me too..." he panted.

She felt the moment he came undone inside of her. His cock pulsed inside of her, his body shuddered, and soon he was moaning her name as he came hard for her. Lola was only seconds behind, her body erupting with white-hot pleasure.

Once again her knees gave out and she barely caught herself as she went down on the bed. Javi snaked one hand around her waist, catching her. "That was—"

"Yeah," she agreed. He didn't need to finish, she knew what he was going to say. Amazing. Earth-shattering. Fucking fantastic.

Javi soon pulled out of her and she whimpered at the absence of him. He got up to dispose of the condom and came back with a bottle of water, which she appreciated.

"Let's rest. For just a moment," she said once she downed the water. She was too tired to wonder if asking him to rest with her was a good idea or not, but frankly, she didn't care. She wanted to be held and aftercare was important.

Javi hesitated for the briefest of moments before joining her back in bed. His warm presence occupied the space next to her and he wrapped his arms around her. She gladly took up the role of little spoon.

"If I'm ever in town again, I'll be more than okay with you rocking my world again," she murmured in her tired state. She didn't hear what Javi said—if he replied at all—because the next minute, she had fallen into a deep, blissed-out sleep.

# Javi

## CHAPTER FOUR

JAVI HADN'T MEANT to doze off, but when he glanced at his phone tucked away on the nightstand, he noticed it was almost two in the morning. He cursed under his breath when he realized Lola was still wrapped up next to him, completely naked.

Seeing her on full display again made his cock twitch with desire. How could he want someone again after just having her? Lola was curvy. She had a body meant to be worshiped nightly, but he only had a few hours with her. It wasn't long enough to fuck her properly, but it took some of the edge off.

That would have to be enough.

Javi contemplated what he should do. He doubted Lola meant to fall asleep for long and she hadn't invited him to stay the night. He also had to pick Camilia up in the morning to take her to school and this hotel was fifteen minutes shy of an hour away from home. Sleeping over was out of the picture.

What they had just done was meant to be a one-night thing and here he was overthinking it. He needed to get up and leave. Now.

Slowly, so as not to disturb her, Javi untangled himself from the sleeping Lola with all the speed of a sloth. He worried he'd wake her and he didn't want to deal with the awkward goodbyes.

Perhaps that made him a coward, but if she woke up, he would want to have her again. He couldn't deal with the rejection of her saying no, or worse yet, her saying yes and him getting another taste of her when he was clearly not ready for a real relationship.

With all the grace of a newborn donkey, he managed to roll out of her bed and onto the floor. He paused, waiting for any signs that he'd woken her, but he only heard the soft snores of a sleeping woman.

Javi pushed himself up, looking around the oversized room to where they'd thrown his clothes. He grabbed his boxers first, finding his jeans next to a vase of flowers and his shirt tossed underneath a leather chair.

He checked to make sure his wallet and keys were still in his pocket before taking one last look at Lola's sleeping form. He understood how creepy he must look staring at a naked sleeping woman, but no one was there to judge him. Lola didn't move much in her sleep and she reminded him of a Latina Snow White. Her full red lips and caramel skin shined in the moonlight. Her black hair was in disarray and her round ass was still tinged red, but that only added to her beauty.

Unable to help himself, Javi approached her once more and leaned down to press the softest of kisses to her forehead. This time Lola stirred, but only to unconsciously grab the covers and pull them over her naked body. She turned away from him, content in her new sleeping position.

"Goodbye, preciosa." He murmured and made his way through her room and down the hallway. Javi left the comforts of their one-night stand and rejoined the real world. Ten minutes and three wrong turns later, Javi was on the road, driving back toward where Camilia waited for him.

# *Lola*

## SIX MONTHS LATER

THE BEST SCENT in the world was old books. Books that had been properly loved with yellowed pages or stains of coffee on the cover. She liked knowing that in her hands she held a piece of history and it always made her wonder who else had touched the book.

Perhaps an elderly man passing the time while his wife knitted. Or a college student who had been told they needed to study the classics in order to graduate with the rest of their class. Perhaps it was a couple in their forties who read together nightly. Sometimes she got lost in all the places books traveled and sat for hours making up scenarios in her mind.

Her love of reading was somewhat of an anomaly. No one in her posh family owned books outside of decorative purposes. The hustle and bustle of work, marketing meetings, business dinners, and charity events stretched their time thin, leaving no room to curl up with a good book.

But Lola had found small moments of peace throughout school, going to the library or reading during lunchtime. It had been her own secret and a time for her to escape to fantasy worlds where dragons existed and Prince Charming was real.

The real world was far less exciting.

"Ma'am?" A gravelly voice startled her out of her memories and caused her to drop the stack of books she held to the ground. They missed her feet by centimeters, sparing her a cracked nail with her open shoes.

A russet-brown face peeked around the bookshelf, large dark brown eyes stared back at her. A feathered brow cocked up, looking between Lola and the burly man standing only a few feet away from her.

"Lo-Lo, you good?" Monique, her best friend since training bras, asked.

"Yeah, yeah, I'm good. Just lost in my thoughts," she assured, knowing Mona—the nickname she bestowed upon her bestie— was quick to jump to her defense. It was a great quality to have in a best friend, but she would rather not displease the contractor she desperately needed in order to get her semi-bad investment off the ground.

"Cool, cool. Sandi and I are going to check out the espresso machine the old lady left behind and see if it works. You need anything?"

"Nope, you and Sandi enjoy," Lola assured and heard a soft meow coming from Sandi. The cat had to be at least ten years old now since Mona was given the calico during her sophomore year in high school. The damn thing was mean but had formed a special bond with Mona, so now her friend took the old feline everywhere. Sandi only tolerated Lola, which was a lot more than most people.

"Can you repeat what you said? I'm sorry, I didn't catch it the first time." Lola used her best, professional voice—aka her white voice she'd inherited from her father's side. Her Mexican mother had adopted the same voice when speaking to any of her father's influential clients so as not to stand out as the brown girl amongst the sea of Caucasians. Here she was doing the same thing.

She would deal with that identity crisis later. Right now she needed to hear the verdict of the nearly dilapidated bookstore she had purchased.

"Well ma'am, it ain't good." The man said in a southern accent, one she didn't hear much in Berkeley, California. "The foundation ain't all that bad, though you have places of rot and mold. You'll want to fix that before you let any customers inside here. You have an electrical problem, too, stemming from your backroom. It's going to need to be completely reconfigured. Your water is also running brown. That ain't what you want."

Leave it to a man to tell her she didn't want brown water running through her pipes. She knew very little about plumbing, electricity, and foundation integrity, but she knew enough to understand brown water wasn't good.

"Okay," she said slowly, her brain already thinking of solutions. The only problem was that nothing was coming. "So can you fix it?"

"Sure, ma'am. But it'll cost ya. And it'll take time."

"How much time?"

"I don't know. Six to eight."

"Weeks?"

"No, months."

Lola's jaw dropped. She shouldn't be surprised. He wasn't the first contractor to come by and give her a large timeline. The thing was that she didn't have six to eight months to wait around. Each day that passed was more ammunition her mother would use against her to remind Lola how awful this purchase had been. Luciana would then remind her father why she shouldn't have given Lola the money—money that was hers in the first place since the account had been started when she was a baby and given over to her as soon as she turned twenty-one.

"There is no way you can do it any faster?" she asked him, trying to hide the desperation in her voice, but failing miserably.

The man, looking like the country version of Jack Black, frowned, shaking his head. "No ma'am. We have a few jobs that we'd be working alongside yours and this place requires the most of our time. This is our busy season so if you want the job done right, it will take time." He shrugged, clearly never having faced a Mexican mother with a vendetta against him.

So, Lola was back to square one. She refused to let this minor setback cause her to spiral into a full-blown anxiety attack, even if she wanted nothing more than to lie down and have a good cry.

"I can see you need time to think about it," the man said. She wondered how much of a wreck she looked like right now to send a grown man scampering away. "I'll leave you my business card and you can call me back once your mind is made up."

The contractor rummaged through his deep pockets and pulled out a bent business card. She took it from him with a tight smile and led him out. "Thank you for your help," she said as he left, locking the door behind him.

With an audible sigh, Lola leaned against the glass, letting her head hit the hard interior side of the door. Her move back to California and the ancient bookstore was not shaping up like she thought it would.

Lola's obsession with books, history, and learning was the driving force that had brought her back to California. Florida had been her home for four years, but Berkeley was where she grew up. Her friends and some of the best memories lived here and she made a promise to herself that if the old bookstore on Addison Street ever became available for purchase, she would buy it.

Florida had been a nice break and helped her get over the sudden loss of her relationship with Archie and the expectations her family—namely her mother—had for her. Expectations she knew she would never live up to.

However, her life in Florida quickly became lonely. She hadn't met many people except coworkers. She liked her previous job fine enough, but it wasn't something she wanted to do for the rest of her life. It was something she did because it paid the bills and kept her busy.

Moving back to Berkeley meant she had to tell her parents where she moved and why, and that hadn't been the best conversation. Her father had been confused but supportive while her mother was simply confused.

Owning a bookstore, specifically Phoenix Books, had been a dream of hers since high school when she got her first job as a cashier here. The older woman who ran this store, Mrs. Sanderson, knew of Lola's home life and understood that Lola stood out like a proverbial sore thumb. She had given Lola the job under the guise of extra credit for her school courses and something additional to put on her college applications.

All four years of high school and well into college, Lola had worked at Phoenix Books as one of the only long-term employees. The day Lola quit had been an emotional decision, but keeping up with her course load and working full time had put a strain on her mental health.

Mrs. Sanderson had been understanding and kept her on as a seasonal employee until Lola moved to Florida for a job in marketing that, admittedly, her father helped her get.

However, two months ago, Mrs. Sanderson reached out unexpectedly and let Lola know she was retiring and closing the store. Lola knew what she had to do. It had taken some convincing to get Mrs. Sanderson to agree to sell, since the store was in rough condition and she had planned to give it over to the city, but in the end, she had talked her way into purchasing Phoenix Books, intending to restore the store to its former glory.

Finding the energy to push herself off her leaning perch, Lola took a quick look around her new store. There was still so much to be done and apparently, it would take even longer than she anticipated, but the inside of the store still held an old charm to it that she wanted to memorialize upon reopening.

Whenever the hell that would be.

"Mona! Please give me some good news!" she groaned, dragging herself away from the front of the store to find Mona behind what was once the register. Mona's back was toward her, but she looked over her shoulder and gave her a thumbs up.

"You, my sweet friend, have a working espresso machine." She smiled triumphantly, holding up a clear plastic cup. Lola had to squint to see the minuscule amount of liquid inside.

"I drank half of it," she said by way of explanation. "The machine did sound like it would take flight, but it made decent espresso. You book people are patient, yeah? So the long-ass time to brew shouldn't be a problem."

"Well, that's something I guess," she grumbled, leaning over the counter. She landed a little too close to Sandi, who promptly swiped at her arm before jumping off the counter. "Your cat is a menace."

"Isn't she though?" Mona cooed and picked up her little devil off the ground, nuzzling the fat cat.

"You realize you have an unhealthy relationship with that cat, right?"

"Only you and my wife seem to think that. I'm thinking you're both just jealous."

Lola scoffed. "Oh yes, Mattea and I are very jealous of your she-demon."

As if understanding Lola's disdain, Sandi hissed at her before wiggling out of Mona's arms and scurrying away, probably to see if she could find any mice in this old building.

"So how'd it go with the contractor? He seem good?" Mona asked, taking a drink of the last bit of her espresso.

"I mean he was fine enough but his timeline is six to eight months. I don't have six to eight months to give," she complained. Her impatience could never allow her to just sit around and wait. She had never been good at being patient.

Mona whistled lowly. "Damn, that's a hot minute. Can we keep looking? I have someone coming into the bakery tomorrow to fix a few broken appliances and an electrical issue I'm having in the bathroom. Want me to scout him out and tell you how he is?"

Lola shrugged. "Sure. At this point, I'll take anything."

"In the meantime, you should really start spreading the word about Phoenix's revival. No use in putting all this money into a place without letting people know. Besides, it'll get your mind off..." Mona paused and looked around the cluttered room. Lola swore she heard a book fall to the ground somewhere. "This mess," she finished.

"And what do you suggest?" She didn't mean to be snippy with her friend, but she was ready to curl up on her cloud-like mattress and binge *Supernatural* until she fell asleep.

Luckily, Mona didn't take offense to her or was simply used to her bullshit that her attitude didn't phase her. "How about you come down to the bakery this weekend? The first weekend of every month, Mattea likes to put on a family day for kids where they make cookies and shit. You could help and read them a story. They would go feral over a good storytime."

Despite her mood, Lola smiled. Children's books had always been her favorite and she enjoyed finding diverse picture books for children who were underrepresented in the media.

"While you're reading, you can make subtle remarks to the parents that you plan on reopening Phoenix. It'll build up some hype." Mona was always the logical one and grounded Lola when her emotions wanted to lead all of her decisions.

"That does sound fun."

"Of course it sounds fun. My wife will make it fun even if it kills us."

"Well we wouldn't want to anger the Mighty Mattea," she deadpanned.

"So, is that a yes, you'll come?" Mona bit her lip, something she always did when she expected the answer to be no.

"Bitch, you know I can't say no to you when you make that face. Plus telling me it's for the children? I'm pretty sure I'd rot in hell if I said no." She laughed, no true malice behind her words.

"That's right, bitch. You'd burn for centuries. Gotta be a good girl and read to them childrens." Mona teased, tossing her empty plastic cup to her. "Now let's get out of here and get some food. I'm starving and ramen is calling my name."

And just like that, her mood increased exponentially at the thought of food.

~

MONA DROPPED her off at her apartment at a quarter past five. The ramen restaurant near Phoenix had been full of college-aged students set up with their laptops on one side and their piping hot bowls on the other. They managed to find a small, cramped booth toward the bathroom, but the table was stationary and gave her little room between the booth seat and the table.

Luckily, the uncomfortable seating arrangement only lasted for about thirty minutes before Mattea called Mona to come help out in the bakery. On her way, she dropped Lola off at the main office in the apartment complex to get her mail. She was expecting a few packages to complete furnishing her new apartment.

Lola had been in her new two-bedroom apartment for a little over a month now. She was adjusting well and often had Mattea and Mona over for dinners and home projects she needed another set of hands and eyes for. They were content as long as she had booze and food, which she always supplied.

As expected, two medium-sized boxes awaited her in the office. She signed for them before walking a few feet over to the mailboxes to gather her neglected mail due to her long hours at the shop. Pulling out a week's worth of forgotten mail was no easy task, especially when the small boxes were filled to the brim. Somehow she managed and made the trek back to her home, only one building over.

When she was searching for an apartment, Lola had called Mona to help her find something big enough so she didn't feel like she lived in a box. Also, she needed somewhere located within the city. She wasn't a country girl and only enjoyed the occasional vacation to less populated areas when she was in need of a break. Otherwise, Lola liked feeling the buzz of crowds and the excitement that inevitably came with city living.

She had sent a few prospects to Mona and Mattea to check out for her, but they had not been thrilled with any of the properties she sent their way. Unknowingly to her, Lola's friends went on a secret mission to find her a place to live and sent her options based on their favorite places. Her current apartment was within walking distance to Phoenix, Mona and Mattea's house, and her friends' bakery. She filled out the application immediately.

Fumbling to get the key into the lock, as well as balancing the mail and packages in one hand, Lola pushed her way into her modern-styled apartment. Pops of pink, yellow, and blue made the living room feel inviting and stylish. She had an eye for colors and bold patterns and never shied away from statement pieces.

Lola dropped the heavy mail and packages onto the bright yellow coffee table after shutting the door with her foot. The mail spilled out over the table, and a navy-blue envelope fell to the floor. She reached for it, but before her hand made contact, she recoiled as if she had been severely burned. The room felt as if it were spinning and she reached back to grip her Tiffany-blue couch, sitting down before she fell on her ass.

She had wondered when she would finally receive it. Her father had been keeping her in the loop about Marisol's upcoming wedding, but she hadn't been quite as prepared as she believed she'd be to get the wedding invitation.

It had been six months since she last saw her family, only keeping in touch with the occasional phone call from her father. Six months since she left their engagement party and hooked up with a stranger. She almost convinced herself that none of it had been real. That her sister hadn't betrayed her in the worst way. Of course, her sister didn't shoulder all the blame. Archie and her mother were just as much to blame for this sinking feeling in the pit of her stomach.

Breathing became a struggle. Her heart raced. Visions of that dinner came rushing back and she didn't know how to turn her mind off. She needed to pick the envelope up off the ground. Did she throw it away and pretend like she never got it? That would create bigger problems with her mother later on, knowing she wouldn't stop calling and guilt-tripping her until she responded. If she responded, then she would have to come to terms with the reality that Marisol was really marrying Archie.

It wasn't as if she loved Archie. She didn't and hadn't for a long time. She recognized that they were two very different people, but there had been a time when she loved him. She had planned a life with the man, only to have the rug pulled out from under her when he said she no longer fit into his life. She had been devastated by losing him, but that pain paled in comparison to the pain of finding out he moved on with her sister.

Marisol had never been a great sister, but Lola would hardly call her a bad one. They did not have the sisterly bond that many of her friends had, and it wasn't for lack of trying. Lola had tried many times growing up to befriend her sister, but the girls were vastly different. It was impossible to find any middle ground when their differences had no commonality.

Despite this, Lola never hated Marisol. She loved her because that was what you were supposed to do: love your siblings because they were family. The fragile relationship and love they may have shared with one another broke the moment she agreed to a romantic partnership with Archie.

She couldn't deal with this alone. She needed to talk this out, to hear her own thoughts out loud, and for someone else to be a voice of reason. Her family was obviously out of the question, so it only left two people. Lola fished out her phone inside her purse and called.

Not even two rings later, a cheerful female voice picked up. "Hi sweetie. Didn't Mona just drop you off? Are you okay?"

Before Lola could answer, Mona's voice piped up in the background. "Don't tell me your dumb ass locked yourself out of your apartment."

Lola tried to find the words, wanting to joke about how many times Mona had locked herself out of her house or assure Mattea that she was okay. But the only thing that left her mouth was an embarrassingly loud sob.

Crying was a vicious cycle. It hurt to fight back the tears, but crying only pissed her off. Instead of making the tears stop, the anger only made her cry harder. Which wasn't fair because once she started, she found it was hard to stop.

"Oh no, sweetie, no." Mattea's sweet voice came through, along with a few sniffles. Mattea was a sympathy crier and would start crying if someone else was, even if she did not know the reason behind it.

"Let it out, Lo-Lo. Talk to us when you can. Are you safe?" Mona's voice was gentle, though worried.

Lola managed to get out a simple, "Yes," because she was safe, just upset. She had not properly grieved the relationship that ended so abruptly. Even now, the hurt felt like an open wound that hadn't scabbed over yet.

Grief was a weird thing. One moment a person could be totally fine, living their normal life, then the next moment the weight of the world could fall upon their shoulders and nothing was good or right.

After five minutes of embarrassing crying, Lola felt some of her composure come back and she could answer their unasked questions.

"The invitation came." She did not need to say more than that; her friends knew exactly what she meant. She heard Mona swear and Mattea mutter something about "burning his white ass in hell" which caused Lola to smile.

"Throw it away. Don't open it," Mona said.

"I thought about it, but I think that would make things worse. You know my family. They're relentless. I'm not getting out of this shit."

"You also don't have to put yourself in situations where you'll be uncomfortable. They obviously don't give a shit about your feelings, so why care about theirs?"

"Mona!" Mattea gasped and Lola heard a light smack, picturing tiny five-foot Mattea smacking six-foot Mona in the arm.

"Babe, you know it's the truth! Lola's gotta have boundaries."

Lola knew Mona was right. If anyone else in her life treated her like this, she would cut them out so quickly. She knew she deserved better and demanded better, but when it came to her family she always felt and acted differently. It was the one area of her life where she couldn't fix it, no matter what she did. Perhaps it was guilt or the hope that things would be different, no matter how naive that was.

"Have you looked at the invitation yet, sweetie?" Mattea asked, causing Lola to look back at the discarded envelope on the floor. With a reluctant sigh, she plucked it up.

"I'm going to look now." Lola broke the silver seal with her nail, unraveling it until a cream-colored paper fell out. As far as wedding invitations went, this one was simple with silver trimming and a photo of the happy couple locked in an intimate embrace. Lola couldn't deny how beautiful they looked together, but it didn't make the announcement any easier.

"Their wedding is four weeks away," she said softly. "In Colorado." As she said that, two other small pieces of paper fell out of the envelope. One was an RSVP note to mail back. She could not help but notice the plus one on her invitation.

Great.

On top of everything else, she would have to figure out who would be her plus one because there was no way she was going to her ex and sister's wedding alone. The other paper was one announcing she was wanted as a bridesmaid. Leave it to her family to drive the knife deeper into her back.

"There's more. Not only do I need to find a plus one, but I will be a bridesmaid in the wedding."

"Shut the fuck up. Shut all the way up. No you fucking aren't." Mona's disgust, despite everything, made Lola burst out in uncontrollable laughter. She had finally lost it.

"This is perfect. Just fucking perfect." She said after a fit of giggles. "Because why wouldn't my family want to torture me a little bit more? I doubt my sister even knows. This screams my mother. She micromanages everything, apparently even my sister's wedding."

"Well, your mother is a royal bit—"

"Overwhelming," Mattea interrupted before Mona finished her sentence. "All of this is overwhelming and will take some time to process. Do you want Mona and I to come over later and we can binge-watch something on Netflix?"

Lola smiled, her heart swelling at Mattea's words. Her family might be garbage but her chosen family always had her back. "As tempting as that sounds," she started, "I think I just want to head to bed early. I have a full day of errands tomorrow and want to take it easy."

"Okay, sweetie. Mona said we will see you this weekend at the bakery for our Family Fun Day?"

"Of course. I'm thinking of books to bring."

"Good." She heard the smile in Mattea's voice. "We love you and if you end up needing us, don't hesitate to call. We will be there."

She knew they would; she was the luckiest woman in the world to have friends like Mattea and Mona.

They said their goodbyes and Lola hung up the phone. She tossed the wedding invitation under the stack of mail to deal with later. Then she pushed all thoughts of weddings and plus ones out of her mind and enjoyed a relaxing night of watching *Supernatural* and doing face masks.

# Javi

## CHAPTER SIX

FOR AS MUCH time as Javi spent in his old pickup truck, one would think he would be better organized. Yet he couldn't find his unopened box of business cards. He thought he had placed them in his middle compartment, but all he found were two Barbies, three pens, and packets of fruit snacks that had long ago melted in the California heat.

Normally, it wouldn't be a problem if he couldn't find his company's business cards for a multitude of reasons. The most important one being he hated his boss, particularly how he took advantage of the hard-working men on his team. Most of the men, like Javi, had families to support and took whatever job they were offered, afraid that they'd miss their opportunity to put food on the table.

Javi understood that. Understood what it meant to worry week by week, day by day, if he would make enough money to cover his family's expenses. Between food, water, electricity, and his six-year-old daughter, money went quickly. He worked like a dog day in and day out, sacrificing his time with his daughter. His father would say this is the price men paid to provide for the family.

He also wouldn't have cared about the missing business cards because his boss always attempted to overprice the simplest of jobs. Javi never felt right charging two times the price for a simple fix, especially when most of the money went back to lining the pockets of his lazy boss.

However, the missing business cards were not his boss's. They were his. Last week he made the scary, but right, decision to put in his two-week notice and leave his job to work as his own independent contractor. He had built up a rather large and loyal clientele over the years and knew that if he was ever going to make the switch, it would have to be now.

Two seconds after he made this life-altering decision, he called his level-headed sister for advice. She had recently moved back to California from Texas with her husband, Maverick, and provided him with more support than he deserved.

Naturally, Ofelia was on board with his decision—he half expected her to tell him he needed to get his head out of the clouds and keep the job with a steady income. Instead, she insisted he come over so they could design business cards.

His sister was a pro when it came to creating shit like that. Javi had shown up at her house, but that was the extent of his involvement. Ofelia took over, asking him a few basic questions like his email, whether he wanted Javi or Javier, and his work cell phone number, which was his only number.

An hour later, she had not only managed to finish his business cards, but also pay for them to be shipped overnight. He insisted he'll pay her back, but Ofelia would not hear of it and requested he let it go. Begrudgingly, he did.

When they showed up the next day, Javi should have put them straight into the middle compartment of his truck, but instead, he haphazardly tossed them to the back so he could drive his cranky kindergartner off to school in a timely manner.

With a sigh of defeat, he pushed himself out of his car and turned to face his client. She had warm tawny-colored skin, with deep-set dark eyes. Her black coiled hair fanned her face, falling to her shoulders. She had a friendly smile and her bright red, over-sized glasses reminded Javi of a schoolteacher.

"I'm sorry. I thought I'd put them in my truck." He mentally kicked himself for being so unprepared after declaring he was going the independent route. He still had a week left, maybe it wasn't too late to beg to keep his job...

The woman waved away his apology. "Don't worry about it. My wife says I would lose my head if it wasn't attached to my body." She laughed good-naturedly and reached into her apron pocket. A moment later she dug out a crumpled sheet of paper and a pink pen. "Can you write down your contact information here? You did amazing inside fixing the water leak and helping design a new cupcake display."

Javi sighed in relief. "Definitely. Thanks for understanding," he said and took the pen and paper, jotting down his information in his best non-chicken-scratch writing. He left two ways to contact him in case one of them was illegible.

"Like I said, it's not a problem. We just need a reliable person to fix shit around the bakery. It's an old building, as you know. I also have a friend who is in need of a contractor. She's trying to open up the old bookstore downtown."

Javi handed her back the paper with his information and raised a brow. "A bookstore? You wouldn't be talking about Phoenix, would you?"

"The very same. Our friend moved back to town and bought it from Mrs. Sanderson. She is hoping to restore it to its former glory but hasn't found a contractor that meets her needs. Love her to death, but she is a hard-ass when it comes to things like that."

Javi wasn't a reader, much to his sister's dismay, but he had been dragged into the old bookstore countless times as a kid. He had hated it at first but eventually found the comic books, which made the visits slightly more enjoyable.

"Oh!" The woman—if his memory served from the job form, her name was Mattea—exclaimed. "She is going to be here this weekend. You could come to the bakery!"

Javi opened his mouth to politely refuse. He had two days off, a rarity for him, and he did not want to spend it doing business. He promised Camilia that he'd spend the weekend with her and he always tried to keep his promises to her. Especially those that involved quality time together.

"That sounds amazing, but I promised I would spend the weekend with my daughter," Javi admitted.

At the mention of his daughter, Mattea lit up. "This weekend we're holding our monthly family day at the bakery. We have cookie decorating and storytime. It's always a hit with little ones. We would love it if you came. Completely free. No pressure on the business side, if you don't want to talk shop while off."

Javi considered her offer. Since his sister moved closer, her mission had been to convert her niece into a bookworm by reading to her, taking her to fun bookstores and storytimes, as well as reading to her each time they were together. It had achieved the desired effect and his Camilia was just as big of a bookworm as her tía.

Add cookies into the mix and he would be crowned superdad. He needed that win. "When does it start?"

The smile on Mattea's face was one of pure genuine joy. "It's Saturday at eleven."

"Count us in."

Mattea clapped, doing a little dance. The woman was pure joy wrapped up in a tiny body. "Wonderful! We are all about getting the community involved. Plus, I love seeing the little ones. I'm trying to subtly hint to my wife that I'm ready for us to start having kids."

He didn't know the woman well, but he could tell she had a big heart and any child would be lucky to have her. "Well, anyway," Mattea said, "thank you again for fixing our bakery issue. I can't wait to meet your little one on Saturday."

"Call me if you find any other problems. I'll see you Saturday." He offered her a wave before getting into his truck. He waited until Mattea went back inside, since it was getting dark, before he took off.

He was off for two days and he planned to make the most of it. He would finally be able to sit and watch his daughter practice cheer, a sport she had been in since she was just out of diapers, and now he could take her to a storytime and cooking decoration activity.

Ten minutes later Javi pulled into his driveway where his father and Ofelia sat outside while Camilia and little Arturo played in the front yard. He attempted to reach for his lunch box, but the zipper wasn't closed properly and his uneaten lunch as well as a white box fell out.

The same white box he had been looking for earlier that held all of his new business cards. Fucking typical.

His body felt tense as newfound stress worked its way through his bones. When he got like this, he knew it meant he was itching for a stress relief. His last relief came in the form of a one-night stand with a gorgeous woman who popped into his head more times than he cared to admit. It hardly seemed proper to seek out another fling when he was clearly not over his last one.

His anger and thoughts of flings lasted a total of twenty seconds though before tiny fists began to pound on the side of his door, accompanied by the sweetest voice he knew. "Papá! You're home."

# Javi

GETTING three full-sized adults and two kids into his sister's minivan had been no easy task. Arturo decided to have a diaper blowout, making Javi thankful that poopy diapers were something he no longer had to deal with. His father, Ruben, insisted on sitting in the third row of the van, which would have been fine if he didn't move at a snail's pace. He was too proud to admit that he was having a hard time maneuvering his body into the back seat, but Javi knew from experience not to stop him. His father would grow angry and impede progress.

Camilla would only get into the car if she could bring along her doll because she did not want it to be scared alone at the house. By this time, Javi was ready to ram his head through the car's door, but he dug deep within himself to find the last traces of his patience.

By the time everyone was finally in the car, buckled up, and in a sour mood, he was ready to throw in the towel and call it quits. Except that would put a damper on their family day and everyone had been excited when he brought it up. Who knew cookies and a picture book would provide so much joy?

His sister was the last in after putting Arturo back into his car seat with his tablet. "Sorry, sorry! Okay, we are all ready to go," she assured, looking frazzled with her messy bun and rumpled shirt.

Javi bit back the sarcastic retort on the tip of his tongue, knowing that would only serve to cause bickering between the two. He loved his family more than anything, but getting them all out of the house in a timely manner was near impossible. He needed to breathe and trust they would make it through.

Though they were in his sister's van, Javi offered to drive since he knew Maverick, his sister's husband, did most of the driving. Today Mav started spring training for baseball and according to Ofelia, he was adjusting nicely to his new team.

Maverick accepted a job with his San Francisco team nearly a year ago. It had been a huge change for his sister who had lived in Texas for the last five years, but she had been eager to move closer to family. She wanted to raise her children alongside their cousins and be near him and their father when Mav had to travel for baseball.

Javi enjoyed having his sister close again. He hadn't realized how much he missed her until she moved back. It was nice having her close so Camilia would have a woman she loved and confided in if she were ever unable to come to him for some reason or another. Especially during puberty, but luckily they were still pretty far off from that.

Not even five minutes later, Javi heard snoring from the back seat. He snuck a glance in his rearview mirror to see his father in the back, mouth slightly ajar and eyes closed. Arturo was slumped forward in his car seat, tablet nowhere to be found as he too slept. Camilia was the only one awake, looking out the window as they drove.

"Well, next time we need to get them ready for nap time, all we need to do is load them up and drive around the neighborhood." Ofelia laughed, snapping a picture of the sleeping duo in the backseat, no doubt sending the picture to Maverick. "I just hate to wake them up," she said as she put her phone away.

"They are like cats. They sleep all the time." Anytime he

walked into the house and Arturo was there with his father, the two were usually curled up on the recliner sleeping. If they weren't sleeping, they were eating something they probably shouldn't be eating. He loved the relationship his father had with his grandchildren. It was special to see him give both Arturo and Camilia his full attention and intently listen to them, even when he had no idea what they were saying. It was a far cry from what he and Ofelia got from him growing up, but he was glad his daughter got this side of his father.

The drive to the bakery only lasted fifteen minutes, but parking would be hell. The bakery was located in the middle of town, one of the busier streets located a few blocks from the university. The only available parking was on the street and so far, he had not come upon a space large enough to fit the van.

After a few times circling the block, a black sedan finally pulled out of a spot and Javi took the opportunity to pull in. The bakery was only a short walk away. He could already smell the delicious sugar wafting from the shop. Camilia apparently could too because she said, "Papá, can I have a cookie?"

"You'll be making your own cookie soon," he answered, which was greeted by a happy cheer.

Getting out of the car did not take as long as getting in, which he was thankful for. His father allowed Javi to help him out without complaint. His sister unbuckled Arturo and placed him down next to Camilia. The two locked hands and Ofelia placed her hand over her heart in awe. "Don't they make you want another one?"

A sad smile touched his lips. There had been a time when Javi wanted more kids, three to be exact, but those dreams died when Estella did. Ofelia clearly noticed his lack of response and shot him an apologetic look. He wanted to tell her he did not need her sympathy; far too many people looked at him with those same sad eyes and it pissed him off.

But his sister meant well. She was in a good place with her husband and their first child. How could she not want more of the ideal family society said they should have. His sister deserved it and he did not resent her happiness, but he sometimes wished things would have ended differently for him.

Not only for him but for Camilia as well. She never knew life with a mother and that, more than anything, pulled at his heartstrings. He wanted to give his baby girl everything, but he would never be able to provide her with the feeling of a mother's love. She deserved that and so much more.

"Papá, let's go!" His daughter's sweet voice made his heart ache.

Despite his changing thoughts, Javi mustered up excitement, which admittedly wasn't that hard when Camilia was a bouncing ball of joy. He reached for her hand and she gladly clasped her tiny hand with his. He wondered how much longer he'd be able to hold his little girl's hand in public.

He really couldn't go down that road of thinking today unless he wanted to bring down the mood of the entire party.

The delicious aroma of sugar and cinnamon greeted them once Javi opened the door for his family. They all trailed in, his father second to last, and Javi took up the caboose. The vibrant pink-and-white styled bakery was packed with so many bodies that made maneuvering from one spot to another an Olympic sport in balancing.

"There's a table over here!" Ofelia called from up front, guiding Arturo and Camilia to the vacant table. Javi took his father's arm out of fear his father would wind up with another family and they'd never see him again. He followed the bob of his sister's messy bun until he made it to the table.

It was a small round table with only three seats, which went to the kids and his father. He did not mind standing and knew his sister wouldn't either, but his father needed the support, or his legs would ache.

"I'm not a child in need of their mother's attention, mijo." His father chastised when Javi insisted he take the seat, but luckily didn't push the matter.

"Javi! You made it!" A feminine voice said from behind them. Javi turned to see Mattea with a giant grin on her face. She carried two plates of plain sugar cookies with icing and sprinkles off to the side. She placed the plates down in front of Arturo and Camilia and pointed to his daughter. "Is this one yours?"

There was no hiding the pride on his face as he nodded. "She is. That's Camilia and my nephew Arturo."

"Well, they are stinking precious. I'm so glad you were able to make it. My wife is somewhere around here and you made it just in time for our story." Mattea's infectious attitude was impossible to ignore and Javi found that he liked the woman. He didn't have many friends, but he could imagine how easy it would be to have Mattea as one.

How the hell did adults even make friends these days? When he was a child, all he had to do was find a particularly nice rock and hand it to the nearest kid and he had a friend for life...or at least for that school year.

A clanging bell sounded, quieting the chatter of the room. Everyone turned to find the origin of the sound and a tall black woman stood atop a chair. He heard Mattea suck in a deep breath and mutter, "She better get her ass down from there. She knows she's uncoordinated." And he wondered if this was her wife, Monique. He had only ever spoken with her over the phone, but all in-person contact had been with Mattea.

"Thank you all for joining us here for cookies and storytime." The woman said loud enough to be heard over the small whines of impatient children and the scooting of chairs. "I'm Monique, co-owner of this bakery. I'm so excited to announce my best friend and the new owner of Phoenix Books—" A few hushed whispers went around the room, wondering when the old bookstore would reopen. He imagined it needed a lot of work before it could open its doors to customers again.

"—Ms. Lola!" Monique finished and a round of applause greeted her last words. She jumped down from the chair to hug the woman who just walked in, carrying a vibrant children's book in her hand.

Javi recognized that deep-golden skin—he'd spent days remembering those curves and the way her ass swayed in the tight pink dress she had worn. He remembered the way she felt around his cock and the way she moaned for him. A warmth shot through his body, reminding him exactly what she did to him.

Standing only feet away, was Lola—the woman he had a one-night stand with six months ago and could not stop thinking about since.

# Lola

CHAPTER EIGHT

WHEN MONA first asked her to read a picture book at the bakery's event, Lola envisioned a handful of kids with a few adults on their cellphones. What she walked into was quite the opposite. The bakery wasn't big by any means, but it held about thirty people, according to the plaque on the wall set forth by fire regulations.

Six circular white tables and a long bench seat holding another four tables made up the seating in the bakery. Each table was full of children, ranging from toddler size to around seven or eight. Lola loved kids and hoped she would one day have a family of her own. Just not now. Now, she needed to focus on her dream of reopening the bookstore.

When Mona called her name, Lola took a moment to straighten out her shirt—a pastel pink V-neck with 'Mattea's Bakery' embossed across her left breast. She paired this with dark-wash jeans and open-toed sandals to show off her painted toes.

Mona's arms wrapped tightly around Lola, as if she were greeting her back from a month-long excursion, rather than the two whole minutes they were apart. She loved that about her best friend though, her unbridled passion and need to show her love for others through physical acts. It was something Lola wasn't accustomed to.

Her family rarely showed outward displays of emotions, though her dad was known to give a hug or two on special occasions. Her sister and mother on the other hand? It would be a cold day in hell if they ever showed their affection like a normal family. Touching her might result in gaining extra pounds through magical osmosis and they simply couldn't have that.

"Knock their little socks off, bestie," Mona whispered into her ear. She then left to rejoin Mattea behind the counter, leaving her alone with dozens of eyes glued to her every move.

Lola had never been a shy person, which was probably due to years of standing out. When one went to the most elite of prep schools and everyone looked as if they just walked off the runway while her left thigh was the size of their torso, it gave little room for shyness.

She plastered on a smile from years of experience attending her family functions and doing business dinners for her father and his clients. She had perfected the smile over the years, making sure no cracks peeked out of her armor. Showing signs of weakness was the fastest way for anyone to home in on one's insecurities and pick them apart until they were left bleeding all over the floor. Metaphorically speaking, of course.

Seeing the excited expression on the children's faces made her own smile more genuine. "Hello, friends!" She heard Mona snort behind her because yeah, she might be laying it on a little too thick, but she just couldn't help it. She was surrounded by cuteness overload.

She perched her round ass on the stool provided for her, taking another sweep around the room as she said, "I'm so excited to be reading to you today a book about—" But her words got lost in her throat. Everything seemed to come crashing down around her as her eyes locked on a man she had never expected to see again. A man who had rocked her entire world in one single night. A feat her past boyfriends could not do even after months of dating.

Javi.

*Holy fucking shit—Javi is here.*

After their time together, she had awoken to find him gone the next day. Sure they were only sharing a single night together and she had not expected him to stay long, but it would have been nice if he had told her goodbye. Instead, she had woken up late the next morning with a delicious ache between her legs and a bed that still smelled like him.

*This is not what I need to be thinking about right now!*

Her internal freakout almost made her miss the beautiful Latine woman next to Javi. She was curvy, not in the way Lola was curvy, but in a straight-sized curvy kind of way. She was beautiful with long wavy brown hair. The woman was hovering over two children, a boy and a girl. One looked like he may still be in diapers and the other one was old enough to be in school. Kindergarten maybe?

Which begged the question: did she have sex with a married man? And did he lie about it when she asked if he had a partner?

Her cheeks heated, anger coiling low in her belly. There were pieces of shit, and then there were pieces of shit who cheated on their spouses, which made them even lower than the lowest scumbags.

Javi continued to look at her, in much the same way she was looking at him, like they were Scrooge from *A Christmas Carol* seeing the ghost of Marley for the first time.

A not-so-subtle cough snagged her attention and Lola turned her head to see Mona giving her 'what the fuck' eyes. Apparently, she had been silent for too long and the audience was beginning to wonder if she needed medical help.

She needed help, alright, but there was nothing she could do now but ignore the sinfully hot man staring right at her.

A sinfully hot man with a fucking family! She had to remember that part of it.

Pushing all thoughts of Javi away—far, far away to the deepest crevices of her mind which she wrapped up with extra strength, heavy-duty chains—Lola turned her attention back to the children. They were the reason she was here, after all.

"This is a story about a young boy getting ready for his first dance recital," she said, not missing a beat and picking up where she left off. "He's very nervous about his performance, but his family helps him through those big emotions."

She could use help getting through her own big emotions right now, but she remembered the calming techniques her former therapist taught her when her anger or sadness threatened to overwhelm her. That was easy enough when she focused on the sweet children's book. She changed her voice for each character to give them all different personalities.

As a young child, her abuelita would read her bedtime stories each time she spent the night at her house. It had been one of her fondest memories as a child and the reason she became so invested in reading as an adult. Her abuelita would create silly voices and act out the books she read. Most of them had been in Spanish, and since she never learned Spanish fluently, she didn't ever quite understand what the stories were about. That hardly mattered because she knew how they made her feel. Now that she passed, Lola wanted to continue her abuelita's fun storytimes with others.

When the story came to a close, Lola took in the captive audience as the bakery burst into a friendly round of applause. Before she could appreciate the situation, Mona magically appeared next to her, leading another round of applause. "Wasn't that the *best*?" Her bestie beamed, getting vigorous nods from the crowd. "There'll be plenty more of that once Ms. Lola gets Phoenix Books up and running again. Make sure to check back periodically for updates and follow Phoenix Books on social media!"

Social media? Who the hell had social media? Because she knew her friend was not talking about her. She covertly nudged Mona in the side, trying to look as normal as possible as she whisper-hissed, "There is no social media."

"Looks like your ass is about to make one," her friend retorted, barely moving her lips as she spoke, to keep up the vivid smile. She then gripped Lola's wrist, not in a threatening way, but rather in a gentle squeeze as she continued to speak to the crowds. "Ms. Lola will be here visiting the tables while you create your dancer cookies. My lovely wife will walk you through those steps."

Mattea took her cue and made her way toward their makeshift stage to lead the children and their parents through the cookie activity. Mona took this opportunity to lead Lola away and off to the side. "You were amazing, Lo-Lo. The kids loved you. Did you have fun?"

Despite her rather tumultuous start, Lola did have fun. "It was amazing. They were so invested in the story!"

"Nah, girl. They were invested in how you told the story. You are seriously a natural. Parents are going to flock to Phoenix if you keep up storytime."

Speaking of Phoenix, she narrowed her eyes at her friend. "Yeah, and now I have to make and run a damn social media account, thanks to you."

Mona was not bothered by her annoyance. She waved her off like she did any time she didn't like what she was hearing. "Everyone has social media. Stop being a grandma. I know you be posting some spicy pics up on your 'gram."

"Okay true, but I can't post pics like that for a bookstore!"

"We will figure it out later, Lo-Lo." Once again her hand moved through the air and Lola wanted to snatch it and shake her. But since there were far too many witnesses in the room, she settled for a good ol' fashion pout.

"Girl, don't give me that face. I already have a wife who pouts to get her way; I don't need another."

"That's only because we know how easy you are." Lola giggled.

"Har har." Mona rolled her eyes. "Anyway, I wanted to introduce you to Javier, the contractor guy I was telling you about."

Lola felt her stomach sink...again. This was not happening.

Her best friend was not about to walk her over and introduce her to the man she had already slept with. She didn't care how good a handyman he was, there was absolutely no way she would ever consider hiring him. Not because she hooked up with him and he left without saying goodbye—she wasn't mad about that at all. She was pissed at the fact that he was married with kids!

"I don't think right now is a good time. Shouldn't we be helping out with the cookies?"

"Nah, Mattea can run these classes in her sleep. She doesn't need us. And you are the one complaining no contractor can finish on your timeline. So let's see if he can."

"But—"

"No 'buts,' Lo-Lo! I love you very much, but if I have to continue to search for the perfect contractor, I might pass away. We're going."

There was no getting out of her grasp, not when Mona had her mind made up. She could be an adult about this. All she had to do was remain cool and collected, pretend his dick hadn't been a gift to humanity, and she would be alright.

She could so do this.

Mona led her toward Javi's table and Lola swore she was having heart palpitations. Mona tapped Javi on the back of his shoulder to gain his attention. The breath was stolen from her lips when he turned around, his eyes immediately locking on hers. She barely heard Mona say, "Javier? I'm Monique, and I wanted to introduce you to Lola."

She could so *not* do this.

# *Javi*

## CHAPTER NINE

SO MUCH FOR attempting to avoid her. Javi cursed his horrible luck, even though he wasn't entirely sure why he didn't want to see Lola. It was not as if they left on bad terms. They had an arrangement, fulfilled their agreement, and parted ways on amicable terms.

She had been a ghost living rent-free inside his head for so long though. Never once had he suspected he'd run into her again, but here she was. His dumb-ass self stood there with his mouth slightly parted, looking like the idiot he felt like, and unable to form a coherent sentence.

"Javi." His sister nudged him, brow creased with concern. She gestured to the woman in front of him as if silently saying, *"Speak, pendejo."*

He cleared his throat, buying himself another minute. Was he supposed to pretend like he didn't know her? As if they were strangers and he had never seen her come before? Fuck, those were not the thoughts he needed to have right now. He was a grown-ass adult. He could be civil around a woman even if she had seen him naked before. Easy.

He opened his mouth to speak, but Lola beat him to the punch. "We've met once before." She said, almost begrudgingly.

Monique shot her friend a look that clearly said they were going to have words about this later. "I just didn't realize you were talking about him."

It clicked for him then. Why Monique decided to bring Lola over. Mattea had mentioned a friend interested in reopening Phoenix Books during his repair visit. But the odds of that woman being Lola? It seemed so improbable and yet she stood in front of him, looking wildly uncomfortable.

Should it be this awkward? Perhaps Javi was overthinking it all. Apart from the split second of apprehension he spotted on her face when Lola noticed him for the first time, she had shown no other signs of tension, making Javi feel like this was one-sided.

In fact, she seemed pissed that he was here, as he came here today to personally offend her. Even annoyance looked sexy on her, which begged the question, what the fuck was wrong with him? He should not be turned on by her pissy attitude, even if it belonged to a beautiful, curvy woman who he couldn't stop thinking about.

"Well, small world," Monique said after a beat of silence, pulling Javi away from his lewd thoughts. She gestured at Javi, reminding him of a farmer showing off her most prized possession. "So, Javier helped out with a few renovations and fixes the other day. He was able to get them done faster and better than others I have hired."

Pride swelled within him. He knew people enjoyed his work from the continued services they booked and the smiles on their faces when he was done. However, hearing praise for him filled him with the assurance and confidence he needed to know he was making the right decision to leave his job and become his own boss.

Lola seemed intrigued by her friend's words, but almost reluctantly so. Her anger had not faded, he could feel it radiating off her as she scrutinized him from head to toe. "How fast can you finish a job?" she asked.

Javi shrugged. It was a nuanced question because each job was different and required different skills. "Depends on the job. I would have to know what you needed."

"And I suppose you have a waitlist too." She sighed.

That he could answer. Javi shook his head. "I don't. I'm in a transitional period right now. I'm leaving my current job to become an independent contractor. Monique and Mattea are one of my only scheduled clients at the moment."

He hoped more would come his way though. So many people he worked for swore to keep him in mind, but he didn't wait for their calls with bated breath. The industry he was in was saturated and any handyman that could do a quick fix at a decent price, no matter the shitty outcome, usually wormed their way onto projects for unsuspecting clients.

A flash of what Javi could only describe as hope gleamed in her eyes, but when she blinked it was replaced with the emotionless shield she had donned earlier. "I see," she said pointedly. "Unfortunately, I don't think that's going to work for me. I need someone who is both dependable and trustworthy. Sorry to have wasted your time."

Leaving everyone with various levels of shock, Lola turned around, her hair hitting his chest as she walked off toward another table. Monique's head swiveled between Javi and Lola, opening her mouth to say something, but then closing it the next second as if she thought better of it.

Ofelia stared suspiciously at her brother, her hand on her jutted-out hip. "I don't understand. Did you say something wrong?"

Bless his sister for always having his back and supporting him, but now wasn't the time to get into it. Every instinct in his body told him to go after Lola and demand answers from her. Why was she acting so cold toward him? What did he do to warrant such a response? It couldn't be because he left her six months ago without saying goodbye...could it? They had an agreement and he was following said agreement.

"I'll be right back." Javi said, ignoring the protests from both his sister and Monique. He couldn't hash it out with them right now. He was never one to wait for an answer to show up; he had always been of the mindset that one had to seek answers for themselves. So here he was, seeking the damn answer and hoping it didn't backfire on him.

He found Lola busying herself at a station for extra supplies, trying to tidy up the already impeccable spread. She was actively ignoring him but he didn't understand why she was so angry. He understood that the situation was awkward, but was it that horrible to run into him? Apparently, it was.

"Lola." He spoke her name, and her entire body tensed.

After a few moments, he watched as Lola reluctantly turned around to meet his gaze. Her brows were squeezed tightly together and her lips were pursed together in a tight line. She crossed her arms over her ample chest, pushing together her breasts. Her cleavage was on full display and he did his best to look anywhere but at her chest, no matter how badly the temptation to peek was.

"Lola," he said again, taking her silence as motivation to continue. "I don't know why you're upset with me, but I clearly did something to piss you off. Want to tell me what I did so I can fix it?"

She laughed, her lips forming a cruel smile. "As if you don't know," she spat.

"I really don't," he said through gritted teeth, knowing if he lost his temper it would escalate the situation.

"Right. You are going to stand here and act a fool when your family is five feet away."

"I'm not acting. I legit don't know what you're talking about."

"You're married, Javi!" Her voice was just loud enough that the table nearest to them looked up. The couple gave them reproachful glances before helicoptering over their toddlers again. Lola didn't notice, or didn't care, because she continued on. "And you have two kids. Do they know their dad is a player? Is that what you are teaching your son? I swear men are all the same. All dogs. Only wanting the next shiny thing that walks by. I should cut off your—"

"Lola!" Javi had to raise his voice to be heard over her tangent. She was clearly not happy to be cut off and sent him a reproachful glare. Her anger made sense to him now. It was almost comical that he had not realized how it would have looked like to her from the beginning.

His amused expression only made Lola more fiery with passion. "Oh, don't you look smug now. Just wait until I tell your wife what a bastard you are. She's gorgeous. She'll find better—"

"Lola! Damn girl, I'm not married. She's not my wife." This time Javi was laughing. Not at Lola, but at the situation. He was so used to doing everything with his sister and their kids now, he never stopped and wondered what it looked like to outsiders. Maybe that was why he wasn't getting any dates. Cockblocked by his own sister.

"Ofelia is my sister," he explained, watching Lola's face heat in embarrassment. "The boy is my nephew. The girl is my daughter though, but I swear to you I'm not married and I don't have a girl-friend. I also didn't have those things when we..." He trailed off, trying to find a word for it that was appropriate for their current public setting.

"Fucked," Lola supplied. So much for decency.

"Yeah." He brought his hand to the back of his neck, rubbing out a knot that was forming. "I'm sorry. I didn't realize how it must have looked until you said something."

It wasn't as if he knew Lola was going to be there or had any time to prepare himself for what he was going to do when he saw her, but he hadn't imagined a second meeting with her going like this.

He waited for her to say something, but she chewed on her bottom lip, lost in her own thoughts. He wondered if this was his cue to leave. He took a step back, knowing both Ofelia and Monique were watching the whole exchange. "I should go. It was nice to see you again Lola. I can give Monique some recommendations on contractors for you." Since she most certainly wouldn't be hiring him. That was okay though. She needed to find someone she would be comfortable with.

Javi turned to leave, but he didn't make it two steps before a hand shot out and wrapped its fingers around his wrist, stopping him. He angled his body toward hers, one brow raised in a silent question.

Lola slowly dropped her hand, bringing it back down to her side. "Do you have any availability on Monday?"

Today was Saturday. Even though he wouldn't step back into work until Monday, his day was fairly light and he could squeeze in a visit. "I do in the afternoon."

Lola hesitated and he wondered what was going through her brain right now. He would kill to catch a glimpse of her thoughts. "Then maybe you could stop by Phoenix? Monique was right. I do need someone to help me get it reopened."

"Am I no longer untrustworthy?" he mused, unable to stop himself from teasing her.

Her brown cheeks flushed. "That is...still to be determined, but I don't want to gut you anymore, so I'll take that as a win."

"As will I. Then I'll see you on Monday."

"I'm not saying this is a done deal. I just want to hear your thoughts. I'm also a hard client to please, so don't think this is going to be easy work."

At that, Javi had no doubt. "When it comes to you, Lola, I have a feeling nothing is easy." He winked at her and headed back toward his sister.

# *Lola*

WALKING into Phoenix Books should fill her with excitement and a sense of purpose. And it did. Mostly. But these days, it was depressing more often than not, to walk in and find there was still so much to do before her dream bookstore could ever operate. Could she open it now? Yeah, probably. If she wanted to get sued, that is, and she did not particularly want to go through those legal matters at the moment. Or ever.

No, Lola had to wait until the store was renovated and ready to go. Everything had to be perfect, just the way she liked it. She was certain her former therapist would say she was projecting onto this store because she couldn't achieve perfection in her own life and relationships, but she didn't care. Lola had a vision and she wasn't going to let a single damn person stand in her way.

The smell of burnt coffee hit the air and Lola looked down to see the mug she made was full. She doctored the drinks, knowing Mona took her coffee in the same way she did. "Mona, coffee incoming," she said once she was finished.

Her squirrelly friend took the hot mug and began to pace. Mona was never one to stay still, especially when juicy gossip was about to be spilled. To her friend's credit, she had waited two whole days—a record—for Lola to finally be ready to tell her the truth about Javi.

After seeing Javi at the bakery, Mona transformed into a bloodhound, sniffing around for answers. Answers Lola was just not ready to give. She still needed time to process the fact that she embarrassingly accused him of being a cheater in front of a family with toddlers.

Sure, she was quick to jump to conclusions, but she blamed that on her own history of poor choices in men. Specifically, the one about to marry her sister. She was working on herself, but she still had so much trauma to process through.

She did owe Javi an apology though, and that was the first thing she was going to do when he arrived later. Right now, she had a best friend who would soon walk a hole through her floor with her pacing if she didn't open up about Javi.

"So I do know Javi..." she started off, taking a sip of her coffee. It wasn't the best, but it was hot and would soon give her the dose of energy she needed to get through the day.

"Yeah, no shit!" Mona rolled her eyes but was unable to hide her bursting curiosity. "How? And are we going bitch mode on his ass? Do I need to cancel him? Because I will. He's a damn good handyman, so it would suck to lose him, but chicks before dicks, amirite?"

"So you remember how awful my sister's engagement party was, right?"

Mona scrunched up her face in disgust. "Yeah, you mean the engagement party you didn't know was an engagement party until you arrived?"

"That's the one." She cringed inwardly. It was just supposed to be a family weekend with a nice dinner. She still couldn't quite believe her sister would betray her in such a big way, but Marisol had never ceased to amaze her. "I forgot to mention when I left the party and went back to my hotel, and I didn't go alone."

Mona's eyes went comically wide. "Shut the fuck up. Seriously, shut the fuck up. You did not just tell me you invited a strange man back to your hotel room knowing damn well how unsafe that is."

"I know, I know! But in my defense, I was sad as hell and wanted to forget. Good dick does that, you know? But I was responsible and took a picture to send to you! I just didn't realize it failed to send. Which is infuriating if you think about it. I paid how much money to stay at that fancy-ass hotel and their Wi-Fi is shitty?" She was getting off topic, but she tended to go off on tangents when she got nervous or excited. Or both.

"Fine, fine. Skipping past the part where you could have gotten murdered, are you telling me that the guy you hooked up with was Javier?"

Mona nodded, walking to the other side of the counter so she could sit precariously on a barstool. Precariously because the moment her ass sat down, it sank lower to the ground. She definitely needed new ones to make them more big girl friendly.

"Girl, you can't just drop a bombshell like that and not give me the details. Was he good? Or was he bad, and that's why you were pissed? I need information!" Mona pouted, discarding her untouched coffee mug on the counter to lean over and prepare for the tea she was about to receive.

A ghost of a smile crossed Lola's face. Leave it to Mona to make anything bigger than what it was. But her moment with Javi had been a monumental experience in more ways than one. She couldn't shake him over the last six months, and seeing him again this past weekend brought the full force of that night back to center stage. She didn't think her vibrator had seen that much action in weeks.

"No, I wasn't mad because it was bad. I was mad because I thought the woman he was with was his wife. Turns out it was his sister and his nephew. The girl was his daughter though, but he said there was no girlfriend or wife in his life. Ugh, I felt like such a fool! I always jump to the worst-case scenario. Why is my brain like this?" Her dumb, over-anxious brain.

"First off, your brain is not dumb. You've just been in survival mode for so long and your brain is trying to protect you. And secondly, I feel like that was an easy assumption to make. It looked like one big happy family. Technically they were, just in a different way than you thought."

"He probably thinks I'm the stereotypical crazy Latina girl." Which was a stupid stereotype to even have. Expressing any strong emotion as a brown girl automatically made you "crazy." It was harmful and rooted in racism.

"I doubt that. But let's get back to what's important here. How was he in bed?" Mona grinned, moving closer. "If I liked dick, I'm sure I would be all up on that one. But I prefer the pretty kitties, so I'll live vicariously through you."

Lola snorted. She had known Mona all her life and her bestie had never been interested in boys. Ever. It was only ever Mattea.

"That's the worst part. It was amazing." Mona let out an excited little squeal as Lola continued on. "He was so confident and sure of himself. He didn't shy away or make a single comment about my body that wasn't wanted. He fucking worshipped me, and I've tried so hard not to think about how he blew my mind. How did I put up with Archie's five-second-sex bores for so long?

"Seriously. I don't think I've ever had a man make me come like that. I usually have to spend time getting myself off afterward, but nope. This man is magic in bed. Fucking magic." She finished her spiel only to hear another stack of books fall to the ground behind her. She groaned and turned around to see where the noise came from and wondered what broke now that she had to fix.

Lola didn't get to make a full turn when she spotted him, standing only five feet away. He wore dark jeans with a simple white T-shirt that had seen better days. Her stomach dropped as she moved slowly up to the man's face. Javi was here, and he was smirking at her. She swore she heard Mona turn around to laugh into a book behind her.

*Fucking hell.*

# Lola

## CHAPTER ELEVEN

Now would be the perfect time for the universe to spontaneously combust so Lola would not have to relive this mortifying moment. The damned smirk on Javi's face would be forever etched into her brain. She also wished her best friend wasn't disguising her laughing fit with horrible fake coughs, but this was her life right now and she had to deal with the consequences.

"You're early!" She accused him like a cheater who blamed their infidelity on their spouse arriving home early and foiling their plans. It was the only thing her embarrassed brain thought of.

Javi took his life in his own hands and leaned against the bookshelf. It creaked under his weight but didn't fold like she thought it would. Apparently, even the nosy bookshelves wanted to stay and watch her humiliation.

"I finished a job earlier than expected, so I figured I'd head over here. I'm glad I did."

Ugh, that infuriating, sexy smile was going to be the death of Lola. Seriously, no one had the right to look that damn good and smug at the same time.

"Have you heard of knocking? Or do you frequently break into people's houses and places of work?" she retorted.

"I knocked. Many times. I figured you didn't hear me. I heard talking so I let myself in. I can wait if you want to finish your conversation though. I think you were at the part where no other man has ever made you com—"

"Oh don't get cocky. You broke my dry spell so I'm just thankful you weren't a dud."

She couldn't believe they only had sex once and he still occupied so many of her thoughts. What spell had this man put her under because she wanted none of it. Unsubscribe her from that brujo fuckery this instant.

"And besides, my last boyfriend wasn't stellar in bed so anyone could have beat him in a competition. Not that this was a competition, but if it was, you would receive a participation trophy."

*Stop talking! Stop talking!* Why was that such a hard concept for her brain? Instead, it felt the need to word-vomit unnecessary things.

"You aren't helping the situation, Lo-Lo," Mona whispered from behind her, loud enough for Javi to hear. "Perhaps, and I say this with all the love in my heart, shut up?"

Yup, that was what she was going to do. Shut up before she dug herself deeper into a hole. She didn't need Javi to know any more about her pathetic love life and lack of orgasms.

For a second, Javi looked as if he wanted to tease her more, if his cocky smirk was any indication. If he actually apologized for her lack of completion in the bedroom, she would simply roll over and die. It had been a good run, but there was no coming back from a blow like that.

Thankfully, Javi seemed to have noticed her discomfort and instead said, "I'll knock next time."

"Good." That was good. It would have saved her from this embarrassment. "So, we should get started?" she added after, hoping to steer the conversation back to the reason he was here in the first place.

Javi pushed himself off the bookshelf, which gave another groan of protest as he stepped forward, doing his best to tiptoe through the piles of books. That was another thing she needed to get around to doing: taking inventory. Mrs. Sanderson had an archaic way of cataloging books, which consisted of a pen and journal. Lola needed to bring this bookstore into the twenty-first century and put the books onto a database. Those were things she could worry about later.

"Let's start with you taking me through the story and telling me your vision," Javi suggested, stopping in front of her. She had to tilt her head up to get a better look at him. He was so tall. Lola wasn't short. She was 5'8". Having been the tallest girl most of her school life and well into adulthood, she couldn't help but find guys who towered over her attractive. She loved her short kings too, they just didn't typically love plus-size women, in her experience.

"That means walk him around the story, Lo-Lo. Don't stare at him and salivate," Mona unhelpfully supplied from behind her. She made a mental note to kill her later. Or tell on her to Mattea. She was unsure which one would be worse.

Lola—who was most definitely not staring—sidestepped away from Javi. She needed to channel the confident girl she had been when she met him the first time. That girl was still in her somewhere and didn't need alcohol to bring her out. She puffed out her chest some, thinking good posture might help, but in reality it looked like she was presenting her tits to him.

"So I guess we can start here. I want a small coffee area for my patrons. Nothing too fancy, but a quiet place to read and enjoy their drinks," Lola began, showing off the pitiful counter area. It wasn't much to look at now, but in time it would be a cozy oasis for readers.

She then led Javi around. Once she started talking about Phoenix Books, she couldn't stop. She wanted everyone to see the vision she had. She told him how she wanted custom-built book-cases, all complete with LED lights built in to add an extra layer of pizzazz. She did not care how extra it was and that it did not serve any other purpose besides pleasing her; she wanted it.

She also wanted to rip up the floors and put in sturdy wood panels. The current wood flooring was decent, but it was long overdue for a face-lift. Along with updating the various lights around the room. Was a chandelier necessary to have in the center of the store? Absolutely not and that made her want it all the more.

Then there were small electrical and water issues she wanted to make sure they addressed before opening. Lola did not want any surprises happening on reopening day.

By the time she finished showing him around, an hour had passed and her throat was dry from overuse. She desperately wished she didn't forget her bejeweled tumbler on her kitchen table.

Once they arrived back at the makeshift cafe area, Lola finally turned to Javi who had remained silent throughout the journey, only speaking up to ask the occasional question or to clarify her vision.

"So," Lola rocked on her heels, trying to hide her nervousness. She didn't know if she could take more bad news. She didn't mind a long time for construction, she just didn't like the waitlist she was put on or the flat-out refusal because she was too needy. "Do you think you can do it? What would the timeline be?"

Lola all but held her breath, watching Javi's face with the eye of a detective on his final case. She noticed the way he scrunched his lips to the side while he was deep in thought and the way his eyes bounced across the room, taking every one of her demands in.

"Well…" he started and stopped.

That one word alone made Lola's stomach drop. Javi was about to turn her down. She braced herself for the hurt and rejection that would surely follow.

## CHAPTER TWELVE

WHEN LOLA SPOKE about her store, her entire demeanor changed. She exuded confidence and Javi easily sensed the budding small business owner within her. She would be a force to be reckoned with and Javi pitied the bastards who stood in her way.

He didn't speak much during the tour. He was far too enamored with her to do much talking and any questions he had were usually answered with her next sentence. He understood why certain contractors would shy away from taking a job like this. It was time-consuming and relied heavily on attention to small details. There was a fair amount of electrical work to be done too, and finding an electrician with open availability was as easy as finding a unicorn in the wild.

Luckily for Lola, Javi was licensed and had a hardworking group he trusted to call upon when he needed the extra hands. Which he would. He couldn't do the entire makeover by himself. There were many moving pieces involved and Javi wanted to give Lola what she wanted.

Except what she wanted would come at a price. A steep fucking price.

He didn't want to let her down. She was bouncing on the

balls of her feet like an excited child about to open their birthday present.

"Well…" he started and that single word wiped the smile off her face. He instantly wanted to take it back, but he didn't want to lie to her either. "This is going to cost you a lot."

The smallest glimmer shimmered in her eyes once again and she perked up at the news. "Okay, cost I can do. That's not a problem."

"It's going to be a lot, Lola."

"And like I said, Javi, that's not going to be a problem."

Damn. What was it like to be so confident in your financial well-being to not even blink when a contractor said a renovation is going to cost you? Good for her for living comfortably, but a small nasty part of him envied her nonchalance.

What did it feel like not having to wonder or stress about paying next month's bills? Or being able to afford new toys for his daughter without having to buy them secondhand? He knew they were lucky to have a sturdy roof over their head and hot meals on the table, but he often wished he could splurge just a little bit.

"I'm more curious about the timeline. How long do I have to wait for you to get started and how long will the reno take? Oh, I should probably also know if you're taking the job." Lola bit her lip, preparing for his answer.

He wanted to suck her lip into his mouth and ease her worry. To pull her into his arms and feel the warmth of her curves against his body. He wanted a lot of things he couldn't—and shouldn't—have.

"A project like this will take me around four to six weeks with my full team. If you are willing to work with me on unusual hours, I can start as early as next week." Seeing as how this job would be the first he took on independently, he would have to work around his crew's hours until he could figure out the times that worked best for everyone. Yet, he could still start work on getting the ball rolling if she was willing to agree to later times.

Lola's wide eyes and slightly agape mouth made him pause.

She stared at him like she was seeing double. He had to look to his sides to make sure he didn't spontaneously grow a third arm. Before he could ask her what was wrong, Lola threw herself at Javi, wrapping her arms around his torso and burying her head into his chest.

He swayed from the sudden impact but soon righted himself. His body acted on instinct as he wrapped his strong arms around her, pulling her flush against his skin. He rested his head atop hers, taking in the sweet floral smell of her shampoo. It fit her.

The way he held on to her, the position of his chin atop her head, and the way that neither of them seemed ready to let go, was far from the professional demeanor he promised to have. But then he heard them talking about their night together and hearing how amazing it was for her, sent pangs of longing through his body. He felt the same way and it was good to know it hadn't been one-sided.

Javi knew he should let go. He had been holding on to her for too long, but it wasn't as if she was in a hurry to pull back either. It was like she needed this hug as much as he did.

A loud cough from someone pretending to clear their throat soon broke the moment between them. Lola snapped away, turning to see Monique smirking at them from the counter. Javi forgot she was there and he couldn't help but wonder what would have happened if she wasn't. How long would they have stayed locked together?

Lola wrapped her arms around herself like she wanted to preserve the warmth shared between them. "Sorry," she murmured and he wanted to tell her to never apologize for hugging him, but she quickly moved on. If she wanted to pretend that she felt nothing when they touched, he'd allow her. For now.

"I'm so excited," she admitted. "I don't care if the hours you need to work are from midnight to 3 a.m., I'll be here. You don't understand how much this means to me. I've been trying for weeks to try and get someone to take on this project, but they kept falling through. Seriously, Javi, I could cry right now."

"But you won't," Monique piped up from the back, moving away from the counter to stand next to her friend. "So what's the next step?"

"I'll need to come back to take measurements and inventory. Then I can give you a better idea of the timeline and pricing. I also need to check with my crew and see what their availability is." Most of his guys he found through working on different projects and often took extra jobs on the side, like him. They were pretty eager to work on new jobs, especially the longer and more profitable ones.

The woman nodded and then Monique said, "Give us one moment." Instead of leaving, they turned around and discussed something in hushed whispers. He stood behind them awkwardly, pretending like he didn't hear them whispering about him. Which was surprisingly easy because he only caught every other word they said.

After a few minutes, both women turned around again to face him. Lola was all smiles and back to bouncing on the balls of her feet, while Monique looked more subdued but equally excited.

"I'm ready to move forward with this. Whatever you need, I'm here for." Lola said, unable to hide her enthusiasm which Javi thought was cute.

"Is there anything else I can help you with? Any questions you have about the process?" Of course, he would go over everything with her tomorrow after he got a better understanding of the layout and his part in this, but he was happy to try and answer anything she might have questions about now.

Lola shook her head no, but Monique spoke up. "Actually, I do," she said. Javi hadn't expected her to speak up and judging by the looks of it, neither did Lola. She raised a perfect brow at her friend which in return was greeted by a wicked grin. "How do you feel about weddings, Javier?"

A look of confusion washed over his face and Javi was rendered speechless. "Come again?"

"Weddings," Monique said like it was the most natural thing

to say when talking about renovating a bookstore. Like she hadn't just stunned two people into silence with her wildly off-topic question.

With a roll of her eyes, she said, "Lola needs a date for an upcoming wedding. What do you say?"

*What the actual fuck?*

Lola

## CHAPTER THIRTEEN

HER BRAIN WAS STILL TRYING to process the fuckery that came out of Mona's mouth. She had not brought up the wedding to her best friend since she got the invitation in the mail a few days ago. The last thing she said about the wedding was she planned on going because not going would be so much worse. She most definitely didn't mention anything about needing a date.

She wanted one, of course, but she didn't *need* one.

"She has a plus one, and knowing her family, everything is paid for. So it would be like a free vacation for you."

"Mona, enough!" Lola couldn't believe her ears. She couldn't look at Javi and see the horrified look she was sure he was wearing. "We need to talk."

"But—"

"Now!" Her words came out forceful and she never spoke to Mona like this. Not once in their twenty-plus years of friendship, but then again her friend had never pushed her this far before.

She didn't wait for Javi or Mona to say anything. She grabbed her best friend by the wrist and pulled her toward the back of the store, well out of earshot of Javi. Hell, she wouldn't be surprised if he decided to make a run for it while they were preoccupied.

"What the actual fuck, Mona?" Lola hissed once they were

alone. She dropped her friend's wrist and settled her hands on her hips, keeping them occupied so they didn't strangle her best friend like she wanted to.

Mona had the audacity to look puzzled. "What? Why are you so angry?"

Why was she so angry? Why *wouldn't* she be so angry right now? "I have every right to be angry with you. What the hell do you think you are doing? What possessed you to think to ask Javi to be my date? In case you forgot, Mona, he is here to remodel my bookstore. That's it."

"Easy. Because Javi is hot and clearly into you, whether you want to see it or not. And I know you, Lo-Lo. I know you don't want to go to your sister's wedding alone. Mattea and I could go, sure, but it's not the same as bringing a date."

"It was one night! He's my contractor, nothing else."

"You obviously have chemistry with him. Who the fuck cares if he is working for you. He can work for you and be your date. Those things aren't mutually exclusive."

Lola had to take a deep breath because she was getting heated. Not just out of anger, but out of embarrassment. How sad was it that she couldn't deal with her own damn love life and find a date to this wedding? She probably looked pathetic and incompetent to Javi, having her best friend ask on her behalf.

She was caught off guard just as much as he was. God, she hoped he didn't think she lured him here just to ask if he would be her date. She didn't need him to think she was loca and for him to stay away from her. She needed him to take this job. Javi was her best bet to open her shop soon.

But maybe if he wanted to also be her date...

No. Nope. She shut down that way of thinking. Why was she even entertaining the idea? It was so unbelievable and unattainable, that she could not afford to put stock into the idea.

"Lo-Lo." Mona's calm voice wrapped around Lola like a soft embrace. She was shaking and hadn't noticed until Mona placed her hands atop Lola's shoulders. It helped center her and from slipping into more gray areas of uncertainty.

"First off, I need you to breathe," she said in a soothing voice. Lola took a deep breath in and slowly exhaled. "Good. Just like that. Now, I need you to look at me when I talk to you. Don't interrupt, just listen. Okay?"

Lola's brown eyes fluttered upward until she was staring into Mona's dark orbs. "Okay," she said softly, afraid of talking too loudly in case Javi was listening.

"I'm sorry I went for it without talking to you first. That was probably not the best way to ask him. But I'm not sorry for playing your wingwoman. This wedding is going to be hard for you and I think you deserve to have some arm candy like Javi. He would be a good buffer between you and your family. I want you to have one person on your side there. I know what a pain your family is and you deserve to have a good time at an otherwise shitty event."

So much anxiety surrounded this wedding. Mona was right. She didn't want to go alone. She didn't even want to go at all, but she wanted to face her mother's wrath even less. Perhaps that made her a coward. The only person she was marginally excited to see was her father. He had always loved her in his own way and his biggest fault was his complacency in their family dynamics. Besides that, he had always been good to her and provided her with money to chase her dreams of opening a bookshop, no questions asked.

A small part of her could picture Javi as her date to the wedding. The way he would look in a tux churned something low in her belly. To be able to spend a week with him all to herself made her squeeze her legs together in temptation. It surprised her how much she wanted that.

Lola let out a half sigh and half groan. "This is a wild idea. He's not going to go with it." If he was even still here. And did she even want to go along with Mona's ridiculous plan? There was no way this could end well.

"It's a tad unusual." Mona shrugged like she was commenting on shorts in the winter rather than a week-long wedding date with a guy she had a one-night stand with. "But I don't think it's such a far-fetched idea. Make it worth his while. Offer him extra money."

"Now you want me to pay for the date? Like an escort service?" Lola asked incredulously.

"Think of it as more of a bonus. Plus, doesn't he have a daughter? I'm sure he could use the extra money as a single dad. Kids are expensive. I've been trying to tell Mattea that forever, but she is insistent on having kids soon."

"Yeah, you'd both make good mamas," Lola said distractedly as she churned the idea around in her head. Of the wedding, not Mona being a mother.

She couldn't believe she was actually considering it. There was no doubt in her mind that she would love to spend more time with Javi in any capacity, but something like this?

But also, what was holding her back? She was a proud, sexy, Mexican American woman who deserved a little fun. Fear had held her back long enough and she was tired of missing opportunities to appease people who didn't give a damn about her in any way that mattered.

"Fuck. I think I'm going to do it," she said at last.

Mona did a weird little excited dance before pulling Lola in for a smothering hug. "Fuck yeah, bitch! Go get him. I'm cheering you on from right here," she said and gave Lola a push forward.

That small push was what she needed to get her feet moving. She needed to do this now while she still had some confidence within her. She prayed to God that Javi hadn't run out, though she wouldn't have blamed him if he did.

When she rounded the corner, escaping the labyrinth of books and scattered pages, Javi was right where they left him with his hands in his pockets. He was pacing quietly and hadn't yet noticed her return.

"Javi?" Her voice sounded small, even to her own ears, but it had the desired effect. Javi stopped his pacing and looked at her. She felt naked under his scrutinizing gaze. The earlier bravado was fading and she didn't want to lose her nerve. "I wanted to talk to you about the wedding—"

"I accept," came his reply before she had the chance to finish. He didn't even know what he was agreeing to and Lola swore she misheard him. But no, he soon repeated what he said, leaving her both stunned and another emotion she couldn't quite place. "I'll be your date, if you'll have me."

# Javi

## CHAPTER FOURTEEN

THE SMELL of homemade tortillas permeated the air, which meant breakfast wasn't far off. His mouth salivated at the thought of refried beans and fried papas tossed with scrambled eggs and sausage. Freshly made salsa would already be placed on the table, waiting to greet him as he walked into his sister's kitchen.

Camilia's tiny hand wiggled out of his and she made a break for it. "Tía Ofi!" she screamed, running into his sister's large kitchen. Before Camilia could reach Ofelia, her husband, Maverick, swooped in and picked her up. Camilia giggled, thrashing around to try and escape the man's grasp as he peppered her little cheeks with teasing kisses and tickled her sides.

"Good morning, my loves!" Ofelia dusted the flour from the tortillas off on her apron that once belonged to their mother. She moved to hug Javi and he—not for the first time—thought about how much he loved having his sister close by. Camilia was a great tía to his daughter and Maverick was proving to be a great tío and father. He was happy for the little family they created and even happier he could experience parenthood with his sister.

"Thank you again for watching, Camilia. I owe you." He said once he released his sister from the hug. He looked down at his dark clothing to find some of the flour from Ofelia lingering on his clothes and absentmindedly wiped it off.

"Nonsense. I want all the time with my sweet Camilia. She's growing too fast, you know."

Oh, how he knew it. Just last week he was wrestling with a rambunctious toddler and now all of a sudden he had a kinder-gartner? He desperately wanted time to stand still, but he also loved watching his princesa grow up and look more like her mother every day. It was a beautiful reminder that Estella was still partly with him.

"How's papá?" Ofelia turned her back to him, grabbing a plate from the cupboard to dish up breakfast for him before he left. No use in telling his sister he was going to a coffee shop and would undoubtedly eat something there, but according to Ofelia, a pastry was not a suitable breakfast item. He was inclined to agree with her.

"He's fine. I thought I would give him a bit of a break this morning." His father was good to watch Camilia in a pinch, but he was getting older and he wanted to respect his father's time. Ofelia loved having his daughter over, so leaving her with his sister was never an issue. He figured she was making up for lost time.

Ofelia handed him a bowl and shooed him over to the table where Arturo sat in his highchair, eggs and ketchup all over his face. He had bits of tortilla stuck in his hair as well. "Mijo, so messy." Javi laughed and ruffled his hair.

"He gets that from me." Maverick beamed, placing a squirming Camilia down in the available seat next to her primo. Fatherhood looked good on Maverick. He picked up his son and whisked him away, probably to clean him up.

Soon another plate of food was placed down in front of Camilia and Ofelia sat down in the empty spot next to her. "So, what are you up to this morning?"

Right. So he had not exactly told his sister why he needed her to watch Camilia this morning because he was still trying to make sense of it all. He didn't know if he was foolish or just plain dumb. Who in their right mind would agree to a whole wedding and be the date of a woman he barely knew and only slept with once?

Lola had requested they meet today to go over the finer details of their agreement. He suspected she meant their wedding date agreement, though he supposed it could also mean her bookstore renovation. Speaking of which, it was unclear if he was still hired on as her lead contractor. He needed to make sure of that.

Ofelia continued to stare at him expectantly, waiting for his answer. He didn't make it a habit to withhold information from her, but he figured it wouldn't hurt in this situation. Soon he would tell Ofelia everything, but he needed to figure out what he agreed to first. No use in getting her worked up for no reason.

"I'm meeting with a client about a remodel. This would be my first big renovation outside my current employer, so I want to make sure it all goes well," he lied easily enough.

The warm smile Ofelia sent him sent pangs of guilt through his body. He needed to remind himself he wasn't lying to her...he just wasn't ready to give her the full truth yet. "Oh, Javi, that's wonderful. You have to tell me how it goes," she said in between bites of her breakfast.

He most certainly would tell her how it went and come clean about everything, in time. He wanted today to provide clarity to something he agreed to without any hesitation. The idea of a sad Lola alone at a wedding was enough to drive him into a fit of rage. She didn't deserve such torture.

Scarfing down his sister's breakfast—which was much better than his father could ever make, but Javi would be damned if he ever told his old man that—he cleared his plate and placed it in the sink, running water in it. "I'll text you when I'm on my way."

"Mav wanted to take Arturo down to the field today so he can see where Daddy works, so we might be there depending on when you're done. If we are, I'll drop her off at your house once we're done."

"We get to see tío's baseball field?" Camilia's head snapped up, bits of egg hanging off her lower lip.

Ofelia chuckled and took a napkin to clean her face. "We do. And I heard the mascot will even be there." Her words were met with more cheers. She would have way more fun with her tía and tío than she would hanging out in the house with her abuelo.

"Thank you again, Ofi." Javi came over to kiss his sister's temple and then gave Camilia a giant hug. She squirmed in his arms but hugged him back. He hoped she would never be too big to hug her daddy. "Be good, princesa. Papá will take you for ice cream later." Ice cream always made him the coolest dad and he will rue the day the simple gesture no longer works its magic.

"Good luck. Happy for you, li'l brother," Ofelia called out to him. He needed all the luck he could get.

THE COFFEE SHOP was surprisingly empty for a weekend morning. Typically, the line was out the door and every table and available service was occupied by a college student or a professional-looking person conducting work from their personal laptop.

Today only a few of the tables were occupied, mostly by friend groups catching up. The line only extended out to two people and for once Javi heard the soft jazz instrumental music playing. Off to the corner, sitting by herself with a journal, two large mugs, and several pens laid out in front of her, was Lola.

She hadn't noticed him yet, which allowed him time to stare without repercussions. Today she wore her curly hair in a half-up, half-down style with little strands framing her face. She wore a pair of blue jeans that looked as if they were painted on her body, hugging her thick thighs and soft belly perfectly. She wore a white button blouse that tied in the front, right under her breasts, exposing the black bodysuit underneath. She was effortlessly beautiful and Javi wanted to take in every inch of her.

He couldn't deny that Lola's physical appearance was the first thing that attracted him to her, but he was starting to learn more about this outspoken businesswoman and her passions. Each facet of her personality she revealed to him left Javi yearning for more.

Lola must have felt him staring, because she soon raised her head from looking down at her journal and spotted Javi. She offered him a tight smile and gestured to the chair in front of her.

"I wasn't sure what you liked, so I ordered you coffee," she said in a way of greeting once he took the seat in front of her. Javi wasn't much of a coffee drinker, but he also didn't mind the taste.

"Thank you."

"Yeah, not a problem," she said before they lapsed into an awkward silence. He knew she was thinking the same thing he was and they would have to address the wedding date sooner or later.

When he left the bookstore the other day after agreeing to her crazy plan, they shared no more words about the matter and she promised she would call him to set up the details soon. He still couldn't believe he agreed to be her date. What possessed him to willingly put himself in a situation that could compromise their working relationship? He couldn't deny the allure of a week with Lola.

After a few days went by and he had yet to hear from her about the wedding or bookstore renovation, Javi began to worry that he fucked up. Until she called yesterday out of the blue and asked to meet him at the coffee shop.

"We should—"

"I want—"

They both spoke at once, laughing nervously, but it eased some of the tension away. "So, I guess I'll start," Lola said, placing both hands atop her journal. He couldn't see much underneath her arms, but he caught a few words and her feminine hand-writing.

"I wanted to give you an out before we take this thing any further. I realize how inappropriate the situation was and under-stand if you are uncomfortable moving forward." Lola looked up at him through heavy lashes. He saw how stressed she was over this whole conversation and he wanted to alleviate that.

"I don't want an out. I stand by what I said. If you'll have me, I'd love to be your date to this wedding." He had no idea whose wedding this was or where it would be held, but he figured those details would be coming soon.

"Well, in that case." Lola grabbed a sparkly pink pen with a fuzzy pom at the top of it and turned to a blank page in her journal. "We need to discuss ground rules."

*Lola*

CHAPTER FIFTEEN

A WELL-PLANNED checklist was Lola's idea of a good time. To-do lists, grocery lists, book lists...there were endless possibilities and it kept her tasks manageable and organized. With so much of her life in the hands of others and her unable to hold the reins, Lola desperately wanted some semblance of power back.

Hence, the checklist.

"So I think we should start with compensation," she said, ignoring Javi's cute, confused face. His brow furrowed and he scrunched up his nose as if deep in thought. She had not been prepared to see him looking all sexy in his denim jeans and long-sleeved white shirt. He made it hard to concentrate while the fabric pulled taut over the muscles he hid underneath.

She had practiced what she was going to say with Mona last night, probably a million times before her friend threatened to call the cops on her for torture.

"I would like to hire you as both my contractor and my date for my sister's wedding," she started, giving Javi a tiny insight into the wedding. She wasn't ready to give him all the details yet, though they would come in due time. "I would like to offer you two hundred thousand dollars. One hundred thousand to one hundred and twenty thousand going into my shop and labor for

451

your workers, and the rest to you for all the trouble I'm causing you. I'll pay you half now and the rest after the wedding."

Javi completely short-circuited. Was he breathing? He had to be breathing. His eyes were the size of saucers, staring unblinkingly at her. His mouth opened and closed but no words came out, none that were coherent anyway. Not even his chest rose and fell with his breathing. Had she successfully broken the man?

"Javi? You good?" She thought about poking him to make sure he was still with her, but felt like that might send him overboard, so she kept her fingers to herself.

"Lola. I—you can't—you—I…" he babbled, his brain going faster than his mouth. She had expected some pushback because it was a lot of damn money. Enough to change a person's financial situation for a while.

"I can, actually," she said as he continued to sputter. "My father gave me access to a good sum of money to invest in my new business. It is more money than I will ever need and I can only use it for work-related purposes. Granted, my father probably didn't think about having my contractor escort me to my sister's wedding as work-related expenses, but here we are. The money is yours, and I'm prepared to give you half now to start on the renovations, and the other half at the end of our deal. Before you say no or try a bullshit attempt at telling me how I should spend my money, you should know that once my mind is made up, I rarely ever change it."

Mona told her she needed to be firm. There was no place for a wishy-washy attitude when it came to this amount of money. It was also important that both parties knew where they stood.

"Please say something. I need to know I'm not wasting either of our time. If you don't want to go through with the date, I understand and still want to offer you the renovation job." Lola's leg began to shake, a nervous habit she picked up in childhood that always made her mother smack her leg to keep from bouncing.

Javi miraculously learned to speak again and put her out of

her misery. "That's a lot of fucking money, preciosa. I should turn it down because I'm getting the far better deal. You don't get much out of this."

Lola snorted, trying not to conjure up memories of the last time he called her preciosa. The way it lit a fire deep inside her, made her wish she could hear him whisper it in her ear.

She quickly shooed those thoughts away. "Don't I, though? I get my dream bookstore and I don't have to lift a finger. I also get saved from endless discussions with my family about how if I only ate more salads and less burgers and exercised every once in a while, I would have a man. The crazy thing is, I don't even like burgers and I do yoga every day!"

Javi rolled his sleeves up, exposing more of his toned arms. His body stiffened and his arms flexed. When she met his gaze again, his lips were pressed together in a thin line, eyes narrowed. "They comment on your weight?"

"I mean, yeah. Mostly my mom. My sister will give back-handed compliments, but my mother instigates it." She shrugged like it was no big deal since she had been living like this her entire life. It was just one of her mother's many quirks.

"And you're fine with excusing her behavior?"

The question was so unexpected and frankly uncalled for that it stunned her, taking her longer to compose her thoughts. "Well of course I'm not okay with it. It's not like I ask my mom to comment on my weight. I'm tired of fighting back. After you've lived with it your entire life, you become desensitized."

There was no mistaking her anger, and Javi had the decency to look thoroughly reprimanded. "Right. Sorry. I just don't like that someone makes you feel inferior about one of the most beautiful parts of you."

*Fucking swoon.*

What person didn't like being told they were beautiful every now and again? To feel desired and cherished. It wasn't a bad thing to want someone to lust for her body and she wouldn't feel ashamed in thinking so.

"You're forgiven, but now you know just a fraction of what I'm up against. Your presence is going to be a big help. Honestly, when you meet my family, you'll feel cheated out of more money. I assure you."

Javi still didn't look comfortable and she wished she could read his thoughts. She wanted to know what was going through his mind and try to help ease his worry. She would never ask him, but she didn't know how much he made and with a daughter, she imagined the bills added up. Being a single dad was a full-time job, and an expensive one, so if this could help him, she wanted to make it happen.

Lola didn't pressure him. She let him stew in his own thoughts as she marked compensation off her checklist. The next thing she wanted to talk about was the wedding dates. She guessed Javi would have to make arrangements for his daughter and she wondered if that was going to be a problem. A small part of her also felt guilty for stealing time away from the girl when his time seemed limited as it was.

"The wedding is three weeks away," she said, looking up at him to gauge his reaction. If he was surprised by the sudden date, Javi didn't show it. "It's being held in Colorado, but airfare, hotel rooms, and most meals will be provided. I booked us separate rooms for obvious reasons. We are going to be there for a week, is that going to be a problem for you with your daughter?"

Javi shook his head once. "No. Camilia will be in school most of the time and between my sister and father, she will be in good hands."

She placed another check in the box and looked at her last topic of discussion. "As far as renovation goes, we can start on your schedule. Mona is going to be helping out a lot so either one of us will be in the shop with you to answer questions or to address whatever you need from us. I'm not good with last-minute plans, but I know there are tons of them in construction, so I'll try to remain as level-headed as possible. This is my apology in advance if I get snippy. It's not you."

There was nothing left for her to say. She had gone over the most important parts of her plan and later—if he agreed—they would have to make a list of things that were appropriate to do as a fake dating couple and things they weren't comfortable with. She didn't have a lot on the not-comfortable list for them, but she suspected sex should be off the table for obvious reasons.

"So, what do you say? Do you agree to this crazy plan or would you rather not associate with my family drama? Totally understandable if you want no part in it. This is so out of pocket. It's not like—"

"Lola, I'm going to need you to calm down and take a breath for me. Can you do that?" Javi grinned, reaching out a hand to place over hers.

She listened, taking in a deep breath and thankful that he had the decency to cut her off before she could babble on more.

"I already agreed to this and I'm not backing out of it. But…I do have one stipulation." That caught her attention and she raised a brow, gesturing for him to go on. "I want to take you out on a date first."

The laugh that left her lips was involuntary and way too high-pitched. "You don't have to do that."

"No, I don't have to. I want to. Think of it as a trial run before the big day. Don't you think we should get to know one another before we pretend we are madly in love in front of your parents?"

"Well, no one said anything about being madly in love." She blushed, but he had a point. They needed to know the basics about one another so they didn't come across as complete frauds. She should at least know his favorite color before presenting him in front of her parents. "Fine, I agree to a date. When and where."

The smirk that crossed his face was nothing short of amused. "You and me, preciosa. I'm taking you to bingo."

"What the fuck. Are we ninety years old? How about you pick me up from my retirement home and maybe I can charm the nurse into sneaking you back into my room I share with Agnes?

The three of us can knit and talk about the good old days before the war."

"You have jokes." Javi took her teasing in stride. "But you are missing out and I would hate for you to have never experienced the adrenaline rush of your first bingo. Do we have a deal?"

This man was odd and damn her if she didn't find that extremely attractive. "We have a deal." She held out her hand to shake, but Javi took it and pulled her hand to his lips, giving it a gentle kiss. This man was going to be the death of her and their deal had barely begun.

*Javi*

CHAPTER SIXTEEN

Two hundred thousand dollars was a lot of fucking money. He had the inkling suspicion that Lola was comfortable financially, but he had *no* idea just how comfortable she was. He not only had more than an ample budget for her renovation, but enough money to catch up on bills, pay Camilia's cheerleading fees in advance, and get his baby girl new clothes and toys.

Yet he still could not help but feel guilty each time he thought about taking the money. Before he left the coffee shop that day, Lola had handed him a crisp check for the amount of one hundred thousand dollars to get started on the bookstore. It still lay atop his nightstand, tucked under the lamp as he grappled with his conscience.

A few days after their coffee shop meeting, Javi had visited Phoenix Books to take measurements and start prepping for renovation. That meant packing up the books and leftover furniture to clear out a workable place for him and his team. There was only one problem: he didn't have a sitter for Camilia. His sister left to accompany Maverick to one of his games and his father was visiting with old friends in town for the day.

He hoped it didn't seem unprofessional showing up to Phoenix with his daughter at his side, equipped with a bag of

457

activities. Today was a teacher planning day, meaning no school for kids. That left Javi with no other option but to bring Camilia along. Lola had noticed Camilia immediately because how could she not? Javi felt his body heat with embarrassment. "Sorry. I didn't have any childcare."

But Lola waved off his excuse and at first, he thought she would tell him to leave, but then she moved and crouched down in front of Camilia with a friendly smile. "Want to help me sort books? I may or may not have candy. We can also read some of them if you like."

Camilia's eyes grew wide at the mention of candy and followed Lola toward the back of the store, disregarding Javi altogether. He didn't know if he should be insulted or impressed that Lola jumped into watching his daughter while he worked and how easily Camilia left him. He went with the latter.

After several hours of clutter removal, Javi finished for the day. He followed the two voices he heard from the back and found his daughter and Lola neck-deep in books. Her hair was tied back in a messy bun with strands hanging out in all directions. The look of sheer concentration on Lola's face—eyes squinted, nose scrunched, and lips pursed—was enough to give Javi pause. He didn't know how he was going to survive the renovation and wedding with her looking good enough to eat, but he would find a way.

Somehow.

"I'm sorry to interrupt, but I'm all done for today," he had called into her office, both girls jumped at his silent entrance.

Camilia made a sound of protest. "But papá, we were just getting to the good part!"

Before he could answer, Lola held out the book to her. "Here. I have another copy and maybe your papá can read this to you tonight."

"Really?" The excitement in his daughter's expression warmed his heart.

"Really. I have an extra copy and I think this one needs to go home with you."

"Thank you, Ms. Lola!" Camilia jumped up and gave Lola a hug. She seemed surprised by this, but Javi watched as she relaxed her body and hugged back. "I'll go put it in my backpack right now!" She giggled and rushed out of the room.

Once alone, Javi took a step closer to lean against the doorframe. "Thank you for entertaining her. I hope she wasn't too much trouble."

"Not at all. Actually, she helped me sort all the children's books, so she was a great help. She earned her prize."

They fell into a natural silence, Javi in awe of how comfortable his daughter was around Lola. From the looks of it, Lola had seemed to enjoy their time together too.

Finally noticing him staring, Lola cleared her throat. "So, I'll see you next week then?"

"No," he said, causing her to frown. "You'll see me Saturday when I take you out on our date."

"Are you seriously going to take me to bingo?"

People slept on bingo and she would understand that soon. He winked. "Seriously." And left without another word. He took Camilia's hand and loaded her into his truck.

He spent the next two days with Camilia, taking her to a park and ice cream after. The distraction helped keep his mind occupied and eased the dad guilt of leaving her for a few hours tonight as he took Lola out on a date that wasn't really a date. Granted, she would be asleep and not even realize he was gone, but still. Being her only living parent, Javi took her safety and happiness into consideration at all times.

Thankfully his papá agreed to babysit and not even an hour ago the two of them waddled with blanket capes around their shoulders to Camilia's room to watch *Beauty and the Beast* for the millionth time. Both of them would be asleep before the credits rolled, snoring peacefully.

Javi needed to get his ass ready and stop thinking about all this damn guilt he was carrying around like a hard hat. His only concern should be what the best shirt was to wear on his non-date date.

Javi thought back to his sister's first date with Maverick. She had called him on the phone and he had to sit for hours, alongside her best friend Willow, to decide on the outfit Ofelia would wear. He would like to think he wasn't that obsessive over his choices, but after the third shirt he discarded with the others, he was starting to worry.

After a solid five minutes of staring into his unorganized closet in hopes that something would jump out at him, Javi settled on a maroon crew neck and his only pair of non-work jeans. After another ten minutes in the bathroom, he was ready to go.

It felt weird not picking Lola up, but she requested they drive separately. She said she liked having her own vehicle in case of emergencies, which he understood so he made sure to give her the address. Thinking of Lola waiting for him at an unfamiliar place made him leave the house twenty minutes earlier than he anticipated, but he'd be damned if she showed up alone.

The bingo parlor was downtown, a few blocks away from Phoenix. Finding it wouldn't be a problem, but rather like anything downtown, parking was a complete nightmare. Luckily there was a garage right across the street to accommodate the various entertainment buildings downtown. Javi parked his truck on the second floor, noting the various open spots for Lola. Then made his way across the street and waited just outside the parlor.

He had been skeptical about it at first until one of his work buddies dragged him here a few years ago. There was a large bar that served beers, cocktails, and wine, as well as a rather impressive menu of street tacos. He remembered dragging Ofelia here a few times after to get her to experience bingo like it should be played. Admittedly, he knew bingo was an odd choice unless you were a ninety-nine-year-old grandpa.

Inside would feel like a small fiesta predominantly full of locals from various Latine cultures. Cumbia music played softly in the background and Javi felt at peace here. Like he belonged. The last thing he wanted to do was walk into a white-dominated bar and get looks because he didn't fit into their perfect little mold.

He hoped Lola felt comfortable too and that he didn't make a mistake bringing her here.

Not even five minutes later, she arrived. Lola was in a black dress and red heels, her hips swayed with each step she took closer to him. Her sweet red lips turned into a shy smile when she saw him. "I think I'm a little overdressed."

Her black dress—he was starting to think black was her favorite color to wear—was skintight, accentuating her curves. She wore her hair down in loose curls. She was beauty incarnate, and Javi felt like a dog, salivating after a particularly juicy steak. He didn't feel worthy enough to be in her presence, but he was damn glad he was.

"No, you look perfect." The words fell from his lips like freely given secrets. The deepening red tint to her cheeks made him obnoxiously happy to know he had made her smile like that. Not another man. *Him.*

"So, bingo. Care to explain why? I don't think I've ever played bingo as an adult," she said, looking up at the building with the flashing neon lights. The parlor itself wasn't much to look at, but the ambiance and food more than made up for it.

"It's easier to show you." Javi offered his arm to her. Lola did not even hesitate as she looped her arm through his.

He opened the door and walked them to the counter where he purchased their bingo cards and markers. The man told them the next round of games would happen in thirty minutes, giving them enough time to get their food and drink.

The bingo man gestured for them to walk inside where a lively crowd had formed. The cumbia music from outside had grown louder, reverberating through his body. Inside felt like a little slice of Mexico, with papel picado decorating the ceiling and terecitas scattered throughout the tables in little clear vases.

"Oh, wow." Lola's voice barely carried over the music, but he could still hear the awe in it. It was how he felt when he stepped foot in here for the first time. Seeing one's culture represented and celebrated in a positive light always left him breathless. He remembered why he loved coming here and made a mental reminder to start coming more frequently.

"Are you hungry?" Javi asked, leading her further inside.

Lola still looked like a kid in a candy store, taking in all the delectable sights and sounds. She nodded at him, though he suspected she was only half listening. "Let's—" she started, but then her eyes went wide and her body tensed.

Javi's own body was on instant alert as he swept his gaze around the room, wondering what made her react like that. He didn't have to wonder long because she said, "Is that...that one baseball player? Maverick Wilson?"

Of course his date would be a sports fan and he not know.

Javi's stomach dropped as he turned in the direction she was pointing out. He sent a silent prayer to God that Lola was mistaken and that his brother-in-law was not here on bingo night. But the moment he looked, there was no denying the familiar face of him and the woman sitting next to him.

"And—holy shit! Is that your sister?" Lola gasped. He remembered she had seen Ofelia once at the bakery.

Both Maverick and Ofelia turned toward him at the same time. His brother-in-law immediately noticed the woman next to him and smirked, but Ofelia's eyes widened in shock. "Javi?"

He was truly and utterly fucked, not yet willing to answer the barrage of questions his sister would undoubtedly ask him about Lola. He wanted to turn around and take Lola to one of those fancy bars he was complaining about. Ofelia must have seen the startled look in her brother's eyes because she moved from her perch at the table and hurried over to him, pulling him into a bear hug.

From over his sister's head, he tried to convey how sorry he was to Lola and how he hadn't planned this at all. But Lola was holding back her own laughs and shrugged as if to say, *"Well, what are ya going to do?"* He supposed this would be their first test in whether they could convince family members they were dating. Javi just wished it didn't have to be right now.

# *Lola*

## CHAPTER SEVENTEEN

IT WASN'T every day you got to go on a fake date and meet a sexy as hell baseball player. She only knew Maverick played baseball because her father was a big sports fan and whenever they were together, he always had a game on or gushed about his favorite players.

Javi had been mortified that his sister and her husband happened to be at the same place, but Lola didn't mind. It actually eased some of her anxiety. She didn't feel like she had to be "on" the whole night and find ways to carry the conversation. Lola thrived in larger crowds because there were always enough people to take the attention off her.

Javi begrudgingly led them over to his sister's table and she reassured him for the umpteenth time that she wasn't upset. Unlike some of her other dates who attempted to hide her or pretend she did not exist. Javi didn't do that. He let her keep hold of his arm as he introduced her to his sister, Ofelia, and her baseball player husband, Maverick.

"Why didn't you tell me you were going out tonight?" Ofelia said the moment they sat down. The table had long bench seats and as soon as Lola sat down, Javi squeezed in next to her. Two large half-drunken beers and untouched carnitas tacos sat in front of her, permeating the air with an oniony aroma.

"Or tell me you had a date with the woman who could hardly stand you at the bakery?" Ofelia continued, whispering the last part. Lola heard it as clearly as if she were sitting right next to her and felt her cheeks redden in embarrassment. She might not have made the best first impression.

"I told you I was going out." Javi shrugged, opening his phone to scan the QR code crudely taped to the table. It brought up a full drink and food menu. He passed his phone over to her with a smile. "Order whatever you like."

"So chivalrous," Lola teased, scrolling the extensive list of alcohol.

"You told me you were going out, but not on a date!" Ofelia chastised like only older sisters could do. At least that was what she thought anyway. She didn't really have a bond with her sister, but she imagined this is what a healthy sibling relationship looked like.

"Baby girl, leave him alone. I'm sure he didn't expect us to interrupt his date," came Maverick's deep tenor. How did Ofelia listen to that voice every day and not want to jump him? Not that Lola did, of course. She was more than happy to be fake dating Javi who made her heart skip a beat with a simple touch.

Ofelia grimaced. "Shit. We're crashing your date. Do you want us to find a new table?"

Javi said, "Yes" just as Lola said, "No." They stared at each other and shared a smirk before Lola continued, "No, please. Honestly, it's fine. It's refreshing to see siblings get along so well."

"Are you not close with your own siblings?" Ofelia asked, cocking her head to the side as if not able to compute that type of relationship.

Lola smiled to ease the knot in her throat. "We've never seen eye to eye." Lola settled on, not wanting to burden these strangers with her family woes. She felt Javi's eyes on her, but she was too much of a coward to meet his gaze. He didn't need to know how bad things were yet. In time he would be able to experience the drama of her family firsthand.

Maverick leaned close to his wife, placing his hand atop hers and giving it a gentle squeeze. "Don't grill the poor woman. We are trying to have fun tonight."

Ofelia's eyes widened. "Right. I'm so sorry. Sometimes I'm so nosey. I haven't had many days away from our son in a long time. Mav's mom is in town and offered to babysit so we jumped at the chance to get out of the house together. I need to remember how to socialize."

"Socialize less, loca, and let us find something to eat," Javi teased his sister with ease and then flashed his smile Lola's way. Her stomach did a weird flip that wasn't entirely unpleasant. One second she thought she was over his charm and the next she was putty in his hands. He was going to give her whiplash.

"Have you decided on what you want?" Javi asked. In truth, she hadn't paid much attention to the menu. The sights, aromas, and chatting had distracted her, but her stomach growled reminding her how hungry she was.

"What do you suggest?" Despite Lola's mixed heritage, her mother went to great lengths to whitewash her and Marisol. White was privileged and Luciana clung to that ideal like a too small dress. The white privilege never quite fit because their skin was a few shades too dark and their hair was too unruly to ever fit the mold, but that didn't keep Luciana from trying. Lola often suspected that was the reason her mother was drawn to her father.

"You can't go wrong with anything, but my favorite is the birria tacos. Super juicy, a little messy, but so damn good."

Lola didn't know what birria was but a quick Google search told her the tacos were typically made from goat meat or beef and she liked both of those things, so that seemed like an obvious winner. She placed the order on the app, as well as a white peach margarita, and handed Javi back his phone so he could place his own order.

Ofelia and Maverick set up their bingo cards. They both had

three each and spread it out among their side to get a good look. Ofelia popped off the lid of one of the markers and placed a neon pink dot on all the free spaces.

Of course she understood bingo but she had never played like this before and was intimidated by the three cards she would have to monitor. At least she had a pretty pink dotting marker to draw with if things went horribly south.

"So, I know about Camilia, but are there any other family members I should know about?" she questioned, raising her brow. Maverick and Ofelia were consumed with each other and not paying them any mind, so she felt now was the proper time to ask Javi about his family. As his fake date, she needed to know these things.

"Just my papá. We don't have any immediate family close by and Camilia's maternal grandparents live in Puebla so they don't see her much." There was a story there, one that Lola was not yet privy to. She wanted to know and wondered how much Javi would tell her, but she didn't feel like this was the place to bring it up.

She moved their discussion into what she hoped was more neutral territory. "Have you always wanted to be a father?"

His features softened, eyes crinkling in the corner. There was a soft peacefulness in his expression and not for the first time Lola wished she could catch a glimpse inside his mind. "I knew I wanted to be a papá, but Camilia was an unexpected blessing. My fiancée at the time, Estella, and I had just fallen in love and were starting our lives together when we found out she was pregnant.

"When Camilia was born, I knew that this is what God, or fate, or whatever you believe in, had in store for me. I was chosen to be her papá and I take my job very seriously. She's been my greatest gift and it's so fun to watch her grow into her big personality."

The love behind each of his words when he spoke of his daughter, tugged on her heartstrings. Every child deserved a father like Javi. "She is a special little girl. I hope she comes around to the bookstore more," she said and was surprised to find that she meant it.

A man with a greasy off-white apron soon approached their table, cutting off any reply Javi might have said. He said something in Spanish that Lola didn't understand, but it made Javi laugh. He then placed down the tastiest-looking tacos in front of her, with a side of broth for dipping. Like a dog, she salivated, nearly panting from the meaty aroma.

Maverick reached across the table and placed a large pile of napkins down in front of her. "You're going to need these." And he was right. The first bite she took after dipping the tacos into the broth, sent juices straight down her arms, all the way to her elbows.

Before she could grab the napkin to clean herself up, Javi beat her to it. He trailed the napkin down her forearm, making sure to soak up every last drop. Heat blossomed on her skin where he touched. There was no hiding the physical reaction her body had for him.

"Careful, preciosa, wouldn't want you to ruin that beautiful dress." Javi's voice sounded right in her ear and butterflies erupted within her belly. Her cheeks reddened and if Javi noticed, he didn't comment—thankfully. She took another bite, more carefully this time, and kept the mess at a minimum.

The music soon died down as a female voice came over the speaker. "Señoras y señores, welcome to another night of bingo!" Loud cheering answered the woman's voice and Lola found herself cheering alongside them. "We will be getting started in just a few minutes. Make sure your cards are out in front of you and your markers are working. Any problems and one of our employees will come to help you. Just raise your hand."

The music turned on after that and begrudgingly, Lola pushed her food to the side to spread out her cards. She must have looked nervous because Javi placed a hand on her thigh and Lola had to squeeze her legs together. "Don't worry. I'll help you. It can be a lot to look over at once."

"Just don't try to cheat me out of my prize."

The man's cocky smile made her forget his sister and her husband were sitting right in front of them. "Oh, I would never."

Her cheeks ached from all the damn smiling she was doing around him. No man had the right to be this smooth. Neither one of them addressed the hand on her leg and she wasn't in a rush to move him away. He brought her comfort and she wasn't one to turn that down.

After a few minutes and once the employees of the parlor made sure everyone had the necessary tools, the woman came back on stage, dressed in a metallic silver dress that reminded Lola of a disco ball. She once again wondered what she had gotten herself into, but since everyone else seemed to be chill with the talking disco ball lady, so was she.

Disco Lady didn't hold back. As soon as she started calling numbers, it was a mad dash to mark them off, and multiple times Javi had to take over one of her cards to make sure that all the numbers were scratched off. She had gotten so close to bingo multiple times and groaned when someone called out a bingo while she was one or two spots away.

The only time Lola had to eat and enjoy her margarita was between passing out cards, and even then it was only a minuscule amount of time. They didn't fuck around with their games here.

The next round of bingo started off slow. None of her three cards had much of anything and she muttered a curse under her breath. She didn't know where this newfound competitiveness was coming from, but apparently, bingo brought out the need to dominate her opponents.

After a few more calls, Lola looked down to realize she was only one away on all three of her cards. Her excitement took over and she accidentally elbowed Javi in the ribs. She ignored his grunt of pain and grabbed his arm, the nervous-excited energy getting to her. Her body buzzed as Disco Lady called out another number. "B-19!"

Lola scoured her three cards and found the number on one of

them. She blinked once, then twice, because... "You won!" Javi beamed, causing both Ofelia and Maverick to look over at her cards.

Ofelia gasped the moment she saw the bingo. "You won!" she repeated what her brother said. "You have to say bingo, Lola. Get your prize!"

If she hadn't just been guzzling the largest margarita known to man between games, she probably wouldn't have been comfortable raising her hand and screaming, "Bingo!" at the top of her lungs. But the alcohol coursing through her veins brought out her extrovert side and she didn't mind all the eyes on her, even some of the pissed ones because she called out bingo before they did.

"We have ourselves a bingo! Let's go check." Disco Lady said, sauntering off the stage and walking over to Lola's table. She shimmied her way between Javi and her, leaning down to check out her cards. Less than a minute passed before Disco Lady grinned and straightened her posture. "A winner!" she announced and the crowd erupted into cheers, Javi and Maverick whistling as if she had just performed an amazing stunt, while Ofelia whooped.

Digging into her chest, Disco Lady produced a gift card. "Here you go, muñeca." She winked, handing over the card that was once nestled between her boobs. Lola tried not to think about that and dampen the moment.

"Congratulations, preciosa!" Javi smiled and then as if acting on instinct, leaned in to place a soft kiss on her cheek. It happened so fast that neither could react. She felt the moment Javi realized what he did because he tensed, slowly pulling back. "Uh, sorry. I wasn't thinking—"

Before he could pull further away and finish his sentence, her own instincts kicked in and she grabbed his wrist, pulling him back and placing a soft kiss on his lips. Just like that. She didn't even second-guess herself. At least not much because it felt right.

"Here, I want you to have this." She handed him the gift card. His smile instantly vanished and it took her a moment to realize how that might have looked. She didn't want him thinking she thought he needed the money more than she did. "For Camilia," she clarified, "let her buy a toy or two. That's a far better use of the money than what I could use it for."

Hearing his daughter's name made him relax. "That is very sweet of you. Thank you. She is going to love it." He tucked the gift card away in his jacket pocket, securing it with his zipper.

"This calls for a celebration. Next round of drinks on me. Lola, another margarita?" Maverick asked, standing up and stretching his tall body.

"Yeah, but maybe something a tad smaller? I still have to drive home." She laughed.

"You got it." He leaned down to press a kiss against Ofelia's mouth before heading to the bar.

Perhaps it was the adrenaline from winning or the margarita from earlier, but Lola laid her head down against Javi's shoulder. "Thank you for bringing me here. This has been so much fun."

"Good. I like it when you smile," he said, giving her thigh another gentle squeeze.

At first, she had been skeptical of the date, but she had never expected to have such a good time, even running into his sister. The rest of the night produced no more bingo winners, but that hardly mattered. She ate far too much and didn't regret it, got to lean against Javi, and laughed until her face hurt. It was one of the best nights she had in a long time.

# *Javi*

## CHAPTER EIGHTEEN

IT HAD BEEN three days and Javi still felt the press of Lola's lips against his. It wasn't a particularly fantastic, mind-blowing kiss. It was chaste and hurried, and yet he couldn't stop thinking about it.

It ran through his head the entire drive to the parent line for morning drop-off. He had a rare morning off and was able to take Camilia to school. She was normally a bus rider, but Javi loved the early moments before school when he could spend some extra time with her.

He helped her get ready for her school day and drove through to get donuts for breakfast, something he didn't do often because Camilia and sugar were a dangerous combination. He felt bad for her teacher, but the smile his daughter gave him was worth it.

"I'll pick you up after school. Papá has to talk to you about some things." The "some things" being him leaving for a week and having to break the news to her.

"Am I in trouble?" she asked, pink icing from the donut covering her mouth.

"No, mija. Nothing like that. I can't stay mad at you."

She gave him a toothy grin. "I know." She had him wrapped around her little finger and they both knew it.

473

Javi pulled up in the line and an older black woman opened the door. He thought he recognized her as the principal, but he wasn't sure. "Well hello, Miss Mendez. No bus today, I see." Her cheery voice rang throughout his truck, reminding Javi that educators did not get paid enough. Who in their right mind could be that cheery at seven in the morning while greeting children?

"No, papá took me to get donuts!" she exclaimed while her principal helped unbuckle her.

He turned his body, catching Camilia before she sprung out of the car. "I'll see you after school. Love you, princess. Be good." He kissed her temple seconds before she swung her backpack around, nearly decapitating him in her efforts to get out of the car.

"Goodbye, Mr. Mendez. We'll make sure she doesn't take the bus." With that, the principal shut the door and Javi was prompted to drive forward. He stayed to make sure Camilia got into the building safely before driving out of the school parking lot, hanging a left at the stop sign.

Although he was off from his normal job, he still had a bookstore he had to renovate. He'd also be lying if the thought of seeing Lola didn't awaken a primal part of him. He wondered what she'd be wearing today. If she had decided to leave the house with makeup or sport her messy bun and puffy eyes. Both were incredibly sexy to him.

He pulled up to the bookstore ten minutes later, miraculously finding parking right outside. He grabbed his clipboard and a few tools he would need to start working on the cafe area. He had a crew coming in tomorrow to get started on the custom built-ins, since those were going to be the heart of the store.

The chime above the door—recently installed—alerted anyone who may be inside to his arrival. He only had to walk a few steps to see that the woman lounging in an old leather chair was not Lola. Disappointment settled over him like the cobwebs hanging from the corners of the shop. He tried to hide his reaction though when Monique looked up from her book and nodded at him.

"What's good, Javi? Lola won't be here today—she's dealing with a dress issue for the wedding. Her family's fucked, let me tell you." She rolled her eyes, letting him know just what she thought about the situation. Curiosity seared through him, as questions burned on the tip of his tongue. It wasn't his place to ask and he doubted Monique would provide much insight anyway.

"Anyway, she left you this," Monique added, reaching for papers on the table and handing them over. Javi looked them over, discovering a plane ticket as well as a note from Lola that read:

Javi,

I'm going to be busy with dress shopping and last-minute wedding preparations over the next few days, so I don't think I'll have a chance to give this to you in person. Here is your plane ticket for Saturday. Please be at the airport early and I'll meet you at our gate. Feel free to text me anytime.

Lola

Holding the plane ticket made their situation a reality. As much fun as they had together the other night, and as much as his body yearned for her, this was a job. She hired him to renovate her bookstore and be her date to a wedding she couldn't face alone. Lola hadn't told him the reason for that yet, but he planned to ask her about it as soon as they were on the plane. It was perhaps a dick move since she literally had nowhere else to go and couldn't excuse herself from answering, but he needed answers.

"Thank you. If you see her, will you tell her I sent over a schedule for the shop for the next few weeks? Someone's going to have to be here while we are at the wedding to answer any questions my guys might have."

"It'll be me or Mattea. I'll have her forward that email to me. Imma head to the back, if you wanna get to work. Just let me know when you're done." Monique grabbed her book with a half-naked woman on the front and a stained mug filled with coffee and headed to the back.

As much as he wanted to see Lola, this at least provided him an opportunity to be productive. He began the tedious, yet stress-relieving task of removing parts of the cafe area to make way for new furniture and counter area. He lost himself in his work, thinking about Lola's vision for the shop and feeling the strain of his muscles with each movement.

SCHOOL ENDED PROMPTLY at 2:45 p.m., but apparently parents started lining up so much earlier. Except Javi didn't realize this, so by the time he finished up with his work and let Monique know he was leaving, it was already 2:30 and the line was wrapped around the school.

One would have thought the president was in town, but no, the mile-long line was full of impatient parents waiting for their children. Though, if there was one thing the school knew how to do, it was getting the kids out of the building in a safe, but fast manner.

It took about twenty minutes before he was pulling up to the same lady from earlier. Camilia stood next to her, Elsa backpack draped over one shoulder as she ate the grapes he packed for a snack. Her entire round face lit up the moment she saw his car.

"Hi papá!" She greeted him as soon as the door was opened for her. "We got to touch frogs in school today! They were slimy and a little smelly." She then went on to list all the facts she learned about frogs today, while her principal finished getting her in the car, waving a hasty goodbye, and closing the door.

"Can we get a pet frog?" she asked as he drove off. It was her thing to ask about any new animals she learned about and Javi was not about to try and keep up with a frog. He could only imagine where it would end up.

"Let's keep frogs at school."

A dramatic sigh from the back answered him, and he couldn't help but laugh. He only hoped his next words got him a different reaction. "Are you hungry? Why don't we go out to eat?"

Camilia's hazel eyes grew wide, her long eyelashes fluttering. Going out to eat was a novelty that they rarely did, unless it was Maverick and Ofelia taking them. Then they would pay the bill after some protests from Javi, even knowing damn well he didn't have spare money lying around to pay for the fancy-ass places they liked.

Lola had given him financial security and although it felt weird to use the money on such trivial things, Camilia enjoyed going out to restaurants. He didn't want to deny her because he was uncomfortable spending money.

The excited hollering coming from the back seat was all the indication he needed to know she liked his idea. The Italian restaurant down the road from their house was one of her favorites and a large greasy pizza sounded like exactly what the two of them needed.

Not even fifteen minutes later, they arrived at the restaurant and Javi requested a booth by the window so Camilia could look out and people watch. Water for him and juice for her were brought to the table and Javi waited until they ordered their half cheese, half sausage with onions pizza before he continued on with their conversation from the morning.

He hadn't yet told her about leaving for a week. Partially because he wanted to make sure it was still happening and partially because he was afraid of her reaction. After telling his sister, only a day after their accidental double date, he was grilled with dozens of questions, each of which he had to answer to avoid suspicion.

Ofelia was smart; his sister knew how to read him better than anyone else, and although she seemed skeptical about the situation, she agreed because she loved spending time with his daughter. Especially now that she had a son she could play with. How a two-year-old and six-year-old played together, he didn't know, but they always had a good time.

"Mija, you remember what I said this morning about having to talk?" Camilia looked up from the Barbie she snuck into her backpack this morning and nodded. "Well, papá has a friend who needs my help. She—"

"What's her name?" Camilia interrupted. "You have friends that are girls?" His six-year-old looked flabbergasted and it made him laugh. She was a perceptive little girl.

"Her name is Lola. Remember her from the bookstore?"

Camilia scrunched up her nose, deep in thought. "Yes, but why does she need your help?"

"Well..." He trailed off, thinking of the best way to tell his kindergartner this, but also not wanting to lie. "She really needs a friend and I'm available. But it does mean I'll be gone for a week." He hadn't ever been away from her for more than a day, so he was anxious about how this would turn out. He trusted no one like he trusted his sister, but Camilia was his daughter and he couldn't stop the guilt bubbling within his chest.

"How many days is a week?"

"Seven."

"Oh." Camilia's forlorn gaze amplified the guilt. She picked at her Barbie's messy hair before her face brightened suddenly. "Wait, does that mean I'll stay with tía Ofi and tío Mavy?"

The tension eased, but only partly as he nodded. "And Arturo. Abuelo will be around too if you need him. You are going to have a lot of fun and I promise to call you every night, mija. But if you don't want papá to go, just say the word."

He waited on bated breath. He didn't believe in making all the decisions simply because he was an adult and excluding his daughter's opinion. She got a say in what happened to her too and if she wasn't comfortable, he wanted that to be known. Of course, that would mean losing out on one hundred thousand dollars and potentially any relationship he might have with Lola, but...

"That's okay. I'll have fun. You'll bring me back a surprise?" Relief washed over him like a tidal wave. Knowing Camilia was comfortable with his trip eased a tightness within him he didn't know he was holding on to.

"Of course, anything you want," he said, which launched her into an explanation of a new racetrack she just had to have for her Barbies and described it in great detail before making Javi pull out his phone and look up the exact racetrack she needed so he could commit it to memory.

Thankfully their pizza soon came out, sparing him another lecture on which racetrack was the best, for the time being. He chose the cheesiest-looking piece and placed it on the plate in front of her, while he grabbed two slices for himself. He couldn't remember the last time it was just the two of them out to eat, but he needed to cherish these moments. They went by too quickly.

Enjoying their night out together was much easier now that he got the secret off his chest and they began to brainstorm everything she needed to pack for a week-long trip to her tía's house. What clothes, toys, and bathroom products she needed.

They ended their dinner with a slice of chocolate cake and once they were done, Javi carried her and the leftovers to the car. They hadn't even pulled out of the restaurant when he heard soft snoring from behind him.

## *Lola*

CHAPTER NINETEEN

ONE WOULD HAVE THOUGHT there was a death in the family with how distraught and erratic her mother and sister were being. No one had died, apart from many of her brain cells and her patience, but dealing with the stress of a funeral would be preferred over dealing with the unnecessary chaos of finding the perfect bridesmaid dress.

More than once, Lola had burst into angry tears after a grueling phone call with her mother and her sister's hysterical voice in the background. "Tell her she needs to find a dress that will fit her before she gets here! I need to see pictures!" It was the same lines from her sister each phone call since her mother had informed Marisol that Lola would be a bridesmaid.

Her mother and sister had no idea how Lola was going to dress her size eighteen body. They insisted she needed someone to make her a dress because *"no boutiques would carry her size."* And therein lay the problem. They only ever stepped foot into high-end boutiques or designer clothing stores, knowing damn well they never carried anything for larger bodies.

So Lola had to have the same damn conversation she had countless times before. Yes she would be able to find a dress, but no she couldn't shop in the same boutiques as them. If her

481

mother didn't want all this added "stress" Lola was supposedly giving her, she shouldn't have made her a bridesmaid.

Lola didn't even bother to mention how hypocritical her family's statement was, considering nobody but her father gave a damn about her unless their image was called into question. She also didn't remind her that Marisol was marrying her ex because it was not a fight she wanted to have.

Finding a dress wouldn't have been so hard if she didn't have a looming cloud over her, ready to rain down and dampen any potential dress she picked. Lola had lived in a curvier body most of her life; she knew which places carried her size and where to find the cutest clothes for her body type.

She started off at multiple bridal stores that carried plus-sizes and tried on an armful of dresses. She video called her mom because her sister was far too bogged down with important wedding matters to pay her any mind. The reactions were much the same, all far too critical and finding something minor wrong with the dress.

The dress hugged her tummy too tightly. This dress was too short. That dress's neckline was too low and her boobs were going to pop out. The list went on and on.

It was on day three when Lola lost her composure with her mother, scaring the poor fitting room attendant in the process. "I have tried on every goddamn navy-colored dress in a thirty-mile radius from my house and not one of them is good enough for you. You get this dress or you don't get anything. Make your choice, right now, because I'm so tired of hearing you belittle me and my body."

As soon as the words left her mouth, she wanted to take them back and apologize. She didn't speak to her mother like this— ever. It didn't matter how snide her mother's comments were, she held the aggression deep inside herself, letting it fester until, apparently, this moment. The screen was a big reason for her newfound courage, but she still found herself clamping her mouth shut with invisible nails to keep herself from taking it all back.

Her mother's stunned expression stilled on the screen with her brows raised high to her hairline and lips pressed in a tight line. Lola thought she was frozen and went to tap the screen as if that would somehow make her mother move.

"The dress is fine," her mother's demure voice said after a moment, shocking the hell out of her. "Get the white heels you showed me earlier. I'll see you at the hotel in a few days." After a curt goodbye, her mother hung up the phone.

Not an hour later, Lola was back at her house, packing two suitcases for her weeklong Colorado trip. Her mother would have thrown a fit if she saw the folded bridesmaid dress at the bottom of the suitcase, so she made a mental note to take it out as soon as she got to the hotel.

The contents of her closet were strewn across her bedroom floor and her bathroom was in complete disarray as she began to pack toiletries and makeup. Sometime throughout the night, she managed to send Javi a text asking if he received the plane ticket she printed out for him.

He replied almost instantly with a thumbs-up emoji.

Make sure to be at the airport two hours before takeoff. You never know what the crowds will be like.

See you then, preciosa.

*Preciosa*. Every time he called her that, her heart did a somersault and she thought back to their first night together and the way he dominated her in bed. No man should have this much power over her and yet, if he asked her to slide into his bed naked, she wouldn't fucking hesitate.

And that was just sad.

Not for the first or second time since Javi unexpectedly came back into her life did she have to remind herself that everything between them was just an illusion and despite the fact that it felt so right, it had an expiration date. Did that mean she couldn't enjoy him while they were together?

Yes. That was exactly what that meant—she needed to push all horny thoughts away and finish packing. She mentally packaged up all thoughts of Javi and filed them away in her mind so she could go back to getting her things into suitcases.

It was nearly midnight by the time she finally crawled into her unmade bed and fell fast asleep. What felt like only seconds later her four a.m. alarm roared to life, bringing her out of the midst of REM sleep.

Her clothes were already laid out from the night before and she mentally thanked her last-night self for the preparation. Lola rolled out of bed, hair wild and matted to her head and last night's leftover eyeliner smeared across her eyes. She relieved herself before washing her face and brushing her teeth. She placed those items into her toiletry bag and gently tossed them into her suitcase.

Lola discarded her clothes into the hamper and put on cheeky panties and a white lace bra that made her boobs look great. The gray sweatpants she chose for comfort and slipped them up her legs and over her ass. The white crop top she made from a vintage band shirt she found at the thrift shop. She completed the look with a black tracksuit jacket in case it got cold on the plane.

Although she was no stranger to flying and airports, she still felt a tremendous amount of anxiety. Flying made no sense to her. How did a giant ass metal bird remain in the sky when all she could picture is plummeting to her death at the slightest bit of turbulence?

The alarm on her phone beeped again, letting her know she needed to get her ass in her car. Mona had offered to drive her but she was barely functional in the mornings, so Lola opted just to leave her car at the airport. Now that she was thinking about it, she probably should have offered to pick Javi up, but she trusted he would meet her there.

Loading up her big suitcase and carry-on, Lola checked once more to make sure she had her phone, chargers, and AirPods. She did. Which wasn't surprising because she checked ten times and each time they were at the bottom of her purse and didn't magically jump out like her brain kept telling her they did.

Her brain was extra nervous today because in a matter of hours, she would be face-to-face with her family. Once again she would have to see Marisol with Archie looking perfect and beautiful together. Marisol was the type of woman who would make any rich entrepreneur happy. Looking back now, she would never have fit into Archie's lifestyle, but she would have tried until it consumed her and spat her back out.

All of her feelings for Archie had faded long ago, so seeing him would no longer feel like a knife wound to the heart; however, being around her family while they flocked around Marisol and silently compared the sisters was enough to bring on the panic attack bubbling near the surface.

She had to remember that she wasn't going to face them alone. Javi would be there and despite the fact that she was paying him to be at her side, Javi liked her. He calmed her in ways she had never experienced before and Lola was hoping that would continue during their week together.

Lola pulled up to the parking area she prepaid for, scanning her barcode before the barrier went up to let her in. The parking area was only half full, so she took that as a good sign and hoped that Javi wouldn't have any trouble finding a spot.

Getting her stuff from her car, onto the shuttle, and through baggage drop-off took twenty minutes, but she had not seen or heard from Javi yet. She sent him a quick text letting him know she was there as she waited in the TSA line. Her nerves skyrocketed when the sleep-deprived TSA agent barked orders at everyone to take off their shoes and remove all large electronic items from their bags. Not really knowing what counted as a large electronic, Lola dumped the contents of her purse out and tossed her carry-on onto the conveyor belt, and hoped for the best. Five minutes later she was through.

Their flight would take off from Gate 20 and judging from the numbers hanging on the walls, she wasn't too far. A small crowd had already begun to grow, all seated with their head-phones on and their noses in their phones. Not one of them was Javi.

Dread began to bubble in her belly as she pulled out her phone to check the time. There was still an hour and a half before takeoff and she had to remind herself that not everyone was crazy like her and arrived well before their flight. Javi would be here. He wasn't the type of guy to just leave her hanging.

At least, she didn't *think* he was...

No, not him. She hadn't known him for long, but from their work interactions and their date, she knew Javi wouldn't just leave her stranded. To put her nerves at ease, she sent him another quick text to let him know she was waiting by their gate. He had not replied to her first text, so she wasn't holding out much hope he'd replied to this one.

Thirty minutes went by and the crowd around the gate began to grow. She expected a full flight and knew it would be a mad dash to the boarding lines, even though they all had assigned seats. It was always that moment when they started calling boarding numbers that her anxiety began to spike and stayed high until they landed safely at their destination.

Lola's knee began to bounce, trying to dispel the pent-up energy inside of her. Another look at her phone told her that Javi still had not responded. If she were being stood up, this was liter-ally the most crappiest scenario.

"Fuck this." She murmured under her breath and picked up her phone to call him. It started to ring immediately. And ring. And ring. And—

"Lola."

Lola jumped in her chair, nearly chucking her phone at the

poor elderly woman next to her. She scrambled to catch her phone and bring it up to her ear. "Javi? Javi, you there?"

A low chuckle came from behind her and a moment later the seat next to her was filled. The familiar scent of citrus and clove filled the air. He wore something similar to her, dark gray sweats that made her eyes wander down to the impressive bulge between his legs. Her body flushed as she averted her gaze up to his long-sleeved black shirt and up to Javi's smug face. Clearly, he saw her checking him out, but she didn't shy away from his gaze.

"Sorry I'm late. I had to drop Camilia off at my sister's and I stopped and picked us up some breakfast. Did you eat?" He reached into the small duffle bag on his lap, pulling out a greasy white bag. How he got that through security, she wouldn't know. Her stomach growled at the sight and she shook her head. "Good. I like feeding you."

Javi unwrapped her breakfast taco and when he asked if she liked salsa and Lola nodded her head, he opened up the tortilla and poured salsa on her taco. All she could do was watch as his man prepared her food. It was a simple gesture, but he still went out of his way to do it for her.

The taco was delicious and she avoided any spills on her shirt. The moment they finished their breakfast, Javi took the trash and tossed it away for them. When he came back, he placed his calloused hand on her shaking leg. "Are you okay? You seem... tense."

"I hate flying. It stresses me out," Lola admitted in a soft voice. She hated that she never knew if the seats would accommodate her, but she felt too embarrassed to say that, even to Javi.

"Ah," Javi nodded his head like he understood. "Well, I've never flown before, but if you need a hand to squeeze, I have two ready."

An involuntary smile spread across her lips. It surprised her that Javi had never been on an airplane before, but she was inexplicably excited his first time was with her. Maybe if she focused on his excitement for flying for the first time, some of her fears would slowly dissipate.

That theory was debunked the moment a woman's voice came over the speaker and announced they would start boarding first class. Lola sucked in a breath and reached for Javi's hand on instinct. He squeezed back gently, getting up and pulling her to her feet. "You ready, preciosa? I'll be right next to you."

His calming voice gave her the strength to move to the line and scan their boarding passes. Javi took the lead once inside the walkway, but he never once dropped her hand. That small gesture made her feel something she had not felt in a long time. Something she was not ready to identify quite yet. Instead, she pushed those new feelings aside and let Javi put their carry-ons away as she took the window seat.

# *Javi*

## CHAPTER TWENTY

Leaving Camilia had been harder than he expected. His little girl didn't cry when he dropped her off, but she did pout and hug him extra hard right before he left. Ofelia assured him that she would be fine, and Javi had no reason not to believe her, but it didn't lessen the hurt at all. He promised to call Camilia tonight once they landed and were settled in their hotel rooms.

When he arrived at the airport—arguably too close to boarding time—the first thing he spotted at Gate 20 was a stressed-out Lola. She jumped when he came up behind her and he hoped the breakfast he brought would ease her nerves. It did for a while, until boarding.

Now Lola sat tucked against the window, hands in her lap, bouncing her leg up and down. He was beginning to realize that was her go-to when she was anxious or worried. She shut herself down, keeping the fears within and he refused to have her suffer alone.

When the plane began its takeoff, he reached for her, tugging her hand to pull her body his way. Her eyes squeezed shut and her breathing became slightly erratic. He didn't speak; he continued to hold her hand, rubbing soothing gestures with his thumb.

It wasn't until they were far enough above the clouds that she finally opened her eyes. He wasn't going to invalidate her feelings by saying takeoff wasn't so bad, so instead, he said, "Thanks for holding my hand. It made takeoff easier."

The surprised smile gracing her face would forever be etched into his brain. He wanted to always be the one to elicit smiles like that. To make her feel safe when they were thousands of feet above the ground. Perhaps this was the machismo in him, but he didn't care. Not when Lola was looking at him like that.

"I'm sorry I'm so nervous. I swear I'm not normally like this," Lola said, embarrassment coloring her features.

It bothered him that she thought she needed to apologize for her very normal human feelings. "It's okay to be nervous, Lola. I want to get your mind off it. How about we quiz each other? We were supposed to do that on our bingo date to get to know one another before the wedding, but then my sister prevented that."

"She did, but I still enjoyed our time together. Hmm, let's see," Lola said, biting her bottom lip while she attempted to think of a question. Javi tried not to notice, but failed spectacularly and had to covertly readjust himself in his seat. All because she bit her damn lip. "Ah, I have a question. Have you always wanted to work in construction?"

"I've always been good with my hands and I enjoy building things. I don't know if I've always wanted to do construction, but I grew up around it. My father worked for various construction companies and would tell me about the projects he worked on. I thought it was so cool. Once I got into the job force, I still felt that way, but I didn't like my management. It's taken me a while, but now I'm in a place to go independent." And now a lot of that had to do with Lola and the amount of money she was paying him for his first big job.

Part of him still felt bad for accepting the outrageous amount of money, even as he finally took it to the bank to cash last week. But another part reminded him how he was caught up with bills for the first time in a long time. He put most of the money in savings to pay for expenses and labor, still unsure if he was willing to accept the entire generous amount.

"Well you're good at what you do, and I'm excited to see what you do with my bookstore." Lola's words filled him with an insurmountable amount of pride. His chest puffed out like a damn peacock, ready to strut his feathers in front of the ladies.

"Speaking of the bookstore, you are going to be amazed at the changes already. The guys are taking care of it while I'm away." He smiled. Lola had been busy for the past few days and Javi had accomplished a lot, like completely stripping the interior until hardly anything from the original store remained. "Also, I noticed the plan you left out on the counter. The one for a large kids area. Will it be for more storytimes?"

"You noticed that, huh?" Lola's eyes twinkled with amusement. "I didn't realize how much fun reading to kids was until I did it at the bakery. I think I'm obsessed now. My grandma would read to me as a kid, and I want kids in the community to be able to experience that as well."

"What was your favorite book as a kid?"

"Oh, that's a hard one. We read so many, but I think my favorite was a book called *The Tortilla Quilt*. My grandma read it to me all the time. It was about a little girl and her friend learning how to quilt from her grandma. It reminded me so much of the relationship I had with my abuelita that I made her read it to me constantly." Lola laughed, a far-off look in her eyes as if she were transported back to a little girl with her grandma. "What about you?"

Javi didn't read much. He wasn't like his sister who could devour an entire series in a week, but he had enjoyed the bedtime stories his mother read to him as a child. "I think mine is *The Giving Tree*."

It was as if he said he kicked puppies on the weekends for fun by the reproachful look Lola glared in his direction. "Absolutely not. Your favorite book cannot be *The Giving Tree*."

"And why is that? I didn't realize this choice was so controversial." It was one of the only ones he remembered his mother reading to him because he liked how soothing her voice was when she read it.

"Well it is!" Lola all but shrieked. "It's a horrible story for kids. Promoting the idea that it is okay to give everything you have and expect nothing in return. Which, sure, a nice topic in theory, but the tree literally gave the little boy everything until she died. Where is the justice in that?"

"Well, damn, I wasn't thinking like that as a kid. I just liked the way my mamá read it to me before bed. It was like our little moment together," he explained. "She died a few years ago, so I try to hang on to her memory in different ways, you know?"

Lola grimaced and sank into her chair. She shocked the hell out of him by leaning her head against his shoulder. The touch shouldn't have felt as intimate as it did. "Well, now I feel like a dick. The book is so terrible, but your mother sounds like she was a wonderful woman. I'm glad you were able to have that time with her."

Javi thought back to the moments he had with his mother. She shaped his entire childhood and although they didn't have much extra money, Javi never felt like they suffered or missed out. His parents had made sure they were well taken care of and loved. He hoped Camilia felt that way, too.

"My mom was a great woman. She loved picture books too. She didn't read much unless it was to us, but I remember her taking us to the library, and Ofelia and I would spend hours with her looking at the books and reading them. Of course, my go-to was *The Giving Tree* before I knew how controversial it was." He laughed, tilting his head to better see Lola.

She didn't respond. Javi waited and watched the slow rise and fall of her chest, accompanied by soft snores. She had fallen asleep. Considering how high-strung she had been, Javi wasn't surprised or insulted.

A smile spread across his lips as he angled his body, moving his arm around her so she could nestle into the crook of his neck.

Lola did just that, not waking up as she made herself comfortable against his body.

Javi leaned down and pressed a featherlight kiss to the top of her head. She smelled of lavender, reminding him of his abuela's house during spring.

The woman in his arms was beautiful. He didn't know what awaited them in Colorado, but whatever it was, he had a strong suspicion her fear wasn't entirely about flying. Perhaps it was what awaited them once they landed. He vowed right there and then to be her rock, no matter what was presented to them. She deserved the best and if her family couldn't see that, Javi would make sure he showed them.

*Lola*

CHAPTER TWENTY-ONE

LOLA HADN'T REALIZED she had fallen asleep until Javi's gentle voice and soft caresses woke her up. She noticed a small spot of wetness on his shirt and was immediately mortified that she'd drooled on him. Thankfully he made no comment as she pushed herself off him and attempted to tame her hair.

Lola reached in her pocket for her phone and to check the time. She quickly turned off airplane mode and her phone buzzed. The screen lit up in her hand as missed calls and texts began to pour in. Most of them were from her mother and sister, but a few were from her father asking if she was able to board the plane okay and if he needed to send a car to pick them up. She smiled at his thoughtfulness and sent him a quick reply that she would arrange for an Uber. A few moments later her father responded with a heart emoji.

When the plane door opened, Javi stood up and stepped aside to allow Lola to get off. She didn't argue with him when he took her carry-on because her mind was clouded with thoughts of her upcoming meeting with her family.

Up until this point she had done a good job at blocking all thoughts of seeing her family, but now that they were only

495

minutes from seeing each other, she no longer had the security of miles between them. How was she going to act when she came face-to-face with Archie? Had she steeled herself enough to face her mother's scrutiny? What jabs would her sister throw at her for stealing the man she thought she would marry?

Her body moved on its own accord to baggage claim. She sensed Javi next to her and felt his gaze bore into the side of her head. She could feel the unasked questions lingering close to the surface and she feared if she made eye contact with him, her resolve would crumble. Like a coward, she pulled out her phone and busied herself with ordering them a pickup to the hotel.

"I'll grab our bags." Javi said after another beat of silence passed between them. He walked ahead of her, and she knew he was giving her space to breathe. She appreciated that he didn't demand answers from her or pry. She couldn't put what she was feeling into words and didn't want to try to untangle the web of emotions dampening her mood. It would require too much back-story and though Javi deserved to know it, she wasn't quite ready to tell him.

She didn't want him to see her for how pathetic she was.

By the time Javi returned with her bright pink suitcase and his sensible brown one, their car was waiting outside. She led him out and slipped into the back while Javi and the driver took care of the bags. A few minutes later, both got in and they were on their way to the hotel.

She hadn't even realized she had been bouncing her leg until she felt a hand on her thigh. She recoiled and Javi pulled back, but not before she missed the hurt expression on his face. Regret and shame washed over her like a tidal wave and she instantly reached for his hand to pull it back to her.

"I'm sorry. My family always makes me jumpy. It's not you." Above anything, she needed him to know that her tumultuous feelings had nothing to do with the man sitting next to her and everything to do with the people awaiting their arrival.

His face was set into a hard expression, brow furrowed, and jaw tense. "What are you not telling me, Lola?"

And wasn't that the million-dollar question? She wanted to open her mouth and blurt out why she was acting like a skittish cat around water, but if she did that, the tears would start coming and she didn't want to face her family with red-rimmed eyes. They didn't need any more ammo against her.

She should tell him. She wanted to tell him, but her lips weren't forming the words. She fought the tears that stung her eyes, avoiding his piercing gaze. "I can't..."

She didn't finish that thought because the car came to an abrupt halt, nearly throwing her against the seat in front of her. "Here," the man said from the front, looking at her through the rearview mirror.

She hadn't paid any mind to where they were and it surprised her how quickly they got to the hotel. It was a typical luxury place her parents would stay at with a slew of valet drivers waiting to park cars that cost more than their houses. It was at least fifteen stories tall and if she had to guess, she would presume their hotel had a spa area and several dining locations. One she was certain her parents bought out for her sister's rehearsal dinner.

Lola was prepared to ignore Javi's question and had her hand on the handle when he reached out and placed his hand on the door to keep her from leaving. The heat of his body radiated off him and couldn't keep herself from looking in his direction.

He was angry, but her gut feeling told her he wasn't angry with her. "Lola," he started again, "are you going to be okay going inside?"

She would have to be, wouldn't she? Lola dug deep within herself and pulled out what she hoped would be a convincing smile. "I'll be okay. Let's get through the initial meeting and I can fill you in a little more when we are in our hotel room."

Javi didn't seem happy, but he released his hold on the door and let her out. She took her opportunity to escape, hearing Javi move behind her. The door to the truck had been propped open and she started getting their things out. Or at least she tried to until Javi shooed her away and got them out himself.

"I can take my own suitcases, it's really not a problem," Lola tried to argue, but Javi shut her up with a searing look that sent her squirming under his gaze and squeezing her thighs together. She stopped arguing after that.

Steeling herself for what was coming, Lola took a deep breath and led Javi into the lobby of their hotel. A giant rock waterfall cascaded down the first floor into a small koi pond. Off to the right was a bar with a seating area, leading out to a courtyard.

Sitting at a circular table in the middle of the bar were four people she recognized. Only her father noticed her at first. Travis Roberts stood up, shaking the table in his excitement. Lola found herself smiling back at her father, a little of the earlier tension easing...that is until her mother, Luciana, and sister, Marisol, turned around.

Sitting next to Marisol was a tall, white man with dirty-brown hair. She had believed seeing him wouldn't affect her because she held no love for Archie, yet her stomach churned, threatening to discard her breakfast from earlier.

Lola could picture his hooked nose and thin lips. The way his eyes reminded her of a murky swamp. Her body froze as Archie slowly turned around. When he saw her, he scowled, before quickly changing his features into a toothy smile he used a lot with clients.

"Dolores, so glad you could make it," his voice—had it always been that smarmy?—greeted her from across the room.

Before she had the chance to address him, her father engulfed her in a hug. She smelled the cigar smoke on him and it reminded her of summer nights at their childhood home in Florida when she would cuddle next to her father under the stars. "Princess, it's been too long." Her father pretended to scold her, but the gleam in his eyes gave him away. "You are such a sight for sore eyes."

"I didn't realize you were bringing anyone." Her mother's voice invaded her senses, coming up beside her father.

Luciana and Travis could not have been more at odds with each other—appearances-wise. Her mother was of Mexican descent. Thick black hair that had been straightened almost every day of Lola's life. She remembered seeing her mother's naturally wavy hair once and how much her mother complained about it. Her mother was slender with soft curves. She had large brown eyes and lashes that nearly touched her eyebrows.

Her father was a white man whose family immigrated from England in the nineteenth century, opening up their own business that specialized in wine production. Her father inherited the company as his birthright and it would now be passed down to Marisol and Archie. Which was fine with Lola, she told her father as much when he tried to make the sisters partners in the business. Lola vehemently refused, knowing there was no universe she could work well with her sister, especially now that she would be marrying Archie.

"Dolores, did you mention bringing a plus one on the invitation? We are only allowed a certain number of people into the venue and—"

"Mother, I made sure to add a plus one." Lola kept her voice level as if the roles were reversed and she was the mother to a petulant toddler. "I sent it back and let Marisol know. I also mentioned it on our phone calls during dress shopping."

Her mother looked affronted as she turned her attention to her oldest daughter. "You didn't tell me this." It was her go-to response each time she wanted to deflect accountability.

"I'm sure I did, but you know I have so much going on." Marisol was the only person who could roll her eyes at their mother and get away with it.

"Ladies, ladies. Enough of the bickering. Our family is together. This is cause for celebration." Her father tried to ease the tension by encouraging them to sit down and enjoy a round of drinks, but Lola could tell her mother wasn't over the fact that she brought a date. The way she looked at Javi made her skin crawl, as if Javi wasn't good enough to be the dirt under her Chanel high heels. Her sister insisted they needed to check on the flowers since they hadn't gotten an update from the store in over twenty-four hours.

Archie, for once, left his nose out of the family discussion and nursed the alcohol in front of him. Lola wanted to dump the contents over his head, but she did her best to restrain herself, even though her sanity was hanging on by a thread.

"Maybe tomorrow, Dad. It's already been a long day and I just want to check into our room and rest."

Her father's face fell, but only for a fraction of a second. "Of course, Lola. Tomorrow we will catch up and I would like to know more about this boyfriend of yours, yeah?" Unlike her mother, his interest seemed genuine and not condescending.

"Right, of course," she murmured and gave him a quick hug. For appearance's sake, she gave her mother and sister an awkward hug and nodded vaguely in Archie's general direction before taking Javi's hand and leading him toward check-in.

"Lola—"

"Not now, Javi. Please." She didn't mean to snap at him, which she had been doing a lot since leaving the plane. She heard his intake of breath, but Javi didn't try to say anything. She didn't know if him talking or not talking was worse.

She let those thoughts leave her mind as she checked into the room. The chipper young woman hummed as she input her information into the computer. "Okay, Ms. Roberts. Your poolside king bedroom is ready for you. You'll be on the sixth—"

"King bed? There are two of them, right?" Lola interrupted her spiel.

The woman shook her head after glancing down at the computer. "No ma'am. Just one bed."

"I booked two queens, though. Could you see if you have anything else available?"

"I'm sorry ma'am but we are booked for multiple weddings

this weekend. This is the only room we have available right now." She didn't actually sound sorry, more like she hoped that Lola wouldn't press her about it anymore.

The dam holding her tears back was going to break any second. She needed to be far away from this lobby when it did. "That's fine." Her voice sounded hoarse and far too small.

"Great. Once again, I'm so sorry about that. You will be on the sixth floor on the left. Please call down if you need anything and thank you for choosing us for your Colorado stay."

Lola turned her back on the woman before she finished, making her way to the elevator. She pressed the up button and immediately expected the elevator to open for her. When it didn't, she pressed it again and again and again...

"Preciosa." Javi's large hand covered hers, pulling her back to his chest. She didn't fight him, she just let it happen. Not a moment later the elevator door slid open and Javi walked them both inside. It was a bit awkward to walk pressed up against his chest, but she no longer trusted her own legs to lead her.

He pressed the button for the sixth floor and let the elevators close. Neither of them spoke after that. She listened to the steady beat of his heart and counted backward from thirty to keep her composure for a little bit longer.

The elevator dinged, signaling they had made it to their floor. This time she pulled away from him so Javi could lead them to their room. She trailed behind him as if each step cost her dearly. She watched in silence as Javi opened up their door, propping it open to allow her in.

The room was beautiful, as she knew it would be, and very spacious. The small hallway held a bathroom off to the right and at the end opened up into a sitting room with a couch and two chairs with a coffee table. A coffee bar sat on the opposite side of the wall. Past the sitting area was the bedroom with one large king-sized bed overlooking the balcony.

And that's when Lola lost it. The stress of the day, preparing to see her family and her ex, and finally the stupid mess up of rooms pushed her over the edge. She couldn't stop the panic attack if she wanted to. Anxiety was stupid and nonsensical. Each hole in her perfectly curated dam had weakened her resolve. Now it was destroyed and she unleashed the bubbling sobs in her throat.

# Javi

## CHAPTER TWENTY-TWO

FROM THE TIME they boarded the plane until the moment they made it to the hotel, Javi had felt the tension rolling off Lola in waves. Each time he attempted to provide comfort, with the exception of the plane ride, she flinched at his touch or snapped at him. He didn't take it personally though because his girl was so deep into her own head that she was barely registering reality.

It just didn't make sense why she was icing him out and that bothered him. Lola had given him very little to go off and though weddings and families could be a stressful thing, the degree to which Lola felt anxious wasn't normal. So what was he missing?

He hadn't expected a welcoming committee upon his arrival, but at the very least he expected more than the reproachful looks he got from her mother and sister. The three women all held a striking resemblance to one another. All had a thick head of midnight-black hair, but Lola was the only one who wore it in its natural curly state. They had the same plump lips and hazel eyes. The other two women lacked the curves Lola had, curves Javi found extremely alluring.

Her father was the only one who seemed interested in meeting him. The only other person Javi couldn't quite get a read on was the other man sitting with the family. He assumed he was the groom-to-be, but Javi noticed the way Lola's body stiffened when she acknowledged him. Javi made up his mind right then that he didn't care for the man.

He didn't get the chance to talk to her between her checking them in, assaulting the elevator button, and entering their room with only one bed. Admittedly he didn't mind only having one bed, but since she seemed uncomfortable with it, he was going to offer to take the pullout couch.

At least he was until he turned around to see full-body sobs wracking through Lola's body. It happened so fast it nearly gave him whiplash. One moment she was quiet, lost in her own thoughts, and the next her cries rang out around the room, nearly bringing him to his knees.

"Preciosa." The nickname tasted vile on his tongue. He didn't deserve to call her that, not when she was crying and shuddering so violently he thought she'd come crashing to the ground.

Not even a second after his thought, Lola's legs gave out and she crashed onto the couch next to her. Her sobs only grew louder, her body shaking as if caught in the cold. Javi crossed the room in two long strides and sank down on the spot next to her. "Lola." Her name sounded like a plea on his lips. A plea for something he couldn't quite put into words.

But now was not the time for talking. No words could form through that avalanche of emotions. He did the only thing he knew how to do, the only thing that didn't need words. She didn't fight him when Javi opened his arms and pulled her to his chest.

There were times when Camilia got so worked up that she couldn't form any words and reasoning with her proved impossible. Javi struggled for a long time because he had always been one who needed to talk things through, but Ofelia helped him realize sometimes emotions were too big, too vast, that no words could break through those barriers.

Nonverbal communication was better at that.

The sobs rolled through her body into his. Lola gripped the

front of his shirt, bunching it tightly in her fists. He rubbed her back, hoping the single action conveyed everything he was feeling and couldn't say. The anger for her family. The frustration with himself for not being able to do more. The curiosity to learn what made her feel so overwhelmed.

For twenty minutes they stayed like this, him just holding her until her sobs turned into soft hiccups. She was far from better, but it was a start. One he could work with if nothing else triggered her.

"When Camilia has had a bad day, the only thing that makes her feel better is a long soak in the tub with her tablet. My mom used to do that for me and Ofelia after we cried on her shoulder. I don't know what it is about baths, but it always did the trick. She would also read us *The Giving Tree*, but I know you have a personal vendetta against it, so can I prepare you a bath?" He looked down, meeting her red-rimmed eyes. She didn't speak, but she also didn't ignore him. A single curt nod was her reply and that was enough for him.

Untangling himself from her, Javi got up and headed to the bathroom. He hadn't gotten a good look at it when they walked in, but now he was able to take it in. The room was two times his bathroom back home, accompanied by a large walk-in shower with a waterfall shower head. The tub was detached and could easily fit a whole family. He sat at the edge of the large tub and turned on the warm water, putting the stopper in at the bottom.

While he allowed the water to fill, he searched the small cabinets and drawers in the bathroom. These fancy hotels always had free shit laying around. Besides the sinfully fluffy white towels, he also found a robe he hoped would work for Lola. It was made from the same materials as the towels, so it would envelop her like a warm hug.

After laying out her towel and robe and turning off the water, Javi stuck his head out to make sure she was still okay. Lola had a vacant look in her eyes, staring ahead at nothing while tears streaked down her cheeks. "Bath's ready." His soft tone still managed to startle her, and Lola flinched. As if in a trance, she got up and walked past him. He stepped aside to give her privacy and as soon as the doorway was clear, she shut the door with a resounding thud.

There was nothing more to say. At least not right now and he knew better than to pry. If she wanted to tell him, which he hoped she did, it would have to be on her own time. She had reached her limit with other people's expectations and he refused to be another stressor in the equation.

To keep his mind off the woman in the bathroom, he took a seat on the bed, letting his back rest against the headboard, legs outstretched. There were a few texts from Ofelia, wondering if he made it alright.

He replied back to let her know he was at the hotel and to let Camilia know he loved her. That resulted in a thirty-minute phone call where she spoke animatedly about the pizzas she got to cook alongside her tío and how he burned his pizza, but hers came out perfectly.

Forty-five minutes later he was off the phone, but Lola hadn't come out yet. He was half tempted to check on her, but then he heard water swishing and someone moving around in the bathroom. He waited and his patience paid off. Lola opened the door, stepping out with her robe on and her hair cascading down around her shoulders.

The tightness of her face from earlier had eased, leaving her more relaxed and although not completely at ease, better than when they started. Her eyes were no longer red rimmed, just puffy from crying. When their eyes locked, her chin dipped down and she grimaced.

"I owe you an apology."

He couldn't have been more shocked if she turned around and showed him she sprouted a tail in the bathtub. An apology? For what? She did nothing wrong and it bothered him that Lola would feel the need to apologize for having feelings. "You don't owe me shit, especially not an apology. I'm worried about you, Lola, not angry."

She seemed to consider his words before nodding. "Still, I doubt you were prepared for me to snot all over your shirt and break down without any warning." She crossed the room to stand in front of him. She hesitated for only a fraction of a second before taking a seat next to him. Her white robe rode up dangerously high on her thighs and Javi couldn't pretend not to notice, not with her smooth brown skin on display for him.

"My eyes are up here, Javier." He heard the smirk in her voice, before he saw her expression. Her lips were upturned, holding back a laugh.

"Dolores, I'm a gentleman. I would never do something as heinous as look at your deliciously exposed thigh. What kind of man do you think I am?"

"Oh, I have a pretty good idea about the type of man you are."

Seeing her smile made him want to capture this moment and lock it away. She deserved to laugh and smile and having that taken from her made Javi see red. He couldn't explain this new streak of violence when it came to Lola, but it made him more curious about what he was obviously missing.

"Listen, you don't have to tell me anything. Nothing at all. But if you want to talk about what happened earlier, I'm here to listen."

The soft hum of the AC was the only sound in the room. Lola rubbed her hands up and down her thighs, seemingly contemplating what information she wanted to share.

"I didn't tell you the real reason I didn't want to go to this damn wedding alone. I had ample opportunity, but I couldn't bring myself to admit it to you. I guess I didn't want you to see me differently. Which is stupid, I know, but my anxiety around this whole ordeal is fucking astronomical.

"So you met my family downstairs. They aren't the most welcoming of people unless your pockets are lined thicker than

Oprah's." Javi snorted. He had the inkling that her parents surrounded themselves with people who used twenty-dollar bills to wipe their asses. And Lola had grown up in that environment. He couldn't begin to imagine what that was like.

"I don't talk about it often because everyone kinda rolls their eyes at the rich girl's problems," Lola continued, "and I get it. I was extremely privileged growing up and I never lacked for anything...well material needs anyway. My emotional needs were hardly ever met and I've been in therapy for it for years.

"Anyway, that's not what triggered the panic attack from earlier. It was seeing Archie."

"Archie?" The name didn't ring a bell to him.

"He was the man seated at the table next to my sister. He's the one she's marrying and..." Her voice caught and a tear rolled down her cheek. A self-deprecating laugh left her lips. "Fuck, I'm not even sad over him! My emotions are just all over the place right now."

He reached over to the tissues on the bedside table, offering it to her. She quietly thanked him and used a tissue to dab at her eyes. "What I'm trying to say is I used to date Archie—don't look at me like that, I was young and stupid. We dated for a few years and I swore he was the one...until he broke up with me and almost immediately started to date my sister. I guess she fit his image better."

It was as if a volcano erupted inside of him, scorching every surface of his body. He had known anger before, most notably after the death of Estella, but that felt different than this. He wanted to wring Archie's neck. Not fit his image? As if the goddess in front of him needed to fit any damn image but her own. A man like Archie couldn't possibly love a woman like Lola properly. He knew men like Archie. Ones who wanted a pretty little wife by their side to advance their own career. Lola deserved better.

"Javi, say something. It looks like you want to break a lamp." Oh, he definitely wanted to break something, but not a lamp.

Simultaneously, he wanted to thank Archie for being a pendejo for letting Lola slip through his grip. She fell into Javi's arms. It didn't matter that he only had this week with her and their relationship was fake; this week was very much real and he would see to it that she was treated as she deserved.

"If you want me to punch him in the veneers, I will." That got a bark of laughter out of her and a smack to his arm.

"Hasn't anyone ever told you that violence isn't the answer?"

"Actually no, someone told me that violence is sometimes the answer." Another smack, this time to his chest. "Ah, preciosa, you don't live by your own teachings."

"Hey, I'm only good at giving other people perspective. My life is a shit show." She shrugged. "But now you know why I have been on edge all day and had a panic attack. Thank you for everything. I've never had a panic attack in front of anyone but my therapist before. You handled it well."

"Camilia sometimes has moments like that. We call it her big feelings. I think she got it from her mother. Estella had bad anxiety, so I tried to learn ways to make it easier for her."

"You don't talk about her. Estella," Lola said softly and Javi's body stiffened. It wasn't as if he didn't talk about Estella. No one ever brought her up and asked about her. He didn't have many friends to confide in and he didn't like the way people looked at him with pity in their eyes. Like he was the one who died and not her.

A soft hand wrapped around his own and he realized he had been silent for a beat too long. "You don't have to speak about her. I just thought since you saw me ugly cry, I could return the favor." Her smile was delicate, but she didn't push. She didn't need to. Javi found himself wanting to talk about her.

"Estella was my high school sweetheart. We met in middle school and hit it off. By ninth grade we were inseparable. When we graduated high school, she went to school for nursing and I started in construction alongside my dad. I wanted to help her pay off her loans and we wanted to start a family eventually."

He remembered the exact day Estella had gotten into nursing school. He had come home from a late-night shift and found Estella curled up on the couch crying over her laptop. Javi's mind immediately went to someone dying and ran to her, pulling her into his arms. But she pushed him away and showed him the acceptance letter she received. They were both crying after that.

"A year later she got really sick, so I took her to the doctor. Turns out we weren't as safe as what we thought we were and she was pregnant."

"Who picked Camilia's name? It's beautiful." Lola smiled, squeezing his hand.

"Thank you, and Estella did. It was her grandmother's name. Estella spent nearly a year with our little girl before she was taken from us."

Lola's eyes filled with unshed tears. Her heart was just so damn big and he loved that about her. He just didn't want her crying for him. "If you don't mind me asking, what happened?"

It was a question he had to answer and hear hundreds of times, but it never got easier. He could recite her death in his sleep for how many times he played it back in his head. "Estella had just dropped Camilia off at my dad's house. He agreed to watch Camilia while I worked and Estella went to school for nursing. She only had a semester left.

"It was a rainy day, bad conditions on the road. From what I'm told, she had stopped at a stoplight and the light turned green. She went to go, but a semi-truck off to her left had lost control of his vehicle or something was wrong with his brakes. I'm not sure which. Whatever it was, he sped right through the light and straight into Estella's car. The first responders said she died instantly, so at least she didn't suffer. The worst part was she wasn't even supposed to be on that road. I should have taken Camilia to my parents that morning, but she let me sleep in. If only..."

"Oh Javi." Tears rolled down Lola's eyes. He was surprised to find his own cheeks wet. Lola moved so she was in his lap, arms around his neck. "You can't blame yourself. It wasn't your fault. You had no way of knowing this would happen. Please don't beat yourself up over this."

He had heard that numerous times from his family. He didn't think the pain or the guilt would ever go away, which is why he worked extra hard to make sure Camilia was well looked after and loved. It was hard not to feel like he took her mother away.

"Javi, look at me." Lola cupped his face and forced him to turn in her direction. Their faces were inches apart. He could lean down and brush his lips against hers, but he held firm. "You are a good man and a great father. Camilia is so lucky to have you. What happened to Estella was a horrible accident. It never should have happened and I'm so sorry it did, but you can't blame yourself. You can't live with that guilt."

Healing was a weird process. It wasn't linear and sometimes it didn't make any sense. One second you were fine and the next you were crying in the arms of a beautiful woman. And he fucking hated crying. It wasn't so much due to toxic masculinity but more because it always made his eyes itchy and his nose run.

"I'll make you a deal," he said, wiping his eyes with the back of his hands. "I'll work on forgiving myself if you work on not letting their opinions dictate your feelings about yourself."

"Well fuck, Javi. That's asking for a hell of a lot." But even as she said it, she held out her pinky to his. "Pinky promise?"

Javi wrapped his pinky around hers. "Pinky promise," he repeated, leaning forward to press a soft kiss to her hand. She smiled at his touch, letting her fingers linger against his before she slowly pulled away.

"Now that's enough soul-searching for one day. How about we take advantage of my father's credit card and order a shit ton of snacks and rent a few movies?" She grinned and reached for the hotel's phone.

"Now you're speaking my language. Let's get our own party started." And that was exactly what they did. Lola ordered far too much food and they watched the first two movies in the *Lord of the Rings* series after Javi found out she had never seen them before. By the third movie, Lola had fallen asleep on the bed and Javi covered her up. He went around to turn off the lights and television before making himself a nice bed on the couch. Not five minutes later he was asleep with thoughts of a certain big-hearted woman on his mind.

# *Lola*

## CHAPTER TWENTY-THREE

LOLA AWOKE the following morning to the sound of soft snores and an empty bed. She was still in the robe from yesterday and must have fallen asleep during one of the *Lord of the Rings* movies, though she couldn't remember which. They all blurred together after a while.

Although the bed was huge, she only occupied a small portion of it, not once moving throughout the night. The bed would have been more than accommodating for the both of them, but she had fallen asleep before they discussed it. Javi, always the gentleman, took the couch and she doubted it was as comfortable as the feather mattress she was atop of.

A soft buzzing sound grabbed her attention. Her phone lay on the bedside table, but it was not plugged in. She hadn't had the chance to get her charger out last night and she was sure it was almost dead. Reaching for it, Lola brought the buzzing phone to her ear and saw that it was her mother calling. She groaned, nearly letting it go to voicemail, but thought better of it last minute and answered.

"Mother, hi," she greeted her as formally as if the Queen of England had called her.

There was a pause on the other end and then the sound of shuffling papers. Knowing her mother, she was still neck-deep in wedding planning, even days before the actual event. "Good heavens, I hope I didn't wake you. It's nearly noon."

One quick glance at her watch told her that yes, she had slept until noon. What the actual fuck? She hadn't slept that late since she was a teenager. Flying and breaking down in the middle of her hotel room really took it out of her. "Oh, I was just lounging," she lied, "did you need something?"

"Yes, I wanted to call and remind you that dinner tonight will be at the second-floor restaurant. Do you need me to send someone to retrieve you when it's time? I know how forgetful you can be when it comes to things like this."

If it were possible for eyes to roll all the way to the back of her head, this would have been the moment. She had been late once to one of the functions her mother had put on, simply because she was out doing errands for *her*. She had yet to live it down and now her mom always asked if she needed to send someone to escort her like a babysitter.

"I think between me and Javi, we'll manage to make it to dinner."

"Oh, yes, the young man you brought with you. He'll be joining us?"

"Yes, Mother." If there was a reward for forced patience, Lola would win in every category. "He's my date, of course he's going to be part of the wedding activities."

"It's interesting we have never heard of him, that's all. No need to get so pressed. Anyway, I actually called you for a different reason. Your sister and I are going out to look for shoes. Can you believe that she hasn't found her wedding shoes yet? You would think everyone is getting married and buying up all the semi-decent shoes in town. But that means I won't be able to retrieve her earrings arriving today. The front desk graciously agreed to keep them safe. Would you be a dear and check periodically throughout the day? You can bring them to dinner. Are you sure you don't need me to send for you when it's dinner time?"

"I'm certain. And yes, I'll get the earrings. Anything else?"

"No, nothing I can think of. Make sure you and your...erm, boyfriend are dressed appropriately."

"Perhaps you want to come in and dress us yourself." Lola tried to hide the bitterness in her tone, but failed.

"Dolores Cecilia Roberts," her mom reprimanded, throwing out all three names like confetti. Except there was nothing celebratory in her tone.

"Kidding. Yes, I promise my *boyfriend* and I won't embarrass you. I'll see you tonight and don't ask me again if I need someone to remind me about dinner. I'm not going to forget. Bye, Mother." She cut the line before Luciana could ask her to do anything else.

"Boyfriend has a good ring to it, don't you think?"

Her soul jumped all the way out of her body, ascending far into the heavens. She could hear her spiritual self now, telling the golden angel that she died of fright. "How long have you been awake!?" She shrieked and pulled the covers tighter around her as if they could protect her from a smirking Javi.

"Long enough for your mother to call me your boyfriend. Though she didn't sound fond of me." Despite having slept on the couch, he looked fully rested and not disheveled like Lola was certain she looked. Her hair alone would take time to tame the bird's nest it probably was.

"Well you are technically my boyfriend this week, so her assumption is correct."

"Does being your boyfriend this week earn me a good morning kiss?"

Despite herself, she smiled at his lame attempt at flirting. "Honey, you do not want to kiss my morning breath mouth."

"Oh, I don't know about that. Just a taste, preciosa. I'll be a happy man." How this man could make her stomach flutter upon waking up, she would never know. She was certain there was a permanent flush to her cheeks now, thanks to Javi.

She flipped over the blankets, freeing her tangled legs and got up to walk toward him. She stopped right in front of the couch and leaned down, placing a swift kiss to his forehead. "That's all you get. Now, if you would kindly stop flirting with me so I can get dressed, that would be amazing. Don't think about checking out my ass when I turn around."

"Never would dream of it. What type of man do you take me for?"

"Hopefully a decent one. Feel free to get ready here. I'm going to be hogging the bathroom for a bit. We're on earring duty, by the way." She turned her back to him and felt his searing gaze on her ass as she walked away. That might have made her swing her hips a bit more dramatically than normal.

MUCH TO HER mother's dismay, Lola had kept her word and made it to dinner alongside Javi and the damned earrings with five minutes to spare, successfully preventing Luciana's beloved lectures. Her father and mother lingered outside the hostess stand, waiting to be sat. Marisol and Archie were nowhere to be found, so her mother pegged the wrong sister as tardy.

"My girl," her father said, wrapping his bulky arms around her. He was the only one in the family that could wrap around her torso and it made her feel safe within his arms. When he pulled away, he shook Javi's hand with a vigorous handshake. "And Javier, isn't it?"

"Yes sir. Javier Mendez. Nice to meet you again."

The conversation lolled soon after that with still no sign of her sister. Lola wasn't surprised by this though. Marisol had always been notoriously late. It was like time held no meaning for her and when she showed up, that was simply the time she was meant to be there. Oh, how Lola wished she could operate like that, but anxiety made her arrive at everything at least five minutes early.

Their stunted conversation came to an abrupt end when the red-haired waiter came by wearing a smile the size of Texas. Working with a population of people who made money in their sleep, Lola too would smile like that in hopes of a good tip.

"Welcome and thank you for dining with us tonight. If you'll follow me, I'll lead you to your booth," he said in an English accent. Lola's stomach churned at the word booth, but she tried not to think too much about it.

Their waiter led them through the expensively decorated restaurant with a stocked bar off toward the right. In the center was a large crystal fire pit with a burning blue fire that added to the ambiance. They were led to a row of booths and she held back a groan.

Her mother's petite frame scooted in first, followed by her father. Her father had a rounded belly that she always loved. The table pressed up against his stomach and he laughed, patting his belly. "Gotta lay off the Oreos," he joked. If Lola made that joke, her mother would have died on the spot, but since it came from her husband, Luciana was all smiles and tickled with laughter.

Lola had said it once and she would continue to say it. Booths at fancy-ass restaurants—or most restaurants for that matter— were not built with plus-size people in mind. They were often placed too close to the table in order to fill more of the space with booths and customers.

Javi slid into the booth first and she sent out a silent prayer as he did. Javi was straight sized, but he was tall with big arms, so scooting down the leather seat had not been an easy feat. Lola felt her mother's judgmental eyes as she slowly lowered herself down to the bench. It was humiliating having her mother watch her as she struggled to wiggle into the tight space. She accidentally hit the table with her elbow, nearly knocking down a wine glass.

Javi snatched his hand out with all the reflexes of Spider-Man and caught it before it crashed to the ground and broke into a million different pieces on the floor, saving her from the judging stares of the other patrons.

When she squeezed in enough, Javi offered her a smile and placed his hand on her thigh reassuringly. Her mother still wore the look of thinly veiled disgust and took this opportunity to not-so-subtly bring up the gym membership she researched the moment Lola told her she was moving. "Have you checked out the gym I sent you, dear? The one with the classes and personal trainers."

Next to her, she felt Javi stiffen, but she clamped her hand around his to ease his temper. "I told you, Mother, I'm loving the yoga studio I go to and have no desire to go work out with a bunch of sweaty strangers. Especially there."

"Oh, but Dolores, it would be so good for you. Don't you want to be healthy?"

It always came back to health. When a fat person existed in a place for straight-sized people, everyone was a doctor. Thin didn't equal healthy and she wished her mother understood that. She knew for a fact that she was in better shape than Mona and Mattea, even if they were both smaller than her. Yet, her mom would only see their size and think they were the epitome of health.

"I'm quite fine the way I am. But if my body insults you, maybe you should work on fixing your own biases when it comes to plus-sized individuals." Outwardly she hoped she projected strength and badassery because inwardly she was freaking out that she even humored her mother in the conversation.

"Now ladies, enough fighting. Let's discuss what we want as an appetizer. Personally, I don't think we can go wrong with a charcuterie board," her father, ever the optimist, said. Lola loved him, she did, but he could be so dense at times. He never saw how her mother treated her and thought to himself that it was wrong. He tried to be a buffer, but she doubted he knew the root of the problem.

"I'm just saying it is something you should consider." Her

mother always had to have the last word. Before Lola could respond, Luciana's face lit up and that only meant one thing. Dread nearly immobilized her body, but she forced herself to move.

She turned in time to see Marisol and Archie head their way. Marisol was in a knee-length red dress that hugged her body perfectly, no roll in sight. Archie wore his standard dark business casual, like he was prepared to go to an interview at any time. Even she had to admit they looked pretty together.

Marisol took one look at her sister, giving her a simple nod before heading over to their parent's side of the table. The booth seat should have only been big enough for three people to fit comfortably across, but both Marisol and Archie slid in.

"What are we drinking?" Archie laughed good-naturedly. He was met by a chorus of chuckles as his father went into a deep analysis of every wine on the menu.

"Did you pick up my earrings, Dolores?" No hi, no how are you, just straight to the point. It was her sister to a T.

Lola searched through her silver clutch and pulled out the black velvet box and handed it over. Her sister inspected it, opened it up, and gasped. "Oh these are perfect! Archie, don't you think these are perfect?"

Judging by his disinterested look and quick glance at the box, Lola didn't think Archie gave a flying fuck. "Yes, very nice. What are they for?"

"The wedding, Archie. The whole reason we are here." Marisol frowned.

"Right. Well, I'm sure they will compliment your dress." He offered her a dazzling smile that might work for his clients, but not a fiancée. Lola felt the anger roll off her sister and, despite their personal problems, wanted to stand up for Marisol. Until Marisol took her ire out on her, the black sheep of the family.

"Dolores, you never showed me your jewelry for your dress. You know I hate those big hoops you wear. Please tell me you got something more sensible."

The night had barely started and already Lola was tired. Between her mother's hurtful jabs at her weight and Marisol's misplaced anger, Lola knew she was in for a verbal beatdown. She just wished Javi wouldn't have to witness these horrendous attacks.

## *Javi*

### CHAPTER TWENTY-FOUR

FROM THE WAY he gripped the table, Javi was surprised that the edge hadn't snapped off in his hand. The only thing keeping him grounded was Lola's hand atop his as he listened to her family demeaning her with every other sentence. How she simply sat there and took their jabs with as much grace and poise as she did, he would never know. Because all he saw and felt was red rage.

"So, Javi. What do you do for a living, son?" Travis's gaze looked him over, sizing him up. Out of all the Robertses, he was so far the most tolerable. At least he seemed to love his daughter, though he was ignorant when it came to how his wife and other daughter treated her.

He had also been the only one to take an interest in Javi. Luciana stared in disapproval, as if she could smell the poverty on him. Not that he was at the poverty level, but compared to these people he might as well be. Marisol only glanced his way a few times but was otherwise occupied by Archie and her phone, which seemed to be an extension of her body.

"I work as an independent contractor," he said, getting a nod of approval from Travis and a furrowed brow from Luciana.

"Ah, good work, indeed. Always a good sign when a man is good with his hands. Never a bad thing to put some grease on ya,"

521

Travis tutted. It was clear the man had a very old-fashioned way of thinking, but it served in Javi's favor this time. Not that he needed his approval or anything since he wasn't technically dating his daughter, but it would make their time together more pleasant if Travis didn't want to run him off.

"He's the one I hired to help me renovate the bookstore, Daddy, remember?" Lola chimed in and he tried to ignore the lurch of his dick when Lola said the word "daddy." Now was not the time to be sporting a major hard-on. "He has a few guys working now and when we get back my bookcases should be nearly finished. Isn't that right, Javi?"

"If everything goes according to plan." He made a mental note to check on his crew later. Just because he wasn't working, didn't mean the guys he hired to take charge of the built-ins weren't.

"The bookstore? What is this about a bookstore?" Marisol's voice couldn't sound more condescending if she tried. Her well-manicured fingers stopped flying across her phone long enough to catch the tail end of their conversations.

With more patience than her sister deserved, Lola explained the renovations taking place back home. He liked the way she spoke about his work, with admiration and happiness. His heart swelled in response, knowing she trusted him this much with her dream store.

"So you opened a bookstore, huh?" was Marisol's only response. Her tone bordered on amusement and astonishment, sounding as if she didn't see the value in what Lola was doing nor understand the concept of a passion project.

Because that was what the bookstore was to Lola. It was a way to turn something she loved into a full-time career. A place where she could spend her days lost in books and the customers. Where she could read to children and find the perfect book for anyone who walked through her door.

"You must send us some progress pictures. I would love to show some of my golf buddies the work you are doing. They were impressed to hear you starting on your own little entrepreneurial path," Travis said, eyes glinting with pride. Marisol narrowed her eyes. Obviously, she had not been expecting that response from her father.

"Yes, you really must show us some progress photos. Such an interesting thing, a bookstore," came a new voice. Everyone's heads swiveled toward Archie. Javi felt Lola tense next to him and he felt his own body move closer to her, as if trying to shield her from the smug smile on Archie's face.

Javi didn't consider himself a violent person, but something about Archie made the hairs on the back of his neck rise. He wanted nothing more than to put the man in his place, but he knew that would embarrass Lola and possibly get him kicked out of the wedding. He wasn't willing to risk that.

"It's admirable. We all have to start somewhere. It is hard to start new businesses these days; most end up failing. But I'm sure that won't be the case with yours," Archie said the last part as if it were an afterthought. Javi hadn't realized he was clenching his hands into fists until he felt Lola's hand covering them.

She was trying to comfort him when it should have been the other way around.

The rest of the table quieted until Travis and Archie launched into work talk about the upcoming grape season. None of it piqued his interest so Javi let his mind wander to Camilia and how much fun she was probably having with Ofelia. To the men back in California working under the watchful eye of Mona or Mattea. And finally to Lola, how she appeared so calm and collected, but how her family had caused an abundance of anxiety.

Their dinner saved him from reliving anymore from yesterday. He hadn't remembered what he ordered until a large lamb chop was placed in front of him, with a veggie combo and a baked potato. His mouth salivated. Lola was given the same except instead of the baked potato, white rice was placed in a single mound on the plate.

Travis and Archie both received similar meat platters while Marisol and Luciana ordered a large salad with what looked to be apricots and almonds, along with a reddish vinaigrette. It didn't appeal to Javi, but Luciana stared pointedly at Lola's plate.

"Sweetheart, are you certain you ordered that?" she pried, even though they had all listened to Lola's order.

"Oh, no. Did I make a mistake?" their waiter asked.

Lola's cheeks tinged red, signaling her mortification from her mother putting her on the spot once again. "No, no mistake. I ordered this."

"Are you sure? I don't mind getting the correct order," the man assured, not realizing he was making the situation worse.

"Looks right to me. Lola was always an...adventurous eater when we were together." Archie commented and it took everything in Javi not to jump across the table and plant his fist between his eyes. His anger only flared when Luciana laughed, seeming to find his words charming rather than hurtful.

Javi saw the panic set in, the way all eyes were on her and how Lola slowly retreated back into her shell. He wouldn't stand for it. "This is exactly what she ordered. Thank you." His voice held a certain dismissal that could not be ignored.

The waiter seemed taken aback by his abrupt answer, but composed himself swiftly. "Of course. Enjoy your meal. Please let me know if you need anything," he said and quickly made his way to a different table.

"Thank you." Her voice came out low, barely above a whisper, but he caught the relief in her features. He, however, was far from relieved. Javi's body tensed up even more than it had been only moments ago. He felt like a too tightly wound rubber band that was about to snap at any moment.

How the fuck could she be so goddamn calm during all of this? How the hell did she grow up in a household that made belittling comments her entire childhood? If Javi had been subjected to that, he doubted he would be half as bubbly as Lola.

Not when he carried so much hurt and trauma with him from the very people who should have loved him unconditionally.

His words should have been the end of it, but Luciana Roberts couldn't read the fucking room and had to make one more comment, not knowing that Javi was seconds away from bursting. "Just remember you have a dress to fit into for your sister's wedding. There wouldn't be enough time to properly alter it now."

Javi had enough and threw his hands down on the table. The glasses and silverware shook and everyone jumped to attention, staring at him with wide eyes and open mouths. "I have only met you guys twice and in that time you have done nothing but make offhanded comments about Lola."

He knew he should stop. Knew that this wasn't his place, but the lava within him had bubbled over and he couldn't stop the flow now. "What gives you the right to police and comment on her body? Because frankly, Lola is the most beautiful woman I have ever laid eyes on. That's the least impressive thing about her though, because she also has a huge heart and anyone would be lucky enough to call her a friend. Which, you would know if you both stopped trying to tear her down for two goddamn seconds and got to know her.

"And you—" his eyes darkened, narrowing to slits, as he turned to Archie "—keep your unsolicited comments and dickhead behavior to yourself. You have no goddamn right to speak to or belittle my girl. Hell, you aren't even worthy enough to be in the same room as her. I highly suggest you keep your mouth shut when she's around."

His passionate proclamation and threat were met with stunned silence. Everyone's faces had different degrees of astonishment, but then the spell broke and Luciana and Marisol began to sputter their retorts back at the same time.

"I never—"

"How dare—"

But Javi didn't give a shit what they had to say. He turned to Lola, barely registering her expression, saying, "I need a moment."

Wordlessly, Lola scooted out of the booth and Javi followed her. "I'm sorry," he managed to say in passing, listening to the chaos he left in his wake. Perhaps he should turn around and apologize for his behavior. Maybe he made it worse for Lola, but going back now wouldn't repair anything. He would only make it worse. Better to beg for forgiveness later when his head was clear.

Javi stormed out, passing disgruntled patrons attempting to locate their seats. He thought he heard someone calling his name, but he didn't dare look back. He didn't stop until he was out of the restaurant and back at the elevators. He found a hallway that only led to bathrooms and hooked a right, using the space to pace back and forth, allowing his anger to dissipate.

Fuck, he blew it. He had always been a hothead when it came to people he cared deeply for and he tended to act first without thinking. If he was a better man, he would walk right back in and apologize and offer to give back the money. The money he needed, but didn't deserve because he wasn't upholding his end of the bargain.

"Javi!"

He didn't know how long he had been pacing when he heard his name. He stopped abruptly and turned toward the voice. Lola stood there panting, eyes blown wide with an emotion he couldn't quite place yet.

The apology fell from his lips immediately, his anger turning into embarrassment. "I'm sorry, Lola. Fuck, did I make it worse? I just couldn't sit there and let them talk to you like that a second longer. I swear—"

"Javi."

He was rambling and he knew it. Lola marched right up to him again after calling his name for the second time. He didn't know if this was the part where she kicked him out. He would go, and although he was embarrassed with how he handled the situation, he didn't regret his words. They deserved to be called out on their toxic behavior.

"If you want me to go, I will."

"I want you to shut up." Her words were a command. One moment she was standing right in front of him and the next she was in his arms, kissing him and stealing the breath from his lungs.

He didn't respond at first, far too shocked to make any sudden movements. But then his brain kicked in and instinct took over. A low growl left the back of his throat and he kissed her back, moving her against the wall. A low moan left her lips as her body curved to his.

This wasn't the reaction he was expecting, but it was far better than he deserved.

# *Lola*

## CHAPTER TWENTY-FIVE

*Because frankly, Lola is the most beautiful woman I have ever laid eyes on. That's the least impressive thing about her though, because she also has a huge heart and anyone would be lucky enough to call her a friend.*

Those words rang through her ears, sending shivers down her entire body. With a few sentences, he had managed to render her senseless, moving only so he could escape the travesty that was her family. Four sets of eyes stared back at her in astonishment, though Archie looked more amused than anything, hiding his smile behind his glass of wine. If only he knew how badly Javi wanted to hurt him. She could feel it in the way his body tensed when he all but threatened him.

As soon as Javi was out of distance, her mother and sister started in on her. "How dare you bring someone so rude and inappropriate to your sister's wedding week. Do you think of anyone but yourself? And for him to insult Archie? Unacceptable." Her mother's scorn cut deep, but she had spent most of her life hardening herself when it came to her. Yet, this time her mother's anger wasn't at her...well, not entirely. When Javi was involved, she found herself steeled against her ire.

To her complete amazement, before she had the opportunity

to talk back to Mom and inevitably make the situation worse, her father beat her to it. "Enough, Luciana. You are always too hard on Lola. Both you and Marisol"—he shot her sister a disappointed expression—"have grilled Dolores since she arrived. Her young man has had enough. Frankly, I have too."

She couldn't have been more stunned if her father had announced he was running away to join the circus. His features relaxed when he turned back toward Lola. "Go check if Javi is alright, princess. And please give him my deepest apologies. This is not how our family normally behaves." Well, she wasn't going to burst his bubble and let him know this was exactly how their family behaved, but she appreciated the sentiment regardless.

"Thank you, Daddy." Lola was tempted to kiss her father, but she would have to lean over Archie and Marisol to do that and she didn't want to be anywhere near them. The only person she wanted to be with now was Javi. If she knew him like she thought she did, he was off blaming himself for his mishap and probably thought she was pissed.

She wasn't upset though, not in the least. What she wanted was him, but getting through the labyrinth of the restaurant had been no easy feat. She maneuvered herself through waiters and waitresses and squeezed her ass through too tight tables and chairs nearly on top of one another. At one point she was certain she hit a glass and knocked it over, but she didn't look back to confirm.

When she finally made it out and didn't see Javi, she got worried. What if he went home? He wouldn't leave her without saying goodbye. Hell, she hoped he wouldn't leave at all. Without him, the rest of the trip would be unbearable. And if she was being honest with herself, she had liked having him by her side for reasons unrelated to her family. She liked the way he made her feel and the safety he offered. She also liked how he looked at her when he thought no one was watching.

Maybe there was something there between them that needed to be explored. She just didn't know how to take that plunge or if she was ready to admit her feelings. It was still too soon; her feelings were too strong and all over the place.

Once she reached the elevators, she found Javi pacing back and forth. He had not noticed her yet, lost in his thoughts. Once again she was struck with a sense of wonder. Standing so close amplified her feelings for him tenfold, passion like she had only felt once before sprang to the surface and she clenched her hands into fists.

Then he noticed her and all the unsaid words he couldn't share came tumbling from his mouth. Her suspicions had been correct and he thought she was mad at him. The whispered way his name left her lips did nothing to stop the onslaught of his tirade.

"Javi." Lola tried his name again only to get the same outcome. He wasn't seeing her. If he was, there would be no question about what she wanted from him. There was only one way to get to him. One way that was a surefire way to get his attention.

Her feet acted of their own volition. Like a hungry viper, she stalked her prey until she was right up on him. One look into his dark eyes and she attacked. Her lips were on his before he could finish his sentence, tasting the dinner he barely touched. Her tongue eagerly parted his lips, exploring the taste of him.

Javi's body went rigid against hers and not in a sexy way. Had she done something wrong? If she read the signals wrong and was accosting this man, she would never forgive herself. Lola went to pull back, but it was as if a light switched on inside of Javi.

His hard body pressed her back until she hit the wall behind her with enough force that it sent tendrils of pleasure and pain through her. His hands went to her hips, squeezing. They were a mess of tongue, teeth, and saliva. There wasn't anything light or sweet about this kiss. It was dominating and rough. Everything she needed.

She felt wanton next to him and when he moved closer, pressing his leg between her thighs. Her pussy fluttered for him. Wetness dampened her panties at the friction his knee made.

"Preciosa." Javi sucked her bottom lip between his, tugging on it. She let out a strangled moan. Any moment anyone could walk by them and see the way Javi had her pinned against the wall and her legs straddling his thigh. They were fully clothed but exposed in so many different ways.

Despite knowing—or maybe even due to knowing—someone could walk by them at any time, it did not stop the proverbial fire that had been lit underneath them. She grabbed his neck to pull him back down to her, kissing him deeply. A long stroke of his tongue met hers and his hands dipped lower to cup her ass.

It was still not enough; it would never be enough. She began to rub herself against his leg, hoping to apply some friction to her needy clit. "Fuck," Javi growled and that's when she felt his hard cock press into her leg. "Look at what you do to me, Lola."

She wanted to show him what he did to her and that started with them getting the hell out of the public hallway. His thigh would not keep her satisfied for long, no, she wanted his head buried between her legs.

"Lola, we should stop." The words did not register at first. Stopping seemed like the opposite of a good idea. They had the chance to chase their pleasure so why wouldn't they?

"I don't want to stop." She couldn't keep out the wine in her voice. It didn't matter that it made her sound pathetic, she was horny and in need of release.

"Trust me, preciosa, I don't want to stop either. But I don't think I would be doing my job if I didn't remind you of our business arrangement. I don't want you to do anything you aren't comfortable doing."

*Business arrangement.*

Those words hit her hard. It hardly seemed fair that she was this close to release, only for her own words to come back and haunt her now. But she hadn't taken the time to consider how this might feel for him. She gasped in horror and shook her head. "Oh fuck, I swear I'm not paying you for sex. Holy shit."

A gruff chuckle met her mild freakout. "No, I know. Believe

me, I want to. But when I get you back into bed, I want it to be because you want me and not because I stood up for you in front of your family and you feel like you owe me."

She didn't feel that way...did she? Fuck, her head was all fuzzy with big emotions and horniness. Damn, this man and his chivalrous nature. "I hate you a little bit," she muttered.

"Trust me, I hate myself too."

"Then I guess we should go back to our room."

"Yeah, it does seem like we should."

"Our room with only one bed."

"Just the one."

"That couch couldn't have been comfortable."

"It wasn't," he agreed with a small smile tugging at his lips.

"Then maybe," she bit her lips, squirming under his gaze. She had just been rubbing herself against him and now suddenly she was shy? Make it make sense. "Maybe you should take the bed."

"And kick you out? Nah, I wouldn't dream of that."

"I said nothing about being kicked out. I said you should take the bed. With me. It's a big bed."

The man was full-on smirking now, his lips plump and still shiny from their kisses. "You want me to sleep with you?"

"Just sleep. As you said earlier. We shouldn't jump into anything right now, but I think we are both mature enough to share a bed and both be on our best behavior."

"I'm nothing if not a gentleman," Javi said and Lola had to keep herself from rolling her eyes. What they had been doing seconds ago was the furthest thing from gentlemanly she could think of.

"Then it's settled. You'll sleep with me and tomorrow I will deal with my family."

Javi's cocky smile dropped. "Yeah, about that. Again I'm sorry —"

Lola stopped him with a smack to the chest. "No, do not apologize for standing up for me after they showed you their true colors. No one has ever done that for me before and I will not let you *"sorry'* yourself out of this."

"Well, when you put it like that, I guess you're right."

"I'm always right. It would do you well to remember that." She winked and slowly—and very reluctantly—began to untangle herself from Javi. Once she put a bit of distance between them and straightened out her clothes, as well as pretending as if she didn't see Javi's erection through his pants, she spoke again. "Now, let's head back to the room and order a pizza since we didn't finish dinner. We can continue watching your silly movie from last night.

"Silly? That's *Lord of the Rings* you're talking about. Show some respect." He winked at her. Lola laughed and turned on her heels, heading straight toward the elevator. She didn't look back, but she heard Javi's footfalls as he followed behind, just like he promised.

# Lola

## CHAPTER TWENTY-SIX

JAVI WAS a cuddler and that made her inexplicably happy. After the terrible dinner incident that resulted in being pinned up against the wall and kissed until their lips were swollen, Lola led them back to their room. Javi immediately went to the bathroom and stayed in there for a questionable amount of time doing God knows what. Her mind conjured up images of Javi braced over the bathroom sink, cock in hand as he pleasured himself to thoughts of her.

A girl could dream.

When he finally came out, dressed in black sweats that hung low on his hips and a gray T-shirt, the explosion of passion from earlier had simmered down to only a mild annoyance. Thoughts of the damn business agreement provided enough of a cockblock for now, but she didn't know how much longer either of them could ignore these feelings.

While Javi got into bed, Lola slipped away into the bathroom. She took off her makeup, making sure to scrub her face clean. Sleeping with makeup on was a big no-no for her because it caused irritation to her skin. She then changed out of the stuffy dress she only wore around family and into her pink, silk, matching pajama set.

535

When she returned to the room, she felt Javi's heated glare on her body, taking in every inch of exposed skin. She made no comment as she made a show of putting away her phone and getting comfortable in bed, all the while feeling his eyes on her.

Lola squirmed under his scrutiny, attempting to hide the blush creeping along her cheeks. "So, we should order that pizza now," she said and dialed room service. Not an hour later, the two of them were in bed, eating a deliciously greasy pizza, and watching a movie.

About halfway through, Lola grew tired but tried to keep her eyes open and attentive. Apparently she was failing because Javi gathered the pizza box and paper plates and got up to toss them away. "We should sleep," he said, his voice gruff but she wasn't sure if that was from being tired or something else entirely.

"Goodnight, Javi," she said right before she reached to turn off the light, leaving them in complete darkness. He didn't respond to her, not at first. For ten minutes they lay in silence, only the sounds of their breathing comforting one another. Lola was certain he had fallen asleep and moved to make herself more comfortable, when two strong arms wrapped around her, pulling her to a hard chest.

She had never been held like this before, where the other person didn't expect anything in return. Hot breath hit the back of her neck and Javi's chest rose and fell in a slow rhythm. His grip around her tightened, not painfully, and not enough to keep her from moving away if she was uncomfortable. The small gesture made her feel important and safe.

She had no problem falling asleep that night.

In the morning, the sun crept through their curtains, cascading rays of light onto her face. The sun brought with it a new day and a new day meant she would have to face her family. If it were up to her, Lola would spend the entirety of their free day together in bed. But she knew from experience that letting unneeded tension fester between herself and her mom and sister would only result in a bigger scandal.

As if sensing her alertness and wandering thoughts, Javi's arms tightened around her and pulled her flush against his chest. Every part of him was awake and ready to greet her and she couldn't stop the slight wiggle she did to tease him. That earned her a groan and lips against her neck. "Don't go."

Soft lips explored her neck and she was inclined to just go with it. Lola let her head fall to the side, exposing more skin to him which he greedily took. "Stay," he said again, his lips brushing against her ear.

How easy it would be to stay here and pretend things like her family or their business arrangement didn't exist. How desperately she wanted to feel instead of thinking about the complicated set of emotions swirling through her brain and heart regarding him.

"I have to go check on my family." The flimsy excuse sounded bad, even to her ears. But she did need to put out fires so the rest of the trip wasn't harder than it had to be.

"Or...you can stay here and we can do more of absolutely nothing." He bucked his hips against her backside and she had to hold back a moan. Wasn't this the same man who told her they needed to cool it yesterday before things got hot and heavy? And now he was instigating something and her body so desperately wanted to give in.

Maybe just a little taste...

"No," she had not realized she said it out loud until Javi's lips and body stopped moving against her. Heat rushed to her cheeks and she quickly clarified. "I need to check in today. I don't like conflict and I know they can be miserable people, but they are still my family. I want to make sure they don't dislike me any more than normal and then I'll be back. We don't have anything planned for today, so we can spend the day doing whatever the hell we want," she assured, hoping that would please him.

His arms dropped from around her and he rolled to his back. The absence of his body was immediately felt and she nearly took back her words. "You're right. If you need to check on your mom and sister, I'm not going to stop you. Do you want me to go with you?" He didn't seem excited about the idea, but it was sweet of him to offer.

"No, you stay here and get some more rest. I don't think it will take too long." She planned to find them, apologize for how things ended yesterday, and make sure they didn't need anything from her. She didn't think having Javi there would help and she couldn't blame him for being wary around them.

"I'll shower when you leave. Then I'll be ready to go when we decide on our plans."

"Perfect." She reached to squeeze his hand before getting up. Last night she had set out simple jeans and a faded black crop top with a pocket on the breast. She escaped to the bathroom to relieve herself and get dressed. Her curls were curling today and there was no taming them. She wore her hair down proudly, thickness and all.

Sending a quick text to her dad, she found out her mother was in Marisol's room making last-minute calls to guests and making sure the rest of her bridesmaids would be landing tomorrow.

"I'm leaving! I won't be too long," she called as soon as she opened the door.

"If you need backup, call me," he said, sitting up in bed now. He caught what she had on and smiled approvingly. "Seriously? There is no reason you should look that damn good at all times."

She hadn't known she needed that boost of confidence and appreciated his words. "Enjoy your shower." She winked at him and left, closing the door without waiting for his reply.

MARISOL's front room was in complete disarray, at odds with the other rooms of her flashy penthouse suite that screamed of Daddy and fiancé's money. She had thought her and Javi's room was lavish, but it paled in comparison to the apartment-like accommo-dations her sister had. On her way in, she spotted two untouched rooms. Who needed two extra bedrooms? Clearly her sister.

Marisol and their mother were seated at a round glass table, the hotel phone and Marisol's purple laptop between them. They ended a call with an uncle she believed to live in Tijuana, but she could be confusing him with one of the many other cousins her mother had. She was a bit surprised her mother considered inviting the extended family since they didn't fit in with her new, flashy lifestyle.

"Good morning." Lola's voice startled both women, her mother's dramatic shriek and hand to her chest as if she just had a heart attack never failed to make Lola cringe. Her mother was extra in the worst ways possible.

"Who let you in?" Her sister's accusatory voice could have been aimed at a poorly trained assassin who announced he came to kill them instead of her baby sister who wanted to make sure they had recovered from yesterday.

"Daddy met me downstairs and handed me a key." She showed the plastic key, holding it up in front of her like a shield that would protect her from her sister's wrath. Marisol continued to look annoyed, but no more than normal.

That had to be a good sign.

"Are you alone?" her mother asked, peering around Lola, no doubt searching for Javi to round the corner at any minute.

"Yeah, Javi's back in the room. I wanted to come down and apologize for how things were left last night. It wasn't my inten-tion to cause a scene at your dinner, Marisol." Did she feel like she did anything wrong? Not particularly. But this was her sister's engagement week and despite everything, she didn't want to taint these memories for her. Emotions ran high last night, but she hoped it wouldn't happen again.

Marisol offered her a smile. Not one that met her eyes, she doubted her sister was capable of a full range of emotions, but a smile nonetheless. "Yes, all is forgiven. Daddy wasn't happy about the incident."

No, she suspected he wouldn't be, though she didn't think his anger extended to her and Javi.

"I still don't understand why you allowed that man to speak to us like that. If you had a problem with our words, you should have come to us. You know we love you and only want what's best for you," her mother cut in.

The thing was, she truly did believe her sister and mother loved her. Or perhaps that was the hopes of a naive girl talking who desperately wanted a loving mother and sister. Their love came with conditions and Lola often found herself coming up short of their expectations for her. She stopped trying to please them long ago, but she would be lying if the thought of giving in to their demands didn't cross her mind every once in a while.

"Javi felt like you were attacking me—"

"Attacking?" Her mother gasped, shaking her head like that was the most outlandish idea to have ever crossed her mind. "Oh, dear, you know that isn't it at all. He needs to better understand our family before he puts his nose into places it doesn't belong. I would hate for that to end badly for him."

"Jesus, Mother. Must you always be so dramatic?" Marisol muttered under her breath, displaying a rare case of sibling support.

Of course, her mother was never one to reflect on her behavior. "That man ruined your entire dinner. I don't think I'm being dramatic when I say Lola needs to pick better men."

A very unladylike snort left her lips. She couldn't escape the irony, could she? "Are you kidding me?" She scoffed, her face grew hot with pent-up anger. "Need I remind you that my last boyfriend is about to marry my sister? So he was only a bad pick for me, but not Marisol?"

"Lola, please. Let's not do this now. This week is not about you, and it's unfair to your sister to bring it up. I thought we were all over it?"

"How can we be over something we never discussed?" Her voice rose with each word. "But it's not even about that. It's about how you two constantly treat me. I'm sick of it and I've been living with it my whole life. Javi was only at dinner for less than an hour before the way you treated me pissed him off. He cares for me, Mother. Openly. Something you could stand to learn from him."

This wasn't why she came into this room, though she knew seeing them would bring along the possibility of another argument. She was sick of being in survival mode all the time. Sick of caring and not being able to let go, even now she had the strong urge to push everything under the rug and survive until the end of the week.

"I said what I needed to and I don't want to discuss this anymore. If you need me, you know where to find me. I'm going back to the kindhearted man who appreciates me and doesn't point out all of my flaws." With that, she spun on her heels and left the room. No one tried to run after her, not that she thought they would. Her goal had been to mend the tear in the relationship, but she only made it worse.

No, not her. *Them.* They made it worse.

How hard was it to be a decent fucking human? Her mom would piss and moan about her attitude and make some offhand comments, then they would go about the same cycle they always fell into. It was toxic, but it was comfortable. All that either one of them knew.

Just once she wished her sister would stand up for her, more than expressing annoyance in their mother. She couldn't quite blame Marisol. Her sister was just trying to survive too.

Lola stormed back to their floor, slamming her key against the reader until the green light shined. When she pushed the door open, she heard water coming from the shower, but that didn't stop her from calling out, "Javi!"

She was on edge and needed to come back down. Needed to experience something other than this negativity coursing through her veins and there was only one man who could help her. A special man she was beyond tired of denying and one who made her feel things she was sick of shying away from.

The water suddenly cut off and she heard him scramble inside the bathroom until the door slid open, exposing a very wet and half-naked Javi, a tiny towel the only thing covering his lower half. His eyes were blown wide with concern as he looked around the room, stopping once he reached her. "What is it? What happened?"

Seeing him, his chest rising and falling rapidly because he rushed to check on her, was the last bit of evidence she needed to know that this man would do anything for her. It was a scary, but exhilarating thought.

"Fuck the business deal."

"What?" Naturally, he was confused by her choice of words, and probably worried. After all, she just stormed into the room and demanded his attention.

"I said fuck this business deal. I don't want to think. I don't want to be around people who can't accept all of me because I'm too much. I fucking want you. This has nothing to do with you being my fake date. I want *you*, Javi. I want you to help me forget. Just like you did six months ago."

Silence met her plea. Heat rushed to her cheeks as she wondered if she had just overstepped. They had been good yesterday, so maybe Javi didn't actually want to be with her. Maybe she had completely read the room wrong and she was making a fool of herself.

But a few seconds later, a low, seductive laugh left Javi's mouth. She watched as his eyes took her in, every inch of her body. She felt herself grow hot from his gaze alone.

Just when she thought the tension was going to be the death of her, Javi stepped closer. "You want to forget, preciosa? I can manage that." In the next instant, he was on her.

# *Javi*

## CHAPTER TWENTY-SEVEN

WHEN JAVI HEARD Lola yelling his name, he didn't even hesitate as he sprung into action. He swore if he ran out and she was on the verge of another panic attack, he'd book them the first flight home. None of this was worth her mental health, no matter how much she wanted to try and reason with her mother. Frankly, Luciana didn't deserve shit from Lola.

Javi barely got the water turned off before he was out the door, grabbing a towel that he tied haphazardly around his hips. One strong gust of wind would send it to the ground, but in that minute nothing mattered but getting to Lola.

He flung open the door, taking in the scene. Lola's cheeks were red and her eyes were glazed over, staring at him with the utmost concentration. Water dripped onto the floor around him, creating little puddles that he would need to clean up later.

"What is it? What happened?" His voice was gruff as he assessed the room for a threat. As if her mother and sister would round the corner and start swinging at him.

But that wasn't what happened and when she spoke, his mind was slow to process what she was saying. *"Fuck the business deal"* repeated in his head over and over like a broken record. A horrible part of him, one that he would never admit to out loud, reverberated through the back of his mind. *What about the money?* And fuck if he didn't want to punch himself right in the face for thinking such vile thoughts when Lola was offering herself up to him.

She wanted him and it had nothing to do with their little deal. She wanted to forget and Javi wanted to indulge her. "You want to forget, preciosa? I can manage that." The words left his lips before he could think them over. There were reasons they shouldn't do this. It would muddy their relationship and leave them with more questions than answers. They had yet to talk about these real feelings they both felt. Were they ready to ignore all the red flags and jump into bed together?

Yes. The answer was yes.

In two long strides, he bridged the space between them, pressing her back against the wall, recalling last night. Only this time they weren't in public and he wasn't going to put a stop to it.

His lips crashed against hers. There was nothing sweet in the way he kissed her. He kissed her to claim her, to feel her heartbeat through her lips. The soft moans he elicited from her went straight to his cock which was hardening against her.

"Javi." She was breathy and panting. It was sweet, tortuous music to his ears. "Please," she begged him as his hands roamed her body.

"Please, what?" Perhaps he was being cruel, but he wanted her to say exactly what she wanted. There could be no mistaking because once they went down this road, there was no turning back.

Lola rolled her lip between her teeth, gaze sinking to the floor. Oh hell no, he was not having any of that. Placing his finger under her chin, he forced her attention back onto him. She was a big girl and could look into his eyes when she asked him for pleasure. Lola stiffened under him but didn't try to move out of his grasp.

"I want..." She trailed off, losing some of her bravado. She wouldn't feel so self-conscious if she only understood what she did to him. Javi rolled his hips against her, his erection digging into her belly. The towel miraculously staying on as he ground into her.

"You want what, Lola?"

"You. I want you to fuck me."

And there it was. The last of his resolve began to crumble and the dam holding back his feelings broke. He was done denying himself and apparently, she wanted him just as much. Javi was prepared to give her what she wanted—but only on his terms.

In one fell swoop, he picked Lola up and threw her over his shoulders. Lola shrieked and pounded his back playfully. It shouldn't have been as arousing as it was, but his cock ached for her. He wanted to be buried deep inside her pretty pussy until she came around him.

"Javi! What the fuck?! Put me down; I'm too heavy."

That statement earned her a swift smack to her ass and once he reached the bed, Javi did put her down. Not because she asked, but because he needed to see her beautiful face when he scolded her. He leaned forward, his arms caging her in on either side, causing her to lean back to get a good look at his face. "I don't know what *boys* you've been fucking around with, but there is nothing too heavy about you, Lola. If I want to throw you over my shoulder and carry you to bed, then that's what I'm going to fucking do. Understand?"

"Fuck, that was so hot."

"Do you understand, Lola?"

"Yes."

He leaned in and kissed her gently. "Good girl." Then he pushed himself up, standing in front of her. His hands went to the towel, but his gaze never left hers as he pulled at the end of the towel and let it fall around him. Lola sucked in a deep breath as she took in his hard cock. All for her. Only for her.

"Do you want something in your mouth, preciosa?" he asked, moving to wrap his hand around his shaft, giving his cock two long strokes. It felt good, but not nearly as good as what her velvety lips would feel like around him.

"Yes."

"Get on your knees." It had been a long time since he got to command anyone in the bedroom and he realized how much he fucking missed it. Lola didn't need to be told twice; she scooted off the bed, sinking to the floor and chased his hands away from his cock. He gave up his stroking as her hand took over.

"Fuck." His groan came from deep in his throat. His muscles flexed and he kept himself from grabbing the back of her head and pushing her down until he was deep down her throat.

As if knowing what he was thinking and wanting to tease him, his girl wore a cute little smirk and brought his tip to her mouth. She flicked her tongue out, spreading the bead of precum around his head. It felt so good, too damn good, and then his brain short-circuited as she took him inside her mouth.

Javi felt like a damn teenager, ready to explode at the first contact with a woman's mouth. Lola's cheeks hollowed out as she bobbed her head to take down almost every inch of him. With her free hand, she reached up to cup his heavy balls and he roared with pleasure. "Fucking hell, Lola, you're going to be the death of me."

She hummed in response, alternating between taking him down her throat to only teasing his tip. Both felt equally good and if she kept this up, he would come in no time.

But he was not ready to come yet. Not until she got what she deserved. His pleasure could wait until he got a taste of her.

Without warning, Javi pulled out of her mouth. Precum and spit rolled down Lola's shocked face. "Was I not doing it well?" The embarrassment was evident in her tone and he quickly shook his head.

"You were doing too good, but when you are with me, you get to come first." Her shocked face told her that she hadn't been accustomed to treatment like this before. It made a primal part of his brain inexplicably happy that he could be part of one of her firsts. "Clothes off, beautiful. Let me see that body you are trying to hide from me."

"I'm not hiding anything from you," she shot back, rolling her eyes but stood up up to do as she was told. He watched as the crop top came off, showing off her lacy red bra. He had never been attracted to a color before, but red looked fucking sexy on her soft brown skin.

Lola then undid her jeans, kicking them off with ease. "Matching set?" he mused, seeing the red thong she sported.

"I like feeling sexy underneath my clothing." She shrugged, undoing the bra and letting her large tits spring free. The last to go was her panties and soon she stood in front of her in all of her glory.

Lola wasn't petite. She had a round belly with the slightest hints of stretch marks. Her thighs were thick, and he wanted to bury himself between them. Everything about her demanded his attention and worship. He couldn't help but notice how she didn't shy away from his gaze but instead allowed him to drink her in.

"You are the most beautiful fucking person I have ever seen." She deserved to be treated like a queen every day and know her worth. Not what her mother and sister tried and failed to drill into her head, but her actual worth. How her body was perfect, a temple to be worshiped by anyone she deemed worthy. He thanked God she chose him.

"And what do you want to do to the most beautiful person you've ever seen?" Her voice was like honey, caressing his senses. He wanted to do a lot with her and didn't know where to start. They had all day, but that didn't seem like enough time to give her all she deserved. Still, he knew where he would start.

Easing her back down on the bed, Javi spread her legs, exposing her sweet pussy to him. It glistened with her arousal and he leaned forward and smelled her sweetness. "So wet for me," he purred, pressing soft kisses to her inner thigh. Lola's legs began to shake and she tried to close her thighs, but he pressed his palms to her, keeping her open. "You stay open for me. You understand?"

"Yes." That one-syllable word held so much meaning to him. So much trust and need.

Looking up at her, Javi licked from her ass all the way to her clit as he let the sweet taste of her fill his mouth. She was tangy and sweet, a perfect combination. The first stroke of his tongue caused her to claw her nails into the bedding.

So she was extra sensitive. Good to know.

With the second stroke, her thighs tightened around his head, unable to stay in place. He chuckled softly into her pussy, not bothering to push her thighs back down. He liked the proximity and full access this gave him.

Javi moved to suck her clit into his mouth, his tongue teasing the already swollen nub. One finger traced the outside of her lips before parting them and pressing deep inside. She was tight, but that didn't stop her from clamping down around him. When he curled his finger inside of her, she let out a piercing scream.

"Javi! Fuck!" She groaned, reaching up to play with her beautiful tits, pinching and twisting her nipples.

"So fucking perfect." His hot breath hit her core and he watched as her entire body shuddered for him. Knowing she needed another one, Javi pushed in a second finger, moving them in and out at a steady pace. His tongue worked on her clit mercilessly.

"Javi, I'm close. Fuck...Oh god!" Her sweet cries did nothing to derail the pleasure he continued to give her. He wouldn't stop until she came undone around him. His licking, teasing, and fingers didn't cease, even as her cries and pleas grew louder. He almost felt bad for the neighbors, but not enough to quit what he was doing.

A few moments later, Lola's orgasm exploded through her, filling the room with her tangy sweetness. Javi cursed under his breath, lapping at her pussy until he forced himself to pull back.

"We're not done," he growled and crawled up her body. "That didn't even begin to take the edge off. It only fueled my addiction to you. Do you see how much you affect me?" he asked and guided his cock through her folds, only teasing. Always teasing because her cries of pleasure tasted like sweet nectar.

Lola was a writhing mess underneath him and he liked seeing her so open and vulnerable with him. "I don't want to wait," she whined, reaching for his cock to bring it to her entrance.

"So needy," he tsked, which earned him a searing kiss to his lips. Lola pulled him down until their mouths connected. He knew she tasted herself on his lips and that made it even more erotic.

Knowing he couldn't hold back for much longer, Javi reached for the small bag on the bedside table that held condoms. He didn't know what made him decide to put them into his bag before he left home, but he was incredibly thankful he did.

With ease, he opened the foil and slid the condom down his cock. As much as he wanted to one day give Camilia siblings, he doubted knocking up Lola now would be the wisest idea. They needed to establish their complicated relationship first.

"I'm not going easy on you. I know you can take it." She had once and he was certain she could again. It was the last warning he gave her before he thrusted inside of her, filling Lola up to the hilt. They moaned in unison, Lola's legs came up and wrapped around his torso. He dropped his arms to either side of her head, curls framing her face on the pillow.

Javi was lost in his pleasure. Lola scratched down his back as he moved inside of her, listening to their bodies move together. He had been so close to coming multiple times and wouldn't last long in this position.

Each thrust sent their bodies crashing together. If Lola needed him to take off some steam from her less-than-impressive family interactions, he would be here to fuck her until she forgot everything but his name.

Reaching down between them, he let his thumb find her clit again. The small moans of satisfaction only increased when he found the right speed.

"I'm not going to last much longer, Lola. You're fucking

incredible." He kept reiterating the fact in hopes of counteracting the negativity her family fed her. He was only one man, but perhaps his words would help. Even if it was just a little.

"Come with me, Javi. Let me see you lose yourself inside me," Lola panted, her legs tensing and he knew she was going to orgasm again soon. It was his goal to pump out all the orgasms he could until she was putty in his hands.

Each stroke brought him closer and closer to the edge. It wasn't until she tightened around him and moaned his name that he finally found his first release of the day, hoping many more would follow after. He came with Lola not far behind him.

Satisfaction and smugness ran through his body. He felt like a king who came back to his quarters after finding the prettiest girl at the ball. Gently, he pulled out of Lola and discarded his condom, before laying on his back next to her.

Neither one of them spoke for a while and he hoped that didn't mean she was having second thoughts. Just as he was about to open his mouth and ask her if everything was okay, Lola rolled over until she was straddling him. A large smirk played across his features and she ran her hand down her chest.

"I hope you aren't tired." She pouted and damn if his cock didn't twitch in anticipation. It was confirmed, Lola would be the death of him and his cock. "Because I'm not done with you."

He liked the sound of that and rolled his hips underneath her. A sultry moan left her lips. "And what else does my lovely date have planned for us?"

To answer his own question: a lot. Lola had a lot in store for them and he was too eager to be the willing participant. "How about I show you?" She smirked and did just that.

# *Lola*

## CHAPTER TWENTY-EIGHT

THERE WERE good ways to spend one's evening and then there was a gorgeous man on his knees in the shower eating your pussy for the third time that night good. How she even held herself up at this point was some kind of sex witchery that Lola didn't understand. Lola knew Javi was good in bed from their one brief night together, but she felt cheated after learning how much of a machine he was.

Orgasms never came as bountiful or quickly from anyone else. Even her small pink vibrator was getting a run for its money. Javi was just so...eager and left her a blissed-out mess, reeking of sex. It was a good fucking scent too.

A delicious ache formed between her thighs and tomorrow she would feel him with each movement. She would carry that around like her own beautiful secret, knowing what they did together in this room. If she thought too hard about it, the guilt and confusion would come and Lola didn't want anything to dampen this moment. It simply deserved to be.

Javi must have noticed the ever-changing emotions on her face and insisted they take a shower. The thought of warm water on her muscles felt good, but she didn't know if she'd be able to keep herself standing when she felt like a sack of potatoes.

The shower started innocently enough with a few touches and caresses. Javi offered to wash her hair and she let him. The next thing she knew, Lola was bracing herself against the wall and Javi had dropped to his knees. His fucking knees! As if she was a damn Khaleesi from *Game of Thrones* and he was swearing his loyalty by eating her out.

With her back pressed firmly against the shower wall and one leg draped over his shoulder, Lola gasped. Her nipples grew hard and she began to absentmindedly play with them, adding more pleasure.

"Javi I can't..." she whined again, but those words did not stop her from riding his far too pretty face with wild abandon.

"You can. I know you can come for me one more time." His naughty tongue found her clit, sending jolts of pleasure straight through her body.

How the fuck was she ready to come again? It shouldn't be possible and yet Javi managed to pull them from her as if he alone held the key to unlocking her orgasms. Damn him and his sinful tongue and thick dick. Until him, she had not known that she could finish by penetration alone.

She was learning so much.

Another tantalizing flick of his tongue had her coming undone in his arms once again. Before she fell on her ass, Javi grabbed her hips, holding her as he leisurely pulled away from between her thighs, wearing her juices on his lips. The bastard dared to smile at her. He was far too smug for what he had done and honestly, she couldn't say she blamed him. He deserved his cocky attitude, at least for tonight.

"Let's get you to bed," Javi murmured once he stood up. They spent time cleaning off the rest of their bodies and giggling like teenagers in puppy love. If she stopped and thought about what they did and how her emotions were changing by the second, she knew the panic would set in.

"I'll keep you up. Come," Javi insisted. She wanted to point out that she did, indeed, come a lot and doubted she would ever come again thanks to him. But no words formed. Instead, she nodded and reached out to him.

With ease, Javi leaned down and scooped her up. Was it insanely attractive that he could scoop her up as if she were a real bag of potatoes? Absolutely. She wouldn't make the mistake of saying she was too heavy again...though the spanking was nice.

Javi was a good man. He was attentive and caring and Lola wanted nothing more than to be next to him for as long as time would allow. But...there were still things she needed to fix about herself before she allowed someone into her life again.

Not to mention that so much money was on the line for Javi right now and although she knew for a fact he didn't spend the last few hours giving her mind-blowing orgasms because she was paying him, she also knew that created a gray area for them as well. No good relationship started out as fake and turned into something real.

But could it?

All of those things were pushed aside when Javi helped her out of the shower and into the bed. "Do you need anything?" His voice was like a gentle caress on her skin.

Next to her bedside table was her water bottle full of cold water—which she remembered to fill after a break between sex sessions two and three—and a half-eaten bag of Doritos. They had expelled many calories and tomorrow her body would demand nourishment, but she didn't want to leave the comforts of their room or have room service bother them. She'd deal with her hunger needs in the morning.

"I'm okay. Hold me?" It came out as more of a question than a command. The bed dipped next to her before Javi's warm, naked body pressed up against hers, pulling her to his chest.

Cuddling felt more intimate than the marathon of sex they just had. Perhaps it was because she was baring herself to him in a different way and letting her guard down. She hadn't done that for a while, scared that any new person in her life would find a way to disappoint her. She was still waiting for the other shoe to drop because what she felt for Javi had to have an expiration date.

Unless...there didn't have to be.

His arms provided the sense of safety she needed tonight to keep the doubts and regrets at bay. She couldn't regret what they did today, but she would need to clarify what they were to each other. This was so much more than cute touches and secret glances, this was...something she wasn't yet comfortable describing.

A part of her was scared to develop anything further with Javi. Was she truly ready to put herself out there again? Javi made her feel like the most interesting person on earth, but was that enough?

But another part of her was scared because she had once thought Archie would never hurt her. The two men couldn't be more different, but putting her heart out on the line again came at a huge cost and she didn't think she was ready to pay it yet.

"Sleep well, Lola," Javi said, pulling her out of her opposing thoughts. His breathing slowed and she felt the soft rise and fall of his chest. Tonight had been amazing, even if the aftermath was scary. The negative thoughts tried to penetrate her mind, but she kept them at bay. Tomorrow she could worry about their future and feel her feelings. Tonight she would let the ignorance comfort her and think of Javi's arms around her.

Within a few minutes, Lola fell into a dreamless sleep.

# *Javi*

## CHAPTER TWENTY-NINE

THE SOFT THRUMMING of a guitar filled the air, breaking the silence of the morning. Lola squirmed in his arms, whining at the sudden intrusion of sound. At first, his sleepy brain conjured up an image of a mariachi band playing outside as if they were sent by their neighbors to congratulate them on their marathon of sex.

When the sound abruptly cut off only to start back up again, Javi realized his phone was going off. His body was wound tightly around Lola's, so extricating his limbs from hers was no easy task, especially because he didn't want to wake her up. He had shown little to no mercy to her yesterday and she needed the rest.

After exiting the bed and hoping he didn't jostle her too much, Javi grabbed his phone. The screen lit up with an incoming call and Ofelia's picture popped up. His stomach dropped as dread and dad guilt threatened to consume him. When he agreed to be Lola's date, he had made a promise to Camilia that he would call her every single day. And he had not lived up to that promise. The past few days came and went without a single call or text.

He wouldn't be winning a best dad award anytime soon.

Grabbing a shirt and sweats from the floor, Javi got dressed at record speed and made his way outside onto the patio balcony in an effort to not disturb Lola's sleeping form. Right before his phone cut off, he answered it. His sister's frown greeted him. "You too busy to speak with your own family?" Her tone bordered on annoyance and his sister hardly ever lost his cool with him.

It was his stupid fault. He hadn't been thinking about anything other than his feelings and the strong pull he felt toward Lola. While he was selfishly taking care of his own needs, he left Camilia to fend for herself with Ofelia. Being away for an entire week was going to be hard on her and yet he had done nothing to make it easier.

"Shit—I'm sorry, Ofi. How is she? Is everything alright? Do I need to come home?" His words were a jumbled mess and he tried to peer around Ofelia's head, hoping to catch a glimpse of his daughter.

"No, no. None of that." She sighed and ran a hand through her hair. "Sorry, Mav's back at training today and I'm alone with the kids. I called papá for backup because Arturo is going to drive me to drink. This morning he thought it would be a good idea to wake me up by dropping a sopping wet towel on me and proceed to belly flop on my face."

Despite his tense mood only moments ago, Javi couldn't help but laugh. Arturo was a rambunctious kid, but apparently so was Maverick at this age. He also made a mental note to buy his sister dinner and books for having to take care of two kids. That sounded like a handful, especially when they were two and six.

"But Camilia has been asking about you. She wants to talk; do you have time?" she asked, and Javi saw his sister move through the house toward the room she had set up for Camilia.

"I have time. I'm so sorry again, Ofi. I should have been checking in."

Ofelia waved away his apology. "Honestly, it's fine. Camilia is doing great, but I know she will appreciate talking to you. Hey, Camilia." Ofelia smiled, no longer looking at Javi but over the phone to where his daughter must be. "Papá is on the phone. Are you ready to talk?"

There was some shuffling and a black screen before a rosy-cheeked little girl popped up. Her beautiful curls were pulled back into a high-top ponytail with a few unruly strands crowning her face. She had on her favorite hoodie he had gotten at a gas station a few months ago with a unicorn riding a bike. The biggest smile greeted him, slamming in the knife of guilt. His sweet girl didn't hold grudges, but he couldn't shake the feeling of fucking up.

"Mija, how are you? Papá misses you so much." A strange lump formed in his throat, but he coughed it away.

"I miss you too. This much!" she said, dropping the phone on her bed and holding her arms out wide. "But tía Ofi is taking us to the movies today. After Arturo has a nap or else he will be a grumpy monster like tío." Javi heard Ofelia laugh outside the camera.

"That sounds like a lot of fun. And abuelo is going too?"

"Oh yes. And it's my job to keep him from snoring in the movies." She giggled and launched into her plan of how she was going to make that happen. While she spoke, Javi listened and nodded his head when appropriate. Inwardly, he wrestled with his guilt of missing out on these small moments, even though there would be plenty more.

Camilia then spoke to him about school and how she was doing with her sight words. How she almost had all of them correct, but still needed to work on a few. Ofelia made sure to read to her every night and Camilia retold the stories they read. Javi couldn't help but smile when his daughter mentioned *The Giving Tree*. He pictured Lola rolling her eyes and explaining how problematic the book was. Still, he wondered if Camilia would ever ask Lola to read it to her.

It terrified him how easily he could picture Lola in his life. Would she be okay with starting a relationship with a man who already had a child? And why the hell was he even thinking about any of this now? Deep down, in the pits of his lonely heart, Javi knew exactly why he could only think of a future with Lola.

How he didn't want any other man to have her.

She was his and his alone.

Perhaps not yet, but she would be soon. If he could sort out his damn feelings.

"Oh, papá, tía wants to talk to you," Camilia said, pulling his thoughts back toward his daughter.

His face relaxed and he smiled at her. "Okay, mija. Tomorrow is the wedding, so I might not be able to call you, but I'll send pictures."

"Oh! Bring home cake!" she said and suddenly disappeared, tossing the phone to Ofelia. The sound of her small feet hitting the floor and running off filled his speaker, leaving the siblings alone.

"And she's gone now. I think she heard the door open and ran to her abuelo. Do you have a minute though? I wanted to talk to you about something. Nothing bad!" she clarified, which was good because he didn't think he had the capacity for anything bad.

When he nodded his head to signal for her to continue, Ofelia started in on her news. "So I've been absolutely killing it being a stay-at-home mom, but I do miss cheer. I called Willow—she says hi by the way—and she suggested I apply as a part-time coach at the cheer clinic Camilia goes to."

Willow was Ofelia's best friend who lived back in Texas. She had visited a handful of times and stayed most of the summer at their house while her husband traveled for work and she was off for summer break. Teacher perks.

"I just got a callback and will be starting next week!" Ofelia squealed. Her excitement was contagious and he was so happy for her. Ofelia had given up a lot of things when she moved from Texas but was eager to be closer to family. She had chosen to be a stay-at-home mom and from what Javi gathered, she had not regretted this decision. But getting back into something so deeply rooted in her soul would be a good thing.

"Congratulations, hermana. You're going to be so good at that. Is Arturo going to go to work with you?"

"Oh yes, he's big enough to run around and play. And

Maverick will be home to watch him at other times. Papá offered too, but he's a handful so I would rather he didn't have to take on the responsibility.

"But, the reason I'm telling you this is because Camilia gets a discount on cheer. I think it will apply to your next payment. I can ask them when I take her tonight for practice. Did you want me to go ahead and take care of the bill?"

She said the last bit as nonchalantly as she could. It was no secret he got bent out of shape when talk of money was involved. He hated that he was like this, but having struggled most of his life with paying off bills, debts, and now cheer practice, it was a point of stress for Javi.

Last month had been hellacious with very little work and worse pay than normal. It was one of the reasons why he wanted to go independent, now that he had worked up a decent clientele. He was behind on his phone bill and a credit card bill and would have been able to afford both if he didn't have to pay for cheer. Camilia loved cheer though. It was in her blood like it was in Ofelia's blood and he would be damned if he made her suffer because he couldn't pay the damn bills.

He had swallowed his pride last month and asked Ofelia to help. She had been all too eager and offered to pay until his new business was off the ground, but he refused for now, hoping that this month brought a more prosperous income. And it did.

But it all hinged on Lola. He was taking so much money from her. Money she was willing to give for his work and pretending to be her boyfriend, but sometime between then and now the lines of faking began to blur.

There was nothing fake about his real feelings for her. The way his heart swelled at the sight of her. How he wanted to see her roll his eyes at him if he said something she didn't agree with or thought was cheesy. The way her cheeks would turn red when she was shy or turned on.

Fuck, things had spiraled so quickly and his heart was leading his actions these days.

"I wrote a check. It's in my bedroom on the bedside table. You can take that," he answered after a minute.

"Javi, I really don't mind—"

"I got this, Ofi. I got this." He worked hard to keep his tone neutral, not wanting to snap at her nor wanting to divulge where he got the money. It would be too complicated and he wanted to sort out his feelings first.

Ofelia bit her lip and looked like she wanted to argue, but soon nodded, letting it go. "Okay, but I'm still going to see if the discount starts this week."

"Sure, that would be very helpful. Thank you."

Ofelia seemed happy with his response and nodded. She then told him about a few things they had done while he was away and from the sounds of it, Camilia was having an amazing time with her tía. Ofelia pried into how his week was going and he gave a brief run down, not going deep into Lola's family because that wasn't his story to tell.

When he finally got her off the phone, an hour had passed and with it, a new uneasy feeling settled over him. Ofelia bringing up the cheer bill reminded him just how much Lola was changing his life, not just emotionally but financially too. If he were a better man, he would tell her he just couldn't accept the money. She didn't need to pay him for dating her when he wanted to date her for real. The money would always be between them.

They still had a few more days together and he hoped within that time he could sort through his feelings and make a better and more informed decision about his money dilemma. For now, he had a woman waiting in bed for him and he wanted to soak up every last minute he had with her.

He just hated feeling like there was an hourglass counting down their final minutes.

# *Lola*

## CHAPTER THIRTY

SLEEP CLAIMED Lola's body last night like a ship in a calm sea, rocking her gently until darkness overtook her. The entire night she slept in Javi's arms and the presence of another person against her back brought more comfort than she anticipated. The hold this man had on her was alarming, but she wasn't yet ready to sever the fragile tethers connecting them.

When she finally managed to rouse herself the next morning, two things hit her instantly. Firstly, the delicious ache between her legs which reminded her of yesterday's activities. She had never had so many orgasms back-to-back and she was sure Javi ruined her sex life completely. How was she to come ever again for any other partner? Just the thought of another man in bed who wasn't Javi left an ache deep inside her chest.

Secondly, Javi was gone. The space he had occupied last night lay cold. The familiar brown, tattooed arms that once squeezed her to his chest were gone, leaving her empty in a dark room. Lola lifted her head off her pillow, trying to locate him. Images of their first night rushed back to her and the memory of waking up to an empty room after a night of passion.

This time was different, and she didn't think Javi would leave her high and dry. He wasn't that kind of man, but she hated the sliver of fear coursing through her body at the thought of the possibility of him leaving. A small part of her brain whispered that he was only with her for the money, but that was her anxiety talking.

But where the fuck was Javi?

She pushed herself into a sitting position on the bed, her muscles screaming in protest. Lola made a mental note to do yoga later today to ease the soreness. She had seen a spacious gym on the first floor and could utilize the space for stretching.

A hushed voice sounded from outside, grabbing her attention. Through the thick curtains keeping the sun at bay, she saw tousled black hair sticking up at odd ends. A smile crossed her face at the thought of her hands gripping those strands.

Javi's posture was rigid at first, as if bracing himself for an argument. She watched in silence as his body went from a defensive stance into a more relaxed posture. She couldn't see his face, but she imagined him smiling at his phone. Only one person made him melt like that.

Camilia.

Fuck, she had been so consumed with her selfish desires that she hadn't stopped and considered his daughter. How could she be okay with keeping him away from his sweet little girl, especially knowing what happened to her mother? She had only met Camilia briefly, but it was easy to tell how much Javi loved her. Being away from her had to be difficult, and she hadn't considered the sacrifices he was making.

Lost in an internal battle, she barely registered the sliding glass door opening. Javi stood in rumpled sweats and a wrinkled shirt that hung loose around his torso. He shouldn't look as good as he did, but Lola had the impression he would look good in a trash bag.

"Hey, I hope I didn't wake you," he said as a way of greeting.

Javi had woken something up in her, but not in the way he thought. These last twenty-four hours had been the best of her life. If she were being honest with herself, the past few weeks she had been able to spend with Javi were easily becoming core memories for her.

If she wasn't so chicken shit, perhaps she could call this feeling for what it was. Love was a funny thing. It demanded so much from a person and consumed their lives, but it could also be broken in an instant and feel like it was never there at all. Only the lingering pains served as a reminder.

Not that she loved Javi. Probably. Maybe. It was just that this feeling growing inside of her felt a lot like it and that scared the absolute shit out of her. He had a whole-ass family to think about and money troubles, since he had agreed to take her up on this wild offer. Not that money was a big deal to her, but it was possible she had actually bought his affection and their relationship was built upon a pillar of lies.

"No, I didn't even hear you leave," she said, which wasn't a lie. She had woken up on her own and then eavesdropped on the entire conversation which sent her into a panic about taking a father away from his daughter.

Javi, oblivious to her internal struggle, nodded before rejoining her in bed. He took up the spot behind her once again and pulled her into his arms, nuzzling her neck. "Please tell me we can stay in bed all day again."

She wanted to. Like, really and truly wanted nothing more than to have this man ravage her body again. But today would be busy with last-minute preparations for the wedding. If she looked at her phone now, she was certain she'd find a list of things she needed to do today. She was but a servant to be bossed around by her mother.

"Judging from your lack of response, I'm certain you're about to tell me you are going to drop everything so I can feast upon you until we are both satisfied and wallowing in our combined plea- sure," Javi said.

It was the furthest thing from her mind, which made her bark out a laugh. She tried to hide it with her hand as if covering her mouth would somehow make the sound disappear but to no avail. "Haven't you feasted enough?"

His eyes darkened with wicked intent and she knew what he was going to say before he even spoke. "Absolutely not. I could never be satisfied after a single night with you."

"Greedy boy." She smiled despite herself. Just a few minutes ago she was worried about taking up his time and set on creating distance between them, but now she was considering his invitation to spread her legs and feast.

No, she couldn't allow that. Not now. The distraction of the wedding would be good enough to keep their horniness at bay.

"We need to feast, but not on each other." She swore Javi muttered something about that being "dumb," but she pretended like she didn't hear him. "There's a cafe on the first floor where we can go for breakfast. And then I'll probably need to run some errands for my sister. You are free to relax since I doubt you'll want to join Archie and his prissy-ass friends in whatever they have planned today."

The look of his pure disgust was all she needed to see to know he had zero interest in hanging with Archie. Not that she could blame him. Archie was a pompous asshole and he and his so-called "friends" would probably find a pretentious bar and talk about how great they were. It didn't seem like Javi's scene.

"Do you want me to help with the errands?" Javi asked instead.

"No, I'm sure it won't be anything exciting and I'll have to deal with my mom and sister a lot. It would be easier—"

"If I wasn't there." She hated the dejection in his voice, but she also didn't know what to say. It would be harder if he were and it wasn't as if she needed him for support since her mother and sister's focus wouldn't be on her. Plus, a little time apart so she could sort through the tangle of emotions wouldn't be a bad thing.

"We can spend this evening together. Maybe we can have dinner tonight?" she asked, hoping her tone was light. The disappointment was evident in his features and it nearly made her cave, but then Javi's mood changed in a blink of an eye and he smiled.

"Sure. We can do it tonight. Let me get dressed and we can head down for breakfast before you go."

He didn't wait for her reply. He kissed her cheek once more and untangled himself from her. He disappeared into the bathroom, leaving her with unwanted uncertainty and the need to distract her ever-changing thoughts.

Once the door was closed, Lola jumped out of bed to find her clothes. She decided on jeans with a fitted, but breathable seafoam-green blouse and sensible booties so her feet wouldn't be hurting by the end of the day.

Lola then checked her phone, only to see her mother's list of tasks for her today. The first thing on the list was to arrange rides for the bridesmaids from the airport to the hotel. Why they couldn't do it themselves was beyond her, but she learned long ago it was better to simply do, rather than argue.

Her duties also included picking up Marisol's shoes from the store, checking in with catering, and picking up the wedding rings from her mother's suite to keep them safe until their big day tomorrow.

She had just finished going over her list and transferring it to the notes section of her phone when Javi emerged from the bathroom, smelling of citrus and pine cones. "Ready to eat?"

"Very." Her stomach growled on command and she reached for her purse, following Javi out the door. Today would be full of unwanted tasks, but at least she would be alone and able to think straight for the first time in weeks. Javi had a hold on her emotions and she was starting to fear for her own heart.

BREAKFAST HAD BEEN RELATIVELY QUIET, but not uncomfortably so. Neither one of them seemed to be looking forward to the day and she felt bad for leaving Javi alone. He was a grown man, capable of taking care of himself, but she still felt responsible for his entertainment.

In the end, Javi had decided he was going to explore the hotel and find something to bring back for Camilia.

Lola took the time for herself to grab another coffee and scroll through her list one last time to make sure she knew exactly what needed to be done. The idea of facing Luciana and Marisol's ire if she fucked up was the only motivation she needed to march her ass out of the hotel.

At least that was what she was planning on doing, until she collided with a hard body rounding the corner at the same time she did. The impact sent her back a few steps before she could right herself.

"Oh, I'm so sorry—" Her words cut off as her brain registered the man standing in front of her.

Archie.

She had done a good job of avoiding him this entire week, only seeing him when she saw the rest of her family, and had planned to keep it that way. But of course, the universe had other plans for her.

Like her, Archie was alone. Unlike her, he looked more put together after the head-on collision than she did. She pressed her mouth into a tight line. The only positive thing was that he didn't appear any happier to see her than she was to see him.

As far as Lola was concerned, she had two options. She could either walk past him and pretend as if they never saw each other, or she can reach deep into the depths of her soul to start a conversation. She knew which one she wanted to do, but she also didn't want Archie thinking he had gotten the better of her.

"Archie—hi." Her voice was higher than she would have liked, showing just how anxious she was.

Archie arched a brow and the corners of his lips pulled up into a smile, clearly amused. "Lola. I have to say, I'm surprised you're here."

"In the lobby?"

"No, in Colorado. At the wedding. I didn't think you would come." He laughed as if he had just finished telling a joke. "I mean, I just know how hard the breakup was on you and I wondered if coming here would make you sad all over again."

It took a Herculean effort to bite back the retort on the tip of the tongue. To yell and scream at him for being a pompous jerk and always making her feel small and insignificant. Yet she knew that was the exact reaction Archie was expecting from her, to blow up and cause a scene. Another scandal, courtesy of Lola.

Instead, she tried to keep her voice calm as she spoke. "Why would I be mad that you dumped me for my sister?"

"Well, you can't help who you fall in love with. And we gave you the courtesy of ending things before we began dating. I knew you would need time to process things." Archie reached out and placed a hand on her shoulder as if to comfort her.

Lola recoiled from his touch. Was he seriously insinuating that she should be grateful that Archie hadn't *cheated* on her with her sister, as if that was not the bare fucking minimum in any relationship? She didn't buy his declaration of love for her sister though. Men like Archie only ever loved themselves.

"Anyway," he said, clearly bored of this conversation. That made two of them. "This man you brought to my wedding. Who is he?"

"I've already introduced him, if you cared to listen. His name is Javi."

"And he's your...?"

"Boyfriend," she supplied, with more confidence than she felt.

"Oh." That one syllable made her tense. It wasn't just an innocent acceptance. No, Archie was deliberately holding his words back, forcing her to ask him what he meant by that.

And because Lola was a glutton for punishment, she asked, "Oh? Do you have something to say?"

"Just that you tend to dive into things without thinking them through all the way."

Lola felt her jaw drop. What right did Archie have to tell her she recklessly made decisions? "How dare you—"

"Does he know you have money?" he asked, his question rendering her immobile. He must have seen the anger in her gaze because he put his hands up to subdue her. "Guys like him prey on lonely, wealthy girls looking for companionship."

This time when she spoke, she couldn't keep the anger out of her voice. "What do you mean 'guys like him?'"

Archie paled, for once looking slightly uncomfortable. But only for a moment before he schooled his expression back into his normal cocky demeanor. "You know the ones. Guys with tattoos who don't know how to conduct themselves in public. Guys like *him*," he repeated.

It was one thing to say something nasty about her, but quite another to say anything bad about Javi. She took a step forward, invading his space. She watched as Archie straightened, puffing out his chest as if to intimidate her.

"Let's be real fucking clear, Archie. I don't give a shit what you think about me. I stopped caring a long time ago, once I learned what a pathetic excuse of a man you are. But say one more disparaging thing about Javi and I'll kick you so hard in your balls, doctors will never be able to recover them."

A beat of silence hung between them as she stared Archie down. He was the first to fold by looking away and clearing his throat. "No need for such dramatics, Lola. I'm simply a concerned friend who knows you and how you jump into things without thinking."

"You don't know a damn thing about me," she spat.

Except he did. He knew some things about her. He had been a crappy boyfriend, but they did spend a lot of time together while they were dating. He was bound to pick up some of her traits.

Was she really that impulsive and not thinking things through?

Well, she was quick to jump into a relationship with Archie. Looking back, there had been so many red flags and yet she chose to ignore all of them. She couldn't help but think about her abrupt move from Florida back to California to open up a bookstore, something she knew virtually nothing about. Then again agreeing to jump into a fake-dating scenario, not allowing herself to dwell on everything that could go wrong.

Fuck. She couldn't help but think Archie might be right.

Not wanting to have this personal crisis in front of a man she held no love for, Lola stepped back. "For the record, I'm glad you broke my heart because it made me realize how much I was settling for a man that wasn't worth my time. I just feel sorry for my sister because even though we may not be close, I still think Marisol deserves better and I hope one day she realizes that too."

She had said her peace and didn't need to hear any futile rebuttal Archie might have. She left him scowling after her, not once looking back as she walked away. It was what she always needed to do and even though it was six months late, she felt lighter with each step. She felt like her Archie chapter had finally come to an end.

Yet as she walked away, she couldn't help but think about Archie's words as doubts about all her recent choices began to creep in despite her best efforts to keep them at bay.

*Javi*

CHAPTER THIRTY-ONE

MUCH LIKE BREAKFAST, dinner was quiet that evening. Javi kept glancing up from his chicken Alfredo to study Lola. Ever since they walked into the restaurant—the same one from the disaster dinner with her family—something had been off with Lola, but he couldn't quite figure out what it was. He didn't want to push her either, since the weary look on her face indicated she had a hard day of errands.

Lola had hardly touched her meal. She spent most of the time moving her shrimp from one side of the plate to the other, only eating about a third of her meal. Javi frowned. He hated seeing her so disconnected and not knowing the reason why.

Javi let his fork drop on his plate, the soft thunk of metal on porcelain drew Lola's attention. She glanced up with heavy lashes and her posture stiffened. It was as if she had forgotten he was there.

"I'm sorry—"

"What's wrong?"

They spoke at the same time and Lola, for the first time that night, cracked a sheepish smile. She finally put down the fork, ignoring her neglected meal. "It's just been a long day."

"Did something happen?" It was a gentle nudge because he

571

didn't want to push her if she was not ready to talk about it. Not knowing would slowly eat away at him, but he wanted to respect her privacy as much as possible.

"I...ran into Archie today. Alone." Her voice was barely more than a whisper, but Javi heard it as loud as if she were speaking into a megaphone. His body grew hot and his leg began to bounce with the new energy coursing through his body.

In the back of his mind, he had wondered if this scenario might happen, though he routinely pushed it out of his mind. He planned on accompanying Lola wherever she went, but she had insisted on running errands by herself. Maybe he should have pushed harder to go with her.

"What did he say?" Each word was a struggle to get out. He didn't *want* to know, but he needed to hear regardless.

Most likely sensing his internal struggle, Lola quickly continued. "It wasn't bad. I mean, it definitely wasn't pleasant, he was being his normal dickish self, but it wasn't anything I couldn't handle.

"I got to stand up for myself, something I should have done in the first place. I might have threatened bodily harm and told him that I thought Marisol deserved better than him."

Despite the agitation building in his body, he let out a breathy laugh. "That's my girl. He deserves to be put in his place."

"Yeah, he did." Her smile slowly faltered as she grew pensive. "But he said a few things that really got me thinking. I guess it's just messing with me."

And just like that, the anger came back at full force. How anyone could find that man even remotely likable was beyond him. He hardly knew Marisol and from their brief interactions, he couldn't say he was her biggest fan, but not even she deserved a lowlife like Archie. He was sleazy and looking for people and things that fit his image.

"Whatever he said was bullshit, you know that, right?" Javi didn't even need to know what he said. Whatever came out of that man's mouth only proved to serve his best interest.

"Yeah, but—"

"No, there's no 'but' about it. He wanted to get under your skin and that's exactly what he did. Don't give him that power over you."

Lola pursed her lips into a tight line, eyeing him like she didn't know whether to snap at him or pull him in for a kiss. He hoped for the latter.

She did neither of those things.

Instead, she let out a deep breath and sank back against her chair. "This isn't about me giving him power or anything. I just can't help but feel that there was a part of what he said that is closer to the truth than I realized."

"And what is that?" Javi tried to keep his tone even. He didn't want to take out his anger on her. She didn't deserve his anger, that was solely reserved for Archie. What Lola needed was for him to just listen and that was what he planned on doing.

"That, well..." She trailed off, hesitating. After a pregnant pause where Javi thought he would have to ask her again, Lola continued. "He said I jump into things without thinking them through. That I'm reckless."

Unable to help himself, Javi scoffed. "Oh, that's rich coming from him. The man who jumped into a relationship right after he broke your heart. Men like Archie aren't happy until they instill doubt in those around them. I'm sorry you had to deal with him alone, preciosa, but I'm proud of you for standing up for yourself."

Javi wanted his words to be a comfort for her, to let her know that this one interaction shouldn't shake her confidence. Though he wasn't sure if he was doing a good job at that because Lola averted her gaze from him, still locked in a battle with her own thoughts.

"Lola," he started, reaching across the table for her hand. Before he could make contact, she jerked her hand back as if she had just been burned. Confusion and hurt rippled through him as he slowly pulled back. A look of regret passed through Lola's eyes, but she didn't try to take his hand back.

"Sorry, I guess I just have a lot on my mind right now," she said and to his dismay, Lola stood up. "I'm just tired. I'm going back to our room to lie down."

"Lola—"

"Can you just charge our dinner to our room? And get to-go boxes? Maybe I'll be hungry later." Once again, she did not look in his direction as she leaned down to gather her purse.

"Sure, but—"

"Thank you. I just need to rest." She cut him off again, not willing to hear what he had to say. Lola finally met his gaze and took a step back. She plastered on a smile that he saw right through.

"I'll be up soon and maybe we can watch a movie," he suggested, trying for an olive branch.

Lola averted her gaze and started backing up. "Not tonight. I just want to go to sleep. I'll see you in a bit," she said and then beelined for the door, leaving Javi alone.

A sense of anxiousness and dread filled the pit of his stomach at the thought of Lola pulling away from him. He didn't like it and wanted to soothe whatever fears that man put into her head. But for now, he let her go so he could finish off his dinner alone.

Tomorrow was the wedding. He just hoped he could last through it long enough to get Lola alone at the reception.

## *Lola*

### CHAPTER THIRTY-TWO

THE LARGE SUITE felt smaller than the last time she had been in here, but that was because four extra women occupied the room. None of whom she recognized at all, not even after an hour of doom scrolling through her sister's socials.

Marisol had plenty of pictures, but mostly of herself, the food she probably only took two bites of, and some of her and Archie. All of those looked posed and awkward. There may have been something akin to lust on their features, but love? No, she couldn't say she saw that.

Lola was noisy by nature and probably a detective in a former life, so she had no qualms Googling the ever-loving shit out of the three bridesmaids while the hairdresser worked on their hair. It didn't take too much digging after she found a tagged photo on her sister's Instagram of a charity event.

The three women stood next to Marisol in the photo, all smiling for the camera. None of their smiles reached their eyes, but rather looked like they were practiced from countless other events.

At first glance, the photo looked like four friends having fun and enjoying the event, but upon further speculation—meaning Lola zoomed in to analyze every angle—their rigid postures and how they angled themselves to be almost touching, but not quite, showed the truth. None of the women looked excited to be there but knew how to wear a mask when cameras were around.

The women belonged in the same social circle as her parents and sister. They were here for appearances only. Though she couldn't say for certain these women—who she believed were named Ashlyn, Vanessa, and Eliza—didn't care for her sister, judging by the lingering silence in the room, she could surmise they were here out of obligation. Just like Marisol would be at their weddings.

Everything was for show.

If she didn't know any better, Lola would think they were getting ready for a funeral. The navy dresses her sister insisted they all wear looked black in the shadows. The mood in the room didn't indicate a blushing bride about to be reunited with her one true love. It felt more like a sterilized hospital room. The only one fluttering around the room working herself up into a stupor was her mother.

"No, no, no. The hair is supposed to be an updo. None of this curling nonsense," her mom spat at the poor woman hired to do their hair. If she had to bet, she would guess the hairdresser gravely regretted taking this job. No amount of payment was worth this nonsense.

She listened to the woman calmly explain the styling process to her mother when Lola's phone buzzed.

She looked down at the phone glowing in her lap and saw that she had another text from Javi. Shame and guilt fought for dominance in her belly at his name. When they parted last night, she had left Javi all alone at their table. There was something different in their dinner date that time, something that felt suffocating when it should have brought comfort. She couldn't pinpoint the exact moment her lust turned to love for a man she paid to date her, but she knew the moment she was in over her head.

The fire burning between them had become an inferno and the only way to put out the flames was to act on the passion.

That, she didn't regret. She regretted losing touch with reality and falling hard for a man she had no business being with. Not when she was still so conflicted over her own feelings. This had to be a sign that she wasn't ready to jump into a relationship yet.

She had jumped into a relationship with Archie and it bit her in the ass. Perhaps it had always been a ploy to get with Marisol. The pretty one. The one that would look good at his side at events.

And maybe there was love between them, even if they showed their love differently than her, she still did not feel like this was the happy ever after everyone raved about. It felt much more like a business exchange. Exactly what she was doing with Javi right now.

> Your father offered to take me golfing three
> times in the last thirty minutes. Does that
> mean I'm part of the family?

Despite her traitorous feelings, she smiled. Oh, how she wished that to be true, but it was becoming more apparent that her own feelings couldn't be trusted.

Another text came in.

> I miss you, preciosa.

Another dagger straight to the heart.

Lola had only seen Javi in passing this morning. She had woken up before him, with Javi sleeping on the far side of the bed. Quietly, so as not to disturb him, she tiptoed into the bathroom. Five minutes later she heard a loud banging on the suite door and peeked out to see who it was.

Javi had wrangled himself out of bed, looking disheveled, and opened the door only to see her father standing on the other side. She choked on the toothbrush in her mouth, gaining both of the men's attention.

Her father had been on his way to Archie's room, and he

wanted to extend an invite to Javi. Poor Javi had looked like a frightened lamb caught in between two wolves. Either he went with her father and left her to her own devices or he stayed and potentially made her father angry.

Lola knew she needed to decide for him. Even if it wasn't what he wanted to hear.

With her being away with Marisol and her bridal party, it seemed only fitting that Javi joined the men. And as she predicted, he wasn't thrilled with the prospect, but he had agreed none-theless.

He had given her a swift peck on the cheek—an appropriate response with her father in the room—before leaving. That was the last interaction she had with him and since then, he had texted multiple times to update her on his endeavors with "stuck-up, rich, white people," as he put it.

Lola had read every message, but not replied. She only hated herself a little for leaving him on read, but she just didn't know how to wrangle her feelings into words yet. Besides, if he asked about it later, she could say she was busy. In a little over an hour she would see him anyway. She didn't think she was prepared to handle Javi dressed up for a wedding yet. She could only imagine how handsome he looked in a suit.

"Dolores! Do you have the rings?" Her mother's voice broke through her thoughts, indicating this had not been the first time she had asked Lola this question.

Rummaging around in her white clutch, she pulled out the small black box. "All safe," she assured, having picked up the rings earlier this morning. She had stored them away, knowing her mother would ask her dozens of times if they were safe.

"Ah, perfect. And you'll give them to cousin Luis when we arrive at the venue? Not a moment sooner. I don't need the boy losing these rings. They cost us a fortune." About that, Lola had no doubt. She didn't remind her mother that she wasn't stupid and wouldn't be giving anything to five-year-old cousin Luis until the very last possible second.

"And my shoes? You picked them up for me yesterday, right? Please tell me you grabbed my shoes from your room." Marisol piped up, looking in the mirror to see her. Her hair was finally becoming the updo her mother wanted and she looked gorgeous, even more so than usual.

"I grabbed your shoes from my room," Lola repeated like the obedient sister she was. "You look beautiful, Marisol." Despite the coldness between them, she still felt the need to say it. All brides should hear it on their wedding day, shouldn't they?

The dress was a tiered ball gown with a plunging neckline, making Marisol look ethereal. Her bodice was covered with lace, spanning down to the skirt of the gown. Small, intricate flower designs adorned the bottom half of her dress, making her look like she just walked off the set of a romance movie.

"Of course she looks beautiful. My girl is beauty incarnate," her mother replied before Marisol could, leaning in to kiss her cheek fondly. She had seen her mother do this before, but it still surprised her every time she showed her sister any affection. The most Lola got was a side hug or a tap on the shoulder, but those were infrequent.

The rest of the hour came and went like a bird passing through the sky. Lola finished applying makeup and helped Vanessa with hers as well since the hairstylist—who was also the makeup artist—had spent far too long on the bride and left everyone else scrambling.

Once again, not her fault.

After intense scrutiny from her mother and being told to fix a smudge of lipstick, Luciana was happy with everyone's appearance. The hairdresser left, and Lola swore she saw steam behind her at how fast she left the room.

"It's time to get married, my baby girl!" Deep within her heart, her mother conjured up a few tears for Marisol who seemed put off by them. What should have been a joyous moment just seemed like a normal Friday. If anyone else noticed the less-than-stellar vibe pumping through the room, they didn't comment.

"Dolores, let's go. We have our jobs to do," her mother said, making a beeline to the door, expecting her daughter to follow. With one last half smile geared toward her sister, Lola left the room. They had a wedding to start and there was a beautiful man waiting among the guests for her to face.

LOLA WAS AVOIDING HIM.

Javi tried not to let that affect him while he was getting ready with Travis, listening to him talk about the different golf courses he had visited last year. He did his best to conjure up the ability to care, even though he didn't give two shits about golf and the only thing on his mind was Lola. She clearly saw his texts but was making the conscious choice not to respond.

She could be busy. It was wedding day after all, and Archie was in the other room, taking a round of shots with his grooms-men, all clad in shades of white. He had the feeling they had all belonged to the same fraternity in college. Javi hadn't gone to college and most certainly never belonged in a fraternity, so he was sorely out of place.

He hadn't wanted to go, but he couldn't tell Lola's father no. Especially when Lola all but pushed him into his eager arms. Something was bothering her and he wanted to know what.

Despite her not answering, Javi continued to text her unabashedly. She was going to hear from him, even if she didn't respond because he needed her to know he was thinking about her.

He texted her when Travis asked him to go golfing with him. Then again to send a sneaky photo of Archie and his basic-ass friends discussing some boring policy in regard to their business. He sent her another message when they were on their way to the venue.

Since Javi wasn't in the ceremony, he didn't have to spend any more time with Archie. Not that the time they spent together mattered much. Archie never acknowledged him when he walked in with Travis and Javi hadn't gone out of his way to congratulate him. Travis also never pushed Javi to talk with Archie, and Javi appreciated that.

They didn't have to go far for the wedding. The top floor of the hotel—which could only be accessed by a special code given to guests—felt like stepping onto the first pages of a fairy tale story-book. The room was decorated in splashes of green and silver. The altar in the center of the room was raised with an arch made of greenery and twine covering most of the platform. Rows of benches that looked like they were sculpted from tree trunks lined the rest of the room with a sheer white runner going in between. If he had to guess, the room would hold close to two hundred people. Judging by the number of people here, Javi assumed the place would fill up soon.

The theme and decor were not what Javi expected for Marisol. He had pictured sleek corners, white and cream color arrange-ments, and flowers that looked to be grown in shops and not in the wild. Though if she was playing up the fairy tale theme because she viewed herself as the princess of the family, she accom-plished that.

Not wanting to mingle with guests who made his yearly salary by simply coughing in the right direction, Javi took a seat in the back. There was still no sign of Lola, but he hadn't expected to see her yet. Though he wanted to catch a glimpse of her soon to see her dressed in her figure-hugging dress, hair and make-up done, looking like the most beautiful woman in the room. While everyone would have eyes on the bride, his would be on Lola the entire time.

As he waited for the guests to filter in and the wedding to start, Javi's mind wandered. He thought of Camilia. He missed her little hugs and the way she would crawl into his bed each morning to cuddle before they had to leave for school or make breakfast.

He thought of the work that still needs to be done on Phoenix. He hadn't heard much from his crew and when he checked in yesterday, one of his lead men sent him progress photos of the shelves. They looked damn good and they weren't even finished. He hadn't seen all the progress in person yet, so he was itching to get back to the store.

Naturally, his mind circled back around to Lola. The way her body moved against his when they made love. For that's what it was. Sometime throughout the night, it had changed from a need to feel one another and get off as quickly as possible, to something that meant more than either was willing to admit. But Javi could admit it now.

He loved Lola Roberts.

The revelation should frighten him. Should have made him fall back into his insecurities and doubts about money. How he was juggling time between being the perfect father and a loving partner, but those fears seemed so trivial now. There was a solution there and he was certain he would find it, but he didn't want to do it alone. He wanted Lola by his side and he hadn't been the best at telling her that.

Maybe that's why she was avoiding him. They hadn't yet had time to talk about how their fake dating turned real so fast. He should be there to help her through her insecurities and fuck out any doubts she might have about their relationship because he wasn't going anywhere. Lola was his.

The opening chords of a familiar hymn started to play. Javi looked up to find Archie and his men at the altar. When did that happen? The grand doors opened up and everyone's heads swiveled around as the first bridesmaid walked in, holding an elegant bouquet of white flowers.

Two other women he did not recognize followed after, making their way toward the bride's side of the altar. The music quieted some as the last bridesmaid walked out. The navy-blue gown hugged her curves like a glove. He loved her body, loved the way it felt underneath him or snuggled up against him. Her dark, caramel hair was pinned in the back with loose strands framing her face. Her eyes had a smokey look, making them look sultry. Despite all the eyes on her, she kept her chin up, looking fucking breathtaking as she commanded the aisle.

Lola was a sight to behold.

Long after Lola went to stand in her spot by the other bridesmaids, Javi didn't look away. He didn't look away when Marisol walked in and made her way up next to Archie. He didn't look away when vows were exchanged and rings were put on fingers. Lola's eyes kept scanning the room as if feeling his stare. It wasn't until the officiant pronounced Marisol and Archie man and wife that Lola's brown eyes meet his.

He locked in on her, the intensity of his stare making her squirm under the heat. It was as if they were the only two people in the room and at a wedding neither of them particularly wanted to be at.

Javi kept her stare even after the bride and groom walked back down the aisle, hand in hand, on their way to the reception. People next to him murmured their apologies as they scooted by him to leave, but Javi stayed in place until Lola descended the dais. His girl looked ready to flee, but he wouldn't allow her to escape him again, not with this new burning need growing inside of him.

Before Lola could dash for the exit, Javi was out of his seat and fighting his way through the crowd. When he was close, he reached out with his hand before she was lost to him, grabbing her wrist and pulling her against him.

Lola didn't struggle, but she bit her bottom lip, looking up at him as if he were about to punish her for misbehaving. And damn if that didn't send a jolt straight to his cock.

He was tempted to do just that.

"You've been avoiding me, preciosa."

There was no use in lying; they both knew it to be true, but she still tried. "I've been busy, Javi. I'm not avoiding you."

"You're pushing me away." And he didn't understand why.

Lola sighed, casting a look over her shoulder to see that the other bridesmaids had left. "I'm not doing that either. Listen, can we do this later? We both need to go to the reception and I need to make sure my mother doesn't have a fit if I'm late. I promise we can talk then."

Promises could be broken. He knew that from experience. He needed more leverage. Something to get him by until they spoke later. "Kiss me, Lola."

"What?" The stunned look on her face made him smile. She was so damn sexy when she was confused.

"I said, kiss me. Let's seal our promise with a kiss."

"Javi—"

"Kiss me." The command in his tone sent shivers through Lola's body. His girl liked his dominance and he was using that in his favor.

She hesitated, but only for a moment before she tilted her head back and waited for him to close the distance. He gladly did. The kiss was different from the bedroom kisses that resulted in them taking off their clothes and falling into bed. This one was searing and full of unsaid words. He felt Lola relax against him, allowing him to hold her for just a second.

After a minute, Lola was the one to break the kiss as she pulled back, her lipstick slightly askew. He probably sported his own red lips from her and made a mental note to wash that away in the bathroom.

"I'll talk to you in a bit. Let me get everyone settled at the reception and I promise I'm yours."

She didn't know just how badly he wanted those words to be

true. Not trusting his voice, he nodded once. Lola offered him one last tight smile before turning away from him and following the rest of the wedding party out of the venue.

If he had to wait a little bit longer for his girl, then so be it. But one way or another, he was going to show Lola just how right they were together.

# Lola

## CHAPTER THIRTY-FOUR

THE RECEPTION TOOK place in the hotel's upstairs courtyard and by the time Lola caught an elevator up, the party was in full swing. Tables were positioned at the edges of the courtyard, spectacular place settings beckoning guests to enjoy their meals. The DJ set up in one corner, rocking instrumental music of popular songs while he waited for all the guests to arrive. A few feet down, waiters in fancy black suits bustled in and out of the kitchen, setting up the first round of appetizers.

What caught Lola's attention was the open bar nestled between shrubbery with nobody yet in line. She braved the cool evening air and headed outside. Her lips still tingled from Javi's searing kiss and his dominant command. It was evident that avoiding him wouldn't work and trying to weave through her feelings right now was out of the question.

What she needed was liquid courage.

"What can I get you, ma'am?" the pretty, young woman behind the bar asked her. Lola took quick inventory of the bottles she had displayed behind her before settling on something that would give her the courage she needed.

"Bone-dry martini, please."

The bartender smirked. "A girl ready to party. I like it." She

587

started to make Lola's drink. "Hoping to find a lonely groomsman to take home?" she asked.

Despite herself, Lola snorted. If only that were her problem. "More like, I need the courage to talk to the one I brought with me."

"Oh no. Sticky situation?" she asked, showing genuine sympathy.

"I guess you can say that. He's perfect and I'm...intimidated. You know how things can feel too good to be true?"

"And you find out it was indeed, too good to be true?"

"Exactly!" Lola exclaimed as if the bartender got a particularly hard test question right. "And I think it's better to protect my heart now before it inevitably gets crushed."

"Preach sister. Protect your heart first. Here's your martini," she said and handed over the glass. "For what it's worth, you seem like a smart woman, so I'm sure you'll figure it out."

Who knew she needed such a pep talk from a strange bartender? What she wanted was to call Mona, but her friend was busy overseeing her bookstore and running the bakery, so that call would have to wait. All she had were insights from a friendly bartender and her muddled thoughts.

"Thank you. I'll be back for another one soon," she said, earning a thumbs up from the woman who moved on to the next person in line.

Before she faced Javi, she needed to check in with her mother. Finding her through the throngs of people hadn't been easy, especially since Luciana wasn't answering her phone. She finally found her mother by the catering table, barking orders at the hard-working waiters.

"Mother, do you need me to do anything?" She came up behind Luciana placing a hand on her shoulder.

Luciana turned her head away from the poor man trying to serve up the appetizers to look over her daughter. She felt the woman's judgment as she took her daughter in. "I see you decided against the shapewear I bought you." Her mother's words cut deeply. If it wasn't a comment about her chosen profession then it was about her weight. Luciana hated how comfortable Lola was in her skin and tried to knock her down a peg at any opportunity she got.

"You saw me while we were getting ready and didn't mention it then. I don't understand why you feel the need to bring it up now."

"Well, I had hoped you would come to your senses, but I was wrong."

Ignoring that bitchy comment, Lola tried again. "Do you need me to do anything?" The patience in her voice should have made her a saint.

"Dolores, must I tell you everything? This is your sister's wedding! Her big day. You should be making sure everything is going according to plan. We need to make this perfect for your sister; she deserves it."

Lola had to grit her teeth. Deep down, she knew her mother was stressed and when Luciana was stressed, her cattiness came out tenfold. Anyone unfortunate enough to be in the way would be open for criticism and Lola was an easy punching bag for her. That didn't excuse her mother's behavior but helped explain it a bit.

"I'm trying to make it the best day of her life, but everything seems to be running smoothly. If there's nothing you need my help with, then I'll make sure everyone is enjoying themselves."

At this point, her mother was back to barking orders at the wait staff, so Lola knew she lost her. "See to that," her mother said off-handedly, signaling she was done with the conversation.

Lola sipped her drink, trying to forget her mother's cruel comments. The dry martini burned going down her throat but also eased the budding anger and panic building inside of her right now.

It was too soon to go for round two of the martini, but not too soon to reach for the glass of champagne one of the waiters served. If it was a different person serving her a drink, it was like the first one never happened. Right?

A loud commotion brought her attention toward the entrance of the courtyard. People began to crowd together in groups, clapping and cheering. It wasn't until she saw glimpses of a snow-white dress that she realized the bride and groom had made it.

The group of people parted for the happy couple. Genuine smiles plastered Archie and Marisol's faces and a ping of jealousy worked its way through her body. Not jealous of Marisol marrying her ex, but the fact that she found someone to spend the rest of her days with. Lola still wasn't convinced that their love ran deep, but hoped her sister truly found love and happiness with Archie. Not for Archie's sake, but because Marisol deserved someone who would truly love her. Maybe it would mellow her out.

The music changed to a slower tune, making her think of far-off places and love that ran deeper than surface level. They were a sight to behold as Archie and Marisol took the floor, commanding it as if they danced together every night.

Dampness coated her cheeks and it took Lola a second to realize she was crying. Why the hell was she crying? Seeing them together shouldn't have made her feel like this. Perhaps this was what healing was. Finally letting go of anger that had weighed her down for so long.

Lola wasn't and would never be the type of girl Archie would come to love and Archie would never be the man of her dreams. Marisol was better suited to that role, but it had taken her until this moment to fully see that. The two of them fit together in a way she never would and she hoped she was seeing genuine happiness on both of their faces. Marisol was just so hard to read sometimes.

"Tissue?" The sound of a deep voice next to her made Lola jump. She had been far too caught up in her thoughts to notice Javi approaching. She gave him a puzzled look, but before she could ask, he shrugged. "When you have a daughter, you learn to carry all sorts of things in your pockets. I have chocolate too, if you're interested."

Actually yes, she was very interested in the chocolate and told him as much. He dug in his pocket before holding out a mini chocolate bar. She needed something in her stomach besides alcohol—which she was already feeling.

"Thanks," she muttered around the first bite.

"No problem. Did you want to sit down?"

She shook her head. Her body was abuzz with newfound energy and sitting down would cause her nervous energy to manifest in leg shakes and overthinking.

"No, how about we dance." She didn't phrase it as a question. She was going to dance whether Javi wanted to join her or not. The first song between husband and wife had come to an end and the music had changed to a more upbeat tune that demanded to be danced to.

Lola took a sip of the champagne before joining the rest of the crowd on the dance floor. She turned her head to see Javi had followed her and she bit back a smile. Her body began to move to the beat, her hips swaying as she backed up against Javi. From this angle, her hips pressed right up against him.

Lola heard an intake of breath and rewarded herself with another sip of champagne. Two large hands landed on her hips, anchoring them together. "Lola..."

Her name was a warning on his lips, but she didn't know what for. With her free hand, the one not holding the champagne glass, she reached around, snaking her arm around his neck. Javi cursed in Spanish and she giggled. "Are you okay back there?"

"I'm more than okay, but why do I have the feeling you are trying to distract me?" Even as he said it, she felt his hips against her ass. Just a touch from this man left her a wanton, needy woman incapable of speech.

"Distraction? From what?" The alcohol was clouding her mind but also made her brave. Before he could answer, Lola untangled herself from him and turned in his arms. Her lips met his with frenzied passion. She moved against him, demanding more from the kiss than what he was giving her.

"Lola…" He tried to protest, but she didn't want to hear it. She didn't want this moment to end and fade like everything else good in her life. She didn't want to think, only feel.

"Javi, please." What she was begging for, she didn't quite know. Instead, she pressed herself closer to him, as close as two people could be with clothes on. She didn't care that they were standing in the middle of a dancing crowd or that anyone could spot them in this compromising position because she frankly didn't care.

"Lola—" Struggle played across Javi's face. Heat coursed through their bodies and she knew a part of him wanted her, but the part of him hesitating seemed to be winning. She couldn't have that, not now. Maybe not until they were done with their wedding week adventures.

Lola leaned in to kiss him again, but Javi backed up, putting a few inches between them. The hurt on her face softened his features, but only slightly. He remained firm, keeping her at arm's length. Her boozy brain wasn't too pleased with this.

"We need to talk, Lola. Now."

*Javi*

CHAPTER THIRTY-FIVE

LOLA STUMBLED when Javi gently took her by the arm and led her away from prying eyes. More than once he had to catch her before she fell on her face, but instead of getting mad or embarrassed, Lola laughed. It was like trying to lead around a toddler who just had their fill of all the sugary snacks inside the house.

Javi had never seen Lola so...out of place. He knew it was from the alcohol making its way through her system, but he had not been prepared for tipsy Lola. And for what? To talk to him? God, he hoped not. He was kicking himself for not being able to see her pain and worry earlier. Maybe he could have helped prevent this.

Still, it wasn't all his fault. Lola had been acting strange around him and hadn't been subtle about it either. If something was bothering her, why didn't she come to him? They could have talked it through like grown-ass adults in grown-ass situationships did.

Javi pulled them to a private nook between the elevators and the entrance to the courtyard. The main party was still in full swing and the only people over here were waiting for the next available elevator, paying them no mind. He pushed Lola up against the wall and not in the sexy way he had done the other

593

night. No, this was to keep her upright so she didn't fall on her ass.

"You got me alone. Has that been your secret plan all along?" Lola giggled, sloppily leaning forward to wrap her arms around his neck. In the span of the two minutes it took to steady her and lead her away from the dance floor, Lola's drunkenness hit a whole new level. She didn't appear to be aware of what she was saying anymore and that frightened Javi. He had wanted her attention, but not like this.

*Fuck*. She was making this more complicated than it needed to be.

"How much have you had to drink?" That was apparently the wrong fucking thing to say because Lola's easygoing smile faded. She narrowed her eyes, lips turning into a deep frown.

"Are you shaming me for drinking, Javi?" Her voice had gone unusually low, sending his body into alert mode.

"No, I'm not, but—"

Just like that, the anger was erased as if it had never been there at all. "Good." She giggled and leaned up to kiss him. He tasted the alcohol on her lips and groaned. His dumb brain wanted more. To press up against her until she was writhing with need for him. But she was fucking drunk and he would never take advantage of her in this state.

He came here to talk, not to fuck.

With great difficulty, Javi untangled himself from her. Lola whimpered, sticking out her bottom lip in a pout. "Do you not want to kiss me?"

"Not when you are too drunk to think rationally," he said, unwavering. Javi sucked in a deep breath to calm down his racing heart before stepping back to put more distance between them.

He hated the pain flashing through her eyes and every part of his body screamed to take her back into his arms. There she would be safe. But that wasn't true, was it? If he held her now, he'd be inclined to forget everything he wanted to say. Everything he needed to tell her.

"Lola, I can't do this anymore. I can't continue when I don't know where we stand." The moment the words were out of his mouth, he knew he fucked up.

Lola balled her hands into fists at her side, her earlier swaying no longer seemed to hinder her balance anymore. "Oh, you can't do this anymore? And what exactly is that, Javi? You can't *do* me anymore?" The anger in Lola's voice carried, and a few guests waiting for the elevator turned to look at them.

"Fuck, no, Lola, that's not what I'm saying. I'm saying I don't like this lie we've made up. I knew what I was getting myself into, but I didn't expect to fall for you the way I did."

"Fall for me?" She huffed, once again doing nothing to hide her voice. He thanked God they were out of most of the public's eye, but he wished she would lower her voice to not warrant unwanted attention.

"Is that so hard to see, Lola? Is it so impossible that during our time together I have fallen in love with you?"

"Don't say that!" she growled, tears springing to her eyes. She put her hands over her ears as if she could block out his words. "Don't fucking say that if you don't mean it!"

"Don't say what? That I care for you? That I want to talk about what's happening between us because I know you feel it too? Tell me, Lola, what is it you don't want to talk about? Because everything I'm saying is *real.*"

She was getting more agitated by the moment and he was pushing her to the brink of explosion, but he couldn't stop. Not now when he was finally getting through to her. He would have preferred it if she wasn't drunk and near tears, but he didn't know if he'd have the opportunity again.

"Lola, please. I want to know where we stand. That's all I'm asking. Let's go back to our room and we can—"

"We can, what?" The tears started to run freely this time and Javi desperately wanted to understand what she was feeling, but she wasn't giving him anything other than drunk anger. He refused to believe these were her real thoughts, he knew his girl and she liked to talk things out. That was exactly what he was trying to do.

"So we can go back and we can fuck and pretend like this never happened?" she continued.

"No, that's not what I'm saying."

"Oh, so now you don't want to fuck me? You didn't have a problem with that the last time you had me in bed!"

"Fuck, Lola, what the hell is wrong with you? Are you not listening to a damn word I'm saying?!"

"If I gave you more money on top of the fucking two hundred thousand dollars I'm giving you, would you fuck me then? It's just a job to you, isn't it?"

Her words rang around him like an ominous finale. The curtains had closed on the tragedy, but something wasn't quite finished. There was more to be said, but emotions were high and running rampant. It would have been kinder if she punched him in the face repeatedly until he passed out.

After all, hadn't he been worried about the same things? He knew the damn money would play a negative role in this, but it wasn't fair to say everything he was feeling and the night they spent together was because of the money.

"Lola..."

He didn't know what to fucking say. His words were not coming and he didn't know how to make this right. He fixed and repaired things for a living, but when it came to his relationships, he was hopeless.

Lola opened her mouth to say something, but her body froze and her mouth fell open in a silent scream. She wasn't looking at him anymore, but rather at what was behind him. Dread washed over him and he didn't want to turn around to see what left Lola as pale as a ghost.

Despite everything screaming at him not to, Javi slowly turned around. Standing there, not even five feet away, was Luciana Roberts. Judging from the pinched expression on her face, she had heard everything. And she was pissed.

## CHAPTER THIRTY-SIX

NEVER IN LOLA'S twenty-plus years of life had she ever sobered up as quickly as she did right now, seeing her mother staring at her. It reminded her of those old cartoons when a character got angry and steam poured from their ears. That was her mom to a T and she braced herself for the onslaught of disappointment about to leave her mother's mouth.

"Dolores, what did you do?" Her mother's voice held no emotion, just a forced patience she had only ever heard once in her life when she was caught skipping class to smoke in the bathroom in middle school with a couple of girls from her science class.

Her mom had been livid then but kept her face neutral the entire time she spoke to the principal. Luciana knew how to keep up an appearance when the time called for it, especially when it would reflect badly upon her. The moment they got into the privacy of their car her mother let her have it. How ashamed she was of her behavior and how those poor decisions could add up. How would that make the family look if she continued to make bad decisions? She had a reputation to uphold and people in their small, posh community talked.

Lola thought her reaction had been over the top then, since she was not the first, nor the last, spoiled rich kid to try smoking at school. She was just unfortunate to be a dumbass who skipped with friends that had the same class. She didn't know how skipping one science class would doom her entire family's wine legacy, but she didn't try to argue with her mother. Even then, she knew it would be a lost cause.

But something like this? Hearing her daughter pay someone two hundred thousand dollars to attend a wedding and pretend to be their fake boyfriend would rate astronomically higher than skipping a class and smoking in middle school.

"Mom, it's not—"

"Don't you dare tell me it's not what I think. Because from my viewpoint, it looks as if I overheard a loud conversation between you and this...*man*," —she spat the word like poison from her mouth— "involving sex and money. Are you hiring an escort service for your sister's wedding?"

The words were said in a hushed tone to not let any passersby hear their damning conversation. The softer tones did nothing to hide the vitriol behind her words. Despite the tension lingering between them, she couldn't help the laugh bubbling out of her throat. She half blamed the alcohol for her outbursts. Luciana pursed her lips together, clearly not amused by the situation.

"He's not my escort," she managed to stammer out between fits of giggles. It was wildly inappropriate to laugh at this moment and yet she couldn't make herself stop.

"Keep your voice down." She huffed, reaching for Lola's hand and pulling her into a room only a few feet away from them. She hadn't noticed it was there, probably because her drunk mind was processing extra slowly. Movement sounded from behind her and she knew Javi was following, she just didn't know if that was a good or bad thing yet.

The door shut behind Javi with a resounding thud and they were left in a small room, barely larger than a janitorial closet. The light flickered on and off, highlighting the animosity brewing in the room. Her mother finally let her go, turning and muttering something in Spanish Lola couldn't understand.

If she didn't know her mother was pissed before, she knew now. She never talked in Spanish. Ever. Honestly, Lola barely remembered her mother knew Spanish. It was a testament to how angry she was when she unassimilated herself.

"Now, let's try this again. Did you or did you not hire an escort to pretend to be your date on your sister's big day?" She emphasized as if Lola did not understand what a wedding was or its significance.

"I didn't hire an escort." Her mother visibly relaxed until Lola went on. "But I did pay Javi to be here."

"Dolores!" her mother shouted, throwing her hands up in exasperation. "What the hell were you thinking?" Now she had her mother cussing. Pretty soon Lola would have her mother in the hospital with a stress-induced heart attack.

"It's not Lola's fault. I wouldn't have agreed if I didn't want to come," Javi, who she had forgotten was there, spoke up.

The redness in her mom's face reached new levels and Lola was quick to intervene. "I don't need you standing up for me, Javi. I got this. This isn't anyone's fault but my own."

Javi looked ready to argue. He opened his mouth and then seemed to think better of it. He cleared his throat, stuffing his hands into his pants pockets. Only the slightest nod of his head was all the assurance she was given, but a part of her was disappointed he didn't try to fight harder for her. Which was a shitty thing to say after the hell she had put him through.

Too many secrets had piled up and not just from this wedding. They weighed heavily on her shoulders and she couldn't carry them around anymore. So she started to tell her mother everything. How this all started with getting the invitation in the mail and knowing she couldn't face this wedding alone. How she had met Javi previously—though she did not explain how they knew each other—and how she hired him to remodel Phoenix. How they came to a mutual agreement on the remodel and the wedding.

"Javi isn't an escort. He's my friend, who also happens to be remodeling my bookstore. I couldn't do this alone. I can't be here and pretend it's not weird or ignore the silent judgment from everyone in the room, knowing Archie broke up with me for Marisol. How it could have been me up there instead of her."

She knew now she never wanted it to be her, but that didn't make the situation any less awkward or the looks any less unpleasant. All she wanted was for her mother to acknowledge this was a weird situation and that her feelings were valid. Perhaps even mention how proud she was of Lola for going through with being in the wedding despite all of those things.

But that was not the mom she was given. No, the woman she was given was looking at her without an ounce of sympathy. Only disgust and anger reflected in her features and the last bit of hope she had for their relationship crumbled. Luciana would never be the mother she needed and Lola would never be the ideal daughter. She saw that now. After years of trying to keep the peace, she couldn't keep doing this anymore. For once, she wanted her mother to fight for their relationship.

It was an eye-opening experience and not one she wanted to have while drunk and uncertain about where she stood with Javi.

"You are sabotaging your sister's wedding for your selfish reasons, Dolores. I knew there might be problems with you considering your history with Archie, and I was prepared to deal with them anyway I could. That's why I kept you so busy in hopes that it would keep you distracted. That was a mistake and I should have checked in on who you would be bringing as your so-called date."

The words cut like daggers through her heart, but her mom wasn't finished. "If anyone finds out what you did, our family will be dealing with cleaning up your mess of a scandal when we should be celebrating your sister's happy day. She is going to be devastated when she finds out her sister tried to sabotage her wedding."

"Scandal? Sabotage?" This woman really thought they were the Clintons and not another wealthy family in America. A bitter laugh escaped her lips as she shook her head in disbelief. "I was trying to survive a fucking visit with this family! I was trying to protect my mental health because no one else would."

"Oh, it's always this same old excuse. When will you give up this idea that you have such a cruel family? When all we want is the best for you."

"You don't know what's best for me and you never have! You only care about your image and I'm too emotional or too fat to fit into whatever impossible box you've built for me. Well, guess what, Mother? I'm so fucking done with trying to please you. I'm done trying to measure up to this impossible standard you have for me because I never will. And you will never change."

Luciana looked taken aback by her words. She had never seen her mother look so thoroughly chastised and at a loss for words. "What are you saying, Dolores? Speak frankly."

"I thought I was speaking frankly. But since you can't see through your own prejudices, I'll say it again. I'm done. Done with you and trying to salvage a relationship that was never good in the first place. I'm done being disappointed by you at every turn and I care about myself too much to continue to place myself under your scrutiny. I'm done with you, Mom. And I hope like hell you get the help you need."

"Dolores!" The complete shock in her mother's voice nearly made her come crawling back and beg her for forgiveness. But she needed to stand her ground for the ten-year-old little girl who never had the strength or the means to walk away. She needed to do this for the woman she had become and who still struggled with the need to have the mother she deserved.

Lola walked right out of the small room, leaving behind a lifetime of pent-up aggression and trauma. With each step, she became a little lighter on her feet, but she couldn't help but mourn the loss of a mother who was still very much alive, just one who didn't deserve her.

As she walked, soft footfalls followed her back to her room.

*Javi*

CHAPTER THIRTY-SEVEN

SHE DID IT. Lola fucking did it. If he hadn't seen his girl stand up for herself with his own two eyes, he doubted he would have believed it otherwise. Not because she wasn't capable, he knew she had it in her, but because he never suspected it to be during her sister's wedding, in a tiny room barely bigger than a closet.

The look on Luciana's face as Lola stormed out of the room was priceless. Her mother's mouth hung open as if stuck on the last word she said. There was a faint twitch in her eye, the only sign she had not processed what happened. In truth, Javi hadn't yet processed it either.

Then, as if a light had been switched on in her mind, Luciana's mouth clamped shut. The fury and rage brewing inside of her turned toward Javi.

"You should be ashamed of yourself! You should—" she started, but Javi didn't bother waiting around to be the recipient of her ire. With each second that passed, Lola got farther and farther away from him.

By the time he made it out of the room and rounded the corner, the elevator was closing on a determined-looking Lola. He jammed his finger against the button and almost immediately the elevator opened...just not the one with Lola inside.

603

Before anyone else could follow him, he pressed the close door button on the elevator, quickly followed by his floor level. The damn elevator took its time descending before it finally reached his level. The doors had barely started to open when Javi squeezed his way out, catching sight of the navy-blue dress Lola was in.

She was only a few feet ahead of him, head down as she made a beeline to their room. "Lola, wait!" he called after her, willing his legs to move faster.

"Not now, Javi," she murmured, fumbling with the key to unlock their door. She found it and pressed the plastic against the reader. Once it turned red, Lola pushed her way inside with Javi at her heels.

"If not now, when?" he insisted, letting the door fall closed behind him. Lola did not stop her speed walking into the room, but instead tossed her clutch onto the bed and vigorously started taking off her jewelry.

"I don't know!" The frustration unleashed in her voice made him pause. He stood a few feet behind her, but didn't dare move any closer. She rounded on him in an instant, chest heaving and looked moments away from crying. Yet, her jaw was clenched and she remained unwavering despite the showdown with her mother.

"I know you want to talk about what just happened and I know you want to talk about us, but I don't have any more to give anyone right now. Please, I want to be left alone."

No, he didn't want to leave this alone and let it get swept under the rug to be forgotten. He wanted to address it now while it was still fresh on their minds. He didn't care that emotions were running high. It was all the more reason to talk about this now.

"I'm not going to leave you alone, Lola. Don't you understand that? You want space? Fine, I can give you space, but I'm not leaving you. You're going to talk to me and we are going to work this out together. But don't you dare think you are pushing me away."

The words seemed to hang between them, but neither made

an effort to fill the silence. What could he say that he hadn't already? She was cutting herself off from him and he was holding on to the fraying tether still connecting them. He wasn't prepared to let go unless she asked him to walk out of her life. Even then he would still fight.

After an uncomfortably long pause, Lola sighed in resignation. She turned back to the mirror and started removing bobby pins from her hair. "I just need time," she said at last.

It wasn't the answer he wanted and didn't help ease the unsteady feelings growing inside of him, but he nodded. He wasn't sure what he was supposed to do, so he continued to stand awkwardly as he watched her unpin her hair until it fell in tight curls around her face.

"I'm going to shower and then we can head to bed. I'll sleep on the couch tonight," she said, gathering her things up for the bathroom and heading in without a look back.

There was no way in hell he was going to let her take the couch and the moment she closed the door, he grabbed a pillow off the bed and tossed it onto the couch. He pretended it didn't sting to have been kicked out of bed with her, but he was at capacity with lying to himself.

While she showered, he changed out of the too expensive tux he rented for this occasion and changed into sweats and a plain T-shirt. With nothing else to do, he planted himself right on the couch and waited for her to get out. After a few minutes, Javi turned on the TV to drown out the voices in his head and to distract his wandering mind.

An hour passed, or maybe two, Javi lost all concept of time as he desperately tried to shut his brain off by watching some documentary about coral reefs, when Lola finally stepped out of the bathroom. The steam from the room followed after her as she walked, sending the smell of clean laundry and lavender to his senses.

She was dressed in a silk tank top and shorts set, giving him ample skin to look at. He couldn't enjoy her body on display, he was too nervous watching her work her way around the room, grabbing her brush to comb her hair, and moisturizer to apply to her face.

The silence was torture.

As if sensing his eyes on her, Lola turned to look at him once she was done towel-drying her hair. "I managed to change our flight to tomorrow at noon." Her words stunned him. He believed they had more time reserved at the hotel and he had hoped that would allow them to talk. But apparently, that was no longer an option.

"I'm ready to go home. I just need to be back somewhere I feel more comfortable, doing my daily routines," she said, answering his unasked question. "And no, I'm not ready to talk. I know I'm being an asshole, but please, let me deal with one problem at a time."

Problem. So he was a problem now? As much as he tried not to take it personally, he couldn't help but take offense to her words. Maybe he wasn't as prepared for the conversation as he thought he was.

"So, that's it? We are going to pretend as if nothing happened?" His words came out harsher than he intended, but he couldn't help it.

He heard Lola's intake of breath the moment before she turned off the lights. "I just need time," she said again, though it sounded flimsy this time. A mere ghost of a promise that would never see the light of day. "But...thank you for being there with me during that. I needed your strength."

"Nah, preciosa. You didn't need me at all. That was all you and I'm so proud of you."

*You don't need me at all.* The words played like a mantra in his mind and he only hoped they didn't come to be realized.

Lola didn't reply and he didn't expect her to. He listened to her breathing and turning in bed, trying to find a comfortable position. His mind was wide awake as he replayed these last two days. Lola had never seemed further away from him than she did at that moment.

Javi didn't sleep much that night, fearing what the morning would bring.

# Lola

BEFORE THE SUN had the chance to fully rise, creating pockets of light that brought with it new hopes for the day, Lola awoke. The only hope she had today was to board the plane without a panic attack and not think about yesterday's fight with her mom until she was home. She just had to survive a little bit longer.

Sleep had not come easily for her; she had tossed and turned most of the night. More than once she had woken up and noticed a light from the other side of the room. Apparently she hadn't been the only one that sleep eluded, for she caught Javi on his phone a few times throughout the night.

When she decided laying around in a lonely bed was no longer an option, Lola rolled out and was surprised to find Javi sitting up. He had dark circles underneath his red-rimmed eyes and his clothes were rumpled from the couch. Their eyes met momentarily and she detected a spark of light inside him. When she didn't address him, the light was smothered out and he looked resigned to the silent treatment.

She needed to talk to him; she wasn't being fair by holding back her concerns. But the truth was, her mind was a minefield of chaos right now and any wrong step would push her over the edge. There was still so much she needed to untangle and the truth of the matter was she couldn't think clearly when she was around him.

Her body and heart wanted Javi more than they have ever wanted anything else, but she had been led astray before. She needed her brain to be in on this too and right now, it was in overdrive mode.

They gathered their things in silence, moving past one another to reach for the items they needed to pack away in their suitcases. Lola had sent a quick text message to her father, asking him to meet her downstairs in ten minutes. Thankfully he was also an early riser and responded immediately that he was getting dressed and would be there soon.

All that was left to do was to gather up her bathroom belongings. She had managed to pack most of her makeup last night, so she just had her shampoos and other toiletries to pack. All of Javi's things were gone from the bathroom when she entered and she couldn't describe the emptiness she felt by not seeing his things next to hers. She was sleep deprived. There was no other reason to be sad over missing toiletries.

By the time she was finished gathering up the last of her things and zipping up her suitcase, Javi was waiting for her at the door. Without asking, he took her bags from her and she let him. "A car is upfront. Do you mind waiting for me out there? I'll just be a minute; I want to say goodbye to my dad."

Javi stared at her and she felt naked under his gaze. It wasn't a piercing hot gaze that eye fucked her. That would have been easier and much preferred over this. No, this gaze was staring straight into her soul, as if seeking hidden truths she wasn't yet ready to give.

The words he seemed to want to say played on his lips, but instead of speaking them, Javi nodded. "Of course." That's it. No preciosa, no kiss, no nothing. He left without another word. Just like she wanted.

And yet it didn't make her feel any better.

Because she was a coward, she waited until Javi stepped onto an elevator before she left the room, letting the door shut on their shortened week. She didn't have to wait long for another elevator and rode it down to the first floor. Just as the doors opened, her father stepped out from the opposite side and beamed at her. His sweet smile nearly brought tears to her eyes. How sad that an ounce of kindness would bring her to her knees.

She met her father in the middle of the lobby, happily accepting his embrace that he always gave her so freely. She knew her father's love never came with strings and it was easy to seek him out for comfort. His biggest fault was his compliance and ignorance of her treatment.

"Hey, sweetheart. Is everything alright? Your mom came back to the room last night in quite the mood. Do you know what that's about?" her father asked once they broke apart.

So her mother hadn't told her father what happened, which surprised her. She didn't think her mother would pass up her chance to belittle her.

"We fought. She's not happy with me. And I left Marisol's reception early." There was no use in lying and her father didn't appear surprised.

"You know your mother. She's a tough woman to please. I'm sure whatever it is, she will get over it soon."

"That's the thing. I'm tired of waiting around for her to get over it. I can't live like that and I'm so tired of the way she treats me, dad." She sighed, shaking her head. "I'm sorry, I know this will cause more problems, but Javi and I are leaving right now."

"Right now?" Her father's eyes widened. The shock on his face was almost comical, but only because he was so deceived by his ignorance. "But tonight is your sister's dinner party. I'm sure your mother would want you there. Let me talk to her."

It was too late for talking. At least the type of talking he wanted to do. Lola needed action because she had been talked to enough of her life and with no actions, their words meant nothing. "I'm sorry, but I'm going. Please give Marisol my best."

Though she doubted her sister would care much. Not with her mother's claws dug so deeply into her.

"Dolores, please. Tell me what happened. Let me try to fix this," her father pleaded and the tears she had tried desperately to hold back began to roll down her brown cheeks. "Oh, sweetheart. Please don't cry. What can I do?"

"Nothing." The words were barely a whisper and the smile on her lips didn't meet her eyes. "I'll call you when I'm home. I love you, Dad," she said and stood on her tiptoes to give him one last kiss.

Her father called her name once more, but Lola was already waking away. Away from the lifelong trauma of her mother and into the car where Javi waited for her. Javi, who she still had no idea how he fit into her life when everything seemed to be falling apart.

To top everything off, the plane ride home was filled with aggressive turbulence that had Lola nearly in Javi's lap, hyperventilating. Despite the wall she had built between them, Lola gladly accepted Javi's comfort on the flight home. Numerous times throughout the flight, the contents of her hastily eaten breakfast threatened to come up. She managed to keep it down though out of sheer spite.

When they landed, she was tempted to join in with the other passengers clapping. She never understood why people—specifically white passengers—clapped when landing and had always made fun of her father each time he did the same thing, but now she was joining them. Motion sickness was no joke and even as they deboarded she still felt unsteady on her feet.

Luckily the nausea went away by the time they reached the baggage claim. She felt Javi's warm presence next to her and despite their cuddling on the plane—which was only to ease her nerves and nothing else—they hadn't said much to each other. A heaviness settled between them and she knew he was waiting for her to be the one who broke it.

Unfortunately, all she provided was more disappointment when she took out her phone and took it off airplane mode, letting the notifications sweep in. She had a few from Mona, asking why she was coming home early and how they needed to talk. None from her mother or her sister, but one from her father asking if she made it home safe.

She sent a text to him to let him know she had arrived back in California before putting her phone away. If he replied, she wasn't yet ready to deal with any more questions or pleas to make up with her mother. The fight with her mother, funnily enough, was the only thing she didn't regret from her time at the wedding.

As distracted as she was, she wasn't surprised that she didn't notice Javi moving to grab her bags until he returned, rolling them up to her feet. "Thank you," she murmured, taking the handle from him.

"Do you need help getting to your car?" His voice was detached, nothing at all like the friendly version she had been spoiled with over these last few weeks.

She opened her mouth to say she didn't when a loud, high-pitched voice screamed behind them. "Papá!"

Both she and Javi whipped their heads around at the same time, seeing a sprinting six-year-old coming to them at full speed. "I thought you drove yourself here." Lola's words came out far more accusatory than she meant them. It wasn't as if Javi deliberately invited his cute daughter here to trap her to talk about her feelings.

"I did...I only told them I was coming home early and..." But he wasn't looking at Lola or paying her any mind. He moved from behind her and crouched down to catch Camilia as she catapulted across the tiles into his arms. She slammed into her father's chest, nearly knocking Javi to the ground. He steadied himself though, wrapping his arms tightly around his baby girl and peppering her happy face with kisses.

"I missed you so much!" She giggled before launching into a long story about everything she did with her tía while they were gone, going into great detail about a painting activity she and her cousin did.

An approaching figure laughed, her curly hair bouncing with each step. On her hip she carried a very tired toddler who Lola believed to be named Arturo. "She wanted to surprise you," Ofelia said to her brother before bringing her gaze up to meet Lola's. "Lola, hi! Did you have a good trip?"

There was no way she was going to get into all the nuances of her trip in the middle of the airport, so she smiled. "We had a good time, but I'm so thankful to be home. I missed my bed."

She laughed at that, obviously buying her half-truths. "Believe me, I know a little about that. When Arturo and I travel with Maverick, I miss my bed and his toddler bed so much. Love my little man, but he's the worst bed buddy. Between him and his father starfishing across the bed, I barely fit."

"Is he traveling now for work? His season starts soon, doesn't it?"

Ofelia nodded. "It does and he had to leave this weekend for various press conferences, so it was just the three of us." She smiled down at Camilia. Javi stood up, holding his daughter in his arms.

"I was thinking we could go out to lunch. Lola, would you join us? I would love to hear about the wedding if you're up for it," Ofelia asked, not realizing the weird position she had put Lola in.

Since she was a people pleaser by nature, she was inclined to say yes so as not to cause conflict or disappointment, even though she wanted nothing more than to go home and lie in her bed, watching her favorite shows on Netflix for hours.

Clearly seeing the panic and indecision on her face, Javi jumped in because of course he did. He was too damn good. "Lola is tired. I think she wants to go home."

"Awe, but next time you'll come, right Ms. Lola?" Camilia piped up, speaking to her for the first time.

Her rigid posture eased some at the sound of the little girl's voice. She still thought back to the fun day they shared at the bookstore while her father was working. Camilia was sweet and a little Javi in so many ways. She was kind and inquisitive. Plus she was interested in reading and any kids who loved reading were perfect in her books.

"Next time," she assured, earning a cheer from Camilia. Though when the next time would be, Lola had no idea.

"Hey, amore, can you go with tía for a moment so papá can say goodbye to Lola?" Javi asked, putting her back on the ground.

Ofelia jumped in, evidently understanding they needed a moment to say goodbye. "Let's go look at the gift shop we passed on the way in. Maybe we can find something to bring back to abuelo."

The idea of shopping sparked an interest in Camilia because she nodded and waved goodbye. "Bye, Ms. Lola. See you soon," she said cutely before following Ofelia off to the gift shop, leaving her and Javi alone to deal with their mess.

When they were left alone, it took a moment for either of them to talk, but instead of letting Javi fill the silence, she took initiative. "Thank you for giving me an out. Your family is lovely and I wouldn't have minded, but I just want to get home."

"I know you do. You have a lot on your mind right now."

It wasn't a question and he didn't say it as such, but she nodded anyway. "Right. So..." She had never had any problems talking to him before, but each time she opened her mouth, she felt like she was sliding a dagger a little bit deeper into his heart. "Can we meet at the shop on Monday? I can give you the last of your payment and we could...talk."

"About the money, Lola, I've been thinking and—"

Before he could finish that sentence, Lola put her hand up to silence it. "Monday, please. We can talk about it then."

Although he didn't look happy, he tensed his jaw and nodded. "Fine. Monday."

"Thank you." Although it was cruel, she leaned up to press one last lingering kiss on his lips. She wanted to remember the taste of him now that she was sober and not trying to throw herself on him. Javi reciprocated and she felt the hope behind his kiss.

She just needed a little time to figure out her feelings. Archie said she jumped into things without thinking them through and that was partly true. Some time apart from Javi would hopefully give her the answers she needed.

When she finally pulled back, the hope instantly vanished from his eyes. Something in her expression must have given her away. "I'll see you on Monday," she murmured, licking her lips to taste the last bit of him. Then she grabbed her suitcase and headed to the car without looking back.

## Lola

### CHAPTER THIRTY-NINE

MONDAY BROUGHT with it a mix of emotions that felt like riding a seesaw up and down. The "up" was arriving at Phoenix for the first time since traveling and walking inside with Mona to see her built-ins. She invited her best friend along since they had so much to catch up on and Mona had been here throughout the process.

Which brought her to the "down." In a little under an hour, she was going to be breaking the hearts of two people. Which seemed self-sabotaging and dramatic—she tried talking herself out of this numerous times—but she always fell back on the same conclusion. She couldn't start a real relationship with Javi because, ironically enough, she didn't want to hurt him. Or herself. Jumping into another big life decision without thinking it through was not what she needed at the moment. Her focus needed to be on opening Phoenix Books.

After all, what type of relationship started as a lie? A paid lie at that. A small part of her still could not wrap her head around the fact that Javi liked her for her and not the large check he was on his way to pick up. She didn't know how she would survive the next few weeks seeing him work in her shop but not being able to have him.

617

Those were problems for future Lola. Current Lola was about to see her shop. Mona parked her car behind the store and cut the engine. "You ready, Lo-Lo? Because your mind is about to be blown." Mona grinned and got out of the car.

Lola's chest was abuzz with nervous energy. "So ready. I still can't believe you didn't send me any photos of the progress, you bitch."

That only earned a laugh from her friend who took the spare key out of her pocket and unlocked the back of the door. "Yeah, yeah, I'm a bitch. At least I'm not the dumb-ass who is about to throw away a perfectly fine man for reasons I don't quite understand."

Ouch. She flinched at her words. Harsh...but accurate.

This morning, Mona had picked her up for breakfast. They went to her bakery and Mattea had a spread of various pastries and juices set out for them to eat. She knew the instant Mona shut the door behind her that both women were going to demand answers about her trip and the reason she came back early and cranky.

There was no hesitation as she sat down and subsequently poured her heart out to them. She told them about the disastrous encounters with her mother, the way Javi stood up for her, the amazing night they spent together, the final fight with her mother, and her reasons to leave early.

Mona, ever the inquisitive, still didn't understand why she planned on ending her situationship with Javi if she felt this strongly about him. It was a fair question, but not one she could easily answer.

She was trying to figure out a lot of things. The relationship fallout with her mother and how it would affect her family. She was trying to sort through her feelings for Javi and it was hard enough when they were forced to spend so much time together in close proximity. And she was also desperately trying to heal from the jabs her mother had thrown at her over the years and unlearn them.

Like she had kept saying before, she needed time and space.

Mattea and Mona had looked at one another, sharing a silent conversation Lola was not part of. None of them tried to coax her one way or another or tell her what she was doing was wrong, but she still saw the hesitancy in their eyes.

"Are you sure you really want to cut Javi off? Just like that?" Mona had asked her.

She wasn't sure and that was the problem. She didn't know what she wanted; all she knew was that Archie's words were fucking with her brain and making her second-guess every decision.

"I think it might be the best choice for now," she had said.

After that, they dropped the subject of her trip and she caught up with what had been going on while she was gone.

And now she was finally at her shop, ready to walk in for the first time. Excitement vibrated through her and she all but pushed past Mona as soon as she got the door opened. "Damn, eager much?" Mona laughed, following after her. "Be careful, I think there might still be supplies out and I don't want you stepping on something and breaking your ass."

"I'm not going to break my ass."

"Not if I can help it!" Came her echoing reply, followed by laughter.

Lola felt the air leave her lungs as soon as she made her way out of the back and into the main room of her shop. All the old brown, decrepit bookcases had been taken down and hauled out of the room. It opened up the room and made it appear bigger than it was. All along the walls were beautifully placed white shelves. Though unfinished, Lola could picture the end product and the books that would soon line each row.

The coffee area, which also served as a checkout, had been stripped of all the old furniture and appliances. Two new, sleek, pink counters stood in its place. They were L-shaped with a small opening for Lola to move in and out of when needed. She shrieked, unable to hide her excitement.

"Mona, have you seen this?!" she yelled though she knew the answer. Her friend had been here the entire week, so of course she saw the pastel pink counter.

"Doesn't it look good? I gotta admit, I was a hater until I saw it in person, but it's so *you* and adds a pop of color. Did you check out the floors yet?"

The last time she had been here, Javi's men were about to start on the floors which made her get her ass in gear and pack all the books. It had been the day Javi brought Camilia. There weren't many worth saving and she had ended up donating many of the books to the library in town, but still had enough to fill the entire back office.

Lola looked down. What was once a reddish, brown wood flooring was now stained a cloudy gray. The color complimented her color scheme perfectly and made the room feel more elegant. "I'm dying! What the fuck, this is perfect."

"And it's not done yet," Mona said, placing her hands on the pink counter before pushing herself up to sit atop it. She crossed her arms over her chest, surveying the room. "It's coming along amazingly though. Your man and his crew do a good job."

Lola's smile vanished and the excitement became tainted with something ugly and uncertain. "He's not my man," she said feebly, but she wasn't sure who she was trying to convince.

"Right," Mona said, the tone in her voice telling Lola that she didn't believe her. "Well, good luck telling him that when he gets here. Do you want me to stay?"

She should say no and maybe it would be easier if Mona was in the car, waiting for her. But she wanted to have a backup in case her emotions got the best of her.

"Stay. Please."

Mona's features softened and she nodded. The lump working its way up Lola's throat subsided, knowing her friend would be there. It felt a lot like relief.

Relief was short-lived though because a moment later, she heard someone knocking on the front door of the store, and her whole body tightened. "I'll get it," Mona said, probably seeing the terror in Lola's expression. She pushed herself off the counter and went to let Javi inside.

Lola waited with bated breath, bracing her body for the fallout that was bound to happen. She heard her heart pounding loudly in her ears. She watched as Mona unlocked the door and swung it open. Lola braced herself, pretending she was ready to see Javi.

However, standing behind the door wasn't Javi as she suspected. Her entire body sagged forward and her face was a picture of shock. "Ofelia?" she asked, not understanding why Ofelia was here instead of her brother.

The pretty woman offered an apologetic smile. "Hi, Lola. I came here on Javi's behalf. Something came up."

"Is everything okay?" Her mind went to the worst scenarios possible. Did he hate her? Did something happen to Camilia?

"Yes, or...I believe it is. He was pretty vague on the details. He said he needed to run an errand," she admitted and stepped inside. Mona let the door close behind her. "Hi, I'm Ofelia. Javi's sister." She offered her hand to Mona.

"Monique. Nice to meet you." She greeted but was unable to hide the skepticism in her expression. Mona kept looking at her as if she had an explanation for why Javi wasn't her, as if she knew the reason.

But she did, didn't she? It was avoidance. Javi was avoiding her and she couldn't blame him. She hadn't given him much hope that she wished to continue this relationship and it was selfish, but she had wanted to see him today. If it was to be the last day they had the opportunity to speak about matters outside of the job, then she wanted this final moment together.

Being stood up by a man you planned on ending a situationship with sucked ass. It felt incomplete, like she couldn't say the last things that were left unsaid. Now they would forever live rent-free in her mind.

"Look, I know you weren't expecting me," Ofelia started,

clearly sensing the confusion and tension in the room. "But...last night Javi came clean to me."

All the color drained from Lola's face. She couldn't imagine what Ofelia must think of her right now. Somehow knowing she knew about their arrangement was worse than Javi not showing up.

"I have to admit I was surprised by what he said. Not the fake dating part, but that he agreed to take such a large payout. My brother's prideful and doesn't like to admit he's struggling. I try to help him as much as I can, but he hates when I offer. I'm trying to respect his boundaries, but it's so hard when he's suffering. You know?

"Anyway, I'm here to tell you he said he didn't want to accept the rest of the payment. Just enough to cover expenses and pay his men."

Lola had suspected as much and was ready to argue the point that Javi earned the money fairly and should be compensated. But apparently, Ofelia was thinking the same thing. "But my brother can be an idiot, so I'm here to accept it and make sure he gets it. If you are still offering. At the very least, he can put the money away for Camilia for when she's older."

"Of course. The money is his to do with what he pleases," she said, fishing in her jeans pocket to pull out the check with the remaining balance she offered to Javi.

Tears began to pool in the corner of her eyes and she had to rapidly blink them away before they could fall. This felt like the final piece of Javi and once she gave that away, they had nothing tethering them together. Sure, he would still be working in the shop to get it prepared for the grand opening, but she wouldn't be his and they wouldn't have time alone.

"Can you tell him something for me?" Lola asked, handing Ofelia the check. Immediately she safely put it away in her purse. When she nodded, Lola continued. "Just that I'm sorry. And...no —just that. I'm sorry."

She had a whole speech prepared, but it didn't seem right

anymore. Not when the message would be delivered by someone else.

Ofelia's kind eyes shined with sympathy. "Lola, for what it's worth, I don't think my brother is ignoring you. He's not that type of man. And even if you claim the situation between the both of you was fake, I saw the way my brother looked at you. He hasn't stared at anyone like that since Estella."

Hearing Javi's former girlfriend mentioned surprised her. She wasn't trying to be his new Estella, but maybe she had played her part a little too well and tricked them both.

"I guess what I'm trying to say is that I know my brother. Don't be surprised if he finds ways to stay in your life. He's a private person and doesn't let many people in, but he's different around you. More...alive." She sighed and finished her explanation with a shrug. "Anyway, thank you. And if it's okay, I was hoping I could still come to the opening?"

"Of course you can. I would love it." Lola was surprised by how true those words were.

Ofelia beamed. "Good. Then I better go. This place looks amazing. I can't wait to see the final product." Ofelia hesitated, but then hugged Lola. She was so surprised that she didn't think she managed to hug back, but when Ofelia pulled away, she didn't seem upset about it.

"I'll see you soon," she said and then waved goodbye to Mona. Lola watched as she walked away, opening the front door and leaving the shop. When the door shut, the reality of what happened settled over Lola, leaving her empty and thinking she had just made the worst decision of her life.

## CHAPTER FORTY

THE MOMENT JAVI left the airport a plan had started brewing in his mind. He understood Lola needed time to sort out her feelings, which Javi could respect...even if he was impatient as hell about it. There was no doubt in his mind that she cared for him, even if she was too afraid to admit it right now. That didn't mean he had to deny the love he felt for her and he was showing his love by giving her what she asked for.

Space.

But space didn't mean he had to sit down and twiddle his thumbs until she realized his feelings. Hell no. Instead, he had things he needed to do and spent the past week since returning back from Colorado getting things in order.

A small part of him feared he was overstepping, but on the other hand, he had not been the one to request the meet-up he was driving to. He saw it as an opportunity and not one he planned on losing, even if that meant Lola would hate him forever. It was a risk he was willing to take if that made just one person understand the hell she put up with for so many years.

That would change today.

Camilia sat in the back seat of his truck, kicking her legs

absentmindedly and watching the world pass them by as he drove. He opted not to leave her with Ofelia today since she had already done him a favor by meeting Lola. Every time he thought of Lola seeing his sister walk in instead of him, it sent a longing pain through his chest. This feeling was temporary and he would make her understand why he had not been there. In time.

No, he brought Camilia along for two reasons. One, he had missed his princess after nearly a week away. He hadn't realized how much that would affect him until he returned and had her in his arms again. And secondly, they needed to talk.

Nearly all her life, it had only ever been the two of them. She had been too young to remember Estella, but she knew Estella had been her mommy and that she was no longer with them. Never in her short life had he brought another woman over or introduced her to anyone out of fear the relationship wouldn't work out, leaving Camilia attached to yet another ghost.

He couldn't do that to her.

But he also had come to realize he would start dating again. Hopefully Lola, if his plan all went accordingly, but at the very least to someone in the future. He didn't want to be alone his whole life and he did want to have more kids one day.

"Mija, can we talk for a second? About something important."

From the rearview mirror, he saw Camilia swivel her head toward the front. She nodded, but it still took him another moment to get his thoughts together. He wanted to make sure he said this in a way a six-year-old would understand.

"So, you know how much I love you, right?" he asked. Camilia nodded, holding her arms far apart to indicate "this much." "Exactly. Well, one day papá wants to find a partner to love that much too."

Camilia tilted her head to the side as if digesting the information. "Like a girlfriend?" she asked, stunning the ever-loving shit out of him.

He nearly jerked his car to the side of the road as he momentarily turned back to look at her. Overprotective-dad mode activated. "How do you know about girlfriends and boyfriends?"

His daughter giggled, finding his flustered mood comical. "I know things, papá. Girlfriends and boyfriends are people you hug and play Lava at recess with. Duh," she said like it was common knowledge.

"Right. Well for adults, a girlfriend is someone you love dearly and want to spend your life with. How would you feel if one day papá introduced you to a woman he loved?"

"Would she be my new mamá?"

Javi had expected this question, but it still knocked the wind out of him. He had to walk a fine line between respecting Estella's memory and also preparing Camilia for the new mother-like figure that would hopefully come into her life.

"Well, let's think of her as a bonus mamá. Your mamá Estella will always be your mother and even though she isn't here, she still loves you and is always watching over you. Anyone I want to spend the rest of my life with is someone you are going to have to like too since she will be in your life." He hoped he made some semblance of sense trying to navigate these new unfamiliar waters.

"Would she read books with me and make cupcakes? Oh, like Ms. Lola! Lola should be your girlfriend, papá. She makes funny voices when she reads—like tía does."

It was getting harder to concentrate on the road with new reasons to fall deeper in love with Lola. Camilia had loved their time reading together while he worked in her shop, a situation he had not meant to put either of his girls in, but it turned out well in the end.

But on the off-chance that he was ruining his relationship with Lola, Javi didn't entertain the idea with Camilia just yet. It was good to know she wouldn't mind it though. "I'm glad you're okay with me one day bringing home a girlfriend. Just know, you always have a say, okay? You are my princesa. My number one. Always remember that, okay?"

"Okay, papá. I love you."

"And I love you."

The conversation had left him feeling lighter. The inevitable conversation had started to feel like an anchor weighing him down and now he was finally free of it. He should have known Camilia would have reacted so well. She was much more mature than he gave her credit for.

The rest of the ride to lunch, Javi learned all about what Camilia was learning in school and how she doesn't like her music teacher because she yells a lot. And then, because no car ride was complete without a little karaoke, they sang Camilia's favorite songs at the top of their lungs.

When they arrived at the restaurant, a popular Mexican place that served California's version of Mexican food, Javi got out of his car to help Camilia out.

"Who are we meeting, papá?" Camilia asked, making sure to grab her purple purse that had her coloring book and markers inside.

Javi hesitated before answering. "A...friend." Friend was a stretch, but he had liked the man enough during their brief moments together. It still had come as a shock when the unfamiliar number popped up on his phone. He almost didn't answer it but changed his mind at the last minute.

And he was glad he did. Equally glad that he managed to trade numbers after a rather serious golf discussion.

Taking Camilia's hand in his, he led her through the parking lot and inside the building. They were ahead of the lunch rush, so the restaurant wasn't full yet. He checked the tables, seeing if he could see a familiar face looking back at him.

"Javi," a deep voice called from behind him.

Standing at the entrance of the old restaurant stood Travis Roberts looking like he stepped out of a golf magazine shoot. He was dressed in khaki pants and a blue polo he had tucked in. The man's eyes went to Camilia and his extroverted girl waved happily.

Travis's features softened. "And who is this pretty girl?"

"Mr. Roberts—"

"Call me Travis, please."

"Travis, this is my daughter Camilia. Camilia, this is Lola's papá," he said, introducing the two.

"I like your daughter. She's nice," Camilia said in a way of greeting.

The man laughed, crouching down to get at eye level with her. "I like her too. And if Lola likes you, you must be one special girl."

"I think so. I get all A's and B's at school and I know how to spell Mississippi."

"Well, you are practically a genius then!" Travis grinned and pushed himself up. His smile faded, but the kindness in his eyes did not. "Thank you for meeting with me. I'm...well frankly Javi, I'm worried about my daughter. As a father, you must know you hurt when your kids are hurting."

Javi knew that feeling all too well. Perhaps it was why he agreed to meet with him in the first place. But also, Lola deserved a cheerleader and he had been around his fair share of cheerleaders —thanks to his sister—to be one for Lola.

"I can only tell you what I've observed, but after this, you are going to have to show up for Lola. Not just some of the time. All of the time. She deserves that. Hell, she deserves so much more than what you have allowed to happen all her life."

For a moment, Javi thought he might have gone too far. Color rushed to Travis's cheeks and his jaw clenched. Javi wasn't here to sugarcoat anything and he told Travis as much on the phone. He agreed then, but had his mind changed since?

After a beat, Travis let out a resigned sigh and nodded. "I see. Well, we should find a table. I figure we have a lot to talk about. I like that you don't hold back. It's a good quality in a man," he said and signaled the hostess. When he turned back to Javi, before they were seated, he said, "I want you to tell me what happened at the wedding and I don't want you to sugarcoat a damn thing. It's time I see what I've been allowing to happen for so long."

Javi hoped this was a step in the right direction and the beginning of the healing process for Lola. Without another word, he followed Travis to their table.

# Lola

DREAMS TENDED to start as nothing more than a seed. With the right fertilizer, a good amount of water, and a little sun, a flower could bloom out of nowhere. That was how Lola felt standing in the middle of Phoenix today, seeing her bookstore come to life. It had started as nothing more than a vague idea. A "what if" that reshaped her whole trajectory.

And now it was complete.

The once-dated bookstore had gotten a major facelift. Out were the old-school browns and beiges and in were the pinks, whites, and grays of her new color palette. The room was more vibrant and open with floor-to-ceiling bookcases. Each section was marked by genre, spanning from romances, to memoirs, to fantasy, with everything in between.

Throughout the large room, various table displays were set up to grab readers' attention. Mona had helped her last night to finish the displays before the big day. Her favorite they had come up with was a book display titled "Not Your Average Romances," where they placed Latinx and BIPOC selections because if there was one thing Lola was doing, it was diversifying.

Off to the side was another small room with the perfect reading nook. When she had worked here all those years ago, Mrs.

Sanderson had used it as storage, wasting precious space. She had always pictured an area for kids, full of bright colors and diverse books that reflected all types of children and families. This was the only space that didn't follow the main color scheme.

A huge rainbow stretched from one end of the wall to the large window. The other walls were off-white, but the rest of the space was an explosion of color. Multicolored bookcases that reached up to her were pushed up against one wall, displaying board books at the bottom and picture books above them.

A larger set of bookcases were placed across the room for older readers who were just starting chapter books and middle-grade books. Her young adult section was within the main room because she didn't want the older kids and adults who read young adult books to have to step through crawling toddlers.

Lola took it all in, the fresh coat of paint, the smell of old and new books, and the sound of the coffeepot making a fresh brew. Serenity like she had never felt before washed over her as she took a moment to think of all she had accomplished. It was so easy to get lost in the hustle and bustle of the daily tasks of a small business owner that it was hard to remember the incredible job she was doing.

Yet, even through the pride and happiness, she could not deny the sadness creeping inside her each time she thought too hard about the last few weeks. Seeing Javi every day and not being able to talk to him had been brutal. It wasn't for lack of trying either.

After the shock of seeing Ofelia three weeks ago instead of Javi, a feeling of wrongness lingered within her. She had been set on ending things between them, but the more she thought about her life and what she wanted out of it, the bleaker it seemed without Javi. Which was fucking scary, considering he seemed to be ignoring her.

The first time he had come in to work on the shop after the wedding, Lola had planned to talk to him. But then she had gotten lost in cataloging books and ordering new ones for the shop that by the time she finished, Javi was gone.

So she tried the next day, but the damn man hadn't been there. According to his crew, he was busy getting more supplies they needed and would be back later. Which would have been fine if Lola hadn't had to go to the bakery to help Mona out while Mattea was home with the flu. She couldn't tell her best friend no, especially after everything she had done for Lola while she was at the wedding.

The third time she tried to corner him ended unsuccessfully and made her look like she was hovering over his crew, waiting for them to make a mistake. Javi had been skillful at avoiding her and hadn't even tried to talk to her.

She had asked for space.

He had given her that.

But space fucking sucked and she regretted that with all her heart. But she also knew when she was being ignored and let down easily. She didn't try to talk to Javi after that, but that didn't stop her from looking at the man. Drooling over him as he worked because there was just something about a sweaty man building a bookstore that did it for her.

A small part of her, though the likelihood of it happening was zero to none, hoped Javi would show up to her grand opening. She was just setting herself up to be disappointed, but here she was—a delusional idiot.

"Hey, you doing okay?" Mattea's voice cut through her thoughts and she looked up. She felt something wet on her cheek and went to wipe it away. That's when she realized she was crying. When did that happen?

She grabbed a tissue from the whale holder it was in and dabbed at her eyes. "I'm okay. These are happy tears." Mostly. "I've been thinking about this day a lot, you know? And now it's here."

It felt significant in a way she had not planned for. Like she was taking back pieces of herself that her mom had tried, and failed, to rid her of. It was empowering to finally do something for herself and not worry about the repercussions. It had been a spurof-the-moment choice that had completely changed her life for the better.

"I get it. Did Mona ever tell you how much I sobbed when I held the keys to the bakery? Not even opened or anything, just holding the keys." Mattea smiled, leaning against the doorframe as she played with one of her braids.

"We had just gotten engaged and you know Mona, she can't do anything half-assed. She knew I wanted to open a bakery. Girl barely had any of my desserts, but she had enough faith in me to forgo the ring and buy me the bakery. I was shocked and cried immediately. It felt so surreal. Like this thing that had been in your head for so long was finally tangible."

"Do you still feel that way? About your bakery?"

"Every single day. Every single damn day I thank my lucky stars for Mona and the bakery. Always feels like I'm living in a dream world."

The women shared a knowing smile before Mattea laughed and pulled her in for a hug. "Today is your day, miss. You get to enjoy it."

"Ten minutes!" Mona yelled, barging into the room carrying a whole tray of assorted donuts. "You know you got a line forming outside, right?"

"What? Seriously?!" Lola gasped, all but sprinting to look out the window at the front of the store. Sure enough, a line of at least a dozen people waited. They were all different ages, but all here for the same reason: the books.

"I have another box of treats in the car. I think we might need them." Mona said.

"Are you sure you and Mattea can afford to be here? Neither one of you need to be in the store?" Lola had pulled them away from the bakery so many times throughout the process, but neither woman complained.

Mattea waved her concern away. "Justina can handle it. She's been begging us to give her more responsibilities at the bakery. She knows she can call if she needs help." Justina was Mattea's nineteen-year-old niece who had been working since she was sixteen. "Besides, I have a feeling we are going to be very busy today. All hands on deck."

"And now we are down to six minutes," Mona called, obviously taking up the job as a talking clock. "Imma get the last box of desserts," she said and made a beeline for the back door.

"Tell me where you want me to go," Mattea said like a soldier waiting for orders.

"Uhm...do you mind running the cafe? We are only selling a few items and all of them are programmed into that fancy cash register. Mona and I can take care of the checkout counter."

"Don't forget to walk around and mingle. Building a community is important. Mona can handle the cash register so you can make your rounds. Trust me, you are going to want to meet and talk to your first-time customers."

"Ugh, seriously Mattea, I don't know what I would do without you." Lola couldn't stress enough how thankful she was for her chosen family. The support and love radiating off her friends had given her the strength she needed to get through these last few weeks.

"You would do just fine, though perhaps have a little less fun." She winked, just as the back door flew open again and Mona came in carrying the pastries they would be selling in the cafe.

"Three minutes," Mona sang, stacking the delicious-smelling desserts away.

Lola took a moment to breathe before making a final walk through the store, making sure everything was in its proper place.

"Two minutes."

She plugged her phone in, connecting it to the speakers to play instrumental music throughout the store.

"One minute."

Heart pounding out of her chest, she swept the room with her eyes as if something would jump out at her. Nothing did.

"And...you're open, babe!" Mona's giddy self appeared beside her. She bumped her hip against hers. "Go open the door and let's get started."

Inwardly, Lola was freaking the fuck out, and outwardly...well she probably looked like she was freaking the fuck out. Mona had to give her a gentle push to get her feet moving. The crowd had only grown in size and watched her with eager eyes from outside.

With a small, awkward wave to her first-time customers, Lola unlocked the doors. She opened up to the public for the first time and was greeted by a chorus of claps and excited cheers.

Ah, she loved book lovers.

"Welcome to the grand reopening of Phoenix Books. We have free donuts, so make sure you grab one on the way in. Our cafe is open and everything is ten percent off today. Now—" She stepped aside, unblocking the entrance.

The first few customers went inside, a few stopping to congratulate her or tell her how excited they are for the reopening. The shop began to fill up quickly, but no one seemed to mind the crowd. Sounds of laughter and excited chatter drowned out the music, but it was a much better sound in her opinion.

Lola's cheeks hurt from smiling so much and as the last person strolled into the store, she got ready to follow them in when she heard her name called. She turned around to see a familiar family and her heart squeezed tightly for a moment. Ofelia and her husband Maverick approached with Camilia and Arturo holding hands.

But just the four of them. No sign of Javi.

That hurt more than it should. She had thought maybe he would be here since he had known how much this moment meant to her. Maybe he would...

No. She had hesitated too long when it came to Javi and she was getting what she deserved.

Even though it hurt, she smiled through the pain. Ofelia had still come like she promised and brought her family.

"I'm so glad you all could make it!" Which was the truth. Lola leaned down to get eye level with Arturo and Camilia. "Are you ready to see all the books?"

"Yes! Ms. Lola, can you read me one? I like your funny voices." Camilia smiled.

"I read too!" Arturo said excitedly.

Lola was overwhelmed by all the cuteness. "I think we can arrange that. I have to make a few rounds, but before you leave, we can read a book of your choosing." The cute cheers from the cousins made her laugh. "Off you both go. There are donuts on the table."

"Donuts? Say less." Maverick grinned and walked inside to find said treats. Ofelia rolled her eyes, but Lola didn't miss the fondness in her features when she looked at her husband.

"I swear that man is a giant toddler sometimes. Anyway, we don't want to keep you. Besides, we will see you later tonight." Her eyes sparkled with mischief and she ushered the cousins in before Lola could ask what she meant by that statement.

What the hell was happening tonight?

Before she could contemplate it more, an elderly woman approached her and asked about book recommendations for her grandson. She soon got lost in helping her customers, manning the second cashier when they had a steady flow of customers, and managing to sneak in one quick storytime that was meant to be for Camilia and Arturo but ended up being for quite a few kids.

After her impromptu storytime and the morning rush of customers, Lola finally had a second to tidy up a few displays needing her attention. The bell to the front door chimed and she looked up to greet her new customer. "Welcome to Phoenix Boo —"

She abruptly cut herself off, blinking once and then twice to make sure her mind wasn't playing tricks on her. Because there was no way her father had just walked through the door. More shocking than that, and even more unbelievable, he wasn't alone.

Marisol had come too.

All of the words she had ever learned in her life magically

vanished, leaving her gaping as she struggled to come to terms with what she was seeing.

"You didn't think we would miss your grand opening, did you?" Her father's boisterous laughter echoed around her. Marisol remained quiet, but for once didn't look disgusted to be around her. She seemed...almost shy. And that was not the Marisol she knew.

"I, uhm, actually did." She didn't have her father and estranged sister showing up to her store opening on her bingo card. Must have missed that one. "I just...You've never...I'm sorry. I'm really surprised. That's all."

"We had to find out the opening date from a friend."

A friend? What friend was communicating with her father?

"I'm not missing my daughter's opening of her own business. What kind of father would I be? I brought your sister for support as well." He smiled and patted Marisol's back.

Brought or forced? She didn't voice that question but wondered all the same. Marisol had yet to say anything, but she saw her biting her lip as if holding back words she wanted to share.

She also noted her mother wasn't present, which didn't surprise her in the least. It still stung though. What surprised her was that Archie wasn't there with his new wife.

"Where's Archie?" she asked, despite herself.

Marisol and her father looked at each other before Marisol shrugged. "Not here," was all she supplied and Lola made a mental note to ask about that later.

"This must be a bit of a shock and I hope us coming isn't upsetting you," her father spoke and for the first time in her life, he seemed nervous.

Was she upset? No, not really. It felt...nice. Weird and a little awkward, but nice. So many questions ran through her mind and she wanted to ask them all, but now wasn't the time for a family meeting.

"I'm glad you're here. Do you, erm, want me to show you

both around?" she asked, suddenly feeling self-conscious. The bookstore was an extension of her and if they didn't like it, she wouldn't be able to feel like they didn't like a part of her.

"We will request a private tour later. Right now, we are here for support. Put us to work," her father said and she couldn't have been more stunned if the books started to fly off the shelf.

"You want to help?" She couldn't keep the skepticism out of her voice. Had her sister ever worked a day in her life?

"If you'll have us," Marisol said softly.

"I—yeah, okay. Sure. Do you know how to make coffee?"

"No."

Lola laughed. "Doesn't matter. Mattea will teach you. I'm sure she could use the help. And Dad, if you wanted to help run the other cash register, I would appreciate it."

Her father saluted her. "You got it, kiddo."

"Not that I'm not grateful, but I'm very confused as to why you are both here. You've never—" She cut herself off. She was going to say they never showed an interest before, but didn't want a fight.

Her father seemed to understand what she was implying and his features softened. "Yeah, I know this seems out of character. And we fully plan on having this conversation, but let's save it until after you close. You have a steady stream of customers and I don't see that stopping any time soon. Is that okay?"

As curious as she was, it was for the best to save this conversation for later. Right now, the only thing that mattered was their willingness to help. If today's opening showed her anything, it was that she needed to hire employees, stat. Something she hadn't thought about and wished she had planned better.

Luckily, her friends and family picked up the slack.

"Sure, sounds good to me. You ready to work?" She grinned, taking some much-needed pleasure in seeing her sister do mundane tasks.

With a single nod and a quick hug from her father, the two of them went straight to work. It was bizarre and unbelievable to see her father and sister jump right into action without complaint, but she couldn't deny the pride she felt seeing them.

So many questions ran through her mind and she wanted answers to all of them. The conversation would be hard, but long overdue. For now, she just needed to focus on her store and keep the momentum going.

She still couldn't help but wish Javi was there to see her first day.

# Lola

## CHAPTER FORTY-TWO

THE REST of the day went by in a blur of books and smiling faces. Lola was sure her face was set in a permanent smile from talking to her customers and helping book lovers find their next story. She barely had any time to pee or eat, though she did scarf down one of Mattea's pastries in the back room.

By the end of the day, she didn't even care that her feet throbbed from running around the store. She was still on cloud nine. Since this morning, they had a steady stream of customers. The bell above the door chimed so many times that she knew she would be dreaming about it tonight.

Yet, each time the bell rang a small part of her was holding out for Javi to be there, smiling at her in a way that made her warm and gooey all over. Her father and sister had come, so it didn't seem too far-fetched.

But he never showed.

The last hour before they closed, things started to slow down and Mona had said she and Mattea needed to go. She was vague on the details but assured her she would catch up with her soon. Lola wasn't the only one dying to understand why her dad and Marisol were here.

It still felt so surreal. The two of them worked hard to help her throughout the store and never once complained. Even when Marisol spilled coffee on her blouse. Her sister shrugged. *Shrugged!* And carried on as if nothing had happened. Lola kept waiting for the second shoe to drop; for something drastic or terrible to happen. It said a lot about her relationship with her family when she expected things to fail.

To their credit, they had stayed within their positions all day. Never once slowing down, besides the occasional quick bathroom break. When it was time to close the store, all three of them sagged in relief. The adrenaline had finally worn off and it was as if their bodies finally realized how tired they were.

"That's it. Day one done," she called out, sitting down for the first time that day. The moment she was off her feet, she groaned.

A moment later the chairs opposite her at the cafe table were occupied by her father and Marisol. Her dad wore an expression she had desperately missed coming from him. Pride. He was proud of her. "I've never had so many paper cuts in my life." He laughed.

"I don't think I have fingerprints anymore. I think they have been permanently burned off." Marisol inspected her hands and then rubbed them against her dark jeans. Marisol looked so... normal. Lola felt as if she stepped into an episode of *The Twilight Zone* and she would soon wake up to realize she slept through her first opening.

Lola was half tempted to pinch herself, but she refrained. Only just.

"I'm so proud of you, kiddo." The pride on her father's face was evident once again. "I always knew you were tenacious. Always knew you had it in you, but seeing you achieve your dreams is an entirely different ballgame. You shined today."

*I'm so proud of you.*

How long had she yearned for her family to give her the recognition she had always craved? Hearing those words as a child would have healed a part of her still desperately trying to please a family who never quite accepted her the way she was.

The only exception had been her father but he had always been complacent in the way she was treated. That shit hurt too and he needed to know.

It was as if a fire was lit inside of her, giving her the strength and grit she needed to reclaim pieces of herself. "Yeah, I did. Didn't I?" The abrupt change in her caught the attention of both of them. "I appreciate your assistance today and the money you put aside for me to do this. I realize how privileged I am to have never gone without and for you to trust me enough to never question the ways I spend my money."

"But?"

There was always a but, wasn't there? Her father had heard it in her words. Marisol tensed, bracing herself for what was to come. She slipped back into the haughty expression she normally wore. It took until now to realize blocking her emotions was Marisol's way of coping.

"But that doesn't excuse the way Mom has treated me all of these years. The way you have treated me, Marisol." For a brief second, Marisol's eyes widened before her mask of indifference took over. But Lola wasn't going to let her hide today.

"You are my sister and all I ever wanted was a relationship with you. We had one once, but then Mom got her claws into you. You were always her favorite and you claimed that spot ruthlessly. You went along with the backhanded insults and never once stood up on my behalf. None of this even begins to cover the betrayal I felt when you started dating Archie almost immediately after we broke up!"

As she spoke, her anger mounted. She was surprised her eyes weren't watery with tears because when she got passionate about something her emotions would overwhelm her and she would end up crying. But not today. Too much had to be said.

"Lola, what the hell did you want me to do? We hardly talked and it wasn't as if you answered any of my calls. You only ever answered for Mom or Dad. Never me," Marisol argued, her voice shaking on the last words.

"So it's my fault you started dating Archie? It's my fault you treated me like shit since I didn't pick up the damn phone to talk to you?"

"No, I'm not saying that!"

"Then what the hell are you saying?"

"Girls." Their father stepped in, but Lola's ire found him next.

"And you"—she pointed a finger at him—"only stood up for me when you got tired of the bickering. You allowed the comments about my weight, appearance, and ambitions as long as it didn't interfere with your perfect family photo. News flash, Dad. It was never perfect!"

Suffocating silence followed her words as they stewed in their thoughts. She searched their features, finding shame and hurt in their eyes. It was something they needed to feel, just for a second, to realize how in the wrong they were.

After a few more seconds, Lola was ready to break the silence, but Marisol's whimpering caught her attention. When she looked back at her sister, she realized Marisol was crying. "Marisol?" Her voice softened somewhat but was tinged with apprehension.

"I'm sorry. Fuck, I hate crying." Their dad reached into his pocket and pulled out a tissue before handing it to Marisol. She dabbed at her eyes, careful of her makeup. Lola couldn't remember the last time she saw her sister cry.

"When Dad called me last week and said we needed to check in on you, I admit, I wanted no part of it. I didn't know how me being here would help you at all. As I said, we don't talk." Before Lola could protest, Marisol put her hand up, silencing her. "And that's largely my fault. It was so much easier to go along with Mom than be the person she pestered."

"I wouldn't call putting me on a diet as an eight-year-old 'pester.' Or shaming me for not fitting in perfectly with this facade she wanted to share with the world 'pestering,'" Lola protested.

To her credit, Marisol looked embarrassed by her words.

"Right. Sorry. You've always been better at words than me. What I'm saying is I knew Mom treated you differently than me. I took advantage of that because I could. It became such a part of me that half the time I didn't realize what I was doing. I didn't think my words hurt you because I had become so desensitized toward you."

"You learned all of this in a week, have you?" Lola muttered, doing her best not to roll her eyes. Marisol was trying and it was more than she had ever done before.

"No. I guess I started noticing the differences once I got engaged to Archie. Mom was so excited for me in a way she had never been for you when the two of you were dating. The wedding brought out the worst in her...in us."

"I..." Lola sighed, pinching the bridge of her nose. She tried to remember the breathing techniques to calm her racing heart and took a minute to count each breath before she started again. "I guess I don't understand what changed. Why you care."

"For so long I always thought you were the problem. That the Mom I got was the same Mom you got, but you pushed her away and deliberately did things to piss her off. After the wedding, once everything settled down, I had time to think. That's when Dad called and I realized I've wasted so much time being mad at nothing. It scared me when you cut Mom off because...believe it or not, I don't want you to cut *me* off."

That revelation stunned her. Never would she have thought that Marisol would be so scared of getting cut off by Lola. Marisol's words from earlier rang through her mind and made her reflect on how she treated her sister.

How many times had Marisol called her only for Lola to immediately put it to voicemail? How many unanswered texts had she left unread?

It wasn't an excuse for her behavior. Not at all. But it did provide some insight.

"I guess it's hard for me to realize we had two very different moms growing up. I couldn't fathom how you could feel so much hatred toward her, but…I'm starting to understand."

"To be clear, I don't hate Mom," Lola said. As much as her mother hurt her, she didn't hate her. Some part understood her need to fit into the society she married into and present this perfect family to the world. She wasn't only a woman, she was a Mexican woman and she had to fight tooth and nail to earn any ounce of respect.

However, her mother needed to work on her own trauma and stop projecting it onto Lola. If she didn't see a counselor, she wasn't sure she ever would. As hard as it was, Lola needed to keep herself safe, and cutting off someone so toxic was the first step.

"And neither do we," her father said. "But we also don't like how she's been treating you. And you're right. I have been pretty ignorant in that way. I thought eventually you two would get along. Your mother can be overbearing, but I didn't see how much she affected you."

Her dad reached over the table and grasped her hand. "Your mother knows we are here and that she was not allowed to join us. Obviously, she isn't happy about it, but she brought this upon herself. That being said, if you would like time away from your sister and me too…well, we would understand."

Did she want that? Maybe she would have wanted her sister gone once, but now? Lola turned back to Marisol. "Just one thing. Why didn't you tell me about Archie? I never understood why you started dating him when you knew I dated him first."

Marisol's cheeks reddened. "Archie had wiggled his way into our family, but especially with Mom. She always made comments about how it was so surprising that Archie and I weren't the ones together. It was constant and got to the point where I just couldn't ignore her anymore. The night Archie broke up with you, he came by the house to inform our parents. Except Dad wasn't home, it was only Mom."

During their relationship, Archie had formed a strong relationship with her parents. She knew now it was because her parents had money and status, and that was the only thing Archie had even been attracted to.

"When he asked to take me on a date a few days later, I said yes because I felt like I didn't have a choice. I didn't know it would lead to him declaring we were dating and I definitely didn't know that it would lead me to marrying him." Marisol's eyes filled with tears, and she looked at Lola as if pleading for her to understand.

Lola had spent so long being mad at Marisol, hating her for being the perfect daughter, without really realizing her sister was hurting too. Only in a different way. Marisol had to live up to the perfection their mother set for them every single day. She always went along with whatever their mother said because it was easier just to do as Luciana asked than deal with the fallout from disappointing her.

For the first time in her life, Lola felt like she actually understood her sister and her heart hurt for her.

She reached out and took Marisol's hand in hers. "Marisol?" She spoke gently, meeting the eyes of the sister she was just starting to understand. "Do you love Archie?"

"No!" Her body began to shudder with the sobs working their way through her. "No, I can't stand that man. I only married him because I just wanted to keep everyone happy but I didn't because I hurt you and continued to hurt you. Lola, I'm so sorry. So damn sorry."

Lola couldn't stop her own tears as she got out of her seat and wrapped her arms around Marisol. They needed this moment, needed to break down and see each other at their lowest to truly understand one another.

Her heart hurt for Marisol and the pressure she was under every day trying to remain the perfect daughter. Hurt for herself for living all these years thinking she didn't have a sister that loved her.

Marisol soon pulled away, eyes puffy from crying and hair disheveled. "Archie isn't here because I didn't want him here. I was too scared to say that before, but I'm not anymore. Not after hearing you stand up to Mom…it made me feel like maybe I can do the same."

There was so much to unpack there and Lola wanted to dive into it all eventually. Marisol shouldn't have to stay married to that prick if she didn't want to be. She wanted to say as much, until she felt a large hand rubbing her back. It took her a moment to realize it was her father. His face was splotchy and red, obviously hurting as well.

"This doesn't begin to right the wrongs we've done. This doesn't excuse the way Marisol treated you or the way I always tried to diminish the situation. But what I can say is that we will try our hardest to make it up to you, if you let us."

Lola rubbed her eyes, slowly untangling herself from her sister. There was still a lot they needed to address, but this felt like a step in the right direction. Now it was up to her and she had to make the decision whether or not she wanted them in her life.

She had acted on fear and let others' opinions influence her decisions. It had cost her the man she loved. She didn't want to do that again, but things needed to change.

"Until I'm ready, I don't want to be around Mom. She has to deal with her shit before we can think about talking and I don't want either of you pressuring me into talking to her. If that means I miss a few family functions, then so be it. But I will not be made to feel bad about it anymore.

"It's going to take some time for us to heal our relationships. If you're serious about wanting to be in my life, then there's a whole lot of stuff we have to work through as well. So be prepared for tough conversations.

"If you can agree to this, then I see no reason you both can't stay in my life." Lola watched Marisol visibly relax and her father nodding his head enthusiastically. Their willingness to try spoke volumes.

"There is nothing more I want than to support my girls.

Through your bookstore endeavors"—he smiled at Lola—"and a potential divorce." The last part was spoken to Marisol.

"No matter how different you both are, I love you equally and am so proud of you both," he said fondly, reaching out for both their hands. "Our Dolores has a backbone on her. Not everyone can stand up to your mother and leave the room a victor."

The nervous energy between them evaporated as Lola snorted. "I don't know if I would say victor. I'm sure she exaggerated some of the details."

"Your mother wasn't the one to tell us about the fight."

"Then who..."

Before she could finish her sentence, a familiar face popped up in her mind. The only other person who was there that night. Who saw everything.

Javi.

The amused expression her father wore said he knew she answered her question. "That's a fine young man you have there. His daughter is adorable. They both speak highly of you."

Javi had gone and talked to her father without her knowing. Knowing him, he did it because he knew she had wasted her last bits of strength on her mom and she doubted she would ever have the courage to speak so freely to her father, much less her sister.

If it weren't for him, she would have never had this moment. Even when she tried to push him away, he still made sure her voice was heard.

"Dad spoke highly about him. I didn't get a chance to talk to him at the wedding, but I'm hoping I can soon," her sister said, the words still sounding foreign, probably to both their ears. Kindness and connection didn't come easily in their bond and it would feel strange for a while.

"I don't think that's going to happen." Marisol's smile faltered at Lola's words. "We aren't together. And it's my fault. I took something Archie said to heart, about me being recklessly impulsive, and I let my doubts cloud my judgment."

She hated admitting her failure and she didn't know when the pain of losing Javi would ever heal. Her feelings had been real. The amazing sex had been real. All of it was the most intense love she had ever experienced and it scared the hell out of her. Instead of facing her fears, she chose to lose it all.

"Nonsense. That boy loves you. No one would meet with a woman's father to berate them for how they treated her if they weren't madly in love."

"Madly in love." She scoffed, unable to keep the bitterness out of her own words. She wasn't sure if she was angry with herself or irrationally angry at Javi for making her fall in love with him. "I can assure you, that is not the case."

"Then you'd be very wrong, preciosa."

Lola had never jumped out of a chair so quickly, whirling around to make sure her mind wasn't playing tricks on her. That the man standing before her was the same man who haunted her dreams night after night. She didn't know how he got in, didn't know why he was here, but he was not a figment of her imagination.

Standing in front of her, dressed in dark denim jeans and his usual black T-shirt, stood Javi. And in his hands, he was holding two things: a greasy bag of food and an old copy of *The Giving Tree.*

Lola opened her mouth, but the only thing that escaped her lips was a sob.

# *Javi*

## CHAPTER FORTY-THREE

THREE WEEKS. That was how long it took for every piece of the puzzle to fit together to create this moment right here. Javi would not soon forget the look in Lola's eyes when she turned around and saw him standing only a few feet behind her. Her eyes were blown wide and her lips didn't know whether to smile or scowl at him. There seemed to be a raging war inside her, probably wondering if she wanted to hug him or cast him out.

There was a chance he only made things worse between them. If she rejected him again, he would have to give her up. He knew when he was fighting a losing battle, but he hadn't failed yet.

Three weeks ago, Javi met Travis for lunch. Out of concern for his daughter, he wanted to reach out to someone who knew what was going on because Lola tended to bottle up her emotions and not feel them until they became overwhelming.

Javi only spoke about the incident he saw between her mother and Lola at the wedding. There was far more that needed to be said, but it wasn't his story to tell. This was how they came to an agreement that Travis would leave Lola alone long enough for her to focus on the shop and come support her on opening day.

Bringing Marisol had never been part of the plan, so it was a pleasant surprise to see her at the shop as well. It made sense

651

though, given their troubled history. Perhaps she was there to patch things up with her sister. The only person missing from the scene was Luciana.

Good.

Travis broke the silence and stood up. "Well, I think it's time for Marisol and me to go." Lola didn't so much as turn around to acknowledge him. "We will see you later for the—"

"Yes—" Javi cut him off, not wanting to spoil the other surprise he had waiting for her. A surprise that was contingent upon her response to him being here.

"Right. We will just see our way out." He winked at him and offered his arm to Marisol. As they walked out, he noticed Marisol's gentle squeeze of Lola's shoulder and the way Lola relaxed her body.

Soon the door closed, leaving the two of them in absolute silence for the first time in three weeks.

"This was you? All of this was you?" So his girl found her voice. Her ever-changing emotions made him want to take all the doubts away. "But how? And what the fuck, Javi? You've been avoiding me for three weeks and now you come in here holding"—she gestured down to the book she hated, causing Javi's lip to quirk up in a smirk —"that damned book and food? Like that's going to fix everything?"

He flinched at her statement. The past three weeks hadn't been easy. More than once he had been tempted to seek her out, just as she did for him. Each time he came up short though. There was still much left unsaid between them, but he didn't want to add any extra stress as she prepared for her opening. Javi had things to prepare for as well and they all revolved around her.

They both needed time apart to find their way back together.

Lola stared at him expectantly, waiting for a response. He took a step forward and her body gave an involuntary shudder, giving away that she was affected by his proximity.

"No, I don't think this will fix everything," he said, putting the book and food on the table. From his experience, food did wonders to calm the most strenuous situations. Ofelia said it was better than flowers, so he took her word for it.

"Javi, did you talk to my dad? What did you tell him? You don't have to continue to stick up for me."

"You still don't get it, do you?" Javi laughed, which only made Lola purse her pouty lips together in anger. "I admit, talking to your father may have been a mistake. I don't regret telling him what happened, but I should have asked your permission first. I'm sorry."

Lola remained stoic, not answering him with words. The slightest nod of her head told him to continue. "He came to me as a father and asked what I would do if my daughter was hurting. So I told him. I said nothing on this earth would stop me from making it right. I wouldn't let my own stubbornness or pride force me to miss out on the best thing to have ever happened to me."

He thought of Camilia and the lengths he would go to for his daughter. Travis was struggling to find his footing and Javi had attempted to give him advice, not knowing what he would do with it, but hoping he'd make the right decision.

Showing up and admitting you were part of the problem was a good first move in his book.

Lola sucked her bottom lip between her teeth. "And my sister? Did you talk to her too?"

"No, I think that might have been your father. He seemed determined to fix a sibling relationship he had a part in breaking. But it's up to you on what you want to do." Not that he needed to tell her this, she had done a good job of standing her ground like she rightfully deserved.

Yet she still didn't seem at ease with him in the room and he was starting to second-guess his plan. "Listen, I'm sorry about talking to your dad—"

"No. Surprisingly, I'm not mad about that." Lola admitted, cutting him off. "I know you did it for me. I'm mostly mad at myself." Her voice came out so small, cracking on the last few words.

Every muscle in Javi's body tensed. "Why are you mad at yourself? You didn't do anything."

"And that is exactly the problem. I shouldn't have let my doubts take over and push you away. I should have fought harder for us and when I was finally ready, I thought you wanted nothing to do with me anymore. Which is, once again, my fault."

"Fuck, this isn't going like I planned." Javi ran a hand through his hair and for the first time, he felt shy around her. He hated that she had thought she lost him and felt guilty.

"How was it supposed to go?" Lola asked softly. When he looked up, he saw that she was only a breath away from him. He needed her in his arms. Except he needed to get out what he had to say before he made the situation any worse.

"I was going to show you the book." He gestured toward his old copy of *The Giving Tree.*

Lola made an adorable, scrunched face that was supposed to convey her anger but just made him want to kiss the wrinkle in her brow.

"You got me the book I hated?" she asked skeptically. "That was your grand plan?"

"No, it's not for you, it's for your store. And I have been thinking about this book a lot. How could anyone hate a seemingly innocent book? And I think it's because you are the tree."

Lola blinked once. "I'm...a tree?"

"Yes." He cleared his throat, thinking back to his sister's analysis of the book. It sounded so smart when she said it, being a former English teacher and all, but he didn't think he could mimic her words but hoped they made sense.

"You have given up so much of yourself to others to keep the peace. Your heart is the best thing about you and you never expect anything in return. When someone shows a genuine interest in you, it scares you because you've had to live in a flight or fight mode for a long-ass time. I understand the need for caution, but I don't want you to continue to give your time and heart away while gaining nothing in return."

"Like the tree."

"Like the tree," Javi repeated and this time cupped Lola's face in his hands. Their eyes met and he searched hers, finding something akin to hope in her expression. It gave him the confidence he needed to continue.

"Lola, I know you wanted time and I gave you that. If you ask me to leave now, I will. But not without telling you what you mean to me. It stopped being about the money the second I took you out on our first date. You remember how nervous I was?"

Lola shook her head the best she could with him holding her. "You looked so confident when we went to the bingo hall."

"I'm glad it came across like that, but I was nervous as hell. It had been so long since I wanted to impress anyone and I wanted to make you smile. I wanted to hear you laugh and I lived for the moments you smacked my arm when you got excited.

"Falling in love with you was easy. I think I loved you the moment I saw you reading with Camilia because that was the first time my daughter ever gravitated to another person that wasn't family. My feelings only grew stronger during our week in Colorado and I wanted to tell you so many times I loved you, but I never knew if it was the right time until it was too late."

Tears rolled down Lola's cheeks now, leaving tracks where her makeup had once been. Even a crying mess, his girl was the most beautiful in the world. Javi was surprised to feel his own eyes burned with unshed tears.

"Lola, I love you. I'm a single dad who works too damn hard and I'm sure I have a lot of other things against me. But I'm hoping you can look past that and consider being mine—"

"Yes!" Lola didn't let him finish his speech before she threw herself into his arms. "I want you. I want your stubborn, workaholic ass coming home to me. I want to read with you and Camilia every night. I want you, Javi and I know you and Camilia are a package deal. If you'll both have me, I want it too."

Nothing could convey the way her words made him feel. No words captured this feeling of rightness that engulfed him the moment she agreed to be his. He let his actions do the talking for him and he swooped down to capture her lips in a heated kiss. He was met with the same intensity he was giving.

"I can't believe your big gesture is bringing that damn book here and comparing me to a tree." Lola giggled, pulling back slightly to speak. Her lips still brushed against his when she spoke.

"I brought tostadas too."

"Fuck, that's so hot."

Javi laughed and backed her up against the counter, caging her in with his body. He saw the moment the humor left her eyes, replaced by desire. He felt his body heat at the thought of her and how long it had been since he last made his girl come.

He needed to remedy that. Even if he still had one last surprise for her. That could wait until later.

"I want you, Lola," he said, his voice growing gruff. His knee nudged its way between her thighs and she spread for him. "Preciosa, I need you now." He needed to feel himself inside of her, remember how her pussy gripped his cock. He wanted it hard and fast, to claim her properly.

Lola whimpered and her hands flew to her jeans. They were far enough into the store that no one walking by would see them. Not that he cared about that right now.

Lola peeled off her skin-tight jeans, scrunching them up on the floor before kicking them away. Part of him wished they were back at his home or hers, but right now he just needed to feel their bodies connect. Judging by the hunger in Lola's eyes, she needed that too.

Javi reached into his pocket to grab his wallet. He had a condom in there, but Lola stopped him. "I can't wait. I started taking the pill shortly after we left Colorado. Please, Javi." The sweet sounds of her begging made his cock stiff. Fuck, he needed her now.

"Are you wet for me, Lola?" he asked, moving his hands

between her thighs. He felt the dampness seeping through her panties and knew she was aching for him even before he pushed a finger into her. He moaned, feeling her wetness on his finger.

Then he made sure she was watching before he slid his finger back out and brought it to his lips. He sucked his finger into his mouth, tasting her eagerness.

"Fuck," Lola gasped.

Javi wasted no time unzipping his jeans and pushing them down until he freed his erection. The look of raw need and desire Lola gave him was nearly enough to make him come on the spot. He didn't think he'd ever get sick of that look.

"Counter. Now," he said in a caveman-like voice, only capable of one-word sentences.

Lola braced her hands on the counter behind her and Javi helped lift her. He pulled her right to the edge, making a mental note to personally clean the counter with bleach later.

"Tell me what you want," Javi said, spreading her thighs again and rubbing his erection through her folds.

Lola gave a shuddering breath. "You. Your cock. Javi, *please.*"

As much as he liked to hear her beg, he was desperate for her. Javi yanked her forward, pushing his hips up and disappearing inside of her. They both moaned in unison, Lola's arms wrapping around his neck.

There was nothing gentle in the way he fucked Lola. It was a sheer, carnal need. He felt her tightening around him, driving him to the brink of orgasm each time. Lola pulled him closer by wrapping her legs around his waist, pushing him deeper inside of her.

*Mine.* Each thrust seemed to say and Lola's gasping breath told him she was getting close. His hand flew to her clit, his thumb rubbing circles around the bundle of nerves.

"Javi!" she cried out. "I'm close."

He was too. He didn't stop his merciless thrusting, his back and arm muscles flexing. They reached orgasm together. Their cries of pleasure echoed around them in the empty store. Javi panted, lowering his forehead against hers.

The only sounds around them were the sounds of cars passing by on the street. He felt like he was in a cocoon of warmth and love and they were on the cusp of creating something great together.

"I love you too, Javi," Lola said after a moment, once her chest stopped heaving. "I don't think I said that before, but I do. And I'm sorry it took me so long to realize that."

"I would have waited for you for as long as you needed," Javi said, meeting her gaze. "Don't apologize. You needed to do this on your own time. So did I."

"Thank you for being patient with me." Lola nuzzled him, shifting her body so he moved inside of her involuntarily, eliciting a groan from him.

"I think you should take me home," Lola purred. The woman was going to be the death of him and send him straight to the grave. She rolled her hips and Javi felt himself getting hard again.

"Fuck Lola, you make saying no incredibly hard," he groaned.

"Then don't say no." Lola giggled, tightening her legs around him.

Javi wanted to give in. He wanted nothing more than to take her on every available surface, but they had people waiting for them. It had taken a lot to organize and many people were expecting them to show.

"There's one more surprise," he said and Lola stopped.

A giddy smile spread across her lips. "What is it?"

"We have to go."

"Well, color me intrigued." She giggled and finally released him. Javi pulled out of her with a grunt. "Just give me a minute to...erm." She looked down at their mixed pleasure dripping down her thighs. "Clean up. Then we can go?"

Tucking himself back into his pants, Javi nodded. "Truck's out back, ready to go when you are." With that, Javi kissed her and smacked her beautiful ass as she walked by. As much as he wanted more of her, he was excited about the next surprise.

*Lola*

CHAPTER FORTY-FOUR

As much as she enjoyed going to bingo for their first date, Lola had to wonder why Javi was pulling up outside it now. The thought of going back to his home and celebrating her opening privately was tempting. Her thighs were still slightly sore from the frenzied fucking from earlier and she wanted more.

"Love, as tempting as this is, are you positive you wouldn't rather go...oh, I don't know, to my bed?" Lola asked.

Javi smirked and cut the engine off, parking outside the building. "That will happen later, but I brought you here to tell you about the money you paid me."

Confusion settled over Lola as she cocked her head to the side. "It doesn't matter, Javi. I already said the money is yours and I wanted you to spend it however you wanted—"

"I know, but just let me get this out." Javi's stricken face gave her pause and she nodded for him to continue. "I was able to give each of my men bonuses for their hard work on your bookstore. Some of the money went to bills that, regrettably, I was late on, and a good portion was set aside for Camilia when she gets older. However, the rest went into making tonight possible."

"I...don't understand. Did you buy out all the bingo cards so we'd win for sure?"

659

Javi barked out a laugh and reached over to undo her seatbelt. "No, but good idea. I'll remember that for next time." He offered her a wink before undoing his belt and slipping out of the car.

Now she was more confused than ever but let Javi help her out of his truck. "So, why are we here then?" She didn't want to sound ungrateful, she just wanted to know what secret he had up his sleeve.

Javi was practically bouncing with excitement but kept his mouth shut. Instead, he led her inside the front door to the check-in part of the bingo hall. No one was manning the booth which she thought was odd. "How do we..."

Her question died on her lips the moment Javi ushered her through the welcome room and into the main part of the building. Beautiful and colorful decorations still adorned the walls and ceilings, but only this time it was accompanied by a large banner reading, "Congratulations, Lola!" in a beautiful, cursive script.

Balloons in various colors of pink, white, and gray were interspersed with the normal decorations of the room and while it should have clashed, it only added to the beauty. Each table had what looked to be bouquets made entirely out of books.

Yet none of that was the most impressive part of the surprise. Standing in the room were familiar faces beaming and clapping for her. Amongst the sea of faces were Mattea and Mona, wearing something different than they had earlier. They had known this the whole time? And kept it a secret? That was almost more surprising than the actual party.

Ofelia and Maverick were there too, holding their son Arturo who seemed dazed but was clapping along anyway since everyone else was.

Her father's face caught her attention next. Among everyone in the room, his bellows of joy rang loudest of all. Mostly because her father was naturally loud and used to speaking over people at business meetings. Next to him was Marisol, changed from her coffee-stained blouse.

A few other familiar faces were there as well. Crew members

who she had gotten to know during construction and what was probably their family. A swirl of pink and silver came charging straight toward her, colliding with her and Javi's thighs. A smiling Camilia looked up, a gleeful expression on her face as she yelled, "Surprise!" Then softer, only speaking to her father, "Did I do it right?"

Javi's laugh echoed around her and he nodded. "Yes, mija, you did good."

So many emotions fought for dominance inside her. Shock, disbelief, and a growing warmth that could only be described as love.

"Do you, uh, like it?" For the second time today, Lola noticed the nervousness in his posture. The way he slid his hands into his pockets, shoulders curving forward as if bracing for an unfavorable response. "I don't know if surprises are your thing. Probably should have asked. You must be tired—"

"Javi?"

"Yeah?"

"Shut up and kiss me."

He expelled a deep breath, shoulders sagging in relief. The smile she had come to love so much returned as the anxiousness wore off. "Gladly."

Brazenly, he took her into his arms and claimed her mouth with his. The hollers and whistles around them didn't seem to deter Javi. Not only did he privately claim her, but this was him publicly declaring their love in front of family and friends. Her heart threatened to burst at the seams with the outpouring of love she felt in the room.

When they broke apart, happy tears ran down her cheeks. Three weeks ago she had gone through the motions of day-to-day living and part of her was excited for Phoenix to open. But her heart had been broken as she thought of everything she had sacrificed to get to that spot. A life with Javi and contact with her family.

So much had changed in one night. More than she could have

anticipated and it would take her some time to come to terms with it all. One thing was for certain. She had a family now. One that she chose for herself. And it started with the man standing next to her and the little girl still holding on to their legs.

This was home.

"Lo-Lo! Get in here, bit—girl," Mona censored awkwardly, seeing as there were children in the room. "And let's drink to a successful opening!"

"What do you say, preciosa? Ready to revel in your accomplishments?" Javi grinned, leaning down to pick Camilia up. He then offered Lola his hand. A few short seconds later, Camilia offered hers with a toothy smile.

There was still a lot that needed to be done. She had to hire full-time employees for her store. The bond between her and her family only had a Band-Aid on it, and there were still a lot of tough conversations that needed to be had. She also needed to process what it would be like to be a prominent figure in Camilia's life and how best to go about it.

But all of these things would take time and patience. They didn't have to be sorted out today and instead, she could enjoy the moment. As Javi said, she deserved to revel in her accomplishments and enjoy the night with the people she loved and admired.

Her people.

With a full heart and a smile stretching wide across her face, Lola took Javi's hand. "I'll follow you both." And she would. Always.

*Epilogue*

TWO YEARS LATER

THE SMELL of fresh cilantro and cumin wafting from the kitchen made Lola's stomach growl, even though she had been grazing all morning. She couldn't help it, she seemed to always be in a snacky mood these days, and with Ofelia cooking in the other room, her snack threshold all but tripled.

"Ofelia, please tell me what I can help you with." Lola entered the kitchen slowly, knowing any sudden movement would gain her ire. As of this morning, her sister-in-law had already shooed all the men out of the kitchen. Normally she was the first to have them help cook, but since it was Father's Day, they had all collectively decided to give them one day off.

"Sure, can you take the bottle out of the warmer and give it to Mav? I hear Violeta crying and I know it's because she's hungry." Ofelia barely looked up from the pot as she added extra seasoning. Lola's mouth watered at the thought of the menudo she was making.

"Oh, I'll do it, tía." Camilia smiled, hopping off the counter where she had been supervising Marisol cutting up the veggies for the salsa. When she passed Lola, she winked, giddy with the secret the two of them shared.

663

"Thank you, mija," Ofelia called as Camilia skipped out of the room. Violeta was the newest member of their ever-growing family, just shy of a year old. She was an adorable little girl with the biggest brown eyes and tight curls that Ofelia had styled into tiny pigtails.

"Lola, can you make the salsa? Yours always tastes so much better than mine." The slight whine in her sister's voice made her laugh. Marisol was many things, but a chef, she was not. She was much more accustomed to other people cooking for her, but Lola gave her credit for trying. Honestly, she was just proud she hadn't sliced off a thumb yet.

"Yeah, just hand me your knife and move out of the way." She laughed and Marisol all but collapsed in relief when Lola took over.

Over the past two years, they had worked hard on mending their broken relationship. Marisol had a lot of trauma to work through along with her divorce from Archie. Some days were better than others and they still went through periods of arguing, but they were trying. It amazed Lola how much she learned about her sister over the years and she loved finding things in common.

Surprisingly enough, they were both huge fans of rage rooms, as suggested by a therapist they saw together once a month. He had thought this would be a good way for the women to get their frustrations out. There was nothing more satisfying than breaking porcelain plates or hitting an old TV with a baseball bat.

She only wished she found a similar outlet with her mother. Their relationship hadn't progressed as much as Lola had hoped. It had taken her a year to even sit down with her mother and talk to her about the pain she'd caused her. Luciana had listened to her daughter, but they were still trying to find ways to reconnect. Right now, their meetings only consisted of large family gatherings and the occasional phone call.

The last time Lola had been on the phone with her mother, three months ago, Luciana had stated she had finally found a therapist that she liked. According to her father, said therapist cost him an arm and a leg, but he thought every penny was well worth it.

It gave Lola hope for the future.

"Technically, I don't have to cook since I'm not married or have children," Marisol said, leaning back against the counter.

"Yeah, but you have a father we are celebrating today," Lola insisted.

"Oh, right." Sometimes her sister was still so caught up in herself that she tended to forget those around her. Lola had long ago stopped being insulted by that. Her sister didn't do it on purpose and she was actively trying to be less self-centered.

It was still a work in progress.

For the next twenty minutes, Lola listened to whatever Ofelia needed her to do to prepare the lunch for the dads. With Camilia and Arturo's help, the three of them got the dining room table set. Ofelia was the only one to have a table that expanded big enough to accommodate the family.

"Boys! It's time to eat," Ofelia called, carrying the large pot of menudo out while Marisol brought out a few other dishes Ofelia had somehow been able to make. That woman was a master in the kitchen and she didn't know how Maverick didn't gain a million pounds with her food. Probably due to his intense baseball fitness regime.

One by one, the men of the family began to amble in. As expected, her father was the first one since he was Ofelia's biggest fan when it came to her cooking. Her mother had come down with the flu and opted to stay home, which was fine by Lola. It gave her one less thing to worry about.

Next came Maverick with his father-in-law Ruben, discussing baseball stats she never quite understood. Maverick held Violeta in his arms, which made Lola smile. He hardly ever put that girl down.

Finally, her husband walked through the door, eyes scanning

the room until they landed on her. The smile he reserved only for her spread across his features and butterflies formed in her belly. She didn't think she would ever get used to that smile. The way he looked at her with all the love and adoration in this world.

"Where are we sitting, Mrs. Mendez?" he purred into her ear, wrapping his arms around her torso. A giggle left her lips when he started to nuzzle and kiss her neck.

Their wedding had been small and intimate. Only a few of their closest friends and some family were allowed to come. Mona had officiated their wedding in a ceremony that took place in Ofelia's backyard. Camilia had been their flower girl and Arturo their ring bearer. It was what they both had wanted. She couldn't believe that had only been five months ago. She felt like she lived a whole lifetime in those five months while simultaneously thinking it was going by too quickly.

"Camilia already called dibs on the middle," Lola warned and gestured to the three seats in front of them. Camilia found her way to hers and eagerly patted the spots next to her.

The last person to sit was Ofelia. As soon as she did, she gestured for everyone to eat. No one hesitated and began to fill their bowls and bellies up.

They didn't often get together. Everyone's schedules clashed, which only allowed for meets ups once in a while. Lola never had a big family and she had not realized how much she wanted one until Javi's family took her in. Two years ago, if someone would have said they would all be sitting down together, sharing a meal on Father's Day, Lola would have laughed in their face.

Yet here they all sat talking about everything from Maverick's games to the small, mundane family moments. Arturo would be starting kindergarten next month, going to the same school as Camilia. Camilia told everyone all about the third-grade teachers and which one she wanted, to which Lola's father said he would write a strongly worded letter to the principal to assure that would happen.

Lola would have to make sure he didn't.

By the time they finished eating, two hours had flown by. Camilia twisted in her seat to get Lola's attention. "Mamá Lola, is it present time yet?"

*Mamá.*

She was still getting used to that. It had shocked the hell out of her when she said it the first time a day after Lola got engaged to Javi. They had only one conversation prior where Lola sat with Camilia and talked to her about how she was allowed to call Lola whatever she was comfortable with. In no way would Lola ever pressure her. She understood and they hadn't talked about it since until she called her mamá for the first time.

"I think it is." She grinned and Camilia squealed. The little girl was bouncing out of her chair. "Remember what to do?" she whispered, just loud enough for her to hear.

Camilia nodded before running off. Javi raised his brow in confusion and Lola waved him off. He would see soon enough. A few minutes later Camilia came back with a small square-shaped box and a zipped-up jacket.

"You cold, Cam? I can go turn the air up," Maverick offered, but Camilia shook her head adamantly.

"I'm okay!" She plopped back onto her seat, keeping the present in front of her. "You can't open yours until last, papá."

"Then I will start." Travis grinned, looking between Marisol and Lola. "C'mon. What did you get your old man, don't be shy."

The sisters rolled their eyes simultaneously but laughed. If there was one thing that their father loved—other than Ofelia's cooking—was presents.

Marisol had been in charge of the present this year and handed him a neatly wrapped box. He tore into it like an over-excited toddler on Christmas. Seconds later he pulled out what appeared to be a scrapbook.

"I felt like it was time you needed some updated pictures. The grandkids are in it too," Marisol explained. Though Arturo and

Violeta weren't technically his grandkids, Travis spoiled them like they were. The adoring smile on their father's face told them he appreciated the gift.

They went around the table, letting each dad open his gifts. Ruben got a new BBQ set from Javi and Ofelia. Camilia made him a cute card with a picture of both of them on it. Then it was Maverick's turn. Ofelia had gotten him new running shoes for training days and the kids—with Ofelia's help—made him a mini book for all the reasons they loved him.

It was all very sweet, but the closer they got to Javi opening his present, the more Lola grew nervous. Which was a crazy thing to feel, but her nerves had been all over the place for weeks. Her heart beat so loud in her chest that she was certain everyone heard it.

"It's your turn, papá." Besides Lola, Camilia was the only other person who knew. Lola had made an appointment at the doctor's after two days of what she thought was a stomach bug. Camilia had gone along with her since Javi was working and had heard the news with her.

They both cried. And laughed. Then promised to keep it a secret until today.

Javi unwrapped the present and it felt like the world slowed down. Lola was certain she was shaking. There was only so much longer she could keep it together.

Javi tore off the remaining paper and opened the lid to the box. Folded neatly inside was a gray shirt with the words "World's Best Dad" in red across the chest. He leaned down and pressed a sweet kiss to the top of Camilia's forehead.

"Thank you, mija. I love it."

"There's more!" Lola blurted out, far too loudly. The room, who had been talking among each other, all stopped and looked over toward them. The blush crawled up the back of her neck, coloring her cheeks.

Javi looked back at the seemingly empty box. She watched as he went from smiling, to complete confusion. Her heart beat faster as he picked up the box, bringing it closer to his face so he could make sense of the taped photos Lola had placed at the bottom. She saw the moment the realization hit and his head snapped to her so quickly, she was surprised he didn't get whiplash.

"Lola. Are you serious?" His words did not indicate how he felt. Was he mad? Fuck, should she have done this in private when their whole damn family wasn't watching?

Before she could say anything, Camilia stood up on her chair and unzipped the jacket she wore to expose her shirt that read "Big Sister."

"Mamá Lola is having a baby!"

Chaos. The whole room exploded with excitement and she was rushed by Ofelia. "I knew it! I had this feeling."

"My baby is having a baby!" She heard her father exclaim, his deep laughter filling the room. Even Marisol came and hugged her and wished her congratulations.

Javi had not moved from his spot, looking down at the sonograms she taped to the bottom of the box. "Please say something," Lola whispered, the tightness in her belly growing by the second. She didn't think anyone noticed his lack of response yet, they were all too busy trying to guess when the baby would be due.

"Javi..." she said his name again, reaching for his hand to try and stir any response out of him. Her eyes flooded with unshed tears and she was seconds from losing it until she saw his first teardrop.

Javi was crying.

She had never seen him cry ever. She lost the battle with her emotions and couldn't keep back her tears. "Please tell me you're happy. Or mad. Or...something!" she demanded.

The shrillness of her voice snapped Javi out of whatever trance he had been in and back toward Lola. His eyes were red rimmed, but she let out a breath of relief when a smile began to form.

"Preciosa, you're pregnant?" he asked again, still in a state of disbelief. He turned toward Camilia. "And you knew?"

"Yup, and I kept it secret. I told you I can keep secrets," she said proudly.

"I'm twelve weeks today. Still early on, but the doctor said the baby is healthy and that—" But she didn't get to finish. Javi was out of his chair and pulling Lola out of hers too, kissing the words out of her.

Her body sagged in relief against his. Javi cradled her face between his hands as he pulled back to look at her—all of her, stopping at her belly. "Lola, you've just made me the happiest man in the world."

"Really?" She was on the verge of becoming a puddle of tears but was trying desperately to keep herself together for just a moment longer.

"Really. You have given me the best gift I could have asked for."

"I...I guess you can finally add on to the house like...like you've been trying to...do," she said in between sobs.

Javi laughed, leaning down to kiss her tears away. From the corner of her eye, she saw Camilia move closer and wrap her small arms around Lola. "No crying, Mamá Lola. Not good for the baby," she muttered, causing an unexpected laugh to burst through her.

"Exactly, mi amor, no crying allowed." Javi wiped his own eyes dry and pulled Camilia closer to them, squishing both Camilia and Lola into a family hug. "My girls, you make me so happy. How did I get so lucky?"

"Remember this feeling when we are waking up at three in the morning to soothe a crying baby and changing messy diapers." Lola laughed.

"I can't wait." The sincerity in Javi's voice made the butterflies return tenfold. The nerves from earlier disappeared. They would come back once she was closer to giving birth and things wouldn't always be easy.

But she learned long ago that sometimes doing the hard

things produced the best outcomes. And she wouldn't be doing this alone and neither would Javi this time. They would have each other and Camilia.

It was all she would ever need.

671

The End

# Bonus Chapter

THE GOWN HUNG on the bedroom door, billowing out in every direction. Lola remembered seeing the dress for the first time after scouring the pathetic selection of plus-size gowns the boutique held. Everything she found was either too simple, too boxy, or simply looked like something her grandparents would have gotten married in.

She had nearly given up, prepared to leave and start the search all over again at the next store, when the dress caught her eye, jeweled bodice begged to be looked at. The gown was nestled between two others, almost completely hidden save for the tulle poking out.

After wrestling it free from the rack, she held it up for further inspection. It was an A-line dress with a sheer sweetheart bodice. Embroidered floral appliques cascaded down the tulle skirt, teasing a sparkly layer underneath.

This was the dress. People always said that you would know if you found your dress by some gut instinct. Lola hadn't believed that to be true until this moment. It was also in her size, meaning the universe wanted her to have it.

That had been nearly a month ago and the day was finally

here. She was about to marry the love of her life. She just needed to remember how to get in her dress again.

The last time she had it on, a team of three people had helped her at the boutique. Right now she was the only one in Ofelia's guest bedroom and she realized quickly that she wasn't getting in the dress without help, so she shot off a quick text message to her friends and future sister-in-law.

Not even five minutes later there was a knock on the door, followed by her two best friends, Mattea and Mona, and Javi's sister, Ofelia busting in.

"Careful with the dress!" Lola called.

"Then why the hell did you put the dress here where we come in?" Mona mumbled, shimming her way through the small opening. She took in the dress and gave Lola a thumbs up. "It's pretty though. The pictures didn't do it justice," she said, gathering up the skirts to heave up so Mattea and Ofelia could enter without damaging the gown.

All three women were dressed to the nines. Ofelia had on a floor-length dress in a gorgeous burgundy color. Mattea's was a little more subtle, but still within the same color family. Mona wore a tux with a crimson-colored tie.

Since this was a small, intimate wedding being held in Ofelia's backyard, Lola didn't really have maids of honor and Javi didn't have best men. No one but her and Javi, along with Mona, would be standing at the altar. The only reason Mona was standing with them was because she was going to marry them.

"You need help getting into your dress?" Ofelia asked and laughed. "I did too. My best friend Willow was the only one to help me and I've never seen a person cuss at a dress so much."

"Let's see how we can do this. Oh, there's a zipper," Mattea, ever the problem solver, sprung into action, grabbing the dress from the door. "Mona, hold that side—no, that's the skirt, hold the bodice, yes. Good. And Ofelia, can you hold the other side?"

"Of course." Her sister-in-law sprung into action as Mattea

undid the zipper. There was still so much material that Lola nearly needed a map to get inside.

Mattea turned to her, with watery eyes and a bright smile. "You already look so gorgeous. But Mona said I couldn't cry because it would make you cry and then you'd ruin your makeup. But sweetie, you look breathtaking."

Lola smiled at the compliment, reaching up to gently touch her hair that was curled and braided away from her face. As a wedding gift, her mother had hired a make-up artist so Lola could have her make-up done professionally. Despite their limited relationship, Lola had invited her mother to the wedding with the caveat that she stay with dad or Marisol, leaving Lola to bask in her special day.

She felt gorgeous. Like a princess, something her father always called her.

"You better not start crying," she whispered, already blinking rapidly to keep away the tears.

"If you both start crying, I'm going to cry. I'm already halfway there," Ofelia piped up.

"No one is crying." Mona gestured to the dress. "But feel free to shimmy on over here so we can get you ready to go. Javi is about to head to the altar."

"He's already finished getting ready?" Lola asked, surprised. She hadn't had any contact with her husband-to-be since last night, when Mona, Mattea, and Ofelia stole her away for a girl's night that consisted of far too many delicious snacks and champagne. But it had been one of the funnest nights of her life. Even her sister stopped by for a few hours and let loose.

"I gave Mav strict orders to make sure my brother was ready by a certain time. Also Camilia is with them and she's going to keep the boys inline," Ofelia laughed.

Lola smiled. Just like Javi, she had fallen in love with that little girl and her larger-than-life personality. But she wasn't the only one to fall in love. Her father was beyond smitten with her and took great enjoyment in spoiling her rotten.

"Let's go, Lo-Lo. We gotta get you married, girl!" Mona's voice brought her back and she hesitated for only a moment before undoing her robe. She only wore white panties underneath since the dress had a built-in bra and although she loved her body, it was still intimidating to undress in front of three straight-sized people.

She got over that quickly though as Mattea led her to the dress and instructed her on what she needed to do. "Step in with both feet and make sure you aren't standing on any of the tulle when you do. Ofelia, Mona, slowly start pulling up."

Mattea continued to instruct everyone until the dress was finally in place. "Now, stand up straight. I'm going to zip you in. You better not need to pee."

"I don't. Girl, I made sure to go like three times before this, so we should be good for a while," Lola assured and did as she was told. The zipper went up with ease and she let out a breath of relief.

All three women stood back and almost immediately Ofelia and Mattea had to turn around, shoulders shaking slightly. Panic set in and she looked down, expecting to see something horribly wrong with the dress.

"What? What is it?"

"You just...look so...beautiful," Mattea managed to get out between deep breaths.

"They don't want you to see them crying," Mona said, but for all of her "no crying" talk, Lola swore she saw her eyes glisten.

The bedroom had a full length mirror and Lola got to take herself in for the first time. She had seen herself in the dress before obviously, but never with her hair and make-up done. She looked...well, she looked beautiful. More importantly, she *felt* beautiful.

*What will Javi think?* She couldn't help but wonder what his reaction would be when he saw her. All she knew was that she didn't want to wait anymore.

"Let's go get married!" Lola squealed and three sets of arms engulfed her in a big hug.

Descending the stairs was her next big hurdle. In movies, the princesses made it look so damn easy, but Lola was convinced she was going to fall to her death. She might have too if Ofelia and Mattea weren't holding on to her.

All women were slightly breathless when they reached the bottom. Mona recovered first and leaned in for one last hug. "I'll meet you at the altar to marry you to your one-night-stand," she teased.

Lola laughed. How things had changed so drastically since then. Best one-night-stand of her life. Now she got to have him every night if she so desired. And she did. Often.

Ofelia and Mattea left shortly after to rejoin the crowd. She had debated whether or not have Marisol with her while she was getting ready and in the end, she was able to see her sister for a brief moment before she was put on mom duty. Her one job was keeping their mother in line and Lola didn't envy her for that.

"Is that my princess?" A jovial voice asked. She beamed as she turned to see her father, dressed in a tan suit, tailored to his proportions perfectly. Her father's face was red, which meant he was barely keeping his composure together. At that moment, she felt like a little girl again, playing dress-up.

"Lola you look beautiful," he said before engulfing her in his large arms. He smelled of over-priced cologne, but it felt like home.

"Thank you, daddy," she murmured, pulling back. Keeping back the tears was becoming harder and harder, and she didn't know how she'd react when she saw Javi for the first time.

"It's your turn, princess. You sure about this? I can cause a distraction if you want to run out. But we'd have to take Camilia. I love that girl too much."

Lola laughed. "I'm sure. So very sure, and I'm ready."

Her father held out his arm to her and Lola gladly looped hers through. The music began to change and she knew it was their time. With one last deep breath, her father began to lead them out.

Ofelia's backyard was an oasis, with a pebbled path leading them to a garden full of blooming flowers and perfectly sheared hedges. Off to the left was a coy pond, the sounds of the small waterfall adding to the ethereal ambiance.

She barely had time to look at the decorations she spent countless hours picking out. Or see the faces of her loved ones come to celebrate. Everything else faded away except for the man in the navy blue suit.

Their eyes locked. Her breath hitched. Javi stared at her and she couldn't look away. He trapped Lola with his gaze and she was helpless to do anything but look at the man she was moments away from marrying.

There was no stopping the tears this time. She let them fall freely and was thankful that her father was there to keep her moving and upright.

It wasn't until she reached Javi did she notice the tears in his eyes. He was just doing a hell of a lot better job than she was.

"I'm trusting you with my daughter, Javier. Please love and protect her," her father said, placing her hand in Javi's.

"Until my last breath," he murmured and helped her up the few steps of the altar until she stood right in front of him. "Preciosa..." His voice came out breathy, taking her in for the first time in her wedding dress. "You're beautiful. And I'm so damn lucky."

Lola knew if she opened her mouth, only sobs would come out and she didn't want to spend the entire ceremony ugly crying.

It was hard to concentrate on Mona as she started off their ceremony, talking about how they met—thankfully leaving out the one night stand and moving to the bookstore renovation. All she wanted to do was wrap herself around Javi and never let go. She was almost tempted to do just that.

From the looks of it, so was Javi.

She finally composed herself enough that when it was time to say her vows, she felt composed enough to speak. Lola felt the eyes of their guests on her, which made her even more nervous to stay what she wanted to, but she looked at Javi for strength.

"Javi…" And that was all she was able to get out. So much for feeling composed and no tears. She was openly sobbing and heard many sniffles from their guests as she stumbled through her vows of love and devotion.

Javi was next and though he was more composed, Lola could see he was barely holding on by a thread. He spoke of their love and how he planned on cherishing her, but stopped every so often to wipe his eyes and compose himself long enough to continue. He was doing well too, until Camilia started crying.

Then they both lost it.

Not even Mona was immune to the heightened emotions surrounding them. She took a moment to compose herself before she said, "with the power bestowed upon me by some sketchy website, I now pronounce you husband and wife—"

The words weren't even out before Javi pulled her into his arms and kissed her senseless. The kiss conveyed everything they already said and felt, but in a way no words could capture.

Five seconds—or hours, Lola wasn't sure—later, they finally broke apart. "I love you, Mrs. Mendez."

Mrs. Mendez.

She was married now. To the best man she had ever met. Not only did she gain a husband today, but she also gained a daughter. Camilia ran to them, hugging her parents around their legs.

"Mamma Lola and daddy are finally married!" She giggled and it was the sweetest sound Lola had ever heard.

"Is this everything you wanted it to be, preciosa?" Javi asked, pulling his daughter close.

Lola looked around at her friends and family who were all wiping away tears. To her father who was blowing his nose into a hankie. To Marisol who dabbed at her eyes, looking happy for her.

Then to her mother who smiled softly at her and for once, Lola thought it was genuine.

Then she turned back to Javi. Her husband for now and until forever. "It's more, Javi. It's more."

# Stay Tuned...

To stay up to date with Anastasia, make sure to subscribe to her newsletter here.

Also by Anastasia Dean

# About the Author

Anastasia Dean is a pen name for Tati B. Alvarez. She lives in Austin, Texas, where she spends most days lost in her own head, creating stories. When she is not writing, you can find her vacationing at Disney World.